The DARK HEART
of NIGHT

Previously published:
(and available from Small Beer Press)

Hound (a mystery) and
A Slepyng Hound to Wake

Available as an ebook only
from Amazon, B&N, Apple IBooks:

I am William McGuire (a novella)

Written and forthcoming:

I imagine my salvation: a Menckenesque
If Blood Were Orange, and other stories
The knight's tale
John Finn
Habits of the Heart

In progress:

A young man from Mars
Benedictions
A Republic of Books
The Gyre

The DARK HEART of NIGHT

by Vincent McCaffrey

Avenue Victor Hugo Books
Abington, Massachusetts

The Dark Heart of Night
Copyright 2015
by Vincent McCaffrey

First Edition

ISBN-13: 978-0692489611
(Avenue Victor Hugo Books)
ISBN-10: 0692489614

* * *

Disclaimer:
The Dark Heart of Night is published by the author and has not been
edited for reasons of length (unhappily for those addicted to the
passionless bits and bytes of a digital romance), political correctness
(human relationships are what they were), or age appropriate
language.

This book is dependent solely on its readers.
If you enjoy what you find here, please tell a friend or friends (as
many as possible). Word of mouth is the only means by which this
story will likely be known.

This story is dedicated to my parents
and the world that knew them.

* * *

My deepest appreciation and heartfelt thanks are given to the
great City of New York and the Department of Records there,
the source of thousands of inspiring photographs from the period,
most especially for "Front Street looking west from Roosevelt Street,
span of El across top," which was on my desktop through much of
the writing, though the photographer is still unknown to me.

I would also like to acknowledge the invaluable help
and assistance of
Cord Blomquist
Pamela Siska
Thomas Owen
William H. Desmond
Adam McCaffrey
Elisabeth McCaffrey
and Thais Coburn
in the preparation of this manuscript.
If I didn't listen, it's my own fault.

The Dark Heart of Night

1. Sunday, March 14, 1937

Now that I'll have a little time on my hands, at least for the next couple of days, maybe I can try this again. There's a lot going on, but it's an easier thing to do if you don't have to get to work.

Depending on what you read in the newspapers, or listen to on the radio, there are about twenty million people out of work in this country right now, give or take a few. The government says the number is only 8 million or so. But like Dad says, it's not the numbers that are unemployed. It's the people. The numbers are doing fine. And I'll bet over a million of those human beings are right here in New York. And even if this is only roughly true, and I think it's shy a few warm bodies, none of the arithmetic accounts for the women, the kids, the cripples, or the old folks. None of that accounts for people working crap jobs, part-time, just to eat the 'day-old' when they get home. None of those numbers account for ruined lives and lost dreams.

But that's not me. Not yet!

I'm named after my dad's little brother, Hugh McNeill, who died of scarlet fever in 1896. He was just a boy and never had his chance. Giving his name to me was done out of respect, I know, but early on I took it to be a challenge—that I was meant to live enough for the two of us. You can get ideas like that when you are young.

They are hard to shake. But then, there are those who don't even want to live the once.

My dad had a fellow who worked at the shop over on Sixth Avenue named Jerry Herzog. I knew him pretty well. I used to help Jerry with deliveries when I was a kid. Dad has customers all over the city because he gets stuff from England and France and Germany, and only the best. French pens are popular. English papers. This Underwood typewriter I'm working on is made in New York, but that is one of the exceptions.

Dad opened his stationery shop back in 1925 and he got a good reputation pretty quick, not for the cheapest but for the best. And Jerry was his first employee. Just a big kid on a bicycle from Staten Island who took the long voyage across the bay water one day to a bigger world. And just as soon as Jerry got himself hired, the guy had a wife and two kids in the blink of an eye. Sheila was a runaway Jerry spotted on the street one day. He told me that himself. Love at first sight. Jerry used to smile a lot in those days and being a few years younger, I looked up to him for the fact that he seemed to never quit, had boundless energy, and a nearly constant good humor.

Even so, when times got tougher in '33, Dad had to let Jerry go. That was even though he'd been paying Jerry half wages for the year before.

Dad stuck Mom behind the counter at the shop in the mornings then. My brothers and sisters and I were all old enough to get by, or in school, and she was the bookkeeper anyway. She looks pretty intimidating with her half-glasses down on her nose and with the way she pulls a crease in her brow. She says she learned to do that from her father, Dr. Dean, who'd been a judge. Dad would be out the door then and making deliveries by himself till noon. But not on a bike. He had a Ford A Model wagon he'd picked up in good times that he used to curse all the winter long for being drafty but it carried just about anything he had, as well as all of us when summer vacations came. He's a wicked driver. (My mom's words, but true.)

By the time Dad had to let Jerry go, I was thankfully on my own. I would get over to the shop when I could, grab anything that wasn't urgent, and drop it off at places as I went about my job for the *Mirror*. I'd already started at the newspaper for nothing except half of Dick Weise's salami sandwich back in 1930, just before the *Mirror* moved uptown from Frankfort Street to 45th. Mom read the *Herald Tribune* and Dad read the *Eagle* but those papers were not big on running pictures and the *Mirror* was the closest tabloid on the other side of the Brooklyn Bridge from Prospect Heights when I first started looking for work as a news photographer and I haunted that place. Mostly I was just playing gofer, but I could walk there in under an hour, no sweat.

Dick taught me pretty much everything I know about a Speed Graphic and a press photographer's tricks and how to make something out of nothing in the darkroom—even though I thought I knew a lot before. Thankfully I still lived at home in Brooklyn until the *Mirror* saw that I was worth the twenty-five a week to be Dick's 'assistant.' Specifically I worked most with Dick because he was already slowing down and the other guys didn't want anyone else looking over their shoulders.

Dick is down in Morristown, New Jersey, now and dying of tuberculosis or lung cancer or both. He practically ate three packs of Camels a day. So they raised my wages by ten bucks, and gave me my own camera to play with, and in turn they got to use me seven days a week and twenty-four hours a day. But it was a job. There were plenty around who didn't have one.

I've managed to raise my weekly take home to all of seventy-five dollars since then. Dad and Mom are still getting by. But Jerry did not. I got to take his picture a week ago.

The cops fished him out of the East River over below Red Hook where he'd gotten hung up on one of the piers in the tide. They figure he jumped off at the Manhattan Bridge the night before. I didn't recognize him when I took the pictures. He was pretty gray and swollen. I only realized who it was when I was in the darkroom. The truth was all in the shadows. You don't see some things when you are looking right at it. It was one of those moments. Chilled me to the bone.

Jerry was a ruddy looking fellow in life. A nice guy. Full of jokes. Liked a good beer when he could manage a few moments. He took me out to a speakeasy and bought me my first shot of whiskey when I turned eighteen. My dad certainly wasn't going to do that. Dad just gave me a bottle of Seagram's instead and told me not to drink it—on the theory, I suppose, that I would be contrary and go ahead and try to drink the whole thing anyway and never want to touch the stuff again. That's his way.

I spoke to Jerry the last time about a year ago. It looked like things were getting better and he had a positive face on. But he was alone. His wife and kids were living with her parents back in Delaware. I could tell he was really cut up by that, though he never complained about anything. Not that I heard. Dad had him doing deliveries again whenever he could. But nothing regular. And then, this year, the economy took another dive. So to speak.

It seems like there are more murders now, but there are definitely more suicides.

The same week, I also covered the death of a young lawyer up in Yorkville. He'd hung himself from the sprinkler pipes in his office with a cord cut from the blinds. Kicked the chair out from under. He was a 'Good lukin' fella,' as Dad would say, and didn't seem the type. The office was well appointed, and it appeared as if he was already a success, even though he couldn't have been much older than me.

Cass Green was the reporter on that one and it made her turn white and not much can do that. Not that I've seen.

Now, on this last Sunday morning, first thing before I'm awake, or I can even think of a cup a' joe and some breakfast, I get a call from my boss, Barry George, to get over to the Hotel Pennsylvania. "They have something there that will suit your artistic nature," he says.

I should have walked, but my bag was feeling heavy and the cold was damp and thick. It's only a mile or so. I went up the steps at the 6th Avenue El on 14th Street instead and waited. And waited.

Anyway, I'm up to 7th Avenue at 33rd street by 7 a.m. Even

with the potted palms, gilt trim and the sparkly chandeliers, the lobby there is a cavern, though nothing like the one in the station across the street. The bellman sees my press badge and just says, "Third floor."

Normally I'd grab some stairs but I'm still only half awake so I take the elevator. The operator gives me a conspiratorial wink when I step in and I see there's a familiar face already at the back, waiting for the door to close. He's with a dame and he dips his head down quick.

I say, "Good morning."

He nods but doesn't speak. I can tell he's worried. But he needn't have been. That's not the kind of stuff I do. And she just offers me a sleepy smile.

When the elevator opens up on three, I can see there's a crowd down the hall. I look for the *Mirror* reporter in among the loiterers and I spot Tommy Sales instead. He's holding up the wall right beside the door to the room in question, where he can get away quick. Tommy's an okay guy if you don't mind that he keeps his brains in a jar on his grandmother's porch so they won't get sullied. Then again, his grandmother owns twenty thousand shares in the Hearst Corporation. And if Barry George sent him out it was because no one else was willing to answer the phone on their half-day off. Of course, I'd been hoping it would be Cass Green covering this one too. I get a big kick out of working with her. She can spin.

But at least with Tommy, you know what you are going to get. Nothing.

All the action was right there on the third floor. No running around necessary. Tommy doesn't even move when he sees me.

I say, "The usual?" feigning boredom over the prospect of taking 4 X 5's of just another bloody cadaver first thing on a Sunday morning. It's always first thing. Murder always happens at night. Saturday night is always special.

He says, "Yeah." This wasn't very convincing. He's outside because the body is inside, and I see he has drawn a picture of Mickey Mouse on his pad.

Now, if it was Cass Green, she would lead me back in the room and say, 'Get me this. Get me that. Get a shot of the so and so.'

So I just went about my business. At least what was left of it to do. The ring of reporters, close like bettors at a cockfight, was still pretty thick for the time of day—probably because of the location. I'll bet half of them never got home last night themselves. All the real fun was uptown these days. But some of the other photographers were already changing out their bulbs and plates and putting the gear away. The quickest of them, like that guy Weegee, would be there and gone. He'd have his pictures developed right out of the trunk of his car and be on the phone in under an hour. Sloppy but fresh. Remember though, it was Sunday morning, and the next edition deadline for me was more than twelve hours away, so there was no rush.

Someone had already pulled a bed sheet over the corpse on the carpet. The word I picked up in the chitchat was that this guy was shot 'in flagrante delicto.' Just a single manicured foot was out there now in the open air for viewing. The cops wouldn't let me close, but the room was one of those big 'Fred Astaire' type suites you usually only see in the movies so there was space to dance around. I got a shot of the naked foot right next to the black brogans of the police sergeant, Hadley Donovan, who was standing close guard over the body. And then the messed-up bed. And the blood spatter on the wall.

The bullet had evidently passed right through an eye and out a soft spot in the back of the guy's head, and the hole in the wall-paper was very neat and uninteresting. No spread to the blood at all. And the blood would register in black and white the same as if it were water. So when it looked like the cops were suddenly about to pack things up and I still didn't have anything worth a damn, I kind of cheated.

I turned my back to the scene and raised my voice to an empty corner of the room.

"Hey! Something just twitched under that bed sheet!"

Hadley bent over in a flash, grabbed an edge and yanked the

sheet off.

At least I got a couple good pictures before he could throw the linen back over the corpse again.

I'd already moved from the spot where I was when I shouted, but the Sergeant was having none of it. He works out of the Tenderloin precinct and they have their own set of rules.

"Was that you, McNeill? Was that you?"

It was better not to lie. It would not go over any better. So I shrugged and smiled innocently.

Hadley says, "I'll have you banished! You hear me! No more shenanigans. You come in late; you take what's left. Hear?"

"Yes, sir."

The corpse had just the one hole in his face. What was left of a face. From the look of the spatter on the wall off to the one side behind, he'd been shot when he was standing right there next to the bed, nearly where the sergeant stood now. At least we were being told he was found right there. The leak of blood on the carpet offered some other ideas.

The Assistant Medical Examiner had already done his initial thing before any of the reporters were allowed through the door. I waited there at the back of the room by an entry closet until the crew from the morgue finally came in, and I managed to get a few more shots of the removal and a stiff arm wagging goodbye from the gurney. Fingerprint powder was on every edge like it was talc in a college locker room. In the developed prints it would make the place look shabby. Couldn't use those. Not for the Hotel Pennsylvania. They were regular advertisers.

The cops had a string tied doorknob to doorknob from the locked doors at either side where the suite could open to the next if they were rented together. That was to keep us birds away from anything they thought was important. I couldn't get close to the bathroom at all. There is always good stuff in a bathroom. Instead, I turned around and looked in the entry closet behind me. The door was closed—a little—but it was one of those folding affairs and just a little nudge pushed it back. I saw a good pair of tan wingtips on the floor. Strawbridge and Clothier, Philadelphia. Size twelves. They looked freshly polished and I figured they'd probably been outside the door earlier. The bellman would know about that. And there was a silk scarf on a hanger—blue paisley—but no overcoat. The scarf was new from Gimbels. No hat. And by the look of the empty closet across the room, with the door already hanging back and a couple of partly pulled drawers on the dresser, no other clothes at all. Then again, most guys don't need much of a wardrobe for a tryst.

According to the sergeant, nothing had been moved since he was discovered by the morning shift. The hotel was booked solid and the stiff had been a last minute check-in early on the evening before. There was a bon voyage party scheduled for the room at noon so he was warned the chambermaid would be there at dawn. He'd assured them he would be gone before 6 a.m. this morning. You could guess they knew what his needs were and there might have been a few extra gratuities involved. He had paid cash, of course. The fact that he was naked now would seem to indicate the object of his last affections had probably been naked at the crucial moment as well and was already on the bed when the shot was fired. And this was exactly the situation as described once more—perhaps even repeated for my particular benefit, in that I was the last one in the door.

Hadley said, "The name he gave was Allen Smith. From Cleveland. But the address is a phony. The 14th Precinct will have a composite sketch available after noon. It would be appreciated if you could run that with your stories so we might get a positive ident- ification sooner than later."

Someone asked, "Any ideas about what might have happened to his duds?"

The sergeant answered that as if he had already said, and was getting weary of it. "Not at the present time."

I wondered then if the Jill had worn them to get out of the hotel incognito.

I asked, "Any other signs from the gun?"

The sergeant took my drift immediately. Guns can leave their own trails.

But again, he said, "That is not established at the present time."

I'm thinking, the victim couldn't have known what was coming. He'd have been moving away from it. Killing him with a single shot might have been a lucky trick, but if the girl was naked on the bed, she must have had the pistol somewhere close.

I got down on my knees and looked under the bed frame.

Detective Jack Barnes works out of Police Headquarters down on Centre Street but is almost always on midtown homicides. I guess it's his beat. He had drifted over in my direction and says to me, "There was a purse under there."

I said, "I figured."

I wondered why they'd failed to mention this fact in the previous rundown and stuck my elbow into the carpet to steady up my camera and take another pic of the vacant spot where the purse was found, with the covered body visible at the back, just for the record.

I asked, "Did it have a maker's mark?"

"Bergdorf Goodman. Bet it cost a week's wages."

I'm thinking, an odd thing to leave, when you're taking everything else.

Barnes is a big lad and was standing so close I couldn't play with the angle for the exposure. That was intentional, I think.

Then he says, "Is Cass here?"

Still on my knees from taking the last shot and looking for anything else I could spot from that vantage point, I give him the look of pity. "No. It's Tommy they sent."

I noticed right then that Tommy was already gone from his post by the door.

Barnes took a big disappointed breath. "Crap. You'd better write it all down then. Tommy won't have a thing when you get back to the paper."

There was some calculation in the tone of his voice. This was doubly funny to me because Jack Barnes himself is the nephew of a police commissioner. He and Tommy are birds of a feather in that department.

I say, "Right. What I already have the pieces for is a Mr. John Doe was in the middle of what he thought was going to be a good time and whoever his lady of the evening was, shot him, maybe before he got to the finish line. Maybe not. He was healthy. Had been. Middle-aged. Balding. Good teeth. Pink skinned with freckles. Red-brown hair—at least what was left of it on the sides. Neatly trimmed." Then I said, "What color was the purse?"

Barnes says, "Black lame."

"Any hair on the sheets?"

"One or two. Black."

"Dyed?"

"Don't know. But they all want to look like Loretta Young now."

"And every guy I know wants to look like Clark Gable."

Barnes says, "We all look alike in the dark." The tone was very knowledgeable. Just like mine was earlier when I spoke to Tommy. But Jack Barnes is probably my age, exactly.

I say, "Maybe. Any guesses about the John?"

He shrugs, "Out of town. Probably some sort of a salesman. The shoes were made by an outfit in Philadelphia. He must have had money for the extras. Toenails clipped. The works. About fifty-five or sixty. Say sixty."

"Anything in the bathroom?"

"Toothbrush."

"When exactly did he check in?"

"Yesterday before dinner, like the Sergeant said." The detective's eyes looked over the scant debris of a relatively clean murder. Then he added, "He had a toupee, but the medical examiner already bagged that up before you got here. The shot could have blown it right off his head."

"And nobody heard it?"

"Not a thing. But there's one of those big jazz bands in the club down below. We figure it must have happened about eight hours ago. Say last night around eleven. The band was in full swing.

No one was in their rooms unless they were sick or had other business to attend to."

Jack Barnes would not give me the time of day if he didn't have a purpose. By the impatient dance in one foot I figured I had already hit the limit of what I could get from him.

I said, "Thanks."

He says, "Tell Cass I was asking."

I gave that a nod, and then went looking for the bellman.

I knew just what I was going to do from there on out. A photo man usually has no part in reporting a story, even though he's supposed to show the story in the pictures if he can. Fair enough. In any case, opportunities to do more than that are few. But I had my job cut out for me if Barry George, or even Stenis, was sending Tommy Sales to cover a homicide. They couldn't be expecting much and this was obviously more than that. The cops were covering up on something here. If I could get that across, I might get George to take more notice. I've been looking to get a crack at my own stories.

It was a chambermaid who had brought the shoes up, polished, around seven the evening before. Mr. Smith was very appreciative and had given her a dime. A real big spender. The news about the tip had traveled on through the night staff, over the two shifts that followed, as a fair warning.

When I was leaving the hotel I saw that the billboard in the lobby blazed with silver and gold letters set out on black felt: 'Benny Goodman and his Orchestra. Exclusive New York Engagement.'

I knew he was there, of course, but I wondered about that sign. I thought Goodman was also playing over at the Paramount Theater as well. Just another proof that you shouldn't believe everything you read.

2. Sunday, March 14, 1937

There is a lot more to tell about that Sunday.

The regular edition of the *Mirror* is hitting the streets by 5 a.m. and George wants his pics in by 10 p.m. the night before, to get a rough on the space, but in this case there was likely to be a need for added info because of Tommy, so I decided to write up the basics I had in my head first thing when I got home—only after I got down a few cups of coffee and something to eat.

When I can, I like to sleep late on Sundays and then go over to Morgy's for the full breakfast. This Sunday, it already being ten o'clock and plenty late enough, and given that I'd been up since it was dark, I went directly to Morgy's from the hotel, a brisk little walk of twenty blocks or so, and sat right down to eat.

Doc had a mug full of black on the counter as I settled on the stool and propped the bag safely between my feet. Then I dumped enough sugar in the cup to raise Doc's left eyebrow and pulled my notebook out of the bag to start writing things up there before anything gets too vague. Got two words out of the pencil: 'black hair.'

Doc says, "Early call?"

I say, "Yeah. Up at the Hotel Penn."

"Murder?"

"Yeah."

"Anybody?"

"John Doe."

Doc threw a few pieces of half-cooked bacon on the griddle.

"Say. You seen Benny Goodman up there yet?"

I lied a little, "Yeah."

"How was it?"

"He was polite."

"What'd ya mean?"

"He was in the elevator."

Doc bowed his head over like he was going to fall asleep on account of my snoozer. So I added, "Yeah. But I really gotta get up there to see him play before he quits town again."

Doc leaned in on his elbows while my eggs sizzled. "My daughter went up to the Paramount to see them. Only cost her two bits. Got up early for the morning show and skipped school. She went nuts. Dancing in the aisles, she says."

"They play loud. Kids like that. That's probably the new guy, Ziggy Elman."

"Him and Krupa and James too. They've all picked it up I hear. My daughter thinks that Harry James is just swell. Southern drawl and all. Plays smooth AND loud. Can't beat that."

"Those Southern boys have an unfair advantage. They don't speak regular American. It's as bad as having a Ronald Colman around."

There is an old fellow in a Greek cap and a navy blue wool peacoat that he has buttoned up even in the warmth of the diner. He's often in the booth at the near corner, and he looks up from his usual study on a mug of coffee and says, "Not the way it used to be. When I was young, the English girls always took a fancy to the Yanks."

By the time that chitchat was done, my eggs and hash were in front of me and I never got the chance to write anything else down.

My apartment on Perry Street is basically two rooms on the third floor front of a narrowish building near 7th. You can tell by the look of it, the real estate there was once an empty backyard to the bigger building around the corner on Seventh that somebody decided to squeeze a little more rent from. But it's cheap. And I like being close to the Village. The subway is a couple blocks away, one way or the other. And so is Morgy's. And Vito's shoe shop. (Vito puts new soles on my Florsheims every few months. With all the walking I do I get an extra year out of them that way). Sal's Produce Market is around the corner on 8th. And Mary's New Laundry. (Don't know where the old one was but I don't think Mary is there anyway. An elderly Chinese woman named Mrs. Lee takes your duds and gives you a tag and in twenty-four hours you have it all back clean and pressed. Pay a dollar extra and you can get them express in four hours or less. Can't beat that.) It's like living in a hotel, but with a little rain between things on some days.

More like a hotel with a hole in the roof.

My bedroom does have a bed. But most of that space is taken up with tables and equipment. The foot of the bed goes right under where the drying rack is. I've blackened the window and use it as my darkroom. Better not to wait in line down at the *Mirror*. True, it stinks like stale vinegar with developing fluid if I haven't washed things down enough, and that happens a lot. So, I tend to sleep in the front room on the couch instead, except when I have to sleep in the daytime and the dark is just what I need. The couch is a fold-up and works just fine. The kitchenette is at the side there. It's good for making coffee and a little oatmeal but that's it. There are only two burners for the gas. The icebox won't freeze anything even if I remember to buy the ice at the corner market on my way in. So I eat out a lot. The toilet works just fine as well, if I don't yank the chain too hard. The tub is good for showers and I have a curtain up in there and use a rubber hose thingamajig for that. The bathroom sink is so small it barely holds my spit when I brush my teeth so I usually wash my face in the kitchen. And that's the picture for that.

I took a shower first when I got home from Morgy's. That washes away a lot more than the grime.

It was not even noon before I was in the dark again, playing with the pictures I'd taken at the hotel. By one o'clock I know I have a few that George would want, but there are a couple that puzzled me and I went back in the room and blew those up to get a better look.

Like I said before, you can see some things in black and white that you don't in living color. It simplifies the contrasts. Then too, when you frame something, it focuses your attention.

Let me make a list.

There was only one pillow on the bed. It was a big bed. A pillow might be good for knocking the sound down on a gun. (Maybe the medical examiner took the other one?)

There was what looked like makeup on the top sheet the cops used to cover the body. I know the difference between makeup and dirt and blood, even in black and white.

There was blood on the bed, right about at the center, and not a splatter. But the guy had fallen over to the floor and bled out there on the carpet.

There were bruises on his body. Like he had been punched in the mid-section. Those marks were very light because the lividity had gathered all the blood that was left at his back, but the hits still showed in the gray.

The guy had a big shvantz. And he was circumcised.

I skipped the subway and walked uptown again, back to the hotel to check with the maid who'd brought the shined shoes to the room the evening before. She was on duty from 2 to 10. I caught her hanging up her coat in the employee room in the basement. She was polite but clearly did not want to talk. She said the police had already spoken to her several times. She didn't know a thing other than that the guy was cheap. I had a buck left in my pocket from breakfast and thought it might help the cause, but she gave me a look like I was a creep for that (though I had the passing thought then that if it were a sawbuck she might have acted differently).

She said, "I just don't know anything."

I said, "I understand. But sometimes people see things they don't know they're seeing."

She says, "Really?"

A hand went to her hip. She was not buying.

I flicked my photographer's press badge on my hat. "Geez. How do you think I make a living? If people saw everything on the first go, I'd be out of a job."

"Why are YOU asking so many questions then? I thought that was a reporter's job?"

"So I'll know what to take a picture of. What do you think?"

Right then I woke up. It already felt like a long day and that was my ready excuse, but a guy ought to notice if he is talking to a good-looking girl. She is an Irish brunette and I have a liking in that category.

I said, "When do you get a break? Maybe we can have a cup of coffee and talk things over then."

She bolted upright with indignation.

"No! All you want is information and I'm not your pigeon!"

She left me after that knockdown. But it was just as well. I had to get out to Brooklyn later for Sunday dinner and I don't need the squeeze on time.

I went up from there to the Bell Captain's stand in the lobby. Best to start at the top, I figure. I asked him if I could get back in the room because I might have left something in there earlier.

He looks at me for the jerk I am.

"What? Your pictures didn't come out?"

"Something like that."

I take the dollar out of my pocket again as a last ditch effort and he raises one eyebrow on me.

He says, "I'm busy," but then takes the dollar with his left hand, steps away behind the front desk and comes back with the key. He does this very surreptitiously. Then says "Don't look for me when you've finished. Just leave the key here on the stand."

My first thought is to question his motives. Looking a gift horse in the mouth is getting to be a habit for me lately. I don't think I am going to last a long time in this business. But a buck doesn't usually buy you diddly-squat in New York and the Bell Captain knew the value of a buck.

Guess who it is in the elevator again. He dips his head a little but there is suspicion in his eyes. There is no dame with him this time.

I say 'Hello' again, and try to sound like an old friend.

In the room, the sheets were off the bed, and the one pillow lay naked on top. Oddly, the room still had the string from side to side between the doorknobs to the adjacent suites at either side. So I duck under that, step over the bloodstain and peek into the bathroom. It looked clean. But there was a faint ring of something dark around the drain in the sink. My thumbnail picks it right up. I could not get a good shot on it though, with the camera, not with all the white porcelain, so I went on to the next thing.

I pulled the desk chair over and stood on that to get an angle down from where the bullet went into the wall. The cops had already reamed the lead out of the hole, but I thought the close spatter had an interesting aspect to it. It looked more like it had been tossed up on there than blasted. I took a shot of that. Looking back down at the bed, I could see the chalk and tape on the carpet where someone had roughly tried to mark the position of the body. But that was all wrong too. The guy was supposedly on his back when he was found. Just like we saw him. If he was shot in the face where he supposedly stood by the bed, he would have belly-flopped. And sure, he might have made an involuntary pirouette, or bounced off the mattress. That would account for the blood on the sheets, maybe. But he was likely dead when he hit the floor. He didn't roll over on his own.

Of course, the medical examiner might have moved the body a little. But I figured that someone had pulled the feet around. That would account for the space, about six inches, between where his body had been when I was there before and the leak of blood out the back of his head. The blood looked dull and black now on that brown carpet. I made a bet to myself that he had just come out of the bathroom when he was shot. I took another pic of the area for good measure, so to speak.

And then, in walks Detective Barnes.

Of course, the Bell Captain had already given me my excuse.

The detective says, "What are you doing here?"

I say, "I was a little rushed before, because I got here late. I had my settings wrong. Nothing came out."

He's not buying that either.

"Right. How did you get the key?"

"I asked for it."

He rolls his eyes like a girl. "Jesus Christ. They were told not to give that out."

I shrugged. "Change of shifts. New guy probably didn't even know."

I kept my own counsel concerning the discrepancies. Jack Barnes wasn't necessarily the one to know about those in any case and he wouldn't be telling me his secrets.

But I had one last thing on my agenda before I left, so I held my camera up like I was going to take another picture from the other wall and instead I opened the window. It came right up with one hand. Good hotels are like that.

Barnes says, "What are you doing?"

I say, "I needed some air. Sorry."

What I saw was only about a seven or eight-foot drop to the inner roof that covered part of the main floor of what they call the 'Madhattan Room,' just below. I figured Benny and his boys would have been pretty damn loud from there. Like a private concert.

I don't think it's pride that makes me say my mom and dad are an unlikely couple. Just the facts of the matter.

Before she was a wife, and a mother, and a cook, Dorothy Ellen Dean was a graduate of Mills College, in Oakland, California, and the daughter of a professor and lawyer who'd been a judge. She's quick tempered and opinionated. She is tall, at least six feet, but so was her mother, and her father was taller still. And because she is not a small woman, when her temper flares, there is an immediate sense of danger. Her hand on my backside is well and fairly remembered. Her voice can go stone cold as easily as it sings a song. She can divide and multiply numbers in her head faster than I can calculate on paper, and a common sound in our house when I was growing up was something like my dad's recent plaintive request, 'Dory. They sell those pens by the gross. They weigh about an ounce apiece. What'll it cost us if they want fourteen cents each and the freight is three cents to the pound.'

Daniel James McNeill is a sailor. He has always billed himself that way. My mom says 'He only calls me Dory because it reminds him of a little boat.' He's the second son of a failed New Hampshire apple farmer and went to sea at an early age, only to come ashore again for good cause. While on leave, he'd met a young girl in Oakland, California, that he could not get out of his mind. He is not six feet tall, but what there is of him is mostly brawn. And this appearance has always been at odds to the fact that for many years now he has sold stationery in a little shop in Manhattan and contented himself with that, though he's never looked the part.

Mom always has Sunday dinner ready at four o'clock. It's up to me these days to make it home to Sterling Place, and I wasn't going to be late for it.

My older sister Kate is married and living in Chicago. My younger sister Esther is away at school in Boston. My older brother Ben is a wholesale buyer for Dad and about a dozen other shops and spends most of his time in Europe (though I suspect that has something more to do with a girl). Ben even has a flat in London, and if I can save a couple hundred bucks, I'll catch a freighter and get over there to stay with him someday, sooner than later. My little brother, Erik, is in the Merchant Marine like my dad once was. He's on a ship somewhere in the Pacific, and he's not good about writing.

I'm home just in time. This is the way that looks.

The table is a long one. It's called a 'trestle' type and it is fairly battered from surviving our childhood, so mom always has it covered with tablecloths. It seats twelve; fourteen in a pinch when Kate and her husband come to visit with their kids, Dorothy and Dan. Right now several chairs are pulled back so we can all breathe easier.

The buffet is set out with a lamb roast, carrots and potatoes, a boatload of gravy, and a fresh loaf of bread. Mr. Oliphant is piling it up on his plate like it's his last meal. He's only a bank teller at Brooklyn Savings and Loan, but he's fatter than a bank president and has the neat little mustache to match.

Stacy White, who is contradictorily very black, and her son Gary, have already served themselves and are sitting down at the other end of the table from Dad and Mom. Stacy helps mom and several others in the neighborhood with the housekeeping. Her chair is next to Mr. Oliphant's at that end and because she's a very thin woman, the contrast with Mr. Oliphant when he finally sits down is more dramatic than a matter of skin color. Her boy, Gary, is a husky lad, just turned nine now and has grown several inches in the past week.

Mrs. Tisdale, sits next to Gary. She is a remarkably petite woman, and an assistant in the children's section at the Brooklyn Public Library. I wonder how often she's mistaken for one of her customers. I calculate that by next week, Gary will be just about as tall as she is.

Across from Mrs. Tisdale would be Norman Jenks, but he is absent—perhaps because he is late again with his rent. Mr. Jenks is an unpleasant man, large headed, but narrow faced, who is often between jobs but never lacking an opinion about work.

Donald Clurman sits in the open chair between Mom and Mrs. Tisdale. He is also not there this day, but when he is, he's generally wearing the same dark blue conductor's jacket he wears at work. He'd wear his cap to the table if he could. He is very bald. He is employed by the Long Island Railroad and his schedule changes week to week, which is the reason for his divorce, as he'll readily say. But there may be other reasons. He's a very picky fellow. And his favorite target at dinner is usually Mr. Oliphant, who sits across from him.

Mrs. Tisdale has finished serving herself, and is very enthusiastically talking to my dad about the drummer Chick Webb and his band when I come in the door. Dad is already at the table because Mom always gives him his plate first, but everyone else serves themselves from the buffet.

Dad just nods at Mrs. Tisdale. He looks more depressed than I can remember. He perked up a little when I came in, but he and

Mom and I had all been over to Jerry's funeral on Staten Island the day before and Dad doesn't look much better than he did then. When I got back in the room from washing up, I figured I should try to keep on the lighter subject.

"I saw Benny Goodman today."

He says, "Yeah?" His voice is totally flat.

Dad likes Benny Goodman. He's liked him since the days of Red Nichols and the Five Pennies. I think Dad's one of the few guys his age who really appreciates the music.

Mrs. Tisdale immediately says, "Oh, I think Chick Webb is much better."

And I have an instant memory of my mom saying that Mrs. Tisdale's husband divorced her because she liked to argue more than do anything else. I can believe it. Mom once hoped something might get started between Mr. Jenks and Mrs. Tisdale, but I'm pretty sure those thoughts are over. That would be two cats in a bag, as they say.

Stacy chips in, "Mr. Ellington has always been more to my taste. I met their singer, Ivie Anderson, once. She was very kind."

Stacy has a Southern lilt to her voice and speaks in such a soft manner that it's hard to believe she is disagreeing.

Mrs. Tisdale insists, "But Chick is the best," just before filling her small mouth with several large pieces of carrot.

I say to Dad, "Doc, over at Morgy's, says that what you read in the paper about Goodman at the Paramount is true. Doc's own daughter was there. They were dancing in the aisles."

Dad says, "Probably were."

Mrs. Tisdale says, "I danced nearly non-stop at the Savoy the other night. My boyfriend, Jack, just loves to dance. That's why we went. Chick Webb is just the best."

Mom rolls her eyes. She is tougher than Dad is, and has less patience. Dad is more the deliberate type. Mom sits next to him at that end and is generally better at conducting the table conversation in friendly channels. But I think she has tired of Mrs. Tisdale over the past year.

Mom says, "Mr. Goodman isn't married, is he?"

Dad says, "No, Dory, I don't think so."

She asks, "Who's the woman that sings with him on the radio?"

He says, "That would be Helen Ward."

"In the paper, didn't they say he was going to marry her?"

Dad doesn't answer. He probably hadn't heard. To his mind, the papers are good for the sports pages and the comics.

I say, "I guess, he's a busy guy."

Dad finally adds, "Why is he going to marry her when he can have his pick on any other day?"

My mom stares at him. This is clearly a set-up. She only raised the subject because she knows he'll likely have a thought about it. It might get him talking.

I say, "He was with a very good looking young woman this morning when I saw him at the hotel. But it wasn't Helen Ward."

Mom clucks her tongue. Mrs. Tisdale smiles.

Dad says, "See. What did I tell you?" But Dad's no fool, and knows when he's being manipulated. He always strikes back. He turns to me to say, "See, the problem is, your Mr. Goodman just hasn't found the right one yet. When he finds her, it'll be like it was when I first saw your mother. There won't be any other girl that'll do after that."

He gave Mom only the slightest glance over his next bite of lamb.

She rolled her eyes again. I thought of Detective Barnes doing the same thing. Mom is more convincing at it. But she was not going to best Dad for blarney. She knows that. She just blows him a kiss across the palm of her hand instead, and went back to eating.

Stacy had just instructed her son again about switching hands when he uses his knife and fork. She watched him now as he practiced with a deliberate clumsiness. He knows that eyes are on him. The temporary quiet however must have brought other thoughts to Mom's mind. She asked, "So how is your star reporter?"

There is no question who she was talking about. Dad's eye came up over his next forkful again in expectation of my answer.

This caught Mrs. Tisdale's attention too. Mr. Oliphant was busy eating. Gary was fumbling and Stacy demonstrated once more, but I had the sense that she was listening as well.

I said, "She's fine."

Dad says, "You ask her out yet?"

"No."

"Why not?"

"I will. At least, I'll ask. She might have other things going."

Mom chips in, "YOU have other things going. You better get going or else someone else will."

"Yes, Ma'am."

She picks up on everything. I guess they both do, but Dad keeps most of his observations to himself. Mom is not so shy. Then again, that's probably how she got Dad.

But Stacy chimes in, "And that's the truth!"

I'd spent most of a Wednesday trailing behind Cass back in January and when I came over for dinner the Sunday after, I said a little too much about her. I was rather smitten, you might say. But I really didn't know anything about Cass then. She was new. Someone in the Hearst organization had spotted her over at the *Daily News* and thought her talents were being wasted. We were in need of another sob sister on our side. They can get away with things a guy can't.

That had been a big week for me. Seeing that I was full of the moment then, Dad had what he thought was a good remedy. "Write it up," he said. But he was not one to talk. He had never written down any of his own adventures. He was right, though. I'd figured before then that it was all in the pictures, but I was beginning to see that it wasn't. So that was the first assignment I tried writing anything about. And most of that was about Cass.

After dinner I took my bag and the latest haul of accumulated pics downstairs to the 'dark room' in the cellar. Why I was keeping them is the question. Even for me. But I have some ideas in the back of my head.

Funny thing about that, even with a few years of accumulated negatives and prints filed away on the narrow shelves that my dad has built down there in his spare time, that one corner still looks bigger than my entire bedroom at Perry Street.

Dad had set me up in the cellar there when I was twelve years old, shortly after I came home from the movies one day gushing over the short travelogue they had shown along with a Douglas Fairbanks feature. That was one of the very first 'Osa and Johnson' adventures to Africa, I think. What inspired Dad to believe I would be happy then with the output of a Kodak 3-A 'Autographic folding pocket camera with range finder' is known only to him. I suspect he wanted one himself. Maybe wished he had one in the old days, just like he regrets he never wrote anything down. The empty box for the camera is still on top of the shelves down there where I threw it in my excitement many years ago and the yellow catches the light first thing when you flick the switch at the top of the stairs. The camera itself is still hanging from the strap over above the table and trays.

I glanced up toward the box and caught a pair of eyes looking down at me through the banister on the stair.

Gary is shy. His mother keeps him indoors too much. But she's worried about what can happen to him on the street, I think. And she's right enough about that. There aren't many negro children in the neighborhood. A few more beyond Atlantic Avenue.

I say, "What's up?"

He says, "Nothin'"

Just about what I would have said at his age.

I was rushed so I took the lot of loose pics I'd accumulated over the past week out from my bag in a heap and didn't file anything away. And the latest of those were copies of the pictures I'd taken just that morning at the Hotel Penn. They were on top so they wouldn't get pressed together and I laid those aside loose then on the rack just in case they needed a little more time to dry.

Gary says, "Is that a dead man?"

I say, "Yes sir. Someone I had to take a picture of today."

Below the counter where my old developing trays are

stacked, there are four or five boxes of the National Geographic magazine. They are always butting at my knees when I work there. So I get a bright idea.

"You had a birthday on Wednesday, right?"

"Yes, sir."

I kicked at the boxes.

"I was thinking, these are going to waste under here. Your mother says it would be fine if I gave to them to you. They're yours if you want them. And if not, you can just leave them back under here."

He is off the stairs and pulling at the boxes before I can bend over to help.

I was on the subway home when I got to thinking about all of that part again.

Some guys think they grow up the day they seduce some foolish lass for the first time. Others think it's simply when they leave home for good. I even knew of a couple of fellows who used to believe they really became men the day they killed some other poor schlub—though they didn't get to enjoy the matter of their supposed manhood for long. They both got the benefit of four-bits of Con Edison's best, up at Sing Sing shortly thereafter.

But for myself, I think I grew up a whole lot just this past January. Better late than never. Starting around that January 13th. Which was a Wednesday.

That's the morning I was up and over on the piers at 32nd Street on the West Side taking pictures for Cass. I figured I had outdone myself with those. In the background, one behemoth of an ocean liner, the *Warren G. Harding*, was just sitting there waiting to leave for the warmer waters of the Bahamas. On our left, the shadow of the new elevated highway laid down some nice contrast.

Sadly, that job was another suicide too, but the light that day was nearly perfect and I hadn't used a flash, even for fill. A risky thing. A matter of judgment. You just have to keep the camera steady for long enough and make a good guess. There was not going to be any posing for the press there. Those guys doing the wet work were already cold enough. And the body came up in the net with the blue evening dress wrapped tight around her legs and the top of it down around her waist, her loose hair had spread across her face and bare chest, and she looked every bit like a Hollywood mermaid, only stiff.

I took half a dozen sides by hanging out over one of the pilings away from the other guys and planting the camera down hard in a fresh deposit of seagull mush. I was very proud of myself over that. I got all those layers into the shot. The hard edge of black from the shadow of the highway—like a knife. For a little subtlety, the dead President's name right there over the girl's tilted head was even offering the warm contrast of imagined Caribbean waters for those who follow the comings and goings of the steam ships and can read between the lines.

I figure I'm the genius now. Gershwin is a genius. Wilder is a genius. Welles is a genius. If everybody else can be a genius, why can't I be one too. Orson Welles isn't any older than me and the paper gave whole pages to him just because he did Shakespeare in blackface. (If I was Paul Robeson I wouldn't be particularly happy with that, mind you). Besides, Eddie Cantor does just about anything in blackface and they don't call him a genius—just a comedian.

So I open the *Mirror* the next day, hoping to see my best shots, and first thing I see instead is that Martin Johnson is dead. His plane crashed in California. And Osa was in the hospital.

To me, this was like a member of the family had died. I was even doing the work I was because of them. I'd been following their careers ever since that first short movie I'd seen as a kid. They were heroes to me, more than Lindbergh or Post, or Hughes. Martin Johnson might be criticized for being a promoter, which he was, but he had something to promote. He had the goods. And he was a great cameraman. People don't understand the difficulty of the shots he got under the worst conditions. And Osa was with him all the way, though she did most the writing. If he hadn't had the sense to make the most out of what he did, I might still be sitting on my thumbs at home. Likely. Or working in a stationery shop on Sixth Avenue. It put things in perspective.

Now, to be fair, my dad had done his own adventures when he was young. He'd been around the world a dozen times in the Merchant Marine. Killed pirates. Picked coconuts out of a tree with a shotgun. And plenty he wouldn't talk about.

But the thing of it was, I'd taken those pictures without the flash that day for another reason. I was showing off. Of course. That was the day I first got to work with Cass Green.

And she'd stood right there on the pier that January day in a stiff wind and watched me and said, "If this doesn't work, you better know how to swim."

And she meant it.

3. Sunday, March 14, 1937

But this Sunday was not about to end with dinner and a snooze.

When I got back to the paper at 6:30 p.m., I wasn't surprised that The Boss was still out. I know he likes the quality of the cigar smoke at the Algonquin Hotel so I went on over to West 44th Street to talk to him there.

This was risky. His dinnertime was usually off-limits. But he had said at least a hundred times that initiative was the thing he wanted from all of us. That, and to use our heads.

On the way, I detoured over to the Hotel Penn to see the chambermaid again before her shift was up. Maybe she had softened a bit. And I'd already pulled a larger bill from my stash at the apartment just in case.

I asked for her at the front desk when I saw that the Bell Captain's stand was empty. The clerk there disappears and comes back with the assistant manager.

This is a roly-poly fellow with a stiff collar and a bow tie and he says, "Molly's not available," before I can open my mouth.

I say, "Her shift isn't over yet."

He says, "We have instructed her not to talk to the press. Or you. You're just a photographer, am I correct?"

I say, "No. Not just a photographer. I am the best."

And then, from behind me, I hear, "Hey Pops."

I turn and Benny Goodman is standing right there.

He says, " So, is the best photographer in the world finally going to take my damn picture?" He winks. I think he is thanking me for not snapping that shot earlier.

I open my bag and take out the beast. It's set. It's always set. That's rule number one. All I have to do is back up ten feet, press the switch on the flash and hit the shutter. Goodman smiles. He's got a funny smile. All reserve. I'm done in thirty seconds. Right there in the lobby at the Hotel Pennsylvania in the midst of the potted palms and marble.

He shook my hand then and says, "Send me a copy."

I had typed up my report, added a couple of thoughts by hand in the margin, and my idea was to give that to Barry George there at the Algonquin, along with the prints I'd made. Otherwise he wouldn't see them until nine or ten or so and that would be pretty late to change directions. Something was going on with the cops and I figure he ought to be made aware of that before he decides on how to handle it.

The dining room there is smaller than you'd think, for all you hear about it. And the tables are not round. The Boss had his back to the far wall and saw me coming across the dining room from the door. There were several familiar faces at the table with him but I tried to keep my focus. I needed to make my case quick and get away.

I squeezed in there between two other tables and managed to get an eyeful down the decolletage of a woman I was sure I knew from the movies, and then put the manila envelope right in his hand.

He didn't speak. He is a plain-faced man of medium height and, sitting at a table, not the first you would take note of. He often speaks without any inflection at all.

I said, "Hi sir. I thought you might want to see this before it got too late. I'll be at the office if you need me," and started to move away.

Without hesitation, he asks, "Did the Empire State building collapse?"

I turn back. "No, sir, it—"

"Did David Rockefeller shoot Mr. LaGuardia?"

"No. Not yet."

With no change of tone he says, "Well then, no, I don't think I will be needing your services. Not now or later. Not at all. Not ever again."

You'd think that would be a blow, but he had fired me several times before.

I just nodded and said, "Yes, sir. Good night sir."

The lady with the fine bust beneath her low cut dress was sitting just behind me there, and given that everyone within a dozen feet had quieted down to find out what the emergency was, she had heard this exchange. She giggled.

I went back to the paper anyway. Just in case he changed his mind. Besides, I was hoping to see someone else.

Cass was at her desk. This is not a common sight. She has a way of being busy, even on Sunday night, but she was there and she saw me immediately when I came in from the elevators and her face was not nearly as severe as Barry George's had been as I came across the floor. With no 'bulldog' on a Sunday, about half the crew was still busy wrapping up and the noise from the typewriters and the chitchat was considerable. My desk isn't near hers but given that she was doing the looking, I took the beeline.

She waited until I was right beside her desk, like a schoolboy called to the teacher.

She says, "Wha'da ya got?"

"A murder over at the Hotel Penn."

"So I heard."

Now I want to know, "What did you hear?"

"A hooker and a salesman," she says.

I give that the shake-off, "No. I'll bet the guy's a politician. Something like that. Washington, maybe. It was a flat-out murder."

"You think? Why?"

I pulled the folded carbon copies of my report to George from my jacket along with a couple of extra 4x5s I'd made to leave in Brooklyn, but then had second thoughts about.

She handed me the hard copy that Tommy had submitted on the murder, and started in reading mine.

Tommy had almost word for word everything Sergeant Hadley had said. At least his short hand is that good.

When she finished reading mine she said, "You have any second sources?"

I say, "Not one. Chambermaid is still out of bounds an hour ago. And that makes it clear that they're hiding something. I was hoping I could get George to run the story with a few more open ends and then give someone else a chance to work on it."

"Like me, maybe?"

"Do you think he'd let you? He just fired me for disturbing his dinner."

That got a smile.

"Yeah. One way or the other. But that's a good sign. You ought to get fired at least once a month to keep things fresh."

I am still standing there by her desk and she has an eye on me and I am feeling uncomfortable.

She says, "Did ya eat yet?"

"It's Sunday. I went home to Brooklyn."

"Too bad."

"But I skipped dessert. Lets go get something. Boss won't be here for another hour."

Her plan was to write the report up from my notes the way I wanted, with all the loose ends attached, and give that to George as an alternative to Tommy's copy work. We went over everything I had done pretty thoroughly and she wrote while I talked. We were back at the paper by nine and she had the thing typed out by 9:15, and in walks George. He sees me standing there right off, but he stops at half a dozen desks along the way and chats with one guy or another.

Let me say something more about Mr. George.

On those rare occasions when his temper flares, his favorite phrase is, "What do you think, I got a glass eye? I can see right

through you." But he does not have a glass eye. His most distinguishing characteristic is a lack of distinguishing characteristics. He
is a plain man of the sort you'll see sometimes in court. The one who
gets away with murder because no one can be absolutely sure of his
appearance, which is always neat; he is neither fat nor thin, short or
tall; his hair is thinning but he is not bald and the color of the hair he
combs straight back with an adequate application of Brylcreem each
day (you know it's Brylcreem because you can smell it) is the color
of tree bark, not brown, nor gray.

Some personal notes of Barry George's biography that I have
collected unintentionally, mostly by being in the wrong place at the
wrong time, are that he is 42 years old and he is of Scots-Irish
extraction. Evidently the extraction was painful. He is married, and
his wife lives in Port Washington. He has no children. He drives
home most nights at about 2 a.m. and returns to work before noon.
He takes one day off per week but not always the same day. He was
a reporter and sports editor at the *Post-Dispatch* in St. Louis for
many years before he came to New York.

While we're waiting, I ask Cass, "Have you ever thought of
being a travel writer?"

She had no quick answer. The half a minute of silence was
amazing. I could see the confusion in her eyes as she tries to figure
my angle. She has very pretty brown eyes.

"Why did you ask?"

"I was just thinking. It would be nice to go places."

Then she says, "Well, now's your chance. The Boss doesn't
look too forgiving."

George is suddenly there, in front of her desk and looking
down directly at her and ignoring me.

He says, "Wha' da ya got?"

She says "I got the piece on the priest up in Harlem who's
taking care of all those dogs while his parishioners are at work." She
hands him about 600 words on three sheets. "And I have a re-write
on the John Doe story from the Hotel Penn."

George says, "Why?"

Now, Cass usually has things set down in her head before she speaks. Not like me.

She says, "The *Daily News* is going to run with the same copy Tommy handed in. Word for word. You know that. It's just what the cops dished out at the scene. I didn't think you'd want that stuff. And a little added mystery might sell a few more papers."

George jerks his head around like something else had happened.

"What? Did I walk into the *Black Mask* office by mistake? This is a newspaper."

"I thought the questions were part of the news."

He grimaces in faux pain. "Then they've got a school for you up at Columbia. Down here we run a tabloid."

She asks, "Did you read Hugh's report?"

Now, I note, George had not looked over at me yet. I was still just three feet away.

"Hugh? You mean the photographer that used to work here?"

She says, "The same." She has a tone in her voice that makes me smile.

He says, "Yeah, I read it. That's just a lot of in one innuendo and out the other. Though some of the pictures will do."

She asks, "You want to read what I wrote?"

"No. I want to put the paper to bed and then myself, in that order."

He turned then and walked on back to his office.

Cass said, "Must have been something he ate. He'll feel better in the morning."

That was when I finally headed on home.

I had not been back in my apartment before midnight in months. Not since I was sick with pneumonia before Christmas. When I'm about a block away, still on the far side of Seventh, I can see down Perry Street to the entrance to my building. There is no light hitting the stoop from the lobby. My eyes go up to the third floor. There's a light on in my front room.

What I should have done is call the cops right then. Probably. There is a phone booth way back by the subway exit on 14th. But if I was being burglarized the police wouldn't get there for half an hour and then just to make a report.

Instead, I walked on and crossed over to the big building on the corner.

They told me when I started my job that my press card opens doors. And it does. You slip that stiff cellulose ticket in the jamb break right at the lock latch and about half the time, voila! I went up to the roof from there, breathing pretty heavily because I was already tired from the day but the adrenaline was in my legs.

The big building is one floor higher but the fire escape goes right down to the adjoining roof and I used my pocketknife to lift the latch and open the fire door to the stairwell in my own building.

I was at my own door in about three minutes and just at the time the guy inside comes out. In his left hand he's holding a large paper market bag stuffed to the top. All I have now is the pocket-knife. He sees me with an "Ah!"

A big guy, he grabs inside his coat with his right hand and I don't want to know what he has to show me. I put a fist in his face and kicked him in the balls. He tumbles right down the stairs from there all the way to the second floor. He was out cold immediately, not from my punch, but from hitting the tiles with his head. The paper bag he was carrying, filled with my pictures and negatives, had broken apart and they fluttered down through the air behind him.

Then I went inside and called the police.

But they were there in thirty seconds. Like they were already somewhere on the block. And they arrested me before they even had their friend sitting up.

I think that about covers everything that happened on my day off. At least what I can think of.

By daylight, the Charles Street Police Station is a grand affair. Granite columns and all. I hear that Teddy Roosevelt built it. But the interior is naturally dark. The cells are like closets. Small closets. And there is a hole in the corner of each cell where you can pee or whatever, if the need arises. That is just about where my nose was when I woke up on the floor in the wee hours, Monday, to nature's smelling salts.

I know that they give you a basin of water and a bit of soap to wash up with and you are supposed to pour what remains down that little hole in the floor to help with the odor, but I think the last occupants of this particular cell had probably swallowed their water instead.

The right side of my face had taken some abuse and didn't want to be touched. I ran my tongue over my teeth and was happy at the complete findings. One eye was in the process of swelling shut but I could still see a bit out of that for the moment. Both arms were sore from being twisted around behind my back. One hand had been stepped on and had the tread mark from a shoe to prove it. I sat back on a bunk that was not quite six feet long. I'm 6' 2". But then again, as tired as I was, I didn't want to sleep.

First thing I said out loud was, "I gotta call my paper."

Now this choice was deliberate. Maybe they didn't know I worked for the *Mirror*, though that was unlikely, but it made the point that I was someone with a connection to an organization that they had to accord a little respect. Besides, I don't have a lawyer.

I said this half a dozen times into the half-dark of the walk-way between me and the cell across. I got a few replies from other cells that are unprintable but amounted to telling me to use my newspaper to stuff my mouth after I had taken care of some other business with it. What I heard in return, besides the aforementioned recommendations, were several snores, and the distant hubbub from the street.

I sat back on the bunk again and contemplated my future. But thankfully, not for long.

A cop in uniform came and opened the door, reached in without stepping any farther into the cell than necessary, grabbed an arm, and hauled me out, dragging me stumbling toward the better illuminated doorframe ahead. Thoughts of another beating entered my brain. Instead, through my good eye I quickly saw the unhappy face of The Boss standing out in the middle of the floor by the main desk.

The cop dragging me along leaves me catching my balance in front of Barry George and says only, "He resisted arrest. We had to quiet him down."

My boss looks away from me in disgust and says to the cop, "Where's the camera?"

Now, that should have been his first concern. Granted. Those things cost a couple hundred bucks.

Another flatfoot rummages around in the accumulated crap behind a side desk and comes out with it, dangling at the end of the strap along with my empty bag, my Florsheims tied together by the laces, my key chain, and my belt.

George says, "Where is the rest of his stuff?"

The first cop says. "That's all there is."

So I knew immediately that I was out the ten bucks from my stash, and my pocket knife, and my new wallet from Christmas, and a swell picture of Benny Goodman.

The Boss waited impatiently, but silently, for me to get the knot out of the laces and get my shoes on before I followed him out. I have been in these situations before, but not on the receiving end. I have only been the observer. I know there is nothing to say.

George was driving a company car from the *Mirror.* I climbed in.

As soon as I get the door shut he says, "You are still fired. Until further notice. You want to go home to Brooklyn or to your own place?"

The odd nature of the statement went uncommented upon by me.

"My place. I don't need my dad seeing this. He'll come down here with his shotgun and get himself killed."

George nodded, "Okay. I suspect your dad knows the score. But you should know that your place is a mess. I saw it."

"How?"

"The police radio said you'd been arrested there. That's how."

"You have a radio?" I looked under the dashboard.

"The one in the wire room. Kelly heard it and told Cass. She told me."

I think I said, "Crap!"

Everyone at the paper would know. Given the perversity of the place, I'd have to buy them all drinks for saving my ass.

Barry George answered, "Watch your mouth."

He had me home to Perry Street in five minutes.

I said, "Thanks," and eased my sore parts out. Every joint of me was feeling it now.

I was already out of the car when he reached into the back-seat and lifted the camera and the bag into the air by the straps and said, "You'll need this."

When I got upstairs, I could hear that there was someone in my apartment. But the radio was on and I jumped to the conclusion that if the cops had come back they would probably have been a little more quiet about it.

I opened the door up to a very nice picture.

Cass was standing there with a broom and a dustpan. She was sweeping up the coffee grounds from the overturned garbage can.

She said, "Holy cow!"

I thought for a split second she was actually going to give me a kiss when she dropped the broom and came right to me, but instead she took my face in her hands and gave it a good looking over. I could smell something like vanilla. I don't cook so I was pretty sure it was whatever perfume she was using. Her hands were a lot softer than I thought they would be. And I also noted that, up close—because this was about as close as I had ever been to her—and through just one eye, she looked even better than she ever did before, which was considerable.

She went to the icebox then and took out the tray with the remaining lump of ice from what I had bought a couple days before and used the pick on that with a vengeance until she had enough chips to fill up a wash cloth and very neatly pinned the corners with a safety pin from a drawer in the counter where I keep my odd stuff. She apparently already knew where things were as well as I did.

I sat on the folding couch and watched all of this with some amazement at first, letting her do the talking.

"I came over with The Boss. He didn't really want me with him going to the Station so I stayed here because the cops had left the place in such a mess. I think it's at least a little better now." She scanned the accumulation of debris she had put together on the table nearby. "I guess you better sort that out tomorrow." Then she looked toward the bedroom door. "Your bedroom is hopeless. They turned the bed over and all the trays. I guess the trays were empty, thank goodness. But it still stinks in there."

"It always does. I usually keep the door closed."

"Where do you sleep?"

"Here," I patted the couch.

At that point she had the cloth ready and came over and pressed it as gently as she could. Still, it seemed an appropriate moment to complain.

I gave her an, "Ouch!"

She said, "Don't be a baby. Hold this."

What I got to hold for just a moment was her hand, which was still on top of the cloth.

I said, "Thanks."

She shook her head at me.

"This is all my fault. I should have been at the hotel this morning."

It was after midnight but I didn't correct that. The day had been long enough.

I said, "You looked a little tired earlier. You probably needed the time off."

"Well, that was it, wasn't it? You know, I was giving a lot of thought yesterday to quitting."

"Why?"

"Because of this!" Her arms spread out at the apartment around us. "Because everything is so cockeyed and wrong. Everything is a mess! And because I'm not really doing anything about it."

She sat down hard in my one wooden chair by the table, with all the mess she had picked up for me piled right there beside her. Suddenly she looked rather dejected.

I said, "What happened? What got you so down? The priest with all the cats?"

It was a feeble attempt at humor.

She ignored that. "Dogs! No. Do you remember that girl in the blue dress they pulled from the water that day over by the docks?"

"The mermaid?"

"Yes. Her name was Florence Roberts. She was from Queens. She worked at Macy's as a salesgirl in the toiletries department."

"I read your story."

"What was left of it, after George pulled out anything that told the truth."

"What was that? What was the truth?"

"She was pregnant. The father was more than likely the floor manager at the store. He's a real slime bag. And she was an only daughter. She was the sole support at home. Her father had worked at the sewer department. He was killed in an accident. Her mother is an invalid. And she was devoted to her mother. That was why she hadn't married. But you saw her. And she was pregnant. And she was a Catholic. I was the one who found the paper bag that she'd left over on the pier. It had her coat in it and a note to give the coat to her mother. The dress was what she had worn to her high school prom. The best thing she ever owned. So, then I went on to Macy's and talked to the floor manger. And he already knew she was pregnant! I'll bet you a week's pay she told him and he refused to help. The store office said she had been fired the previous Friday."

I said, "Now, that's a story. Why didn't George use it?"

"Macy's advertises. That's why. You know . . ."

"Right."

Then she says, "Though, you know, I was thinking that you got it right. In that picture of the drowned girl with that big luxury ship there in the background. Why did she go all the way over there wearing her best blue dress? It seemed to me that she was looking at that ship and thinking about the life she'd wished for herself before she jumped. The one she'd never have."

"Lost dreams."

Cass nodded and caught a breath. "And then I went to the funeral a couple days ago over at Linden Hill for that young lawyer, Sam Schechner. The one who supposedly hung himself. I spoke to the father again. And the mother. And his brother. There was quite a lot of family there. You know they're Jewish right off. Religious. Very close. And the father cried right in front of me again. He couldn't stop himself. It was like everything he had ever worked for was lost. But the one thing they were all very positive about was that Sam could not have committed suicide. That was not in his nature."

The ice was sending a sharp pain from my cheek to my brain. I tried to keep my head on the more important subject.

"What do you want to do? You think there's more of a story there? Maybe something about what can drive someone to do a thing like that, especially when they're otherwise so unlikely for it?"

She said, "George isn't interested."

Then she looked at me for almost half a minute in silence. In spite of the pain I pressed the cloth a little tighter to my cheek as some defense against her scrutiny. I didn't want to ask.

She answered my silent question anyway. "Because, just another suicide won't sell papers. But there was something else to it, Hugh." She paused again. Whatever the matter was, the reluctance was pretty visible. And finally she says, "Did you know that I was Jewish?"

This fact had never entered my mind. There was no cause for it to. She never even took Saturdays off—except yesterday. Though pretty clearly, she hadn't been practicing that faith recently. Not that I was aware of, and it was clear enough she had been affected by the religious service she'd attended.

"Did the funeral bring back some memories?"

"No. No. I wasn't raised as a Jew. My father's name was Greenfeld. He left Poland when he was still a boy. He changed his own name at Ellis Island because he didn't want to be a Jew. He wanted to be an American. He liked to say he had more faith in Joseph Conrad than he had in any Rabbi he ever met. And my mother—she was a schoolteacher. Being Jewish wasn't really a part of the culture she knew as a girl either. Her father owned a shoe store in Cleveland."

I tried to make something more positive out of it.

"We have that in common, then. My dad doesn't read much, but he reads Conrad."

Thankfully, she ignored this comment too.

She says, "But being there with those people the other day was an odd feeling. With all the weeping and unhappiness for Samuel Schechner's death, it felt like I belonged there."

I said the obvious. "Then maybe you did."

Her reaction to that was sudden.

"What?"

I said, "What you felt is as true as what you know."

She looked oddly skeptical at my simple statement of fact.

"That doesn't say much for reason, does it?"

I suspected she knew a lot more about this sort of thing than I did. I just laid out all I had then.

"Sure. From what little we know. We do our best. But I've been listening to Hendrik van Loon on the radio. He says mankind is just at the beginning. Just starting to sort things out. I guess there's a lot left to understand about all that. About how we think. Why we do."

She squinted at me for just a moment. What was it she saw? I figured my hair was probably up in a riot from my previous activities.

But what she said was, "Do you ever read? I don't see a single book in here."

She had me there. "Not much. Mostly just the papers. And those story magazines you piled up over there." I looked at the stack on the table. "I never did get into Dad's set of Conrad."

She took a very long breath on that, as if it was a primary fault on my part, and it was a difficult matter for her to overlook. I immediately reconsidered going to the library more often.

Then she says, "You ought to know, The Boss is running our rewrite on the John Doe."

I liked the way she said, 'our' rewrite.

I just said, "No kidding?"

"Yeah. He's upset about the cops taking an extra interest in this." She scanned the room. "But, right now, you better get some sleep. Do you have any aspirin?"

"No. But I do have some Seagram's."

"I saw that!"

She went to the cabinet and pulled it down, but then had some trouble opening it. I'd never touched it since Dad gave it to me. That was the challenge. The cork came out at last and she poured a juice glass full.

I said, "Pour something for yourself. I think you probably need it as much as I do."

She did pour a little into another glass, but she looked long and hard at me after she handed me mine.

She said, "I can't stay."

It was funny how she said it.

I said, "Then call a cab. But sit down first and tell me a little more about what you were thinking before."

Again the hesitation. This is not like the Cass Green that I'd gotten to know in the last few months. She studied her glass. I took my first sip then and practically coughed myself to death. My ribs were sore and the convulsion doubled it. This was prohibition whiskey and not the stuff you get now. It had a steel edge to it. But at least it got her hand onto my shoulder for a minute.

When I'd settled and taken my second bite of the dog, she said "Which thoughts? About Sam Schechner?"

"Maybe. You'll have lots of time to work on that. I'll help you, if I can. If you'll let me. But what about your idea of quitting."

The drink went right into a fairly empty stomach and then directly to my softened brain.

She sighed. She does not sigh much that I've noticed. Not like my mom can.

She said, "There has to be something more than this, Hugh. This is a game. It's just an everyday sort of game. All of these unfinished puzzles. Just the pieces we find spilled on the floor after the fact. And then we're off to find another."

I offered, "Maybe The Boss'll give you a feature now and then." It was a weak encouragement, but all I had.

"Maybe. But I just wonder how it matters. We can never tell the whole story anyway. No one really wants to know the whole of it. They only want the parts that fit easily into their own expectations."

"Like what? What story? Tell me a story you want to tell."

Even as I spoke those words I knew my brain was not communicating very well with my tongue. The load from the day and the whiskey were holding hands in my head.

She said, "You're right. I would like to know what happened to Sam."

At least I remembered that much in the morning.

4. Monday, March 15, 1937

Cass was gone when I awoke. This was a funny feeling, because I wanted to see her there when I opened my eyes again, in the worst way. My eye. The left one was swollen shut.

I called in sick. Stenis gave that a laugh. Son of a bitch. I was generally in pain, from head to foot, but I was actually feeling pretty good. My shoulders ached the most. I used the last of the ice Cass had broken into the tray on my face and went over all of this and that in my head. Then I took a cold shower because I needed it. After that I hummed a few Benny Goodman tunes to myself and cleaned up most of the mess on the table. The reason for my mood was pretty pathetic, of course. Fact was, Cass had come down to the apartment last night because she was worried about me. Facts don't lie. (Though I have heard they can be easily misinterpreted.)

The fact of it was that the guy I had punched and knocked down the stairs was a cop. What he would have shown me in his coat, if I had waited, was a badge. He didn't have a warrant, it was true, but they had cause for a search. I had been caught earlier at the murder scene where I wasn't supposed to be.

Rule number one: never hit a cop—unless. Not unless you have to.

The guess was, why were my pictures so important to them? What did they think I might have gotten?

Thankfully, the search they made of my two rooms had not turned up my stash. I still had the hundred dollars I keep aside, minus the ten.

With my face looking like one of those unfortunates I take pictures of all the time, I was not going back to the office. Dark glasses don't cover much. And besides, I was still fired. So I set out another plan for the day.

I wanted to know about some other things. And people.

Starting with Cass Green.

Even with my body feeling like I figured it might some day about fifty years from now, if I survived that long, I had to get out of my rooms. It suddenly felt very small in there. However, walking far was out of the question. I had a nasty stoop going on from when I'd landed on my back right after the cops showed up.

I grabbed the subway at 14th and headed up to the New York Public Library. At least nobody would know me there. I'd never even been inside the place before.

And I hadn't shaved, so with the green of the bruises I must have looked a little suspicious. A young towheaded woman at the desk there made me fill out a sheet to get a card so that I could use their archives and then called the *Mirror* right in front of me to make sure I was who I said I was. She kept looking at my face, while I filled in the blanks, like she was inspecting a used-car for dings.

Finally I said, "You should have seen the other guy."

Best I could do.

You have to understand that reporters—and I'm including photographers in this—only know what they know. What they need to know. And seldom what they shouldn't. Plumbers don't spend a lot of time learning carpentry. That's why they cut a lot of ugly holes in things for their pipes. Good cooks don't take time to learn how to run a business until they make the mistake of opening their own res-taurant. And then, if they aren't quick about it, they're back on the short-order line.

The problem is, you are usually too busy to look around and make broad assessments. I'd told the guy at the hotel that I was the best. But that was just a defensive brag. I don't know the fact of that. I see the other tabloids everyday—at least the *Daily News* and the *Pos*t. And even the bigger broadsheets like the *Journal-American* and the *Herald Tribune* because they use a lot more photo work on the inside pages nowadays. I take a quick look at some of the others. Not to compare. Just to see what I missed. And mostly the photography. I usually don't give a crap what else they are doing. Half of what you read is wrong. Or some sort of promotion. Or politics. Most times, the only place you might see a little bit of the truth is in the pictures.

My whole attitude is to do what I do, the best I can. That's it. And I think that's the case with most of the others in the business as well. It's not a competition. No assignment is the same. You just do your job and keep learning new tricks as you go.

But I'd been reading Cass Green in the *Mirror* for three months now. She is the best. The copy editors all love her, and when she gets it wrong, she doesn't howl. I've even heard her say 'thank you.' Not a common thing in the City Room.

When Phil Winks on the copydesk saved her from embarrassment after she misspelled the name of one of a Governor's Education Council members, her third day on the job last January, she bought him a bottle of good Scotch and told him he could take a drink every time he caught her out. Phil was already on the wagon at that point so he shared it around with the rest of the guys and it didn't last the night. And she doesn't yell for the copyboys every time she needs something, but she seems to know all their birthdays. And I wanted to know why the *Daily News* had gotten rid of her and what it was she'd done there that made them let her go.

The morgue at the library is divided into parts. Any newspapers more than a couple of years old are bound up into big folio volumes, each more than two feet high and weighing in at about fifty pounds. They're a pain to handle off the shelves if your shoulders are sore. And my knuckles were still too stiff for turning those big pages gingerly.

I spent most of my time with the more recent stuff kept in binders with wire rods down the folds. They weigh a lot less.

I followed the *Daily News* backward from the end of last year. At first I couldn't find anything Cass had written. Not until I got to October. From there, it seemed like she was in nearly half the issues all the way back to the bound volumes. I started reading.

The matter with Cass was really that she was too good. Most of her stuff was fairly short and sweet—or bitter, as the case often was. She covered the usual range of building fires, school board meetings, car crashes and lost dogs. Even the lost dogs. She seems to have a soft spot for the dogs. (No more comment is necessary there.) But she definitely wasn't just another female fashion reporter. She had come over to the *Mirror* on the promise of getting better assignments than she got at the *News*.

One story she followed for several weeks concerned a Soviet GUGB agent, named Gregory Pesko, who had been recognized by a 14 year-old Russian immigrant girl, Olga Ostrovsky. Olga was living in Brooklyn at the time with her aunt and uncle. The Soviet agent had apparently been the very one who had taken the girl's parents away from their apartment in Leningrad four years before, but no one would believe her. The girl was then found dead in the street one day. Hit and run. The agent had disappeared. But it was Cass who had gotten his name in print.

And nearly every week she would pick up on one particular matter. Prostitution. That seemed to be her regular beat. And the last of those longer pieces appeared on Wednesday, October 28, 1936. Under the heading 'Lost and Found:'

> When Marley James was found dead by police summoned to 304 Mott Street, on June 3rd of this year, the grim discovery did not make the front pages of any newspaper.
>
> You might have seen the inch and a half of copy the immediate facts received on our page twelve the following day. Just another drug death. Virtue lost. Another cadaver destined for the potter's field on Hart Island.
>
> But Mary James, known as 'Marley' because of a childhood speech impediment, had been a flaxen-haired beauty raised in the quiet precincts of Strawberry Lane in Cape May, New Jersey. Her father was a fireman and constable. It is the

sort of town that still has constables. Her mother was a teacher at the local grammar school. She had three brothers, two in the Navy. Theirs was a happy family by all testimony, and not a lot goes unnoticed in such a place.

How was it then that she ended up dead in a drug den on Mott Street, with her body pocked with abuse? Perhaps that had something to do with the fact that Marley used to wait on tables at the Fairweather, a restaurant close by Cape May's Congress Hotel. She had done this since she was in high school.

In the summers, Cape May is a playground for city dwellers from Philadelphia and New York who can afford the price. But such a place, with loose money flowing, can be attractive to certain other characters uninterested in the sunlight and fresh air.

A Mr. Victor Neims was staying at the Congress Hotel in July of 1935. He is a dapper fellow by all reports. He frequented the nearby Fairweather every morning for breakfast. That much is certain. That and the fact that Mr. Neims has long been associated with the Lucky Luciano organization.

The day that Victor Neims checked out of the Congress Hotel was the day that Marley James disappeared. This fact was duly noted and Mr. Neims was questioned by the New York police. But no direct connection was found to Marley at that time.

However, the address on Mott Street where her body was found less than a year later has been known as a house of prostitution. It has long operated at that address as an SRO and survives with little more than the occasional inconvenience of a police raid. Specifically, the real estate is registered to a Mr. Charles Neims. Charles is Victor's brother.

You will notice that any connection to Mr. Luciano is circumstantial. This has often been the case against the best efforts of Mr. Dewey and Mr. LaGuardia as they sought to bring that man and his cohorts to justice in recent years.

But the dead do not testify. Not in words. It is words that have merit in a court of law.

Marley James was found only through the indiscretion of a Fordham University senior engaged in an ill-advised fling after graduation. He had awakened from a drunken slumber beside his dead 'bride' and reacted not as others might who would flee the premises and remain quiet afterward in shame. He had called the police. At least give him that credit.

And Hart Island is not the worst of destinations. The remains of Marley James might instead have ended with an anonymous mingling in the sewers beneath Mott Street, or in the festering swamps of Dead Horse Bay, to be consumed in all the other offal of our seven million lives. But on her ankle the police had found a charm bracelet given to her by her mother at the time of her own graduation—from high school. That object was then traced through the good diligence of the New York Police Department. Her body has now been recovered and is resting at last in St. Mary's Cemetery only a few steps from Strawberry Lane in Cape May.

Mr. Luciano is presently in jail and waiting further assignments for his conviction on pandering charges. Mr. Neims remains at large.

The report, her last by-line at that paper, appears to have caused some difficulty for her editor. Perhaps the Cape May Chamber of Commerce had threatened to pull their summer advertisements. Or the family of Marley James might have had other connections, which they resorted to in their embarrassment. For whatever reason, there were no more by-lines for Cass Green afterward, though I checked all the dog stories and I thought I could detect her flair in a few of those.

For my own part, after I had been banned from City Hall by the Mayor himself about year and a half ago, I had begun spending more time with the crime reporters. That particular restriction had begun when I ran into Mayor LaGuardia during the Macy's Thanksgiving Day Parade at Herald Square—literally run him down in the midst of several hundred people as I tried to get around to the front of the temporary podium where he was to welcome Santa Claus to the seasonal mercantile bacchanal—and he had not forgiven me. The Mayor is a man of usually predictable movements, much like his politics, and though not tall, of large enough width to see easily in a crowd. But he had stepped to avoid something on the sidewalk just as I was distracted by a very attractive elf in Santa's entourage. It was only a momentary calamity and I was even able to help the Mayor back on his feet, but the next day when I went over to City Hall on another assignment, he must have spotted me from afar. Echoing across the lobby from the great stairs I heard that squeaky voice bellow like a phonograph played in a tunnel, "You! *Mirror*! Get out! I don't want to see your face around here again."

Barry George thought to fire me then, and actually did for a few hours, because to be banned from City Hall limited my usefulness, but instead he stuck me on call, covering the homicide squad. Lucky for me.

Which you could say, given the circumstances, is how I finally got the chance to write all this down. We'll see how far I get with it this time.

5. Tuesday to Wednesday, March 16 and 17, 1937

Unexpectedly, just a couple days after the 'John Doe' at the Hotel Penn, there was a message from the Mayor's office, hand delivered to Barry George. The Mayor wanted to see "The Mermaid Man."

At that point, the phrase had come up several times before, all deriving from the one photo I took of the drowned girl in the blue dress.

I appeared at City Hall as directed and waited an hour or two and then, as it seemed I was being ignored, left. Watching coat-holders come and go, and the usual kith and kin of the bureaucracy begging for scraps and preferences, is not entertainment for me. I tend to get angry at the sight of it.

After midnight then, George calls me at home and tells me I should get along to the Mayor's office. I mention the time. George is silent. I say, 'Yes, sir.'

I was at City Hall about 1 a.m. The place was still busy. LaGuardia is a known pain in the ass about the hours he keeps.

As soon as he sees me falling asleep on a bench in the wait-ing area, he says, "I thought it was you!" and waves me back into the office.

Most of the photos in the paper are credited to 'STAFF.' By-lines and individual credits are reserved for feature material. He couldn't have known that I had taken the pictures of the dead girl. But I wanted to think he did.

What the Mayor wanted from me now were pictures of his

police department in the midst of routine night work. "The kind of stuff you see in that new *Life* magazine," he said. "With some art to it. Romanticize a little, like that gal Margaret Bourke-White does. It's not all murders and mayhem, ya know. Show something more comforting to the citizenry. It's all about keeping people safe in their beds, you know."

"Sure."

His eyes examined my face for just a second.

"And don't walk into any more walls."

"Yes sir."

The meeting was three minutes. Then he was suddenly talking to someone else about school textbooks. It was clear to me then that I was not to be one of those who would be safe in bed at night for some time.

For the next several weeks I went out with individual officers on the beat. I did my best. But in the end, the result was adjudged too grim. No matter the settings I used on the Speed Graphic, the night has a way of looking dangerous even when it's a picture of a police officer just standing by a lamppost.

However, there were a few other problems caused by this project. The first was with the cops themselves. In several cases I was running around with the same faces that had taken their revenge on me that Sunday night. They were not particularly friendly, even by the standards of the day between the press and the police. Not a word was mentioned of the incident, however, until I happened upon the fellow I had punched down the stairs at my apartment. He was at a desk and still wearing a neck brace and he appraised the fading bruises on my face with acute interest. Nevertheless, there was some sense that bygones were to be left in the past.

The second problem was a matter of sleep. George kept me on call for the ongoing escapades of the homicide squad. The deal there was that whenever I wasn't following patrolmen around on their beats, I should be ready to answer my phone.

The third matter was with Cass. I barely got to see her.

But for the most part, the assignment wasn't so bad. It was a good excuse for prowling places I was not used to going, during hours I'd normally not be there, and I got to see a lot of things I'd never noticed before. Like laundry.

With your head back, laundry can look like the signal flags of a hundred different human nations strung out on a web of lines across an alley above, all of them fluttering with simple messages in a late afternoon sun: I am a clerk; I am a mother; I am a postman; I am a young boy; I am a widow; I am a buxom girl.

One particular day, the muttering of the fabric in the wind overhead was so constant it nearly obscured the voices of the officer I was with—and the mother, an abused wife that he was questioning just within the open door. I did not want to hear the details, but I heard her baby crying. The mother doesn't want me to see that she has been beaten and I must stand outside. A neighbor, probably the one who wears the several pink cotton slips that wave at me just beyond my reach, had called the police. She leans on her own windowsill and looks skeptically at me. A domestic quarrel had occurred. The husband has since stormed away. The mother has a red welt on her bare arm and another on her face and she had ducked away after she answered the door and saw me there behind patrol-man Andrews. I figure now that the neighbor, appraising my own bruises, is hoping I got the beating I deserved as some sort of general compensation for her friend's misery.

I took a picture of the laundry instead along with the neighbor's scowl.

At a grocery store one morning I stepped gingerly across the debris of a nighttime burglary. I got a picture of the cop speaking to the owner. The man sat low on a stool behind the counter with his head in his hands. The cop had a pad and pencil at the ready but the page of his notebook was blank. What was there left to say? The shelves around looked sparse enough. I suspect the business would not absorb this final indignity.

There were two fires in the one week. I was kept away to the perimeter at both. The police take their orders from the firemen in those cases. At the first one, a dense white smoke, illuminated by searchlights from the trucks, exhaled from all the windows of the place into the dark of the night, as if manufactured and unreal, but spewing from an otherwise normal looking brownstone. There was that artificial look of it in my shot. At the second place there was little smoke at all to see except the gray curtain-rise up at the roofline. But red glared from the windows in multiple devil-eyes. Unfortunately, the red does not register in black and white. Instead, I caught the 'rope-pull' on the hose as it was carried toward the building by half a dozen of the burly fellows from Ladder Company Three. The orderly progression of firemen somehow made me think of a procession of Bishops.

Most nights there was nothing of note. Just the words of the cop I was with registering in a short echo from the closest brick wall.

My best work of the second week could not be used, I was told. I was present in the room when a baby was born. It appeared as if that cop's big hands, sleeves pushed high to his elbows, had taken the child directly from the womb; and with the blood marbling the white of the flesh, as if he and mother and baby were all one being. Too graphic! I was told. Instead, they ran the picture of the baby swaddled to his nose in his mother's arms. A shot you've seen a thousand times.

The third week in March, I was sitting at the 14th Precinct Station on West 30th. I had been on my feet since midnight and it was six o'clock. Dawn hadn't really cracked over the distant crest of the Heights of Brooklyn. Then gloom wafts through the door. In walks Jack Barnes. But he is not alone. He has Cass with him.

She sees me there on the side and gives me a wink and then goes on about her business. Barnes is oblivious, I think. But he is clearly quite taken with her and showing her off to anyone that might notice. All smiles.

You know something is wrong when you are 25 years old and the first thing that comes into your head, when you see the woman you're in love with, are the words of your mother. 'You better get going or else someone else will.' No kidding.

When I got back home that morning, first thing, I get a call from the office about a body found at a single-room-occupancy over on East Houston. I had just taken my shoes off, and then I was up and out on the street again. The fella who died had been drinking cheap alcohol and hadn't eaten in a week or so. That was my diagnosis. There was no crime other than neglect. I took some pics and went home again. George would not be using them. It was too common a story.

I had my shoes off again by nine o'clock and I was asleep by 9:05.

Cass called at 10.

She says, "Did I wake you."

I say, "No. I was just reading some Joseph Conrad."

This gets a laugh. She says, "I couldn't sleep, myself. Not after I saw you."

I said, "Long night?"

It was the wrong thing. It had baggage with it. But I was too tired to think better.

She just said, "Yeah. How about you?"

"They had me up patrolling the Tenderloin last night, all the way from Bryant Park to the Flatiron. The officer I followed was a talker. I now know his life story. I couldn't get him to understand that the words were not going to appear beneath the pictures."

I didn't want to ask her what she was doing. Mom's words were in my head again. So I just said, "Can I take you to dinner tonight?"

She said, "I have an appointment."

I said, "After the appointment?"

She said, "It's a long appointment."

I said, "Before the appointment?"

She said, "I'm going to be eating later, so I better not."

I said, "It's going to be a great day. What if we just get some ice cream at Coney Island and then go watch the planes take off at Floyd Bennett Field?"

I got a pretty serious hesitation on that. And then, "Yes. Let's do that."

I told her I would meet her at the office. That was my mistake.

George had another assignment for me as soon as I was in the door at 45th Street. I left a note on Cass's desk, apologizing, and then did what I had to do.

6. Sunday, March 20, 1937

The following Sunday, when Cass hadn't answered her phone at home for a couple of days and it was likely she wouldn't be coming to dinner, I went to see Dick Weise in the sanatorium in Madison N.J., before heading over to Brooklyn. Dick looked terrible. Worse than the last time. Every breath was a shallow noise. His face was sallow but his eyes were still sharp.

Right away he asked, "How's The Boss?"

"A pain in the ass."

"Good. Keeps you awake?"

"When he can find me."

This was the start of most of our conversations. Then I asked about his kids and got a full report. He didn't mention his wife directly because they were not on terms since he stopped working. She had been forced to take a job at Woolworth's and was not happy with it.

He asked, "Are you okay again with the cops now?"

"I think so. They've had a little fun with me lately."

He slapped at the bones beneath the thin fabric over one knee.

"So I've heard. The word is, the Mayor even got in on that. 'Revenge is a dish best served cold,' they say "

I asked, "Didn't The Boss's friend Miss Parker say something like that once?"

Dick is a reading man. So, he told me, "No. No, I think it's French. But it works one way or the other. I'll bet it was Barry

George who dreamt up the idea of putting you out on the street with the cops for awhile. He and the Mayor might even have cooked it up together. A way to kill two birds with one stone. But at least you'll be able to cover City Hall again."

So that was the real deal. I was so tired, I'd totally missed the bigger picture. Now that it was clear, I felt a little better about it. You can't fight the accidental, or plan for the unintended, any more than you can bank on the fortuitous. But the thing of it was, I had to find a way now to return the favor to both of those guys without giving myself any more pain.

Suddenly I thought of something else.

"Tell me, why is it The Boss doesn't ever want to go home to his wife? Is she a harpy or something?"

Dick laughs again and this causes a coughing fit and I have to wait until he gets his breath.

"No. It's because he's afraid he might kill her, like Charley Chapin, the City Editor of the old *Evening World* did to his. The Boss told me that himself."

"But Chapin was crazy? The Boss is the sanest man I've ever met. Is it his wife who's nuts?"

"Sure. Must be. She married him."

Funny thing about Dick Weise—I have often thought of him as a sort of father figure. Certainly he is a patient man (as he was to me) and the sort of fellow who would be a good dad, though I don't know his kids (he has four), and never met his wife. But on re-flection, I realize he had very little in common with my own father at all. Both are stalwart. Both are honest men. But I cannot imagine Dick working the wet on the deck of a ship in a storm. He has a nervous and skittery side to him, especially around deadlines. In a heavy rain, Dick would head for the nearest coffee shop and sit it out. He is bony thin, always a little stooped as if ready to pull a positive from the tray, and would've had trouble with the lines on a ship. And I never noticed him to be remarkably steady on his feet. But those are merely physical characteristics. Most men are shaped in some way by the flesh and blood they're given but what there are beyond that is something else.

Because he was gone for so much of the time, my dad was more an imagined figure at the beginning of my childhood. Once the war started, he did not come home again until I was seven, and prior to 1918 my earlier memories of him were like snap shots taken on those visits he managed every few months while in the Merchant Marine. Kate and Ben have their stories of him from that time, but those are not much more substantial. In a given year he was home for three months and gone for nine with an occasional visitation in between. To me, because of the gifts he'd bring with him, he was like a Santa Claus who'd lost his way as well as his sense of time.

It was Mom who shaped our thoughts of her husband, rather than the man himself. A frequent refrain would be, "Don't do that. Your father would not like to know you were doing that."

This was a true double negative. It said that whatever we were doing was wrong, and that we would disappoint Dad if he knew about it (including the implied possibility that Mom would be writing to tell him in her next letter.)

We were instructed to write Dad once a week and these notes were placed in a larger envelope and mailed off with my mother's letter. But we were always cautioned not to worry him as it might take his mind off his work. And once a month or so we'd get something back from him. Usually this was a short reply saying all was well and hoping for our own continued health. Not much more. No tales of pirates. No narrow escapes. No fabulous storms. Only notes such as this one I have found, "Belfast. The ship appears to be sound after a little beating we took. Should be in Stockholm next Wednesday. Hauling finished lumber to Marseilles. We have a load of cork in Barcelona waiting to be taken out to New York. Will see you the first week in May. I love you all."

There was never a hint about any of our transgressions.

A few years ago, when the family was together one holiday, just after Kate's marriage, Dad admitted to how much all this harmony had worried him. Mom had never written a word about our misdeeds and mischief. Not a word. And this fact had caused him the greatest concern. He worried over it constantly and was ready to quit the Merchant Marine in 1917 as a result. What could be wrong with his kids, he wondered. When he was a child, he had lived with the daily threat of being sent away to the reformatory. His own father had been free with the belt, and he "still had some of the welts to prove it." (He referred to those welts several other times, but none of us ever saw any sign of them).

But in fact, pleasing him was the yearlong ambition for all of us. Getting that wind-stiffened face to smile was a constant goal. I have no idea what a burden this was to Mom. We never heard a complaint.

When, at last, Dad was there each morning to caution us about the streets and home again every evening at 6:30, nothing seemed to change. Ben said as much to me once. It was as if he had been there all the time and we had merely overlooked his presence. And that was all Mom's doing, I know.

The thing of it was, I think, he was the same man there as he was away.

He denies this. He has said to me that he could not have been a good father in the years just after they were married. He had not grown up yet. And it is his contention that he "grew to fit the pants your mom had sewn for me. Just to please her."

I think it is more likely she saw the man he was from the start.

7. Wednesday to Saturday, March 24 to 27, 1937

I read that last entry over just now and see I'm missing one thing.

As kids, there was never any doubt in any of our minds that my dad could do violence if need be. This was not a threat he made. He was not given to making those. It was a fact we simply understood. Though we never feared that he would do anything mean to us, we knew his anger would greatly upset Mom. And we were witness to that on a few painful occasions. The incident with the coal man comes to mind. And such an event had to be avoided if at all possible. Avoid trouble when we could, he said. But the menace was made a little worse, I think, by his repeated cautions to us.

"Don't be letting the other fella take his chance," or, "If he throws his punch first, you might not get an opportunity to plant your own," and "Be ready. Think what comes next before it happens. Don't be waiting."

Such advice was always given with his added concerns about acting too soon, acting hastily, or his favorite, "jumping the gun." The point was not to be a casualty before the battle had even started. "Anticipation is forethought, not eagerness," he'd say. Imagine the consequence before it happens and know you can afford the price. But always avoid problems if you can. "Trouble has a way of being its own worst enemy. Don't stop the thug from damaging himself. They usually do, in time."

'Thug' is a word he often uses.

That's more than one thing, but then I can think of others too.

Still, none of that was on my mind when Cass called me about ten days after my close inspection of the holding cells at the Charles Street Police Station.

She says, "What'cha doin'"

I say, "Thinkin' about you," which was the truth.

She says, "This isn't a good time for that, Hugh. There are other things going on."

I said, "Not for me." I tried to think of something witty to add and couldn't. A little frustrated, I added, "But it's your nickel. Tell me what can I help you with?"

She says, "I need you to go with me to a rally up in Yorkville on Saturday. With your camera."

Now, there were not a lot of rallies going on around town. Some strikes. Some sit-downs. A riot now and again and a mob or two here and there, but the only rallies I knew about were of the German American Bund kind. I had gone to one of those the previous October over in Brooklyn and taken some photos. The *Mirror* had run a couple of them with the caption, 'Young Thugs at Meeting of like Minds.' My name wasn't attached to the pictures, but I figured after that, the *Mirror* wouldn't be welcomed.

I say, "Sure. That should be fun," and added the first thought I had. It was nonsensical, given what she was asking, but I'd been holding this out as something for some perfect future moment. I can be a little impatient at times. And my instincts told me to strike while the iron was just off the stove so I added, "And how about you come over to my parents' house on Sunday for the big Easter feast."

This seemed to discombobulate her again. I thought that I was at least getting a handle on doing that much.

She asks, "Do you know what's going on Saturday?"

"Nazis?"

She says, "Okay. If you'll come with me on Saturday, I go with you on Sunday."

I say, "Tell The Boss, so he doesn't stick me on something else."

She says, "I already did."

The rest of that week was taken up by the all-nighters with patrolmen on the beat. Chinatown, Chelsea, and Hell's Kitchen. On Wednesday I had a car crash right off a newly opened portion of the elevated highway on the West Side. This ended in spectacular fashion on 24th Street, but thankfully only killed the driver. On Thursday I was called out for a four-alarm fire on Avenue A that killed three people smack in the middle of the day. They'd been asleep because they'd worked all the night before—just like me.

The Bund was going to be a piece of cake.

I met Cass at the paper at 3 p.m. This was a blessing. I had gotten nearly six hours of good sleep and eaten a fine lunch at Morgy's and I was ready for what the thugs might bring.

Cass looked pretty great. She was wearing something a little nicer than the usual, a long green dress full of plaits that made your eye notice the curve of her hips as well as the turn of her calves below the hem. The jet-black of her hair was done up high on her head beneath a wide brimmed yellow spring hat to shade her eyes. I figured her plan was to knock'em dead.

Right off she says, "Let me do the talking. Please. I expect you'll hear some things that make you want to speak. But don't, if you can help it. I want to keep control of the conversation as much as possible. If I have to answer for you as well as myself, it's going get messy. But you'll have the camera. Take lots of pictures. Get the pictures."

No argument from me. I really had nothing to say to those guys.

Besides, nothing happened. It rained and we were forced into a school gymnasium where there was no room to move. And very little air. Perspiration was visible on faces in most of the exposures. Cass got through to the front of the crowd, probably because almost any guy would make way for her, and asked a few leading questions.

A big fellow there named Kuhn, dressed in a tan-brown shirt and black tie and black slacks, his hair cropped close enough to see that he was balding, was apparently in charge, and he answered all inquiries in a thick German accent with what sounded to me like memorized lines. He didn't want anyone else speaking to the press and said so loudly after getting some silence after our arrival. The way he tried to control his voice in a lower register made him sound like the actor, Conrad Veidt. Cass baited him. He snorted, and passed on the questions that were impossible, like, "What instructions have you received from Herr Goebbels," asked while he directed the ranks of neatly uniformed youth on the floor of the court with sharp commands at each change of formation. They march very well for a bunch of kids. At one point they sang the National Anthem and then something else in German I had never heard before but I assumed to be the Kraut equivalent.

The American flag hung conspicuously high against every wall. At the front side, this was paired with the colors of the German American Bund, which were mostly red with a small Nazi insignia at the center. I couldn't get a good shot of the insignia because of the way it hung from the staff and there were no more of those 'swastikas' visible in the room. At either side of these flags were large portraits of a standing George Washington and a sitting Adolf Hitler. I could not help but get the sense that Hitler was posed just like a picture I had seen once of a sitting Napoleon. Washington looked like he was a supplicant. Unfortunately, what with the lack of light from the gray skies coming in the high windows all around, I was fairly certain that little of that would be captured by the flash.

I got a few good pictures of the assembled boys and girls. Most of them were clearly in their teens. Parents were gathered at either side against the brick and I got several sides of them attentively watching from below the two flags, but because my pockets were already full of unused plates, I had to slip the exposed frames back into my case. Those shots then disappeared while I was getting more pictures of the youth assembled on the floor; this after being forced briefly to set the bag down in order to get to the front of the crowd. The fellow who took them did not bother to hide himself. He was standing over the bag when I turned. He just smiled. But his hands were empty. His tie was neatly tucked into his shirt and I thought to reach and pull it out, but restrained myself.

With rule number two broken, I couldn't complain. At least I hadn't broken rule number one and let go of the camera.

And then we were asked to leave.

Cass argued. It was the gymnasium for a public high school, after all. Kuhn produced a letter attesting to the fact that the space was rented from the City for private use at the cost of $20. He then summoned a police officer hired for special duty and that fellow escorted us out the door into the rain. The patrolman looked happy to do it.

Cass called me that night and begged off going to Brooklyn the next day. She apologized. She said she was very tired and needed the sleep. Given that she was probably only working eighteen hours a day, same as me, I was disappointed.

8. Sunday, March 28, 1937

Let me tell you something about the house I grew up in. It's narrow and not the fanciest building on Sterling Place. They used brownstone on the outside of the first floor to spiff it up, but it's plain brick on up from there. Four floors. Three bigger rooms are on the first: a kitchen at the back along with a dining room and then a parlor beyond the stairs at the front.

One large room is at the back of the second floor. That's my parents' bedroom. There are two small rooms at the front on that floor which were always the bedrooms for the youngest in the family and that's where Erik and Esther both still have their stuff, even though they're away, because they haven't settled in anywhere else. Above that there are two rooms at the front and two at the back all the way up to the top. Kate, Ben, and I had once each occupied one of those on the third floor and the other was always called the 'guest' room. The fourth floor was for the boarders. Usually, and during all the years of my childhood, those rooms were filled, and the passing parade up the stairs was a constant source of fascination and education to me.

Those extra tenants were an important source of income to my parents, and they suited the building, which had been a rooming house before and during the war. My parents had bought it for a good price with a 'loan' from Dr. Dean during the 'little depression' in 1920. (The remaining sum of that loan, as I under-stand it, was converted to a belated wedding gift in my grandfather's will, so that took a lot of financial pressure off.) But the true benefit of the building's previous use was that there were bathrooms at the center of every floor, directly across the passage from the stairwell. I did not fully appreciate the glory of this semi-privacy until I later lived in a rooming house over on Henry Street and had to endure the damp remains of physical absolutions and the odors of various necessities from nine other people, just as intimately as they had to become accustomed to mine.

Importantly, my mom always offered 'Room and Board.' She does not want to share her kitchen and refuses to have any cooking in the rooms. But kitchen visitors are also discouraged. For instance, it has always been against the law for anyone to open the icebox door without a writ. Looking more like a steel-strapped wooden safe, this multi-door behemoth still sits beside the newer refrigerator and is kept busy with the odd item. (My dad brings home the block of ice only once a week now). It is easier to raid the refrigerator because it has a light inside, but getting close can be the problem. And this has usually meant that our dining room table and the long buffet is a busy affair. Typically a dozen at mealtime. Two pitchers of milk in the ice tray. The oatmeal in the mornings always fills a large crockery pot. When I was a kid my prank was to stack the toast in one tall pier just to bother anyone looking for a piece browned to their personal liking, but there is now a toasting contraption and the bread is cut on the board. Guests are welcome, with the usual warning. And because of Mom's abilities in the kitchen—something she credits to Fanny Farmer and some months spent up at the Boston Cooking School shortly before she was married—there are constant visitors. An Easter dinner typically fills every chair.

Mom was as disappointed as I was about Cass not being there. She had prepared things a little better than usual I think, which is saying something because there are only three big feast days in our house and Easter was always a good one because there was nothing else to it. Sort of a spring Thanksgiving, with no other worries, obligations or expectations for us kids. Not even the High Mass a few of my friends and some of the boarders might have endured at

St. Joseph's.

I had already told Mom that Cass was Jewish and so she had replaced the traditional ham with a roast beef. All sorts of flowers had migrated indoors from the Terminal Market. She'd baked her special sweet egg-bread the evening before. The usual canned vegetables had been transformed with honey and almonds and raisins and spices.

I had to call and tell her the bad news first thing that morning.

Mom asked, "Is she sick?"

"She's tired."

"What's she afraid of? She thinks we bite?"

"I don't think she's afraid of anything."

"Meeting the parents. Commitment maybe?"

"We haven't even been on a date yet."

"It was too soon, then."

"I think so."

Later, at the table, Mom had another thought, summed up succinctly.

"She's a career girl."

This is a pejorative in my mom's view and was said with a certain resignation. The whole idea of a 'career' for women was something she scoffed at. She wasn't terribly fond of 'careers' for men either. Work was work unless you were a professional. A doctor, or a lawyer, or a farmer could pass muster. But the idea that I wanted to be a photographer had always struck her as a little absurd. As if photographs were a passing fancy. Like telephones.

I answered, "Maybe. I'm not sure. She's told me she's not happy about what she's doing."

Dad said, "Writing about dead people. Mayhem. Misery. Murder. Nazis. What's not to be happy about?"

One of the boarders, Norman Jenks, put in his two cents. Rumor has it Norman has found work again at the shipyard, but we will only know the details of that when he is laid off again and complaining of life's injustices.

He says, "That's what caused the Depression, ya know. Too many women working."

This was a well-placed comment. Mom disagreed with just about everything Norman said, so it might make her reconsider her position on the issue in Cass's favor, if only a little.

Then the phone rang. Dad said, "Let it ring."

But I got up anyway. I was still hoping Cass might feel better and reconsider.

It was Cass, but not for the reason I'd hoped.

"Hugh! Really sorry to bother you. It wasn't my idea. The Boss can't get ahold of Jerry or Pete. He needs you uptown. There's a triple murder at 318 E. 50th. I'm on my way there now."

So that was the end of my Easter dinner, in any case.

Mom can hear the voices on the phone from ten feet away. When I turned around she was already off to the kitchen and stuffing some roast beef between slices of bread. She gave me two paper bags by the time I got my coat on.

She says, "The other one is for her," and gives me a kiss.

The place on 50th was fairly mobbed when I got there. Late again. It's a wide five-story brownstone and brick, with fire escapes out front like brackets on either side of the face. Behind the iron grillwork it looks like my parents' house, only stretched double. Even in the broad daylight you could see the flashes going off in the fifth floor windows. Weegee was already on his way out the door when I arrived. He had an unlit cigar in his mouth and his hat tipped back and he smiled at me like a cat who'd just swallow a bird.

He says, "I liked the mermaid, kid. The mermaid was good."

I nodded but he knew I was in a rush and there was no time to chat.

Despite its size, the place was not as spacious inside. Cops are posted all over and picture taking was a matter of shouldering yourself between two people who don't want to give way. Weegee can do this a little easier than most because, by earned reputation, he doesn't bathe more than he has to, wears the same clothes to work and to bed, and always stinks of cigars and sweat and the sardines he eats right out of the can. People simply pull back at his approach. Regrettably I was getting little allowance for space until Cass spots me and says, "Hugh!" from down a hall.

She had a corner staked out near the kitchen and I pushed my way there without being polite about it. In the kitchen a detective is talking to an older fellow who looks stone-faced. Cass whispers, "It's the father." I snap a couple pictures before an arm reaches around and shuts the door on that. In the bedroom at the back there is a dead fellow in his underwear who hadn't been covered over yet and looked like he was used for target practice, except that he's been stabbed. His name was Frank Byrnes. He was deaf and another reporter speculates that he probably never heard the one who killed him. I grab a couple shots of that, but I know there isn't much they'll use because it's too messy.

In another room there is the naked body of a girl. A blonde. This was Veronica Gedeon. She had a sheet pulled over, but even so, a clear shot wasn't going to be good for a newspaper like the *Mirror* anyway, so I just get an angle on the form of the body beneath the sheet. I couldn't see any blood there to give it a hook other than that she was very obviously nude.

In another bedroom there was the body of an older woman, Mary Gedeon. Her face was exposed for just a moment while she was being shown to someone else and I got that and some blood that had come through at one side of the sheet they'd draped over the body.

When I circled around a second time, the door to the kitchen was open again. Another fellow was in there alone and appeared to be waiting by the rear stairwell. He was holding tight onto a small hairy dog they call a Pekingese. He looked to be stunned and kept stroking the dog's back a little too fast, probably out of nervousness. The dog had his tongue out and was panting happily at all the goings-on. I spoke to the fellow, just a 'Hi, how are ya? Do you live here?' until I caught another glimpse of Cass and waved her over. His name was Charles Robinson. He was the upstairs neighbor and loaded with information about the family. Cass got to quiz him for at least five minutes before another cop came and led him off to the Station House for an official interrogation.

When they started closing the scene down I followed Cass out to the stoop next door to sit for a second. She was headed back to the office to write up what she had before going on to the precinct station. She looked to be a little pale. Maybe she had been feeling sick, after all.

There would likely be no additional information on the murder for a few hours anyway unless somebody confessed. The betting appeared to be on the father for that. He was estranged from the family. Divorced from the wife. He was known to have a temper. He had supposedly discovered the bodies when he'd come over for Easter dinner.

The upstairs neighbor seemed to think the murders had taken place early that morning. He had heard the girl come home very late. The whole family had something of a reputation for being a little 'irregular.' The parents were both Hungarian. The girl worked as a photographer's model. Another sister had recently married and was living elsewhere.

Before Cass headed back to the office, I pulled one of the paper bags out.

"You eat yet?"

She just says, "You're kidding."

"From Mom."

This got that look again on her face. Confusion.

I was now getting the idea that the only way to stop Cass in her tracks was to confuse her.

She said, "Thanks. I'll eat it at my desk," but looked more serious than happy about it.

I went back to my apartment first and developed the best shots I had right there.

When I got back to the paper myself, things were popping. Word had seeped out that the dead girl was a model and this one titbit had caught everyone's fancy. The dead John Doe at the Hotel

Penn had merited a yawn and a page six column using only one of my shots. Of course that might have had something to do with the location. Advertisers don't like bad publicity. But these Gedeon murders were headed right to the front page. Sex sells. Sex and blood sells better. Just about everything I handed in was used.

But when I got back to 45ᵗʰ Street from my place, Cass was already gone up to the 17ᵗʰ Precinct station house. The Boss took the pics right out of my hand and sorted them, resorted them, and then disappeared. I had no other orders at that point, so I sat down at an empty desk and read the beginning of a book called *Youth.* It was the one I'd grabbed in the parlor on the way out the door that afternoon from my dad's shelf of Conrads, and this was my latest ploy for dazzling Cass. If I was going to wait for her to get back, I had better get to it.

The problem with the Conrad is that I was a few chapters in, and totally oblivious, when Cass came in the City Room again. She slipped up right behind me and looked at what I was reading.

"Trying to impress somebody?"

This was said close to my ear and practically knocked me out of my chair.

Thankfully, I had the presence of mind to say, "Only you."

That got a nod and she went back to her desk and typed up whatever else she had gleaned since I had seen her, and then came back.

It was nearly midnight. The paper was closed.

She says, "You want to get a drink?"

I didn't need to answer. Better, she let me walk her home afterward.

There was no goodnight kiss. No holding hands. Just a couple of good smiles. But at least now I'd found out a little more than I knew before about my 'career girl.'

I chalked that one up as our first 'date.'

9. Thursday, April 1, 1937

My friend Izzy Baerz worked at Radio City for a time after it was finished. He worked up in the tall building, on the 32nd floor. The elevators there are fast, but not big enough for the crowds so they run them in a smooth rotation to manage the traffic. The problem is this: Izzy's claustrophobic. Always has been. He won't even go on the subway unless he has to. That's why he lives in a basement apartment now even though it's over in Hell's Kitchen. Fewer walls and he can walk to work. When we were kids, he and I used to walk everywhere together. Not just to save the nickel.

Now you have to understand Izzy. He was brought up by very strict parents. His mother always calls him Isidor, pronounces each syllable, and says it with a mother's pure love, even when she's angry at him. Which is most of the time. I seldom saw his father because the man worked twelve hours a day at an office and then came home and worked a few more hours in the closet under the back stairs for private clients. His father is a bookkeeper and Isidor is now an accountant and earns several times what I do. But every time we get together he wants to hear every detail about my work and bemoans the fact that he never learned to use a camera. Which is funny, because he can play Gershwin on the piano and I can't.

Isidor went to New York University on a scholarship. He is very smart, but knowing the guy as I do, I don't understand how he survived there. He is a prankster. Which brings me back to the elevators at Radio City. Most days, squelching his panic in confined spaces, he got by with closing his eyes before the doors closed. But for those times when the attendant started to really pack them in, Izzy had discovered a fine tool.

In case of emergency, he has a small thick red rubber balloon he has often used for other similar purposes and he blows that up beforehand to about the size of a baseball and holds it shut with his thumb, stashed in his coat pocket. The elevator attendants at Radio City are very orderly, and they close their doors in a proscribed manner every few minutes or so to keep things flowing smoothly. But if the elevator car has gotten too full for Izzy's comfort, about thirty seconds before the door closes he will let a little air out of the balloon. The subsequent noise would usually change the minds of half a dozen or more of the occupants who would then flee to the next car.

Izzy would typically stand in the center of the car floor, forcing everyone else to fill in around him. That way, if his ploy was made necessary, it was difficult to tell who made the sound and Izzy would look around for the culprit just like everyone else. I feel like I was there to see it because he dilated upon the subject to me on several occasions when we would meet for a beer.

This had worked like a charm for about two years. But I suppose there is a certain attrition of patience that takes place. The last time, when forced to use his device yet again, a large fellow at the rear of the elevator pushed forward, grabbed Izzy by his collar, and tossed him out with an accompaniment of descriptive phrases concerning 'cabbage eaters' and Jews.

The embarrassment for Izzy was enormous and he described this in detail to me over hotdogs and Dr. Browns while sitting outside in the sun one day and watching the workmen putting up yet another building close by. He had climbed up a hundred plus flights of stairs to the thirty-second floor the day before, and that morning he had arrived more than an hour early to avoid the usual crush on the elevators.

We both had our eyes glued to the pivot of a thirty-foot beam of lead-colored steel as it soared skyward on a thread.

"What is it with people?"

"I don't know."

"Sometimes I think there is no sense of humor left."

"Worn out."

"Jews aren't the only ones who eat cabbage."

"Russians. Germans. Poles."

"What's with the Jewish thing? Do you hear people talking about Jews at the newspaper?"

"All the time."

"What's with that?"

"I don't know."

He ruminated over my answer a moment, as if it meant something. Then he said, "I did the balloon thing once when we were waiting in that long line for ice cream at Coney Island. Re-member? Everybody laughed."

"I remember."

Another pause. Long enough for him to finish his hotdog and half his soda. He was obviously in a contemplative mood.

Then he says, "I don't know if I can keep working here."

I said, "People forget. There was probably no one around to see it that you know."

"At least a dozen. Almost half of them were from my floor. Including the blond with the boobs who works for the Comptroller."

"She probably wasn't paying attention."

"She giggled."

I had to admit, "You know, I hate the giggling."

He sat there for a bit longer and stared at a stream of workers as they climbed an open stairwell in the construction like ants. I had nothing to say. What could I say? There were a lot of stupid people in the world?

Izzy finally added, "But when they look at me, do they see a Jew? Is that it? They can't forget that?"

I looked at him for a second. The kind of critical look you give a piece of food on your plate that you don't recognize. Then I said, "I think it's because you have the nose for it."

He laughed.

This incident might seem trivial. Izzy subsequently took a job with a firm that occupied the lower floors of a building on Fifth Avenue and had no need of elevators. But talk about Jews had increased noticeably in the previous couple of years. And not just at the paper. You even heard it on the radio.

It finally dawned on me that Cass might have some reservations regarding my own interests because of her being Jewish. She had even said as much, hadn't she? I was being thick.

Then something else happened. This was a day or so after I had seen her come in the precinct house with Jack Barnes.

It was dinnertime and the City Room ranks had thinned. I saw Cass at her desk and moseyed over to chat. It couldn't hurt. No more than it already was.

She had her head down typing up some notes.

I hit first, "What cha got?"

She said, "Just a follow up. What about you?"

"A lotta smoke. No fires." But then I couldn't help myself. I added, "That seems to be the general situation for me."

She hasn't looked up at me yet except for a nod. She says, "Maybe you're answering the wrong calls."

I say, "Guess so," but I was feeling a little worse for wear. Just sore enough to say too much. "How about you? Is Detective Barnes on the right track? Should I be looking for my own story elsewhere?"

This got her to stop typing in the middle of a word and push back in her chair.

She narrows those brown eyes at me and says "Is it that easy with you? A little competition and you just back right off?"

I peek around and see that there is no one close by to hear.

I say, "It's not about the competition. It's about you."

She says, "And you think I'm the kind of girl who'd be interested in Jack Barnes?" And her voice rises at the end of that. It's a question. I'm instantly encouraged.

"I don't know what to think. Some guys are different when

you get to know them."

"Really? You think Detective Barnes has subtleties that might intrigue a girl?"

"Don't know. I'm not a girl."

She shook her head at my hopelessness.

"I will tell you this though. He is not as stupid as he looks. He has an idea about something and no one else has picked up on it."

"What's that?"

"There've been four naked bodies of men found since Christmas. Four John Does, not including the one at the Hotel Penn."

"I hadn't heard."

"That's because it's not news. Back page stuff. They were all dumped. Mostly in the river. By the time they washed up they were in pretty bad shape. One was found over in the rail yard. He was under a load of ties and nobody noticed him for at least a week. The rats found him first. But they all had a few things in common. For one, they were naked. For another, they think they were all middle-aged. And they all died since Christmas . . . And they were all shot."

"That seems like a lot of coincidence. Is it the Mob? Why hasn't anyone else picked up on it?"

"Because originally it was thought to be random. Then it was thought to be mob related, but now the cops have identified one of the corpses. Paul Reagan. He was from Mt. Vernon. He actually worked at Metropolitan Insurance downtown. And it's an insurance investigator at the Met who tagged his toe, not the cops. Mr. Reagan had a very healthy policy with his own company. He was separated from his wife. Kids were grown. I would say he was your average lonely guy."

"Maybe his wife had him killed for the insurance?"

"Well, that was a theory the investigator from the Met was following. Then Detective Barnes got put on the case because he was the first one to do the math."

"And Barnes thinks they are all related to the Joe Doe at the Hotel Penn?"

"Yes. That's what he thinks. Because of one other thing. The others were all shot in the face as well. Right in the eye. Two of them more than once. Not all the bullets were recovered but those that managed to rattle around inside the skulls were all .22 caliber."

I'm thinking another thought. No clothes and no face, no identity, unless they'd been previously arrested for a felony and there happened to be fingerprints available.

"How about you? What do you think?"

"I think that, for a guy who knows his way around a camera, you seem to have a tough time getting the picture."

That shut me up. And she still had one eyebrow up, waiting for me to say something. At least I knew what my dad would do. Attack.

"You know, it's not just *The Shadow* who can cloud men's minds. You're pretty good at that yourself."

She shrugged but only offered me a blank face. "I do my best. But I have to say, no guy has used that particular line on me before."

"You should be happy I'm only half Irish. Otherwise, you'd be begging me for mercy."

She says, "I'll bet." But that finally got a smile.

It was now up to me to lead the conversation away from all that tar.

"Have you told The Boss about this?"

"He okays my paycheck. Sure. I've written it up four different ways already. But he keeps putting a hold on the story. There's not enough there yet. And for now, no one else is on to it but me. Murders are a dime a dozen. Maybe he's just waiting for someone to get the right picture to go along with it?"

I say, "What kind of picture do you want?"

She says, "We'll know it when we see it."

But I wasn't about to lose the moment. And it was already late.

"Want some dinner? We can go down to Bleecker and get some Pizza at John's."

And she says, "Sure! As long as we get back by eight. I've

got a story due on another appeal from Luciano's lawyer. Living at the Waldorf Astoria all those years spoiled him. But at least he seems to like the food at Dannemora better than Sing Sing."

With that, she's up on her feet and didn't even finish the sentence she was typing.

In the cab I asked her, "Do you think the murders have anything to do with Luciano? Maybe there's some reorganization going on, now he's gone."

She looks up and sees the cabbie staring right back at us in the rear view mirror.

"You better hush. This guy is going to have an accident if we talk about that stuff here."

The cabbie shoots back with a line I'm sure he's used before. "I got two eyes, Miss. The license says I only need one to drive."

Cass answers, "As long as we're entertaining you. Wouldn't want you to fall asleep at the wheel."

He says, "What? Now I can't amuse myself by watching the customers? Is every newspaper working for LaGuardia now or something?"

LaGuardia has been all over the cabbies for one thing or another. Mostly for having dirty vehicles. The Mayor had even threatened a five dollar fine for each cigarette butt he saw on a cab floor. Now he'd signed the Haas Act and made every hack get a regulated license.

This fellow had picked us up right out front at 45th Street so I figured he must have an idea about what we do for living.

I asked, "What do you think? Is Luciano still in charge?"

The cabbie has his answer ready. "Until they kill him, he's in charge. And they tried that before. The others all end up like Dutchie Schultz."

That seemed about right to me.

Cass asks him, "Is the 'trade' still the same with Lucky gone?"

He says, "The girls? That's been the same since Moses, Miss. You can't stop that."

"But do you think anyone else has been moving in on that lately, now Lucky's in prison?"

He gives us both eyes in the mirror as he heads down Second Avenue.

"You want a full quote, or just a couple of words on that?"

"About 800 words will do."

He nods his head with his body. "It's the same as ever. There's always some independent operators. They might last awhile. But they're usually at the bottom of the heap anyway. No competition there. The sharp elbows are all at the top. And maybe there's something going on up there . . . Seems to be a little chill going on up there."

"What kind of chill?"

"Can't say. I had a high-priced girl in here the other day that works out of the Biltmore and the Roosevelt mostly. Says she's lost some regular customers. And she's heard talk of that kind of thing around. But then she says there's always gripes and always somebody else waiting."

In that it was just the two of us and this was not happening while we were on the job, I had to consider going out for the pizza to be our second actual date. I had even left my camera bag safely under my desk.

The date was April 1st, so I figured I was the fool, and happy for it.

10. Friday, April 2, 1937

So I get a call just before 6 a.m. from the Assistant City Editor, Brad Stenis, to get over to the Fish Market. Of course, I have to go into the office to get my camera first, and Cass is already there, waiting.

She says, "We've got another floater."

Now given the time of day, and the haste of getting dressed, I am probably starting to look a lot more like Mr. Weegee, but Cass is wearing a pair of loose brown slacks like you will see on Claudette Colbert or Katharine Hepburn. Let me tell you, in the flesh, she hits the eye even better than those two. So I have to tell her, "You look swell and an awful good sight for sore eyes so early in the morning."

She ignored that and gets ahead on the aisle.

The place is pretty empty at that hour but there are a couple guys at the circulation desks and they hear me and one of them whistles.

She says to them, "In your ear," and then tells me to be careful what I say and where I say it.

I am well aware of what happens to office romances at the paper.

There was a reporter named Davis who was here a few years back. He was totally smitten by the theatre critic. The problem with that was she was already married at the time. Her husband sued for divorce and even named the *Mirror* in his complaint as cores-pondent, saying the paper had allowed the affair to happen right on the premises. Or so the husband thought.

The Boss had to go give his deposition to the contrary. But the bother of it resulted in George's threat to us all that any extra-curricular activity in the office was forbidden. Anyone caught would be fired.

It still went on, of course, but the thing was to keep it on the q.t.

I grabbed my bag and some extra ammo for the camera from my desk and happily followed her out the door. The slacks from behind were something else.

The guys at the Fish Market were not so polite. The whistles were louder and fairly constant. Shouts were mingled in, but the words were thankfully unclear. The only thing to do was to ignore it amidst the bustle of trucks and carts. We followed our eyes instead of our noses, right down to the dockside where the *Daily News* photographer, Ted James, was practically on top of the body, with his flash going. The cops had no perimeter on this. The body, in the water for at least a day, was totally naked. The bullet had entered right beside the guy's nose, and that plus his mottled color made the poor fellow look like a monster for the cover of *Amazing Stories,* even though the green would not be appreciated in black and white. In that there was some seaweed in around his neck, I concentrated on the sea monster angle. The paper was not going to run anything below the waist in any case.

With the nasty work done I took a couple of extra pictures of the bridges in the morning sun and then, when she wasn't watching, grabbed a couple more without the flash of Cass talking to an officer.

We walked both ways from the El to the Fish Market, so there was time to chat.

On the way over, I had suggested that there was a nice little Italian restaurant opened up on Second Avenue. Maybe she was free for dinner?

The previous September the theatre critic for the paper (this being the guy George hired to replace the one whose husband was

was stepping along.

By the time we got back to the office, The Boss was already there and I went down to the darkroom to get some prints of what I had while Cass spoke to him. When I brought those upstairs again The Boss waved me into his office and took a look at what I'd gotten of the corpse, the shots of the Brooklyn Bridge and Cass were tucked in my jacket pocket.

"Grisly," is all he says.

I said, "There was nothing else to grab. The rest of him was off limits."

He says, "Yeah? What's that in your pocket?"

"Just some random stuff."

"Lemme see." He rubs his fingers together impatiently. I handed them over and kept quiet. What's to say? Cass looked pretty great. He studies them for about a minute. Stone-faced. Then hands them back and says, "Keep that on the outside, will you? I don't need anything going on in here that I can't print, smoke or drink."

"Yes sir."

He says, "Everybody is nuts over the Veronica Gedeon thing now. There's no good playing another murder off against that for the moment. And you may be right about a connection between this one and the Mob. I told Cass she can keep her eye on this along with the others and keep me posted. And for the time being, you're off the night beat. I think the Mayor feels he's gotten his pound of flesh on that one."

But I was pretty well pleased that Cass had told him it was my idea about the mob.

I added the pictures of Cass to my growing collection as soon as I was home. At this point I only have about thirty. None taken with the flash. She is very naïve about cameras and I am pretty certain she doesn't know I have taken even one. Or else she doesn't let on. I'm not sure.

I picked up a nice little album at my dad's store and started filling the pages and adding a few notes from things she had told me about herself. But I actually don't know a lot, because she's pretty reserved. I know she was born and raised in Cleveland. Her father has a shoe store there. On that first date she told me he came to America from Poland and went to work at The Peerless Company as a metal worker—the very same thing he had done before in Danzig. Her mother is a high school English teacher. Her mom was born there in Cleveland, and she'd met her father, soon after he arrived, when he advertised in a local paper for a tutor to help himself learn English. A determined man, he had married his teacher. They had been married for over thirty years and Cass has three brothers.

Now, three brothers—that's enough to toughen up any girl, or else turn her into a weeper. Cass was no weeper.

Right after the war, when steel work was slow, her father had opened the shoe store in downtown Cleveland.

I had asked her, "What did he knew about shoes?"

She told me, "My mother's father sold shoes. He probably did it to please her, but when someone would ask that, he would say 'Everything! I've been wearing them all my life!' But he must have been good at it. It was a success. I worked there when I was a girl and he was always a happy salesman. I helped him by getting the boxes from the back room. I learned my fractions that way. I know he liked the smell of leather far more than the smell of steel. He'll often say that too."

So I know she had worked in her father's shop, just like I did. An important point, I think.

But mostly she wanted to talk about her work. I thought that this might just be a way to distract me from asking more about herself.

First I wanted to know what got her in trouble over at the *Daily News*.

She says, "Mrs. Roosevelt."

This sounded like it would be a good one. I could only ask, "How was that?"

"I'd done this piece on a dead girl that caused a stir. It was just part of a series I was doing on the prostitution rackets. Some of the fellows upstairs thought this was rough territory for a female reporter. But even after they cut them down by half, the pieces caused a few problems. So they decided to send me down to Washington to interview Mrs. Roosevelt instead and see if I would fit in there. And that didn't work out so well. It's a regular coffee klatch there at the White House. All women. All 'sob sisters.' And they just adore 'Eleanor.'"

Cass took a breath to consider her next words. My guess was she wanted to say something she knew would not go over well with some people.

"But she's really an incredibly ignorant woman, full of opinions and advice about almost everything, even though she has no experience doing anything. She's supposed to be a feminist but she hasn't done a thing that isn't on her husband's coattails. She's never had to earn a living or go without a meal. Never gone without, or had to make ends meet. She can speak three languages but can't make sense in any one of them. Basically I said so, as politely as I could. And they didn't run it. My editor decided that I'd written this as some kind of ploy to get out of the assignment and get back to New York. 'How could anyone not love Mrs. Roosevelt?' he says to me. So he put me on lost dog duty instead. But then I started doing those like you would for a human being who's missing or died. And they were popular. That only caused more trouble. The *News* couldn't wait to get rid of me."

Mrs. Roosevelt was on the radio quite a bit and the person Cass described matched the voice I had heard once too often. To change the subject, I wondered then how her inquiries concerning Sam Schechner were coming.

"I've been talking to his clients. One by one. His appointment book was right there on his desk. The police didn't even bother to look into it except for the last few days before he died."

"Why not?"

"They had their own ideas, I suppose. Minds made. He'd been seeing a woman named Norma Lenz. She's married and came to see Sam for a divorce. The stupid ass had gotten involved with her

himself. Very dumb. But it appears she'd come to see him the day
before to say she was going back to her husband. I spoke to her
about this myself. She was still rattled about it, I think. It was clear
what had happened. Men get some sort of protective instinct going
about women, when they see a woman crying. And she was very
good looking. But I don't think she understood how much she had
meant to him."

"And she had told this to the police?"

"Yes. She had too. She'd been showing up at his office a
little too often."

"Could her husband have killed him?"

"It was the first thing they looked into. But they seem sure
the husband hadn't known anything about the affair until they came
to question him. He was very shocked by it. Especially with his wife.
But the husband was at work when Sam Schechner died. Henry Lenz
is a ticket agent at Grand Central Station. A very public place. He
was there."

"Why did she want to divorce him?"

"The usual reasons. He was fooling around too."

"Fooling around on a beautiful wife?"

"I hear looks aren't everything."

"Really?"

"Men are goats."

"Really?"

"Really!"

"So why are you pursuing it?"

"Because, I don't understand it."

"Curiosity, then,"

"More than that. It doesn't make sense."

I said, "A guy kills himself because he's going to lose his
girlfriend. It happens everyday."

"Really? It happens to people who don't have anything else
going on in their lives. Young girls, mostly. Ones who aren't whole.
Or the ones who haven't done anything on their own yet and think
they need a guy to make their lives complete. They're afraid to live

without someone else. Young guys can be that way too, I suppose. But I think it happens that way more often to girls. The 'Juliets,' I call them."

"Don't forget that Romeo did himself in as well."

"True, but all that was more about young love, I think. A kid in love can be pretty stupid because it's the biggest thing that's ever happened to them."

I had to be wondering if she'd ever been stupid once, but there was no way I could be asking about that.

"And Mr. Schechner doesn't fit that bill?"

"No. I'm pretty sure he'd been around the block a few times before."

"So you think someone killed him. A Secret Agent maybe?"

"You're making fun!"

"No!"

"Then why did you say it that way?"

"It's the title of the Joseph Conrad book you saw me reading. That's all."

Still, she looked at me very suspiciously. Like she didn't think I even knew who Romeo and Juliet were. But I'd seen the movie. Leslie Howard was a chump. Though Cass does look a little like Norma Shearer without the cross eyes, only better.

But that was a different Norma altogether.

11. Friday, April 9, 1937

The night is the right time to sleep. The lack of sunlight helps. No kidding. I was out on the couch again and I liked that better than the bed in my darkroom anyway. Never mind the smell. But the sudden addition of sleep to my daily routine was a shock to my system. I was suddenly feeling tired all the time.

Other than the weight of the bag, the most tiresome part of the job is the waiting. Some days you just have to sit at your desk and hope for somebody to kill someone. You almost pray for it. That, or to burn something down for the insurance. You can stand by at the courthouse for hours waiting for a jury that should have been able to do their math in five minutes. Guilty or not. The cigarette smoke in the hall is thick enough so you don't have to buy your own. Then there's a brief crush of time in a doorway or a stairwell when being a little taller than the others is to some advantage. Afterward you wait again at the paper while Eddie or Frank do their work in the darkroom. Frank is faster and you can only hope he's the one who comes through the door when your turn comes. If they got it right, you can carry on. If not, you mark out what you want with the grease pencil and tell them to try again. Then you go drop the results off at the assistant city editor's desk and head back to your own.

I share the desk there with a fellow named Tom Reilly. He works City Hall almost exclusively because he gets sick at the sight of a corpse. But he's good with the politicos. He can tell you which side is the good side for almost the whole crew over there. They are a vain lot. And they much prefer him to me.

Most days you take a look at the board where they post assignments and take your pick. Sometimes there is a note waiting at the desk from The Boss to do this or that. And sometimes you just have to look hopefully at your calendar. In the springtime, that's likely to be something like a Polish American Parade, or an Easter egg hunt at City Hall Park, or a Flower Show at the Armory. If so, you head out then to find the reporter assigned to that piece of fluff. (It's never Cass. George knows she's better than flower shows. He gives her the dog stories just to give her a break). And you must understand, the reporter you want is never at their own desk. Odds are, they're in the hall near the toilets, puffing up a storm along with half a dozen others and trading in smoke-cured gossip. You wade through a fog in there even when the window is open at the far end. But it's always a good excuse to say you were going to the toilet and just happened to see them.

When you find the scribe you're after, you have to pull him by the collar, about like you'd get a dog by the ear, and lead him away to pick up his own gear and then you're finally out in the fresh air. If you're unlucky, you're in the office again in under two hours and there's likely a note from The Boss telling you to go get a picture of the aftermath of the fire on 14th Street that's going to lead the front page unless there's more important news—say something like, 'Slay Suspect Irwin Sighted," because the Veronica Gedeon murder case never seems to end (just an unconfirmed report, naturally). The other standing heads like 'Italians invade Ethiopia,' 'Japs invade Chinese territory,' 'More Stalin Show Trials in Moscow,' 'Germans to Sterilize Colored Children,' (or 'the Mentally deficient,' or 'Alcoholics,') or 'Scottsboro witness recants'—that's all pushed back to page two, four and six. If they don't have a fire or a murder for page one, they might even go with 'Earhart Leaves for Record Flight.' She, or Hughes, always seem to be good copy with the public. Or, as a last resort, there is something humorous, like 'Texas Size Popeye Unveiled.' Everybody loves Popeye. Problem is, none of that uses anything I've shot.

After a couple of days of regular sleep, I'm totally exhausted. No flower shows. No parades scheduled. So early one morning I hunt up Cass. Besides, it's Friday and she might be free now for another date. I want to get my bid in early. But she's off somewhere on a story.

Now I can't ask The Boss to tell me where she is. He might not know and that's two of us embarrassed. I have to use some common sense. It's Friday.

I head uptown to the Park Avenue Synagogue where that young lawyer, Sam Schechner, used to go. I figure she's up there talking to the family again, or if I'm wrong I might head over to the Metropolitan Museum of Art and pick up some odd facts about this or that and maybe drop them into conversation when the opportunity arises. Cass is always mentioning the names of painters to me that I've never heard of. "The inside of that bar looked like a Velazquez painting," she says. Who's he? But I don't say that. Everybody knows Rembrandt. That was an okay movie. A little slow. But who knows from Vermeer? Cass says that when I don't use the flash, I catch the light sometimes like a Vermeer. I want to see that.

The Rabbi there at the synagogue was already preparing for the evening service and didn't want to talk, but he'd just spoken to Cass about half an hour before. He thought she might be over with the family.

Yorkville is a nice area of town. Well kept. You'll actually see people outside of their apartment buildings sweeping up the street. Not much crime there. The mix is a lot like Brooklyn. Mostly Catholics and Jews. Some Italians, Irish, Hungarian, Polish, Czech and Russians. A lot of Germans. The works. Besides having to walk the night circuit out of the 19th Precinct along with a patrolman named Finch (a guy who looked more like an owl), and not counting the German American Bund, the few stories I've been up that way to cover in the last year or so have been for émigrés from Germany and Czechoslovakia. A lot of people are getting out of those countries. New York is home to the world, or so says The Mayor.

They have renamed old Avenue A along there, York Avenue,

after the hero of the Great War, I suppose because it matched up well, but these are people that Sergeant York would never recognize from the backwoods of Tennessee—though they are just the type he might have met at the Argonne Wood. And you know, Yorkville is also the original home of the Marx Brothers.

Cass is right outside when I spot her. She is talking to a young fellow on the stoop of the house where Schechner had lived. I stand off a few yards and smoke a cigarette and study the pigeons until she's free.

When she's done she says, "What'da ya got?"

There is a little something sharp to the edge of her voice.

Now I had been thinking this through for the last hour. Cass does not want me hanging onto her skirt. If she wanted to see me, she would have called. So I started working up a cover story of my own. Actually, I started on that particular angle the same week the young lawyer had died. I could see that Cass was affected by it. I thought if I could come up with anything extra on Sam Schechner's death to make sense of the thing, she might appreciate it. Very calculated, I know. It's a very mercenary world out there and you have to make your own opportunities. Besides, it was interesting stuff. A lot more interesting than just listening to a night beat cop tell me about his mother-in-law.

Pat Finch, the cop, is Irish on both sides, so when he tells me his mother-in-law is German, I ask him what's she like. He says she's like the mother in the Katzenjammer Kids and then proceeds to offer some examples for the Sunday pages. Only she uses a wooden spoon instead of a rolling pin to get her way. Very colorful. So then, figuring on some insight, I work Pat around to telling me if his mother-in-law has a problem with Jews. He says, "Are you kidding? That's all she talks about." I ask him if he has heard a lot of that kind of talk? Now, as he is well aware, that's leading the witness. He wants to know why I'm asking. I tell him it's for a story I'm on. I need pictures. He asks about the story. I tell him about Sam Schechner.

Pat Finch informs me he wasn't on duty when that all happened but he knew the guy. The suicide surprised him too. I ask him if he knew any other reasons for it. He says no. Then he tells me, "I do know that young lawyer was working with some of the people in the area. The ones just off the boat and can't afford legal help. He was a good guy for that. They all went to see him. And he'd gone to bat for a number of them in court that I know of."

So Cass wants my excuse for butting in.

I tell her, "It's a great day! The flowers are blooming all over Central Park. You can even smell them way over here."

She says, "That's cabbage," but she means something else. Those brown eyes are flashing.

So I get right to the gist of it, "I was talking to a patrolman, Pat Finch, the other night. Actually all the night long. And it was raining."

I paused then because I was trying to gather my story up in a coherent manner.

She says, "Is the weather report important?"

I say, "Just a matter of why we had the time for conversation, standing in doorways, like we were, for much of the time. And Pat told me about his mother-in-law. Hildegard is her name, for the record. And because he doesn't like her and she's much on Pat's mind right now with another baby coming and her living with them in a four room on York Avenue, he was happy to tell me all about her foibles, one of which is a strong dislike for Jews."

I paused again. I can see she is listening now.

I say, "One thing leads to another then, and I mention the young lawyer, Schechner, and he tells me that Schechner was a good guy. He was helping out with legal council for a lot of the newer immigrants in the neighborhood. A go-between you might say. Important, because a lot of them are afraid of the police."

She says, "Yes, he was."

"And then you know there was that story last year about the Soviet GUGB agent who was recognized by the young girl over in Brooklyn and no one would believe her."

Cass perks right up. "That was my story! I wrote that for the

News." Then she frowns at me. "I thought you didn't read."

"I read that."

"Just happened to."

"Just happened to. Anyway. So what if our young lawyer, in the course of helping someone, has come upon something that the Nazis around here don't want him to know? We know they're all over the place. Like termites. Is it possible that they could have killed him?"

She doesn't answer me right off. She squints at me. Like she's sizing up the picture. And then I can see she's got the focus. I can tell she's not surprised at my idea but more skeptical at my telling of it, so now I know for sure she's already been working that particular angle herself.

She says. "You figured that out on your own, or did you talk to The Boss?"

She knows the answer, I think. She was likely keeping George well informed about her pursuits. But I have to answer anyway.

I say, "The Boss and I are on good terms again. He tells me what to do and I don't talk to him unless I have to. But I figured this one out on my own."

She sighs. I think she knew right then and there that it was a hopeless matter between us, but maybe it would be a while before she would have to deal with it.

She says, "And you came all the way up here to tell me that?"

"No. I came up here to ask if you wanted to take a walk in the park. Maybe go over to the Museum and look up Mr. Vermeer."

12. Tuesday, April 13, 1937

There were a string of fires down around by Tompkins Square Park the next week. No doubt about it being arson. Just a matter of finding the culprit. But that wasn't going to happen. I hear the odds are one in twenty. One arsonist caught for every twenty fires. And then judges give them ten years and they're out in five, or three.

There were four buildings involved here, each with a different owner. Six firefighters had been injured. Two people were dead—an elderly Italian couple who reportedly couldn't hear the alarm and slept through it all to the end. That was the story that ran. But one of the fire captains told me on the side that they had found the couple huddled in a closet beneath the stairs. Afterward, I asked George why he didn't print the real story. He looked at me for the fool I am.

"When exactly was it that you saw the real story on one of our pages. I must have slipped up."

That was the truth of it. Nobody wanted the real story. If it did not involve sex, or the Mob, they all wanted the LaGuardia version now. The hopeful version. The better tomorrow version. The version where the government was going to find a solution to the problem—just you wait. The detectives would find the arsonist. Just give them some time. Who wanted to think about their mom and dad huddled beneath the stairs in their last moments?

Even though they almost never find the arsonist, they always assure everyone that they will. And everyone seems to believe them like that lie was never told before, and then they go on about their lives.

I was sitting there in Tompkins Square Park on a bench, about ten o'clock on a cold gray morning, just after the third of those fires. I hadn't had breakfast and I'd been up since five or so for the third night in a row. It's when you're tired that you get bad ideas and I'd just grabbed some pictures of the bodies as they were carried out a few minutes before and that had taken the legs out from under me. Sort of hung me up by my own dark thoughts. 'What was the use,' kind of thoughts. Maybe a hundred people stood between me and the engines, like a human picket fence, and half of them were only dressed in what they could grab on the way out of the building. With me on my arse and nothing to see over the crowds, it was all just the stink in the air, and the growl of the fire engines backing out to Avenue A, and a fireman yelling 'hey, hey, hey' to keep the trucks from running anyone over. I'd changed out my film and bulbs, but suddenly I wasn't so sure I could get up again to watch any more. There might be a picture there, in those faces, but I was tired from the inside out. And it just wasn't my legs—because with no cabs at 5 in the morning, I'd run a couple of miles to get over here. My head was tired from the inside as well.

Nor had the sun deigned to shine down on any of it. Too unimportant in the larger scheme of things. Just another gray day. Another stinking gray day. The First Avenue entrance to the El was farther away than I wanted to walk. The corner was farther than I wanted to walk. So I just sat there, behind that wall of people. And that was right where Cass found me. I don't know how she did that.

First thing she said was, "You look sick." She didn't even say 'Hello.'

I said, "I think I am."

"What happened?"

"A fire."

"No. I mean, to you?"

"Just another fire. Feels like the whole fucking world is

burning down."

She had never heard a cuss word out of my mouth, I think, maybe, so that was the first one. She was stooping to look at my face when I said it, and that word stood her right up again.

She's very perceptive. She says, "So you aren't really sick?"

"No. Just tired. Just sick and tired."

"What are you going to do?"

"Sit here awhile."

"I mean, after that."

"Head over to the El."

"You want me to stay."

"Sure."

"You want some coffee?"

"I'll get it on the way. There's a place on the corner."

That's when she sat down right there beside me. A funny moment. Just sitting, side by side. Both of us sizing up the rear ends of the crowd in front of us. But even through the stink of the fire I could smell her.

After a long minute, a lump of curiosity finally bubbles up and I say, "Why did you come over? I saw Harris. He's already here. I know he already talked to the Fire Chief."

"I was looking for you."

That got some blood moving. "How come?"

She says, "I was wondering if you still had any of those Annie Oakleys."

Now that's what funny moments are for. I knew damn well she wasn't there to ask me out on a date. She had some other business in mind. But now she was feeling a little pity for me. I thought through the situation, and that much was clear enough. She was worried about me! But you don't want a girl feeling pity for you. Not a girl like Cass.

I said, "I'll get ahold of some tickets, but only if you tell me first why you came all the way over here?"

She was quiet for maybe a short minute more.

"You're right. Like you said to me, one step at a time. I

wanted you to go uptown with me. I have an interview with that fellow Kuhn."

Last fall, during the campaign, I got some fine pictures of FDR. He's usually up at Hyde Park when he's around, but he was at a function the night before and was staying over at the Hotel Roosevelt, (which might as well have been named for him and not his cousin for all anyone knew these days), and that particular morning he was climbing in his limousine with his wife and his son. The fellows that are always with him had his arms, and he followed his wife right into the seat, easy peasy, but George wouldn't use the shots because they showed that the president is crippled. As if that particular fact is some sort of secret. Like everyone from Washington to China doesn't know it. But politicians are funny too. It's all image. The substance of the man, overcoming his catastrophe is not enough.

I said, "But everyone knows it!"

George said, "Pictures are louder than words. People don't want a cripple for President. He doesn't want that shown. Beat it back out there and get some more. The campaign's got him out at the Yonkers Raceway around four o'clock. Go get some clean shots there. I want a picture of a President, not a cripple."

This is all part of the great mystery to me now. I had started out believing that pictures only show what is. That was my philosophy. But I was wrong again. Pictures can also be used to show what you want people to see. Good and bad.

And I know now that the deal with Mr. Roosevelt is the exact opposite of what we will be looking for with Mr. Kuhn.

Our appointment had been made by Cass. She'd suggested to someone at the German American Bund that the foul weather of our previous visit might have soured the situation and she would like another chance to speak with their leader.

Now I was charged with getting some shots of this thug again. I didn't need it said that I should skip any moment where he was smiling, laughing, or in the least way pleased with the interview.

What George wanted was the thug. If the guy hadn't shaved closely that morning, I should try to capture some of the sinister shadow of that in his cheeks. What was wanted was a glare. A scowl. A leer. A grimace. At least a nice frown.

But Mr. Kuhn was in good spirits. His skin was shaved to the pink. Where the sun had refused to shine on those who had lost their homes down on Tompkins Square that morning, now it glowed like a gold coin in the mists and warmed all that it touched.

He rose from his desk and shook hands with us both, and then ushered us outside to a small garden at the back in order to take advantage of the light. He is smart about photographs. Fritz Kuhn is a large man and bluff and could easily appear to intimidate. Instead he raised his face toward the light to look at the branch of a small tree growing there and made a theatrical notice of a group of sparrows that clustered above us in the sun on a limb already clotted with the green of new leaves. I took some pictures of that just to please him. Settle him down.

He said, "Our winter wait is over. Our spring time has finally come."

There was no doubting his double intentions.

Cass started her interview with questions that were benign, and worked her way to the darker matters. Where at first he had simply smiled and offered a little detail, by the end of the half-hour he was laughing and translating each of her inquiries into a joke and extrapolating from that. The accent in this voice was like a singsong of spoken lieder throughout. And at the end he took some time to restate his meanings to be sure he had made his point.

"Why do we hate the Jews, you say? Why should you hate the Jew grocer with his thumb on the scale, I ask? Why would you hate the Jew banker who holds your money back for an extra day because he knows it will be worth less if he does? Anger is the word you want, not hate. We are all human in that way. Are we not? But this is incidental to the life of a people. Anger makes you smaller. True? It diminishes you. You cannot build on anger. The German spirit is not contained by anger, but set free by exuberance! You would see that much very clearly I think if you came to our youth camps in the summer. And notice! Our organization is devoted to just such projects, and not to hate, or even anger. Our purpose is to educate. To enlighten. To build! And if the Jew bankers will not loan us the money necessary for that, we will start our own bank. Already we have established a savings and loan just a few doors away from where we sit. And if some grocers choose to charge usurious prices, we will open our own groceries. We have already done so. We are everywhere! Germans are industrious, you see. We build! And if some newspapers will not report the truth of what we accomplish, we print our own papers. As we have now done! We will not beg for the indulgence of others. We shall make a better world with or without them."

And with this he arose from his chair. He was done with us. I had taken a dozen shots that I knew were worthless. I needed something better.

I could see that Cass was not pleased with her effort, just as clearly as the look of smug confidence radiated from Mr. Kuhn.

I said, "When America goes to war with Germany, what side will you be on?"

It was the sound of my voice that startled him. I had not said a word before that. Anger flexed his jaw for just an instant. His brow folded downward to a sudden scowl.

He answered, "I was born a German."

That was the shot I wanted.

Cass was quiet when we left. She gave one quick look at me when I spoke up to Kuhn, and then nothing. Outside there was a roar from the shadows above and we ran up the stairs and quickly caught a local on the Second Avenue El right there at 86th. The car was crowded, and we didn't really talk again until we got off to walk the rest of the way to the office.

She said, "You just wanted the shot."

I said, "Yes."

She considered that for a moment before speaking again. "Do

you think I should have been a little tougher?"

"I don't think so. He would have just ended the whole thing as soon as you did. As it was, he came off as a happy megalomaniac. I might have gotten my own shot in sooner, but then you would have gotten less yourself."

"I didn't get much." She was unhappy. "Do you think I should have mentioned Sam Schechner?"

"No. I'd save that for when you know more. At least until you already know the answer."

She nodded at that. But it was just common sense. Asking questions when you don't know what the basic facts are will get you nothing but what the other guy wants you to know, while letting him know where you are going.

But then that suddenly led to a thought of my own I'd had once before and never managed to slip in the conversation. I asked Cass how it was that she decided to become a reporter.

She smiled, but not happily—'wistfully' is the word for it I think—before she answered, "It was a mistake."

"How was that? Did you apply for the wrong job or what? You know, I've done that myself."

"No. I had a scholarship to Ohio University, but they had no courses for someone who wanted to be a Willa Cather. Or an Edith Wharton. The only writing courses they had were in 'Journalism.' And Ernest Hemingway was already the biggest writer around and he'd worked at a newspaper first. And John Dos Passos. And a dozen others. They were all newspapermen. So I signed up for journalism."

There were at least a dozen other things that this answer made me want to know.

"So you want to write novels?"

"No. Not now . . . Not right now, anyway."

"But you don't like being a reporter."

"But I do. I just don't like some of what I have to write about."

"That's what a reporter does, right? You don't get to make up the news. You write about what comes."

"Do I? Really? That fellow Kuhn—if all you knew about him was what you saw today, you'd never believe he was capable of murder."

I suppose I was being glib with my answer, but I meant it.

"We are all capable of murder, don't you think?"

She didn't answer. She tried a misdirection instead. One that worked.

"So what was the job that you took by mistake?"

The story for that was involved but slightly entertaining, I thought. "That happened before the *Mirror* anted up their 25 bucks a week. The winter of 1931. Dad was having serious trouble and could not really pay me and Jerry Herzog as well. And I was still living at home. I decided to take what I could find. One day I was delivering some boxes of letterhead and such to an address on Sutton Place. Nice. Marble portico. Crystal chandeliers. The woman who takes the package looks like anyone's mother. She has a slight accent, but I could not tell what that was. So I just give it a go and asked her if they needed any extra help with things. I can saw a pretty straight cut in a board, paint, plaster, fix a pipe, wire a light. And I could take the trash out. That's what I tell her. She asks my name and when I say that, she knows who I am because she's bought from dad before, and always orders the best French paper. She tells me her name is 'Miss Em.' And she says, 'Fantastic!' the way the French do and I'm thinking she's French then as she explains they've just fired their janitor for being drunk one too many times. If I can mop floors and sweep, as well as doing all the rest, I have a job. AT FIFTY DOLLARS A WEEK! Fifty bucks, and I'm just nineteen. They even have a room in the basement where I can live. I say, 'Great! Fantastic!' I'm pretty excited. I get back to the shop and tell Dad all about it. He just stands there and lets me tell him everything without a word. And of course, I notice he's being sort of quiet so I finally calm myself down and ask what the problem is. He says that she is not French but a Russian Émigré. He tells me that the place is a brothel. The woman I spoke to is one of the oldest Madams in town."

I had to laugh then at my own story.

Cass gives me the blank stare. "Did you take the job?"

I see the problem now. "Are you kidding? Mom would have killed me."

I got my pictures from Eddie and Frank downstairs and handed those in and then sat at an empty desk out near the elevator and read my Conrad and waited for Cass to hand in her story. I'd called earlier and my friend had left our tickets at the box office, so that was all set.

But time came and went.

It was nine before she left her desk and carried a few sheets in to George.

Then she wandered up the aisle between the desks, slinking just a little like a shy dog.

She said, "Sorry."

I said, "So am I. But a girl's gotta do what a girl's gotta do' as my sister Kate likes to say. How about some Chinese food instead?"

She said, "How about that!" Like she meant it.

And I got to walk her home, after.

That was the night I got my first kiss.

13. Wednesday, April 14, 1937

Whenever I was in the neighborhood, it was my habit to stop at my dad's shop on 6th Avenue, just off the corner of 19th. The El there goes right above the shop and the stop is only a block away so it's a cinch but my mom always appreciates the visit. She likes to think I've gone out of my way just to see them.

The trouble with this is she wants to chat. If I've bothered to come so far, why don't I sit with her a while and talk a little.

And then, right away, she is onto the one topic on her mind.

"So how is your girlfriend?"

I say, "She's not my girlfriend."

She sits up in mock surprise, "Have you asked her to marry you already?"

"Not yet."

"Then she's still just your girlfriend."

The logic is unarguable.

"She's fine."

"What amazing thing has she done this week?"

I look hurt. "You don't want to know what I've done?"

She says, "I know what you do. I want to know what she's up to."

"I don't know. She's busy with something but I don't know what it is."

Of course I was worried that she was seeing Jack Barnes.

"Have you asked her?"

"Not yet."

"She might think you don't care."

Again. Unarguable.

I caught Cass going in the doors at the paper as I was leaving and turned in my tracks and followed her back to the elevator.

"What da ya got?"

"Just a story."

"What about?"

I had her in the elevator alone, except for Sid, the operator. I figure Sid has seen it all and wasn't interested in our shenanigans. He has a wheeze from getting gassed during the War and generally doesn't speak, but like a lot of elevator men he's good with a nod and a wink.

Cass reaches over and gives Sid something that he puts right in his pocket at the same time as she is answering me.

"I'm not supposed to be talking about it."

"Even with me?" I put on the same hurt face I have often used on my mom.

"Especially with you."

"Why especially?"

She says, "Oh, God."

And I see a catch in her eyes. She has given something away.

As the cage rises, the elevator wall at the backside opens to a balcony above the floor of the pressroom where a second floor should be. Those big mat presses are grinding away there. The noise comes gushing in, so Cass doesn't say anything because I wouldn't have heard her anyway.

Sid opens the doors again at the City Room on three. Several reporters are standing there getting ready to leave for dinner together. They all look at Cass and me and then at Sid and then smile to each other. I figure Sid has given them the wink.

When we are out and they are in, and just before the door closes again, Herb Dent, a sports writer, says loudly, "You see the look on her face? I think there was some hanky-panky going on there. What'd a ya bet? What about it Sid?"

The doors closed on that, but I doubt if Sid answered.

Cass says, "Oh, God," for a second time.

I followed along to her desk.

I say, "What's going on?"

She gives me that look she has started using with a tilt of her head whenever I've said something hopeless. It's very cute.

Then she looks back into The Boss's office and she says, "Give me a minute." And she's gone. I pulled a chair from an empty desk and sat there and waited. On her desk I can see she has at least six stories started with the notepaper clipped on the typed sheets. I think about peeking but then think better of it.

She's looking grim when she gets back.

I say, "The Boss doesn't want you to tell me?"

Again I get the tilt of the head but this time the look is far more serious.

"No. He says I can. He says I should."

"What's the matter then?"

"You are going to want to be in on it."

"And that's not good?"

"Maybe. Maybe not. It's my story Hugh."

"What's the problem with that?"

"Because it started with you, that's all."

Funny, I knew immediately what this was. I'd thought about it everyday since. But I've developed a tough skin for these sorts of things. Whatever the best picture was that I'd taken, it was almost never the one used. When I first started I would argue with Dick Weise and even with Barry George about it until I got it into my thick skull that the best picture was not what was always needed—that one was the picture that had the right information for the story they were telling—the one that would confirm the words—and that was also the one that would sell papers.

But after The Boss had gotten me out of jail that night, a few weeks ago, I knew he would not take the matter lightly. I just couldn't be sure how he'd handle it. Now I knew what he'd done.

And Cass sat there looking at my own face and she knew I was doing the math on that.

She said, "I wanted to know why the cops went to all that trouble to burgle your apartment that night. I wanted to know what was going on. I told The Boss and he gave me the lead. He had the feeling it was some sort of cover-up. And on the other side of that would be a story that might be good enough to file away. Something that might stop them the next time they decided to rough up one of our guys. And that's exactly what I thought too." She looks at the piles on her desk and shakes her head. "Look, I gotta hand in a piece on an old lady who passed away this morning—she was the daughter of a Civil War vet. Good story. Let me write that up and then we can go get something to eat and I can tell you the rest of what I've been doing about the John Doe."

I went off to my own desk and pulled out the Conrad again. She was done in less than an hour and then we went looking for some spaghetti.

The story was this: she had gone back to the hotel to speak with the chambermaid herself, but 'Molly' no longer worked at The Hotel Penn. The management was doing the stonewall. Fortunately, another chambermaid had offered the helpful hint that Molly may have been 'traded off' and might be working up at the Hotel Astor now. Cass goes up to Times Square, finds her, and in sworn confidence greased by a sawbuck, gets the info that before his murder, the John Doe had been something of a regular at the hotel. Came once a month, usually staying the one night and always had a different female companion. Nobody knew who the guy was but that he was a cheapskate, and that one particular fact had made him notorious given that he always took one of the larger rooms.

After that, Cass returns then to the Hotel Penn to get some more info from the Head Bellman. But the police have ordered him to keep his nose out of the matter and his mouth shut. A little grease won't change his mind. It would be better for the hotel if the incident was quickly forgotten. Cass then gets the okay from The Boss to investigate further and goes out on the town a couple of times with

Detective Barnes to gather what information she can. She gets him drinking, and along the way he spills the fact that the John Doe was a Philadelphia cop. Barnes had heard another officer tell the Sergeant that fact when they first turned the body over and found a large and very distinctive purple birthmark on his arse. The guy used to call it his 'purple rose,' and bragged that women were crazy about it. The officer who related the fact, and the John Doe, had both been police recruits together just after the war. Detective Barnes had 'missed' hearing the name, but with that much in her pocket, Cass quickly discovered his actual identity.

'Allen Smith' was actually Michael Allen Deems, a great-great-grandson of Ethan Allen, a decorated war veteran in his own right, and most recently a Captain on the Philadelphia police force. He was also a thoroughly corrupt individual. He had repeatedly been accused of taking bribes and giving false testimony, but never convicted. He had used the Hotel Penn for his pleasure many times before. And he had always used the same phony name for his escapades.

But the cover-up by the New York Police department had been a little half-hearted, there being some animosity between the two forces at the moment over conflicted interests in several other cases. LaGuardia had refused a special request from the City of Brotherly Love to offer the press some misinformation concerning the murder—at least until the killer was found. Nevertheless, the body was soon shipped back to Philadelphia where it was reported in the papers there that Captain Deems had suffered a heart attack at home while his family was away. He was quickly buried without ceremony. The important point that there had been no more than a private service and not the usual fuss over a fallen officer of the law, was even made in the *Philadelphia Daily News*, but they had attributed the fact to the body not being found for several days. Nevertheless intimations were also made that Deems might not have been the most honest member of the constabulary—descriptives used in his obituary were 'unconventional' and 'unorthodox.' And, most notably, the fact that his wife of eighteen years had left him months before and was in the middle of divorce proceedings was not mentioned.

A little more poking and the application of some common sense made it clear that Deems would not have wanted to be seen cavorting about town while his wife was suing him in court, and certainly would not have traveled with his female friends any farther than was necessary. This might indicate he had picked up his new best friend somewhere in close proximity to the hostelry he was using. The big room at the Hotel Penn was to impress them.

That part of midtown has fewer saloons and restaurants beyond the hotels but several of those possibilities had bars that were frequented by ladies in search of a free meal and some paying companionship. Soon enough, Cass discovered that Deems often picked his girlfriends up at a local tavern called The Shaw's, where he would usually eat first (probably to avoid the cost of another meal), and then choose from the display of desserts arranged on the stools at the bar, before bringing one of them back to the hotel. He did this about once a month and his habits were well remembered by the headwaiter there. Just as he was also noted for not tipping well at the hotel.

To the waiter's best recollection, which Cass thought was even better than she could have hoped, the girl that night of his murder had black hair, and was a looker. Prettier than the usual. She was not a regular, and not one of the more common gals who were there nearly every night and looked the worse for the wear.

So The Boss's project had been a success.

But there was no point in rubbing the collective noses of the police in their own foolishness. The *Mirror* had to work with them everyday. It wouldn't pay. Instead, The Boss had used the newly acquired knowledge to bargain for privileges and a little inside dope on the other deaths. But the fact was, they had very little additional information on those, and could only promise that they would keep Cass informed. Even better, Barry George had told her that these murders were her story from there on out.

Otherwise, it seemed that the police had been correct about

much of what had happened that night at the Hotel Penn, and what they had offered the press to begin with was a reasonable starting point. Deems was likely shot by the woman he had brought back with him to the hotel. The woman in question was not seen leaving the hotel afterward, but there are various fire doors and exits, and after the Madhattan room closed for the night, things quieted down around there considerably, so the shooting must have occurred earlier. The hair sample found on the bed had indicated one more possible reason for her not being recalled by any of the staff. The woman in question was probably not a brunette. The hairs found had been dyed. Speculation was that she might have been wearing a wig.

Two other pieces of information dangled. Capt. Deems had been carrying his Smith and Wesson .38 caliber revolver, and that weapon appeared to be missing along with his clothes. The other and more fascinating detail was he had been shot, not with a .38 but with a .22, just as the several others had. A very unusual murder weapon. More common in poorer neighborhoods. Low calibers were often used for defense but seldom for a planned homicide. Killing the victim with the lower caliber was simply not a certainty. Not usually.

I insisted on ice cream after the spaghetti and that was only available at that hour at a place I knew very well, Patty's Parlour on 6th Street. This was not a purposeful attempt to get Cass any closer to my apartment, though I saw a look pass in those eyes that made me think the thought had occurred to her. But she likes ice cream. It was an easy sell.

Besides, I had another couple of questions to ponder. "How did the cops know I had developed the pictures at my apartment?"

Cass was clearly perplexed by that. "Who else knew?"

"The Boss and Brad Stenis knew. Tom Reilly knows because we've talked often enough about the joy of waiting in line for Frank and Eddie to develop the photos at the office. And Frank and Eddie knew, of course."

"What about Eddie." she says.

"What about him."

"His brother is a cop."

So Eddie might be the police informant at the paper, keeping the cops up to the minute on what the paper was doing. Spying. They couldn't be paying him much. Cops never do. His loyalty had to be bought on the cheap. A brother could do that.

On that note Cass let her spoon drop into her dish—only half done with a double scoop of strawberry ice cream and chocolate syrup and with my own dish already long empty. Her eyes examined the top of the little three by three table we were at like it was covered with writing instead of shellac.

I said, "What's the matter?"

In that distant voice I've heard a couple of times now, she says, "It looks like a sort of Bruegel . . ."

She hesitated, so I piped up, "Mahogany I think. But just veneer."

Her head titled off toward her shoulder again, and she smiled at me sweetly that time. Hopeless or not, I know my woods.

She says, "I mean the Flemish painter. It's as if there is something else going on everywhere you look. Too much going on. Even if we catch one thing, there is something else in the background that we don't even know about."

I see she still has her mind on darker stuff. I say, "That's the fact of the matter, isn't it? You can't cover everything. You cover what you can and hope someone else is taking care of the other thing. Otherwise the ocean of troubles just swallows you up and no one is saved. That's what Dad likes to say about it when they used to come up on a sinking ship. Take things one at a time and do your best. Doing too much will mean more will drown. Right?"

She sits up straight. "Yes. You're right! As you're always saying, I have to keep my focus."

"I say that? I think that all the time, but do I actually say it?"

"Yes. You do" The head tilts again. Twice in one minute. That must be a record. But then she says, "It's getting late. We should go."

"Don't you want to finish your ice cream?"

"I'm full."

"Can I have it?"

She gave me that sweet smile one more time and I ate what was left in about half a minute.

I finish with, "One more question."

She says "What?" I can hear that she is getting tired by her voice.

"What did you give Sid in the elevator?"

"Two bits."

"Are we supposed to be tipping Sid now?"

"No! I borrowed twenty-five pennies from him for the poker game on Thursday."

I flagged a taxi right out in front of Patty's Ice Cream Parlour and sent Cass home before she got to worrying any more about my motives. I paid the cabbie in advance just to salve my own conscience because my intentions were in fact not the best.

At least I got another kiss for the effort.

14. Tuesday, April 20, 1937

One of my night patrols during the past week was into a new piece of real estate called Knickerbocker Village. This is an R.F.C. development that was built on the old 'Lung Block' in the middle of an ancient slum of tenements that used to fill some rat infested acreage between the butt ends of the Brooklyn and Manhattan bridges, just up the street from the old *Mirror* office. It was originally supposed to be for the people that were kicked out of the stew of brick tenements along there on Hamilton Street, and so it was financed by all the taxpayers for the benefit of the less fortunate, but it's fully occupied now by all the lawyers and paper pushers who work a few blocks away over around City Hall and knew the bargain when they saw it. No sense wasting those neat one and two bedroom apartments on a bunch of filthy wretches who were going to die of tuberculosis anyway.

The modern design of the place was appealing enough on its own. Very sharp lines. Very clean. But fifty bucks a month got you three or four big rooms and a full kitchen—brand spankin' new. I pay $35 for my two smaller rooms over on Perry Street. The wait list at Knickerbocker Village is a couple of years. That is, if you know someone.

When I was over there recently with a flatfoot named Lorimer for a disturbance call, I briefly got to see the inside of one apartment. Very nice. But this was under a dark circumstance. The lawyer who lived there, a Henry Broome, had been knocking on his wife and kids. A neighbor had called to complain. Because I was assigned to that beat for the night, I had simply followed along when the patrolman, Lorimer, said, "Jesus. Mercy," into the call box like he meant it.

The elevator up to the ninth floor was nearly elegant with chrome appointments, maybe more than one needs that's not in the Chrysler building, but there is no operator. The halls are narrow but with high ceilings and not as airless as some of the newer apartments you see these days.

At the door, there was whimpering audible. Lorimer knocked with his nightstick. Broome opened the door abruptly as if already close on the other side. But when he spotted me standing there behind the patrolman he went berserk again even though I had no intention of taking pictures at first. Patrolman Lorimer, who is not a big guy, had to whack Mr. Broome with his nightstick once or twice to calm him down. Then Broome's wife begun wailing again from somewhere out of sight. A couple of kids were crying as well. This was one sad scene at two in the morning. Lumps of food—mashed potatoes, carrots, and some sort of gray meat—was scattered on the floor and had apparently been thrown there by the husband in anger a few hours before.

I supposed the wife was not a good enough cook to satisfy the man's tastes—that's the sort of joke you tell yourself to keep your legs steady. But I could not imagine that he'd been raging for so many hours. This was madness. One of the children looked stupefied. The youngest had crawled into a corner and fallen asleep amidst the chaos of several pairs of shoes.

I also told Cass about this recent encounter over our spaghetti. That was a larger mistake. Her stories seemed so much more interesting, and I was just trying to give my own efforts a little color. She had promptly asked The Boss about it the next day and this becomes the start of another piece for her to follow up on.

I imagine the occupation of the Knickerbocker Village by middle-class bureaucrats was hard to sell as a scandal. Just another example of inside political favoritism, given all the other misappropriations of public monies going on. But this particular incident had the simplicity of a basic human drama to it and the cardinal numbers were all set out against a nice, clean looking background and that was what Cass played with when she spun the case to George. I didn't exactly hear that, but I watched him listen through the glass to his office.

Fred French, the fellow who had designed the Knickerbocker Village, keeps a high profile. He is actually responsible for several projects around town. All of them very nice looking. And that makes him an easy target, given that he's living large from his contracts with the government in hard times. In the office, I could see The Boss nod his head repeatedly. But Cass did not come out smiling. It seems that Cass was upset with me for not taking any pictures the first time I had been over there. I suppose she could have used them for her argument. Now she asked me to go back to the place with her.

First she told me to wait, made some calls, and then came back in less than an hour. Time enough for me to catch up with what was going on with some of the new players in the Dodger lineup.

We grabbed a train and were down to Chatham Square in less than twenty minutes. Figuring the husband to be away during mid-day, Cass knocked on the door and the wife answered directly. She had a black eye turned green and swollen and looked like she might be a relative of mine in that regard. But at the sight of us her good eye went large immediately. Then we heard the voice of the husband from the kitchen. This was two o'clock of a Tuesday afternoon.

He says, "Who is it?"

Mrs. Broome is obviously afraid to answer and has her arm raised immediately to hide her face so Cass speaks up.

"The *Mirror*. We'd like to ask you a few questions."

Mr. Broome was at the door in a second and already talking.

"I don't wanna talk to the damn *Mirror*."

He tries to slam the door but I had my shoe in place on the jamb.

I say, "How did your wife get the shiner?"

Mrs. Broome had already fled somewhere out of our sight. I could not hear the kids.

He says, "I'll sue your asses," while trying to shut the door. But I'd moved in a little so his second attempt could not get any momentum.

Cass says, "You work for the Parks Department. We called and they said you were out someplace talking to a vendor about a contract."

Staring down at my foot on the doorjamb, he points down with a stiff arm, "That's trespass!" and repeats the words while trying to kick my shoe out of place. Instead he gets a lick on my shin, so I put my fist in his chest and he went right down on his butt. The door opened wide then all by itself, but we stayed right where we were. I had my camera out in my left hand and took a shot on that, but I didn't have the right picture yet. I wanted the wife and the black eye. It was a lot to ask. Thankfully, the husband stayed where he was. I could see his mind working. He was probably just hoping for something out of us that he could take to a judge.

Cass says calmly, "The police have been called in here more than a dozen times. You're getting quite a reputation for knocking your wife around. I was wondering if you had anything to say in your own defense?"

He says, 'I've got nothing to say. Get out!"

Cass says, "The *Mirror* is filing an amicus brief with the court. You will be charged with assault and battery as well as the endangerment of minors—by the way, where are your kids?"

"I have friends! I know people! Robert Moses'll hear about this! He'll sue you and your damned paper for defamation!"

I was thinking, if Robert Moses heard about this, he would likely fire the guy and toss him in the East River with his own hands. But I repeated Cass's question, "Where are your kids?"

We heard a thin voice from back in the apartment.

"My father came and got them."

Cass's tone of voice changed right there. The calm conciliator disappeared. She says, "Then why are you here Doris? Why are you even here if your children are safe?"

The wife's voice came again, "He said he'd get them back if I left." We could see her shadow then at the rear of a short hall that lead to the bedrooms.

Mr. Broome sat bolt upright and twisted himself briefly toward the hall, saying, "Shut up! Shut up, bitch! Stay back there! I'll kill you if you say anything!"

He sat there motionless then for a moment with his butt planted on the parquet and legs splayed out like a doll. It was as if he had no idea what to do next. The confusion on his face was clear. I could not smell liquor. I thought right then for certain that the man was in fact crazy.

I toned my own voice down, "You're not going to kill anyone, Mr. Broome. That's not what you want."

Cass says, "Doris. Come with us. Your husband is dangerous. He could hurt you. He won't be able to get the children now. He'll be in jail. And your children need a mother."

Mrs. Broome didn't answer.

I said, "We can drive you wherever you want to go, Mrs. Broome. Get some things together and we'll take you there."

When I looked again, Henry Broome's face had suddenly fallen. The tight knots of anger had collapsed. He continued to sit as he was, but now the upper portion of his body was hunched and he started to cry. His upper body shook

Cass said, "Please, Doris. I can take you home with me, if you don't want your family to see you."

Mrs. Broome came fully out in the hall where we could see her then.

Cass said, "Please. Come home with me."

There was a moment's hesitation and then Mrs. Broome disappeared briefly. When we saw her again she had stuffed some clothes in a cloth bag and came up the hall toward us, growing more hesitant as she approached the spot where her husband sat crying.

Suddenly, as she came closer, he sprang up on his feet and turned on her.

Again he said, "I'll kill you!"

I dropped my bag and was through the doorway pretty quick. I let the camera fall down on its strap into the crook of my elbow and grabbed his arms from behind.

Doris started a scream but with Cass reaching toward her, she took hold of a hand, and Cass lead her out toward the elevator.

I had a good grip on Henry Broome, but he did not try to break away. He stood there, as if frozen. Every muscle tight. When I heard the elevator door open I let go and retreated into the hall, closing the apartment door behind me.

The elevator was not fast, but in any case, Henry Broome had reached the sidewalk before us. It was not the picture I wanted but the one I got.

15. Friday, April 23, 1937

When it's slow, I sometimes end up playing pool with the guys upstairs at Julian's Billiards on 14th Street and drinking coffee at the Horn & Hardart right downstairs. We play for nickels and the guy that wins has to buy coffee for the others. Works out fine unless you can't handle a stick. And the place is centrally located between 45th and City Hall, so if something happens there is a phone booth just outside. We can hear it ring and they call us there for a fire or whatever, George is not shy about calling just to give us indigestion.

While I'm there, I usually grab myself some beef stew, or if I have the extra buck, a Salisbury steak and mashed at the steam table, along with a dish of the rice pudding. But it's the coffee we actually go there for. It's better than the greasy spoon around the corner at 45th Street.

The Friday after Mr. Broome's fall, I was just started on my Salisbury steak. Suddenly somebody grabs my right ear between two fingers and tries to lift me out of my chair from behind. But my nose works fine and I don't have to turn around to see who it is.

I say, "Can I at least finish?"

She says, "You didn't tell me you were going off."

Across the table is Reilly and he's smiling too broadly for his own good health.

I say, "Did you tell me you needed me for something? I missed it."

She still had my ear.

Reilly is having a fit, he thinks it's so funny. He's about to lose a mouthful of coffee.

I turn and I see she's smiling. It's her little joke.

She says, "No. I was just hungry."

And then she heads off to get some nickels and visit the steam table. She's back in a jiffy. "Who won?" she says, referring to our game of eight ball.

Reilly says, "I did."

Cass has the macaroni and cheese. She digs in quietly and I have time to consider the situation. I know she didn't come all the way down from 45th Street for the macaroni and cheese.

I say, "What'da ya got?"

She raises an eyebrow and keeps eating.

I say, "You're still tiffed at me for tracking you up to Yorkville the other day. This is revenge."

She shrugs and keeps eating.

Reilly is still there nursing his coffee and watching for developments. He says, "He, ho!"

I say, "Let me guess. John Doe?"

She stops chewing just for an instant and I know I'm on to her.

This does not require professor Einstein. A few days before she'd asked for my copies of the pictures I had taken at the hotel that day. The ones I left in Brooklyn. But I see the way her jaw works. I'm getting to know that jaw very well. It tightens up just a mite and goes a little square when she is going to be contrary about something.

Reilly finally says, "Well, then. I'd better be getting back to work. I'll see you kids later." And he's gone.

She says, "I wanted to do a follow up on Henry Broome. I thought you'd like to come along for the ride."

That was an easy call. I just smiled back.

Mostly it would be a matter of speaking with the wives. The husbands were more likely away at work given the hour—just as we had thought Henry Broome would be the other day. Nevertheless, Cass was sure that was the best strategy. The women would be more willing to speak to her.

What was clear to me however, and very quickly, was that most of the women who answered their doors had other things on their minds.

Our first call was an immediate neighbor on the same hall, a small blond woman with a very large hairy mole on her chin and a high voice.

After getting her name and assuring her that it would not be used in print, Cass asked, "Do you have any idea why Henry Broome became violent so often?"

The neighbor said, "He was a Leninist. Very unstable."

Not the sort of answer we might have expected.

Cass said, "Then you think his politics drove him to beat his wife?"

The small woman with the mole said, "Certainly. He was recidivistic!"

We moved on.

At a door on the opposite side, an overweight woman answered who was nearly as tall as I am, and looked me in the eye as if I were a mortal enemy. She appeared to have just awaked to our knocking. The air of the apartment was stale and smelled of her sweat.

After introducing ourselves, Cass says, "I am doing a follow-up on Henry Broome's death."

This woman says, "Why?"

Cass says, "To understand how the situation came to be."

The woman, "Why does it rain? Look Miss, I was the one who called the cops. I was always the one who called. No one else cared. He beat on her all the time. I went over there one night and told him that he should try that with me. I would break his neck."

Cass, "How long do you think it had it been going on?"

The woman: "Years. Since Adam an' Eve."

The woman looked directly back at me as if I had been doing

this sort of thing as well.

Cass, "Did you know Doris?"

The woman, "She wouldn't speak to me. He told her he'd kill her if she spoke to me."

Cass, "Do you have any insight into what might have caused this?"

The woman, "He's a man. What can you expect?"

Cass took down her name and what she did for a living. She worked as a night operator at Bell Telephone. On her own behalf she added that she was divorced.

I could not control myself and asked, "Did your husband ever beat you?"

This seemed to surprise her. I thought the question was pretty funny myself. But she looked at me as if I was a fool, "I would have wrung his neck if he tried, for the bantam he was."

Another woman on the eighth floor just below admitted she had heard Doris fall several times to the accompaniment of Henry Broome's voice—the voice was barely muffled by the building. This neighbor was a bleach-blond with half an inch of dark roots who might have been under forty but I bet otherwise. Not really bad looking despite the roots.

Cass asked, "Why didn't you call the police?"

The blonde said, "It's not the sort of place."

"Why?"

"I have to live here."

The woman craned her neck out into the hall to see who else might be there to listen.

Cass asked, "Can we come in for just a moment?"

The woman stood back and let us in. I noticed then that she wore leather slippers run down at the back. No socks. She had on a dark blue house dress that fell well below her knees and this was decorated with a pattern of bright red flowers, but apparently very little else beneath. We had probably gotten her out of bed as well.

With the door carefully closed, she whispers, "They're all Boshies here. Always arguing. Yelling. The Trotskyites hate the

Stalinists and they both hate the socialists and the fascists. We actually have several fascists, you know. They've had excrement thrown at their doors. I don't know why they stay—No. I do. It's cheap here. Everybody likes it on the cheap."

Cass asked, "Do you have children?"

Blonde woman, "Me? No."

Cass, "What do you do for a living?"

Blonde woman. "Whatever I can."

She very purposely looked at me then.

Cass, "Does your husband work."

"I suppose. I haven't seen him lately."

I had immediately picked up on her meaning, but only now I saw that Cass had also taken the hint.

"Did you know Henry Broome?"

"Is this for print?"

"No. Just background. Your name won't be used."

"Yes. We've met, you might say."

"Did he ever try to hit you?"

"All he wanted was the sex."

She looked again at me to see what response the statement of fact had gotten. I don't think I gave her much to see.

Cass asked, "Did you know Doris?"

"Yes. We spoke. A number of times. She's nice."

"Did it bother you that he beat his wife?"

"Sure. But at least he didn't do it for a while after he'd come down to see me." She winced immediately, maybe realizing what she had said. "Look. I don't work for the Salvation Army. It's just high finance with me. Henry was a very rude person. He would come down here knocking and when I looked through the peephole he would hold up his five-dollar bill and wave it at me. Very rude. But when he beat his wife, he usually raped her. You can tell when a woman is being raped. Not like she was enjoying it."

Cass's voice dropped so low it was near a whisper. "How often?"

"How often did he come knocking? Once a week or so."

"How often did he beat Doris?"

"Hard to tell. I'm not here all the time. I don't usually conduct my business here, you understand. I work the hotels mostly. My name is in with all the bellboys and concierges. I get calls. Maybe not like I used to. But I'm not as young as I used to be."

She tugged at her dress at both sides of her hips. What was revealed beneath the tightened fabric was not unappealing.

Now suddenly the story had turned. There was a thread here to the death of John Doe. This was clear to Cass as well and she did not hesitate.

"You've read about the murder at the Hotel Penn?"

"Sure. It's bad for business. Papers even say it was probably one of the girls. I don't think so. Not likely. The girls have enough on their minds. Someone is always bending your arm for a piece of the action. The bellmen are the worst. They're all hooked up with the Mob. You can't lie and say you didn't answer a call."

I could see on her face that Cass was trying to sort the information in all this. But I was curious. I asked, "How did you get this apartment?"

She shrugged like that should be obvious. "One of my regulars over at City Hall set me up."

16. Monday to Tuesday, April 26 to 27, 1937

Because the nature of it was not exactly family fare, The Boss held the story back until Monday. Page six.

Monday, just after noon, I get another bright idea. The Boston Bees are the worst team in the National League and the Dodgers are playing them at 1:30. This may be one of the few teams that Brooklyn can beat this year, so I go up and tap Dan Parker for a couple of passes and then corner Cass at her desk. And so it's nobody else's business, I have a note written out on the back of one of the pictures of a black and white cocker spaniel in the arms of a fireman that I took about a month ago. Cass is busy typing something, but the picture gets her attention. Then the note. It took her about thirty seconds longer than I wished it had but she finally says, "Sure," pulls the sheet from her typewriter and grabs her coat.

The ballpark was nearly empty and the air was raw. A good reason to sit close. Some girls near the dugout got a couple of songs going to woo their favorite players and those went around the park and gave Cass and I a reason to sing a couple show tunes to keep warm between innings. The Dodgers lost. That's okay. But naturally I find out there that she is a diehard Indians fan. With them in the American League, I might have to endure a few Yankees games to satisfy that.

By Tuesday we know LaGuardia has gone nuts over the story. He sees it as a disparagement of both government workers and the Knickerbocker Village, which he calls one of the City's finest public works projects.

Cass had laid the facts out as the incidental discoveries made while looking into Broome's suicide. But the fact was that the *Mirror* was a Hearst paper and Hearst had been in a nearly continuous battle with the Roosevelt administration since before the first inauguration. Never mind that Mr. LaGuardia has taken up President Roosevelt's cause here in New York.

To be fair, Hearst had frequently attacked Hoover's inept attempts to solve the economic crisis when the President passed a truck load of government programs—as if some bureaucrat is going to know how to grow corn better than an Iowa farmer—but when Roosevelt then went on to pick up the worst of Hoover's measures and not only carry them forward but add to them, Hearst's criticism increased dramatically.

Speaking about all of this to me, Cass is pretty explicit. And I was pleased that she thought she could trust me with her thoughts more than I would be bothered by the politics of it. I don't care for all that and she knows it.

She says, "Hearst is the boogey man now. When he opposed the Roosevelt gang instead of going along for the ride, the White House took the gloves off. It didn't matter that Hearst had opposed Republicans before. Or that he had criticized Hoover before. Any criticism of FDR will not be allowed or go unpunished. The purpose of the press now is to support the President's program. You see it everyday. They're even putting plays on Broadway that are financed by the Federal Theatre Project that go out of their way to take shots at Hearst. That fellow Orson Welles you were talking about the other night is a part of all that. He may be a genius but he gets his wheels greased because he says the right things. He's expected to be just another promoter if he wants to work. It seems like everyone is a shill for something. But all of them are just two-bit Babbitts. It all gets so tiresome to me."

I wondered, "If you don't promote what you do, how's anyone going to see it?"

She was perplexed by the very idea, "I don't know. Just do it. If it's any good, someone will notice." You'd think she's Italian when she gets excited about something. Her hands start moving. She says, "Maybe it's just a matter of a line that gets crossed, Hugh. The difference between saying this is what I can do, or here's what I've done, instead of saying this is the best, or this is the greatest or this is the only way. Everything is a Barnum & Bailey circus now. Everything is the biggest. It's a whole way of thinking, now. Everything has to be the biggest. Everyone has to be the brightest. And if it's not the biggest, it's not worth a damn." She looks fierce when she on a ride. I try to stay quiet. She says, "But who takes the measure of all that? Who gives it the first place medal? You look behind it and all you see is it's just the same old people putting everything else down except themselves, or their friends. The kid who wins the essay contest is the alderman's son. The girl who wins the beauty contest just happens to be the Mayor's daughter."

I had a feeling and I had to ask about that.

"Did you ever lose an essay contest that way?" I immediately wondered if she had ever lost a beauty contest, if only to get the chance to say that the judges were blind, but just as the words started from my lips I knew it was the wrong choice. She would never have entered such a thing.

She smiled at me for that. I think she had read my mind and appreciated my choice.

At least she laughed, "In high school. It was a civics essay. I've never recovered from the bitter disappointment."

"Maybe that was the difference, then. You wanted to be the best and you just wouldn't give it up."

"Maybe. But I think it was more likely my father's idea. He was often angry. I worried about him sometimes. He doesn't take losing very well. He could never accept the injustice of things."

I already knew that her father used to give away shoes. He could not stand the sight of children in the streets of Cleveland, especially in winter, without a good pair of shoes. Thankfully, though he never advertised the fact, his generosity had become well known and his business had only prospered as a result.

Still, I was worried about Cass for much the same thing.

I said, "You write about that. I can see all that outrage in what you say. But I don't think you always get the wrong of it. You want someone to be the cause. You want something to be responsible. That's not always the way it is. If what you're looking for is black you'll never see it in the dark. What you have to look for is in the shadow."

"You! You and your pictures! Everything is about the shadows. But Hugh, some things ARE black and white! Some things are simply wrong and others right."

This begged a thought I had fairly often. "How can you be so sure?"

But it didn't take her a second to consider. Probably because she has asked herself the same question too many times before.

"Sometimes, just by the reaction. When you stick a snake, it squirms. If you write something critical about the politicians, and they come after you. If you had it wrong, they'd ignore you. But when the paper gets letters by the bucket load, you know. George gets a call from upstairs wondering what's going on. It may not be as bad as what they're doing to some of the guys I've heard about on the radio these days, but nearly. It's the intimidation that shuts everyone up."

"Except you."

'Well," she starts, but she knows I'm complimenting her and she's feeling a little embarrassed by it. "I've managed to be more creative about it lately. Don't you think? George has taught me that. Just in the short time I've been here. He's seen everything. He knows all the ropes! Or at least the strings to pull." I can see her mind working on a self-defense. She does not want to be thought of as righteous. She knows the pitfall there. "But you know, I think it's not all that different than what you do with your camera. You move the focus. You don't make it all about the stupidity of the guy who drove his car into the post, but the foolishness of what he's done. Or the meanness of the scene. Like the opened can of evaporated milk you got into that picture of the kids sleeping on the fire escape last summer. You could see the jagged edge of it. You knew that those kids had fallen asleep hungry and the edge of that metal can on the side said it all."

This caught me by complete surprise.

"How did you know I took that picture?"

"I asked."

"When?"

"When the fellow from the Hearst organization first called me to see if I'd be interested in leaving the *Daily News*. The *Mirror* ran that picture a couple weeks before. He didn't know anything about the picture, but he looked into it for me. It gave me a chance to think about the offer."

What an extraordinary thing!

I had to tell her, "And the funny part of that was, someone wrote a letter to the *Mirror* about that picture. They objected to it, saying it was a set-up."

"Why would they think that?"

"Because it's like what you said about Barnum & Bailey before. So many things are phony. They see all those photographs of suffering people that come out of the Works Progress Administration and they know half of them are staged. Now, why do they have to do that, when it's all around them? Why did Mathew Brady have to arrange all those bodies on the battlefield for his Civil War pictures? You can see it right off. And even if they're not sure how, they can feel it. So people start being suspicious of everything they see."

She's giving me her cutest frown. "They thought you'd put those kids out on the fire escape?"

"No. People sleep out on their fire escapes all the time when the heat gets bad. It was that milk can. That jaggedy can. The letter writer wanted to know why they'd open it like that instead of just punching a couple of holes like everybody else does. Like I would know the answer to that. I took that picture from the window across the alley. I never got a chance to go back and ask."

The night we went out the second time—the spaghetti night—I had not wanted to talk about anything too removed from the subject at hand—which for me was Cass herself, of course. But somehow the matter of spies had come up because of what she had been doing, looking into the death of Sam Schechner. This was a fun topic for speculation. Especially as it might concern the German American Bund. There was a lot of worry around town concerning those fellows and about the Soviets too, and what either of them might be up to.

In my life, I had only ever known a single person that I thought was a spy, and I mentioned him to Cass that evening. That was Mr. Shinn. He was just one of our many boarders at the house during the years when I was growing up. But Mr. Shinn was our mystery man. We actually never learned what he did for a living, if anything. He was always very polite. He was quiet. And he stayed with us for just a year. He spoke excellent English and that was the only way we had to determine he was a foreigner. We understood him to be vaguely Jewish in background but religion never entered his conversation. Nor did the word 'God' ever make an appearance.

If you deal with strangers that way, over a period of time, it's almost impossible to avoid getting to know them. People have their quirks. Their habits. And those little things are always tied to larger ones. A picture is always drawn for you. But Mr. Shinn had none of that. Other than being polite and soft-spoken and always coming and going at the same hours. Mom and Dad were puzzled and even disturbed by it. I heard them talk about it several times.

In the end, Mr. Shinn's revealing moment came when it was obvious by his dinner conversation that he had taken a fancy to one of our other boarders and this was confirmed the evening he made some sort of proposal to her and she slapped him so hard we all heard the crack of it throughout the house. Like a firecracker! Neither he nor Betty made any comment about the incident after the fact, but Mr. Shinn's face had borne the evidence of the offense for the week following. Like a 'scarlet letter,' my mom said. And then he left us for good.

Cass said, "Having boarders in your house must have been fascinating. Tell me another story. Tell me about this 'Betty' you've mentioned."

The little voice in my head protested, but then I just had to tell her about Miss Betty Malone.

"She was a successful actress. Not famous, but she had a talent for 'types.' Mimicry, they call it. So she was always needed and always working. Her great game was to sneak her boyfriends up to her room without my mom and dad knowing. Her room then was directly across from mine on the third floor because my older brother had already moved out and I was well aware of her shenanigans. But watching her accomplish this was a great fascination to me. Betty was always getting home late from her work at the theatre. I would hear her on the stairs and would peek out from my door. I think she knew that, but I never told on her.

"One thing she had down like an acrobat was in walking up the stairs with whomever the fellow was that she'd brought home with her that night. They would take the steps exactly in unison, as if they were shadow dancing. I suspect they were all actors themselves and used to that kind of choreography. Also, she could plot Mom's movements downstairs by the sound of her step. She knew the precise time when Mom went out to the market in the mornings and that was when the fellow would make his escape. She knew when Dad got home, and just when he would go down to the basement to shovel the coal into the furnace. He couldn't be hearing a thing when he was at that and we all took advantage of the fact in our own ways through the years. But she had everything timed to the instant. I imagine that stage work requires this. And it went on for years. At least until we got the oil furnace put in.

"Eventually she married one of those fellows and moved away. But the joke was this. My mom had known about the sub-terfuge all along. I heard her speaking to Uncle Robert about it one evening during a visit. Mom had made the pretense of keeping a watchful eye over the doings of all the boarders but, having made the mistake of renting the room to Betty back in 1920, the first year they took in lodgers to help with expenses, she had also taken a liking to the woman and could not just throw her out.

"Betty was a great fabricator and had endless tales about the stage and about the various stars she'd met. Very entertaining. She knew John Barrymore personally, she told us, and we all had an idea what she meant by it. For years, we would look forward to dinner-time on her nights off. But Betty did have her 'predilections' as Mom would say. She was very much given to a physical approach to anything. And Mom has admitted she was afraid that 'Betty might take it into her head one day to seduce one of my boys. So letting her have her way with the fellows she brought home was a good preventative to that I think.'"

I knew at that instant Cass's interest had suddenly changed. This was clear in her eyes. There was nearly a frown, but only enough to darken her eyes a shade. I stopped talking and waited for whatever the matter was to work its way out.

Finally she said, "Did she? Did Betty ever seduce any of your mother's boys?"

"No, never. Ben was crazy for her, but Betty had her own code. And besides, he was ten years younger."

It was the first time I had the idea then that Cass could be jealous. And I was astonished to think that I might be the object of that worry.

17. Wednesday, April 28, 1937

But like I said, LaGuardia was unhappy with both Cass and myself for the story about the Knickerbocker Village, as well as at the *Mirror* for printing it. Thus, I was persona non grata at City Hall again.

And this led to another occurrence that was even more of an outright disaster for me, even if it was of little importance to the world at large.

Somehow, in recent weeks, I had gained a little standing in the eyes of the police. They were just trying to be helpful then, I think, when they bothered to drop a paper bag off at the *Mirror* filled with all the photographs they'd previously confiscated from my apartment. I was happy to have them back, of course, except that some of the lot were the ones that I had kept there purposely so that my dad (and mom) would never see them.

This needs more of an explanation.

My dad does not advertise in the newspapers. From the beginning he has cultivated a specific clientele through the use of a device he conceived of himself: The Pocket Officemate. This is a small book with flexible covers, which does in fact fit easily into any pocket. The stiff cover is a high quality faux vellum, and the interior is printed on the very same heavy 32 lb. French stock that is used as stationery by Miss Em, the madame on Sutton place who had first offered me a job.

The Pocket Officemate is a simple enough idea. On the right

side page is a graphic instruction for accomplishing some difficult office task, such as replacing the ribbon on a typewriter or properly filling a fountain pen. The instruction is clear and concise and the pictures, as graphic as the cartoon panels in the funny pages, make sure the words are easily interpreted. On the left side page is an advertisement for the relevant ribbons or pens offered at my dad's shop. Page after page. And the book is usually about 200 pages long. Most of the copy is humorous and intended as such. The fellow pictured there struggling with the task is clearly a caricature of my dad. The secretary who always comes to his aide is just as plainly my mom. From the very beginning Dad has hired a fellow sailor he knew in his Merchant Marine days to do the graphics—a man who had once entertained a hard lot with his cartoons of fellow crewmen and now works installing oil furnaces. My mom wrote the text.

Each October, Dad distributes his little book to 'select locations.' Miss Em's is just one of those. So are the offices for some of the best advertising agencies and the better hotels. The book has a limited run of 2000 copies. Because of the quality of the thing itself, with a sophisticated cover design not so subtly stolen anew each year from some poster originally made for one of the Paris art exhibitions, and always printed in two-colors, as well as the useful advice and the humor on the inside, Dad's little book is usually kept at hand by his customers throughout the year.

Dad never sends the books through the mail, same way as he seldom ships items to his customers through the post office. The person to person contact is the key to the entire business so far as he is concerned.

In October, 1933, Dad was sick with pneumonia from running about and making deliveries himself after he had let Jerry go. This nearly killed him, given the economy and his state of mind, so Mom had the responsibility then of keeping things together during the worst Christmas of our lives. Naturally, I took on the job of distributing the Pocket Officemate that year. As difficult as that might seem, given that I was then employed full time at the *Mirror*, the whole project was something of a lark for me. I'd already carried hundreds of copies through the years to new customers who'd requested them and I had Dad's client list in hand and used the 'street-finder 'down in the circulation department at the newspaper to locate the addresses I was unfamiliar with beforehand to save time. There were 1680 addresses on the customer list. Intermixed with my assignments for the paper, and some indulgences by Guy Fredericks (who was City Editor then and aware of my project and the reason for it), I managed to complete my rounds just before Thanks-giving and kept my job too.

Now this is the story, and pretty much, what I wanted to tell Cass, if she let me.

It was a rather cold and wet November day of that year when I finally reached Sutton Place just before noon. I tapped with the brass knocker—a squirrel with an acorn in his paw—rather gingerly, still remembering my first use of it when I had even shocked myself with the reverberation. And Miss Em answered the door just as she had a couple of years before. (I was unaware then that there was a discreet window at the side, which allowed her to review her callers in advance.)

She is a small woman, slightly plump, with her hair short and dark, and has a terrific smile, but she appears somewhat older than her years. You don't realize her height at first because the entry floor is raised a full step, so she is more at the level of her visitors when the door opens. That day she was dressed in a bright green kimono laced with gold thread and something very yellow peeking from the edges beneath. And she welcomed me immediately as if she knew me.

"Well hello to you! Hugh, am right?"

It is very pleasant when someone remembers your name.

I said hello and that I was delivering dad's little book around to all his customers.

"Come in out of the rain then!"

This statement was delivered as a command. Her Russian accent was suddenly sharp, resisting any argument.

Immediately she offered some hot tea. I told her I seldom

drank it. She said to try hers and that it would change my opinion of the stuff. (And it did, but I haven't found anyplace since then to make it in a similar fashion—in a tall samovar of brass and decorative blue and white porcelain. The teapot sits at the very top like a crown.)

She sat me in a parlor where there were several small tables arranged around a coal fire which was very welcoming on that nasty day. One other person was there already, a large man in a housecoat and he was reading the papers in the light of the window. He nodded at me. He is a famous author with a distinctive voice and I suppose he thought to conceal his identity by keeping his mouth shut. I have since encountered him elsewhere but it is not fair to say his name.

Miss Em, having already taken my wet coat and noted that I held onto my large bag rather jealously, sat across from me and asked. "Is that filled with those little books?"

"No. It's my camera. I work for the *Mirror* full-time now, as a photographer."

This seemed to instantly delight her. "Are you any good?"

The direct way she asked this begged me to brag. I think it was the turn of her voice. But I controlled myself.

"I'm learning to be."

At this point I was aware that the fellow reading the paper had an eye in my direction again. The thought that I might have taken his picture as he sat there at Miss Em's must have thrilled him.

She asked, "Do you have anything you have done with you now?"

Of course I did. I had half a dozen of my best prints. You never know when you might have to impress someone who does not want their picture taken—or a girl.

The fact was, I had seldom been asked. I pulled the envelope, with each of the photographs in their own glassine wraps. She examined these very carefully. Almost solemnly. And then, she surprises me when she hands them over to the fellow reading the paper. He goes through them, and nods again, and hands them back to me.

Miss Em says, "Can you take outside work?"

I had never been asked that myself. I had no idea what rules governed my job at the paper. (In fact, I've found out since that I'm not supposed to). But I said. "Yes. I think so."

"Would you take some pictures for me?"

I said, "Sure! When?"

"Sunday. Come on Sunday afternoon."

The following Sunday was thankfully brighter. The air was crisp. The rain of the week had left the autumn air as clean as it ever gets.

On the previous visit I had not even asked what it was I would be taking pictures of, but in my own defense, despite already knowing then that Miss Em conducted a high-class brothel, I had not thought anything of that. I think I assumed somehow I would be taking pictures of Miss Em herself.

Instead, after she opened the door, I was greeted by half a dozen young women, each of a different complexion and height, and dressed in robes of various colors and texture and length, though all vaguely similar to the one worn by Miss Em herself, and appearing very expensive to me. Some of these were velvet. Some were satin. But all the women were flat-out beautiful and the mood was rather happy from the first moment. Several appeared to be near giddy at getting their pictures taken. I must have been smiling ear to ear. The talk was almost continuous.

The first few of these were 'family portraits' of them all together in front of the white marble hearth at the coal fire. After that I was to take several shots of each of the girls separately except in the case of Jenny and Pearl who wanted theirs to be together.

I asked their full names, as I always did for my subjects when working for the paper. Only first names were offered. But they all wanted to know about me. Just the sort of encouragement that goes right to your head when you're my age and talking to a pretty woman. It was a clear object lesson to me in that regard. And perhaps, now that I think of it, probably the cause of my immediate attraction to Cass. For months she had acted as if I did not interest her.

Over the following four hours or so on that November day, until dusk—so long as there was sufficient natural light to give the photographs any of the substance that would show those women at their best (remembering that I had no studio light to work with there), I took dozens of photographs of each of the girls in various poses and various states of 'dishabille.' This was a word I first learned that day. Miss Em speaks French fluently but her Russian accent gives her words in English as well as French a sound distinctively her own and always provocative. And I should note that in none of these pictures were the girls actually nude. Thankfully, that was not wanted. However, they all posed as if removing their clothes would be their next endeavor.

When the job was done, and Miss Em asked me to stay for tea, I refused, saying I had to get home to dinner in Brooklyn. I think I could have too happily remained and missed my Sunday dinner, though the prospect was nearly as terrifying as it was thrilling to me at the time. And I admit that, in the odd moment, I've regretted the missed opportunity more than a few times since. Nevertheless, I did not stay.

I returned with the developed pictures several days later. Miss Em seemed very pleased with them. And it was then that I saw my very first $100 bill. That was, in fact, to be the beginning of my emergency stash, which I still keep to this day.

But unhappily, copies of those same pictures had been part of the haul taken away by the police during that raid on my apartment in March.

So, when I came off the elevator into the City Room, I was immediately aware of some change in the air. Or I imagined I noticed, after the fact. Where, as a mere photographer, I would normally pass unobserved through the rows of desks, now I had the eyes of at least a dozen reporters as I crossed the floor. Cass was at her desk at the back and totally ignoring me.

Because they had been trying to be helpful by returning the pictures, given the recent truce between us, and being well aware of the Puritanical tendencies of Mayor LaGuardia, the cops at the

Charles Street Precinct had thought to divest themselves of the evidence lest he get wind of it. Lamentably, they had themselves taken a greater interest in the pictures from Miss Em's, and those photographs were at the top of the open bag delivered to the *Mirror* offices that day.

18. Wednesday, April 28, 1937

Cass ignored me for the remainder of the day and, the same way I'd felt the awareness of eyes when I got off the elevator, now I was distinctly conscious of those same eyes running between Cass's desk and my own.

There was no pretending about it. No possible pretense of a mistake. The thing to do was to fess up. But she did not allow me to explain. Every attempt was met with an "I'm busy," or a quick exit for a supposed assignment. I called her that night and there was no answer.

And this was the same the following day. And the next. And for several days after.

And then, just as suddenly as it had started, the cold-shoulder was off. And this was only because of a matter of severe embarrassment to me.

The previous Sunday, while I was home in Brooklyn eating a lamb stew and avoiding or deflecting Mom's questions and enduring Stacy White's repeated suggestions that I must have broken up with "my girl" (along with various ideas on how I might remedy the situation and win her back), Cass had gone to Sutton Place to interview Miss Em concerning the current situation in 'the trade.'

I have no idea what Cass said to Miss Em to get her to speak openly. She has that talent to see the soft spot in people and go to that immediately. I think she likely approached the subject from the fact that she had written so much about the prostitution racket for both the *Mirror* and the *Daily News* and her articles might have been read at Sutton Place with some sympathy.

With her face just as solemn as it had often been during those recent days, Cass came by my desk on Wednesday and asked me if I would have lunch with her. When she was out of sight, Reilly hit me on the shoulder.

"You are a dead man now. She has something up her sleeve. She'll put the screws on now. You'll see." Reilly has a fiancé and is a known expert on all matters concerning women. At least he thinks so.

Cass wanted to go over to Bo Bo's in Chinatown. The clientele there is mostly first generation Chinese and thus I immediately assumed the worst. She had chosen the place because whatever she might have to say would not be easily understood by others. At least that part of my assumption was totally wrong.

In the cab going over I attempted conversation. She answered my inquiries with a 'yes' or 'no' or a series of nods and shrugs. The cab driver shook his head in pity and kept his own mouth shut.

Bo Bo's is a narrow and deep hole in the wall with a counter at one side and small tables at the other. Eavesdropping is difficult. The lights are almost never on except after dark, and every time the kitchen door opens at the rear, the brilliance blinds you if you're facing that direction, which I was. The waiter poured us small mugs of nearly clear tea and Cass pointed to something with a number on the menu and I said, "The same." I had no idea what it was until later.

Then she started in. "I don't think I can drink this now. It's too thin. But I had the most incredible tea just the other day."

"Tea? Really."

"Yes. It was made in something called a 'samovar.'"

You would have to see her eyes at a moment like that. The color brown does not do them any kind of justice. But I knew immediately where she had discovered this 'incredible tea.' Clairvoyance was unnecessary. It was written in her eyes.

"You met Miss Em."

"I did."

"What did you think of her?"

"Very winning. I think I can understand now just how she's managed to be so successful for so long. Very forthright."

"Are you going to write something about her?"

"No. I promised her that I wouldn't. She doesn't want the publicity. Or need it. But I can use the information I got. Besides, what she's doing there is very different than the sort of thing I've been working on."

"I thought you said that all prostitution was the same."

"I did. You're right. But I think maybe I'm wrong about that now. I think I've come around a little to your way of thinking about all that. What you said to me once about everyone selling themselves for shortchange and so many people prostituting themselves in other ways, everyday, is something to consider. Why is that any different than what they do at Miss Em's unless it causes harm? Most of it is an evil and ugly trade in human flesh, and I suppose there is an aspect of that there—but that's not the way she conducts her business. Not at all. I met several of the women who live there. They've already been through the worst of it. Yet, they look happy now. I've never seen anything like it."

"Like a club," I offered that because it was my own thought.

"Yes. A little. Like a weird sorority. An odd sort of family. Like the story we ran about the wives of the French soldiers who were killed in the war and live together now for comfort. As far as I can tell, those women at Miss Em's are not forced to do anything. It is a profession for them—a job." She stopped, stricken for a moment as if she had caught herself doing something wrong. "You know, now I don't believe I'm saying this. It's the same sort of excuse I've heard men use a hundred times. But Monday I started checking up on some of the things Miss Em told me. I might disagree with her but I could not find a single lie. So I must assume that what she told me about you is true as well."

Now at first this was an enormous and sudden relief. But

then, just as quickly, I realized what it might also mean.

My day at Miss Em's had been a constant struggle to keep my attention on what had to be done. I took forty-eight photographs in all, using all the film I had. I could have made fewer shots perhaps, but many were spoiled. The difficulty for me had been a near constant interrogation which seemed to entertain them all about as much as it rattled me.

It started innocently enough. Miss Em had asked if I had a girlfriend. I said no. She wanted to know why not. It was as if I was suddenly speaking to my mom. Then the others began their questions. In no time they had figured out the truth of the matter. And that's when the real fun began. Each of them in turn tried harder to impress me as I took the pictures. But I knew the pictures were good, so I couldn't object too loudly. Not that I wasn't enjoying the attention.

Cass rather smugly watched my reaction. I knew of course that she'd barely begun to relate her revelations. And then she said, "One of them, Hazel I believe, was telling me about her family. Like so many girls I've met, she was abused when she was very young. In Pittsburgh. She'd run away from home at the age of fifteen and lived with an older man for a time. And run away again, and come to New York. When she was telling me about the earlier parts of her life, she didn't smile once. I would say the color had gone out of her face as she spoke about herself. But then that changed on a dime. By some luck she had met Miss Em. She pointed up at the fireplace mantle where her picture was framed with the others. 'I didn't look like that when I came to New York.' She said, 'I looked like a cat in a bag. That picture was taken later.'

"I said that the photographs were beautiful. I ask who had taken them. Hazel says, 'Oh, V.B. took all of them. Aren't they swell.' So I said, oh, he must be a professional! But I've never heard of him. And she said, 'Oh, that's not his real name. We just call him that.' 'Why,' I asked. 'Because he was so funny,' she said. 'How is that,' I asked? 'What does V.B. stand for?' She laughed at the question. They all laughed. 'Virgin Boy,' she says. I say, 'Why is that?' And she says, because we found out he was a virgin. He had never even been with a woman before.' I said, 'Then he must be very young.' Hazel said, 'No! In fact he's a year older than me. Can you imagine?' She was simply astounded by the fact. So I said, 'How can you be sure? Did he tell you that?' And she said,' No! You just know these things.' And Miss Em was right there laughing at the account. She said, 'It's true. He was a lamb!' Well, I said, 'So, I imagine you took care of that situation easily enough.' And Miss Em said. 'Ho, no. Virgin Boy wouldn't stay to dinner. All the girls tried to seduce him. But he went home instead.' Somewhat astonished by that revelation myself, I unconsciously said aloud, 'To Brooklyn?'

"Well, Miss Em caught on to that slip immediately. She said, 'I smell a rat! You know that boy, don't you?' And I admitted it. I admitted to her that you were the reason I was even there. And she gives me a look. You know. When her lips go flat in a line. And then first thing Miss Em says back to me is, 'Is he still a lamb?' And I had to say, 'I think so. But I don't know.' And she said, "Well, maybe you should find out.'"

By that time I was nearly under the table. Our food was cold. And the several customers closest to us were sneaking peeks. I asked the waiter to put the food in a carton so we could leave with it.

Cass sat there in Bo Bo's as if she was unaware of the additional attention. She just looked at me with a silly grin. Finally she pouted her lips and asked in a little girl voice, "Is it true? Are you still a lamb?"

But I wasn't going to answer that while under any scrutiny. There was a laugh. And then another chuckle. And then others as the story was retold in Chinese from one table to the next.

I reached the sidewalk ahead of her. I didn't even hold the door. She came out carrying the cartons of food right after me.

She said, "You're angry."

I said, "Wouldn't you be?"

She said, "Probably. But with a woman, it's always assumed, isn't it?"

Like my dad before me, I was not going to stay back on my heels.

I said, "Well, are you?"

Cass gives no quarter. She looked me square in the eye and said, "Isn't that for you to find out?"

19. Monday, May 3, 1937

I've created a file for some of my better pictures at the apartment now so they'll be safer and still be close at hand. This will also make it easier to show them to Cass if she comes by. But I'm fairly blind to any other interpretations of my own work than what I had intended. I've always been that way. Like someone once said, 'a blind photographer would be God's fool.'

This particular lot is now in a cork-insulated metal box designed for milk bottle deliveries. I don't get milk delivered, but I acquired the container at the hardware store after I got home with that bag of photographs that the cops had returned—specifically to keep my better stuff safe from the moist heat on summer days and the dry heat in winter. They were all looking a little worse for wear after being kidnapped, not just the ones from Miss Em's.

Most of the pictures I've put in the box are ones I have done for myself, not just copies of things I've done for the paper. That includes many of the shots I'd taken at Miss Em's as well as my collection of candid photos of Cass in action. However, I've taken several of my favorites of Cass and framed them up and hung them on the walls in the apartment.

I spent a fair amount of last Friday evening just listening to the radio and cleaning the place down. I put all my sheets and things in at Mary's New Laundry and picked them up Saturday morning. I bought a flower in a pot at Gino's market. I still don't understand the name for it. The Italian woman who sold it to me repeated herself several times but I just didn't get it. It's purple. Very pretty. You can smell it when you open the door. And I've put a curtain on the window in the main room.

I went down to Rienzi's and picked up a bottle of the chianti that Cass said she liked once before when we went there for spaghetti. Then I had a bright idea and asked them for a couple of empty bottles like the one they put on the tables for the candles—the ones with the straw covering on the outside. I bought a box of candles too. I even stacked the tables up in the bedroom and left the window there open wide to clear it out a little. I admit all this. I had plans.

Saturday night, I took Cass up to the Savoy Ballroom. I took her out to dinner first before I was suddenly struck with that brilliant idea. Of course I had been thinking about something like that for days. And she was game. We both wanted to learn how to do the Lindy-hop. But when the cab dropped us off up at Lenox Avenue and we saw the lines of people waiting to get in, and some of them already dancing and it looking like a street party there beneath the strings of lights above, I was disheartened. It was after nine o'clock and we could get no closer than the corner. Naturally. This was the busiest night of the week. But Cass was undaunted. She marched right up to the side door where a rather large fellow was keeping watch on the tail of the line and she whipped out her press card. I had mine as well, even though the camera bag was back at the paper.

In we went.

Cass can dance almost anything within minutes. She can swing. I did my best. Chick Webb was fantastic. I had to admit that the boarder at my parents' house, Mrs. Tisdale, had a point about Webb. I still like Goodman's music better, but Webb hits the beat harder and it's easier to dance to. Especially for me (though it's hard to imagine Mrs. Tisdale doing the jitterbug).

The Savoy is enormous. Maybe bigger than Roseland. It feels bigger. The ceiling is high and the lights are lower. But Saturday the place was packed and the real dancing had been divided off into a couple of areas near the bandstands and those kept filling up so tight you could hardly move. We did our best but then watched as much as we danced. Still, it was great fun. This was a happy crowd and no one seemed to mind if you found yourself mashed up against some other guy's date now and again.

They have two bandstands there and when one outfit took a break, another would start up and the action would shift in that direction. Even with rests, we were about done by midnight. Several big fans were blowing air, probably to keep the skirts flying, but you can work up a decent sweat just looking at a jitterbug. Because of the crowd out front, we left the way we had come, by the side street and there was a cab right there waiting—probably for one of the dignitaries of that musical world—but we took it.

I started to give the fellow directions and Cass speaks right up and says, "19th and Third."

Now Cass has a roommate. Ellen. She is a very nice girl. But as I understand it, she is always home. Cass read my mind.

She says, "Ellen went to her parents' farm in New Jersey for the weekend."

Of course, I was thinking that this was even better than my own plot.

When we were paid up and out of the cab, I was a little anxious, of course. I started to move but Cass didn't budge. She was up on the curb then with me still standing on the bricks. Eye to eye she was just about irresistible. So I kissed her quite a lot right where she stood. Then she took me by the hand and lead me up the stoop, unlocked the front, on up the stairs and opened her apartment door. She did not let go of my hand once the whole time. At this point I was just about crazy. She didn't have the light on at first, and that was fine, but I wanted to see her. She was wearing a green and white spring dress that looked great but all I really wanted was to see her take it off. I admit that too. Then, somehow, she found a hand to turn on the light.

And with that, like it was attached to the light switch, the phone rang. She ignored it a moment, but then picked it up to stop the insistent racket and we could both hear The Boss's voice talking to the air.

She sighed and put the receiver to her ear. I couldn't understand the words.

Standing there for the first time in her apartment and looking around I had a nice surprise. She had several of my photos up. One, of a string of big dogs being walked by a small woman in Central Park that The Boss wouldn't run, and another shot of the Brooklyn Bridge first thing in the morning when the metalwork looks like it's made of gold.

Though it's only big enough for one person at a time, she has a real kitchen with an actual refrigerator, and also what they call a 'dinette,' though that's only a wide place in the hall. The living room is hardly big enough for sitting, and the two closets at the back are likely referred to as 'bedrooms' in the classified pages because they each have a window. All of it looked very trim. My sisters' rooms at home were never as neat as this.

When she hung up the phone she says, "He's been calling for an hour. He's looking for you, too." My first thought—no, my second—was that I didn't have my camera. Cass can see that written all over my face. She adds, "He says to tell you to go on along with me. He'll put your camera in a cab and send it up."

Another naked body had been found where the construction for the West Side highway ends. There's a mess of equipment parked in there, and earthen embankments, piles of rock, and the stacked steel for the finishing touches. On the river side of that are several short rock jetties.

Close by, just beneath the elevated concrete slabs of the completed highway, there is a small hobo jungle of fifty or sixty of the luckless. It's mostly men but there are some women too. This settlement was twice the size when I first visited last year to take pictures around Thanksgiving time, along with a crew from the Salvation Army when they were delivering turkey dinners to a local church. But LaGuardia has been cutting it down in preparation for the highway dedication ceremonies that were scheduled for the Fall.

Just after nine o'clock, about the time Cass and I were starting to dance, a hobo by the name of Fred Bellows saw a car drive in at one of the jetties and back around. The driver had gotten out, opened the trunk and pulled a body by one arm onto the rocks.

Fred had been engaged in a personal activity down by the water's edge at the time and had taken umbrage at being interrupted. So he yelled at the interloper. The driver immediately stopped what they were doing, got back in the car, and drove away. Shortly after that, Bellows had called the police from a booth in front of a bar on 72nd street.

Unlike telling a cabbie that you want to go to 19th and 3rd, when you say you'd like him to drive to the very end of 72nd, he says, "Why?"

I got cute, "We have to see some cops about a stiff."

At least he was reassured by the number of police cars that were jammed into the broken street. Having been there once before, on foot I took a short cut beneath the elevated highway and you could smell those people under there in the dark. Their candles were out so the cops would leave them alone and all you could see was a glint from an eye or a silhouette against the darker sheen of the river beyond.

Near the jetty I spotted a patrolman with whom I'd spent a fine evening not long ago and asked him what was up, but it was just a minute or so later that the cabbie sent by The Boss found me and handed over my bag. Knowing how cheap Barry George can be, I gave the guy a couple dollars tip myself. He seemed to appreciate that.

Cass had gone on to the location of the body ahead of me. That ghastly heap lay twisted to one side as if trying to rise up across the uneven rock. His legs were folded under in an awkward crouch, likely from time spent in the trunk of the car. The limbs were clearly stiff, so he had been dead for a few hours at least, but probably less than a day. An assistant medical examiner, Melvin Furst, was standing guard there against the reporters and cameramen. His hat was pulled low against the bright illumination from the police cars and he was smoking a cigarette and apparently enjoying the night air and the more delicate display of lights across the river over in Jersey.

I got behind him and took a good shot of that—the dark standing figure hovered over the pale naked body with Melvin's pants legs hiding what would otherwise have to be cropped. From that angle you could see the gaping hole in the victim's head where an eye should have been. Blood had dried in his hair. There was blood streaked across much of his upper torso, and my first thought was he must have had his own pants on when he was murdered because he was clean from his belt line down. He was overweight. Brown hair. I figured him to be between forty and fifty years old.

Simpson, the patrolman I knew, whispered at my ear.

"It wasn't just one shot. I heard Grimes say it could have been three or four. All in the same spot. No powder burns. Grimes said it was 'Some fancy shootin.'"

For a short time, Fred Bellows sat on a large block of granite at the side of this convocation, apparently pleased at the commotion his phone call had made. He had tied a blue scarf around his neck and turned his collar up against the night air and looked almost jaunty with his hands clasped at one knee and a short pipe clinched in his teeth. I grabbed that shot. And then he was gone.

About the time the guys from the morgue had the cadaver loaded and out of there, Cass and I hitched a ride as far as the Station House with a Captain from the 20th Precinct. It was nearly four a.m. I found another cab from there and saw Cass to her door anyway.

She says, "I better go up and get some sleep. I'm beat." She kissed me but then puts a hand on my shoulder as if for some serious talk. "Listen. I want you to be ready the next time. You're handy with things like that. Before we go out on a date again, I want you to go down to the wire room and sabotage the damn police radio."

I said, "Sure," just as seriously, even though I had no idea how to do it. But at least I did get another good kiss out of that.

20. Tuesday, May 4, 1937

I'd dropped the pictures off at the paper by noon on Sunday. But Cass wasn't there. I called her and didn't get an answer, and then hung around a while longer, just in case, before heading out to Brooklyn.

She answered Sunday night. We talked for an hour or two. Not about anything in particular. Not about business. Just talked.

On Monday she wasn't there when I got to work. I found out afterward that there was an anti-German rally in Brooklyn. Stenis had already called me at the apartment first thing so I was off then taking pictures of a building collapse on 41st Street. This was not much more that a hole in the ground that suddenly got bigger. The *Daily News* guys were all over it because they were right next door. Meanwhile, some pro-Nazis had shown up in Brooklyn and there were some nasty fistfights. That was the better story, but I missed it entirely. Carl Jonas got that assignment because he happened to be sitting on his thumbs at the office at the right moment. I got to read Cass's account of the matter in Wednesday's paper. The picture with it was of a crowd. A few sneers but not a fist in sight. In fact they looked a lot less enthusiastic than a bunch of fans might at a ballgame between the Giants and the Dodgers.

I caught Cass later at her desk.

She says, "Where have you been?"

This is a joke we all use. You're not supposed to answer. But I did.

"A hole in the ground. And an apartment fire on 32nd, but that was out before I got there. So I took the C line up to 72nd and went over to see Fred Bellows."

That got her attention. Not that she was ignoring me or anything, but she was doing two things at once. She stopped typing.

"What did Mr. Bellows have to say?"

"He's pretty certain the person who was trying to dump the body in the river was a woman."

"Did he tell the cops that?"

"No. He said the cops weren't interested. It cost me five bucks."

"Money well spent."

"There's more. It happened that I only had a fiver on me at the time and so I just anted that up. He would have told me about it being a woman for a buck. For a fin he told me his life history."

"Anything about the murderer?"

"This. She was not big. And she was blonde. He was rather taken with her physical strength. He said he'd been married to a girl like that in Pennsylvania once. A farm girl."

"Anything else than her physical attributes?"

"Yes. But that part is important I think. Whoever we are looking for is obviously no spring flower."

"What else?"

"She was driving a Buick. Black. Fred told the cops that the car was black, but not the make. They didn't want to give him the time of day so he shut his trap. Just another tramp, one of them said. But Fred says to me that he isn't a tramp. He was hurt by the accusation. Anyway, I gave him some of the nickels I had left over from Horn & Hardart's and told him to give me a call if he saw anything more."

Cass did not seem happy.

I asked her, "What's wrong?"

She said, "I should have followed up on that myself."

I shrugged that off. "So I did it for you. That's all. You and I are the only ones that know anything about it until tomorrow morning's edition." Not exactly the truth, but close enough. I added, "We work pretty well as a team, don't you think?"

At least that got a passing smile.

Cass told The Boss that I was the one that did the interview with Bellows, even though I told her she shouldn't.

At this point I was feeling very guilty about my attempt to take advantage of the situation with Cass. It's not just a guy's feelings that gets to running hot in a situation like that. It's chemical, I think. Hormones. And a cold shower isn't going to take care of it.

On Tuesday morning I went across town and saw Izzy. Izzy's brother is in the diamond trade and works for an outfit on 7th Avenue. When I told Izzy what I was after, he takes a break from work and walks me over to see his brother himself.

Izzy is given to being a very emotional guy. He laughs at his own jokes and cries at the movies. Always has. He immediately looks like he is more excited about this thing than I am. He's laughing and crying all the way over there.

"Is this the Jewish girl?"

"Her parents were Jewish. She's a reporter."

"Do her parents know?"

"I've never met them. They're in Cleveland."

"They might object."

"Maybe. I hope not. I'm going to marry her anyway."

"How come you find yourself a nice Jewish girl and I can't?"

"I wasn't looking."

"That's the worst kind. When it hits you like that—when you're not looking."

"How do you know? You've only had one girlfriend in your whole life."

"It happens to some people when they're younger. That's all."

"You were twelve years old!"

"Doesn't matter."

"Why aren't you married yet, Izzy?"

"When Mabel married David Gross, my love life was over."

"You're only twenty-five, for Christ's sake!"

"Even Christ would have given up on the Jews, I think. I feel like an old man."

"You know what they say. You're as old as you feel."

"Older."

Izzy's brother Phil is the exact opposite. He's a large fellow. He moves very slowly and deliberately. Phlegmatic is the word for this, I think. He wears a black suit with a black tie and a black yarmulke and he reminds me of the Rabbi back in Brooklyn who used to come to Izzy's house to visit with his sister all the time, before Naomi ran off with the actor. Phil talks in a low voice that is just above a growl. He looks like he's fifty. He is twenty-eight.

The front room at Steinmetz and Co. is not well lit but the rings are laid out on black velvet inside thick glass cases with lights inside. At the bottom of each row there is one that is set up in a clip with a diamond already in place, or two, or more. Just the first sight of them tells me I can't afford anything.

After Izzy fills his brother in on important details, like my budget, Phil says, "She's Jewish?"

I say, "No. She's a reporter."

Also unlike his brother, Phil has no sense of humor. He gives me a stone cold face.

"Do her parents know?"

"They will."

"So. What we should do here is get you a ring that you can return if things don't work out. I'll ask my boss."

Phil disappeared into a back room. After a couple of minutes he returns, following a small man, maybe a little over five feet tall, wire thin, with a wide head and small glasses that sit at the very end of his nose, which is also quite small. This is Mr. Steinmetz, his boss. He is half the size of Phil. He has on a white shirt with his sleeves rolled up and his tie tucked away. His yarmulke perfectly covers the bald spot on top of his head but his hair sticks out on either side and this, regrettably, gives him a look like a clown. Only, he is not interested in being funny.

First thing he says is, "Maybe you should wait."

I say, "I can't."

He says, "That's the way all young men feel. They think they can't. But they can. Your whole life is ahead of you. A rash decision now will change everything."

"It's already changed. It wasn't a decision. It just happened."

"Have you spoken to your priest?"

"I'm not Catholic. I'm a photographer."

The old fellow looked at me without a twitch in a blank face for nearly thirty seconds. Izzy and his brother both stood quietly at his back. Izzy's eyes are rolling.

Finally Mr. Steinmetz says, "Alright, smarty. But don't bring it back in here after twenty years and tell me it didn't work out. You got thirty days."

Phil picked out a very nice ring for me. The diamond was not as big as I hoped, but the setting disguised the fact nicely.

My next hurdle was choosing the right moment. And the sooner the better. Then, on Thursday morning, I got a brilliant idea from reading our own paper. The *Hindenburg* would be passing over Manhattan on the way to a docking at Lakehurst, New Jersey, that very afternoon. This was a German enterprise much ballyhooed by the local Nazis. There had even been a poster up at Kuhn's office in Yorkville. Both Cass and I had other things going on later in the day, but we could call this excursion 'work' and go up to the top of the Empire State Building to watch the mighty symbol of the Third Reich go by. I had seen the *Graf Zeppelin* a few years ago and that was truly magnificent.

More importantly, the observation deck up there is a very romantic spot.

When we get off the elevator, the deck looks packed, inside and out. But everyone is clustered on the south side hoping to be the first to spot the floating behemoth through the afternoon haze. I lead Cass around and over to the North side where it's totally empty.

Even though we're in the shade there, she's squinting at me. She knows something else is going on. I say I want to show her something. I casually give her the little box like I'm passing over a pack of cigarettes. 'What's this?' is the look I get. By the time she has it open, I am down on my knee. I kept it simple.

"Will you marry me?"

She caught a breath. The squint is gone now from her eyes and they're open wide.

And then she says, "Yes!"

Done! Just like that. Except for the kissing.

And the rest of our lives, of course.

Watching the *Hindenburg* float by was nothing after that! But we practically missed it.

The airship is a fat perfecto of silver that appears to move in slow motion. The low-voiced buzz of the distant motors wafts with the changing of the breeze, the sound frequently overcome by the tinny whine of traffic on the streets below. This does not have the urgency of a plane, but appears to be aloft on its own terms and not in need of any speed or pilot or permission to keep it in the air. The size, at our distance of more than a mile at the closest approach, was not so impressive as the thought of it. The gleam of metal is as deceptive as the size—the skin is just canvas and paint and dope. An illusion. The real metal of the skeleton is hidden within. Perhaps that is some of its magic. It has the sense about it of a living creature, with bones within, and not a shell—meant for the sky and not a projectile thrown there against the gravity of the earth.

Afterward we walked back to the paper. There was talking to do. Cass has a thousand ideas about a wedding, and before I can make a single comment she knocks them off, one after the other. She wants it small. Just family. And few friends. Maybe forty or fifty. Or sixty.

She says, "October would be nice."

I say, "How about June?"

"It's already too late for June."

"How can it be too late? It hasn't happened yet!"

"We have to make plans."

"Give me a list of names. I'll call everyone. They'll come"

"It's not that simple. It takes some time just to get a license."

"I think I read somewhere that it's faster in Delaware."

"I want my parents to be there."

I thought it would be nice if my parents were there as well.

She says, "I'd like to go away. A honeymoon. I don't want to be anywhere close to a phone."

"The moon?"

"I'd like to go to Paris."

"They have phones there."

"Or Italy."

"Mussolini."

She finally says, "What would you like to do then?"

I tell her, "I've always wanted to go on an overnight train. Like the *Zephyr*. Or the *20th Century Limited*. Like those ads in the magazines. I've never slept in a Pullman. "

"Go where?"

"It doesn't matter. Just go"

Nothing more substantial than that.

She gives me the squint. She's hoping I'm kidding.

The joke is that poor Cass works with a bunch of guys. She had that ring on when we got to the office and managed to keep her hand up in a very physical display of the facts, but the average reporter at the *Mirror* was half-blind from overwork in that dim light, or else the diamond was too small. No one caught on until Barry George comes out with some notes on an assignment for a Republican Women's Association meeting that Cass was supposed to cover that evening.

George did not get to where he is by overreacting.

"This is the stuff on Dewey. He'll talk their ears off but he won't say anything so you better have this to fill in." Then he flicks a finger in the direction of her hand and says, "So I take it, now if I fire him, I have to fire you both?"

But he did offer his congratulations.

21. Thursday to Friday, May 6 and May 7, 1937

Hal Henry, another press photographer, works for United Press. He mostly covers politics, and because all that stuff gives me the creeps we don't see that much of each other except for an occasional game of 8-ball, but he has always been a decent guy to me. He was the one who told Cass about the *Hindenburg*, while Dewey was jabbering on in front of a room full of warm ladies, and she was busy trying to scarf some free Republican food off the buffet.

Hal comes over to her and says, "This is someone's lucky day, but not ours."

She says, "I don't know. I was just thinking it was very lucky for me that those lettuce leaves fell down on top of that roast beef so nobody else saw it. And today Hugh proposed to me. I'd say that was pretty lucky too. Though you might debate with yourself which of those two things is the better."

Now, Hal only laughs at jokes that involve bodily functions. But this was a perfect example of Cass's sense of humor. You have to be there to appreciate it. She likely said it with a straight face. When she tells me later, she runs through it without a hitch in her voice.

And Hal is not a sentimental fellow either. Besides, his mind is on what he came over to tell her. First he says, "Where's Hugh now?"

His worry is simple enough. He wants to know if I happen to be in Lakehurst.

Cass says, "An induction ceremony at the 4ᵗʰ Precinct."

Hal says, "Well then, for him I'd say it was certainly a day of mixed blessings."

Cass says, "There's no food at induction ceremonies."

Hal says, "So, he got himself engaged. Congratulations to both of you. But he missed the big one, didn't he?"

Cass says, "I could gain some weight, I suppose."

At this point, Hal is a bundle of frustration. He had wanted to fly by and drop his bomb in her salad. He had not bargained for anything more than a 'Hello.' So now he just lets it go.

"The *Hindenburg* has crashed. Burst into flames at Lakehurst. Could be a hundred people are dead. Whoever got the pictures for that will be in every paper tomorrow, coast to coast."

Cass gets to a phone with the roast beef still clutched in her fingers. The induction ceremony took half an hour so I'm already back at the paper and the word has come upstairs and everyone is running around like steel balls in a penny arcade. She correctly assumes that The Boss would be hard to reach and called through to my desk. Tom Reilly finds me in the wire room looking at the first pictures and pulls me over.

She says, "Tell The Boss that you and I can be out there in an hour."

No need to explain where 'out there' is. No need to advise her that it's a two-hour drive. I tell her I'll get a car and meet her at the Houston stop on the El. Of course, the regular company cars that the *Mirror* keeps on the side are all gone. One of those had been taken by Gene Sisk, the reporter Barry George has already sent out to the site. The other had been grabbed by one of our photographers, Carl Jonas, because he happened to be smoking down in the hall by the toilets when Stenis went looking. But Bill Toomey, who works in circulation, drives in from Queens everyday and has his sedan stashed over near the big trucks at the back. I beg him, and forgive him for screwing me out of Dodgers tickets last summer. He drives an A Model and I've driven my dad's wagon often enough so his clutch is a cinch.

When I get down by the Houston stop, Cass is standing at the curb and we're gone. She's inside maybe a minute before she realizes again that everything is different between us now. She leans on over and plants a pretty good kiss on me as soon as we got to the first red light.

While I am breaking various speed limits, she tells me about her encounter with Hal Henry. It happened that he had just called in a 'hot' item on Dewey from there at Insomnia Hall and got the first report from Lakehurst as a gift. Our luck.

And perhaps thankfully it was getting late. We were on the move by 8:30. Traffic on a Wednesday night is not so bad. I hit the Holland Tunnel less than ten minutes after she's in her seat and I'm on Route 9 in half an hour in spite of a motorcycle cop in Perth Amboy who had his eye on me and made me slow it down.

We were in the traffic jam near the airfield before ten. I managed to get a little closer using a gravel access road to where we can see the wreckage silhouetted against the lights across the grass of the field, so I pull it over and throw the 'Press' sign in the windshield and we climb the fence right there. The grass is wet from the rain and I'm glad I have on long pants but Cass is in a dress that only comes to her calves. She doesn't seem to mind. I see then that she has her shoes off and stuffed in her coat pocket.

The run was a good half-mile and most of the ground there is rough with only the dim cast of the distant lights to see by. The sky is still cloudy. She was ahead of me the whole way. Of course, I have the bag to carry. At least that was my excuse after the fact.

Police have a cordon along the far side where the small terminal is. The lights there, mostly from the police cars and navy vehicles, are blazing. The empty mooring mast, a naked construction of steel like the top of an unfinished skyscraper, sits to our left and is a mere outline in the dark. The face of the big dirigible hanger is farther over to our right but reflecting the orange of the emergency lights in a neat arch over the open door and black within, where the great ship should have already been safely asleep for the night.

The air was harsh and I think this was the stink of rubber or whatever it was used on the fabric of the inner cells to hold the hydrogen before the gas had burnt off so quickly in the disaster, and not the doped cotton from the outer shell of the airship. We had come up from the backside and the *Daily News* guy, Phipps, is also there in the shadows as we approach.

He says, "Reminds me of a circus fire I saw once."

There was no fire still burning but smoke or steam continued to arise wherever the sailors had used their thin hoses to spray the charred wreck. Still, I knew what he meant. It was the skeletal remains of something enormous that has suddenly collapsed and burned down to very little. Most of the narrow duralumin girders of the great ship were bowed and broken like the frame of a crushed basket and appeared almost delicate against the lights. Skewed and bent at awkward angles to the ground, they lack any of the expected architecture of flight and are not even immediately disturbing. Only the bow of the ship spoke of the shape it had been.

A cop who was clearly tired of being accommodating, kept us back with repeated barks—but we are so far away that my flash was going to get me very little against the brighter illumination from the other side. Cass had already drifted off on her own. When a pale plume of steam began suddenly to rise from within the ruin, I got down and braced the camera hard on a metal track from a rail set into the field and grabbed one good shot of that against the lights and then scooted around to the other side where at least I'd have some better illumination on the wreckage.

From there, I see better how the neat knot of steel at what had been the bow of the airship remains, tying off the useless cords of twisted metal scaffolding that restrained the volatile hydrogen gas cells used to keep the Zeppelin aloft just a few hours before. I got a good shot on that. I heard one voice nearby remark on the charred bodies found there, part of the crew that sought refuge by coming forward. Their bodies had already been removed. But the busy American sailors, the white of their hats tracing in the dark, offered no steady chances for a shot with a more human element, so I walked beyond to the terminal.

One fellow in a white hat and blue blazer stood near, hands on his hips, looking over the wreckage like he might be observing a cricket match. This offered no drama either, even in contrast.

An ambulance sat halfway, red light on top turning insistently round and round, doors open, waiting as if another charred body might be discovered any moment, but the attendant was sitting inside on the stretcher, smoking. Nor did that seem to have much relevance to the event. Not that I could squeeze into a frame.

Some of the surviving passengers had been taken to a hut where a yellow school bus stood idling in front of the door. Policemen there would not allow me to get closer but I took a picture of several getting on the bus together.

In the dark there was little to see beyond the skeletal wreckage that caught the emergency lights. That mess itself lacked any reference to something people might find interesting. The average house fire had more going for it.

By that time, I had caught sight of Cass by another, smaller building, speaking with our *Mirror* reporter, Gene Sisk. Probably comparing notes. She spotted me immediately and pointed to one dazed looking fellow sitting on a box to one side.

"Get a picture of him for me, will you?"

He was young. Hatless. His light gray suit was badly soiled, or perhaps scorched. He bent forward from his perch at the edge of a wooden crate and stared blankly at the wreckage with his hands folded together and his elbows on his knees. I took my first shot from right where I stood because it was good enough to capture the stunned moment. But the flash surprised him and he started to move away. I followed, asking if I could take a better picture of his face. He fled ahead me into the dark, saying "Nein!" or "Keine!" or both.

Cass shook her head at me unhappily as if I had done something wrong but continued her conversation with Gene.

I still hadn't seen Carl Jonas and could not assume he had gotten any shots on the emergency morgue. There were no police there at that moment, so I pushed my way inside through a cluster of reporters and others at the door.

The injured had already been ferried away by ambulance. But inside that building, the lights were mostly off, out of respect, I think. It has the look of a temporary sort of structure from outside— a sort of barracks—painted gray. The word 'Snack Bar' was stenciled by the door. The bodies of the less fortunate, at least those that had been recovered so far, were still there and laid out beneath neatly squared army-green rain tarps in several rows.

In the lower light, the green appeared appropriately black against the lighter gray of the wood, but the sight of it oddly reminded me of Boy Scout camp where we slept on the floor of the largest cabin in bad weather. I was maybe twelve years old and got up early one morning to use the latrine. This was a scary enterprise in the dark and the smell from that place and the lye they used there was nearly suffocating. The sounds of the woods and a constant dripping of run-off into the black hole had me so panicked I could hardly do my business. No explaining the working of the mind. I hadn't thought of that in years.

The opposite horror of this scene was at once obscured and yet magnified by the plainness of the painted wood and bare windows. But somehow the pictures I took of it did not carry the same emotional weight as the one in my head.

Gene Sisk, as the assigned reporter, was going to stay there through the night, so Cass came and got me there in the morgue. She stood at the end of one row and I was tempted to take another shot of her shadow, cast by the light from the door where it reached out over the bodies, but I thought better of it. She was already angry with me for something else now and it might make things worse.

I'd taken more than enough shots of the general wreckage by then, and no more interviews with passengers were in the offing so I asked one of the uniformed Navy personnel standing by a truck who was apparently in need of something else to do, and he drove us back across the field. Cass worked at her notes even against the jostle of that short ride.

I did not wait to find out the cause of her being upset. First I got the car turned around on that little road, between the two rain filled gullies, and then got right to it.

"What did I do?"

She was staring out toward the lights clustered around the wreck on her side and I could not see her face.

"What do you mean?"

"You were shaking your head at me."

She turned to me, surprise. "Oh no. Not you. That boy. He's was so scared. And I couldn't help but think he was frightened about something else."

"The wreck wasn't enough?"

"He was shaken. Sure. But it was something else he said. When I found him he was in the room there with the bodies. He was sobbing. I talked to him there. Just a little while. I asked him where he was from. I asked what his job was. He said he was a wine merchant. Of all things. I was just trying to make conversation then and I said he looked too young to be a wine merchant and asked where he had learned about wines. He said his father owned a wine shop in Dresden. Because I was there once one summer just after college, I told him that. But he wouldn't say much more. I asked if I could help by sending a message to his parents to let them know that he had survived. He became very agitated at that idea. 'No,' he says. But he was clearly upset about something else. Not just the crash. He said he had to meet somebody. But he had lost his letter of instruction in the fire. He had to meet them that evening or all was lost. There would be no point in sending a telegram. He repeated that to me. He had to find them or everything would be lost. He said it that way. 'All is lost.' I asked him if I could help in any way at all. That got nothing at first but then he asked me if I knew where 110th Street was. I assumed he meant New York City so I said it was at the top of Central Park. He said, 'Ya! Ya!' and went outside again as if he were headed right then for New York. I followed him there. The Red Cross had a table with water set out and I got a cup of that for him. But he wouldn't talk to me anymore. After that, Gene Sisk showed up and we traded notes and then you showed up."

At the local newspaper office in Freehold N.J., the lights blazed with the activity spawned by the event. The old gent in the dark room was pulling shots from the trays still limp and dripping, one after the other. We were able to wire a story back to the *Mirror* for Sisk as well as a side-bar from Cass, along with a couple of the best pictures I had. Cass called again to the *Mirror* office to make sure that all came through before we left.

The drive back then was a little more leisurely. The dark made a sort of confessional booth of the inside of the car when we were in the long haul across the meadowlands—with the feel of a tunnel there through the tall grass that was still mostly dead from the previous winter, and us playing catch up with the puddle of our headlights on the road ahead.

That was where Cass told me a little more about her family. Her grandparents had immigrated to the United States in the 1880s, following yet another pogrom in the city of Kiev. Both of her grandparents had lost at least one brother, or sister, or parent to that. Her grandmother, still alive when Cass was younger, described being the only living relative that remained and just twelve years old at the time. And she had been brought to a temporary morgue to identify the bodies of her family.

"They were 'laid out like they were sleeping in the dark, but they would not answer her cries,' Grandma said."

There is a rise along that road where the illuminated island of Manhattan lies below and adrift in the dark of the river, at one gauzy end of the Milky Way where it falls down from above. I stopped there long enough to hold her awhile and just catch our breath.

I drove Cass directly home then and had Bill Toomey's car back in place well before he left work at five.

22. Friday and Saturday, May 7 and 8, 1937

"Was it sabotage?"

That was the very first question Tom Reilly asked me when I got to my desk late that morning. It was an interesting thought and hadn't even occurred to me yet. There have been so many accidents with airships, especially the ones using hydrogen, I'd immediately assumed it was just another example. Perhaps I don't have enough of a conspiratorial mind.

Mr. Verloc, the 'secret agent' in the Joseph Conrad book I've been reading seems to lack that sensibility as well. You can see everything that's going to happen before he does. As if his fate is sealed. That's the way Mr. Conrad wanted it, I suppose. But the matter is this, how can such a thing as sabotage be carried out with so little idea of the consequences? Most of what will happen as a result of a bomb cannot possibly be known. What might be expected from the start is that people will be hurt who had nothing to do with the cause that was pursued by the anarchists—or whoever is re-sponsible for the deed.

To my mind there was a good contrast to such a thing already in mind. For all the grisly fact, those five men who had been shot in the face had suffered a fairly neat execution. Or at least it appeared that way to me. Was that better than being blown to bits? Or crushed within the 'fiery holocaust' of a burning Zeppelin?

I told Tom, "I don't think so. That doesn't make sense, does it? Not unless the idiot was on board the airship and intended to kill himself as well, if he had to. Like the Professor."

"What professor?"

"Just a character in a novel. It doesn't matter."

I buried my head in our coverage of the disaster in the *Mirror*. Most of the photos were from United Press, as expected because they had been on the scene from the first moments. But there were two of mine in the mix. I wondered aloud what Carl Jonas had gotten.

Tom offered a hunching of his shoulders in answer. He appeared to already know more.

Naturally, the one photo I took of the skeletal remains of the airship, silhouetted with the lights bleeding through the steam, was one that George had used. It showed very little detail but the ominous shadows spoke loudly, as he would say. The photo of the young and hatless crew member was mid-column along with Cass's piece on the aftermath. The main story by Sisk started in 18 point bold on page one, but it was pretty close to what was in another reprinted from the Syndicate on page three. The shorter piece by Cass was mostly about the crewmember and briefly related his firsthand account of escape as the fiery wreckage collapsed about him. My picture was to the right of that.

I read it all through, and only then, for the very first time, actually realized an obvious fact—that Cass could speak German. Of course! What had I thought before? What had I assumed about her conversation with the young wine porter? I hadn't even thought about it. And that made me figure it was probably about time that I learned to speak another language than American.

Cass was still away from her desk so I went to find Stenis. I was wondering again about the shots taken by Carl Jonas. Stenis looked at me like I was making a joke.

"The fool said he was caught in traffic. Couldn't get close to the wreck until nearly midnight. The Boss fired him as soon as he came through the door this morning."

I was okay with getting rid of Jonas, but this might mean I'd have to cover more police induction ceremonies and parades and the like until they got a replacement. Not a pleasant thought.

Cass shows up about eight o'clock. She'd been uptown at an appointment and had already eaten something along her way so I would have to skip out to the Horn and Hardart on my own.

When she looked comfy and ready to write, I slipped up on her, "What language do you think I should learn to speak?"

She appeared flummoxed.

I said, "German?"

She got the point. "French. If we are going to Paris on our honeymoon, you ought to learn to speak French anyway."

"We're going to Paris?"

"I thought you agreed."

"I wanted to go on the *Zephyr*. That doesn't even go to Montreal."

"I thought you were joking."

She knew I wasn't joking. This was her ploy.

I said, "Well, from what I saw in the *Tribune* last week, the Maginot Line isn't going to keep them out, so if the Germans are going to invade Paris, maybe I should learn to speak both."

She was having none of it. She started typing.

There were no reasonable assignments on the board for me.

The hall by the restrooms was empty except for one copyboy smoking his cigarette in the corner so I drifted down to the wire room then to offer a little more color to the dry stories floating around the office about our adventure of the evening before. One of those had it that I had stolen Bill Toomey's car. That wouldn't hold up. Another that I had been chased most of the way by the cops out of Perth Amboy, which is why I was there so fast. I chose that one as the easier to embroider. The idea of a car chase in an A Model offered some interesting possibilities for absurdity.

But I had only just started in on this project when a call came in on the police radio concerning a body found. A man had been shot and the cadaver left in an ashcan in the ally just off Fifth Avenue at 9

West, Central Park North.

I went directly up to get Cass and told Stenis we were on it.

We grabbed a cab at the door. Cass sat there quietly beside me and I held her hand until she pulled it away. This was not going to be a coincidence. We both knew it. For the offer of a couple extra bucks to the cabbie we arrived shortly after an assistant medical examiner. He wanted to keep us away and said so, loudly directing several patrolmen. Two police cars had their light on the area. Cass got a Sargent to understand why we were there and he removed the tarp for her to make the identification.

I let her do the talking while I took the pictures. A couple of other reporters were there as well, including a young guy from the *Daily News,* and they were writing down everything she said, so she kept it brief.

The trash barrel had been turned over and the blood that drained into it from the body had then run out again in a neat black seam between the paving stones of the alley. The galvanized steel lid of the barrel had been run over by a car and lay mangled now at the middle. The body was to one side of the barrel, but folded into a fetal position and stiff with rigor mortis, with the head forward and chin against his chest. He was still wearing the same clothes we had last seen him in, minus the jacket. The white shirt was now soiled at the arms. One shoe was missing. There was no identification.

I could see that his cheeks were smeared with grime and the imprint of the hands that had dragged him to the barrel after he was murdered. I asked about the other shoe and the sergeant said it had been found in a basement apartment behind us. The door there was open. It was not hard to identify, with the skid mark from the barrel giving a near solid line across the bricks all the way from the door. I imagine they had first tried to drag him by his feet before the shoe had come off. We agreed they must have killed him earlier and come back for the corpse after dark.

Lying there in the lights from the police wagon he looked aged by the pale white and not at all the young man we had spoken to hours ago. The several holes in his back had made his death fairly quick, I think. The fabric of the shirt was dark and glistened with blood that was not yet completely dried. That was the better picture but The Boss might think it was too much for people eating breakfast in the morning. I took a few others.

Cass looked pale but angry as we listened to the first police report from the Sergeant for the reporters present. The apartment had a bare mattress and some cigarette butts in the sink. Otherwise it was empty. Whoever had occupied it either didn't live there or they had moved out previously. Neighbors were being questioned, but so far there was nothing else from that. One neighbor had heard the sound of someone moving the trash can and came outside to investigate. Bums frequently left a mess from their scavenging. He saw a car there, idling, with the headlights off and the trunk open. The neighbor had yelled at them to stop. Then someone else had called out from a window across the ally. The two men who had been struggling with the barrel, as if trying to dump the contents into the trunk, had climbed in the car quickly and sped off. No car make was identified. No license. One man was taller than the other was the only remark made. The barrel had fallen over in their attempt to move it and they had left it where it fell. It was the first neighbor who had come over to turn it upright and found the body.

There was a flex in Cass's jaw. I knew her thoughts.

I said what I could, which wasn't much.

"There was no way to know."

"I should have tried harder to get him to speak to me when I had the chance."

"That wasn't going to happen. He did not want to speak. He was on his own mission. Besides, you were worried about pressing him, given what he'd been through."

"I should have tried harder."

But I had another and darker thought in mind. Worse. Did my picture of the fellow, in the *Mirror* that morning, make him an easier target?

The story of the murder hit the Saturday edition.

"*Hindenburg* Survivor Murdered," made a good headline.

The young man had never given Cass a name, but his statement to her about being a wine merchant's son from Dresden had been forwarded to German authorities.

23. Sunday, May 9, 1937

I can imagine the dread Cass felt about going to Brooklyn for Sunday dinner. Perhaps more than I felt myself. But I was proud of her for facing it immediately and not putting it off. It had to be done, and the sooner the better.

Except for the fact that my mom welcomed her immediately with a kiss, and there was a mercifully quick and prejudiced appraisal of the ring, there was not a lot of talk about marriage while we were eating. Mostly she was grilled with questions about her family. Dad asked about the business of selling shoes and then, told of Mr. Green's success, suggested that perhaps he himself had chosen the wrong thing with stationery. Mr. Oliphant had once been to Cleveland. He didn't like it. Stacy had an aunt who lived there. A good church going woman, she said. Her boy Gary kept looking over at me waiting for some response to one comment or another. I kept my mouth shut except when I was filling it with roast beef. Mrs. Tisdale had heard the winters were very cold. Mrs. Schumacher had only been through there after her honeymoon at Niagara Falls, thirty years before.

As soon as the meal was over I escaped to the quiet of my darkroom at the front of the basement. From long experience, I knew I would be unable to hear even the murmur of voices there from that star-chamber in the dining room. Dad found an unfinished cigar and took a walk. Mr. Oliphant fled to his room on the fourth floor. Young Gary was quickly sent down to their apartment at the back of the basement. Stacy White, Mrs. Tisdale, Helen Schumacher, Mom and Cass remained at the table with coffee and some orange russe. Mom had invited Helen to dinner as well, not only as a best friend, but as a widow and a font of endless advice concerning marriage and men.

Regrettably for him, Gary's bedroom is just below the dining room and because it was raining outside he couldn't retreat any farther into the backyard. The Dodgers were in Philadelphia but that game was over, and in the quiet I busied myself sorting photographs onto the shelves Dad had made for them. Gary found me.

"You said you were going on an adventure someday."

There was just a small note of accusation in his voice.

"I will."

"But you're getting married."

"Maybe I'll take Cass with me."

"She'll be having babies."

"We'll take the babies too."

"Babies can't walk."

"We'll have horses, like Mr. Tschiffely."

He considered that possibility for a moment. I had given him all my copies of National Geographic and some weeks ago had pointed out the account there of Aime Tschiffely's ride from Buenos Aires to Washington D.C. Stacy had told me since then, Gary had taken to reading the magazines cover to cover, over and over again. She was already worried now with the thought that he would take it into his head to run away. I told her not to worry. I had done the same thing and with those very same issues that were now looking the worse for the wear.

Gary moved closer to look as some of the unsorted pictures on the pile.

"Why don't you just go on your adventure first?"

It was a good question. Fact was, that had been my plan—to save enough money to go wherever I wanted and to take pictures of whatever I found and earn a living at that. Gary had already heard about all that several times.

I said, "Plans are not promises. Plans are made to get you going in the right direction. But if you keep your eyes open, you learn about new things as you go along. You can't expect to be keeping old plans you made when you didn't know about something better."

He was instantly incredulous, "Getting married is better than hunting dinosaur eggs in the Gobi Desert?"

I had to confront that head on.

"I hope so. I am going to be married a long time. I might only get to the Gobi Desert once."

He clearly did not believe me. Roy Chapman Andrews and his expeditions had set a very difficult standard for the rest of us to follow. Thankfully, the loose photograph of the *Hindenburg* I had taken from the top of the Empire State Building caught his interest.

"Did you see the crash?"

"No. I saw the mess afterward. Cass and I were there later."

Gary pulled another edge from the pile, a picture several weeks old.

"What happened to this guy?"

"He was shot."

"Dead?"

"Dead."

"In the eye?"

"In the eye."

Gary wiped his forehead of imaginary sweat. "Whew! Bull's-eye! Just like Annie Oakley."

The thought of that somehow lingered with me. It was more than just a murder, wasn't it? It was some sort of fiendish target practice. A kind of fetish.

After leaving, I made a suggestion regarding this to Cass as soon as we were out of the wet of the evening and onto the El. Cass looked like she was in need of a distraction following her ordeal. We were both holding the straps and I moved in close so she could hear me over the racket of the tracks, but also just to be close.

I said, "It might be a way to get some attention for those John Does. It's an angle. That's just the sort of thing George might need to make it work and give it a little more space. You could call them the 'Annie Oakley Murders.'"

She seemed to ignore the idea. Her mind was on more important things than mere murder.

"Your mother thinks we should get married at St. Joseph's. In the Chapel. She thinks the priest would allow us to get married there even though we're not Catholics."

"Maybe that's a key to the thing. You see! Look at it from a whole different angle. How many people are good enough with a gun to hit someone in the eye almost every time?"

But she had heard me after all.

"You'd be surprised. I think. Besides the one at the fish market was shot in the nose."

"That was a Luciano hit. He's not a part of this."

She twisted her face up at me with phony disbelief. "Do you want to get married in a chapel?"

I kissed the pout on her lips.

"No. I was thinking we could have a party at my parents' house first and then we could just go hop aboard the *Normandie* and the Captain could marry us."

"I thought you wanted to go on the *Zephyr*."

"It's the '*20th Century Limited*' from New York. It's the '*Zephyr* 'from Chicago. But I changed my mind. I want to go on the *Normandie* first."

"Will that boat be here in October?"

"Or some other ship."

"Does it matter?"

"The *Normandie* is a ship. A boat is a smaller matter. But I figure we'll be in the cabin most of the time anyway."

She shook her head at me. "I want my parents to be there."

"Wouldn't your parents want their own cabin?"

"Don't be silly."

"Did you speak to Mom about this?"

"No. Is that the way to get your mother to come around?"

"You're right. I usually say, 'maybe.' She hates 'maybe.'"

Cass was struck with an inspiration. "Maybe the Captain of the boat can marry us right here in New York Harbor, and then they can all leave on a tugboat!"

I had to bring her down to the truth of it.

"I was just joking. I don't think it would be legal. My dad told me that when he was in the Merchant Marine, the Captains would often perform 'marriages' for the sailors when they were in port just to keep them happy. Those were never legal."

"Did the girls know that?"

"Probably not."

"That's horrible!"

"I'm sure it was great fun for all concerned. Why would a girl assume that a sailor she had just met was going to stick around to be a good husband?"

"That's not the point!"

"Sure it is. If they both wanted a little connubial bliss, they got it."

"Is that all marriage is about? Sex?"

"Mostly."

This conversation was recorded with the typewriter on my desk at the office within half an hour of its occurrence. It went along just about exactly that way. But then Cass stopped speaking to me after I said 'Mostly.'

On Monday morning there was a new article by Cass, linking the 'Annie Oakley Murders.' That one finally got picked up by the Wires.

24. Tuesday, May 11, 1937

Being old hands at this now, having done it once before, we went up to the Savoy again on Tuesday. This time we arrived early. That was the evening Benny Goodman and Chick Webb were scheduled for what was boldly advertised as 'The Musical Battle of the Century,' and as before, my plans were all made.

The deal at the Savoy was that each band would set up and play alternately until one was declared winner by acclamation. There had been a number of these battles previously but this one had gotten a great deal more press attention after a mention in the Walter Winchell column that ran in the *Mirror*. The problem with that was, the regular *Mirror* critic and an assortment of his cronies had just arrived ahead of us. The big guy at the side door took one look at our press cards and said, "No dice."

We were on our own. And the crowd out on Lenox Avenue was already stopping traffic. Certainly, no one inside would be leaving until the main show was over. But the night was still young.

In keeping with the romantic occasion, Cass and I had been discussing the whole idea of the newly christened 'Annie Oakley murders' since we left work, and so the next thought was a natural. I found a phone booth and called my good buddy Jeremy Stern for a pair of tickets. I knew the chance of him being home was slim, but he answered. At first I thought he might be sick, but he was simply glum. His bride, Lois, the girl from the chorus line at the 1936

Ziegfeld Follies for whom he'd fallen so hard, had recently landed a larger role in a new musical called *Sea Legs* and was filing for an annulment rather than risk having his baby and spoiling her career. He told me he could return the wedding pictures, if I wanted them. I told him to toss them but keep the nice leather album. It was English and the best one my dad sold. But then, having no mercy, I asked for one last favor and promised more pictures the next time he lost his footing on the path of true love. Given the short notice, he said he couldn't manage anything for one of the newer openings that night, but he could probably swing some complimentary tickets to one of the older shows. I asked for his recommendation.

You Can't Take it With You by Moss Hart and George S. Kaufman was going strong at the Booth Theatre down on Broadway. We grabbed one of the cabs that were still unloading hopeful jitter buggers and managed to arrive just in time for the 7:35 opening.

This show is a screwball comedy more than a romance, but it has sufficient fervor to put us both in a good mood—for an argument.

Contrarily, it was Cass's contention that because nothing in the improbable plot was really resolved, the play was incomplete.

"Why does Alice stay? Has anything really changed? Would she? Really? She might love her family, but the crazy way they live doesn't make her happy. And now the guy she loves is throwing in with them instead of following her. Do you actually think Mr. Kirby is going to change a lifetime of bean counting for a bunch of nutnoodles? Is Mr. Kirby going to divorce his wife? And what's Tony going to do for a hobby? The snakes and the fireworks are taken. And bricklaying is an actual job! Maybe he can take up printing political slogans along with Ed. He's a little old for taking up ballet, don't you think? And do you truly believe the IRS is going to settle for the idea that Grandpa Vanderhof just isn't going to pay his taxes because of a name mix-up?"

I said, "Well, she's changed her mind. And yes, she might. Maybe. True. He could, because he's obviously not happy bean counting on Wall Street. But his wife is probably a lost cause. As my dad likes to say, spiritualism is a dead end. (He always laughs then at his own wit.) Maybe Mr. Kirby'll pick up with the Grand Duchess Olga Katrina if he likes her blintzes enough and Mrs. Kirby can find happiness with an astrologer in need of a home planet. I'm sure our guy Zolar could give her some advice on that. But as for the Internal Revenue Service, I think you might have a point. That problem is a stickler. They're going to find out sooner than later that the mix-up in names is a trick. Then again Mr. Kirby might be able to pay Grandpa's tax off as the price for his share of Vanderhof Shangri-La. My quibble would be about how he gets away with it in the future."

"That's not a resolution! That's a fix!"

"It's a comedy, for Christ's sake!"

"It's ridiculous!"

"I don't know. My parents' house has been pretty topsy-turvy now and again. Some of their boarders have even been nuts. And they have a negro housekeeper just like the Vanderhof's."

"Stacy only works for your mother part of the time . . . and your father pays his taxes, doesn't he?"

"I don't know. I never asked him."

She wasn't finished. The real matter remained to be dealt with.

"Do you think I'm as flighty and inconsistent as Alice?"

There were two wrong answers. I grabbed at the lesser one.

"No. Not at all!"

"I'm a fuddy-duddy then?"

"No! You're a free spirit who knows what she wants. That's all."

Cass saw through my contradiction but let me wiggle loose.

We stopped at the Gaiety Delicatessen afterward for a couple of fat corned beef sandwiches on rye. It was there, at a small table in the tight squeeze of the after-theater crowd, that I learned Cass had her own personal connection to Annie Oakley.

"You asked me before if it was likely there were a lot of people who could shoot like that. Did you know that my mother was an 'Official Annie Oakley Sharp Shooter?' She has the certificate to prove it, framed, and signed by Annie herself. She and about a hundred other girls went out to the Cuyahoga County Fairgrounds one time to see a demonstration of Annie's amazing skills and then paid one dollar each to receive personal instruction on the art of marksmanship."

I was greatly impressed at this. I said, "Now, there is a promoter!"

Cass was indignant. "Maybe. But she had the goods, didn't she. Annie Oakley was actually the best!"

"But did your mother learn anything about shooting?"

"A great deal! Miss Oakley spoke to each girl as they took their first shot. One after the other. And then again with their second shot. And then again with the third. Twenty shots each. They had all brought along their own rifles, or their father's, or brother's rifles. They stood in a row, a dozen at a time, with the targets clipped on a rope about ten yards away. They took aim, and fired when Miss Oakley set her hand on their shoulders. It was her belief that every girl ought to know how to shoot well. My mother has told me many times that it changed her life. And you should know right now that my mother taught me everything she learned, so you had better be careful about getting any more funny ideas, like those sailors you told me about."

I said, "I think we should definitely rule out the chapel in that case."

We took the subway downtown. And again, my intentions were not the best. But Cass did not object. And most importantly, when still looking forward to a night of swing with Benny Goodman and Chick Webb, I had taken the hopeful precaution of disconnecting my phone as I left for work that morning.

Sadly for me, and us, Barry George had sent one of the stringers out to slip a handwritten note under my door.

I managed to get Cass over to 45th Street around eleven thirty, just in time for her to write a short additional piece reconnecting five of the murders for the next edition.

The 'Annie Oakley' version of the John Doe story had not

only been picked up by wire services, but one of Barry George's spies had passed him the word that the *Daily News* was scheduling a full page for the morning edition and that they were using the head 'Annie Oakley Killer' in twenty-four point.

George intended to see that card, and play the first picture I had taken of Fred Bellows with it, to up the ante. And even better than simply matching them on point size, he would use a new Gothic Bold type font the guys downstairs had just added to the inventory. The *News* had a larger circulation and George figured whatever he did, they would only up the pot later in the day, but he had some new thoughts on that matter as well.

Another battlefront had been declared in the ongoing war between the *News* and the *Mirror*.

My assignment, as well as Cass's, was to go back up to 72nd Street first thing in the morning, the earlier the better, and speak again with Fred Bellows. He was the only eyewitness and our best bet was to see if we could put him out of reach for a few days while the story developed.

To make sure this operation ran smoothly, Cass went home with me again, but this time with other intentions. She slept on the couch and I slept on the bed in the room with the trays, all alone.

25. Wednesday, May 12, 1937

But Fred Bellows had not been seen since late Sunday morning.

We arrived at that concoction of wooden crates and canvas tarps tucked beneath the new West Side highway even before the sun had skirted the warehouses along the river. The hobo jungle was quiet in the half-dark, sheltered from the wind off the river. Not knowing exactly which hovel was his, I had no other choice but to yell out Fred's name into the instantly hollowed echo that returned from the concrete ceiling. There was no other answer at first, before a pale face appeared where a tarp door was bent back.

A graveled voice said, "I think Fred must have caught the West Bound."

'Taking the West Bound' was known jargon among the hobos for someone having died. I asked the face that was still unconnected to a body in the dark of the opening, "Why's that?"

"He left his gear. His favorite cup. He told me his mother gave him that cup."

I could tell then that the voice, hoarse as it was, belonged to a woman.

"Where can I leave a note for him just in case he comes back?"

"Right here. He stays with me."

Other figures began to emerge then, one by one. Some of the men were wearing union suits with pants or overalls pulled on quickly. One fellow, his bare feet inserted in a battered pair of wingtips and wearing baggy trousers hung by loose suspenders from bare shoulders, neatly squared his hat as if it would hide his other omissions before he spoke.

"Fred ourta haf kep his mouf shout," was the sound of that.

A thin and pale skinned woman wrapped to the neck in the oversized folds of a man's overcoat, her bare feet and toes curled against the cold ground, stood half-hiding behind this fellow.

The small amount of cash I had remaining from the night before brought forth several statements concerning Fred's possible whereabouts, but all of them conflicting.

The woman who had first spoken, her unkempt brown hair streaked wildly with gray, now stood outside the squatting frame of the hut, clutching her arms around a green wool coat as if it were winter. "When he went out he said he was on his way over to Bill's—over at 72nd Street." I knew that was where Fred had originally phoned the police the week before. She looked then from Cass to me. "He was intendin' to get hisself a beer and an egg and a pack of cigarettes as soon as they open at noon. He still had a few dollars left from when you was here before. Said he'd bring me back somethin' but he never did."

One fellow was certain Fred had family somewhere in the Bronx. Or possibly Yonkers. The first woman, who called herself Barb, had shifted over to the warmth of a first slice of early sunlight, but still shivered within her coat. I could see that her legs below the hem were thin and white and she wore house slippers that had probably never seen the inside of a home. Barb had disputed the other accounts as they were proposed. She said that Fred was from 'Bal'imer.' His family had all died from the influenza some years before. Now she stood there in that sun, face turned up and her eyes closed, with the silver streak in her hair gleaming, and on any other occasion I would have taken a picture. But I was fairly sure she was praying.

Cass dispensed the few nickels she had to encourage anyone who saw Fred to call us. There would be a reward if Fred were found.

And he was indeed found later that day. His body was discovered in an empty warehouse near the water at 69th Street by two of the hobos, Larry and Gill, who had been encouraged by the reward to go looking for their friend.

They had called Cass first. She tapped George for a couple of sawbucks from petty cash and I went uptown with her to check the situation out.

The low brick building was one of several close by the new elevated highway that were now scheduled for demolition, and except for the accumulated windblown trash of vagrants, they were otherwise empty right down to the cinders on the floor. A pair of rusting rail tracks led outward through wide-open sliding doors at one end. Fred's body was just below a window on the riverside where, my guess was, he had tried to escape at the last moment. He was not naked. But he had been shot—several times. The blood had not traveled much beyond the body and outlined it at one side. I took that picture because it appeared as if he were lying on his own shadow. His hat had fallen loose and lay in a clutter of refuse at the wall. By the small wound visible above the darkened collar of his shirt, my guess was that the bullets were likely .22 caliber, but that would be determined soon enough. His blue scarf was not around. The tobacco stained pocket of his jacket had no pipe.

Cass gave each of the fellows a ten and I gave Gill an extra nickel to call the police.

We stood there silently then in the gray light and thought our own thoughts. No need to express guilt for having exposed Fred Bellows to this fate. That fault belonged to us both. Remorse could be allowed for later. But my thought that he had tried to escape whomever it was that killed him, and not moved quickly enough, led me backward to why he might be there at all. Had she picked him up on the street and held a gun on him as she drove? Not a good bet. Would he have gotten into the car in the first place? Maybe, if she had a gun pointed at him. But I did not think Fred was a stupid fellow. Getting in the car would have been accepting his fate.

An afternoon wind picked up against the roof and sang a dirge in the overlapping metal.

Pretty soon, a police car pulled up at the open bay door, and then another. Both vehicles were there, sitting in the sunlight, when another thing occurred to me. The police car bumpers are black but the bodies are green. However, at night those cars always looked entirely black. What if the car that picked Fred up was green and not black at all, as he thought? In the sunlight, it might not have occurred to him that it was the same one he had seen before. I was only supposing now, but I did this aloud as the cops walked toward us, their heels grinding the cinders into echoes with each step.

"And she could have been wearing her wig again. She might have simply asked him for help moving something heavy. He still had his pride."

26. Friday, May 14, 1937

The unintended consequences of the things you do begin adding up in your mind as well as in fact. The arithmetic is relentless. Merciless. I'd thought several times about Henry Broome and whether he would still be alive if we hadn't gone over to the Knickerbocker Village that day. You can argue that he would have killed his wife or kids instead, crazy mad or not, but you can't be sure of that. I think Fred Bellows would certainly be alive today if we had not reported his name in our first story about the Annie Oakley murders.

But another thought occurred to me. Slow as I was. How had this killer known what Fred looked like? My photograph of Fred had not actually run in the *Mirror* until after he was dead.

Cass was off at a school disturbance in Harlem, so I went up to 72nd Street again on my own. And there I found another consequence of what I had done. The hobo jungle was gone. The earth beneath the highway was newly scraped clean and raw. A pile of fresh gravel awaited to one side, ready to be filled over any remnant of the lives that were there just days before.

I walked beneath the highway, too aware of the imprint my shoes left in the loose soil—like walking across the fresh ground of a grave. On the far side, a bulldozer sat near a ramp and a fellow in the seat there was eating his lunch in the sunlight and enjoying the view across the dance of the tide in the river.

Our conversation felt more informative to me than the words

allowed.

I asked him, "What happened?"

"What do you mean?"

"There were more than a dozen hobos living in under there."

"They're gone."

"I can see that."

"The Mayor doesn't want any bums setting up shanty towns. They moved them out."

"Where?"

"Who cares?"

"I do. Do you know where they moved them to?"

"How should I know? They scattered. Scuttled away like cocka'roaches. That was yesterday. Public Works sent us over with some trucks and equipment and we just scooped all of it right up. It was nothing. Just a load of trash. But I don't run a truck, so I don't know where they took it. They probably dumped it over in Staten Island. That's where most of it goes."

'They,' had become one of those words used too often now-adays that I didn't like.

About to leave, I noticed a gleam of metal and dark blue enamel from under the windshield.

"What's that?"

"What?"

"The cup."

"I found it. Over there."

He pointed at the bare earth. My own footprints were all that remained to be seen there now.

"What do you want for it?"

"Two bits?"

I gave him the quarter and dropped the cup in my bag.

At Bill's Tavern I found a small crowd of denizens who looked as if they'd grown there in the semi-dark the way mushrooms do in an abandoned basement. The smell of spilled beer was thick. There was no music and the talking quieted when I came in, the better to listen, I supposed.

I asked the bartender, "Is Bill here?"

Someone laughed.

The bartender smiled. "No bills here. Cash only."

More laughs. I couldn't manage the humor. I went right to my questions.

"Do you know Barb?"

"Who Barb? You mean the old whore from over at the hobo jungle?" He paused a beat at my nod and then added, "You don't look like the type."

I'm proud of myself for not hitting him. I was already in a bad mood and that would have made me feel a lot better. At least temporarily.

I pulled my press card out of my pocket and stuck it in the band of my hat for the clown effect.

"Our dear Mayor moved them out yesterday. I wanted to talk to her."

He shrugged, "No one left a forwarding address with me."

There was some more laughter.

I tried again.

"Did you know Fred?"

"Bum that was killed?"

"He was supposed to be coming over here last Sunday to get an egg in his beer and a pack of cigarettes."

"Yeah. He was here. He came over every Sunday for the same thing. What about it?"

"Did he leave alone?"

"Yeah."

"I'm trying to figure something out. Was anyone else in here asking about Fred?"

The bartender stared at me, dumb faced.

I said, "What are you thinking?"

He said, "I read that story in your paper. The one about the 'Annie Oakley' killer. I just didn't put two and two together."

I said, "Arithmetic is like that. If you don't add the numbers up, they stay the same."

"There was a woman in here last week. Black hair. Scarf. Cheaters. Good looking. She was asking about Fred. She wanted him for some day labor. She said he'd done some work for her once before, but she couldn't remember his name."

"You told her where to find him?"

"You kidding! I'm not going to send a dame over to that jungle. I told her he always comes in here on Sundays at noon to drink his breakfast."

"How tall was she?"

"Not tall." One hand rose up to the level with my shoulders.

"Built?"

"She had a coat on, but I'd guess she was built."

"Would you recognize her if you saw her again?"

"Maybe, if she came in dressed exactly like that. But I'm not going to testify to anything if that's what you're looking for. My mind isn't what it used to be. I forget things. Especially as they might concern ladies that shoot their victims in the eyes. I want to keep seeing what I can."

Later, at the office, Cass gave me that look again, when I told her about this encounter.

All I could say was, "I couldn't wait. I was curious."

She said, "That does seem to be one of your faults. You just can't wait."

I said, "I don't know. I figure I'm doing pretty good, if you ask me."

She knew what I meant. She gave me the tilt of the head that goes with the look.

27. Sunday, May 16, 1937

First thing Mom said was, "Where's Cass?"

I was prepared for the question. I just wasn't prepared with an answer.

"I don't know. Home, I guess."

"Did she have a headache?"

This was definitely a case of leading the witness. Having a 'headache' always meant one thing with my sisters—that it was the wrong time of the month to go down to the park with me and play ball.

"She's never mentioned having any headaches to me. She says she has laundry to do."

Mom rolled her eyes beneath arched brows and pursed her lips. I have always known her to use that same facial expression about other delicate matters, and I wondered if I had stumbled upon another of the same sort of pretense as the headache.

I defended her. "Are you expecting Cass to come over every Sunday now? She still has her own life. We're not married yet. At least give her a chance to get used to the idea."

Mom wasn't buying. "Maybe it's you who needs getting used to it. You didn't even ask, I bet."

"But I did I ask. She said she had to do her laundry."

Mom was in a bad mood. This is a sometime thing and I have long supposed that it might just be a matter of one of her own laundry days when it happened, but this time the situation was simply the burr of having read another lofty pronouncement from Mrs. Roosevelt. We usually avoid politics at the table, but this was to be an exception to prove the rule.

Soon after we are all seated she took aim at her target.

"That smug woman who thinks she was elected to the Presidency along with her husband has done it again this week."

In his most calming voice, Dad says, "What was that, Darlin'? " He knows a storm when he hears it rumble.

"I read in the *Herald-Tribune* today that Mrs. Roosevelt has decided a mother should be paid a fixed salary like any other worker. It is her grand opinion that 'A woman who works to give her children the necessities and some of the advantages of life should have her workday limited to eight hours.'"

Having described the cause of her bother, she surveyed the table for reaction.

I looked at my dad, and he looked back at me, and we both kept our mouths shut.

But Mrs. Tisdale was quick to the breach, "Isn't it wonderful! Can you imagine if women were paid the same wages as men?"

Stacy looks a little surprised that Mrs. Tisdale would take such bait and ducks her head a bit while offering Gary some encouragement over his turnips.

It is Mr. Oliphant who foolishly answers that.

"Who'll be cutting the checks? Who signs them? Drawn on what account? Those would be my questions."

Mrs. Tisdale answers back immediately, "Why, the government! It could be administered exactly like they have proposed the social security program."

Mom set her fork down and leaned forward toward Mrs. Tisdale.

"And where would the money come from?"

"They would print it, of course."

"But then all the rest of the money would be worth less as a consequence of the inflation. And who would decide which mothers were paid—and how much? A good worker earns more than a bad one. Is the government going to be firing bad mothers? Are their sufficient single women out there who want a child to take on that demand? Or perhaps you would like to take care of a foster child who has been taken from an incompetent mother?"

"I have a job! I couldn't. Bad mothers could be sent to a reeducation program."

Mom says, "Well, that's something else to pay for then. Mrs. Roosevelt has never worked at anything but her opinions. She wouldn't have any idea how to judge the motherhood of another woman."

Mrs. Tisdale's voice rose, 'She has five children herself!"

Mom answered, "And at least that many servants to take care of them."

Mrs. Tisdale says, "She is a brilliant woman!"

Mom said, "So she thinks. And that everyone else has a right to her opinions. But I can't imagine the government running motherhood. They have enough on their plate with the CCC. And I certainly can't imagine the responsibility pared down to an eight hour day—not unless you yourself want to be taking care of someone else's children during the off hours. Who takes care of the colic at three AM."

At this point no one was eating. My mom's voice had taken on that tone of absolute authority that I must have first obeyed as a baby. Mrs. Tisdale's voice had risen from mezzo-soprano to a full soprano.

"Why shouldn't there be equality between the sexes?"

Mother said, "Perhaps because they are not equal to begin with!"

Mrs. Tisdale then announced, "I am the equal to any man!"

At that my mom had both eyebrows raised and simply let the words fade into the corners of the room. She said nothing but smiled and took up a forkful of turnips.

I was very glad Cass was not there.

Actually, I don't know what Cass would have said. I am going to have to find the right time to ask her. But I'm pretty sure that Cass does not think men and women are equal. She is certain that women are superior.

After dinner I went downstairs and turned on the radio thinking I'd listen to a little of the Jack Benny program and relax a bit.

Benny's okay. I like Fred Allen better, but that show's on Wednesday nights when I'm working. I don't get the chance to hear it as often. But what Benny has on his show that's better than Allen is the band. Phil Harris is the bandleader there, and he's good. Allen's jokes are better but the music isn't so much. I twisted the dial until I was sure. But Benny wasn't on just yet.

When I looked up, Gary had shown up behind the banister again. He holds on to the spindles like he's behind bars and stares out pitifully. He's doing that more and more lately. On Sundays he has to stay home and he must be bored out of his gourd. This is the curse of the only child, I suppose. When I was his age I had too many brothers and sisters to play with to ever be at loose ends. My one object in life back then was to be left alone.

And then the idea popped into my head from out of nowhere.

I say, "You want to learn about photography?"

"What about it?"

"Do you want to learn how to take pictures?"

He's down the stairs in a flash.

"You mean it?"

"Sure. Maybe you can help me out now and again."

I'd been taking my latest copies from the big bag and he stared open mouthed at the beast that was now exposed beneath.

"I can use your camera?"

"No. Not that one. That one belongs to the *Mirror*. This one." From where it hung above the table, I lifted the neat black case of the Kodak down on its strap.

"It's not as impressive as the Speed Graphic when it's closed, I admit, but opened, it has all the glory of a smaller flower of the same species. A mechanical orchid, a friend said to me once. And orchids come in all sizes."

When I snapped the button to release the cover and the bellows opened on its spring, his eyes went just as big as expected.

I'd received the Kodak for Christmas years ago, and unimpressed with any of the subtleties of winter, I had immediately taken it to the only place I could think of that was filled with beauty and color—the translation to black and white occurred in my brain before I ever snapped the lever with my index finger.

I asked Gary, "Has your mother ever taken you over to the Brooklyn Botanical Gardens?" He shook his head. "No? They have real orchids there, and that's where we'll go. Next week. Before dinner. How about one o'clock? We'll need a couple of hours anyway. But I warn you. If I get a call from The Boss, I'll have to beat it back to work. Don't be disappointed in me. Be patient and we'll get it done. For tonight I want you to pull that little yellow box from up there off the top and get the manual inside. Before we take a single picture, you'll want to know all the parts and what they do. Once you know that, the rest is a cinch."

I stayed a little later Sunday night to see if I could sweeten the pot for him. I explained what I could of the principles without using up any film. For all his wide-eyed takes on the things he doesn't expect, he is a very cool customer. Very shy, very patient, and a quiet student.

When I got home there was a note from Cass.

"Missed you. Ellen was making dinner for her boyfriend so I went along to the office to see if there was anything else cooking there. Bad news. I am sorry. Dick Weise's wife called earlier. Dick passed away this morning. The funeral will likely be Wednesday. Call me later. I'll be home by nine."

My first thought was, it's a lucky thing Izzy Baerz managed to get the black suit for me that I wore to Jerry Herzog's funeral when he did. I was going to get some good use out of it. The thought was in Dick's voice and I even heard him laugh.

And that put me right back to thinking about orchids again. Dick had won my complete attention the very first day on the job when he had compared his camera to that flower. I told Cass all about this and some of Dick's other funny ideas. I didn't get off the phone until sometime after midnight.

28. Tuesday and Wednesday, May 18 and 19, 1937

Mr. Conrad is depressing. The stories are fine, but his characters all have problems with themselves more than anything else. A lot of the stories involve men at sea, but I've never thought of Dad being like that during his time there and I know he isn't that way now. But maybe he was once. Before he met Mom. Though I know she wouldn't put up with any of that tar for a minute.

I mentioned this much to Tom Reilly, and how Mr. Conrad's stories make me glum, and he tells me his favorite author is Kenneth Roberts. I'd heard this guy writes about frontiersmen. Tom was never even a Boy Scout, so I can't figure it. But I decided to go up by the old Wanamaker's store on Broadway on Tuesday afternoon after getting some fresh shots of Wall Street for an article one of the fellows upstairs is doing about the effect of all the steel strikes on the stock market.

I got a nice shot over the tops of a row of stones in the Trinity Church graveyard with the near end of Wall Street in the background. There was a crowd of pigeons surrounding some guys wearing homburgs and pinstripes who were busy eating hotdogs from a wagon instead of chowing down at Delmonico's. Maybe they like hotdogs or maybe they are all suddenly short of cash. I was still down there at three when the banks close and I caught a nice spill of suits in a hurry to leave. As an afterthought I stood up on a trash can and got a standard fix of the Wall Street sign with some perspective behind it. So you can guess which one of those The Boss chose to use.

With that done and things quiet, I went over to Wanamaker's and prowled around the book department. Kenneth Roberts has several other books out but the best seller at the moment is called *Northwest Passage*. It's too thick to keep at the office so I just took that directly home and decided to a read a chapter or two before I turned out the light at night to go to sleep. This worked fine except that it was four o'clock in the morning before I managed to turn the switch.

On Wednesday morning I went down to Dick's funeral in New Jersey. We had a fire to cover down on Water Street and a sit-down strike up at Chrysler Building, but Stenis sent some stringers out on those and The Boss and a couple of Dick's other friends and I all piled in a couple of company cars and went to Morristown. It was a fair assemblage of the sorts of people he knew through the years. Even Bill Phipps from the *Daily News* and a couple of the other Hearst guys from the newly combined *Journal-American*. The man was well liked.

Cass and I went out to dinner that night. This was a little subdued, but Dick had a good run and there was nothing too tragic about it. I told her a couple stories Phipps had reminded us about while we were standing around in the parking lot after the funeral. Cass had a few tales of her own about *Daily News* photographers. Not Phipps. But one of them who had his private collection of pin-ups in the darkroom for the entertainment of the other fellows that worked in there. She had gone in unannounced to oversee some shots taken for one of her stories and had a good laugh at their discomfort.

That was when I also found out from her own lips that she had something of a reputation as a prude. The idea had never occurred to me, but I suppose it derived from her ongoing concern over white slavery and the prostitution rackets and with the series of articles she had written about that subject for the *News*.

29. Sunday May 23, 1937

Before Stacy and Gary, or Mrs. Williams and her cats who lived there before them, but for all of the years of my childhood after we moved to Sterling Place, a German couple rented the two rooms at the back of the basement. That couple, the Sterns, seemed very old to me then, but were likely the same age as my parents are now.

Those basement rooms have their advantages. The rent is cheaper. They're rented together and that makes them a little more private. They have a direct entrance to the backyard. The yard is small because dad's A Model is parked on the other side of the fence by the alley. But in good weather that yard is like a third room. On the minus side, the ceilings are lower and it's colder in the wintertime. They're quiet, except when things are too active upstairs in the kitchen or the dining room. You can't hear the furnace because it's up front by the old coal chute and even now, with the oil, that can make my little darkroom uncomfortable when the beast is roaring. In fact, it was the racket of the pipes in the wintertime that always used to drive me out of there. Like a hammer on a spike.

Mr. Stern did odd jobs. Mrs. Stern did pretty much what Stacy does now. She was a housekeeper. Mrs. Stern was plump. Mr. Stern was thin. What they did together mostly was argue. Bicker. I could even hear them from upstairs sometimes. Mr. Stern was a devotee of Karl Marx and could evidently quote whole passages at the drop of a dime. Mrs. Stern was a Lutheran. I have no idea what brought them together originally, but I knew that in their past they had at least one more child than my parents, because that subject had come up. Why all of their children had remained behind in Germany when the Sterns had emigrated was a mystery alluded to many times in my parent's conversation. My dad's German was good, though he seldom used that language after leaving the ships except to haggle at the market. He heard nothing. Still, I came to understand that it was their politics which had made them come. Mr. Stern had even been arrested for a time. But the real importance of this was that two of their boys had later died in the War, fighting for 'The Fatherland.' The hurt of that loss was ever-present in the fact that neither of the Sterns could manage much of a smile on the best of occasions. Mrs. Stern always looked sad. Mr. Stern looked grim.

When you are young and just learning the meanings of words, it strikes you as a revelation and not a coincidence when you discover that a person's name perfectly matches their temper. For me, 'stern' was a German word and has always had those two faces attached. But because they argued in German, I never knew what was actually being said, though the tone of their voices was clear enough to me.

This all comes back to mind now because of an interesting development.

When Gary and I returned from roaming in Prospect Park on Sunday, we had a surprise visitor waiting. Gary's father.

I had thought the man was dead.

Mr. White is a tall fellow, and muscular. It had been my previous understanding that he once worked for the Norfolk & Western Railroad. But Stacy had left her home in Virginia and come North without him about three years ago. And though I assume my parents knew all about it, I had been reluctant to ask if they were divorced or what had become of him since. Some answers you just don't want to know.

Stacy had looked to her son immediately when we came in, and it was clear she had been crying. Gary had taken one look at his father and become stone-still.

Mom introduced him as Gareth White. She had invited him

to dinner, which he had evidently accepted. Stacy remained standing back by the buffet where she had started to fill two plates as she always did. I could not see her face then.

Gary made no move toward his father, but his demeanor was obvious.

Dad's face said it all. He was already sitting and looked up at me with that squint he gets when things are a bit raw, and then back at Gary, "Go get washed up, boys. Food's getting cold."

As I turned with Gary to leave, Mr. White stepped forward and with one hand on the boy's shoulder, took the closed camera from Gary's hand and extended it to me. Gary's head was down nearly into his shoulders as his fingers released the strap. He did not look up.

I said, "Gary has to take the film out later to develop it first, like I've been teaching him to. But I guess we can do that next week."

"Won't be a next week. Gary's leaving with me."

"I haven't heard anything said about that."

I looked to Stacy but she had not moved. Her face was turned away to the wall.

Mr. White said, "That's the fact."

I asked, "What about that, Stacy?"

She still didn't answer. I got the feeling she was shrinking in size now, right where she stood.

Mr. White said, "That's Mrs. White, to you. She has nothing to say. I'm the boy's father."

Mom interjected, "We can talk about this after dinner."

Mr. White gave a short and definitive shake of his head, "This is none of your concern."

Dad said, "Stacy is part of our family here. It is our concern."

There was a flinch in his cheeks, and Mr. White showed some small confusion in his eyes. He had mostly been keeping those eyes on me, but now he looked down at my dad.

"You mean she's your maid."

But Mom answered. "Stacy helps me with the housekeeping.

If that makes her a maid, then call it that. It's a job, just like any other."

Now, to see this correctly, you have to understand that Mr. Oliphant is standing behind Stacy with his empty plate in his hand. He'd been breathing with some impatience before this, but now he had gone completely quiet. Mrs. Tisdale, was already at the table, hands in her lap, looking straightforward across her food to the windows. Her eyes are wide. Mr. Clurman, who was also sitting, fork in hand, was ready to start eating as soon as the rest of us were seated. He shifted his eyes between Mr. White, Dad and myself as if trying to see us all three at once.

I said, "I don't know what the law is about that, but if Stacy says Gary's staying with her here, that's the fact."

The man had a full inch on me. I was not in a position to intimidate him. Alternatives were not coming to mind.

Now, my dad is a man of very specific habits. He has said, perhaps too often, that you can't get sloppy aboard ship. Every one and every thing has its place. He is not exactly mechanical about this philosophy. It's just what he does.

At that moment Dad stood up.

In twenty-five years I don't remember my dad standing up at the table with a plate of food in front of him. Maybe once. But's that's another story.

Dad's a couple inches shorter than myself but he could probably take me in a fight to this day.

He says, "Mr. White, you've been invited to dinner. You're still welcome. But if you are going to be rude you'll have to leave."

There was time for a couple of good breaths there, but you could not see Mr. White doing any breathing. Without comment he finally turned and took one of the two plates still in Stacy's hands. I ushered Gary toward the hall so we could wash up.

When I got back, Gary was already sitting in his usual spot by his mother. Mr. White had taken the chair next to Stacy. Mr. Oliphant turned from piling food on his plate, seemed flummoxed for just an instant and then took the chair closer to me than our guest.

Mom passed the bread and initiated the small talk immediately, asking Mr. White a few questions. I watched Stacy as she
coaxed Gary to start eating. To my knowledge, he had yet to speak a
word to his father. After three years.

"What do you do, Mr. White?"

"What I can."

"You're not with the railroad any longer?"

"No more."

"Where do you live?"

"Been. In Virginia."

"Whereabouts?"

"Roanoke."

"What are your plans now?"

"I've come to get my boy."

"Yes. I think we understand that part. What else were you
thinking of doing?"

"California, . . . maybe."

She let up on her inquiries with that answer and ate her own
dinner. Gary looked several times at me, but not at his father.
Everyone else was unusually silent. Mr. Clurman had yet to say one
disparaging word to Mr. Oliphant.

Dad says, "Where did you grow up, Mr. White?"

"North Carolina."

"You don't like it there?"

"Not much."

"You have family there?"

"Yes."

"What do they do?"

"Farm tobacco."

"They must have work. I see everybody smoking cigarettes
these days."

Mr. White looked up as if some insinuation was being made.
"Slave's wages."

Dad didn't hesitate, "I can imagine. Fieldwork is long on
pain and short on gain. Most the sailors I ever knew were born on

farms and happy to be gone. I remember, just after the war, there was no work anywhere. The Influenza had everyone down. I'd already decided to leave the Merchant Marine years before, but then the war came. In 1919, I took my papers right here in Brooklyn, where there was no work to be had at all then. A friend of mine— " He looked to Mom for confirmation, "You remember Sully? He knew some people in New Jersey that needed to have their strawberries picked. Those three weeks were the hardest work I ever did. Harder than any apple harvest because we were always bent over."

I had actually never heard that story. I said, "How did you get out of that, Dad?"

He said, "The strawberry season was thankfully short, or I'd still be walking around with a stoop. But your mother had you kids to take care of and I wasn't looking to leave her alone again like she was during the war. And I'd spent just about all I had, so that was a fix. I tell you." He started to take another bite and halted mid-air. "Well, I took my hat in hand and went to see Dr. Dean—" Dad looked at the others at the table. "That's Dory's father—and I asked for his advice."

Dad paused then to eat what was left in his plate. I think he was anticipating that Mom would want to have her say.

Mom rolled her eyes and looked to me for understanding, "He did not ask my father for his advice! He simply told him that he was flat broke. He went up to Boston on the milk train and confronted your grandfather bright and early one morning, right there in his office. His intention, the best I can guess, was to have my father offer to take us in, at least until he could find another job, but he hadn't consulted with me about it! Not a word. Male pride is a wicked thing. And father was not interested in having a house full of kids again because mother had passed the year before. So he asked your Dad, 'What can you do, other than tie a knot?' And with typical candor, your father said, 'Not a darned thing'—only he didn't say darn. And my father said, 'That makes you a bigger fool than I thought you were.'"

Dad cleared his throat and held up a finger to defend himself.

"And I answered, 'But you have to admit, I was smart enough to marry your daughter!'"

Mom waved the comment away and finished the story. "Father says, 'I suppose I have to take some of the responsibility for the fact that she was foolish enough to marry you. Now that it's too late for an annulment, we'll have to solve the problem some other way.' And the two of them sat down together right there and figured it all out without a word to me. My father loaned us the money to buy this house first and then later, in his will, what we used to start the business. But when Daniel came home that night from Boston he presented it to me as a done deal. I could have killed him, right then and there and been justified."

Dad sat back.

"Now, Darlin,' you picked this house out yourself. You said you liked the name of the street, 'Sterling Place' because of your own grandpa."

She waved her hand again but said nothing.

This was all fresh material to me, but somehow I knew to keep my trap shut for the moment.

But then, it was Mr. White who asked Dad, "So, what did you do after the strawberries were picked?"

And I suppose that was where he had intended to go anyway because he picked his story right up.

"Well, I got a job at Fleischer's. Answered a classified ad, just like I had a hundred times before. They were an old stationery company on Pearl Street, downtown. They needed a deliveryman. Between deliveries I worked in the stock room. It was clean work and kept me out of the fields you might say. But it really didn't pay enough to take care of Dory and the babies. At first it was Dr. Dean who made that possible. That was before he passed on in 1921. And I kept looking for other work, but it was a difficult time after the war. It wasn't long then before I knew a little something about the stationery business. Even thick headed as I am. And when things started to improve again, I was already making a little more than I could convince anyone else to pay an old sailor who knew his knots.

Well, then Mr. Fleischer went and died the summer of 1924, and I could figure what was coming next. So I talked Dory into the idea of using what was left from Dr. Dean's bequest, found our little spot under the Sixth Avenue El that was cheap enough, and got Mrs. Fleischer to let me take over their old stock and furniture for a percentage of sales when they closed their business that winter."

I wasn't sure of the point Dad was trying to make. But I knew he had a purpose. And I could see that things had calmed down a little as they all listened.

Mr. Clurman ventured a comment.

"You were lucky, don't you think, Mr. McNeill?"

"Luckier that I had a right to be. Fortunate, I'd say. Not many women would have carried the weight that Dory did for all those years."

Mom wasn't going to sit for any blarney.

"You do what you have to do. Of course, during the war, I had someplace where I could run off to with the children when Daniel was away. Most people don't. And my father was a Yankee in more ways than one. His own father was in the Navy, and his grandfather had been a sailor, and a captain. And his great grandfather before him.' She turned to the rest of us. "Dad was more tolerant of Daniel for that reason alone, I think."

I knew about all that part, of course. It was family lore. But there was a darker strain there and I suddenly worried that this topic might suddenly open up.

Mr. Oliphant continued to eat with a very deliberate preoccupation but Mrs. Tisdale had calmed enough to address a question to our guest.

"You've heard Chick Webb haven't you Mr. White?"

"No."

"Really! You must. He plays at the Savoy. Everyone goes there to dance."

Stacy actually spoke then for the first time since I had arrived.

"Gareth is a Baptist. He doesn't believe in dancing."

Mr. White ignored this comment and turned back to my dad. He said, "Did you have a reason to be telling that story about yourself Mr. McNeill?"

"I did. Indeed. More than a couple reasons. If you'll let me explain."

Evidently, Dad had been arguing with Mr. White before Gary and I had shown up. I could only imagine that.

Mr. White nodded.

Mom lifted the bread plate toward that end of the table.

"This will go well with that gravy Mr. White."

He took a piece and then passed the plate around.

Dad cleared his throat in the way that commonly meant he had collected his thoughts.

"I suppose there isn't much more work around here today than anywhere else. But that's a point. If you're going to be looking for a job, it might as well be close to where your wife already has good employment. And a home. And I want it to be clear to you that if you would like to stay here in this house, you're welcome. The ceilings downstairs may cramp your style a little if you like to dance, but seeing that you don't, that won't be a problem. I'm pretty sure there are odd jobs you could pick up here and there. And if you persist, maybe you'd even find something with the railroads. We have several hereabouts, as you might know. Why, Mr. Clurman might even be able to help in that regard." Mr. Clurman's face showed immediate alarm at the idea. Dad went on, "Or maybe not. But work is work and it only matters that you do it well. My point is that you aren't much younger or older than I was when I left the Merchant Marine and had to learn a whole new way of getting along. I got along. With a little help, of course. And you could too."

30. Sunday, May 23, 1937

You'd think that my dad's attitudes might have been shaped by his years as a sailor, after shipping to the four corners of the globe amongst "crews of every color and size of man to have ever pleased the eye of God," as he's said more than once. But you'd be wrong. Any impulse toward broadmindedness he has always credited to my mom. I've known from childhood that these beliefs were naturally hers, and I have learned since that they were impressed upon Dad after the fact by events and his own stubborn attachment to her. But perhaps both things are true.

Because this is such an unusual circumstance, I ought to explain it better.

On my dad's side, it is a simpler story to tell. He left New Hampshire as a young man of nearly seventeen and set out to see the world. His own father, James McNeill, had been born in Ireland and had left the famines there to come to America around the time of the Civil War. Grandpa McNeill worked as a farmer laborer for others during most of his shortened life, was an unsuccessful apple farmer, and died of tuberculosis the same year my dad first shipped aboard a freighter 1896. Dad did not meet Mom until ten years later, shortly after the San Francisco earthquake of 1906. The steamship *Far Wyoming* was one of the thousand ships carrying relief supplies to that city and Dad had taken a quick liking to the place and stayed behind there for 'just a week too long.'

The accounting on Mom's side is a more difficult history.

Parker Dean was the son of a wealthy Boston maritime family that made its fortune in the molasses and slave trade. Those facts are known. And it is this knowledge which seems to have troubled the young man in just about the same way as such thoughts can corrupt the lives of characters in Mr. Conrad's novels. Upon graduation from Harvard in 1878 he had fled his tainted inheritance and gone west.

For a time Parker had worked as a cowboy and was then known as 'Professor' to his associates around the campfires. A natural reticence to speak only confirmed the belief in others that he was a man of great knowledge. I have seen letters from old friends addressed to him in that way in later years, as well as his own brief accounts of his wanderings, told in correspondence to his mother.

Eventually Parker ended up in California, sometime around 1880. Penniless, he took a job on a ranch there near Sacramento. It happened that place was owned by 'Silver Jack' Lawrence, a former prospector who had himself gone west from Boston during the gold rush in 1849 and then floundered about for some time.

In 1859, heading home in defeat, Silver Jack had stopped to dally awhile with a 'Paiute princess' along the banks of the lower Carson River in Nevada and picked up some work there with the 'Washoeites' in the gold diggings just to the north. It was there he stumbled upon something else entirely when the Comstock Lode was discovered, practically beneath his feet. Wisely, having learned his lesson before, he had stayed amidst that fevered rush for only one year, but long enough to accrue a small fortune.

Silver Jack married his woman of 'unknown origins' (as she was later described on a Sacramento census in 1880), named Nelly, bought himself some land in California that he had admired once before in passing, and settled down to producing daughters and cattle. And it was one of those daughters, Bertha May, who had eventually married Parker Dean.

Bertha May Lawrence was my grandmother. In one letter, Parker writes to his mother that "old Jack Lawrence is hungry for stories about Boston and keeps me up into the wee hours telling him all the news I know, which is now at least ten years old. Please write and give me the details on something colorful but more current." Thankfully he was not reluctant about transcribing his own adventures as well.

Going back over that again, it is pretty well established by family tradition that Bertha's mother "Nelly" had taken her name from a popular song of the time and that she was very likely Mexican, or Paiute, or both, which at least accounted for Mom's darker complexion. Also, that she had made her living 'the best way she could' in and around the silver camps of Virginia City after her first husband, supposedly a Paiute chief, was murdered over the price of a horse.

I suppose it is easy enough for me to dismiss that inheritance in the same way that Parker Dean walked away from his own past, but I have always liked knowing it. Especially the irony, if that is the word, of Parker running away from all the ghosts of the men and women who had suffered for his family's wealth, and then, by marrying a rancher's daughter, finding himself better off once again.

About the time he married Bertha Lawrence, Parker Dean passed the California Bar and began to practice law. Soon after, he had risen to the status of Judge. And this was also the cause of his then being called 'Judge' for many years after by other friends. I have seen letters to that effect as well. His own correspondence was obviously prolific and the cause of constant responses, but we have only those letters he sent home to judge him by. He was a man of many parts and unusual ideas for his time.

Dorothy Dean was born in 1888.

It was in the year 1908 that Parker Dean had confronted the anti-miscegenation laws of the state of California by publicly officiating at the marriage of a white friend to a Chinese woman. And then, apparently unsatisfied with the furor that resulted, or perhaps to make his intentions all the more clear, he had compounded the matter by doing this a second time, marrying a white woman with a Japanese man. The furor promptly resulted in an attempt by a mob to burn him out of his home, the dissolution of his law practice when his partners abandoned him, and then the recall of his judgeship.

By 1908, Parker Dean's father had died, and his mother was an invalid. I suppose that Parker decided it was finally time to return home, take care of family matters, and face his own ghosts. The letters he had so regularly sent his mother end there and leave us only to guess his motives. He took a job in Boston, teaching at the Latin School (which is a public high school with some higher stand-dards than the usual), and perhaps resigned himself somewhat to the evil tendencies of his fellow human beings as well as the need 'to persist in order to triumph.' This was his pet phrase, which I likely got to hear from his own lips about the time I was learning to walk. I don't remember it, though I suspect there are many former students of Boston Latin who remember those words very well. I do recall a reserved man who wore black suits and high starched collars, smoked cigars and smelled of tobacco and whiskey. He was fond of whiskey. His joints ached from the abuses of his youth and it was a needed salve. As much writing as he did, he was not a man to speak too quickly. And he was never comfortable speaking to children. Bertha May, famously affectionate, had passed before my memories of that dark house begin. And the Judge died in 1921, when I was nine years old.

But thankfully, in that previous year of 1908, my dad did not take Parker Dean's withdrawal to Boston with his daughter as a per-sonal rejection. Dad followed Mom there and married her the first chance he got.

"Stole her away to the exotic precincts of Brooklyn,' as he says.

I did not stay for long on Sunday. Matters appeared to be much subdued following dinner. I went down to the basement and unloaded some more pictures and then had another thought.

I was thinking about Cass, of course. I'd seen her the day before when we went to a Russian restaurant on 3rd Avenue near Murray Hill. Cass had been up to see the Schechner family again on Friday, and that was a lot of what she had to talk about. She would not let that matter go.

Neatly filed away in the basement at Sterling Place I had the photos I'd taken at Sam Schechner's office the day he hung himself. I hadn't looked at them since.

Within those 4 by 5s, a piece of thin rope still dangled from the sprinkler pipe. The chair he stood on had been picked up from where it was overturned and now sat in the shadows to one side. The body lay on a carpet, already stiffened and in much the same pose as it was found hanging when cut down by whoever found him. The darkened tongue was partially out in a final gasp for breath. His jacket sleeves rode high from his shirt cuffs at either side as they might have been if pulled there by a last attempt to reach up to the noose and stop what he had begun—or perhaps in a desperate bid to stop what was being done to him, especially if his arms had been held until the noose was secure. His tie was askew, but his collar was buttoned. I had seen men who had hung themselves before. Not many. But all their collars were undone so that they could get the rope placed. On the desk, just above and behind the body, several items were shifted in from the edge toward the center. As if someone might have sat there, perhaps to hold an unwilling victim. Or stood to set the rope on the sprinkler pipe. The ceiling was high. The chair alone would not have been sufficient. Even the desk might have been a difficult reach for a shorter man. Had he tossed the end up and over he would have used a hitch knot of some kind, I supposed. The knot in the rope at the pipe did not look common to me.

I took that photo upstairs along with my magnifier to where my dad had an apron on and was doing the dishes in the kitchen.

"What kind of knot do you think that is?"

Dad squinted at the picture.

"Looks like it might be a bowline. I taught you that one when you were still a child."

"I thought so. It's stretched out a bit. Looks odd."

"It's odd because it's an odd knot to use that way. It's not secure to the pipe, you see. Too much play. I'd have used a couple half-hitches on that pipe myself. Simpler."

"He might have not been thinking straight."

"Who's he?"

"Fella named Sam Schechner. Maybe a suicide."

"Funny rope to use."

"Cut from the window blinds."

"Hasty! What would have made a man so hasty about killing himself."

That was the thought that had not occurred to me but was begged by the fact that his collar and tie were not undone.

"He was distraught?"

"Even so. I've seen a man kill himself after getting a bad letter from home. But I've never heard of it done on the spur of the moment. There's always some brooding to do first."

"My thought was this. If the end was thrown around the pipe and then tied to itself with a bowline at that point, it wouldn't slip. It might give you some idea of how tall the person was who tied it."

"Might."

"Just might."

31. Tuesday, May 25, 1937

I have a couple of friends from the old neighborhood who are cops. I touch bases with them when I can to stay on top of what's going on, but they have their own lives now and even if we live in the same city, this place feels damn big sometimes.

One of them I often see, Danny Seger, was thinking about quitting the police force again recently, and I'll tell you why. He's honest. This puts limits on what he can do, or what they'll let him. And a lot or most of that limitation is put there by himself. An honest cop is not trusted by the ones who are on the take. Rising in the ranks can often involve pay-offs of one kind or another and many of the Captains are corrupt.

But Danny is smart and he did not take long to make detective. He's young, he works hard, and he went to Brooklyn College when that place opened up—about the same time a lot of us other dopes were too quick to grab the first paying job. Danny's dad runs Seger's Fresh Produce Market on Flatbush Avenue and was not about to cover Danny's tuition at college because they don't take apples and bananas for barter there. Cash only. So he paid his own way at school too, full time for a couple of years and more lately at night school. He just recently graduated with some sort of a 'B.S.' diploma and he doesn't leave you to guess what the B.S. stands for.

Danny decided to become a police officer because he grew up working in his father's store. He had to watch his Dad pay off somebody nearly everyday of each week just to keep his windows in one piece and his fruit stands upright, or get a fresh delivery when he needed it. That was mostly due to the protection rackets, but it included just about anyone who could do any harm. With most kids I knew growing up, they would have figured that was just the way of the world and gotten used to it. Not Danny.

Just like I did at the *Mirror*, Danny started hanging around the 78th Precinct House when he was still in high school. He made friends. Because it was only a couple of blocks away, he was a gofer there whenever he wasn't hauling potatoes out of a delivery truck. And he used to tell me stories, though he keeps more of those to himself these days.

Even though we grew up in the same neighborhood, we actually only met in high school. We played basketball together and we were in a lot of the same classes at that time. But that's the way it is in Brooklyn. I can't tell you the name of the family that lived on the other side of the alley from us, though I knew their dog pretty well. You get to know the people you need to know.

So recently, Danny was thinking of quitting again. I got a call back in February, late one night. He knows when I get home. He wanted to talk, so we talked then, and the next day I went over to see him. He's right there at the 78th Precinct on 6th. And he didn't pay anyone off for that assignment either—but it did help that he knew the Chief there from when he was a kid. And this was the same Chief who sat Danny down a couple of days before and told him the facts of life.

I don't need to go too deep into that tall grass. It was about what you could expect. The Chief was having trouble keeping Danny on duty. No one wanted to work with him. This Chief is not a bad guy, you understand. He might be the best police chief in New York for all I know. And Danny wasn't passing judgment on him. Not to me, at least. But that guy works within the system, and the system is corrupt from the inside out. Danny had made detective on the merits and because he had a college degree, but he was not likely to get much farther. Too many people in the department saw him as a danger to their own interests.

You understand, Danny was not hearing this for the first time. He did not go into the police department blind. He had just hoped that he could work around it. Like everyone does at the start, before they find out the facts of life.

This gave us a lot to talk about. That and the fact that now Danny has met a girl he wants to marry. Now he's thinking that maybe he should change jobs for the sake of her alone. I was having something of an exact opposite reaction just then myself. That day was the first time I admitted to another human being that I was pretty well crushed on Cass, and I had told him all about it. He thought that was pretty funny because I hadn't even asked her out on a date yet. But still, he thought I would understand his situation with the police department because he had heard some of my own complaints working at the paper and he hoped I might have some words of wisdom.

What I told him was this: that if he quit, he would regret it for the rest of his life. He would be a miserable husband because he was not doing the very thing he had set out to do. I had even watched once one afternoon as his father paid off a driver to get a better load of bananas. Right there in the broad daylight. Just part of doing business. And if Danny was ever going to do anything about all that, he was going to have to hang in there. Then I reached for the rosy glasses and reminded him that LaGuardia had recently signed off on direct cooperation between the Federal Bureau of Investigation and the New York City Police Department. This might be nothing but a political show, but change is happening. The days of Jimmy Walker and Tammany Hall were waning. And as that came about, the Department would have to be looking in their own ranks for the officers they could trust. This is what his Chief should have told him, but didn't.

And except for the bonus fact about the F.B.I., this was all just a rehash of what Barry George had lectured me about the first time I told him I wanted to quit that one time after I had covered a Christmas fire and saw the kids all laid out in their pajamas on the sidewalk, which was the saddest thing I had ever seen in my life up to that moment. "Things will only get better if the good guys stay at their posts," was the way George put it. George was an officer in the army during the war and he talks like that.

One extra note on all that: my dad was a big fan of Jimmy Walker's. This was a matter of some heated discussions at the dinner table on many occasions. There are those who believe that Walker only worked with what he had and didn't believe in the government telling people what they could drink or much of anything else. Maybe so.

So, this morning, I get to work and I see in the paper that Danny Seger has been shot in the line of duty the evening before, while investigating an assault, and he is lying in the hospital in critical condition. I gave my apologies to Stenis and went right back out the door.

Danny wasn't in any condition to see anyone, but his girlfriend, Gail, was there in the waiting room with Danny's mother and I talked to her. Danny had shown me her picture in his wallet and now I saw she was a good deal prettier even than that.

And now here's the joke.

Gail tells me that before he says anything else, he asks her to pass a few words on to me, because he figured I'd be there sooner or later.

I'm floored.

Danny has already calculated that I was going to want to take some blame for his still being out there on the police force and in the way for getting shot. He wants me to know he was doing what he wanted to be doing, however it comes out. That's the way his mind works. Always two steps ahead.

I tell Cass all this over hotdogs that evening and she is out the door pretty fast. She went right over to talk to Gail.

32. Wednesday, May 26, 1937

I was thinking about Danny when Cass and I went over to the Knickerbocker Village again. Cass had a nice piece about him in the paper that morning along with the latest word concerning his medical status at the hospital. It appeared that his condition was now stable. The doctor was thinking he had a good chance at recovery. But the reason he was on my mind at that moment had more to do with Henry Broome. We were headed over to Knickerbocker Village because a complaint had been filed with the police concerning our conduct on the day of Broome's suicide. The complaint had been filed by Doris Broome.

The Boss thought it likely that the complaint to the police was just a preamble. A suit would be brought shortly and the grieving widow and mother was going to make a play for damages, due to our interference in a private matter, and set herself up against the coffers of the Hearst Corporation. That sounded to me about like what we should have expected, but it surprised Cass. Even an out of court settlement could be considerable, and maybe you couldn't blame Mrs. Broome if she was thinking about her kids. But for all her tough exterior, Cass is a softy. On the way over she repeated one fact out loud, "Doris Broome even slept at my apartment that night."

We headed over late because our first appointment was to see patrolman Lorimer who was coming on duty at 4 p.m. and was going to meet us near the call box at the corner of Catherine Street. We wanted a fair rundown of his own knowledge concerning Broome before someone paid him to keep quiet.

In fact, Patrolman Lorimer had already been spoken to—not by anyone connected with the Broome family, but by City Hall. La-Guardia had his nose out of joint at Cass's portrait of the place as a refuge of hacks with little room for the poor that it had been built to help.

Thankfully, we again encountered some integrity. Ted Lorimer even laughed about the call he had received from a councilman at the behest of the Mayor, and told us there was a reason he was just a patrolman after twelve years with no chance in hell of ever making sergeant.

"They'll probably be shifting me to a precinct in Harlem when they find out I've been chattin' wit youse."

And there was that evil 'they' again. But he confirmed Cass's previous account and cited days and times to look for the calls on the precinct record book. And then he gave us a little more.

Lorette Fine, the large woman across the hall who had made the original calls complaining about Broome's beating on his wife, had been spoken to as well, but in this case it was Doris herself who had come to her neighbor. When Mrs. Fine opened the door she immediately told me that if I took my camera out of my bag, there would be an accident. No 'might be' about it. Mrs. Fine refused to say more than she already had and suggested we had previously taken her words out of context.

Grace Williams, the aging call girl who lived in the apartment just below the Broome's, had been spoken to as well. Her identity was concealed in our story but Doris must have figured that much out easily enough by simple deduction. Grace did not want to speak to us and said outright that she would lose her apartment if she did.

"Why don't you go talk to one of the other working girls around here. I'll bet Broome knew them all."

Cass asked if she could give us a couple of names.

She couldn't. And then she had another thought.

"Why don't you talk to the new girl, Lucille Whatsherface

across the courtyard there on the fourth floor. She moved in the first of the year. I hear she bills herself as an artist's model, but she got her place the same way I did, I'll betcha."

There was a keen edge on the voice.

"What makes you think so?"

"She's home days. In warm weather she'll open all her windows up wide to let the sun in and then she strips down to her birthday suit and sunbaths right there where everybody on this side of the courtyard can see her. Broome would have to be blind not to have noticed that."

The mail box in the lobby said 'L. Beinecke.' When we knocked on Lucille Beinecke's door we could hear someone come to the peephole and then walk away. It sounded like bare feet on the parquet to me. Cass knocked again, but there was no answer.

33. Thursday, May 27, 1937

Cass and I talk over the things we're doing at work a lot more than we should. Sometimes I'd prefer anything else, in fact. But Cass has that one flaw. She's what they call an 'obsessive.' She has to finish things. The good news for me in all of this is, she's wearing my ring. Eventually she will get around to me.

She's still deep into the Annie Oakley murders, and at least three of the piles of paper on her desk must concern that alone. One of those had to be for the randy cop, Michael Allen Deems. Another is for the Insurance salesman, Paul Reagan. And I imagine there's a third for Fred Bellows. In addition to that, I figured a fourth had to be for Sam Schechner.

The widow of Paul Reagan had separated from her husband several months before his death, which was just as soon as their youngest child had gone off to college. She was now living with her parents. Cass used one of the company cars and drove up to Poughkeepsie to visit with her.

Tom Reilly was sick that day with the not unexpected results of his own bachelor party, which I had only looked in on briefly for a free beer, so it was me who got to follow Thomas E. Dewey all over town instead. That little man could put a cricket to sleep with his speeches and his delivery, but he is non-stop. Relentless. And that's how he got Luciano. Though, I think he should shave his mustache. Makes him look like a gigolo. And he'd look ten years younger in the pictures.

This fact did remind me to find out how tall Sam Schechner was. Not tall, was my guess, and this was good. He was five feet, eight inches. Now I needed a measure on the sprinkler pipe.

That night I had to settle for a peanut butter and jelly sandwich and the electro-fried tones of a phone call about nine. It's the one Wednesday night I'm home and Fred Allen is off somewhere else and they are playing amateur-hour stuff on the radio.

When she finally calls, first thing Cass says is, "I think I've got something."

Now, given that this is sort of a last ditch effort to keep her Annie Oakley story running, it's gotta be news. Barry George was not operating a detective service, and the *Mirror* could not be paying her salary to run around looking into something that wasn't still twitching on its own accord—five or six murdered or not. That's what the cops are underpaid for. Most of the material was now weeks old. We had even talked this situation over a little just the day before. And it came down to the fact that, assuming Mr. Bellows to be collateral damage, she only had the two names so far to work with—Paul Reagan and Michael Allen Deems. Both cases appeared fairly obvious to us. The other victims were still unidentified, and those two had nothing in common that we could readily see. Except for knowing who'd shot holes in their eyes. The Annie Oakley act needed some new polish.

Given that Cass had gone off for a ride by herself in the country that day and I had been made to squeeze into the press pool car with six other guys, the first thing I say to her when she calls is, "What'd a ya got?"

Cass says, "Listen! Mr. Reagan had some funny ideas. Let me tell you!" She's excited. At least that was encouraging. "Up front, I told Mrs. Reagan why I was there. The kids are all grown up and gone and her own mother was serving us ice tea so we just sat on the porch and chatted like a couple of old friends. I think she's needed someone to talk to. Probably for a long time. The mother didn't seem like the communicating type. But at least the tea was good and she had cookies. Good cookies. I got the recipe. And Mrs.

Reagan told me a lot about herself that won't be good for what we're doing, but I had to let her unload or else she wasn't going to open up about her husband. She really doesn't like talking about him at all. She's still angry, even with the idea that he's dead.

"When the time was right I finally asked her why she thought he'd been fooling around on her, and she says, right out and very defensively, 'I never said no to him. I always gave him what he wanted. He had no good reason.' So I decided to go back a little further and I asked her how they had met. I figured to start at the beginning. Turns out it was at a college mixer. She was a live-at-home scholarship student right there at Vassar, and he was at Columbia. He started coming up on the train to see her after that. She never graduated. She got pregnant, instead. But evidently he'd made a lot of progress with her that very first night at the mixer. She admitted that. She was really taken by him in more ways than his sexual interest. 'He was full of ideas,' she said. She'd never met anybody before who was so full of ideas. So I say, what kind of ideas. And she gets a little coy with me about that and then after a bit of a run around she admits it.

"Evidently he had told her never to talk about all this. To anyone. But, 'now that he was dead, what did it matter?' she says.

Cass let a pause slip through to give her words a little more oomf. I tried to be patient.

"Paul Reagan was a Communist. He even belonged to the Communist Party for a number of years since the 1920s. He'd been traveling around as a salesman on the Metropolitan Insurance Company dime but apparently was doing work at the same time for the Comintern. He was a direct contact with the local labor unions."

Now I know a dozen commies. Brooklyn is full of them. I went to school with them. I got yelled at by their parents for breaking windows. I learned to swim at Long Beach with Carey Geddis who is still a commie to this day, though he runs a successful retail business for the Burroughs Adding Machine Company downtown. What was I supposed to say to the idea that Paul Reagan was a commie?

"So?"

I get silence on the other end of the line.

She finally says, "Have you been keeping up with the news?"

I say, "Probably not as much as I should. What did I miss?"

"There's a struggle going on between the factions inside the Communist Party."

"You mean Stalinites killing the Trotskyites?"

"Right. So you do know about that. And Paul Reagan was a Trotskyite. Devoted."

"So you think that had something to do with all this?"

"Yes, I do! It's one of those things. Just a hunch—"

"Female intuition, you mean?"

She raises the level, "You know I don't believe in that."

I say, "Yeah. But I do. Where would I be without it?"

She comes right back with, "I don't know. There was always Betty down in the wire room."

That caught me off guard. "What do you mean, Betty? I never even flirted with Betty!"

Cass does a mock tone in her voice "Betty says different. She says you used to go down there all the time, especially on slow news days, but she hadn't hardly seen you since January . . . Betty was the first person to ask me if we were officially 'going out.' "

I was curious. I asked, "When was that?"

"Some time in February, I think."

February? I hadn't even told myself in February. And Betty was cute. But not like Cass.

I say, "I still don't see a connection between the other murders and Reagan being a commie."

She says, "It's there, and I'll find it. I'm going down to Philadelphia tomorrow."

34.   Friday, May 28, 1937

So Cass is off to Philadelphia before dawn, to dig more up on Police Captain Deems. No place for me on that trip either. I had to go out to Hempstead in Queens to cover an Eagle Scout badge ceremony. I knew that when The Boss got rid of Carl Jonas it would mean I'd have to do stuff I hadn't done since my first couple of years at the paper. I'd long since risen to the level of police induction ceremonies, after all. But looking around at the other guys on the staff, I could see that I was probably the youngest amongst them once again. I couldn't be complaining.

And she's back by six o'clock and clearly not too happy when she gives me a wave and goes in directly to see The Boss.

I took her out for spaghetti after that. Nothing lifts my mood like a plate of spaghetti. And some Chianti.

The deal in Philadelphia was that, even with some ready contacts that The Boss had, she could find no communist connections to Deems at all. He took his graft from all sides. Non-partisan. His one predilection seems to have been for prostitutes, and their political affiliations didn't seem to matter.

The Boss had now lowered the boom.

He told her, 'Keep your eyes peeled, but don't spend any more company time on the matter unless there are other developments.' This of course had a key word buried in the middle, like a dime dropped in a toilet: 'company' time.

Given her disappointment, I figured this was the right

moment to bring up Sam Schechner. I pulled the pictures out of my pocket that I'd been carrying around with me since Sunday.

She took the bait like a carp on a scrap of bread at the Fallkill Pools in Prospect Park. Though it was true The Boss had okayed her ongoing interest in the activities of the German American Bund, he had never given her any extra leeway for the Schechner case. Not specifically. She was already on her own time for that. What I showed her in the photos was not enough to take to George now for any extra allotment, but it was plenty to get her wheels turning in that direction again.

And then, out of the blue, another random thought flashed at me once again. Why did all the Annie Oakley murders start in January? Granted, we might not even know yet who else was murdered, and we had asked this same question before and not come up with a reason. Not every body dumped in the sewers of New York or some vacant lot is ever found. They turn up odd bones at construction sites all the time. But somehow this seemed important again—but then perhaps this was for lack of any other direction to take.

I said, "Maybe we should look at that again. What about the timing? And was it a coincidence that both men were separated from their wives? That might be incidental to their appetites, but it might not."

In any case, this time, talking about so much murder over plates of spaghetti seemed somehow appropriate.

35. Saturday, May 29, 1937

It is in the nature of the job, with me hauling my butt home through the empty streets at midnight or later, to get a regular whiff of the seamier nightlife. The odor of flora and fauna that blooms after dark lingers on the air, but just as often it is in the sounds as the smells. Most nights it's just a cab or two, slowing down as they pass me with a shout out, "Hey buddy, looking for a good time?" Or it's one of the pimps by the phone booths down on the corner of 14th— though the tall one there knows me now and he does the spiel with a smile on his face just to tease me.

"Young stuff? Clean? Lollipops! You can pick your color!"

I avoid the streets that are a little too dark and a little too quiet. Mostly if I feel like walking to settle things out in my head, I go from 45th Street over by Grand Central and then down Madison, or 5th or 6th. Just a little more than a couple of miles to Perry Street. Forty-five minutes or so with the bag. If I'm tired or the weather stinks, I grab the El on 6th, but that still knocks half an hour, even without a wait.

You get to see the girls along the way. Most of them are young. Just girls, really. Younger I think than the ones who work for Miss Em. White, black and yellow. Most are white but you see more of the Chinese girls at the downtown end. The white girls are more common uptown. More black girls along 6th. One of them even stands right in the shadows at the door of my dad's shop. But you see them all the way. And if I can see them, any cop can too. That tells you something right there.

I knew a fellow named Havey. Not Harvey, Havey. I think his father was Bulgarian, or at least I heard that said. He was on the basketball team with me in high school and a good outside shooter but the coach liked an inside game so his talents were wasted except when we played for fun. Havey's father was a lawyer who was never home much. I think his mother might have been the problem with that. But I know he was an only child. And I know that Havey was the first kid of my acquaintance who ever had sex with a girl. Not that he was a Romeo or anything. He just wanted the sex and he got it wherever he could.

Havey was also the first person I ever knew who got syphilis.

In our senior year, one of the gym teachers at the high school handed out this little flip book to all the guys in 'Health Class.' Pretty crude stuff, but it was effective. The line drawings were like the funny pages, with no color and no humor at all. The fellow in the story starts out strolling down the street with his hands in his pockets and whistling a tune. Then a girl whistles back at him from an alley. Next thing you know he's in a bare looking room with a skeletal looking bed and the girl is naked but you can't see a whole lot because he's on top of her. A couple of frames later he's in a doctor's office getting some bad news. End of story. One of these was given to every guy in the class at the same time as about a half-a-dozen nine by twelve photographs were passed around, one at a time, which showed the graphic results of V.D. The photos were more effective.

Afterward, I think every guy in the class, including myself, speculated that if it was us, we could get away with it 'Scot free,' so to speak. There were at least a dozen remedies we'd heard for scabies, or the clap, or crabs, or 'the syph,' all of which we bandied about with great authority. Garlic was favored by the Italian boys. Epsom salts was a favorite with some others, or apple cider vinegar, kerosene, cayenne pepper, and zinc cream. We were assured by one older brother that you could get both tea-tree and neem oil in Chinatown, both of those were ancient and reliable remedies, no questions asked. Not one of the guys suggested aloud that not screwing around was a possibility. It probably didn't enter our heads. What did occupy our brains for hours and years afterward was how to have sex and not get caught at it, as well as the gruesome consequences of 'not getting lucky.'

But that particular time, as we all flipped the pages of our book-lets and a couple of the more artistic fellows started to doctor the images with pencils, it was Havey who snapped his fingers and held up his other hand and said, "All you need is one of these."

He held the hand high above his head. We all stared open-mouthed at a dull beige-colored latex oval, captured between his thumb and index finger, which he then flexed slightly for added drama, and it looked to us to be mysteriously translucent in the streetlight. Apparently he always carried a condom in his pocket these days. Or so he said. We were all speechless until someone thought to ask if he had ever used it. That got a hard laugh. He said, "Fool! It's a 'one-time Charlie," and laughed again. I had never seen one before, and I don't think half the others had either. But over the following weeks he sold one 'rubber' to each of us for fifty-cents each. He was stealing them from his father and I suppose that had to be done carefully. But they were more expensive back then and he couldn't have been making any profit off the transaction. He did it for the prestige, I think. And in addition he entertained us with details of his own sexual adventures as he did so.

Well before graduation in early June, Havey was gone. He simply disappeared. No explanation. For all we knew, he might have been killed by one of his 'whoores.' That was his word and we all repeated it exactly that way for a time. But he did return to school the following spring and got his diploma. And though we were gone our own ways by then, the word got out quickly soon after that. Havey had gotten a 'dose,' and had been through some sort of terrible medical procedure in order to be cured. The rumor was that he looked terrible. No longer like a kid at all. But I never saw this. I never saw him again.

I heard back then that they got a slightly different flip book at the girl's high school. It was all about getting pregnant out of 'wedlock.' And the joke that went around—told by a girl, mind you—was this: 'What kind of tool do you need to pick a door lock, and what kind of fool do you need to prick a wedlock.'

I have not told Cass anything about old Havey, but some of all that business has coursed through my mind this week. For a reason. More than one.

For one, on Saturday morning Cass and I are on the New Haven line headed out to Larchmont on our way to a wedding. She is dressed to the nines and has her hair pinned up with silver clasps. I was in my one and only formal navy blue suit, which needed a little pressing but was good enough. I couldn't be wearing the black one without someone making a comment about funerals.

At the small stone rail station there, a fellow in a gleaming silk top hat, driving a hansom cab and a horse, (both of them festooned and garlanded with carnations) picks us up and trots us all the way through the village to a place called Manor Park. This is a swell place. Stately homes and broad avenues lined by soaring elms and massive oaks that look as if they might have escaped George Washington's ax. The park is trimmed and combed like a hundred Italian barbers have had a recent go at it. The sun is shining. The water was dancing with diamonds. The breezes are tempered and sweet with the smell of roses. The birds are tweeting. Women are dressed in clothes you only see in magazines. But Cass looks better than any one of them, and she's wearing something blue and white that she bought off the rack at Macy's just that week.

Tom Reilly is dressed in black and gray tuxedo and looks like a stiff but he is upright and fidgeting. I advised him that it would all be over soon and then he could get back to work. But this was wishful thinking. He apologized to me for having to cover for him the next four weeks while he is off to Europe. In fact 'Stutz' Murphy, one of our regular freelancers is doing most of the filling in around City Hall. LaGuardia doesn't want to see my face there. I was handling the chores on the outside, and given the election coming up, that will be enough. But my guess is that Tom Reilly will soon be quitting. He is getting hitched to a girl whose father can afford to rent a public park and an entire hotel and dining room (a small and quaint hotel, but nevertheless), and to truck a fleet of hansom cabs out from the city to meet the guests at the station. There will shortly be a better job offer for Tom to consider.

Folding chairs were set in neat rows to face a gazebo wreathed in red and white roses. A small orchestra assembles magically on the grass and plays Mr. Mendelssohn.

The ceremony was very pretty. But one look at Cass tells me she thinks it's pretty fine. Tom could hardly get his words out of his throat. The bride, a round-faced blue-eyed blond could be heard very clearly all the way at the back of a crowd of two hundred or so, even above the sound of the seagulls who have discovered the event. Cass has got my hand in a lock the whole time.

I brought my camera, mostly for Tom's sake, so I can get a few shots that he'll want to show his own friends, but some of the guests think I am the official wedding photographer and keep striking poses for me and I have to oblige because it's faster than trying to explain.

Afterward we were all herded away by ushers beneath the temporary arbors and trellises of flowers to the nearby Bevan Hotel, which is right there at the edge of the park. Both Cass and I ate as much as we could hold before heading back to work.

Miss Em had called Cass late on Friday. On Saturday afternoon, right off the train at Grand Central and still dressed in our wedding duds, we head straight up to Sutton Place for a chat. At this point Cass has been talking for the last forty-five minutes straight on the train. She has a lot of new ideas about weddings. I was looking forward to the tea to settle my stomach.

You have to appreciate the situation. The piece Cass had previously done on Miss Em had been tough. But Cass had not given out the name or the location. Miss Em appreciated that. I wasn't sure at first why I was being included on this second visit, other than the fact that Miss Em seemed to like me and she knew I was stuck on Cass. The thing of it was that I could not take any pictures while I was there, and so I found myself paying more attention to the details in front of me than I might otherwise.

The niceties were quickly dealt with. Miss Em offered an exaggerated appreciation of the ring, congratulated us, and asked when the event was planned for. She then promptly sat us down, poured the tea in small flowered porcelain cups that hung from the brass hooks on the samovar, and got right to business.

Miss Em was wearing something very loose that looked like light blue satin pajamas with big sleeves and this put a flourish on every movement of her hands. She was smoking short little cigarettes pulled from a light blue wrapped pack that might have been chosen to match her pajamas. She offered the cigarettes to us both. They were French and a little bitter and I didn't catch the name, but then I was thinking more about how much better Cass would look in those pajamas.

She said, "I need a little help. Maybe you can do something." She nodded her head down low between her shoulders, as if it were a shrug. "There's this fellow shaking me up." I'm sure she meant shaking her down, but then, maybe not. "He was one of Lucky's guys, but he's not working for Lucky now. Probably one of the others." She flicked a finger off her thumb into the air dismissively. "But I don't think he has the balls to be doing this on his own. Not from what I've seen of him." The Russian in Miss Em's accent was stronger now than I had noticed before and I could see that she was tired. She said, "He's trying to fill the spot—the empty place—with Lucky in prison." She nodded in that exaggerated way again. I had not noticed her make this gesture before and it surprised me as if it were something copied from another person. "Now, you should know, Lucky and I had come to an understanding long time ago, during Prohibition. I was here even before he started working with Legs Diamond, back when Dutch Schultz was mostly running the numbers on the West Side here and living off the vigorish from his loan sharks. I had been for four years in Paris after the war, before I came to New York in 1925."

She was speaking in such a deliberate manner, I was certain

she was unhappy to be relating all of this to us and was choosing each word.

I offered, "That was the year my dad opened his shop!"

She smiled and waved at the air with her palms and the sleeves flapped in the circles of smoke, "Yes. Yes. I was one of his first customers, you know that. But this is another story." She took a sip of tea. "In 1925 I had a place just over at Kips Bay. Jimmy Walker used to come to see me there. And Arnold Rothstein. Arnold was the first to bring Lucky in. And Lucky appreciated that. And later I understood, maybe before anybody else because he used to talk to me about it, that he was trying to put a syndicate together that would cover everything. 'Everybody,' he said. He trusted me. Men are usually foolish to trust most girls, but I'm not like that and he knew it. He was tired of the feuds. He was tired of the killing. He told me that himself. I believed him." She took a breath and looked at Cass and nodded differently, as if appreciating something else. I think that was because Cass had not pulled out her notepad. "Fact is, Lucky took twenty percent and never asked for more. In seven years, Lucky never once asked to see my books. He could have demanded fifty percent! He got that from most of the other houses around town . . . But at those rates he saw them all cut back to make the business pay and he knew I would have to do that too. I always had the classiest operation in New York. The best! A man could come to me and not worry that he'd be taking a little dose home with him to his wife." By her tone, she might have been talking about the common cold. "My girls have never had crabs or clap or any of that. Ever. Not in twelve years! Lucky appreciated that. That's why he came here himself." She inhaled the smoke from her cigarette back up through her nose each time she paused. This was done in a way that I had seen her do before and appeared very affected to me, but somehow it was in keeping with her personality. A theatrical sort of gesture. "Dutch wasn't so keen on my independence, though. He tried to make trouble a number of times but Lucky stopped it. I don't keep books you see. I always say, 'this is just a rooming house. My girls pay me rent. That's it!' The tax man can squeal like a pig but he's not going to get anything else. And I pay my dues. The Precinct gets theirs. The inspectors get theirs. Every month. And at the end of the year, they are all invited to the Christmas party!" Her head went up and down again. I thought a moment that this was perhaps her way of appearing apologetic for the facts of her life.

She paused to drink some tea, with one finger flared away from the others holding the handle and finally, I see it. She's acting. This is a performance! It might all be true, as far as the words went, but she was doing her best to place all of this mischief in a different light. Just a matter of doing business. As she always has. She is an amazing person, no matter what she has done.

Suddenly she sets her cup down, with a loud clink, and says, "Now this pig shows up! He wants fifty percent and he wants me to keep a record. He wants me to charge a regular rate. I told him to go to hell! I don't 'charge' Ever! There is no rate! That's why we've always done so well. We don't ask for a dime! Our guests give a girl what they want to give. A gratuity. A present. That's all. That's our rule. But I can tell you this: what my customers give is a great deal more than any other house has the nerve to ask. And I'll tell you this also, the last vice cop who came through my door left without paying a red cent! Because he was never asked! During Dutch's time, I was arrested several times. The little bastard was needling me. But the judges threw the cases out the door!"

Another sip of tea. She was even righteous!

Suddenly she held both hands up, palms toward us and shook her head. "And now this. He was here yesterday. This pig! I didn't sleep last night. I am sure he's going to pull something. With Lucky away, he'll try to use me for an example to the others. If he can whip me into line, the others will fall in too."

She sipped her tea again and then looked at us both in turn. "You don't remember Casper Holstein, do you? No! You're too young. He was the King of the Numbers in Harlem. A good man. An honest fellow. He practically invented that racket, you know. Made his fortune. Then Dutch moved in on it and forced him and the others out. Anyone who stood their ground, Dutchie killed. All except for Queenie and Bumpy, of course. Those two hooked up with Lucky first and kept their own business going. But I don't have the money they had. And now with Luciano taken out of the picture, who knows."

Cass was quiet the whole time and probably thinking it through, but I had to ask Miss Em, "Why do you think we can help?"

"Ah! Because, your Miss Green wrote something about this character once before. She knows about him. She might be able to write something that would make some spectacle of him. Make him run from the light like the cocka-roach he is. Maybe make his friends think twice."

"What's his name?"

"Victor Neims."

36. Saturday, May 29, 1937

Cass had gone silent during the conversation and didn't have
a lot to say as we left Miss Em's either. Victor Neims was villain
enough to occupy her mind, of course. Her story last year about
Marley James could not be forgotten. But I was sure there was another matter mixed in and I'm busy guessing what that is and
keeping it to myself.

It was just about six o'clock and we are still all dressed up so
I ask if she wants to go someplace around for dinner and catch the
movie over at Radio City. But she can't. She has an appointment uptown. Between a couple of kisses, I slipped in the idea that she
should come to Brooklyn tomorrow for Sunday dinner and she
agrees to that just as she scampers away. She scampers very nicely
in high heels. Sometimes you wonder why women wear them but not
when you see something like that.

I spotted a phone booth there on the corner of 57th and called
into the paper, but according to Stenis I had no assignments, and The
Boss is already gone, and with no 'bulldog' to worry over and most
of the Sunday edition locked up early, he's not likely to be back. I'm
free!

For a minute I thought I was at loose ends. I'm just standing
there looking down the open street and across the East River at Welfare Island. It's a dismal place that looms out of the gray flow like a
ship in a low fog with the Queensboro Bridge passing over top. The
prison there is empty now that they have Riker's finished, but there

are still a couple of hospitals. Renwick is for charity patients and Metropolitan is for the insane. Renwick used to be used for the smallpox cases and looks strangely like a small castle—as if a defense from outside attack would have been necessary. I took some nifty pictures over there for a story a couple of years ago. But there are never many lights and now, in the dusk, the mist has made a ghost ship out of it. I quickly got my camera out and opened and set down firmly atop a fireplug to keep it steady, guessed the aperture and snapped a shot. And just as quick as that, a car that was parked across from me at the opposite corner pulls out, tires squealing, and turns down Sutton. I pivot the camera, guess again, and grab a shot of the tail end of the car.

It was a brand new Ford coupe and my first guess is that whoever was driving was watching me. But from right there, they could have seen Cass and me come out of Miss Em's. More likely, they were watching Miss Em's and not us.

And another thought occurs. Miss Em might not be able to pay for the protection she needs, but she just might be able to get a little of that for free—and if a reporter and a photographer from the *Mirror* were seen entering her place it might even stall some hasty actors. Miss Em is no fool.

And then I got another brilliant idea. The calculation is simple. What's the worst that can happen? I get fired again? I figure Barry George is over at the Algonquin about now cutting into some rare roast beef, and I head over that way for a quick chat.

To my mind, Miss Em is in a pickle. She would not have called Cass if she had an alternative. As long as Luciano was around, Miss Em was okay, and with him gone, she was now at the mercy of whoever had the strong hand. But on the other side of it, Cass would not be happy with the idea of simply helping Miss Em to conduct business.

I have about fourteen blocks to get my excuses in order.

My idea is that the paper could do a series on the Mob re-organization in progress now that Luciano is off the street. This piece could even speculate on who the new bosses would be. And it could name Mr. Neims as a key suspect. Miss Em could be referred to a little more carefully, without giving away her identity, but making it clear to those who know about such things. This just might get Neims in hot water with the other Luciano henchmen who were supposedly still in control. It didn't matter if he had their backing in making a move. The publicity was not the right kind. And Luciano might not like the idea of Miss Em getting squeezed. With a little effort we could probably have the first piece ready for the Monday edition. Sex sells. We could even spread the coverage over the whole week. With the Annie Oakley business on hold, Cass could knock out the whole series herself. She had the background detail in her head. She hadn't really done a series like that for the *Mirror* yet.

Of course I hadn't asked Cass about any of this, but I thought she might come around, just for the chance to shoot a few arrows at the prostitution rackets.

But like a face card in a marked deck, the first person I see in the dining room at the Algonquin is the writer who'd been there at Miss Em's on that cold wet day some years ago. He's by himself and has half-glasses on to read his menu and tilts his head to look over the frames, right at me standing by the door.

The Boss is not there. The Maître d' says he hasn't come in and I turn to go but I hear a voice. It's a voice you'd know if you listen to the radio. And it was booming.

He says "Young man. Young man!"

The writer is waving me over. The whole dining room has turned to look.

"Can you stay a moment? I'd love to chat."

I was at loose ends, remember, and I was dressed for the part. He was just ordering his dinner, and asks if I can join him. "It's on me, of course," he says. There was no refusing to do.

Right off he tells me that the fish is on special that night. Fish is always on special Saturdays, wherever you go. It's what wasn't sold to the Catholics on Friday, but I've already eaten pretty well that day, so I oblige him.

He's a large man, just less than fat. Neat mustache. Balding.

The suit looked like something made in England.

Perhaps it was because I thought I already knew more than I wanted to from hearing him on the radio, or because other matters were on my mind, but I couldn't think of much to ask him. Maybe I'm just not cut out to be a reporter. Thankfully, he appeared to want to know more about me, and what I was doing. He tells me he liked the pictures I'd taken at Miss Em's. He refers to her as "Our mutual friend." On an impulse I picked that thread up.

I said, "I think our mutual friend is in trouble."

He dropped his fork. That's a movie prank, but I suppose he was surprised at the direction I had taken.

He says, "Goodness, you'd think they knew enough by now to leave her alone. But then I suppose every new politician has to mark his territory, like every dog must tag his tree. Who is it, La-Guardia, this time?"

"No. One of Luciano's old crowd."

"But he's in prison, I hear."

"They aren't."

"Ho! I see."

I offered a little explanation, not sure of where I was headed. I tell him, "I was just over there this afternoon, and she was talking to us about it."

An eyebrow arched high into a forehead crowded with a sort of reverse frown.

"Has the 'Virgin Boy' progressed to being a rake?"

It looked as if my reputation had extended far beyond Bo Bo's in Chinatown.

"Not exactly. I was there with my fiancé. She's a reporter."

The forehead dropped just as suddenly to a real frown.

"Miss Em is speaking to reporters now?"

"I don't think so. Not regularly. But about this she did. She needs help."

I had a beer with my fish, a thick slab of cod, which evidently wasn't the right choice of beverage given another frown I got. But my host was full of many frowns at that point. He was drinking a white wine and started smoking in the middle of the meal, something that would never have been allowed at my mom's table, so in matters of etiquette we were about even I'd guess. The situation at Miss Em's had clearly changed his mood. He apologized for not knowing about this problem before. He has been in Hollywood a great deal lately and lost touch with the old haunts. He pined a moment for past days, by which I think he meant Prohibition. To his way of thinking, things were simpler then.

He sighs and slumps into a cloud of cigarette smoke.

"Everything has changed," he says, "All of a sudden. Overnight." I hear theatrical pity. "In the blink of a false eyelash. Now the thing everyone is talking about, even on the West Coast, is drugs. Hollywood is loaded with the stuff!" And then adds the afterthought, "And the gin too."

I keep my trap shut. Finally he sits back and announces his own appraisal of the situation.

"As much as it pains me to consider it, I think it may be about time Miss Em retired. Like a few of us that are left, she's a relic of the old school. But she must have enough socked away to spend the rest of her days on the coast—the Mediterranean, I mean. Maybe entertaining a local fisherman now and again just for the sport of it. I know of just the place for her, near Antibes."

Without knowing half as much, or anything at all about France, I had something of the same thought.

In the morning I found out that I had been saved from any worse transgressions at the Algonquin by mere circumstance. Barry George had gone all the way out to Long Island and had dinner at home for a change. His wife had demanded it. But I had told Cass about my idea first, on the phone that night. I managed to phrase it in the best possible terms. And then I got myself in hot water anyway, when I told her about eating cod and not getting a single word of copy.

37. Sunday, May 30, 1937

I've gotten a good sense of Cassandra Green now, after only a few months, which is uncanny. I know what she's thinking. Well, sometimes. Maybe not uncanny, but still surprising to me because the idea of what she is thinking always comes to me without trying—just out of the blue. If I could only stop my own mouth long enough to look ahead, I could tell easily enough when she was going to be unhappy with me.

We were at my mom's table on Sunday and Mr. White was telling us about tobacco farming because Mom has asked, and none of us know anything about that subject anyway, including Dad, and the whole time I can see the look on Cass's face. She's not eating, but her lips are apart just a little. Her face and eyes are almost vacant. Almost. But not quite. And those brown eyes are wide open. She has gotten an idea for a story. I suspect Mr. White is the subject.

Mr. White is not comfortable talking about himself, and he has to be encouraged.

Dad asked, "What was the pay for work such as that?"

"Fifty-cents a day, when you work for others. But I worked mostly for my Papa. I got four good meals and a feather bed."

"Four meals?"

"The day is long. Breakfast at dawn. Dinner at dusk. And two in the fields. Just cornbread and buttermilk and fatback fried to a crisp. What my momma would bring out to us."

"You had machinery?"

"Later. Papa fixed up an old model T to haul a sledge, but before that, nothing much."

And when his shorter answers had frustrated our inquisitiveness, Gary was the one who kept it going.

Gary says, "Tell about the snakes!"

Obviously, for him, the week has been filled with family stories.

His father says only, "There are snakes."

"Tell them about the ones that lived under the shed."

Mr. White nods in resignation to his son's enthusiasm for it and says, "Papa kept snakes under the drying sheds and corn crib and let everyone including the mice know it, so they would leave his crop alone."

Mrs. Teasdale was immediately interested. "Wasn't that dangerous?"

"In truth, not too much. Copperheads won't bother you unless you bother them, and they prefer the vermin. The mice will eat the corn crop down to the cob."

Cass suddenly said, "The schools in North Carolina must be very good—but, they're segregated, aren't they?"

This inquiry clearly confused Mr. White and he seemed at a loss to answer. I would bet everyone else at the table knew the drift of her question.

Stacy spoke up for him, "Gareth went to the Harris School in Roanoke. With me. It's a colored school. That's where we met."

Mr. White shot a hard glance at his wife, and then back at Cass.

He said, "Why do you ask?"

Cass was in gear now and after her point. "Because, you're so well spoken! The schools here, for white or colored, don't produce students with the command of the language that you have. Or Stacy for that matter. I thought that same thing before when I spoke to her, but I didn't ask. I'm sorry if it sounds rude, but it is extraordinary."

Stacy says, "That's because of Miss Lucy Addison. Harrison

is her school. She doesn't allow for carelessness of speech. Her students are meant to go to college, even if they can't afford it."

Mr. White adds, "My Aunt May lives in Roanoke. Papa sent me off there each year as soon as the crop was in. The colored schools in North Carolina are truly pitiful. Ours at home was an old counting shack. Mud chinked. Cold. It was set up off the ground on piles of rock that were always coming undone and it sagged at the middle. If you rolled an apple up the center of the floor between the desks it likely came right back and that was a game we played when the teacher wasn't looking. The cracks in the floor let the wind blow unabated and we lost a few of our apples that way. The books were the cast offs from the ones they had used in the white schools in Winston-Salem. After the second grade, my father sent me off to Aunt May in Roanoke each year."

More questions were asked and the answers shortened again.

Mrs. Teasdale inquired, "You say you've been traveling. Where did you go?"

Mr. White answered reluctantly, "Here and there. Where there was work."

Gary said, "Tell them about the tornado!"

His father smiled. This was perhaps the first smile I had seen on the man's face. He said only, "There was a tornado when I was working on a farm in Kansas."

My dad was quiet through most of this. It appeared to me he was doing what he often does and simply listening and keeping his eyes on the face of the speaker. He seems to hear twice as much that way.

Mom said, "Oh, my. I've never seen a tornado. Never once."

Dad turned to her, "You saw the water spout that time on the ship. Same thing but bigger. But we aren't giving Mr. White a chance to eat. Mr. Oliphant! What have you been up to this week?"

Mr. Oliphant swallowed a mouthful in surprise.

"The same as always. Nothing ever happens at the bank."

Dad pursued him with a cheery voice. "Any robberies?"

"No. No. Not in ages."

"A fraud, maybe? Any of the tellers get themselves arrested for missing funds?"

Mr. Oliphant's voice rose an octave. "Oh, no, no, no. That sort of thing doesn't happen."

I was suddenly worried about Mr. Oliphant.

After dinner Gary wanted his father to watch as I instructed him on developing his pictures. Mr. White stood at the door to the space, almost invisible under the red light. Gary did most of the work himself. It's a simple process and he had it down from the start. He'd read the book, more than once, and his pictures were quite good. He has a sharp eye for the balance of light and dark.

38. Tuesday, June 1, 1937

Barry George has lectured me about the paper not needing another reporter before. They don't need copy from me, he says. They need pictures. But I had suggested again that it might be worth putting me in a few situations where I could write some things up. I had a couple ideas about that, not the least being that I could be helping Cass.

He says, "People will always look at a good picture even if they don't have time to read the story. Reading is too much trouble for most. Generally speaking, that's why people are so stupid, and also why guys like Fritz Kuhn are so effective. They appeal to people's ignorance. They don't want to think, because it might disturb them. Makes them uncomfortable. Makes them aware of their own failings. People won't ever think about anything more than themselves unless things become intolerable. But they will react. They'll see a good picture, and they'll react to that. You take a good picture and I'll put a few key words under it to give the reaction some direction and that'll do more than a thousand words every time. We'll let Cass take care of the German American Bund boys on her own. She can handle them. You can write well enough, Hugh. But she writes better than you do. And she can't take your pictures."

"I'm worried about her running off on these things alone, all the time."

"That's her job."

"How about Annie Oakley?"

"That murderess seems to have something against guys. But whoever she is, you think she'd kill a reporter? Isn't that asking for it?"

"But how about the Mob?"

"There's nobody there who's stupid enough to kill a reporter, I can tell you that."

"Maybe you've never met the ones—."

His voice changes tone and he interrupts, "I have known more gangsters than you've had wet dreams! Don't tell me about gangsters. Look what happened to Dutch Schultz when he got too big for his britches. The Mob doesn't need that kind of publicity. There's plenty of gravy for them to slop up as it is, without any of that. They're pigs, remember, and they know where the slop comes from. And they don't want to work too hard for it. They sure as hell aren't going to kill the farmer."

"How about Jake Lingle?"

"That was Capone. Lingle was in bed with those guys. And that was Chicago."

"How about Joe Rosen."

"He wasn't a reporter. He was just a witness. Look. If Cass can't stick her neck out she can't do her job. Same as you. So drop this load of BS before I tell her you were talking to me about it and she breaks your neck for me. Eat your steak."

He told me this over a small table at the Palm. This is a known ploy. The Palm is one of the favorite eating places for the better-off reporters. Especially the kind who think to call themselves 'journalists.' The food is first class. And it's The Boss's Maginot Line. When he wants to make his point once and for all, he takes the troublesome employee out to lunch and a beer. He makes his case again. If you don't take the hint, he fires you for good. He doesn't want ingrates in the ranks.

Just above my head on the wall is a large cartoon of Ganzi and Bozzi, the two Brooklyn-Italian owners of the Palm. The walls around us are covered with various flights of fancy by the resident Rembrandts from all the papers and the news services located in this part of town that frequent the place. This particular one is drawn by a favorite of mine, Al Capp. In this cartoon our startled restaurateurs are both dressed *Li'l Abner* fashion and staring down at the ground in such a way that makes it seem they are looking right at the table where we're eating, and one is saying, "I think that steak is too rare!" and the other says 'That moo you heard was not the steak. It was the chair. Tell Felix to wax the floors again, but this time he should wait until the customers leave. We don't want these cheapskate newsboys slipping by the cashier.'

I gave George as pitiful a shrug as I could manage for an ingrate with 8 ounces of sirloin still under his nose. I say, "But I can't draw pictures with the camera like Capp does. And I can't say what's on my mind."

He gives me the sneer he usually reserves for the mention of politicians.

"What'da ya think. I got a glass eye? I can see right through you! What's on your mind that's so special? You think you're the only one that's worried about the Nazis? You think you're the only one that wonders about who Mr. Stalin has decided to kill this week? You have concerns about Mr. Roosevelt's bullying the press, do you? Or is it just that you feel ashamed to be here eating a steak while someone somewhere can't get a crust of bread? Heh? The world turns. It's not all about you. What you do is up to yourself. You can cry about all the pain and nobody is going to read a word you write. You can take a picture of some poor wretch on the street with a toe peeking out of his shoe, and they will quickly turn to the sports pages." He gestured up to the picture on the wall. "What makes Mr. Capp here so good is he has a real sense of the human condition and he sees the farce in it. He doesn't whine. He makes you laugh till it hurts." The Boss leans in over his plate so far he's practically on top of mine—like he is going to either share a confidence or scarf a piece of meat off my bone. "If we don't run the sports pages and the funny pages, we won't sell any papers. But the thing of it is, if we just fill up on Al Capp and Lou Gehrig, we couldn't sell any papers either. The Dodgers may have beaten Carl

Hubble and ended an historic winning streak, and that's news to more people today than give a damn about the opening of the Golden Gate Bridge. But who will even know who Carl Hubble is in a dozen years as they drive to work across that bridge? I ask you!"

I jumped to the defense, "But that's really big news! Twenty-four games! Why do you want to run a story about opening the Golden Gate Bridge? That's in California! This is where the Brooklyn Dodges put a stop to Carl Hubble's shenanigans!"

George is not sure whether I'm kidding him or not. I let it play.

He says, "But sports alone is not enough to pay the bills. You might think I could sell twice as many papers if I could put War Admiral on every front page, but I can't. People still want to think they buy the papers for the news, even if what they really want is entertainment. They know there's bad news out there and they need to know about that too, but they don't want a diet of vegetables. They want some steak with that."

The Boss usually gets his way with that plain face of his. It's deceiving. You never know if he has gotten the joke or not. But he might have lost me with the comment about the vegetables if you couldn't see that point made right there on his own plate. His bone was clean and his steak and potato were gone and the green beans were untouched. (As my dad often says, every Irishman knows that the potato is a meat). For Barry George, steak is the equivalent of the sports section and Al Capp is dessert. He'd been happier as the editor for the sports pages at the *American* when he was younger and you had to feel sorry for him now, having to deal with all the grim gray stuff on the front pages, day in day out.

He'd been stuck with those city room chores by the great Walter Howey himself. That was with Hearst's backing and despite the publisher, A.J. Kobler's objections, but done to balance out the more lurid sensibilities of Mr. Gauvreau, the Managing Editor. Gauvreau was an old Bernarr Macfadden man from the *Graphic* and never saw a two-headed chicken he didn't like. But George has done well at it, despite the handicaps. And I was not about to second-guess him. Or the one-eyed Mr. Howey for that matter.

Mr. Howey has become something of a living legend and far too famous for being the proto-type city editor portrayed by Adolphe Menjou in the movie, *Front Page,* a few years back. He's in charge of the Hearst picture service now. And that's good for me, at least. Getting your work sent out to all the papers in the Hearst Empire is a feather for any cap. I don't mind that at all, even when I don't get a line of credit.

39. Thursday to Saturday, June 3 to 5, 1937

On June the third, somewhere in France, the newly designated Duke of Windsor married Mrs. Wallis Simpson. I didn't read the story beyond the headline, so I cannot tell you where in France that was and I was too tired to investigate it further. Hopefully it wasn't Antibes, or Miss Em might find the price of retirement has risen. But this 'news' was in all the papers. Everyday. Before and after. You might have seen it.

It was a long week for both me and the Duke of Windsor. Four school graduation ceremonies. A strike at the new Consolidated Edison. A murder on Fourteenth Street at ten o'clock at night that I just got back from, by the skin of my teeth, in time for the morning edition. Only two fires. And on the same day that the Duke married his Duchess, Josh Gibson hit a ball 580 feet in Yankee stadium. This is prodigious. He plays for the Grays in the Negro Leagues and none of the regular sports photographers were there so Stenis sent me out to take a shot of the spot where it landed. That shot didn't make the cut, but I saved a copy for Gary to see. Right now, what the Dodgers need most is a hitter like that, but they'll never let a negro play in the big leagues.

Most of the big news was from places too far away for me to travel and I was glad for it. I wasn't sleeping well. Cass was up to something and wasn't talking. I worry about her now pretty much all the time. But I can't tell her. She'd blow a gasket, if she had one.

I took her out to dinner on Thursday and she says to me,

"What's eating you?"

I was in the middle of a plate of raviolis so big it could have choked a horse, so I thought this was funny and laughed out loud, but she was serious.

I say, "You're up to something."

She says, "I am," and nods her head once for punctuation.

"And you aren't talking."

She says, "Do I have to tell you everything now. We're aren't married yet."

"You might as well get some practice."

"I'm teaching you patience."

"I've graduated that course."

"Then why are you so surly."

"I'm not surly. I'm worried."

"About what?"

"About that car I told you I saw."

"What about it."

"Stenis says the plates were stolen."

She shrugs it off. "So you were taking a picture of Welfare Island and a guy with stolen license plates thought you were taking a picture of him and panicked. That's all."

"No coincidences. He was watching Miss Em."

"Maybe. But she can take care of herself better than we can. I did my part."

"The piece you wrote was pretty short."

"It needed a picture. If Miss Em doesn't want her picture taken, it's pretty hard to cover."

"But you're working on something else."

"I am. Two or three things."

"What."

"I'll tell you later."

"Sure. So now, I can be surly for good reason."

"There's nothing for you to be surly about."

"Then it's got to be something pretty unimportant, so why not tell me."

"No."

Cass can exhaust me faster than a mile run.

But she's coming to dinner again on Sunday. At least there's that.

On Friday, nothing else is breaking in the morning and near lunchtime all my paperclips have been counted and the pencils sharpened and turned in the same direction. In my haste to get out the door this morning, I'd forgotten to bring something new to read along with me to work. With the coast clear, before noon I headed out to the Scribner bookshop on Fifth Avenue to see what I could find.

This is a fine looking place with tall windows, a wide space inside made larger by high ceilings, and a balcony. Down-stairs, in the last row of the new fiction there is a broad shouldered fellow in an ill-fitted suit and an odd beige cloth hat with a wide brim. He's got his glasses dangled from one hand and his face turned down close into the pages of a book. By the way he was standing close to the shelf, I assume he was hoping not to be noticed. But I know the face right off. This is the author Ernest Hemingway and it surprised me to see him there in the shop because I'd read in the newspapers that he was in Spain, covering the civil war there.

Some of the pictures I'd seen of that war in the newsreels were terrific and sad. But his articles in the papers had seemed a little cold to me, as if he accepted the deaths as a cost of achieving certain goals. This did not seem right because it wasn't him paying the price. He was getting to watch it like one of those bullfights he writes about but hadn't even bought a ticket. He was getting paid to watch, and there is an easy French word for that but it doesn't come to mind. I'd read that he was now the highest paid newspaper cor-respondent around. True or not, he is obviously well fed, and clean shaved and had a good healthy mustache going.

Unhappily, I am at a disadvantage because I haven't read any of his books yet. However, there is no crowd around him so I have to take the opportunity.

I say, "Hello, sir. Sorry to interrupt you. I'm a photographer for the *Mirror*. Is there a chance I could grab a picture?"

He looks at me grumpily and says, "Sure," but then he does not pose and instead continues reading. In his hand I can see that the book is *Northwest Passage.*

I grab the picture and then another for the angle on the book. But I need a caption. The Kenneth Roberts book is my only wedge, so I say, "It's a little slow in parts but it's a great story."

He looks up at me again and says, "What?"

I say, "The Roberts book. It's a great story. A kind of adventure and history rolled in one."

He says, "Maybe. But the man has no style."

"Style isn't everything, is it? Not if you have a good tale to tell."

He smiles but that is not in his eyes. "Are you a critic too, or just a press photographer?"

I wasn't sure exactly what that smile meant.

"No, sir. I've never had a lot of use for critics. I just like things that work."

After a hesitation, he says, "Fair enough."

I thought I'd better get him to say something useful before he's lost patience with me. Smartly, I ask, "Do you have a new book coming out?"

His head goes back a little and he says, "In a few months." But then he stops a second and studies me out of one eye. I wasn't sure why. I kept quiet and held my notebook up where he could see that I'd write down whatever he had to say.

"*To Have or Have Not* is the title of that. It's a novel. But I'm in town now for a picture we've made, *The Spanish Earth.* It's a documentary about the war over there and what it's doing to the people."

And that's where I stepped onto the soft ground. I should have known better. I don't know much more about the politics that's driving that particular piece of misery than I've heard Cass talk about. I was just looking for something to prolong the conversation.

I say, "It looks like the people there lose either way."

He squints at me then and his voice goes flat. "The sides are not the same."

Now, I wasn't going to be able to carry on any sort of conversation with this man about Spain and I didn't want to seem flustered for something more to ask, but I say, "Once they're dead, what side they were on doesn't make much difference, does it?"

He gives me both eyes. "That's moral equivalence."

I could guess what he meant by that.

"I guess I didn't know such facts could be moral. I thought that was all in how people made use of them, or what they did to cause them in the first place."

He nods at me and says, "And that's simplistic. It's gone beyond that now. The choices are made."

I couldn't help myself, "From over here it looks like the politics of the war are what's immoral. The ones who are causing the fighting. The ones making people choose sides who don't have a stake in the thing."

Taking a deep breath, he is clearly unhappy to have been drawn into this, "People always have to choose sides. The rest doesn't matter."

"But killing people for their politics can't be a moral thing."

"All choices are political."

I said, "I don't think the bodies I've seen in the newsreel belonged to people who wanted to die. I'll bet most of the choices they made weren't for political reasons at the start. They were likely made just so they could live."

He shook his head at me, "They were, whether you know about it or not."

I knew I'd stepped in it now, but I was also sure by then that he'd gotten it all wrong.

"What if they're made by someone who's never thought about the politics before? Never even knew about all that. They only knew about carpentry, or running a shop, or maybe even fighting the bulls. Isn't it important to actually find out just what it is that made them choose the way they did, instead of interpreting the whole thing for them? Understanding something isn't likely if you're trying to make it fit your own ideas. Like those farmers you wrote about in one of your articles, most of them didn't give a damn about the politics. They're just trying to survive. It sounded to me like they cared more about a loaf of bread that politics."

He has a wide face and I see a bit of a flush. He says, "That's why things are in the mess they're in. Ignorance. Expediency."

I answer, "Maybe they're a mess because some people are trying to make other people's lives fit their own purposes. People would get along just fine without the politics."

He sighs at that and he tells me, "I knew a woman in Spain that thought like that. She's dead."

I said, "I don't know, but it's more likely that politics killed her than that she killed herself."

Suddenly he looks very impatient with me and closes the book that had been hanging open in his hand and slips his glasses on but then he has a new thought and says, "Have you ever known anyone who killed himself?"

I said, "Yes, but it wasn't politics that caused that. It was confusion, and bad choices, and desperation, and forgetting what matters."

Mr. Hemingway says, "And what's that. What is it that matters?"

"I'd say being true to the people you care about is one thing. Looking after them first and after yourself second for another."

He squints at me again and raises his chin, "So this person you know who killed himself wasn't true to someone else?"

I answer, "He was confused. He thought it was the money that mattered."

Hemingway doesn't answer right away. First he sets the Kenneth Roberts book back on the shelf. Then he says, "My guess is we aren't so far apart on that point."

Hemingway didn't put his hand out so I didn't shake it. He just half waved a salute at me and went on back to an elevator at the rear of the place.

I went directly back to the paper to get the photo developed.

The fourth floor has fewer desks and responsibilities are less obviously defined amongst the columnists there and you can wander around a bit if you don't know where you're going. It is not considered good form to ask who is who. Everybody is somebody. Unluckily for me, Dan Parker wasn't at his desk to give directions. But I know the usual guy for book reviews is named Stanley and I finally track him down flirting with one of the fashion writers.

I abbreviated the tale of my meeting by ninety percent and hand him the better of the two shots and say, "I thought you might like this."

Stanley looks at me skeptically and then at the photo and says, "I hear he's made some sort of a movie about the fighting in Spain."

I say, "Then you probably know he has a new novel coming out too."

Stanley takes that blank-faced. It's what we call 'The *Mirror* look.' Half the guys in the building don't know what they're there for unless you give them instructions. I write down the particulars that Mr. Hemingway told me, and let it go at that.

I took Cass to Radio City on Saturday to see a Stanwyck movie and it depressed us both. It was stupid. The cartoon made more sense. I thought it was going to be a romance. Cass thinks Robert Taylor is a dish—if a guy can be a dish. The title had me thinking there would be a little adventure too, and with Stanwyck and Taylor making the news every week with their shenanigans, I thought that was what was needed. Instead, we get a movie about President McKinley trying to catch a gang of bank robbers—not even Teddy Roosevelt. McKinley! And he sends in a secret agent to foil these evildoers. But he hasn't told anyone about it. No? A secret agent to foil bank robbers! And that's Mr. Taylor. And Stanwyck is the sister of the chief bad guy, and she's singing in his nightclub, but she's still a good girl. Right? And Taylor ends up in a prison cell with the only guy who can save him. Happens everyday . . . There are a lot of good cops out there doing their jobs and I know that they are not as stupid as this guy, and 'good' girls don't sing in sleazy casinos. But meanwhile we read every week about the depredations of the Brady Gang shooting cops dead out in Ohio, Police in Puerto Rico shooting protesters in the back, and the Chicago Police gunning strikers at Republic Steel. There is a lot going on. Why can't they make movies about the real stuff?

I told her then about meeting Mr. Hemingway. I told her that he had made a movie about the war in Spain. And I told her about the argument I had with him.

Cass had her mouth open through this entire rendition. As if it were something important instead of just me putting my foot where it doesn't belong. But when I was finished, she only has one question.

"Was Gellhorn with him?"

I only vaguely knew the name.

"I think he was alone."

"That's the wag. He sleeping with Martha Gellhorn now. They were in Spain together, and his wife is down in Florida or something."

"What does that matter?"

Cass looks at me with disbelief.

"Gellhorn! She's the best female reporter out there now!"

"Except for one."

Cass is an easy mark.

40. Sunday, June 6, 1937

You could tell Cass had something up her sleeve on Sunday, but she came. Then again, I had something up mine as well. June 6th was her birthday. I knew this because she'd let it slip once before, but I hadn't let on as the day approached, except to tell Mom so she could make her trademark orange and coconut cake.

I went over to Cass's apartment to pick her up on the way to Brooklyn. But she wasn't ready yet so I sat in the dinette and talked to her roommate, Ellen. Ellen Bennett is what you call a 'healthy' girl. Actually good-looking in her way, but not a girl you want to cross. She has obviously tossed a few bales of hay in her time. Though I'd already met her in passing, we had not really spoken, and she took this opportunity to give me the third degree.

First off she starts to whisper to me that it's Cass's birthday, and I have to stop her with some gestures and a wink, and she puts her hand over her mouth and says "mum's the word," but just a little too loud. Then she starts her interrogations. "Cass says you have two brothers and two sisters. Same as me. But I'm the oldest. How about you?"

"In the middle."

"You get a better grab at the food on the table from the middle."

"Mom wasn't strong on grabbing."

She straightens right back. "I didn't mean it that way."

She has very rosy cheeks and when the smile suddenly goes

away, they are immediately splotchy. It makes her look very hurt.

I say, "I'm sorry. It's just that we always served ourselves at a buffet. The food wasn't laid out on the table."

She smiles again.

"That's smart! Why didn't my mom think of that! Cass says you live in a rooming house."

"Not exactly. We have boarders. The place used to be a rooming house."

"You think you'll live there after you're married?"

"No."

"Cass wants to keep working. Maybe your mother could babysit."

What do women talk about amongst themselves?

"We'll get to that, sometime, maybe. We'll have to work something else out, because my mom works too."

"If you lived with your parents, you could probably save more money. You could buy a house sooner."

I suppose the facts of life are just everyday fodder to her, and Ellen is addressing this stuff like it's all the obvious, but I hadn't thought much about it. Suddenly I was worried even more. Frankly, I'd only just looked about as far into the future as the honeymoon.

Cass has heard this conversation, of course, but she didn't say a word about it on the way over to Brooklyn. She has something else on her mind.

"I spoke to The Boss about something and he's given me the okay."

I'm already standing so I'm ready for anything. "About what?"

"I want to do a story about Lucy Addison and the Harris School in Roanoke. The schools here in New York need some better examples. They're not educating the kids very well. Imagine if they could turn out students like Stacy and Mr. White without spending a lot more money?"

As much as it seemed like a terrific story, I was immediately worried. "Have you spoken to either of them about this?"

She heard my doubts. "You don't think it's a good idea?"

"It's a great idea. But if they don't like it, you're going to have a problem."

"Why wouldn't they like it?"

"Mr. White seems to be a very private sort of fellow. He might take this as some kind of intrusion."

"I'll have to convince him, then."

She started in on the convincing almost immediately after we were all at the table.

She says, "I was very impressed by what you told me about Lucy Addison last week. Teachers like that don't get the credit they deserve. And we need more of them, especially up here."

Mr. White says, "Sure," but you could hear the caution in his voice.

Stacy says, "That's so true."

Cass presses right on, "So I was thinking about taking a train down to Roanoke to see the Harris School. Get some details and interview the teachers there and some of the students. Maybe do a story on what makes it work."

Stacy and Mr. White look at each other. There was more surprise on Stacy's face and she says, "Why, that would be wonderful. But you understand Miss Addison's retired now. She's living with relatives in Washington D.C. I suppose you could see her there if you wanted. I know that some of her students go to visit all the time."

Mr. White's face grew darker, if that was possible.

Mom was quite impressed by the idea, but I could see my dad's eyes studying the look on Mr. White's face. And once Stacy realized her husband's response, she grew quiet again as well.

Cass said, "You aren't so happy with the idea, Mr. White?"

He looked over at Gary before he spoke.

"No. It's a good idea. It would be good if you can do that. The schools here are not what they should be."

Nothing more. Certainly no enthusiasm.

After dinner, Mom asked everyone to stay seated for a moment. She had Gary come into the kitchen with her and together they lit the candles and he then held the swinging door as she carried the cake out.

Cass was completely surprised. Her jaw was dropped for half a minute. But as soon as the cake was on the table and before she blew them out, she reached out and grabbed one of the lit candles and made it disappear.

She said, "I'm going to stay 27 for this year."

That got a good laugh.

41. Monday, June 7 to Wednesday June 9, 1937

A quiet week so far. Nothing much happening in our baili-wick. Miss Jean Harlow is dead. And I am sorry for the woman's family and Mr. Powell, and all concerned, but by my count more than several other women died recently and you can't find much in the papers about any of them. To the world at large, their lives and works are anonymous, while Jean Harlow's face occupies the space above the fold on every paper in New York. To me, if they are going to play that tune, they'll have to admit that this is only because Miss Harlow was born with the body of a high-class hooker. Nice to look at but a difficult thing to excuse on the front page of *The New York Times*, even if it fits well into the scheme of things at the *Mirror*. She had a way that made her appear nude to the male eye even when she was somewhat dressed. But what did she do that wasn't make-believe? She couldn't act. Not like a Bette Davis. Not like Stanwyck. And she couldn't sing. Not like Alice Faye or Ruby Keeler. She couldn't dance, like Ginger Rogers or Eleanor Powell. She just looked swell in satin.

Of course, Sunday is more important to me now because it was Cass's birthday, and because of the astonishing fact I found out that she's 28 years old. Her age had never actually occurred to me. I've been well taught never to be that specific about a woman's age, but it's a total surprise that Cass is almost three years older than me. I would have bet she was younger. And there is something even more mysterious about that. I have no idea how mom discovered this.

Mom won't tell me, either.

I guess the important matter to me now is that I have a few more reservations about working at the *Mirror*—or any newspaper for that matter. I'm already 25! My father had been around the world a dozen times by the time he was 25. And after all, like Cass has said, our work there is just a game. And to think, Cass is 28! No wonder she worries about wasting her time.

I was just thinking, newspapers are all alike at the center. Some newspapers are filled with more facts but there seems to be little truth to be had in any of them. Jean Harlow is dead, but what did she do? A press agent supplied the details, for all they're worth. The pictures are all set-ups. All pose and no fact. All the papers cut their corners and make their deals. 'If it bleeds, it leads,' as one pundit noted. Probably a Hearst man. Yet even that's only part of a truth. Some blood appears more valuable than others. And it looks to me like we learn nothing from the sensational stuff at all. It's just a distraction from our own lives. A circus, as The Boss calls it. Worse, we're thrilled by it in just about the same way we're thrilled by the dimpled silver of satin as it stretches tight over the bosom of Miss Harlow on a screen that makes it appear to be fifty times larger than the reality. Though I admit her bosom never killed anybody, even if it might have knocked a few eyes out. But the news that's not reported each day kills millions. Or certainly will, as time goes by.

When I was a kid we used to get the *National Geographic* magazine. Dad was rather critical of the articles, but he thought it was at least a cheap introduction to the world he'd known firsthand and he renewed the subscription every Christmas because we all liked it. For my part I was quickly attracted by the fine photographs to be found there of naked native bosoms. That was even before I succumbed to the rougher charms of Roy Chapman Andrews. And after gorging on one issue or another, I used to challenge my dad at the dinner table based on the things I'd read. He'd actually been to many of the places in the articles, so this was tough—at least when it came to any of the ones that was touched by an ocean. And he often had an anecdote to sum up his experiences in this port or that. (Though he was reluctant to discuss any lack of clothing he found within earshot of my mom or sisters.)

But then I stumbled on the first article written by that madman Mr. Andrews and his expeditions into deepest China in search of dinosaur eggs. Andrews had encountered bandits in the desert there just the same as my dad had encountered pirates on the ocean. Those accounts really stumped Dad. He had no knowledge of Mongolia. And then, even crazier than that, there was the great Swiss fellow, Aime Tschiffely, and what he wrote about his ride from Buenos Aires to Washington D.C. along with two Argentine ponies as his only comrades. Dad could not imagine the feat and would not challenge the veracity of the account. Nor did he add any color to those exotic places. Tschiffely had simply wandered too far from the water's edge.

I should note that when Tschiffely's book of those adventures finally came out, I did read that longer account and then kept the volume around my apartment for some time. Cass might have seen it there when she was cleaning things up for me that night, and not thought of me as a total illiterate, if only I hadn't loaned it out to Boris Lensky in the pressroom at the *Mirror*. He never returned it.

My one reservation about Tschiffely was that he didn't have much of a camera with him. I would have taken 10,000 pictures on a journey like that—at least one for every mile. But the thing of it is, I want to write about doing things like that myself someday. And better than that, I'd like to take pictures of all those places. And someday I will.

Sadly though, I can't see this happening too soon. The chances for me to travel very much of the same world that Martin and Ossa Johnson, or Aime Tschiffely saw, right now, seem pretty remote. Likely, I should have set out first thing after high school, like Dad had done in his time. So what if I didn't have a dime? I could have walked and lived off the land. Just me and my trusty

Kodak. And I could have pretended there were not a hundred other young fellows just like me out there looking for jobs along the way.

Probably not.

Another thought: a few weeks ago I was in a dentist's office awaiting my turn and I picked up a copy of *Time* magazine. That publication is often a difficult slog for the way they pretend to be 'objective' about one matter or another while they're using words that are cocked and loaded. In describing a recent Saturday assembly of the German legislature, they had this: "Looking like a parliament of soldiers, the uniformed Reichstag waited 30 minutes for its Messiah to arrive in flaring black military breeches, well-shined boots, and unadorned brown shirts. Up jumped the Reichstag to salute and 'Heil Hitler.'"

That is a very effective picture in words. I wrote it down in my notebook because it was. The problem is, as we all know, the British and the French will do nothing to stop this clown and he won't be outdone by the Soviets who are killing their own people in advance of any conflict just to keep them in line. And on the other side of the world, the Japanese are invading China. They've already grabbed all the coal in Manchuria and busy themselves now enslaving the people they need in order to mine that fuel for their engines of conquest. War is coming. Everyone talks about it and I can see no other possibility. No one will stop it until it gets to us.

But while China falls, we do have proper coverage of the Bronx borough school committee hearings, even if the parent I photographed there testifying this week could not find Manchuria on a map if he was asked to. He'd attended those same public schools in his own turn and he wants to make sure they do as fine a job for his children. Really? Cass was kind enough in her story not to point out that he was pretty ignorant and his children would be no better off if things weren't improved.

Still, in that very same issue of *Time* that I read at the dentist's office there was a letter that ran counter to my own complaints. It was written by a 'Willie Weaver' from Curityba,

Brazil. Mr. Weaver was taking issue with a previous letter to the magazine's editor. That one had complained about the dire state of things, and the world in general, and the ominous doings reported in those pages. These things had caused the author to wish he could take refuge in a monastery. In response, Mr. Weaver criticized the cowardice of the previous letter writer, not by saying as much, but by showing him. And he did this by describing his own recent experience during a difficult jungle journey.

During that adventure, Mr. Weaver had attempted to save the life of a local woodcutter who had, to his amazement, been happily living alone in the forest he loved. Weaver wrote:

> It's too bad entirely if there are any monasteries left. I stood one Sunday afternoon at the head of a gigantic waterfall on the Rio Parana, looking down on the gorgeous rainbow the sun had painted on the gauzy curtain of spray which seemed to serve as a fairy robe to the river, veiling its lower reaches in a thunderous mystery. On the very edge of the rocky gorge, a tiny hummingbird, that most marvelous jewel of nature, hovered about a gorgeous spray of boton d'oro—a glittering emerald set in a golden crown. And seeing, I said, 'What monk can say what God hath wrought? What dull cap and gown can bring a smile to the lips of a dying man who has seen God's creatures in all their splendid livery, marshaled in the battle of life under the starry ensign of heaven?

Such an anthem should be enough to set anyone out on their own adventure. I cannot use the excuse of a mere Stalin, or Hitler, or Hirohito to keep me from posting such letters on my own adventures. Sooner than later I have to get to it!

But now I have a new concern. Or maybe it's Cass who ought to be concerned about me.

And another thing. The inky news that's soiling these great

sheets of paper that roll through our presses is no more true to the facts than the gossamer fabric worn by Miss Harlow. But what did the woman think, and why? What did she actually do? And why is that make-believe so important while war approaches, along with the misery and destruction and death that will follow.

And I wonder what will Cass want her role to be in all that?

So, nothing has happened in the last few days. A few more deaths. A few more births. Is that news? The shoe store where I buy my Florsheims went out of business. Even the guy next door doesn't know what happened. So no news there. But you really know that nothing important has happened because Jean Harlow is still front page.

42. Friday, June 11, 1937

What has happened now is very confusing.

Cass has been covering the school board hearings on a regular basis. I understand that she has some of her own ideas about
these matters, and some strong concerns. But her sudden interest in
the Harris School in Roanoke took me by surprise.

On Monday morning she was long gone on her way before I
got to work. And she had left a note for me. Oh, very sweet. But it
did not explain a thing. And she hadn't said a thing about it on the
phone the night before. I can guess why.

She did call me every night she was away to say she was
fine, and when I asked what she was doing, she said, "Talking to
people. Just a story on the school and how it works." That was about
it. She spent Monday night and Tuesday in Washington D.C., and
Wednesday and Thursday in Roanoke. She returned by a couple of
night trains. Friday morning she was already at her desk when I
came in so I couldn't even give her a kiss. She looked a little
rumpled. Not her style. And she doesn't have time for lunch. She
doesn't have time for dinner. She is typing like crazy.

Evidently The Boss somehow got an okay from upstairs for
Cass to go beyond the usual geographical perimeters of the City
Desk, but they had okayed it only because she was also required to
interview the two New York Senators on her way through Washington.

She had already called those stories in and the interview with

Senator Copeland had run on Tuesday and Wagner on Wednesday. She'd also spoken to Congressmen Marcantonio and O'Toole. The interviews with the Congressmen ran Thursday and Friday. But while she was in Washington, she had taken the time to speak with Miss Lucy Addison at length. The aging teacher was evidently not in good health. After that, Cass took the train to Roanoke and received a guided tour of the Harris School.

I imagine then that she had a lot to write about. Plus she had follow ups for her interviews with the Senators and Congressmen. I had to be patient again.

My own week was less inspiring. It began when I got a good shot of LaGuardia laying the cornerstone for a new high school in the Bronx, and then one of the commencement speaker at a graduation ceremony up at Columbia University. This guy managed to keep talking for nearly an hour without saying anything. (I hung around to see if he could accomplish this feat or if some of the graduates might form an ad hoc committee to strangle him first. That would be news.)

Tuesday I grabbed a nice photo of a garbage truck that had taken a curb at high speed and spread its contents out in front of the Schubert Theatre, just beneath the marquis advertising *Babes in Arms*. This disastrous dumping had blocked all traffic on 44th and drawn a swarm of seagulls and pigeons that extended all the way down the block to the Great White Way. The rotting milk kept onlookers at bay so the shot was uniquely for the birds. On the same day I got a good one of four impatient kids playing hooky, jumping into the cold waters at Coney Island in advance of summer, and just an hour later I snapped a shot of a bullet hole in a car window, which was all that remained to be seen after a young fellow was murdered up on 125th Street.

On Wednesday morning, bright and early, I got a crisp photo of the husk of a human body that was once a man named Michael Palmer, now dried from the inside-out by too much cheap alcohol. This fellow was lying in an alley off Houston Street. They won't run it. He was not 'somebody' and his tale is as threadbare as the seat of his soiled pants. But Michael Palmer's demise has been duly recorded. On the way back to the office I caught a line of commuters waiting for a replacement bus during rush hour. The scheduled vehicle had broken down and the result was a mob scene that made Park Avenue look like Herald Square during a Gimbels January sale when the new bus arrived. This did it for me. I went upstairs and talked a pass out of Dan Parker and went to the ballgame. The Dodgers lost to the Cubs, 4 to 8.

And on Thursday, four hours standing in the rain on White Street at the back of the Tombs got me a picture of a man who had been wrongfully accused of murder as he was ushered to a waiting car a few hours after it was finally discovered he was innocent. He looked a little worse than I had after my few hours at the Charles Street Jail. I suppose the delay with his release might have been that it took them a little longer to clean him up before he could be presented to the public. George wouldn't run that one either because it made the cops look bad for no good reason. "Everybody makes mistakes," was the caution.

After I finished my own chores today I sat myself down next to Cass's desk about nine o'clock and told her I was going to wait her out so I could walk her home. She let me. But she would not tell me much more about her travels.

43. Sunday, June 13, 1937

Cass is a willful woman.

This, in and of itself, would be enough, but she has been well tutored lately by Barry George and they have conspired against me. Apparently my expressed concerns about Cass putting herself at risk unnecessarily has resulted in the heavy-handed decision to simplify matters and not inform me of her assignments until after the fact. And this has now gotten me into hot water for the perverse reason that I have told Cass she was being unfair, which was evidently sufficient cause for her to get angry at me in turn for being angry with her. Keeping me uninformed was for my own good, you understand. To keep me from worrying. Figure that out.

There was a little yelling.

Most of this conversation took place on the stoop of her apartment building on 19th Street with her roommate Ellen watching attentively from the dark of an open window above. Very uncomfortable. I figured Ellen was about to come down and knock me in the head at any moment.

But the key moment to that was when Cass tried to lay some of the blame off on The Boss because he had advised her not to be telling me so much about what she was doing. She dutifully reported that, "What I didn't know wouldn't hurt me," were his exact words.

Which explains, in another way, why George doesn't go home to Port Washington for dinner unless he is commanded to.

Cass hardly spoke to me on the train as we made our way to

Brooklyn. Still angry at me being angry, I supposed. We were leaving early because I'd promised another stint of camera instruction to Gary and she wanted to speak to Stacy and Mr. White before dinner. She only informed me of her larger plans when we were just a couple of blocks away from my parents' house. This stopped me in my tracks and required another discussion in the open theatre of Sterling Place. In Brooklyn they don't stay back in the shadows to listen when there is free entertainment to be had. They open their windows wide and lean out to get closer to the action.

At least Cass lowered her voice somewhat then to frustrate onlookers. I can only hope the sound of the traffic coming from Flatbush Avenue was loud enough to help cover the difference in mine.

She says, "Look, before we get there you better know that there are some problems."

"What kind of problems?"

I can tell she has rehearsed something in her head to say to me and now she is even having a problem with that, so I add, "Just tell me what's going on and cut the bullshit."

Now, I knew she would be immediately angry with me for using foul language, but I really wanted her to cut to the chase. She could get to the point without a lot of funny business. No more run around.

She clinched that jaw of hers a couple of times before she could speak and then the effort to keep her voice down only served to make her tone that much harder. "Mr. White—Gareth White—is not Mr. White at all. His name is Darrell Anderson. He is an escaped convict."

She stopped there to see what my reaction would be.

I kept it cool. "And you didn't think I should know this until now?"

"I was going to tell you earlier but you got on your high horse about me going off and not telling you anything!"

"You could have told me yesterday."

"I was still checking things out yesterday. And anyway, I

don't think it's anything to worry about."

"Well, if your idea of the way to treat me is like a child who can't be told anything, then maybe all of this is worth the extra price after all."

"What do you mean by that?"

"I mean if you can't be upfront with me now, maybe getting married is the wrong idea."

Anger took over again. I'm not sure I spoke as precisely as that.

This stopped her. Her face lost any expression. For at least a minute I think she didn't know what to say, so I picked up the tattered end of it.

"What did he do? Did he kill anybody?"

Cass got her voice in an even lower register. "No. He supposedly stole twenty dollars. But it was his own twenty dollars! He went home during August a few years ago to help his father during the tobacco harvest and he was arrested before he even got there for some robbery that occurred locally. And then the man who'd been robbed identified him, even though Mr. White wasn't in the vicinity on the day it happened—he was at work in the Norfolk & Western train yards in Roanoke the day before. But with the testimony of the victim, they wouldn't even check Mr. White's story. The testimony of a white man against a black man. They just threw him in jail."

I couldn't help myself when I said, "Actually, it was white against White."

She didn't give me the flicker of a smile. "And evidently the sheriff there was being a little rougher that week because there'd been a murder in the area as well. And that was just about the time the Supreme Court had reversed the Scottsboro decisions, so tempers were already high. The summer heat just brought out the flavor of the sweat and the blood. They beat Mr. White up pretty badly. And the jail itself was about what you might expect of a place that puts children in a school like the one Mr. White—like the one he described." She took a breath. I had already failed to lighten the situation so I kept quiet. She added, "The thing of it was, he couldn't take that for very long. He escaped from a road gang. He went back to Roanoke and told Stacy to take Gary with her and get out as fast as she could, and then he went on out to Chicago by himself to find work. And that's where he's been for the last three years."

Funny thing was, as she told me this I could hear the bare bones of the story she could write—but probably wouldn't. At least this put a little distance between my worry over the way Cass was acting and what else had to be done.

"So what is it you've been concocting for today?"

Badly said. Her tone turned sharp on me again.

"Nothing! I'm not concocting anything! I just wanted to talk to him about it. And I think you should probably be there."

This was not a good plan. There were already too many cooks in the kitchen.

"And Dad and Mom and Stacy. No. You talk to Mr. White— Mr. Whoever, along with my dad. He'll know what to do. I'll take Gary out with the camera. I'll leave you alone to finish what you've started. I guess it's not really any of my business now anyway."

I turned away from her then and walked on to the house. She yelled my name rather loudly in anger and then followed up behind me.

The thing of this was, I think my own anger over certain matters had been growing more than I knew. Whatever was going on with Mr. White, things were not right between Cass and myself. I'd ignored this for the most part. This whole thing only put a head on it.

Then, to further complicate Cass's scheme, when we arrived, Mr. White was not even there. He had already left town.

I took Gary out with the camera anyway. The kid looked pretty unhappy about the state of affairs, so I thought I might be able to communicate with him a little better away from home. I left Cass to explain matters to my parents.

Talking to Gary, I managed to at least get an understanding of what his parents had told him. In light of what Cass had been up to about not telling me anything, it was interesting that Gary already knew about the whole deal with his father. He even informed me of a few additional things.

He told me, "Gareth White was my uncle. He died before I was born. He died up at the New River coal mine when a tipple collapsed. He was only eighteen. I was named after him. And my dad took his work card and his name so the sheriff wouldn't be able to find him."

Given my own dead uncle, Gary and I had something else in common.

I said, "You've got something to live up to, I think."

He nodded and then shook his head. "What's Miss Green going to do now?"

I told him the fact, "I don't know."

He shook his head, this time slowly, in the way of someone much older who was taking stock of an endless misery. "Daddy has run away again. He doesn't want to go to prison."

I was afraid the boy was too young to understand all that was going on, no matter what he had been told.

"Your daddy didn't run away. He left. He got out. It was a bad deal. Getting out of a bad deal is not running away. You can't face a bad deal and make it better. There is no win to it. Mostly, fighting it can only hurt you more. You should just get out. If I was in his place, I hope I would have had the smarts to do the same. But I know it must have hurt him to leave you and your mother again."

The kid started to cry at the point and we never did take any pictures.

Things were not as dark as I expected, however. When Gary and I got back to the house in time for dinner, there was an obvious change of mood.

At the start of dinner, Dad promptly made the announcement at the table.

"Mr. White has been called away on business, Hugh. Hopefully he'll be back soon," and as quickly, he changed the subject and looked at Gary. "How was the picture taking business? You fellas get anything good over at the park?"

I looked at Cass but she wasn't looking back—probably still angry at me for being angry at her. In any case, Mom was glaring at me as she does when I've done something wrong.

Gary could not seem to speak to answer, so I said, "Not so good. The light was a little hazy. Maybe next week."

On the way home, Cass explained some of what she had discussed with Stacy.

As I expected, Dad had come up with a plan almost immediately. He and Mom had realized something was wrong about Mr. White from the start, but had no way of knowing what his tribulations were until Cass explained it to them in the kitchen that day. Stacy only confirmed what Cass had told them and added some detail. An old friend of the family in Roanoke was the go-between for their letters until just recently. Unfortunately, the friend has died. With no more letters coming, Mr. White had shown up in Brooklyn not knowing what to expect. Stacy was waiting for a letter from him again, even now, so that they could make new arrangements.

My dad had an idea. Why didn't they just stay? What would change? Cass was not going to write anything about this matter. She would be writing about the Harris school and Miss Addison. Who would know about any of the rest of this but them?

Cass had learned most of the story she told us from Lucy Addison while she was in Washington. No one in Roanoke appeared to know what had become of Stacy or Darryl. Or else they weren't talking.

Overall, it was a topsy-turvy day.

44. Monday, June 14, 1937

I went to the New York Public Library again on Monday morning. I was not sure of my purpose with this. I just wanted to read a little bit more of what Cass had written at the *Daily News* before she came to the *Mirror*. I had a couple of thoughts about that but mostly the more I knew about what mattered to her, the easier time I would have trying to figure Cass out and maybe find a way to help her.

I wasn't there ten minutes before I came onto the story again about the girl who had been hit by the car in Brooklyn. I read it a second time:

> On Saturday, April 18th, Olga Ostrovsky was run down and killed on the sidewalk where she played at Ocean Avenue near the corner of Quentin Road. She was 14 years old. The two friends with her were narrowly missed. The chalk lines for the hopscotch fade but her blood remains darkly etched on the cement there.
>
> Onlookers have testified that the car in question, a dark blue late model Chevrolet coupe, had started moving very suddenly from where it was parked nearby. The smell of rubber was in the air. Everyone on the street, including the girls, had turned to watch as it quickly gained speed. Olga Ostrovsky was looking directly at the automobile when it unexpectedly swerved from the street onto the sidewalk, 'as

if on purpose,' onlookers reported, immediately striking the child. Olga must have seen the driver's face at the moment she was hit, just as clearly as he must have seen her.

According to witnesses the driver was a smallish and middle-aged man in a black coat and a brown felt hat. He was clean-shaven and wore dark glasses, even though it was a cloudy day. The car never hesitated or halted, but afterward sped up Ocean Boulevard and turned onto Kings Highway.

The driver of the murder car has not been otherwise identified. The license plate appears to have been one stolen Saturday morning from another automobile in the Fort Green neighborhood.

But there is more to this story. It has been additionally established that on the morning of March 14th of this year, Olga Ostrovsky and her Aunt, Natalia Strenko, went to the precinct police station in Brooklyn and told the on-duty officer there that Olga had just seen a man who fit the exact description of a Soviet Secret Police agent, Gregory Pesko, who had come to her parent's apartment in Leningrad, sometime in December of 1931, and taken them away at gunpoint. Olga was certain of his name and appearance now because he had previously insinuated himself into the family group as a friend.

It was this man, Pesko, who had been lingering that morning at a corner market in the neighborhood of Ocean Avenue. He was described to the precinct Captain as 'smallish and clean-shaven, wearing a black coat and a brown felt hat.'

There have been other and repeated reports of Soviet OGPU and now GUGB operatives in New York, as confirmed during recent House Subcommittee hearings at the Federal Courthouse in Manhattan. In addition, the Federal Bureau of Investigation has issued its own report to substantiate this increasing presence.

Olga's parents were never seen again. Their little girl had come to America as a political refugee via Helsinki, Finland, along with her aunt and uncle in 1933.

It cannot then be incidental that her uncle, Nathan Strenko, a haberdasher, was killed in January of this year. Mr. Strenko was reportedly pushed from a subway platform onto the tracks ahead of an arriving train by an unidentified assailant. However, the testimony of an eyewitness to this incident was discounted in the police report as 'speculation.'

The disturbing pattern of these deaths does not appear to command the attention of the New York Police Department. Despite subcommittee hearings, and FBI reports, Police Captain Morris Philbrick has informed this reporter that there is no ongoing investigation into either death.

The death of Nathan Strenko has been classified as an accident. The death of Olga Ostrovsky now appears to be destined for this same obscurity. Mrs. Strenko has gone to live with friends, but she has supplied and confirmed many of the details of this story and Olga's later complaint at the precinct station house has also been confirmed.

Given that the testimony against the man seen in the market was obtained from a child, and depended upon a memory of incidents that were several years old, it was automatically regarded by the police as vague. Olga's complaint about there being an OGPU agent in New York was not investigated further. The marginal comment in that police report includes the words "an unpleasant and hysterical child."

It is supposed then that the N.Y.P.D. will now be satisfied knowing this hysterical child can no longer be a nuisance.

I was more than a little surprised that the copyeditor at the *News* had let that last line slip through. It sounded unnecessarily provocative. But then, whatever behind the scenes political battles had been waged in the editorial offices of the newspaper at that moment in time, were well beyond my knowing.

Tuesday was a splendid day and with some coaxing I got Cass away from the office and over to Central Park for lunch. We happily ate hotdogs heaped with sauerkraut and then stood around to watch the seals get their meal tossed at them from a bucket and had some sympathy for why they were so diligent at catching the pieces of fish in the air—the gray water looked filthy enough to poison any meal. Then we watched the chimpanzees pick their noses and nibble from their fingers, and the lions eat slabs of beef that were festooned with flies as fast as they was thrown onto the blood stained cement. Our lunches justly spoiled, we went back to the Paper and attended to our own business.

45. Wednesday, June 16, 1937

On my way downtown on Wednesday I stopped by my dad's shop to say hello and I see immediately that my mom has got something to say and she makes me wait until a customer had left so she could lay it out cold.

"You can't make her think like you. You think too much like your father. To him, everything is just the way it is. You think you can deal with it that way too. But you can't. Not when it involves another person. She'll have her own idea of the way things should be."

"Mom, what are you talking about?"

"You're angry with Cass."

"Yes."

"Because she hasn't been talking to you about one thing or another."

"Did she say that?"

"No. I can see it."

"You can see amazing things."

"She is a very independent woman."

"Very."

"You're lucky."

"I thought so. Maybe not."

"Take my word for it."

"She doesn't trust me."

"She trusts you. She's in love with you."

"She doesn't tell me what she's doing."

"You can't know everything. Listen to me. Who are you to know everything? You are a smart boy, but you can't be that smart. Listen to me! Don't look out the window. Look at me. When your father was working on the boats, he wouldn't tell me anything. I said, 'Why did you marry me if you can't tell me anything.' He said, 'Because you'll worry.' I said, 'I worry anyway because you don't tell me. At least I want to know what I'm worrying about. Tell me what you do.' And so he told me. And then the worry was twice as much. Then I wished I didn't know. I wasn't any happier. But at least maybe I understood a little better then."

This was hopeless. "You always say that. I've heard you say that a thousand times. 'I don't want to know.' But then you always ask anyway. You always made me tell you what I was doing when I was a kid."

She waved that off like a poor excuse.

"At least, you're lucky. I couldn't go on the boats with your father. I had to take care of you and your brothers and sisters. At least you know what's going on with Cass. You work in the same business. At least you know something. You should understand."

This flaw in my own thinking was too obvious.

It was time for some tactical maneuvering.

I said, "Why do you always call them boats?"

She shook her head at my misdirection.

"Because your father thinks it's cute. It's a habit now. You can't keep Cass from doing what she thinks she needs to do, but at least you can help her when you can."

I shrugged at my own helplessness. "I'm not sure I can do that. Cass wants to make the world better. It's very brave and very pointless. I've told her that, but we argue about it. I've told her that she should just do her best work and let the world take care of itself. But she doesn't think that's enough. I've told her what Dad always says. 'You start trying to change the world and you'll soon begin telling other people how to live in it. That's a road littered with the bones of the idealists and the ones who wouldn't listen, or simply had their own ideas. Right or wrong, you can't tell the bones apart.'"

Mom nodded at Dad's frequently repeated phrase.

"What did she say to that?"

"She doesn't say anything. She's very righteous. She's full of ideas from college. From the way she describes it, they were all very sure there that they had the answers and they could end all human suffering, or end all wars, if people would only listen. Ohio University sounds to me a lot like the sort of school Fritz Kuhn would have appreciated—just a different set of ideals."

This is exactly the sort of stuff that's on my brain when I'm sitting at my desk a little later and Stenis catches me shooting rubber bands at the flies on a half-eaten sandwich nearby. There were five or six possible assignments on the board and I could have taken any one of those and been out and gone but I was feeling a little down.

The problem for me is this: What's so difficult about right and wrong? It sounded to me like a lot of the philosophy I hear spouted here and there isn't about what's right and wrong. It's about getting people to do what other people want them to do.

And then, out of the blue, just after eight o'clock, Stenis palms a rubber band in mid air and says, "Get your arse in gear and see if you can catch Mr. Welles performing his latest stunt. He's just set out from the Maxine Elliot Theatre with a crowd of actors and a big part of the audience that were waiting there to see his new show, *The Cradle Will Rock*. Seems the Federal Theatre people have closed down the preview performance, locked the doors, and the actors and musicians unions won't cooperate with Welles, or his friend Houseman, about letting them put on the show anyway. They tried to cancel it but Houseman has found a venue uptown at the Venice on 59th. Welles is leading them like Moses up 7th Avenue. The whole 20 blocks. Get me some pictures."

A quick guess and a cab ride had me at 49th Street just ahead of the crowd. Welles has his hat off and a full swing to his arms as he's striding along. His jaw is set with a determinedly serious look, but the glint in his eye tells me he's smiling. He winks at me as he

passes. I got that and then half a dozen more of his followers as they
weaved through the evening crowds on the street. I followed along
for the ride.

A young woman wearing high heels and trying to keep up,
says to me, "What going on?"

I say, "That's what I'm here to find out. What do you know?"

She shrugs a little and says, "I was just down on 42nd on my
way to the subway and there they were. I say, 'Liddy, you gotta find
out what's going on.' So here I am."

There were a lot more like Liddy.

The place was already half full when we got there—likely a
few of them used public transportation. The Venice is a huge barn of
a theatre. And it's pretty much packed by the time things started
happening. I find out later it's over 1700 seats. The stage however is
empty except for a lone piano and a frumpy looking and mustachioed fellow in a suit and tie, sitting on the stool nervously eating
peanuts by the handful and looking out across the lights at the
spectators as he chews at a mile a minute.

About 9 o'clock, Welles heads up on stage, says a few words
I could not make out as the crowd begins to quiet, and when he
scoots off a spotlight catches the fellow at the piano. This turns out
to be Mr. Marc Blitzstein, the guy who wrote the show. He starts in
playing the piano and begins to sing solo. I was over against the wall
in the orchestra by then. Suddenly a thin girl in a green dress stands
up in the audience and starts to sing as well and Mr. Blitzstein shuts
up, but he keeps playing. This turned out to be Olive Stanton, one of
the scheduled performers who's playing the part of Moll, a prostitute, in the show. The audience is wide-eyed with the turn of events
and starts to clap even as Mr. Blitzstein goes right along into the next
piece. Another member of the audience stood then and sang with
Miss Stanton, picking up the words to that number. Several times
Mr. Blitzstein sang numbers by himself but it appeared that most of
the cast was there and thought they were obeying some union rule or
another by remaining off the stage, doing their parts from where they
were, and this gave the whole thing a feeling of spontaneity that was

infectious.

No matter how serious the number, all of the show being about prostitutes, corrupt cops, greedy unions, evil bosses, and the steel industry, some of the audience could not stop smiling with the feeling of being in the midst of it all. I spotted Liddy at the back, half way through, and her mouth was open in awe. At the end, the crowd was in a frenzy and the applause went on and on.

I took pictures at every break, but the shot The Boss ran with on the front page the next day was the first one I took of Mr. Welles winking at me on 7th Avenue.

46. Friday, June 18, 1937

The film star, Warren William, always strikes me like a long nosed dog—like Asta, in the *Thin Man* movies with Myrna Loy. Doesn't matter how tough Mr. William plays it, the nose is the first thing I see and I think of that dog. This is the way the mind works, I suppose. And then I think, if he'd grown up in my neighborhood, that Roman nose would have had a few twists. But it's the sort of nose that makes him a good bad guy, which is what he plays best. He's also been a lawyer named Perry Mason a few times, sticking his nose into things like no lawyer you ever knew. He was Julius Caesar once, and he wore his Roman nose well with that. I just think he should have done something a little sooner there about Cleopatra's asp. And *Don't Bet on Blondes* was very good. But the Warren Williams movie I liked the best was *Satan Met a Lady*. Bette Davis is the Lady and Satan had no chance. But here's the thing. Maybe because Mr. William usually plays it so serious, when the guy smiles, you've got to figure he's okay. The smile really lights things up.

I'm thinking about this because of Cass. She's always way too serious. I make the jokes, for whatever they're worth, but I can hardly get a smile sometimes. Almost never a laugh out-loud. I've been taking her to the movies as often as she'll let me, and except for a couple of sappy romances, and one very stupid melodrama, almost all of them are comedies, and she'll laugh for a minute but not a lot. The best so far, for this, is the one I took her to last night, called *A*

Day at the Races. She did laugh out loud. More than once. She couldn't help herself. And then after that, when I walked her home, hardly a smile again, even with the ice cream.

The Marx Brothers do some very funny stuff. Regrettably, before the feature and the cartoon they had a newsreel with pictures from 'The Battle of Madrid.' With human bodies sprawled in ditches and piled up like cordwood, this was not the right subject for her frame of mind, or mine.

Afterward we went looking for some 'Tutsi Fruitsi' ice cream but had to settle for strawberry and then we managed to get in another argument right out on the street before I could get her home.

My point was only that the Marxists and Fascists were flip sides of the same coin. They were both more than willing to kill anyone who got in their way. Madrid is falling to the fascists because they had the better guns—German guns that come direct from Adolf Hitler. Joe Stalin wants to get by on the cheap and won't even supply his Republican side with all the bullets they need to kill everyone who disagrees with them. And they were both killing the students and the professors first in order to cut down on any more arguments. In the newsreel, the bodies were actually piled up. A sad sight. No need for more idealists than they already have.

Cass insists that her ideals are better than that. She was actually offended and upset with me for believing she'd force anyone to do something they didn't want. I said I knew it but when she gets the sort of government she's looking for, with the laws to take care of all the world's problems, she won't be the one who'll be holding the key or the gun. I say, what difference does it make, anyway. Neither of those political philosophies have anything to do with the real world. They're just fabrications. Phony baloney.

She insists her ideas for perfecting the world are rational. Historical. I insist that the world is naturally imperfect and any attempt to make it ideal is an unnatural act. That's history.

And that was the sum of the argument. At least as I saw it.

She says, "What about corrupt politicians and crooked police? How do things get better if we don't stop them?"

I say, "We should try to stop them the best we can by telling everyone who'll listen or bother to read about it. But we can't keep them from being corrupt, any more than we can keep people from being stupid. All we can do is shine a little light on it and step on the ones that don't run for cover fast enough. But the way I see it, the real problem is that a lot of them are corrupt and crooked because we set it up to be just that way. We give them the power over our lives to do it. They're no better than the rest of us. It's a problem of our own making. We make the rules they break. Most of the time the cops and the judges get to be corrupt just from trying to do the impossible—trying to keep people from drinking or gambling or having sex. It's like the stupid Marihuana Tax Act they just passed. Who's going to pay the tax if having the stuff is illegal to begin with? I hear the price of ganja has already doubled again. The gangsters will make a fortune out of that, just like they did from Prohibition. Trying to keep other people from doing what they want is the real problem. There was always ganja around when I was a kid. Who needed it? It was for losers. Now every kid on the block who wants to show off how tough he is will be spending his pocket money to burn a common weed. How are the cops going to stop that? And that leaves the cops with no time for the real stuff. The murders. The robberies. The bunko. It's not like the guy says on the radio. Crime does pay. And most of them will never get caught. The cops can't cover even a small part of that if they're running around peeping in bedroom windows and sniffing the smoke at doors. And the frustration from trying to enforce all of the laws leaves them with very little patience for the pleading of an 'hysterical child' who thinks she's seen the boogeyman. But it is the boogeyman they should be after, and not the numbers runner or the prostitute."

That was my speech. No laughing matter there. And not a smile from Cass. I barely got a goodnight kiss. And all the way home then, I'm thinking about Warren William and how I could ever get Cass to smile again if I'm talking about stuff like that all the time. I've got to figure a way to light things up.

47. Sunday, June 20, 1937

Stacy hasn't heard from Mr. White. She's worried, but she's a very quiet person and only gets quieter when things go wrong.

I got Gary out to the Zoo for a couple of hours to show him how to get an easy focus on a subject that's likely to move. This went well. It took his mind off other matters.

I know that Cass evidently had one of those long 'woman to woman' discussions with Mom, because Dad fled the premises and barely got back in time for dinner. My suspicions are, given that my mom's primary topics of conversation are the foibles of her husband and her children, Cass now knows as much about me as I know about myself. It couldn't have taken more than an hour to cover the topic in full.

The big news at the dinner table was that Mr. Clurman has got a job lined up in the engine house at the Long Island Railroad. He said it was mostly cleanup to start, but the fellow who has the job now is moving on up to a position as a mechanics assistant and if Mr. White comes back soon the open job might be his. Mr. Clurman has already put the word in for him.

Stacy nodded at the idea, but had nothing to say. I think she wanted to be happy about it but how could she under the circumstances? I suspect Dad has been leaning pretty heavily of Mr. Clurman.

On the way home, I tried to get Cass to tell me about her own faults because I don't have such easy access to her mother's store of information. I'm just looking for some fun facts. Some cute stuff. I don't figure she'll tell me anything really horrible, like she used to play the ukulele or anything quite as bad as that. Besides, I only played the ukulele for one summer before my brother Eric accidently sat on it.

Cass says right out, "But you already know I have no faults. You told me I'm perfect."

I say, "I know that, but because I'm not so perfect myself, I still can't be sure. I think I need some solid evidence. Maybe some hands-on demonstration to prove it to myself."

She isn't giving any ground. "For the time being, you'll just have to take my word for it. I don't lie either."

Ellen hears us on the stoop and comes right down. She is clearly unhappy. She's breathing heavily, and she's sweating.

"Someone was just here, looking for you."

She says this looking directly at me and not at Cass.

I say, "What was his name?"

"Garvas. Robert Garvas. He said your name and he told me to tell you he came here looking for you."

Now this is not difficult stuff to figure. Whoever Robert Garvas was, he really wanted me to know that he knew where Cass lived. This would carry more water than just following me home some night and getting my address at Perry Street.

"What did he look like?"

"Big fella. A little pale. Dark haired. Had a suit on, but his hands looked pretty rough."

I don't know any hoods named Garvas, so I asked to use the phone upstairs and called my buddy Danny Seger. I know Danny's number right off the top of my head because he's still living at home with his parents while he recuperates from getting shot a few weeks ago in the line of duty, and I used to call him there all the time. Danny is an encyclopedia for this kind of stuff, but he never heard of the name. He tells me he'll pass it around at the station house.

Then I call Stenis. I'm supposing it's better not to bother The

Boss now on a Sunday evening. Stenis had never heard the name either but I guess the door is open behind him because he calls into the Boss's office and the next thing I know I'm talking to Barry George.

"Where did you get that name?"

I tell him.

He says, "The only Robert Garvas I know of has been in prison for maybe twelve years. He used to be a strong-arm for Dutch Schultz. Fixed bets at the track. He was away for second degree murder, last I heard."

Now, my easy estimate is that this probably has something to do with Miss Em. So I call my mom. Mom knows the phone number for every customer my dad has. Not in her head, of course. She has an account book she keeps at home so she can work there when she doesn't feel like going into the shop.

But Mom first wants to know why I want that number. I remind her that she always says she doesn't want me to tell her about this sort of thing. But she insists. So I tell her I'm feeling a little lonely. She doesn't think that's very funny. I see Cass standing there while I'm talking and I get the full eye roll. She's learning.

I called Miss Em. I get a young woman who works for her and it takes a minute to get this person to understand that I am not a customer with any specific physical needs. This at least got Cass smiling.

I finally get through to Miss Em and tell her about Garvas.

Right off she says, "He's a nasty fellow. He came here last week. He was with Victor Neims. I told him, 'Gladys isn't gratis anymore.' He wasn't happy with that. He saw I had my gun in my sleeve and went away."

Now, I know exactly the way The Boss would want to handle this so I call him back and give him the latest news. Immediately, he wants to speak with Cass. He wants her to write up a short piece on this as an attempted intimidation of a reporter. He tells her to call it in and give it to Bob Raites, one of the copyeditors, as soon as she can and that he'll tag on some background there at the office. Maybe they even have an old file photo of Mr. Garvas. They'll have the piece up front in the morning edition and see how that suits them.

Now I already know that Cass doesn't have a gun. Not here in New York, so I ask Ellen. Ellen is not shy about it. But all she has at home in New Jersey is a shotgun she has used for shooting ducks. She wants to bring that in. I tell her that's fine, but it's closer quarters in the city. Then again, most of what I know about shotguns is from my dad who used to carry one along with him in the Merchant Marine. He called it one of the 'tools of the trade.'

She says, "That's good. Then I won't be able to miss. You should have seen the way he was lookin' at me. He's a pervert."

I told her Garvas probably was that, but worse, he was a pervert who'd been in prison for a dozen years for killing someone.

48. Tuesday, June 22, 1937

Joe Louis beat Jim Braddock. Knocked him out in the eighth round at Comiskey Park in Chicago. The 'Brown Bomber' is heavyweight champion now.

A lot of photos came into the office from the Hearst photographers and stringers assigned to the bout and the *Mirror* only used a few. Some great stuff. I grabbed off copies of the best of those and put them aside for Gary. I got to hear the contest on the radio and it was a very impressive performance. Standup boxing. All in all, it was a good finish to a long day.

Earlier, Cass had a story to do on a war hero who'd become a recluse. He'd been found dead in his nest of an apartment up on Columbus Avenue. After that, because the weather was perfect and the smell of the apartment had been thick, she decided to walk east on 86th to Central Park and from there across to stretch her legs and get some fresh air in her lungs before putting a little more time into the Schechner investigation. She never noticed that she was being followed.

I got to go with her as far as the apartment of the recluse for some pictures of that. People love stories about hoarders. Especially the pictures. It's a New York thing, I think. I can imagine wives, or husbands all over town the next day holding the page above their heads at the breakfast table and saying that it looks just like their own basement or attic. But I was supposed to be back downtown to cover a Shriner's convention at the Hotel Pennsylvania, so I left Cass there at the door and went over to grab the Broadway local.

This is a funny thing. My dad has always said to listen to the hairs on the back of your neck.

Now, first I'm thinking someone is following me and I keep an eye out. Then I suddenly realize what the situation actually is, just as I get into the subway, and so I am already out the nickel. From there I started running at a good trot. You can't run very well with the bag. I look for a cab and don't see one for a couple blocks and then I see two sitting there on the corner at Columbus again and the drivers are chatting and I'm on my way. I tell the fella to put his foot down but then go slow across the park. Cass doesn't usually dawdle but it's that good a day, she just might. The sun is sharp and I'm looking for a flash of green from her dress amidst the trees and bushes. It's a strain. By my guess she's at least halfway across, just below the reservoir. And we catch up to her a little beyond that, where the road sinks for the overpass. There is a guy closing on her as she goes into the shadows below, maybe ten yards behind. The only bill I have is a five and I drop it over the back of the seat and tell the cabbie to stop right next to him.

The eyes of the guy that's following Cass go saucers when he sees me and then he turns around to run back the way he came. But he didn't have a chance. He starts moving at a lope and I swing my bag out in front of him and hit him from behind at the same time and he goes right down under me. His breath is gone and his face is already bloody from hitting the stones on the wall because the walk is narrow there and he tried to keep himself upright. Still, he tries to throw a punch and kick me in the groin at the same time. That was a real mistake, given the situation. I knocked his head back against the cement and his eyes went blank.

Then I took the wallet out of his pocket. He had his prison release card right up front. Mr. Garvas obviously had to report to someone recently. He also had a gun in his jacket pocket. Not even a holster. This was a short-nosed .22 caliber job.

Suddenly I get a tap on the shoulder. It's the cabbie. A round faced fellow with a ready smile. Even then. He wants to give me my change. I tell him to keep it if he'll go call the cops.

Cass of course was long gone. She had no idea what happened. I got to tell her all about it back at the office later on that day, after I'd made it down to Herald Square and caught the Shriners in full regalia.

But she wasn't happy about it. She got quiet, like she does.

We went out for spaghetti before the real fight between Louis and Braddock.

49. Friday, June 25, 1937

The papers are full of the Veronica Gedeon murders again. Robert George Irwin, the "Mad Sculptor of Beekman Hill" is now in police custody. Reporters for the Hearst papers captured him in Chicago and then gave themselves the exclusive for at least twenty-four hours by keeping him under wraps, but the story was still picked up by everyone, even the *Times*. My heroic action in the apprehension of a murderous thug, who was now on his way back to prison for violating his parole for having a gun, was only a filler on page eight at the bottom. But at least it had a great picture.

I had the second day of the Shriner's Convention. Cass had a piece to cover talking to the guys who paint the metalwork on Brooklyn Bridge. Stenis assigned Billy Dorn for the pictures on the bridge. That was a real waste. I've taken some swell shots along there and I could have done it better.

Friday evening Cass and I went to see the movie *Slim* with Pat O'Brien and Henry Fonda. Now, that is a movie about something worth talking about. The life of a lineman. Electric power! No phony baloney detectives who always forget to look behind the door when they go in a room, or cowboys who shoot bullets like their six-shooters have magazines or have romances with no consequences. Cass liked it too, but not as much as me. She wanted to see the new Cary Grant and Katharine Hepburn picture.

We were having a good discussion about this while I was

walking her home and suddenly I feel the hair on the back of my neck again. Twice in two days is something else. I took her into a break between the buildings there on 19th and checked back behind us but didn't see a thing.

She says, "What's the matter?"

I tell her, "Something's wrong."

She says, "How do you know?"

I say, "The hairs on my neck."

She's giving me the look then, like, 'Not again.' And I'm looking down the street, parked car to parked car, for a shadow, or someone walking, or crossing at an odd angle. Nothing.

She says, "I didn't know you were superstitious."

I tell her, "I'm that, too. But this isn't the same."

This is the back of my brain trying to tell me something. This is the sense of things that don't add up. Or maybe the addition you forgot to do and your brain did it for you without being told.

Cass says, "You're full of this sort of thing, aren't you?"

The thing she meant was what I told her is the one thing I didn't like about the movie we'd just seen—that Slim would never have made a play for Cally, because she was Red's girl and Red was his best friend. Slim should have walked out right when he first saw her, because he knew right then she was trouble.

Cass had said, "He couldn't know that!"

I said, "Sure he could. You saw it! But even if you didn't, he'd know. Like I knew, the minute I laid eyes on you, that you'd be all the trouble I'd ever want."

This puts her back on her heels a little.

She says, "Did the hairs stand up on the back of your neck when you first saw me?"

She doesn't understand this. The hairs on her neck are silky and long and don't stand up. What she gets is goose bumps. I've seen this. I only get those from the cold.

And so I told her, "That's a different kind of trouble. What I'm talking about is what Mr. Van Loon was talking about where the saber-tooth tiger is tracking you down, or he's sitting on a ledge around the next bend in the trail." She'd heard this theory from me repeated at least once or twice before.

Now, this conversation had taken place a little earlier but it was probably what was in her mind right then while I was making a quick study of 19th Street from there in the dark about halfway along the block between Irving Place and Third Avenue. The Elevated is ahead of us. Cass's building is up about thirty yards on this side. A train passes and the sound of it fills the street for just a second. This draws my eye in time to see the glare from a car headlight at the corner as it turns beneath the tracks. The light sweeps through the windows of a dark coupe parked over on the opposite side from Cass's door. Somebody in there moves. The hairs on my neck are all at attention. I take Cass's hand and put it on the back of my neck then and gave her a kiss and told her to stay put. I said that as firmly as I could in a whisper. Then I walked out onto the sidewalk again in the direction of her stoop, trying to keep a side-eye on the open places.

I realized this was a chancy situation. Whoever was in that car now—and I had an idea who it might be—he could be looking to shoot somebody. He was probably angry at me for taking out Mr. Garvas, his gunsel, and at Cass too for talking about him in print. He might even know what I look like. But maybe not. And maybe not well enough in the dark. The couple of trees along the block there shadow the streetlights too well. But if he moved I was pretty sure I'd see it and I thought I could get down quick enough to scoot around behind the parked cars on this side. There is a police call box on the corner, just below the tracks of the El.

I only got about as far as Cass's door. The side window of the car across is open and I don't see a thing before the flash when he fires. He just ain't Annie Oakley. I get down quick enough then and start to scramble toward the corner but there's a fire hydrant and an open space of about thirty feet that looks a little too much like a shooting gallery at a carnival given the distance across to the car where the bad guy is.

Another train passes above on the El. The rattle of it is coming down on me like rain where I was, doubled by the echo from the buildings. And in the middle of that noise there is a boom. This sounded a lot like a wrench on a steel drum. I peek around at the shooter's car from where I'm lying on the cement of the sidewalk and I see nothing. Then another boom. This time the windshield glass pops out across the hood in a thousand pieces. The train has passed and I can tell the boom was from up above me. There I can see the barrel of Ellen's shotgun on the window ledge just as she pulls it in to reload. The car starts up, slams into the car behind it, and then pulls out and screeches up the street. Two minutes later the cops are coming around the corner from Third Avenue, one car after another. Quite a scene.

Neims abandoned his vehicle a couple of blocks away on 23rd Street. There was blood in it, but not much. Maybe just from glass cuts. It was presumed he grabbed the subway from there.

Naturally Cass had not stayed put. She'd run down the break to the alley and gone in the back door of her building. But it was Ellen who'd done the firing.

Robert George Irwin, the 'poor' sculptor, has got himself a high-priced lawyer and he's not saying much, but the papers are talking for him. Someone has gotten ahold of Veronica Gedeon's diary and they're running quotes in both the *Mirror* and the *Journal-American* with different photos from her days as an artist's model. For the second time in a row our little misadventures only make it to the bottom of the page again, but at least this time it's moved up to page four. Because I didn't have my camera with me, and I was preoccupied with police questions at the time, Billy was the one who got credit for the picture of the car with the windshield blown out and the glass all across the seat. Couldn't see the blood but still a good picture.

50. Monday, June 28, 1937

So, here's the problem. The Boss has switched sides on the matter. He has decided to assign me to just about everything Cass does from here on. And Cass is not happy about that at all. Worse than not happy.

Cass wants to be Nellie Bly.

Now, there is someone to make a movie about. I'll tell you that. Bly went around the world in seventy-two days, long before Amelia Earhart or the aeroplane was even invented, just to see if the French author Jules Verne had it right. She beat him by eight days. She got herself institutionalized at the Bellevue insane asylum so that she could report on the disgusting conditions there. And I can remember clearly now when Bly died of pneumonia. I was just a kid at the time but my mom had read the tale of her exploits out loud, right from of the obituary in the old *New York World,* over Sunday dinner. Even my mother was impressed.

Barry George told us about his decision on Saturday. He tried to candy-coat it for Cass. She spit it out. She actually swore. She said out loud she couldn't do her job with me on top of her. Made me think. George said that was probably true, and looks at me quick, eye to eye, but adds, "Especially not if you're dead. But while you're still kicking, I want you to make an honest effort."

Now, I was feeling a little guilty over all this because, if I hadn't kept walking the night before, there would have been no 'Shootout on 19th Street,' as the *Mirror* called it. I should have just gone around to the alley along with Cass and called the cops from her apartment. But I wasn't used to getting shot at, and somehow it had all happened a lot quicker than I thought it would. I could just as easily be dead now myself. But I didn't say any of that. The Boss did, in his own way.

After he tells us both what he wants us to do, and Cass has quieted down, he turns to me and says, "And if you pull another stupid stunt like that I'm going to fire you for good. I don't want to pay for the funeral. The budget's tight." Funerals were on his mind, I guess.

That same day we had the funeral of Councilman Edwards to cover at Woodlawn Cemetery and after that I got Cass to walk with me over to the gravestone for Elizabeth Cochrane Seaman who was the real 'Nellie Bly.' This is a simple granite marker. You wouldn't know that the woman had done so much by the size of the stone.

I told Cass then, "If you want to be Nellie Bly, that's fine by me. I'd just like to go along for the ride. There ought'a be some good pictures in that."

I figured it was as close to an apology as I could come.

And right there, Cass up and says, "What I really need to do is to be taking flying lessons! If I knew how to fly I could have been the second person on that plane going around the world right now with Amelia Earhart, instead of Mr. Fred Noonan. That's the story! And you can see in the papers they all want to give the 'real credit' to Noonan. Drives me nuts."

This was the first I had heard of this. I knew Cass had interviewed Earhart down in New Jersey for the *Daily News* last year, but she'd never talked with me once about flying.

All I could ask was, "So why haven't you done it?"

She hadn't expected me to ask that, I suppose. She was just getting a little frustration off her chest. She looks at me then with real hurt in her eyes. For a moment. I thought I'd done something else to disappoint her. But then we're still standing over Nellie Bly's grave. It wasn't a place to tell a lie. And she finally says, "I'm afraid of heights."

There were tears there but she looked away and used her sleeve. This was clearly more important to her than I understood. She doesn't tear up all that easily.

For my own part, I'd been dreaming about playing the part of my hero Martin Johnson for far too long without doing a damn thing about it. I said, "They say the trick there is not to look down. We can go over to Mineola next week after we cover the World's Fair diggings for The Boss. I know a guy there. He cuts the grass. We can both take flying lessons. I'll bet he'll cut us a deal."

She just shook her head at me for that one.

I walked her home from Third Avenue that night and I stayed around on the street there for a while. There was nothing doing. But I couldn't be hanging around outside of her apartment all night.

I talked to her on the phone when I got home. She assured me Ellen had her shotgun loaded.

And Cass didn't come to Sunday dinner in Brooklyn. She called Mom to apologize. She wasn't feeling well. Maybe she had laundry to do. Mr. White was still not back and there was nothing to be done about that either. I gave Gary an assignment that I thought would keep him busy for at least a couple of weeks and his mind off other things.

Now, here's the other part of the problem. A good-looking woman is used to being stared at. That's the fact of it. They just don't react to things the same way as a guy does. This is basic common sense. At least The Boss knew it. And even though Cass didn't have the intuition to deal with the problem if the guy looking at her was a murderer, she was not about to admit it. She'd tell you instead that she can spot a phony as fast as anyone. Because, that's what she told me. And I told her, I thought that was right enough. But the way she did it was by talking to them. That was her way. She liked to talk to people. It was what made her a good reporter. But the guy she really had to watch out for was not interested in a conversation.

Basically, I wanted to be around her twenty-four hours a day. That was my problem.

51. Wednesday, June 30, 1937

Roosevelt Field is as wide open a space as you'll find anywhere close to New York City. It's like suddenly being in Kansas.

We had a company car because there was no train service
into the construction at the World's Fair site and that made it a cinch
getting over to Mineola afterward. My buddy there is Paul Higgins.
He doesn't fly, himself. He's afraid of heights too. Thing is, he runs
the tractor out there to keep the grass cut. He'll tell you, he cut the
grass before Lindbergh took off for Paris. Lindy couldn't have made
it without him.

Paul tells me the right guy to see is Paddy Ryan. The best of
the best instructors. And our good luck is, Ryan's already down on
the ground for the day. He does all his flying in the mornings. I find
this guy in one of the huts they use for a terminal and offices and
he's already started drinking so he's loose.

I make my appeal to his better nature while Cass is off investigating one thing or another in the next building.

Mr. Ryan is not tall. He does not look like you imagine a
pilot should. Like a Hughes, or a Lindbergh. He's paunchy and balding and I get a peek at that when he takes his cap off and wipes the
sweat from his brow. Drinking booze on a hot afternoon will do that.

Mr. Ryan says, "Everyone wants to fly! Now, with Amelia
making the papers everyday, every other housewife wants to get
away from her husband and tootsie with the clouds. I'm booked solid
right into winter. I can talk to one of the other guys for you. But

that's the deal with all of them. Lessons are 10 bucks an hour. That's per person. You gotta book in advance. We're looking at January right now. After I get back from my vacation in Florida. Winter's the best time to fly, anyway. Trouble is, your buddy Paul has to keep the runways clear, and if we get a lot of snow that can be a bitch. There is a three lesson deposit in advance. No refunds."

I say, "I'll have to think about it."

Just then Cass comes in the office and Ryan takes a long gander at her before she even speaks and he adds, "You might want to sign up now in case we have any cancellations."

Cass is ahead of the whole thing. She introduces herself and says, "The *Mirror* is thinking of doing a series, what with all the interest in the Earhart flight. Something like, 'A woman learns to fly.' That sort of thing. But the paper doesn't want to pay for the full freight. They figure the free publicity ought to be worth something. Do you think any of your friends might be able to help us out at a better price? How about the instructors over at Fitzmaurice Field? The coverage couldn't hurt business—unless, of course, you dropped us in the ocean."

There is a total octave change in Mr. Ryan's voice. To the high side.

"I can do that! I'll just shuffle the schedule around a little. Can you get here on the early side. Say 7 a.m.?"

"What would it cost?"

"Five dollars an hour plus gas."

She says, "I'll talk to my boss and we'll get back to you."

There are some benefits to working for a newspaper.

52. Friday to Saturday, July 2 to 3, 1937

There is a lot to tell about all this, even if it doesn't yet make a lot of sense.

On top of it all, Miss Amelia Earhart is missing. Her plane has disappeared and the papers are regurgitating the same small lot of information over and over again with different ledes. Everything else starts on page four. That, and the Fourth of July, makes it a good time to be out of the city. If you can get away

Thursday and Friday were the usual beats. There was one bloody murder on Thursday in the Bronx, but the *Mirror* bought a shot from Weegee for that because I was already out and about and they couldn't reach me in time. Friday, I was down at the Navy Yard with Cass taking some pictures of the *U.S.S. Brooklyn*, a new battle cruiser almost ready for commission, while she got a personal tour from a very eager Chief Petty Officer. Later there was an accident on the new Triborough Bridge that backed traffic up in Brooklyn, Queens, and the Bronx. It appears they still have some kinks in that particular traffic plan to work out. I got a couple of good shots on it at a distance from the roof of the old State Hospital on Wards Island and then climbed a 50 foot maintenance ladder up one of the piers, which was almost fun except for the pigeon crap, but what I needed was Miss Earhart's Lockheed Electra to get above it all to really capture the chaos. Cass stayed back at the office to write up her naval adventures of the morning and do follow-ups.

On Saturday, Cass got herself an invite out to a place called Camp Siegfried at Yaphank, Long Island, where the German American Bund is training their young Nazis for the summer. The invite was for 10 a.m. And we got the use of a company car again, so we left early.

It was a great day and I worked hard at getting Cass to go with me out to Long Beach for a swim afterwards. I came close on that.

In Yaphank, the sign where the pavement ends just off the county road says 'Camp Siegfried. No Trespassing.' The 'No Trespassing' was larger and bolder than the name of the camp. Ominous enough, but the smell of beach roses blooming everywhere made the air sweet and sour at the same time.

This place looked fairly straightforward. Like your average Long Island summer colony of the kind advertised in the back pages of the broadsheets every week from March to August. But there is a high fence. At the gate in the fence there is a little gatehouse, stripped red and white, candy cane style, like something you'd want to hang on a Christmas tree because it's only big enough for a tin soldier.

Two kids dressed up in matching semi-military costumes of tan and brown, but both wearing dark shorts on very white legs in need of sun, step out and meet us there. I couldn't help wondering what they were doing so close together in that little house before we arrived. They waved us to a stop behind the closed gate. I snapped a picture of that for starters.

Holding up a piece of paper, Cass says to them, "We have an appointment."

The boy has a scowl on, perhaps because I took the picture, or likely because we had interrupted something else. He grabs the letter out of Cass's hand rather abruptly and runs up to a large white house set back in the trees maybe 100 yards along the turn of the same road. Two flags flap lazily at the front of this place in the sunlight. One is the American. The other is an angry red with the thick black scar of a swastika that makes me wish I had color film.

The porch there overlooks a short dock and the water of a lake at the other side. A couple dozen canoes, rowboats and small sailboats nuzzle in a light breeze that dimples the water. But no one is in the water, so I got a shot of that.

While we waited, Cass turned to the girl, "Do you like it here?"

She has brown pigtails and enough of a bust under her shirt to be fourteen, but she does not look happy. When I was a kid, getting away on vacation was the highlight of the year. A week of pure delirium.

She says, "It's okay. I'll be able to go home soon."

I look at Cass and she is already looking at me.

From there the place appears pretty much like any summer camp except there was something that was wrong besides the angry flag. It was 9:30 on a sunny Saturday morning, and it was very quiet.

Cass has her note pad out, "Have you been here long?"

The girls says, "A week."

"What's your name?"

"Elisabeth. With an 's.' Elisabeth Dietrich."

"Where are you from?"

"Garden City."

"Why do you come?"

"My father says it's good for me."

"What does your father do?"

"He works for Doubleday. He works at the press."

She delivers her answer, still without a smile. Maybe a little worried to be talking with strangers.

I said, "Do you sail?"

She says, "It's not permitted."

After a few minutes the boy returns and tells us to wait.

Cass asked his name. He shook his head.

Beyond the house, the road curves toward the far side of the lake beneath a row of older sycamore and pine. From that direction we began to pick up the hum of a cadenced song and the tromp of feet on the gravel road.

Just then a man steps off the porch, adjusting his cap on a balding head and pulling his tie straight, and comes hurrying in our direction.

He started speaking before he reached us. "No pictures! Your invitation was for one! A reporter, not a photographer."

Cass spoke up immediately.

"It doesn't say that! It says 'You are invited.' The *Mirror* is a newspaper with pictures. We don't do stories without pictures."

The fellow halts directly in front of Cass. Maybe a foot away with only the bar of the gate between them. It appeared to be an attempt to intimidate her. He is possibly two inches taller than she is. She stood her ground without a flinch. He seems to be ignoring me.

"No pictures! If you want a story you'll have to leave your cameraman here, with your car."

Just then a column of kids in uniforms matching the two at the guardhouse and marching in unison come into view on the road near the house. I worked the focus and got a shot of that before the fellow's hand came up to block my lens.

His voice rises, "No pictures! For that, your appointment is cancelled!"

Cass argued briefly, but it was obvious this rooster had his roost and wasn't making allowances.

I snapped a shot of the guy with the snarl. Good shot. And another with him standing there in the road with his fists planted on his hips. It was the one with the snarl The Boss used on the story this morning because the Nazi flag at the house was fully visible over his shoulder. That made it to page eight. Wire photos of Earhart and her Lockheed Electra were page one, two and three along with a brief statement from her husband, Mr. Putnam, all of which contained very little new information.

As we drove away from Camp Siegfried, Cass had another idea. She recalled my complaint that I did indeed have one book in my apartment before that time when she had first gone there and tidied up the mess left by the cops. That was the Tschiffely tale I'd loaned to one of our pressmen at the *Mirror*.

In the village, by the fire station, I found a payphone and called Boris Lensky. I ask him if he knows any of the guys at Garden City Press. In fact, he does. A guy named Richard Sullivan. A couple of nickels later I get ahold of Mr. Sullivan. Sullivan says he knows Dietrich. Dietrich lives in Hemp-stead and he gives me an address.

While I'm tracking that down, Cass is talking to someone in the drugstore across the street. She comes back with a couple more pages turned in her notebook. Seems everyone in Yaphank has an opinion about Camp Siegfried but the woman in the drugstore has actually been out there in person.

The Dietrichs live in one of those new low brick townhouses in Hempstead that always have the word 'modern' attached to the description in the papers. The sort of place you'd be hard-pressed to tell apart if you'd had more than three beers on a dark night. But no one is home.

We were sitting out front of the address in the car and making other plans when a woman comes drudging up the sidewalk from the bus stop. In the hot sun, with two paper bags filled with groceries, she looks like she's having a hard time of it so, hoping to start up a conversation because she must live nearby, I jump out and offer to help. Maybe I can get a little extra information on the Dietrichs, anyway. She's reluctant to let me help at first but Cass gives her a smile from the car and the woman hands me one bag and asks me to put it by the door there, just up the walk, so she doesn't have to bend over. This then was Mrs. Dietrich herself. A brunette like her daughter. But more than a little overweight. She's wearing a dark blue cotton dress with small pink print flowers the exact color of her bulging calves below the hem. The blue is streaked to black by her sweat in inappropriate places.

Cass is immediately out of the car and talking. "Hello! My name is Cass Green. I'm from the *Mirror*. We are doing a story on Camp Siegfried and we just happened to speak to your daughter, Elisabeth, there this morning. Nice girl. Do you have a moment?

We'd love to get a parents' perspective."

This interview offered some good small detail to the story that we ran. Mrs. Dietrich is very proud of her daughter. The girl is apparently quite an athlete and the camp supposedly stresses physical discipline. And moral discipline. She says, "It is very hard to keep young people out of harm's way these days. Especially in the summers, when they need to exercise both mind and body."

I could imagine those words in italics on a brochure, but then I was thinking about the two kids in that little candy cane guardhouse. I imagine a fair amount of discipline would have been required under those close circumstances.

Even though we were near to Roosevelt Field, Cass is not ready to commit herself yet to the flying lessons. We were back in town by four and I ask her if she wants to go to the movies again as soon as she gets the story filed. She gives me the look. No. She doesn't. She says I go to the movies too much. I should go home and read a book. I ask her if we can read a book together. She doesn't bother to answer that.

I walked her home at least, and with orders received, I came back to my apartment and read some Kenneth Roberts. *Northwest Passage* is a very long book and I'm only halfway through it. Luckily, given the heat, I fell asleep after a few chapters because, when the phone rang, I was rested.

And this is where the day got complicated.

It's about midnight. Cass is at the 13th Precinct Station. I'm still dressed so I get right out the door and even remember to grab my bag. At least that much of my brain was working. I caught a cab at 14th and I was over there to the Station House pretty quick. She's already finished with the cops and she and Ellen are waiting. We took the same cab back to her apartment. All the while she doesn't want to answer any of my questions and Ellen has been ordered to keep quiet. The cabbie looks grim. Details can be worth a little extra dough to a cabbie if they're sold to another paper and Cass doesn't want the *Daily News* to scoop us on our own story.

A patrol car is still at the corner near the call box beneath the El and the officer there watches us go in. The several holes in the thick glass of the front door are neat and random, like stars. There was still a lot of blood all over the foyer floor. Cass tells me then, on the stairs, that while they were waiting for me at the Station House, she'd already called Stenis at the paper and given him the details. Just in time for the morning edition.

The story is this: after I'd left earlier, Cass and Ellen decided to go out for some Chinese food. A good plan, really. Only I wish I'd been with them. But at least I've had some positive influence on Cass, neck hairs or not. As they left the apartment, Cass is pretty sure they were being watched. The street is busy, but she didn't see anything. "It was just a feeling," she says and turns a lip up at me. Then they hopped on the El at the corner.

After their dinner it seemed like another good idea to go for some drinks. They were not back home until eleven or so, and right away Cass gets that feeling again of being watched, this time at the front door. They go inside and start up the stairs and by then she says it felt like alarms are going off in her head. She's never felt anything like it before. I told her I never had alarms. Just some stiff hairs. Ellen doesn't think any of this is funny. She keeps adding in the details you'd expect from Cass.

Ellen waves away the foolishness and interrupts. "So Cass says, 'We've got to get out of here. Now!' And I don't know what she's talking about. I have to use the toilet. But Cass is ahead of me on the stairs and she turns and starts pushing me back down. I can see her face. She's serious! So I turn too and then there is this guy who's come right through the front door behind us. He has a gun. A little pistol! Pointed right at me! He says, 'Stop. Turn around!' And when I turn around to look at Cass, I see another guy up the stairs on the second floor at the landing, waiting for us. HE HAS A PISTOL TOO! But his is a funny one. It has a long, fat barrel. Never seen one like that. And the guy who's come through the front door is right behind me then on the steps and he sticks his little gun in my back. The next thing was just a reflex. The metal was cold. I twisted back around and punched him in the nose with my fist. He goes back sprawling onto the tiles. His gun goes flying up in the air like a toss. Blood was spurting out everywhere in a flood! I went right over him then and out the door with Cass right behind me. The guy with the funny gun was the one who shot the holes in the glass."

I asked the obvious, "What did that sound like?"

"That sounded funny too. Not like a bang. Like a slap."

Cass says, "It was a silencer. The detective at the station was pretty sure the gun had a silencer. They found the other gun behind the radiator in the foyer. It was a .32."

"What make?"

"A Walther."

My immediate thought had been that it was Mr. Neims again. Trying to finish the job. But my second thought then was that this was all wrong. The mob isn't into things like silencers. Not that I've ever heard about. If they want to eliminate someone, they tend to do it fast and dirty. They usually get rid of the gun afterward, anyway.

But a Walther? That's a German gun. This is a fact too easily interpreted to ignore. Especially because the gun was not left intentionally. The mob would use a Colt, or a Smith & Wesson. At least something that was common and readily available.

It's on my mind right then that now the Bund is unhappy with Cass's attentions. The Nazis have probably been reading the papers too. They're aware that Cass had been attacked by a mobster recently. This is their opportunity to get rid of her and have the blame fall on someone else. And the only visible reason I could think of for that would have to be because Cass was getting too close to something in her investigation of the murder of Sam Schechner. They want to bump her off and put an end to it.

I wanted to ask a couple hundred questions right then, but Cass's eyelids are at half-mast. She's had a long day.

So I slept right there on the couch, in my clothes again. I'm starting to feel like Mr. Weegee. Probably end up smelling like him sooner than later.

53. Sunday to Monday, July 4 to 5, 1937

We had Sunday breakfast together for the first time over at Morgy's. The three of us. Doc is in high spirits with his flag flying out front and very happy to finally meet the source of all my troubles. And he and Ellen get along very well right from the start and begin trading information back and forth about the two of us while we are sitting right there in front of them.

Now, by this time Cass is already coming around to my way of thinking about the Nazis. Something about the two fellows that tried to murder them the night before was unlike any mobster she had ever seen before. The fellow up the stairs had not spoken but the one below with the newly altered nose did not have an accent.

Ellen had an opportunity to tell the story all over again to Doc.

Inappropriately, after that, Doc is feeling a little too familiar under the circumstances and says something he shouldn't have.

"Does this have to do with that Jewish lawyer that killed hisself up on the East Side?

Cass looked a little like she'd been slapped.

"What did Hugh tell you about that?"

I tried to defend myself. "Nothing! Just this and that. Doc is a good listener."

Doc sees he stepped in it and turns his back to us to hide, scraping the iron of his griddle with a vengeance.

Cass stares at me.

I say, "I'm sorry. I needed someone to talk to. You have your own ideas about the thing and I wanted to try to make sense of it myself. What was I going to do? You wouldn't talk to me. Remember?"

This brings a fair moment of quiet to our little group, and just then the old fellow who always sits in the corner booth speaks up. He's not wearing his coat, but he's still wearing a red check flannel shirt, even in the heat, and his cap is on.

"So, what the hell happened? I been waitin' to find that out for months."

It was me who said, "Oh, geez!" but it was on Doc's face as well.

Cass was still glaring at me. No one else in the place looked like they cared one way or the other.

Ellen starts toying with her potatoes and singing a little song in a girlish voice,

"He's not the only one. Not the only one. Not the only one. She talks to me, too. She talks to me, three."

Cass says, "Be quiet!" and turns away, stabbing a large piece of egg in a dollop of ketchup with disgust. Finally she says, "Okay! Alright! So, tell me what it is you've been telling Doc?"

It was the easier thing just to get to the point.

"I think it was Sam Schechner who killed himself, after all."

She says, "You and the cops both."

"But it's not that simple."

Ellen says, "It never is."

I say, "Let me tell you about something. I know I told you a little about this before, but let me tell you again. Jerry Herzog was my friend. Solid as a rock. Good humored. He worked for my dad off and on for more than ten years. I worked with Jerry, myself. He had a wife he adored and three kids. In the end, he had everything but a job. When you boil it down, that's really all he didn't have. But he killed himself. Why would a man do that? What was he thinking? He didn't just hurt himself, he hurt a lot of other people he loved by doing that. What for?"

Doc poured some coffee and took another order from down the counter. I finished my breakfast.

The old fellow in the corner was the first to speak.

"Alright. What for?"

I shrugged, because the answer was too simple. "He lost his mind. And that happened because he let things get the better of him. His emotions took over and he couldn't see straight anymore. He was ashamed for not being able to provide for his family. He thought it was his fault. He blamed himself. And he couldn't stand being without them after Sheila went home to live with her parents. After all those years of struggling week to week, when things started getting worse again, he thought there was never going to be a way out of it for him. In his mind, he'd lost everything. But he still had some part of his pride. He'd always been able to provide before, ever since he was a kid. There might have been other matters I never knew about, of course. I know that his teeth hurt him and he had a busted knee from a fall he took once from his bicycle when a cab hit him. But the pride was something I saw. A lot of times. And suddenly he'd lost that. He was ashamed. And I suspect he'd been drinking. He liked to drink a little too much."

Cass said, "You think that has something to do with Sam Schechner?"

"Yes. Everything. But the question to ask there is, why? You couldn't see a reason for him to do it, so you assumed it was someone else that did. That makes sense. But what if there was a real reason?"

"But what about your idea that the guys who tried to kill us last night were connected to that?"

"Right! That's what I'm thinking now. How are they connected? If they'd wanted to kill Sam they could have simply shot him, I guess. Or run him down, maybe. But hanging him in the middle of the day? That makes no sense to me. Trying to make it look like a suicide? They could have done a better job of that."

Cass said, 'Well, it worked." She gave me her blank face. This was serious. She was thinking this through. "So you think we should be looking for a connection between Sam committing suicide, and these idiots who tried to kill us?"

"Yes!"

The old fellow in the corner groans, "Jesus, Mary, an' Joseph! You mean you still don't know?" I looked over at him. But what could I say? Then the old fellow barks back, "They're all damned spies! You know that! Your young lawyer friend there might'a given'em somethin' he shouldn't. Right? He was ashamed! Just like your poor buddy, Jerry."

That seemed to be the best direction we had.

We all three just looked at Doc then, I suppose because he was standing there in front of us. Doc looks back at each of us in turn and says, "Don't look at me. Timmy could be right!"

At least I now knew the old guy's name.

Then, out of the blue, Cass asked an odd question that had never occurred to me before.

"Why do you call it Morgy's. Why not 'Doc's'?"

Doc shrugs, "My daughter named it. My wife is German and she always says 'Guten Morgen.' When she was little, my daughter thought it was funny to say 'Good Morgy,' instead."

Because it was on my mind then, I asked him, "What does your wife think about Herr Hitler?"

Doc's smile vanishes and he says, "She thinks he's insane. She's sure there is going to be another war."

That was very sobering.

54. Sunday, July 4, 1937

It's not just the Germans, of course. The Russians are making lots of noise too. The Japanese are already busy in China. It feels like another war has already started.

I walked Ellen and Cass back to 19th street. Ellen ran a finger around the bullet holes and stepped over the blood that was dried brown on the white tiles there and said she had about enough of the shooting for the time being. She packed a bag and went off to her parent's farm in New Jersey for a few days. With mobsters and Nazis hanging around, I wasn't all that sure I wanted Cass staying in her apartment alone. It was a difficult situation to figure. Well, not difficult for me, but for her. I asked her to stay at my place. She gave me the look. With that ruled out, the other option I figured was Brooklyn. At least she agreed to that.

Cass had a couple of things to write up, back at the paper. She packed a bag and we headed up there first. But I wasn't in the office for two minutes before Stenis sent me out to Coney Island. The Ferris wheel was stuck again—always good for a human interest picture, especially if kids were involved. It was three o'clock before we were both on our way to Brooklyn together.

This was funny, however, because I had not called my mom in advance. She had no idea about our plans. No idea. From the kitchen she heard us come in and practically met us at the door, takes one look at Cass with her suitcase, and says, "The front room on the third floor is empty. You can take that."

The news at home is that Mr. White is not back yet but he has finally sent a letter. He has a job in a tool shop in Detroit and he wants Stacy to come out there now. She has written him back, telling him about the job here that Mr. Clurman has lined it up, as well as my dad's idea about other arrangements.

Stacy and Gary took a walk with Cass and me over to Prospect Park after dinner. Gary is already a little happier now with the recent news about his father, and he led Stacy off by the hand to show her how he takes his pictures and that gave Cass and me a chance to talk.

Cass didn't let a moment pass. "Do you really think Sam was that ruffled over his relationship with Norma Lenz?"

I'm even more certain of it than before. "Sure. But that's not all of it, either. Like I said. As soon as we can, I think we should find out what it was that agitated our Nazi friends. Why did they attack you last night? Sure, the story was in the paper about the shoot-out with Victor Neims. That was a good excuse for doing it when they did, but why do it at all? I think the answer to that is what I've said before. You're getting too close to something. And probably it's something you've done just recently that sparked it. Something . . . Who were you going to see the other day when I was busy playing with Garvas in Central Park?"

She thought about that for a minute while I watched the play of kites that people had flying above the slope of Prospect hill.

"I've been going back over his appointment book. One name at a time. I spoke to several people that day. A woman named Etta Wertheimer. Schechner had just recently gotten her a visa. She seems like a perfectly average person. She only came by that day to give him ten dollars against her account. Which appears to be all he charged her. She's already working now down in the Garment District. And William Lehman. He's another lawyer. He's with a Madison Avenue firm. Schechner had an appointment with him the day before as well. I know they talked about visas. The State Department is not issuing visas as easily as they were. There are people that

Sam Schechner appears to have had the names of on a list. Several hundred, I think. And they're all waiting to leave Germany right now."

"Where is that list?"

"Lehman has a copy. He says he does. But he also says it's private information."

"Where's the original?"

"I don't know. It wasn't around in Schechner's office. I looked for it even before they packed things up."

"What did Lehman have to say about that?"

"He didn't say, exactly. But it seemed like it was a touchy subject with him. He was being careful. The list was Schechner's. Lehman only had a copy so that he could work on it with his contacts at the State Department."

"We should try to find that list. You might have missed it in all those files. Schechner's office is closed now? Where is everything that was there?"

"In his father's basement."

"I'd like to go up there with you and poke around. If you'll let me."

She didn't answer quickly. But she said "Alright."

She wasn't sitting close to me on the bench and I had made the decision not to move over closer myself. She looked like she needed some room.

I said, "What else have you done recently? Have you spoken to Norma Lenz again?"

"No. She's back with her husband. I know that."

"What else?"

"I spoke to a fellow named Dunner. He saw Schechner earlier that week. He has a relative in Prague who was trying to emigrate.

"Anything in that?"

"No. Nothing to do with Sam Schechner. But I did find out that Mr. Dunner's cousin has been arrested. He'd heard that from yet another cousin." Cass and I were already looking directly at one another when she offered this detail. She got that blank face of hers. Then she added, "What I need to do now is to make my own copy of Mr. Lehman's list as soon as possible and try to find out how many of those people have been arrested too."

I said, "Right."

But nothing really was.

55. Monday, July 5, 1937

I went with Cass up to Yorkville late Monday morning. In terms of assignments, it was a quiet day. Under the circumstances, I think The Boss was taking some of the load off. I'd appraised him of what we were up to and he agreed with the most of it. With a couple of additions.

He said, "If you got married sooner than later it would be a lot easier to straighten out your living arrangements."

And then, "Marriage is not what it's cracked up to be in any case. There's no reason to wait until you're married to set up housekeeping. This is the Twentieth Century, you know?"

I told Cass about both of those comments. She did not even bother to give me her usual glare.

The elder Mr. Schechner was not looking well. He had clearly lost weight since I had last seen him, and he'd already been a scrawny fellow then. But we found nothing in Mr. Schechner's basement other than hundreds of briefs and files for past cases. All of it was clearly labeled. His son had been a busy man. Interestingly, most of those files involved visas. That appeared to be a specialty. Schechner was intent on getting as many people out of Germany as he could. My guess was most of them were Jews.

Just before we went home for the day we caught Mr. Lehman at his office on Madison Avenue. Lehman is a tall gentleman, gray suit and bow tie, with that nasal sound atop a deep voice that you hear from prep school boys trying to talk like their fathers. He has a

Harvard Law School certificate of approval on his wall. He has a relaxed manner and pretty obviously a razor edge of mind.

Right off, he says to Cass, "I thought you'd come back. You're the persistent type. And I saw the story about your encounter with a gunman in the *Mirror*. My secretary ran in with it this morning. Very exciting. It's a matter of two and two, I think. So I called a friend of mine in Washington. He's looking into the matter."

This statement was made as we sat down and immediately after Cass introduced me. She had not yet explained a thing about the reason for our visit.

Cass said, "What exactly is your friend looking for?"

"What's happened with those visa applications on the German end. It's all we can do. The Germans are very efficient with their paperwork. If the applications are still active, we will know fairly quickly."

"And if they're not?"

He bit his lip with regret. "We'll lodge a complaint, of course. But there is little else we can do."

"Is it possible you can give me a copy of the list?"

"I'm sorry. As I mentioned before, that's confidential."

Brightly, I asked, "Even with Sam Schechner dead?"

I could hear the added patience in his answer. "Yes."

But Cass had no patience left at all. She sat forward to the edge of the leather chair.

"Here's the deal. What we need to know is if anyone on that list has been arrested. That should be public information. Shouldn't it?"

"It could be."

"The reason I was attacked the other day is probably because there's someone who thinks I'm getting too close to something that they don't want known."

"I understand."

"What I'm now thinking is, that might involve the names on that list."

"If you're worried about someone getting those names—they

wouldn't get them from me. But, I can see that it might be a matter that would somehow involved Sam's death."

I asked, "How many of the names on that list were Jews?"

He took a breath on his answer. It was carefully worded. "I can't know that."

"How many do you think were Jews?"

"It would just be a guess. Of course. And not for attribution. My name should not be attached to any of this except perhaps as the usual 'reliable source.'"

Cass said, "Yes."

He said, "All of them."

Cass said, "But wouldn't the Germans already know that?"

Mr. Lehman's voice dropped another notch. "No. That's the point, isn't it? Jews are not permitted to emigrate. If they do leave Germany, they have to leave all of their personal property behind. There are many people who have been living their lives privately in Germany—all over Europe for that matter—without publicly attesting to any religion for years. For generations in some cases. The Nazis are determined to ferret those families out. At the very least, to confiscate their wealth. And worse. And if these people have attempted to leave Germany under false pretenses—a vacation, or a business trip, for instance—or say, with the pretense of visiting relatives but with no intention of returning, they would be breaking German law."

56. Thursday, July 8, 1937

You hear old-timers use the phrase, "Back in the day," and you turn away and head for the door as fast as you can because you'll only be getting a heavy dose of misinformation. What The Boss calls "lies dressed up like a promiscuous parlor maid." Or, as one assistant editor once dilated upon it to me, "just another photographer in spats." I suppose, when I'm old enough to use words of the kind myself, I'll have better things to do. For now, and for me, 'back in the day' is yesterday, or maybe the day before.

Five years ago I spent the election year of 1932 working the night shift with 'Fancy' Frank Futterman. Barry George was still in charge of the sports pages then and the City Editor was Guy Fredericks, an old-timer who'd known almost everyone that ever lived—so long as they were currently dead and unable to correct the reminiscence. The word was that Fredericks had once even been on speaking terms with Jesus Christ, which was why that name came up so often in conversation.

At the time, Hearst was more intent on our matching circulation with the *Daily News* and thus we had a smarter budget. Nowadays, The Boss mostly uses stringers to cover the eleven to seven shift, which is not the best arrangement. It means that, with no willing alternative available (as is too often the case), I might be home and in dreamland and I get a call from whoever the unlucky soul is who was left on duty that night to polish the gravestones, telling me I have to get my butt out to Canarsie because some fellow has come home from carousing and found his wife in bed with the baker.

I only say the 'baker' now because of the famous case of Dan Wright, 'the Doughnut Man' who is likely the father of several dozen unsuspecting New Yorkers and was shot on election eve in 1932 for casting more than one ballot at the home of an alderman. An alderman Jones had returned early because of the lopsided vote in that election taking away any drama after his flask was empty. I myself arrived at that scene around three in the morning and took the pictures and got the names, returned to the office and then went home again, only to wake up at noon the next day to the phone ringing and loud praise for not only the cover photo on the morning 'extra' but for the headline too: "The Hole Story on Doughnut Man Murder." I had evidently (and unintentionally) used the line on my notes when I handed in my plates. I'd meant to write 'whole.' So much for my public school education.

But this is how legends are made, as they say.

Take 'Fancy' Frank Futterman, my fellow staff photographer at the time. He is known by that appellation to this day because, soon after he started working at the *Mirror*, he came to the office one evening wearing a white linen suit and spats. This got him a great deal of attention only an hour later while out on the street taking shots of a taxicab that tried to climb a tree in Gramercy Park. And I happen to know the true cause of this wardrobe change. Frank had failed to pick up his laundry that day, but he'd recently been given a box of goods by an aunt to donate to the Salvation Army whenever he got around that way. The box contained some dress clothes from an uncle who had died of the influenza a dozen years before. In some desperation, Frank had put the white suit on, even though summer was well behind us and the fit was not exact.

The consequence to this happenstance was astonishing. The attention his duds garnered were cause for him going back regularly to the Salvation Army and buying up anything donated that he could find of a better stripe. (In those days, bankers and stockbrokers were jumping out of windows willy-nilly and leaving excellent wardrobes behind). More improbably, Frank began to shave everyday, and bathe more than once a week. And even though he was only the lowly press photographer at any event, he was almost always better dressed than anyone else in the room. This meant that he was often noticed and even consulted at the scene. Several times he was even quoted by other papers as the 'anonymous observer.' (His greatest interest at the time though were the women who would cross a room to speak to him in the midst of some momentary chaos or another). Within a couple months Guy Fredericks had rescheduled Frank to days only.

Briefly then, I considered heading down to the Salvation Army thrift store myself, but Frank is of medium height and build, and more easily fitted to a larger number of castoffs. And besides, those heady days when great fortunes were being lost overnight and thus better wardrobes abandoned in the fall, soon ended, and we were left with the dreary repetitiveness and more common failures of the overly cautious (and men with lower sartorial standards) that continues to this day. A story about a jumper is more likely to draw attention now if accompanied by a picture of the dog that was being walked by the maid and just narrowly missed by the body of the deceased there on the sidewalk.

Now, Frank is a perfectly good photographer and always worked for what he got, but this one change in his sartorial ways was akin to winning the lottery. About a year after that, The *Daily News* stole him away from the *Mirror*, and two years later he'd become a Republican and was married to an heiress. But I'll give Frank credit. He's still at his job at the *News* to this day, even though the heiress has moved on.

I remember one particular instance, back in those days, when Herbert Hoover came to town. Usually this was to meet with business leaders. But this time he was also met by a well-organized delegation of the unemployed who had been rounded up by one of the unions and given a dollar each to express their heartfelt opinions on the matters of the day.

Given the number of dignitaries, Frank and I were both

assigned to that event, which was held outdoors at Union Square. Despite a large crowd of Republican supporters, Mr. Hoover never got a chance to deliver his full speech because the Bronx cheers were constant and the paid audience had gotten fully into their roles. Enthusiasms quickly boiled over into the street. The cops were caught unprepared. Pretty suddenly, poor Frank was mistaken for a swell and set upon by a committee of toughs. His press card seemed to offer him little protection—or only magnified the emotions.

Naturally, I had to enter that fray, if only to help Frank get his camera put away before some harm was done to that. We had a fine time of it. Neither of us had anything more than our own fists. The thugs had all come equipped with short lengths of wooden staves and fencing, which they'd secreted up their sleeves. Nonetheless, the result was a bunch of fine photos of the sort of angry faces you still see too often nowadays. Guy Fredericks ran several of these shots from each of us in the next edition. But the triumph of the moment for us was when Hoover himself came over, mistaking Frank for a constituent (Frank's hat had been knocked to the gutter) to inquire about Frank's health. Frank got a short interview out of it and we both got several good photos of the President to go with the rest of the story.

During his brief stint as a husband, Frank had gone to Europe on his honeymoon. And because his own father had been born in Frankfurt, he'd gone with his bride to Germany then to see the tailoring shop some of his relatives still ran there. This was in 1934, and Frank discovered that the shop had recently been burned out. His relatives were already packing up and getting ready to move to America. Frank got some excellent shots of the remains of the shop as well as of the two thugs who had come along to threaten him for taking the pictures. These ran in the *Daily News* shortly after that and I managed to get some of this story directly from his own lips.

Frank was certain then that the mood here in America was not far behind what he had seen in Germany. He even cited our run-in with the thugs at Union Square as evidence.

So naturally I thought of Frank and called him on Thursday

to get his take on things in general and the situation with Jewish immigrants in particular. We had hotdogs and sauerkraut together in Bryant Park, behind the library.

Frank is decked out in a nice light gray summer suit and vest and because of the temperature he has taken the jacket off and I see he has French cuffs despite the heat.

I say, "That's ridiculous."

He says, "Feel the fabric. Light as a feather. Made in India."

"How can those ink-stained wretches over there at the *News* stand being around you?"

He shrugs that off. But first thing, Frank wants to know is, "Just how did you manage to score with Cass Green?"

Evidently, she had been the object of his attentions for some time before she left the *News* and he'd been unable to make any significant headway.

I said, "Maybe it was my sunny disposition."

He said, "I should have known."

So I asked him if he knew anyone in Germany that might be helpful concerning the subject of Jewish immigration.

"Not any more. The people I knew there before, are all of them right here in New York now. Peter Grodin and his wife live in Bensonhurst. Mr. and Mrs. Kantor live somewhere in Queens. But I do know it's a lot worse than it was. And I know it's going to get worse, still. I tried to get a visa to go over last year for the Olympics. They delayed it until I was already involved with another assignment."

"Could you give me some names and addresses?"

"Sure. Is Cass working on this too?"

"Yes."

"Say hello for me."

"Sure."

"Sure you will. You rat."

Cass and I went over to Bensonhurst to see Mr. and Mrs. Grodin that afternoon. Mr. Grodin works the night shift for the

Sewer Department, and he was home. Mrs. Grodin works in a dress shop in Manhattan and would not be home until later. The conversation was very polite but he was reserved and seemed wary of saying anything too specific. Cass picked up on this right off and pressed the matter.

"How did you get here?" and "How did you pay for that?" and "Who was your sponsor?" That sort of thing.

My patience ran out after awhile.

I said, "Who are you protecting? What are you hiding? What you've done is perfectly legal. You talk like you're afraid of something."

Mr. Grodin says, "You don't understand."

I say, "Make me understand!"

"I could be deported."

"What? Are you going to rob a bank? Have you swindled someone?"

"No. No one!"

Cass was quiet through this part and I figured she was giving me free rein to play 'bad cop,' so I went on with it.

"What's going on then? You were sponsored. Right? Who is this Mr. Finckle who sponsored you?"

"My cousin. My mother's nephew."

"Should we talk to him?"

"No! Please."

"What if we talk to him without mentioning you?"

"He'll find out."

"You said he's a haberdasher. What kind?"

"Notions. Buttons. Mostly buttons."

"What's wrong with that?"

Mr. Grodin shrugged at us. He had nothing more.

We tracked down Mr. Finckle on Houston Street near Avenue A. His business occupies the second floor of a six-floor granite and brick building that must be over hundred years old. The sign simply says, 'Buttons."

When you pull back the heavy metal door on the hall, the first thing you notice are the eyes. Like gleaming buttons in the dark. My second thought was that these eyes were sweating in the heat. Twenty-two women sitting at broad tables littered with what appears to be debris. Much of that is cloth, cut into small bits. Along with crimping tools, there is a pot of glue and various little boxes with small disks of brass, shapes of glass, and heavy brass wire.

The young women are all dressed in soiled smocks and hunched over the tables with their faces turned up and staring at us as we stand at the door waiting to be noticed by someone in authority.

Mr. Finckle finally appears from a back room. He is a short and bullish looking man, large headed and clean shaven. He is bald down to a fringe of hair at his ears. The trim of hair somehow makes his head look larger. He has on a light blue shirt and he is stuffing this down under his belt as he comes forward, as if punching it into place.

"What do you want?"

Cass shows him her press card. Mine is in my hat. She says, "The *Mirror* is doing a series on the haberdasheries. We were told you were the man to see about buttons."

He smiles. "That's me! I'm the button man! They all come to me. What do you want?"

"You make buttons for some of the better shops, we hear."

"The best!" He turns and waves at the women. They all duck from the sudden attention. "It's a small operation. I don't do anything for Macy's, or Gimbels, you understand. You'll only find my buttons on a few of the better things at Saks, Bergdorf's, or Bonwits. You want a sample?"

He reaches into a metal bucket pegged on the wall by the door and pulls out a handful of various types and sizes and extends them to us on the palm of his hand. I took a picture of that, with the girls behind for background. He had a large smile until he saw what I was doing with the camera and then put his other hand up too late.

"I don't want any pictures."

Cass asked, "Why?"

"It's my business. No pictures. Put your camera away."

I knew immediately then that I should keep my mouth shut. Cass could handle the interview without my interference. I looked out over the room instead.

Cass begins with the usual, "How long have you been in business?"

Her voice had dropped to that false calm that I knew.

This is what I saw in that room: There were five rows of four tables each. A cord dropped down from the ceiling above each table with a single cone-shaded bulb, but these were all turned off. The only light was from the five narrow side windows, one illuminating each row. At the side away from the windows a line of small barrels were filled with the raw materials, and every couple of minutes one of the girls would get up and carry a smaller container from her table over to that side and fill it. The floor was littered with bits of the remains. The girls at the tables had all turned their heads down to their work again after Mr. Finckle came into the room from the back. There was no conversation among them. After several minutes another girl came through the same door at the back where Mr. Finckle had first appeared, and settled at a bench on one side.

Cass says, "I take it from your accent that you are German?"

"Austrian! Vienna."

Cass fingered the button she had plucked from his hand. "This is fine work. Where do you find the craftsmen?"

"All my girls are from Europe. Germany. Poland. Czechoslovakia. You can't find the people to do such work here."

"How much does a button like this cost?"

"Materials? A few cents. Labor. Much more."

"How do you find such talent?"

"I go to Europe every year. I find them."

"You are their sponsor?"

"Yes!"

"You say you go to Europe every year to find them. How long do they stay here working for you?"

This question brought a new frown to his face.

"Why do you want to know that? What does that have to do with buttons?"

"It's a matter of how they are made."

"I told you. You can see. This is how they are made."

"Can I speak with one or two of the girls?"

"They don't speak English."

"I speak German."

"I don't want you bothering them. It's enough. I have to get back to work. Go, now."

At that command, Cass spoke out into the room, loudly and in German. I know a part of that was her own name and the name of the newspaper, and later she told me that she'd simply said who she was and what she was doing and how to reach her.

Immediately Mr. Finckle explodes. His face and head turned pink as he yelled. "Stop! Stop! Stop it! You have no right. Get out!"

I took a picture of that face as we left, as well as one of the room in general and all the faces that were turned up at us again, mouths open, eyes wide.

Mr. Finckle reached for my arm as I did this. I hit his wrist away with the knuckles of my right hand as it came up and his arm pulled back as if he were bit.

He screamed louder. "I'll have you arrested!"

Cass said, "We'll wait, if you'd like to call the police now."

Instead, he jerked the metal door open with his other hand and yelled again for us to get out. And we did. Trespass is only a misdemeanor but it can take unnecessary time at the station.

57. Friday to Saturday, July 9 and 10, 1937

On Friday evening, after we left the Paper, I took Cass to the movies. Primarily this was to get out of the heat. The movie was just so, so. *You Can't Beat Love.* Joan Fontaine is a dish but she's a bit reserved for being in a comedy and Preston Foster makes a wooden Indian look soft. Afterward we had some ice cream and I told Cass more about talking to Frank Futterman, and that he had asked me to say hello.

Cass doesn't want to hear my gripes about the movie anyway and says, "Poor Frank. If ever there was an argument against advertisements that say 'The clothes make the man.' He's not a bad guy. Smart. But he doesn't read, and his biggest passion is jazz. He has a record collection and he invites every girl he meets over to his apartment to hear the latest thing."

In fact I had been thinking better of Frank Futterman, especially by comparison to Preston Foster the moment before when I'd remarked that Foster looked a little like the sort of clothes dummy you see in the shops. At least he's dressed well. But Frank wears the clothes like they were meant for him and he's never stiff unless he's put away half a bottle of Teacher's.

So I say, "Is that from personal knowledge"

And she shrugs and says, "As a matter of fact."

I didn't want to know anything more about it.

I said, "How about Frank's friend's cousin, Mr. Finckle. Did you find out anything else about that guy today?"

Cass says, "What you'd expect. He's a creep. No one thinks any more of him. But he produces good buttons and on time. That appears to be about all that counts to the buyer at Bonwit's."

On Saturday morning, Cass was in the office before me. This turned out to be important because she got a call there. This was from a Greta Sturmgart. She wanted to meet us on Sunday afternoon, but Cass spoke to her on the spot, in German, for as long as she would stay on the line. I picked up a little from that. Miss Sturmgart was from a town named Kiel. She was 23. She was a Jew.

Later Cass explained that the girl's father had paid for her passage just to get her out of the country. Mr. Finckle had promised her work. She did what he asked. But she had never been paid. Supposedly the money was being saved for her. It was also clear that Mr. Finckle often used some of the girls 'badly.' At the moment of the call, Mr. Finckle was at Temple and Miss Sturmgart had snuck out to a drugstore to make the call. Somehow, Cass got her to say her address and then told her specifically what to do next. She was to act like she was very sick and stay in bed if Mr. Finckle returned before we got there.

This was a fast cab ride to East 3rd Street. We were there in less than twenty minutes.

Miss Sturmgart was living on the third floor, at the rear of the building, along with several of the other girls from the button factory, but Mr. Finckle answered the door. He did not get it shut again in time. I kneed it open against his weight and when he took a swing at me I hit him directly in the chest and that set him down, gasping, long enough for Cass to find Miss Sturmgart. The girl already had a fresh bruise on her cheek when we arrived. We stuffed what she said was hers into a pillowcase, with at least four other girls screaming and wailing around us. Cass kept repeating in German that any of them could leave with us, but none moved to the offer and we left with Miss Sturmgart in the same cab we had arrived in.

All the while, Mr. Finckle was screaming as only a man can do in a rage.

"You'll be sent back! I'll send you back. Your family will know! The authorities will know! Whore!" That sort of thing, but in German. I had to have Cass interpret that later.

The Boss was willing to pay for a small room at the Clarke Hotel, only a few blocks from the office and that's where we checked Miss Sturmgart in. Cass interviewed her for the rest of that day between frantic episodes of panic and remorse. Evidently this was the first time she had allowed herself to express her fears. I was assigned to bring food. And we found an elderly woman from the Jewish Aid Society to stay with her for the time it took them to find a family to take her in later in the week. The promise Cass made was that if we could not find someone better, she would act as a sponsor herself and that the Paper would pay the legal fees to fight Mr. Finckle with the immigration authorities.

Cass's first story on all this made the Sunday edition. The series ran for three more days, mostly centered on Miss Sturmgart's testimony, but with various corroborations and several additional photographs from a few other visits to local sweatshops.

58. Tuesday to Thursday, July 13 to 15, 1937

On Tuesday I was on another assignment when Cass went
out to Queens to see Frank's friends, Mr. and Mrs. Kantor. The
husband, Aaron, is out of work and he was the only one home. The
wife has a job as a chambermaid at a hotel in Manhattan.

Mr. Kantor had been a machine parts and gears salesman for
the Bemmel Metal Works Company in Hamburg. For many years
after the war he had the luxury of being able to travel throughout
Germany and he'd watched the changes that had come over that
country with growing fears. He was bitter now, having lost everything, and this made the interview difficult because he easily slipped
into rants about one evil or another.

I read Cass's notes. She had no story to go with it for the
time being.

Mr. Kantor had said, "Maybe I should have stayed. But I was
afraid. Even though I knew that running away was not an answer."

"Why did you leave when you did?"

"I was let go. Fired. After twenty-two years! But I'd seen it
coming and when they closed our account at the bank and confiscated our savings, I knew it was time. Then they took our home. It
was my father's house. We had to pay rent if we wished to live there.
It was just a matter of time before we would be trapped. Like so
many others. If you have the money to leave, they take it and then
tell you to go, if you don't like it. But you can't buy a ticket! You
have no passport! Nothing! But I saw it coming. I had purchased

gold coins for years. The old marks. Mostly on the black market. I had a friend who manufactures steel dies in Belgium. I would send him some machine parts and a little gold at the same time. I started doing that in 1932. By the time I was fired, we had put away a considerable sum. One day we went to the beach for a little walk. And we kept going. And when we got to Antwerp, I went to see my friend. But he wasn't my friend anymore. Which is another of life's lessons. As it happened, my wife was the smart one. She had kept some of the smaller coins aside. This was for gifts, she told me. But she sewed them in our clothes. Our children are grown and my son lives here and my daughter is married to a man in California. Even my wife's mother is now in California. But I don't get along with her. Even before we left, my son went to school here at Rensselaer when the University in Germany rejected him. He is now an engineer. He always loved gears. So we are here."

We both agreed with Mr. Kantor, his was a very fortunate circumstance.

The evening papers have stories about George Gershwin and how he was too young to die, alongside speculations that the crash of the *Hindenburg* was caused by St. Elmo's fire. St. Elmo could not be reached for comment. But everybody on that airship was too young to die. Nobody will know any of their names in another week but everyone else will still be whistling Gershwin. Life and death are both funny.

59. Saturday, July 17, 1937

Dog days.

Not much is happening. But Dewey is busy giving speeches. LaGuardia is out at the Summer City Hall near Flushing, and Roosevelt is up at Hyde Park on vacation. The President had a little chat with reporters which cost me a couple extra hours on the train. But I gave The Boss the pictures he wanted, and the better ones I kept. I got to go out on my own to cover two fires, both in Brooklyn, and a drowning at Coney Island.

I'd asked The Boss for permission to go down to Alabama to cover the trials of the Scottsboro Boys on several occasions starting way back in '31. I did not have the seniority then for it but none of the other guys wanted to spend any time in Alabama. It was too much of a national story however and a couple of guys from the *Evening Journal* and *The American* got tickets instead.

Yesterday, the wise jurists of that state, figuring I suppose that two negatives make a positive and dismissing all the evidence to the contrary while apparently ignoring the shifting and contradictory testimony of the two girls involved in that supposed assault and all the witnesses to the contrary, have convicted Clarence Norris of rape yet again. Haywood Patterson was already re-convicted in January, so this is no surprise.

This legal fiasco has gone on long enough to make another point that should be obvious to every citizen—that our legal system, and especially the courts, are broken. And just as clearly, the sad fact of it will not change for the better anytime in the foreseeable future—not at least while the courts are just another political branch of government subject to party appointments. What bothered me personally though was that Hearst did not bother to send another photographer down to Alabama for this latest absurdity. All of Hearst's New York rags are still using the same file photos today from years ago, mixed in with a few pics supplied by stringers or local papers. Though, I imagine this is not Barry George's decision. It could go all the way up to Kobler on the 5th floor, but my guess is it's a call by Mr. Gauvreau, the managing editor. He's always more interested in the 'three legged baby born to bearded lady.'

Cass and I were talking about all this again when we were in Dad's A Model on Sunday, even before the latest decision. Dad let me borrow the car and I got Cass and Stacy and Gary to Long Beach for the first time. I thought I might get Stacy to say something about the Scottsboro travesty in the privacy of the car, but she was quiet and I gave that up. If Gary had any thoughts on the matter, he kept those to himself as well.

The sun was actually too hot to lie down in, so we spent most of our time getting battered and scrubbed by the waves. Cass burned herself pink. I was red. (She put the zinc ointment on my back, which was some compensation at least.) Gary was afraid of the waves at first but then transformed himself into a fish and spent the three hours in the water, non-stop.

At dinner, Mom was very dismayed over the whole thing, and lets us know it. (Our beach excursion, not the latest Scottsboro decision. She is of the opinion that sunlight is best in limited doses.) Nevertheless, I avoided any analysis of the jury system at the table.

The word now is that Mr. White will be back within the week. Mr. Clurman says the job at the engine house is still open.

Mrs. Tisdale apparently has a new boyfriend named Bill. Bill doesn't dance. He is an opera buff and she has been over to the Metropolitan Opera House several times in the past month to hear recitals. I figure Bill must be very well off if he can afford the tickets.

After dinner, with Stacy and Gary gone, we got to talking about the Scottsboro case and Clarence Norris again, along with the new testimony from Victoria Price. Ruby Bates, the other woman involved in the supposed assault, has already recanted her testimony but Price is more adamant than ever. Cass cannot explain it. The idea of a woman saying she was raped when she wasn't makes no sense. Cass thinks it may be that Price had been raped before—perhaps more than once if she has been working in the trade—and the woman is desperate for some sort of revenge.

Mom then says she has seen such things before. Some people commit themselves to a thing and cannot give it up, no matter the cost. Somehow it means more to them than anything else. For Victoria Price, the case against the Scottsboro Boys and her desire to see Clarence Norris, Charlie Weems, Haywood Patterson, Andrew Wright and the others executed on her account, seems to have become the great purpose in an otherwise very sad life.

I look over to Cass to see if she has any thoughts about that, and I see the blank face. Something has occurred to her. I quickly think back over what's been said. Only one thing stands out.

I say, "Do you think our Annie Oakley murderer might be another Victoria Price with a gun and a good eye?"

Her face told me what I wanted to know. But she didn't answer.

This conversation was conducted in the kitchen, after dinner, while dad did the dishes. His only comment was that people believed what fit their own beliefs. Good and bad. Clear thinking had little to do with it. And the courts were no better than the people themselves, especially when they had stepped outside the limits of their own laws. They would not easily admit to making an error. Yesterday's verdict appears to confirm Dad's opinion.

60. Tuesday, July 20, 1937

On Monday, Cass spent the day on the phone. But she confirmed my own guess. She was doing a lot of calling to Philadelphia.

On Tuesday we went on the train down to the City of Brotherly (and Sisterly) Love, together. She held my hand most of the way, which she doesn't do often enough. And she said something interesting. She said, "Wouldn't it be grand to just keep going." And before that, when we were in Penn Station and we looked up at the big board to find our track number she had said. "Look at the choices!"

She had three appointments lined up. One was with a police Captain who had known the stiff from the Hotel Penn, Michael Allen Deems, very well. They'd been buddies in the Philadelphia Police department for many years. What Cass had said to the Captain on the phone that got him to open up was simple enough. She promised not to use his name, or any reference to him, in her story, but told him that she was going to find out who killed Deems with or without his help, and she had thought, given his personal ties, he might be interested in having a hand in on the case.

Captain George Parker is clearly an alcoholic. He has the nose of W.C. Fields and the lazy tongue of a man who starts his drinking before noon. He's large headed and nearly as bald as Mr. Finckle, the button man, but almost a foot taller. He is now assigned to a desk and you can readily see that his belly has the same curve as his head. Cass had spoken to him at least once before and gotten nowhere. Now she presented her case to him a little differently.

"Captain Deems liked the girls. We know that. And one of those girls killed him. That's the probability. But why?"

Parker shrugged, "Maybe he got a little rough?"

He said this with a raise of his eyebrows at Cass as if perhaps she would know about such things. She ignored it.

Parker looked at me and smiled outright.

Cass said, "Can you tell me if any of the murders in Philadelphia in the past two years involved shooting out the eyes of the victims? Specifically with a twenty-two caliber pistol."

He shrugged this off as well. "Not that I am aware of."

"Who would I see about that?"

"Coroner's office."

"They won't talk without a specific warrant. Do you know anyone down there who will talk to me off the record?"

Captain Parker looked at me again, so I spoke up.

"Deems was your friend, you said. But maybe not that much?"

Parker sighed a little, weaved in his chair, then fingered a small notebook he pulled from his drawer and held it out in the air far enough to read without his glasses.

"Stanley Sheetz. With a 'z.' He owes me."

Then he made a call. Ten minutes later we were down in the cool of the basement.

Sheetz is a tall man. Thin. Soft spoken. He is dressed in a white shirt and bow tie when we meet him. On the way to his windowless office we passed two open doors where naked bodies lay out on tables. One of those cadavers was opened up like a sardine can with the metal key still wound in. Sheetz' office was next to that and his soiled green apron was across the back of the only other chair in the room so I did not sit down.

He says, "I was just looking at my files. I would need more time to tell you if there were more than two but I know of at least that number, just off the top of my head. Eyes shot out is a distinctive marking."

Cass asks, "Were they both middle-aged men?"

He says, "Yes. How did you know?"

She says, "Don't you read the papers?"

Apparently he did not read the *New York Mirror*. And the *Philadelphia Daily News, Record* or *Inquirer* had never reported the information about the New York murders, nor the more grisly facts of the two found dead in Philadelphia. But perhaps it was not so common there to give away the details of a murder to favored reporters—at least not the ones under current investigation.

We went back upstairs again and caught Captain Parker just before he abandoned work early for the day. He already had his hat on to leave.

Cass did the questioning while I stood in the door. This was funny, actually—trying to hold a police captain captive in his own office. I smiled back at his scowl.

Cass stood between us. "Come on! Please! Just take a minute. Just tell us if Captain Deems worked on either of these two cases?"

She handed him her note pad.

Deems scowled over her shoulder at me again and then reluctantly took it.

Immediately he says, "This one. Josephs. Mike worked on the Michael Josephs murder. I'm sure of that one."

"Can you tell me who Michael Josephs was?"

"A jeweler. He was robbed."

"Where would I go to find out something more?"

"Talk to the guy's brother. Likely. The shop's somewhere on Sansom. Now, you'll excuse me."

I stepped aside just in time to avoid getting a heavier shoe on top of my own.

Mark Josephs looked a great deal like an older version of Izzy's brother, a large man with the smell of garlic still on his breath from lunch. He was not happy to talk with us.

He says, "What good does it do?"

Cass said, "We may be able to find his killer."

"Then what? If you could prove it, you'd have the cops over here now. You're just doing a story. Right? All you care about is your story. Right?"

I said, "Wrong! The killer is still out there. Killing other people. How do we stop that?"

He closed his eyes on my question.

His shop was narrow, just one in a small arcade of other jewelers. Another man dressed in the same white shirt and black slacks came to the door and looked in.

Mr. Josephs leaned to the side of his counter to see around me.

"It's okay, George." The other man disappeared before Mr. Joseph's continued. "I told the detectives everything I know. I don't know what else to add to that."

Cass cut to the chase, "Did your brother have any strong political beliefs."

Josephs looked at her blankly for a moment. The answer he gave was reluctant.

"Yes."

"What."

"He loved Karl Marx. He could quote Karl Marx until the cows came home."

"How about Leon Trotsky?"

"Trotsky too. Always Trotsky this and Trotsky says that. Why does it matter? He was robbed."

"Maybe. But he wasn't killed for the diamonds, I think. How long had he been involved in the politics?"

"Since he was a kid. Twenty, twenty-five years. What do you mean? Do you think an anti-communist killed my brother?"

"No. I think another communist killed him."

This was the first time I heard Cass say this thought outright.

Since Sunday's excursion to the beach, I have shed the skin

off my body like a snake and lost more sleep than I did during the nights after Cass and I went on our first date.

61. Wednesday, July 21, and Thursday, July 22, 1937

Mr. Lehman called Cass at the paper on Wednesday. He had some bad news. All of the visa applications on the Sam Schechner's list had been withdrawn.

I think it dawned on us both more certainly then that the list might be the key. If somehow those names had fallen into the wrong hands, it would have been devastating to Sam Schechner. That and the end of his relationship with Norma Lenz might have been enough to make him lose his grip on things—especially if he suddenly realized that his relationship with her had been the first cause.

We were both at the office when Mr. Lehman's call came in. I'd been fiddling at my own desk, working out some worthy project for myself now that The Boss had hitched me to Cass's wagon, at least figuratively. She came over and sat down in Tom Reilly's chair and looked across at me with that blank face, her mind working over the facts so that I was not sure she even saw me. I waited for her to speak.

She finally says, "What do you think about Norma Lenz?"

"I've never met her."

"If you had, you'd probably say that she was blessed by the chest fairy. You'd say that to The Boss, of course, not to me."

"Okay. I'll take your word for it."

Cass nods. "And I know that some good looking women go for ugly guys. We've all seen that, but Mr. Lenz is as homely as they come."

"Luck of the draw. But he might have a Dale Carnegie personality."

"He's a cold fish. Very surly. I've talked to him twice."

I asked her why she was talking about this now and she tells me about Mr. Lehman's phone call.

It takes about two seconds then for me to catch up with her line of thought.

I say, "Then, maybe we should go talk with Mr. Lenz again?"

"No. I want to talk to Norma first."

And we were off.

This was the middle of the day. Almost noon. Working hours for most people. But Cass had called Mrs. Lenz a couple of times before and gotten hold of her midday so we took the chance and just showed up at her apartment. She was there. And not alone.

She was obviously surprised to see us at the door but didn't open it more than a couple of inches. I couldn't get my brogan far enough in on the doorjamb.

She looks at Cass and says, "Oh. It's you. I don't want to talk to you anymore."

Cass says, "Just a couple questions . . ."

Norma Lenz says, "Enough! I've talked to you enough already. Go away! I'll call the police!"

Cass says, "Why would you call the police, Mrs. Lenz? What are you hiding?"

At that point, Norma Lenz put her shoulder on the door and slammed it.

Now, Cass and I had talked this over quite a bit by the time we got up to Seventy-Third Street, which is where the Lenz apartment is, just off York Avenue. We agreed, it being a man's world and all that, Norma was probably just the go-between in all this. Or perhaps merely the bait.

The likelihood was, she'd gotten hold of the list from Schechner's office, but the key to guys who were trying to kill us had to be her husband. Henry Lenz was in the best position, working at Grand Central and issuing tickets for travel coast to coast. He would be a crucial contact for others. I got myself into the phone booth on the corner and called the office. The Boss has a friend at the F.B.I. by the name of Fred Pell. I figure they ought to be alerted to the possibility that Henry Lenz is a German agent—and likely providing tickets for spies in need of transportation to and from New York.

The Boss tells us, "Avoid any shootouts. Will ya?"

While I'm there in the booth, Cass is standing by outside, and she says, "Golly! Looky there!"

Up the block we see a fellow come out the door of the Lenz's building in a rush. A tall fellow. Thin. In a gray suit. And Cass says "I'll bet my bottom dollar, even at this distance, that is the nice gentleman who was at the top of the stairs shooting at us the other evening."

She is being very arch about it. There wasn't a whole lot we could really do. Especially if he happened to be carrying his gun.

We stood back a little in the booth so as not to be quite as obvious, but he saw us anyway. He actually stopped in his tracks. He looked both ways then, not to cross the street I figure, but to see what his best opportunity was. Then he broke into a flat-footed run toward the stairs at the El on the next block.

I had nothing better to do, so I followed him at a trot.

I have my bag, of course, but I was moving along pretty well. I couldn't hear the drone or screech of a train coming so there was a chance this guy would have to wait for his ride anyway. But he must have had the same thought. At the next corner, he stepped out in front of an off-duty cab and grabbed that.

Cass was right behind me and saw the whole thing. But she's already thinking ahead.

As the cab pulls away in front of us she says, "Let's go down to Grand Central. Maybe you can get a picture of Mr. Lenz."

Thankfully, we could hear the train by then.

Fifteen minutes later, Mr. Lenz was indeed still behind the

brass grill at his counter. He looks up at me first with no clue when my turn came in the line. I got a nice picture of his surprise. Cass stepped up there beside me.

He says, "Why did you do that?"

To the back of the booth I see another of his fellow ticket agents on the phone. From the conversation, I'm pretty sure this guy is placing a pool of bets with a bookie. I'm very grateful for the fact. Mr. Lenz has not been forewarned.

Cass says, "I'd like some more information please."

Lenz is still frowning. "What about?"

There is a round hole in the grill and I got my camera up just right then and got a second picture of him without the bars. But The Boss used the one with the bars, of course. It had a graphic touch to it.

At that point Lenz really knows something is wrong and he jumps up from his stool and heads out. I hustle around to the side and clocked him as he came through the door. This wasn't really fair of me. He didn't have his hands up yet, but I was holding the camera and didn't want a tussle. Where he had sprawled on the marble floor, I held his arm behind his back and kept my knee on his spine, Cass called the cops, but the other ticket agent had beaten her to that.

First thing the cops wanted to do is charge me with assault. Lenz was raising Cain. But at least they kept hands on him as well. I let Cass do the talking, and pretty soon Mr. Pell and another F.B.I. agent came down to the substation there at Grand Central. Before four o'clock, I was released 'on my own recognizance.'

Mr. Lenz is now being held somewhere by the cops. The *Mirror* was the only paper in town that had pictures.

Thursday, I thought we should celebrate and I took Cass to a ballgame at Ebbets Field. Naturally, the Pirates demolished the Dodgers, ten to one. A truly sad affair. This comes a day after a one run win in the tenth on a Winsett single that you would have thought from reading the *Eagle* was a gift from God. But this day, Burleigh Grimes can't manage to get out of his own way. Cass tried to make me feel a little better about it by telling me the hotdogs were a great improvement over the ones they had in Cleveland. That only tells me that the hotdogs at League Park in Cleveland must be the worst. But I didn't argue. I was thinking other things by then.

While she's gone to get the hotdogs I see the empty seat next to me has a copy of a newspaper folded over and left there in a gap. I open that up to see what story someone had found of interest and at the top I see that a Brooklyn lad who had lived right across the street from the ball park, Vincent Rinkunas, has been slain while fleeing the scene of a burglary. The kid was 16 and was evidently already a well-known troublemaker. It is being noted here that his mother stood in her doorway and wept at the additional news when Church officials denied funeral rites—perhaps on the grounds that the boy had gone to his reward unrepentant. But I'm thinking, perhaps the Church ought to have some sort of rites for the living, instead. The dead are beyond caring. And this gets me wondering who Brad Stenis had called to cover that piece of unhappiness. I'm feeling glad just then that it wasn't me.

At this point, below the fold, I see that two 18 year old negro youths, Richard Hawkins and Earnest Ponder, were shot to death by four masked men around 3 a.m., a couple nights earlier, after being forcibly taken from their jail cells just a few blocks from the capitol building in Tallahassee, Florida. The suspected crime of these fellows was breaking and entering and the consequent serious stabbing of the police officer who had first tried to question them. The four unidentified killers of the suspects had paper bags pulled over their heads, but evidently no other distinguishing characteristics for the authorities to follow, even after requiring another policeman to travel the several blocks with them from the station house to the jail and open the six doors between, as well as the cells—and all of this before leaving said policeman (and only witness) bound and gagged. The motive for the murders was clearly explained by five crudely printed placards later left with the bodies, warning all other negroes about harming white people.

And that story was one column over from a smaller lede

about the Scottsboro jurors, in their equivalent wisdom, giving Andy White a sentence of 99 years.

I stashed the newspaper back under the seat where Cass couldn't see it. Sort of takes the bloom off the rose of a day.

62. Monday, July 26, 1937

My next bright idea, I should've had long before. I took Cass down to see Eddy Kim. Eddy's father once worked with my dad on a freighter out of San Francisco. This particular fact I only discovered a few years ago, after I started taking boxing lessons from him.

Eddy Kim is not like most trainers I've seen—stolid fellows who have taken one too many hits in their own time. Eddy is cheerful and always moving and he is seldom in the path of a punch. As he says frequently, in one way or another, his purpose is not to impose rules on the unpredictable, or teach you to win, but to instruct you on the ways that will get you out of a fight alive and in one piece. He is not interested in the 'sport' of doing bodily damage.

One of Eddy's ploys was to talk to you as you sparred with him. The idea there is to distract you. He says, if you can hold a conversation and overcome the distraction at the same time, you can defeat an opponent, or at least have the chance to avoid being defeated yourself. You must always be thinking. And I try. But I have never won a match against Eddy.

When I was fourteen and I'd lost another street battle with someone or another in the neighborhood, my dad had taken me in the door one day and looked at my bloody lip, opened my mouth to check my teeth, and then said, "It's time you went to see Dong-gun Kim."

I knew this name, of course, but by his tag. My older brother Benjamin had been sent to 'Don Juan' before me. It was a rite of passage. It was part of Dad's determination that his sons could handle themselves in a fight.

Dong-gun Kim, better known as 'Don Juan,' has a shop down near the old Fulton Ferry station. He sells various goods there but in the back he conducts a gym for boxing and such. By my time, he no longer taught lessons himself, but had passed this knowledge on to his son, Eddy.

I went there every Saturday afternoon for two years. And it was nearly at the end of this time, when I once thought I might finally have the better of Eddy, considering that he was on his fourth or fifth lesson of the day, that I thought I had a chance to beat him on points. And that's when he says to me in the middle of a round, "My dad once saved your father's life." This got just enough of my attention for Eddy to put me on the mat with a nice whack on the side of my head.

I found out later from Dad that this was true.

The story was this. Evidently, 'Don Juan' had very easily earned his nickname in those days. In 1902 he was in Shanghai with my dad, waiting for a cargo of 'bric-a-brac' to be loaded for their return trip to San Francisco. They were both working for Pacific Mail at the time. Dad would have just turned 21. He'd been newly made second mate on the trip and was celebrating. Don Juan was third mate and there had been some rivalry for the higher posting on the *S.S. Acapulco*.

In some manner which Dad failed to remember quite as clearly as he did the details of the battle itself, he and Don Juan had gotten themselves into trouble with a local dock gang. This resulted in the vessel being caught in port by an attempted extortion—a demand for extra payments for loading the cargo. After negotiations had failed (the additional cost would have come from their own pockets for having caused the rift), they had lost patience and hired a different crew of stevedores to get the job done on time. The replacements were all Koreans, previously abandoned there by a bankrupt Japanese company in Seoul. These fellows had been dis-covered by Dong-gun Kim and Dad during their own carousing in the city. Now, with Seoul being their next stop anyway, the *S.S. Acapulco* offered the Koreans free passage home if they got the job done.

To guard the way during this operation, Dad sat on the pier with his trusty Browning shotgun—the same one he has to this day. It would seem that at his tender age he'd already acquired a reputation for being fierce. Nevertheless, after a short while, the dock gang had finally reconsidered their own position (losing face among the other gangs) and challenged him. The problem was that the guarding with the shotgun was merely a bluff. Dad knew that a shooting would have created an incident involving the Shanghai Port authorities. Those officials were British at the time and already un-happy with the rising American competition for trade. The whole thing would have been blown totally out of proportion.

Instead, Dad had bargained against the Chinese gang's pride, offering to pay a specific sum to any of them who could beat him in a fight without weapons.

For a time then, Dad had defeated individual challengers, one by one in hand to hand combat, while Kim had looked on, holding the Browning 12 gauge. And when Dad had finally faltered, Kim had dispensed with those remaining few. (Only, in Dong-gun Kim's version, it was he who had handled most of the challengers while Dad had done the watching.)

Eddy taught something called "Gungdo,' to some of his Korean customers, which was a sort of archery with a small bow, but to the others he taught 'boxing.' Not Marquess of Queensberry boxing, mind you. Korean boxing—though enough like what Jack Dempsey did to recognize the general form. The most obvious difference was in the use of feet. The biggest difference was in the intent. Korean boxing is ostensibly for self-defense. It was some-thing devised to survive the reality of the ongoing Japanese occu-pation of their nation, while weapons like the bow were illegal. But in fact, it was very offensive in nature, and the purpose is not to put on a show. The simple intent was to overcome an opponent in the fastest way possible. Speed was of the essence. Rules were out the window when your life depended on it.

I should mention that Eddy is five feet, four inches tall.

I should also say here that it was my inspiration that Cass should take lessons. We had already talked about my buying a gun. This is not a bad idea either, but I figured that at least once she might not have me with her—on the steps at her apartment for instance. In any case, in exchange, she had already promised to teach me to shoot. Or at the least to shoot better than I can now.

However, by the way she talks about it, you would not know that this was my idea. She took to the thought as if it were her own. I expressed the notion on a Sunday afternoon and she had me taking her over to Fulton Street on Monday after work.

It is also a matter of note that, after Eddy got over the surprise of her request, that he informed us that she would be the first 'white girl' he ever taught.

It was a fine evening and I walked her home to Sterling Place after her first lesson. We were talking about things in general and what little I knew about Korea in particular, and the conversation naturally shifted over to what was in the news. Not the local news. The larger news of the world that seemed to be getting darker by the day. What with Japan already occupying both Korea and Manchuria and their invasion of China underway.

I wondered aloud if what we were doing was really worth it. Reporting on the lesser failures of civilization didn't seem to matter in the scheme of things. There was always more and more, day by day, and on an ever larger scale.

I said, "We're small potatoes."

She was having none of it. She said, "Speak for yourself, buster."

But I think I'm right.

I said, "True enough. You're a tomato. But me, I'm just a spud. Looking around, I see a whole lot of people who don't give a damn, one way or the other—or else they believe everyone else ought to think the same as they do. Whatever they can get away with is fine, and screw the other guy. Or screw the other guy because he's not one of them. Some days I don't want to read my own paper anymore. Don't want to even look at it. No wonder you like dogs so much."

She wasn't going to back down. Instead she became more vehement.

"I like dogs because they're simple. No questions. You get back what you put in. But dogs aren't saints. They'll stick their noses right up another dog's rear end. They'll eat another dog's food. They run in packs as vicious as any human gang. A male dog will take advantage of any bitch he can catch. A dog will kill another dog for standing up to him. A big dog will kill a small one for the sport of it. Small dogs will kill whatever they can, just for play. Dogs have to be trained to be good. It doesn't come naturally. In the pack, they do what the other dogs do. They do what works for the moment, good or bad. But if you treat a dog well, it'll return the favor. They're honest that way, at least. Humans are not so simple. You treat a person well and then turn your back on them at your own peril. They're only as good as they have to be."

This sounded to me as if matters were getting under her skin too. I aimed in another direction.

"Hah! I thought you were the idealist. I thought you were the one that was after a better world and it was me who was—what did you call me? A pragmatist?"

"Yes. But no. I was wrong, Hugh. That was all backwards. It's you who thinks you can find the truth in things. You're the one who tries to keep things square. You just don't want to tell anyone else how to live, not as long as they leave you alone. I thought that was just your way of getting along. Avoiding things. But it's a philosophy with you, isn't it? Don't laugh! You're the philosopher. Not me! I don't learn from my mistakes. Comes down to it, I'm not all that much better than the rest. I want people to act the way I think they should. And I've been too willing to try and make them do what I want if necessary. That's not good."

That was more tall grass. So I changed direction again. I

couldn't see any safe ground.

"My dad always says, 'Beware the failed reformer. They never blame their ideas, just themselves or someone else for not doing it the right way.' Is that you?"

"I guess it is."

I said, "Then, it's too late for me too."

She knew what I was saying. Whatever she did, I was along for the ride. It just wasn't the right moment for a kiss.

She said, "What do we do?"

Never take yes for an answer.

I said, "Even if we can't find out what happened to Sam Schechner—not for sure—we can put some light on it. We can let people know what's going on. I may not want to tell anyone else how to live, but if they threaten me, or what's mine, I have a right to protect myself. What Sam Schechner proves is that Herr Hitler and his Germany is not so far away. They're already here! And those John Does that Annie Oakley killed might have had it coming, somehow, but I know that Fred Bellows didn't. And it's people like Fred Bellows who'll get squashed if they get in the way of Mr. Stalin's latest scheme. It's pretty obvious that what's good for Mother Russia now is what's good for Stalin. What kind of human being would want to live at the whim of a monster like that? What kind of father wants his kid to goose step for a Hitler? Do Japanese mothers really think it's just swell to kill the Chinese until they do things the way the Emperor wants? It looks to me like there are a whole lot of people who think that way."

This was a sort of kitchen sink dumping of all the things that were on my head just then, and when she didn't give me a smack for it right off, I even tagged on another dark little thought I'd had a few days before.

"I was just thinking that people do the same sort of stuff in Peoria. I was reading about all the bystanders who got killed and hurt when Mr. Baby Face Nelson decided to rob a bank. Yet some idiot always took the guy in afterward and covered for him. People used to talk about him like he was a Robin Hood, just because he'd spread other people's dough around. Same with Bonnie and Clyde. And some crooked flatfoot took short money to look the other way. Or an insurance company paid a ransom for the bank bonds that Nelson stole so there'd be no questions about what they had to cover. And a politician buys himself a house in Florida on a clerk's wages for passing some law to give them all cover. It's all the same game, isn't it? It may not be my bank that was robbed, but no one deserves to die because they went down to the Savings and Loan for grocery money and happened to be in the wrong spot at the wrong time. It ought to be safe enough to walk down the street, don't you think? And it doesn't make the arithmetic that much harder to see that it's the same for a whole country as it is for one person. If the Japanese think they have the right to take as much of China as suits them, should they be allowed to do it? Who's going to be next? The Russians want Finland. The Germans want Czechoslovakia. And they both want Poland. And like my dad said, when he was a young man, Hawaii was doing pretty fine before the U.S. got there. And what the hell are we doing in the Philippines, all the way on the other side of the Earth? Stupid nonsense! People dying for nothing but politics! Maybe you can't turn back the clock, but when does all that stop?"

Cass stops right in the middle of the sidewalk there on Flatbush Avenue by the Con Ed building and stares at me like I've gone completely mad.

Finally she says, "Maybe we need some ice cream so you can cool off before we get you home."

63. Wednesday, July 28, 1937

Wednesday was a pretty stupendous day. But it started slow.

Cass wouldn't go to the flying lesson with me. She said she had work to do. And this made me think that I had to be setting some example, so after a phone call, I headed out to Mineola by myself. This required taking the BMT to Forest Hills, a bus to Floral Park, a wait there and a change to the Garden City bus, and then another change to one going out Old Country Road by Roosevelt Field. This was about an hour and a half of my life, all told, and offered me little encouragement for my coming adventure.

Roosevelt Field is a triangle open on the long side. The larger hangers are off to the left toward Roosevelt Raceway. The empty grandstands at the raceway are barely visible there in the distance. Out toward the open side are several strips of narrow asphalt crossing at odd angles. To the right are smaller hangers and offices. I headed that way.

The flight instructor, Mr. Ryan, was busy. If Cass had been with me he would have been Johnny on the spot, I'll bet. Ryan passes me off to a fella who introduces himself as 'Digby.' This is a guy with an accent that sounded Australian to me at first, but wasn't. His full name is Chauncy Digby. You can't make up a name like that. He's an old Brit who'd shot down half a dozen of the Kaiser's best in 1917 before he lost a leg. Now he teaches. He's also picked up what he calls "the fine American habit of chewing my tobacco instead of smoking it." This he spits out into the slipstream just before he speaks, and it makes you happy he's behind you in the plane. Mr. Digby is thin to the bone, narrow faced, long toothed like a horse, and funny as hell. He likes to tell dirty jokes. I'd never heard any of them before, so the education was not lost, but he tells me he learned every joke he knows from the American pilots who were stationed in France during the war. True or not, that was another crew I would like to have known. But most of them are long dead.

The plane we go up in is an aging Standard J-1, with enormous wings. It's about fifteen years old and looks every minute of it—a gaunt skeleton of wood framing and faded fabric. The fabric was stained in splatters by what I thought at first was oil.

Listening between the lines of Mr. Digby's ground instruction, I get the idea that he takes first timers like me up in one of these older planes to find out if we have the stomach for it. If I feel the need to empty the contents of my particular stomach, I can easily lean out. Just keep my face down, he says. Digby doesn't want any of that backwash. He says the Hispano-Suiza engine is quiet as a humming bee and I'd be able to hear instructions, but I suspect right away his preference for that motor and that plane is because they use less fuel than others. That, and it 'waffles' nicely, as Digby also says. If I passed my first test, next time up he'd do some rolls to see if I could still keep my stomach out of my lungs. More encouragement. After that it would be no time before I could solo. He promised and spat on the grass at our feet to make a fact of it.

The weather was near perfect. The only way that I knew we were off the grass was when the shudder in the frame stopped. He didn't pull up until we were nearly at the fence line and I watched that approach with some amount of worry. The arc of the rise was not as bad as a Ferris wheel. But that only became a roller coaster when he let the plane dip again. Up again. Down. Perhaps this was just a further test of my fortitude. However, we gained a little each time. The sky soon became a hard blue as far as the eye could see. The horizon sunk to a dark charcoal line. I can see the breakers filing in on the beach at Fire Island in close military order. Cars are bugs on a ribbon. The 'waffling' appears to be the buffeting of the afternoon breezes that we hit one after the other like bumps in a road. Digby tells me to take the control stick the way he'd shown me on the ground. But unlike before, the thing is shaking now—more like a shiver and this shiver goes right into my spine. He tells me a dirty joke about that and I laughed involuntarily. "Don't jerk it around," he says. "This old girl doesn't like it." I manage to ease it forward to his satisfaction. Digby says, "You can hear'er breathing harder now, can't you? Pull it back slow again. They like that." We gained altitude once more. And to that he says, "The silence you hear is our girl in dreamland."

But there is no silence. The smooth running of the engine that he must hear is still just a roar to my ears. He teaches me next to play with the flaps, and adds, "That keeps her interest while you're making other plans." I bear on the stick like he says and we turned somewhere above Oceanside. The streets are neat there and all the white houses are just going butter yellow in the late sun. Digby tells me I fly like a natural. But I think he is already looking for the income on his next lesson. My right hand was shaking on the stick from holding it too tight, as if I had a palsy, and my knee caps are dancing all by them-selves. But his jokes are good. He yells them forward and it keeps me from remembering I'm going sixty-five miles an hour, a thousand feet above a hard crust of earth. My one stomach bounce was when Digby turned us in for the landing. He told me afterward that the landing was often when first-timers lost it. Like the last moments when you have to pee and you've been holding it for an hour. A lot of first timers don't make it.

Afterwards I sat in a very steady chair in the office, feeling a little numb. In a little while, my kneecaps steadied as well and my ears cleared and at last tuned into the lonely striking of the keys on a single typewriter. It's then I hear a young woman's voice behind me, gushing my name to someone else, and I turned to look. But she's not talking about me. She's talking about Howard Hughes. Evidently he has a plane being repaired in one of the hangers. It's getting late, but this was a nice opportunity. I grabbed my bag from the locker and went out looking for number '7.'

That is the last and smallest hanger in the row and a good quarter-mile away. My legs are still a little rubbery but the walk across the grass felt good, and the solid ground was reassuring.

The bay doors at number 7 are open to the late sun. The silver-aluminum skin of the plane—a mono plane with a flared nose that looks much smaller than the Standard J-1 that I was just in—is brilliant in the glow. This was the great record-breaker itself. The 'Silver Bullet.' The fastest thing on Earth. I had seen it before at Lakehurst in January when Hughes had broken the coast-to-coast record. Fast but pretty too. Now a cover at the right side of the engine is folded up on a dark interior. There are no sounds of repairs being made. No one seems to be about. I took my best shot then.

Suddenly, with the flash, I hear a "Hey!"

An unkempt fellow who looks like a mechanic in stained overalls rises from a wooden crate against the wall at one side.

I start my usual line of excuse and say, "Hi. I'm from the *Mirror*."

He says, "I don't give a damn who you are. Get out!"

As he comes forward, I can see just who this is. He is a tall fellow, and thin. He hasn't shaved in several days by the look of him. Or bathed, I think. He has the look of someone who has skipped a lot of sleep.

I've always had my own way of dealing with this sort of thing.

I pulled the plate from my camera and handed it out to him.

"Sorry. I didn't mean to intrude. I was just taking the chance."

He stops about five feet away and stares at me.

"How did you know I was here?"

"I just came down from my first lesson. There was a girl in the office who was saying to someone else that your plane was out here being repaired. I just took the chance."

"You came out to see the plane?"

"Yes, sir. She's a beauty!"

He turned on the craft.

"Well, right now she's just a big silver rock."

"You'll get it fixed. You always do."

He looked back at me with a side-glance.

"People have more faith in me than I have in myself, I think."

I said. "Nah. If you can't do it, no one can. You know it. If you didn't, you wouldn't be here."

Which is what I thought was true.

He let out a, "Hrumf," at that. He probably thought I was just trying to butter him up. Then he asked, "Did you like it?"

I knew immediately what he meant. I said, "It was swell. I'm pretty sure there are some things better in life, but I haven't done them yet."

He nods at that, still looking at his plane. "Remember it. The first time is the best. With all the awkwardness and the sweat, it's still the best. Remember it. It gets you through."

He turned away.

I said, "Thanks," and extended the plate to him again.

He looked back and said, "Keep it," and went back to the shadows.

I walked back toward the office feeling pretty good. A fine brick red had come up on the horizon. The low buzz of late arriving planes, and the high-pitched singing of crickets in the grass were among the few sounds to be heard against a steady offshore breeze in my ears.

I was waiting at the bus stop, just a sandy pull-over on Old Country Road, for nearly an hour, before I noticed the small posted schedule on a wooden sign against the fence and realized I'd missed the last one. So I started walking. The crickets by then were louder there than anyplace I have ever been. A real racket. And a nice chill fell in the dark. The odd scattered lights on the field were mostly hidden by the growth along the fence. The sky was a bowl of new stars. I had to stop to look at that. You don't see all of them like that when you are in the city.

But I hadn't really got my bearings enough to be sure what was Jupiter and what was Saturn when a Lincoln limousine with that long hood you see comes up the road with lights blazing and then stops abruptly just beyond me.

A window rolled down and the darkened but familiar face of a woman I'd seen before more than a few times peeked out from behind the steering wheel.

"Do you need a lift? Howard seems to think you might need a lift. Climb in the back."

She talks just like she does.

Whatever conversation they were having before I got in, was ended. You could smell the sweat of Mr. Hughes as plainly as the perfume worn by Miss Hepburn.

Mr. Hughes barely nodded. Miss Hepburn looks to him and then doesn't wait.

"Where do you live?"

"In Manhattan."

"Gosh. That's a long way to come for flying lessons. But I think we can take you all the way home if you like." She looked across at Hughes, but again he said nothing. She asked, "You're a photographer then?"

"Yes."

"How long?"

"For the *Mirror*, about seven years."

"No! You look too young!"

I didn't know what to say to that, other than my usual, "I started early."

Mr. Hughes suddenly spoke, "What made you want to learn to fly?"

What was the true answer to that? To impress Cass?

"Martin Johnson, I think. Maybe Osa."

Miss Hepburn said, "Didn't flying kill him?"

I said, "Yes, but first, I think he lived a whole lot more."

Mr. Hughes let out a full cackle at that. It was slightly shocking given the confines of the car.

Miss Hepburn gripped the steering wheel a little tighter. I suspected this touched on some matter between them.

After a brief silence, Mr. Hughes says, "You'll need your Osa. Don't forget."

And I promptly answered, "I've got her!"

In the front seat the two silhouettes turned to each other.

I reported all this to Cass on the phone last night.

Cass was quiet through most of the telling. Her sentences get short and her voice dips and rises when she's angry. She was angry mostly at herself, I knew. She wished she had gone with me.

Cass asked me, "Did you like it?" I told her what I had said to Mr. Hughes and I got silence to that. Then, "Did you get sick?"

"No. Almost. Once, at the end."

"What was it like?"

I told her what I could. This was not yet digested for better words.

She only interrupted me once, when I told her my answer to Mr. Hughes (with as much drama as I could manage without going on a stage about it), and he said, 'You'll need your Osa. Don't forget.' And I told him, 'I've already got her!'

And Cass answered, "Yeah, I guess that's so. You got me."

64. Thursday, July 29, 1937

Cass was actually pretty burned that I had gotten to meet Katharine Hepburn and not even taken a picture. Maybe that more than for missing the flying lesson. She knows how I think about all that, but I could tell it bothered her. She was less impressed with my meeting Howard Hughes. She thinks of him as a playboy and a tycoon. I haven't been able to change her mind on that. But then again, I find it hard to see Miss Hepburn as anything but a celluloid flame.

Miss Hepburn was very polite in the car on the way into Manhattan. She did most of the talking. Mr. Hughes seemed to be very tired. Exhausted, I think. By pestering me with so many questions, I believe Miss Hepburn was avoiding the awkwardness of my asking anything of her. She is the public figure, of course. Too much is already known, I'll guess, and much of that is likely wrong.

She caught on to the corners in my voice right away and asked, "You were raised in Brooklyn?"

"Yes, Ma'am."

"What does your father do?"

"He and my mom sell stationery and office supplies in Manhattan."

"Ah," she says "but the shopkeeper's life is not for you!"

This sounded a little unfair, so I told her, "Dad was in the Merchant Marine for twenty years and had his fun before he made it through the war. I wouldn't mind doing a little of that myself. But the photography got a hold on me first, I guess."

I could hear Mr. Hughes chuckling at something and then he mumbled, "Osa and Martin, here we come!"

Miss Hepburn asked, "What does your girl say to that?"

"She's already a reporter at the *Mirror* now. I think she likes the idea."

Mr. Hughes chuckled again. His reactions appeared to irritate Miss Hepburn and she said nothing for a time. In the dark I had a moment to appreciate the feel of the fabric of the seat I was on with my hands. A silky velour. The smell of it was not like any car I had ever been in and it came through right between the sweet of Miss Hepburn's perfume and sour of Mr. Hughes' sweat. For a stretch on the Jericho Turnpike she must have been doing sixty, but it was quiet inside. Only the whip of the air at the windows. None of the hundred squeaks and squeals of my dad's Ford.

All of a sudden Miss Hepburn asked, "Does this mean our little ride will end up in Winchell tomorrow?"

I said, "Not unless you ask me to tell him. I don't think this is really news, is it?"

Mr. Hughes, his eyes already closed, says, "Ha!"

This was all very nice to say, but I did keep the ride to myself—and Cass, of course. I handed in the photograph of the 'Silver Bullet' and was pretty happy with that because I was able to lighten up part of the background and found Mr. Hughes still sitting right there, eyes wide, just before he yelled. I gave that to Stenis with the explanation that the plane had only been there on a brief stop-over, but they ran it anyway. Hughes sells papers.

And another thing.

Miss Hepburn asked me if I knew Margaret Bourke-White. I said I'd met her once, but that she moved in different company than I did.

Miss Hepburn came right back at me for that. "What kind of company do you move in?" The skepticism was in her voice.

"Reporters, mostly." I said, "And cops."

"You don't think Margaret is a reporter?"

"With a camera, she's the best!"

"What did you mean then?"

By Miss Hepburn's tone, I figured the quick remark had gotten me in some kind of jam. How was I going to explain something like that?

I said, "She doesn't have to go out at dawn and take pictures of stiffs. She's made it onto a higher rung."

Mr. Hughes laughed a little again, though I had the sense that he was falling asleep. His head had drifted to the side. But my answer seemed to satisfy Miss Hepburn for the moment.

Then she asked, "Does your girl have to write about the 'stiffs?'"

"Yeah. That's how I met her!"

"How romantic."

Somehow, all this had another effect on Cass than I could have calculated, much less expected.

The next afternoon, Cass got me outside for a hotdog and we found some shade at the stoop of a brownstone on 46th Street, beneath a gnarly old tree. The trunk of that tree was encircled by a flat iron grill, and the bark had grown into it so that the metal was imbedded and this somehow bothered me. I know that grill was intended to protect the tree but it seemed that now it had imprisoned it. And this occurred to me as a harsher metaphor. Cass loves metaphors. And I was expounding on this very point. But she wasn't answering me as she usually does.

She already had a funny look on her face. I did not yet know what was on her mind but I had my guesses. First off, she didn't want to be living at my parents' house in Brooklyn, even though she was grateful for that. And she had not yet given up her apartment on 19th, even though Ellen had already informed her that she was not coming back. I still had my place on Perry Street and was sleeping there but not very well. Every odd sound had me up off the couch. I had a bar on the door now and an exit plan for the fire escape. Dad had offered me his Browning shotgun, just in case, but I refused that because I hadn't fired it but a few times before. It has a kick. I might hit the wrong thing.

Just about then I realized Cass was talking to me in that tone of voice that she has reserved for special occasions. When she's feeling romantic. Like that night we first went up to the Savoy. But here we were sitting on a stoop on 46th Street.

I had mustard on my lip, and suddenly she kissed that off.

Then she says, with no extra explanation, "I was thinking that maybe we should move in together. Now."

I'm not sure what was on my face just then besides mustard but I imagine I looked like a fool with his mouth open. All my guesses had been wrong. And I had about a dozen thoughts on this at once. But they couldn't all come out of my open mouth at the same time.

One thought was this: why had she chosen that particular place and moment to say this? If it were me, I would have made a little more of an elaborate production around the occasion.

Another thought was about whether she'd been talking to Barry George lately, because this had been his suggestion to me. And what would my mom think of the idea. Or did she already know? Or guess?

What about Cass's father? I knew from her own stories that he was a man of fairly strict principles, religious or not. However, I also knew that my own father would simply say, 'That's fine!'

But I also knew she wanted a full wedding. Why was she giving that idea up?

Then again, I had thought the same thought, at least a hundred times a day, for months. Long before we had the Nazis and the Mob gunning for us. So what could I say?

Essentially, it all came down to one answer.

"Great! I think that would be great! We can get married at City Hall. Maybe I can even get my friend Fiorello to officiate."

Now, she looks rather stunned, as if I might have said something else. Or maybe she had worried that I would. So I kissed her back. I sort of picked her up then I think. As suddenly as I had all those other thoughts, I was not thinking a whole lot about anything else.

And just then an old gent in a homburg comes out the door above us and grunts and says, "Pick up your garbage!" as he slips by.

Half of Cass's hotdog and the wax paper and both our pickles had fallen on the sidewalk at our feet.

Now this is the actual story.

Cass got the idea that we ought to speed things up only about two minutes before she came over to my desk to ask if I'd like to step out for something to eat. The inspiration for it was all of those things that were on both our minds, I guess, but she could not tell me exactly why it came to her the way it did just then. I think she'd even surprised herself. Spontaneously. I was just happy it did.

We picked up our garbage and went down to City Hall together and got the license, and I called over to Doctor Raymond who had been the family doctor for about twenty years and made an appointment and then we went back to the office.

All hell had broken loose there.

A perfectly calm summer afternoon had gone completely nuts—just about as fast as everything else had changed for the two of us again, once Cass had made up her mind.

There was a four-alarm fire at 149th Street. Three buildings were involved. And a tugboat had accidently rammed a private yacht in the East River and the yacht had gone to pieces and sunk. There was no accounting yet for who was on board the yacht, but a Wall Street broker and three other people had been picked up out of the water. The tugboat had sustained little damage.

And a mobster named Victor Neims had been found dead in the trunk of a stolen car parked in a vacant lot in Hell's Kitchen.

Cass and I went over to Hell's Kitchen to confirm the death of Mr. Neims, first thing. Most of the additional details unknown to us already amounted to the fact that he had been dead for more than a day and the sun on the trunk of that black car had done a fair job of cooking his remains. We smelled it before we saw it.

Because two of the copywriters were out 'sick' (vacation time being in short supply during the summer), Cass did the re-writes on the fire and the collision in the East River that were handed in by stringers. I went uptown for a couple extra shots on the fire, just in case.

We were both free by nine, when The Boss got back from his dinner, and we went in to see him together.

The date set for the event was now Monday, August 9th. I wanted at least the two weeks after that off. The Boss cursed, and then offered us one. This was an impasse that had me ready to quit. I appreciated George's predicament, but no job was worth every min-ute of my life. The longest vacation I'd had in memory was when I was knocked on my back for a couple of days by the cops. Cass looked grim, but said nothing. I did all the arguing.

He says, "What'dya think, I got a glass eye? I can see right through you. Paid honeymoon! Where's the end of it? I saw this coming. I should fire you both for canoodling on the job."

Then, out of the blue, Cass says to George, "We could do a travelogue. 'Coast-to-Coast on the *20th Century Limited*'"

George quickly informed her that the *20th Century Limited* stopped in Chicago. "Of course, given the budget, you might want to walk the rest of the way."

Cass looked at me sheepishly and objected, "Why doesn't it go coast-to-coast?" But then recovered a little dignity with a better wording, "How about 'Coast-to-Coast *in* the Twentieth Century.' We could fly back on one of those new DC-3 sleepers. That would broaden the reader interest of the piece plus save a little time."

Despite this previous tone, George sighed loudly at last, gave the mess before him on his desk a pat with both hands at once, and then said, "Right!" He said that with all of the unhappy resignation he could muster.

I was wondering myself just how much privacy there was in a DC-3 Sleeper Transport.

65. Friday, July 30, 1937

First thing in the morning, Cass went uptown to do a follow-up story on the families who had been displaced by the four-alarm fire in the buildings on 149th Street, and I went along with her for more pics.

On the way, Cass tells me she called home to Cleveland the night before and told her mom and dad the news. Her dad had immediately insisted that they would buy their tickets today and be in New York on the 7th of August. They wanted to be here for the event, even if it was at City Hall. Besides, they wanted to meet my parents. And me, of course. Mr. Green had also asked his daughter to find a clean hotel with reasonable rates for them. Cass said she knew of a nice place in Brooklyn at the right price. I asked if her mother was very disappointed with the fact that the wedding would be small. She told me that her dad and mom had gotten married by a justice of the peace in Girard, Pennsylvania, because they wouldn't wait the extra week in Ohio.

After that I went down to Grand Central Station to see about our own tickets.

One other thing: *The Normandie* has been in port twice in recent weeks and Cass has asked me about that. It would be in port again the second week of August. Should we spend the additional money and take the extra week to go to France?

This was sweet of her to ask. She would have done it, if I'd insisted. But we couldn't afford it. And Barry George was already in a fix to cover for us at the paper on such short notice.

And a funny thing. I had to go to the very same window to get our train tickets that I'd been to recently to take a picture of Mr. Lenz. The other ticket agent who'd been helpfully on the phone that day by placing bets was the very one who helped me now. I gave him the hundred-dollar bill from my stash plus a few fifties I'd taken out of my savings account and got the private compartment for both legs of our journey, New York to Chicago and Chicago through to San Francisco. He examined those large bills very carefully. Counterfeiting was the new rage in some circles. The Germans were printing up a storm according to the papers. And the whole time, he's giving me the eye, wondering where he has seen me before. That's what I thought, at least.

We left the office together around eleven. Cass said she had to do her laundry, and I wasn't tired, so I gave her a kiss at the steps of the Third Avenue El and walked home from there. It was a good night for it anyway. Above the streetlights, you could almost see the stars.

But Friday nights, things are happening all over and there is much else to see. People are dressed up and in a hurry to get some-place. Heels tap briskly against cement. In the summer, and without coats, the costumes that pass for dress are often gaudy with color and sequins or sleek with black silk. Every gal appears in the shape of her promises. Every guy is a gentleman. The nightclubs are busy, and each one with waiting lines that stretch out the doors and onto the sidewalks and present a gallery of the best and worst—in and out of fashion. Romeos loosen ties for the duration and Juliets undo buttons and bend to slip tight shoes loose from pinched feet. It's a sight repeated half a dozen times on my way.

Add to that, there are a couple of hookers on nearly every block. The newly arrived (or re-arrived from a quick bit of business) among that number, stand up straighter, with a hand on a proud hip, and offer a worthy presentation of their natural gifts. The less fa-vored are slouched against the available mailbox or across the fender of a parked car. Except for the taxis, cars on the street are all agleam in the lights as they pass.

The paper said it was going to rain the next day and I guessed they were right for once. There was a cold chill rising off the harbor to break the summer heat. The trouble with that was I had goose bumps pretty quick and hadn't taken notice of the hairs on the back of my neck for awhile.

When I was suddenly aware, it was as if I'd been tapped on the shoulder. My second guess is that I'd been followed all the way from 45th Street, but only first noticed when I turned off Madison onto 34th. What I saw then was just a shadow that moved out of sight a little too quickly as I looked back. The Empire State Building is dead ahead and the lights there are up high and cast a glow on the street, but it's brighter that way in any case and the traffic is steady. I was going to turn again on 5th Avenue but I got the bright idea to go down 6th because I could grab the El from there, first chance. This turns out to be a bad idea, not only because I hear no trains coming but because it's darker under the tracks there. The streetlight doesn't travel as far beneath the steel structure of the El and the signage is that much lower and obstructs much of that.

I stopped several times to catch some other glimpse of what might be behind and thought I saw something at least once again. But when you stop, if there is a hooker close by, she'll come your way immediately. Maybe two, from opposite directions, both look-ing for the same business. It confuses the situation. This night, there seemed to be more of them in the shadows than usual. But then again it is Friday and lately, while things in the country have generally taken a turn for the worse, I have been too busy most Friday nights to notice.

I did walk a little faster and by the time I get to 19th Street I have another idea. I always have the key to the door of my dad's shop and I turned in there, only to get my wits knocked out of me almost at once by a woman in an overcoat huddled there against the glass. She says, "Hello sweetie. Come to keep me warm?" She might as well have said, 'Gotcha!' I let out a fairly loud yell in surprise, probably more of a shriek. This scared the poor woman half to death and she scurried away, heels clacking.

Inside I called the cops. The conversation with the woman on the other end of the line is humorous, only if you're in the mood. I give her my name and the address first thing.

She says, "What's the problem?"

"I'm being followed."

"Who's following you?"

"I don't know. It may be a Nazi spy."

I actually said that. What was she was going to think of that? When I realized how stupid this sounded, I tried to cut through her next questions, which were asked in a tone of someone dealing with a lunatic, and I said my name again, and told her that I worked for the *Mirror* and I had reason to think a Nazi spy might be following me.

Five minutes later a foot patrolman is at the door tapping the glass with his billy club. I start to explain the situation, but then a patrol car pulls up behind him. It's suddenly become a street party outside, with the curious passersby stopping to see what the show might be.

The officers in the patrol car offered to drive me the rest of the way home and I accepted, though the fellow following me had probably moved on.

The phone was ringing when I opened the door on Perry Street. It was Cass. She was worried because I hadn't answered before. I'd already decided not to tell her the details of my own adventure until the next day. Besides, the phone at Sterling Place is in the front parlor and you can hear conversations up the stairwell all the way to the fourth floor. But she had her own story.

There was a fellow on the subway platform at 42nd Street. She'd caught him looking at her in an odd way and ignored it at first, but suddenly realized he'd managed to get directly behind her just before the next train arrived. She quickly stepped aside then and looked him directly in the face. There were a dozen people close-by, but he had actually moved toward her a little before reconsidering and then walked away and down the steps again. He was a non-descript sort of man. Not tall. With a mustache. A dark tie. His hat was pulled low on his forehead.

This was my theory in practice. Some women don't think twice about a man looking at them. But I'd already expressed this bit of wisdom to her more than once and kept the thought to myself under the circumstances.

66. Saturday, July 31, 1937

My chief worry, of course, is for Cass. True, she's become a little more savvy, but not nearly enough. Then again, I'm not as sharp as I should be, either.

Saturday afternoon I covered another funeral, in the rain; this one for a woman whose distinctions were read aloud to the assembly at the graveside. She may also have been a good friend, a loving mother, and an adored wife. But none of that was said. She appears to have belonged to every civic organization on earth. She evidently bred horses and dogs and was well known in the best circles at Belmont Park and a ribbon winner at the Westminster Dog Show. Unluckily, I could not find a wet eye in the crowd, even in that drizzle, and was forced to play off on the dampened scenery there at Woodlawn for a decently somber picture of the assembled.

Cass worked late again on Saturday, with the intention of cleaning up a couple of the piles on her desk before our departure. There were no more assignments on the board for me so I sat nearby and read my book. This is something short, called *Of Mice and Men*. The length is the reason I picked it out after finishing *Northwest Passage*, but it's a nasty little story and I wish I was back with Rogers Rangers and only worried about getting scalped.

It is a fact that the sight of someone reading gets Cass's eye faster than a hard stare. She kept looking up from her desk and me.

I say, "What's wrong?"

She says, "I haven't even read that one yet! You're reading

more than I am now!"

I say, "I don't work as hard as you do. But don't let that discourage you. I'll be needing your support when I become a professional layabout and wanderer. I still have a lot of reading to catch up on."

She says, "There's no time for it, lately. The world is going around too fast."

I say, "Someone should really invent a time machine—but one that just makes more time."

She says, "And what would you do if you had it?"

And I say, "Spend more time watching you."

But she is not buying my blarney tonight.

We left the office after midnight. I went up the steps at 42nd Street with her and waited for the train. There are a lot of people about but not one that causes a single hair on my neck to rise.

As I write this, I know I should have gone at least as far as 14th Street with her. But it's such a strange way to be thinking. The idea that someone might be looking to kill you for what you know is hard to understand. No more I guess than someone wanting to kill you for what you believe. But I have to make myself see things differently now.

67. Sunday, August 1, 1937

Mr. White is back. He's looking fairly worn-out and I don't know if that is from his job, wherever he had been working recently, or his traveling and lack of sleep.

The interesting thing is that, unlike our first encounter, he shook my hand soon after I came in the door. The less happy thing, perhaps, is that he will be taking Stacy and Gary back to Detroit with him. He is working at the Ford plant in Dearborn and says he likes it there. (He works at a furnace pouring molten metal for parts. This cannot be so pleasant.) And he's found a house for them to live, in a nearby town called Inkster. An actual house. He says it's pretty small, but there is a yard. Stacy looked uncertain but hopeful.

I left Gary to his father and spent my time before dinner pestering Cass. Cass was already in the kitchen trying to help Mom with the cooking so this was no simple matter.

Most weekday evenings, my mom will let Stacy help her, but otherwise no one is allowed in the kitchen when she cooks. Today she is moving a little more slowly and saying everything she does out loud so that I hear her first in the hall before I realize that this is done so that Cass could follow along. Meanwhile, Stacy is not there and Cass is chopping whatever she is given to chop and stirring whatever she is told to stir. This is all very domestic and it has got my complete attention. But I cannot resist occasional smart remarks.

I say, "Why are women more beautiful in the kitchen?"

This is easy bait. I figure it will get a bite from both Mom and Cass.

But Cass gives it a good leaving alone and says, "Maybe it's just the flush from the heat."

I say, "Wait! I've got to get a picture of this! Let me get my camera. I never expected to see you in a kitchen. Maybe it won't happen again."

Mom says, "Be quiet, Hugh. Maybe you'll learn something. Wash your hands and peel the potatoes."

I protested, "But I already know how to peel potatoes."

She says, "After that you can take out the garbage and then set the table so that Stacy has a little more time with Mr. White."

Despite the beauty of the scene, as soon as I could manage it, I went looking for my dad. He was in the parlor, reading the paper.

First thing he says is, "The Japanese are in Peking."

There was no refuge in that. After a few dire predictions from him and as few words as I could get away with, I went along to the basement to file some of the pictures I have taken in the last few weeks. The pile there is thick. Besides, it's cooler down there. The fan that I use to blow the heat away when the furnace in the winter is switched on and this also knocked down the sounds from the various conversations going on.

Gary came along soon afterward. I said hi, but he stood in the door quietly and didn't seem to know what to say to me.

I said, "I hear you're going to Michigan."

He says, "Yup," The glum on his face was unavoidable.

I say, "You'll have to send me copies of your pictures so I can keep up with your progress."

This seemed to confuse him. I figured the reason.

"If you can, you better haul some of these trays and developer with you too. It'll fit together very neatly in a box about this big." I held up my hands. "You think you can carry that along? I'll ask your father."

He gets the drift now. "I can keep your camera?"

"It's yours, now. I thought you knew that."

He's an emotional kid and he gave me a hug. We sat on the

stools then until dinner was ready and I wrote up a short list of the things he'll need and then a program for him to follow. He still had trouble with shots that were too bright and too dark because he wasn't using a flash for fill. The bulbs cost too much. I gave him the name of a company in New York where he could write away for a gross at a time to make it cheaper whenever he had saved enough for it. This was my big advice of the day: never pass up a job you can handle, and always save a little.

68. Monday, August 2, 1937

Monday morning George waves me into the office. Cass is already there. The Boss tells me to close the door.

Cass is sitting away in the corner and gives me wide-eyes as I come in. She's got her pleated green dress on and she's looking pretty swell.

George begins, "I have decided that it would be in our best interest, given this latest business with you being followed, that we make some adjustments." That was his preamble.

At this point I figure he is about to fire us both. The word has come down from upstairs that the budget cannot bend enough for our little adventures and he has to let us go. I actually maybe thought that for at least an instant. George gave me plenty of time for the idea while he lit up a cigarette and inhaled the first smoke down into his toes. He seems to be enjoying his little calculation, whatever it is.

I winked at Cass anyway, and say, "So, what's up?"

George, who is usually not lost for words, starts some verbal dancing.

"It's like this. You have to give a little on some things. Or a lot, on others. That's just the way it is." I figure this was his excuse. He puffs on his cigarette and looks thoughtful. Then, "Hearst has this *Journal-American* merger going pretty strong now, right off the blocks. But they're looking for more talent." That was the set up. He shrugs, "I told Gauvreau about Cass's idea for writing a travel piece. I knew that was going to be a squeeze for us. We don't usually do travel pieces unless they're for people going to Atlantic City or the Poconos. But no! Right off he says 'Fine.' So I figure there is something up with that, and he knows I know, so he lets me in on it." This was the dodge and feint. Now the left hook. "He tells me that the Hearst people have their eye on Cass for the *Journal-American*." Another pause and a puff. His eyes slide back and forth between Cass and myself. Cass has not changed her expression and is giving me more attention with her eyes than George. He says, "It will mean a substantial raise, you understand. And a by-line. Feature work." But he's reading my Irish face like a postcard. "Unfortunately for you, they don't want another photographer over there just yet." And then the other qualification. "However, if Cass goes quietly, they'll loosen the purse strings on this end," and, finally, his justification, "and I'll be able to hire two reporters to replace her."

Cass looks quickly out the window at a pigeon on the sill. I can see the guilt rising in the color of her cheeks. I feel like the pigeon.

Now I'm supposed to buy the idea that The Boss would think any two reporters he can find will be as good as Cass?

I say, "Well, if it's okay with Cass, I think that's great! But we're still getting married in one week and we'll be gone for the two weeks after that."

George heaves a heavy breath, "Thing is, they really want her over there today."

This was pure posturing. I hear the word 'really' inserted in that sentence and know it's a phony. And he knows I'll know it. He's just doing his duty on the part of the Hearst Corporation. The tightwads in accounting can't complain that he didn't try.

Cass finally speaks, "No deal! I'm getting married next Monday. Either that or else I'll already be dead."

George is obviously not the least surprised at the answer. Not a flinch. But his face is now a little more serious.

He says to Cass, "By the way, I've hired a guy named Flynn from the Byron Agency to keep an eye on you for a while, especially evenings, at least until after you leave."

I say, "What kind of guy?"

"A private dick. He might be able to spot whoever it is following Cass around."

I say, "Don't I get my own private dick? They're following me around too."

The Boss gives me one of those looks you can't measure.

And then suddenly I have the picture.

I say to Cass, "What did you say before I got here?"

She wags her head back and forth. She knows I'm onto her. "I just said I liked the idea, but that it was up to you."

George steps right in on that. "Look! It's a good deal, all right. Even better! For both of you! The only thing is you won't be working together. Not for awhile at least." He sees us looking at each other for some more answers, so he adds, "I said better! So let's cut to the chase. Here's the sweetener. Something I think you'll both appreciate. I was supposed to negotiate this out and give it up only if you both refused." His smile is as false as his frown was before. "They'll give you the two weeks for your honeymoon, and two weeks more. FOUR WEEKS! Take your time. See the sights. A paid vacation! Except for the series of travel articles you'll be doing, of course. Remember to keep your notes on that. File your stories as often as you can. But you've got through the first week in September. You should be getting pretty tired of each other by then."

All of this is sounding pretty good to me, but my dad's rule is that nothing is free. Everything costs somebody something.

I say, "And what else?"

George delivers a sorrowful sigh. As counterfeit as he can make it.

He looks at me. "Gauvreau wants to see how you'd handle a little close-up work. Personalities. That sort of thing."

I tell The Boss what he already knows. "I don't like show people."

"You don't have to like them. Just show them."

It was a fair request. At least for the moment. But there was something more.

"What else?"

The Boss has this all down like there'd been a rehearsal.

"Gauvreau wants to see if you can get along with Winchell."

Nobody gets along with Winchell. Not even Gauvreau.

"You mean before they fire me?"

"No. If you do this for me, I promise I'll take you back if it doesn't work out. In the meantime, it'll mean an extra ten bucks a week."

I took Cass to lunch at The Palm to celebrate. We didn't have the dough to pay for the extra two weeks honeymoon, but I figured we could borrow it. Every good marriage starts out in debt. That was the American way, wasn't it?

We stayed at the Palm about an hour too long. The waiter got antsy. But there was a lot to talk about, and not much eating or drinking—even with the steak and wine. Cass thought the whole thing with the job offer was ironic, so I add to that, and I tell her about another of Miss Hepburn's comments on our long drive from Mineola to Manhattan. This one concerning Margaret Bourke-White and recalling the first meeting between the photographer and the actress. It was a titbit I had not related to Cass before because she already has an idea I have a crush on Bourke-White (which I do—or did), and she might have taken it the wrong way. Once before, I had mentioned that it was a great coincidence that she and Miss Bourke-White were both from Cleveland, and Cass wanted to know why that would even qualify as unusual much less a coincidence.

Miss Hepburn had said to me, "When Maggie was assigned by Mr. Luce to take pictures of all the new young things who'd turned up in Hollywood that year, for *Fortune Magazine*, Maggie hated the assignment." (She actually called her 'Maggie,' so I knew right away that they must be friends now.) "That was 1932, you must remember, and there was grim news all around. Maggie was used to photographing machines and powerful men who stand and make things, and she thought we girls were all a bunch of ninnies. But she took the best pictures of me that anyone has ever managed to do. I wish I looked as good in real life. Producers were always disap-pointed when they actually met me after seeing those photos."

I was surprised. I admitted that I'd never seen these pictures myself.

Miss Hepburn had tossed a hand in the air as if to say 'of course,' a sweeping silhouette against the blaze of oncoming lights on the windshield. "They never ran them in the magazine, I think. Just like Hollywood never uses the best take. RKO passed them around like crazy but Mr. Selznick thought they made me look too regal. Maggie sent copies to me with her apologies."

I admitted to Cass that my urge to reject the offer when The Boss presented the idea of me taking pictures of 'ninnies' had been stifled by knowing that Bourke-White had been able to handle the same assignment in her turn. Cass gave me the skeptical eye.

That evening I kept an eye all around as we walked down to 42nd but I don't see any private dick in the shadows. There seemed to be nothing doing, but I went with Cass on the train as far as 14th Street.

69. Tuesday, August 3, 1937

Cass spent most of the day over at the *Journal-American* getting her introductions. She was back at her desk at the *Mirror* around four o'clock and we went out then for coffee at the new Horn & Hardart on Madison and ate rice pudding. Rice pudding calms her down.

Along about six, on his way out to The Algonquin, the Boss stops by her desk and tells her that Flynn, the private dick, has called him to say she ought to be getting off at a different stop on the way home every night. If the bad guys are waiting, Cass doesn't want to be making their job too easy.

That seemed like good advice to me. She shakes her head, but she'll start doing it.

For dinner I bought her a corned beef sandwich and she ate that at her desk so that she could catch up on more of her work before our great adventure.

We left the office for home at ten, moving pretty fast because suddenly I wasn't feeling very calm at that point myself.

Again, I didn't see a thing. And no private dick.

We stood back on the platform by the rail. There is an emergency stair at that end which is closed off at the bottom and that seemed like a reasonable escape. I studied everyone else waiting along the platform in front of us. This was about as average a lot of heathens and criminals as you would encounter at any subway stop. Not one of them appeared to have more than a passing interest in us.

And this seemed a little odd to me.

One of the guys, about ten feet away, is young. Likely in his twenties. He's reading the paper. And he hasn't taken so much as a peek at Cass. If I were in his spot, I would have peeked several times. Cass is holding onto my arm and not gently because she sees I'm a little worried.

I stick a cigarette in my mouth, tell Cass I'll be right back, and go over to this guy and ask him if he has a match.

He looks me right in the eye then and says in a real soft voice, "Go back over there with Miss Green, will ya, and stay away from me." Then a little louder he shakes his head and says, "I don't smoke."

At least I got that one right.

70. Wednesday, August 4, 1937

Cass covered a piece about refugees today. This is annual fare. It was just her turn, I guess. There is always an argument going on about who they are letting in and how many.

We went out to Ellis Island and sat in an office for several hours waiting for some sort of 'okay' to speak to a few of the people being detained for one reason or another. There are a lot of stories floating around these days about this. Her piece was supposed to be about Italians trying to escape from the new paradise in Mussolini's Italy, but it ended up being a rough piece on the idiot Director who is managing the office and makes everyone's lives more miserable after they get this far. When she interviewed him, it comes out pretty quick that this fellow doesn't like 'wops.' And when the story appears, it's going to be hard for him to deny he used the term. I was there. But the pictures were nothing new because we were not allowed to roam. I filed an objection to that immediately but that likely never made it beyond the round file next to the desk where I left it.

Otherwise, I'm getting a lot of reading done even though I have been picking up on any loose assignments that I can. My name has not been on the general assignment board in several days.

71. Thursday, August 5, 1937

I went over to the Scribner store on Fifth Avenue today and bought four new books in preparation for our trip. I figure we can't actually be making love all the time, and looking out the window is not going to keep us occupied after dark, so I picked up a few novels. For myself I got *Beat to Quarters,* which looks like a nifty sea story, and a romance for Cass called *Out of Africa,* and in the spirit of things I couldn't refuse either book but both are fairly light weight and easy to carry. The good-looking clerk who recommended the African story seemed a little less happy when I told her it was for my fiancé (I could tell this girl was from Brooklyn too). Funny how suddenly I'm noticing a lot of other choice girls. That's got to be some kind of perversity given that I've already found the best.

I also found a volume of poems by Robert Frost with the hope that I could get Cass to read some of them aloud to me. I saw Norma Shearer do that to Frederick March once in a movie and it seemed pretty romantic. For Cass I also bought *Women Called Wild*, a collection of true stories about ladies who didn't stay in the kitchen, by a journalist named Rosita Forbes. Just for the title alone. But it looks like just the kind of thing she'd like.

Cass covered a school committee hearing concerning the fall budget. LaGuardia was supposed to be coming in from his summer residence to address this bunch and I couldn't bear the thought of it and managed not to be around when she went off. One of the stringers followed her and was happy for the chance because the air-conditioning in the office at the *Mirror* is on the fritz.

Instead, I went downtown to cover a protest over the banning of organ grinders and hurdy-gurdy men. It seems you hardly ever see those old fellows these days anyway, though at least forty of them filled the plaza out in front of City Hall, each of them churning up a storm. A couple of the monkeys got in a tiff over some bit of food and that was a comic scene that brought a tight crowd. Cass would have liked this story a lot better. The streets will not be the same without those guys and their tricks. And this reminded me that I haven't seen a potato man in years. Used to be that the smell of roasting spuds was what gave any autumn breeze some flavor. Chestnuts are not the same.

Pelligrini, the Potato Man, with his floppy, broadbrim hat and wide, hand embroidered, suspenders was once a fixture over by the War Memorial at the Grand Army Plaza and this was a regular stop whenever Mom took us to the zoo.

I remember a time I was scared out of my wits by one of those monkeys.

Likely I was about five or six years old and feeling mighty. The organ grinder's capuchin was performing nearby on the paving stones, dancing from one to the other like they were pieces on a checkerboard. This little guy had a red and green jacket on and a jeweled hat that appeared to be glued to his head the way it stayed in place with every jump. Suddenly one of the potatoes that Pelligrini was handing out—I think that one was for Kate—practically leapt from her fingers, so hot it burned her through the newspapers that the old fellow liked to use for a wrapper. The spud burst open on the stones with a puff of steam when it hit. Kate squealed and I stooped to grab it up but the monkey beat me to it and turned his ancient small face up at me, only inches away, bared his teeth and hissed. I let out a yelp that had Esther immediately laughing but this only hurt my pride at being so easily frightened. The organ grinder was saying something loud in Italian to the monkey, while Pelligrini was saying to us, "You have another! I have another!" And my mom was advising, "Let the little beast have it!" But I was determined then and I snatched at the potato again with my left hand while distracting with my right, and retrieved it. At that, the monkey, in the most theatrical fashion, turned his head down as if shamed.

Suddenly I felt like a complete bully for my action and set the spud back. But the little beast wasn't the least bit thankful. He must have been used to winning his battles with that act. He simply began dishing the white meat out into his mouth by the handful while ignoring me.

It was a good memory. I even recall that the monkey had bad breath and several darkened teeth.

But this is Mr. LaGuardia's doing again. He doesn't think the organ grinders give the right image to Italians and he has banned all such permits. In the meantime we haven't heard a peep from the Mayor concerning the jerk at Ellis Island who doesn't like 'wops'—that story appeared this morning and Cass tried in advance to get a comment out of City Hall.

On Broadway near City Hall, and right in front of the Woolworth building, I got a nice shot of three old fellows who'd set themselves up in a row with their monkeys—one had a parrot—and at least five cops right behind, about to arrest them as soon as they turned a note. Stenis thought it might make the front page tomorrow.

72. Friday, August 6, 1937

It rained cats and dogs in the morning. Even the dogs didn't make Cass any happier. Still no assignments on the board for me so I volunteered to go down to Coney Island and take some shots on the washout there. Sad young ladies in bathing suits and holding umbrellas in the rain were a sure-fire interest. But before I left, Cass gets a call from one of our guys in Staten Island. There was a body on the beach at Princes Bay.

Stenis told her not to take it.

The Boss told her she should leave it to someone else.

It took her about two minutes to get halfway to the door. I think she's stir crazy. But this was a schlep. I tell her it's a couple of hours by subway, ferry and bus. In the rain it would be worse. Cass turned on her heels and begged Stenis for a car and he okayed it without asking George, and then we were out the door. It meant going through the Holland Tunnel, down route 27 again, and around to Perth Amboy. Longer as the crow flies—only 45 minutes on a sunny day, but an hour and a half in traffic snarled by rain.

By the time we got there, what remained of the body was on ice in a temporary tank in the basement at the 123rd Precinct station house in Tottenville until the City Morgue could send out a truck.

The matter of interest with this was pretty obvious. The dead guy had both his eyes blown out. And he was naked. Given the condition of the body, it was hard to say, but the Sergeant there estimated the fellow was between forty and fifty years old. Definitely not young. One foot was oddly shaped and missing the large toe. And one additional thing. He had a tattoo on his upper right arm.

I took a couple of shots on the tattoo in different light. It was the sort of thing that kids get in the navy. Maybe even cruder. Perhaps done aboard ship by an amateur. What might have been difficult to read before was now near impossible. But the skin over the flesh of the guy's arm had gone translucent and just beneath the surface the ink had held up pretty well. Well enough.

Many sailors get markings such as this, for some reason— I've heard it said they do it so that their bodies can be identified after the fact, if the ship sinks. Like a cattle brand. And with the positive still wet, you could see this one had a single star above a name, 'Norman,' and then 'USS Wyoming.'

By the time we had that much to go on, it was four o'clock, and Cass was already on the phone trying to catch anyone at the Navy Department who had not yet left work for the weekend. Within half an hour we were going through the phone book by a process of elimination. By five, Cass had reached George Norman, who lives on Prospect Avenue in the Bronx. He has not seen his brother Charles in over a week. He agreed to talk to us.

The rain had quit and the late sun was yellowed.

George Norman is a decent looking sort of fellow. A little overweight. Clean shaved. Balding. By his speech it's pretty clear he was born and raised right there in the Bronx. The house is a small white clapboard sandwiched among a dozen just like it. A nice neighborhood. There were kids already playing stickball on the street. Mr. Norman let us in immediately.

His first words after hello were, "Is he dead?"

When the door was closed, Cass said that it was likely. We had seen a body and she described the tattoo.

"Yeah. That's him. How did he die?"

There was no emotion in this question. But I thought that might only be a front. He looked at me, when he asked this, so I answered.

"He was murdered."

There was no immediate reaction to that either—at least no emotion on the man's face.

Cass said, "I'm sorry."

Mr. Norman said, "He was asking for it, ya know. I told him that. He was hanging around with the wrong sort."

"Criminals?"

"Nah. Not exactly. Rabble rousers."

We were standing in a small foyer. Pictures of an older couple and more than a dozen children flanked us on the wall by the stairs. In one of the older pictures, two young boys look at the photographer with grins of mischief. I was immediately thinking these were the two brothers in happier times. At the other wall, a grandfather clock ticked into the silence of the house. The ticking marked off several seconds before Mr. Norman continued. I was very sure then that his composure was willful.

He tells us, "Charlie was injured in the Navy. Crushed foot. He had a pension but it was small. Not enough to cover much. As he got older he became, what you'd call, bitter. Patrice—his wife—left him. She couldn't take it. I was the only one in the family he ever spoke to. Mostly to argue. He had to borrow money almost every week and every week he got into an argument with me about some damn thing or another. I think he actually wanted me to refuse to help."

I knew that she'd ask the question anyway, but I was impatient. Actually, I was hungry. I wanted to get this part done. I said, "What kind of rabble rousers?"

"Ah!" Mr. Norman flailed the air with one hand. "A bunch of Reds."

Cass asked, "What kind of 'Reds,'"

Mr. Norman went across the room to a bookshelf and pulled off a volume of Leon Trotsky's essays. "This guy was his idol."

I had to talk Cass into stopping for some pizza on the way back to the office because I was feeling weak. Sometimes it seems like she can run on spit alone. She wanted to get right to work. I told her to slow down, and this got a spark of anger.

She says, "What are we doing? We shouldn't be running away, with all this still going on."

I tell her, "We're not running away. It's our honeymoon, for Christ's sake! You just did your job. The rest is up to the police. That's not your responsibility."

"The police haven't done 'diddly squat!'"

I had to smile a little, "That's Dad's expression. You've already picked that up in just a few days."

She says, "I picked it up from you, for Christ's sake! It's a good one."

I liked the way she'd added Christ to the mix. I say, "You should be proud of yourself. Well, maybe not proud, but at least content. Your hunch was right. It's all politics. You've got three dead people with one thing in common."

Holding up her end of the bargain, first thing when we get to the Paper, Cass calls Detective Barnes and relates most of what she's learned. Then she wrote up a rough of her story and got that okayed by Stenis. The Boss was out of the office but she had the piece written by eight when he returned.

73. Saturday, August 7, 1937

Mom called at seven o'clock and woke me up with some nice news. My younger sister, Esther, will be in town for the wedding.

Before she got interested in the Law, Essy studied English at college (which she already knows better than anyone else in the family, so this puzzles me), but now she has a job there in Boston working at a legal firm. She has the job because she can type like a demon, something she learned to do as a kid at the stationery store where she had to spend most summer mornings with my mom. Typewriters were among her first toys. Now she can make sixty dollars a week any time she wants.

My older sister, Kate, is in Chicago and has her kids and her husband's schedule to deal with so she won't be able to make it. Luckily, we have a six-hour break in our train connection there and we'll try to see her then. My brother Ben is somewhere between London and Paris on a buying trip and the mails won't catch up with him until next week, at the earliest. Erik won't find out until his ship makes port in Seattle sometime next month.

Cass has also called her brothers.

One of them, Robert, still lives in Cleveland and works there as a manager at a coal processing plant. He won't be able to make it, even though business is slow, because he can't risk being laid off for leaving his desk just now. David, the youngest, is still footloose and could not immediately be found. Stanley, the oldest, is a lawyer in Chicago and has a court case in progress. But at least her parents would be there.

Actually, they were there already.

On Saturday, Cass was supposed to meet them at the train station, but unluckily, with our lark to Tottenville and then to the Bronx afterward on Friday, we'd missed a call from Mr. Johnson in the legal department. The suit against Hearst Corporation by Mrs. Broome has progressed and it appears we are required to meet her lawyer next Thursday for a deposition. This command was in carbon copy and left on our respective desks. We found it waiting for us on Saturday morning and sent answers back separately with our own responses concerning the fact that we would not be present. Mine was not as colorful as Cass's. However, one portion of this had us concerned. The judge assigned to the case was unhappy with both the police department and the Hearst Corporation for dragging their feet. It seems Patrolman Ted Lorimer, who'd already been asked to appear, had missed two previous appointments.

Another phone call established the news that Lorimer, who lived only a few blocks over from Cass's apartment in Manhattan, had recently been reassigned to a different precinct and a new beat out in Astoria, Queens. This was probably the punishment he pre-dicted to us for being willing to tell the truth about things at Knickerbocker Village. But he had not shown up for duty in Astoria either and was now under official suspension for dereliction of duty.

I told Cass the situation would work its way out while we were gone. She argued that it would work its way out while we were gone a little easier if we were to go speak to Patrolman Lorimer first. If I didn't want to go with her, she was going by herself. And that was why we were both at 18th and Avenue B on Saturday at noon.

Lorimer did not answer the buzzer in the vestibule. I used my trusty press card to get by the front door latch and we went up to the third floor and knocked. Again, nothing.

This was Cass's call, but I decided to relieve her of the guilt she sometimes feels about stretching things too far and jimmied the door latch there with my pocketknife. If the dead bolt was on, this wouldn't mean a thing but it wasn't, and the door slipped right open.

Lorimer's apartment is a simple shotgun set-up: kitchen (bathroom to the side), second room, third room. The ice in the ice-box has melted and the milk is bad. Other than that, it looked as if Lorimer had just stepped out for a breath of air and never returned. I smartly calculated his absence to be about eight days. There was a date stamped on the milk bottle cap. Sheer genius.

There are a couple of old photographs on the wall—the kind that fade away at the edges. Nothing newer. Also a stack of news-papers from over a week ago. A back window was partially opened onto the fire escape, but there were no marks in the soot on the sill and it was my guess he had left it that way himself.

A comfortable looking chair is close by the Philco and I suspect his primary entertainment is listening to the radio. There is a Catholic Bible with black leather covers worn to orange at the corners, but no other books. He did have some copies of *Life* magazine in a rack behind the chair. These were well thumbed.

I said it to Cass right then, standing by that chair and looking at the picture of an old gent on the wall who was likely a grandfather. "I think he's dead."

Cass wondered, "Who would kill him?"

"Maybe he did it himself."

"Did he look like the type?"

"No. Though, I haven't been too good about seeing that kind of thing lately. But I can tell you this: if his only friend was the radio and he figured there was not a whole lot to look forward to in Astoria he might have done it."

We were about to close up and go knocking on a few other doors when someone knocked on his. This was a sudden jolt, with us standing right there. I opened it up on a woman who looked to be about forty, neatly dressed, with a smile that disappeared when she saw me.

All she could say was, "Who are you?"

Cass stepped up and explained why we were there. When she asked how we had gotten in, I lied and said, "I just jiggled the knob a little. It came right open. We were worried because he'd sort of disappeared since we'd spoken to him before and so we came over to talk to him again."

She seemed to accept that. I wouldn't have, but then I think she already had darker thoughts on her mind.

This was his downstairs neighbor, Jane Phelps. She is a secretary at the J. Walter Thompson Advertising Agency. She'd been concerned about Lorimer and come right up when she heard the sounds we'd made prowling around. She told us she'd knocked on his door a number times before, during the past week.

"He's always bringing me the pastries that people give him on his beat. But I haven't seen him since last Thursday."

The worry in her voice was obvious.

I was a little happier for the guy then, but definitely figured the suicide angle was less likely when she said they often went out to the movies together on Saturdays.

"He is a sweet guy." She said. "He shouldn't be a cop. He's too nice."

Cass asked, "Has he mentioned anything he's working on?"

Miss Phelps didn't answer that. Instead she said, "If you're from the *Mirror*, then you must think something's happened to him."

By the tightening of her voice, she was obviously beginning to consider the worst.

Cass could only express the obvious. "We think so. But we don't know that."

I asked again if there was anything he'd said to her about his work recently.

Miss Phelps shook her head. "He never talked about his work. 'Rule number one,' he called it."

We went back to the office without a lot to say. Neither of us had any ideas we wanted to toss around. Mine were pretty half-baked anyway. All I had was the thought that coincidences don't happen without a reason, which makes them something else. Cass called in to the Precinct and reported our conversation with the neighbor. It was up to them to track Lorimer from that point.

Again there were two messages waiting for us at the *Mirror* when we got back, one for each of us. The first was from Cass's father and it said they had arrived at the station. This was a little over two hours old. The other was from my mom and was about ten minutes old. It said, 'They're here. Where are you?'

Stenis said, "Go on. Both of you. I'll call if we need anything tomorrow. But bring me back a picture of Bette Davis from Hollywood—in a bathing suit. Will 'ya. I haven't seen one of those yet."

74. Saturday August 7 and Sunday, August 8, 1937

That Sunday seems like a very long time ago now and difficult to sort.

Actually, this should start with that Saturday night. There
was nothing particularly important about that evening, but it pleased
me a great deal and I've thought about it a number of times in the
weeks since just for that reason, and about the characters that were
there, and because it was such a good beginning to things in general.

Mr. Green is the real character. His stories are as short as my
dad's are long. He delivers them like a radio comedian, all pauses
and timing, and you can barely detect his accent, which at first
simply sounds like most of the Jewish people in Brooklyn. But it's
not from the Yiddish. It's the Polish. He and dad have almost nothing in common but they were clearly best friends from the first. They
do laugh at the same kind of jokes, however. That helps. Thankfully,
they know different jokes. And they both smoke cigars, which gives
them the time to chat as they walked outside that night. My dad is
not tall as I have said, and though he is not fat, he is a burly fellow,
and Mr. Green is oppositely thin and wiry and tall and the two of
them stepping along Sterling Place, side by side beneath the curl of
their smoke, is a sight.

Mrs. Green is stout. There is an old saying that if you want to
know what your bride will look like when she ages, look at her
mother. Cass would have to lose a foot in height and gain fifty
pounds to make that true. Not likely. But Mrs. Green has a good

strong face. Where Cass looks my mom directly in the eye, Mrs. Green will actually bow her head a little and look up over the top rim of her glasses, which gives her the appearance of always being skeptical. She and my mom appeared to have far less to talk about than our dads. But then, most of the time, when I was there to watch, my mom was in the kitchen and there was little for Mrs. Green to do but sit on a stool by the old icebox. That situation was only made worse by the fact that Essy pays no attention to Mom's commands to leave and took over most of Stacy's chores, even while chatting with Mrs. Green about one thing or another.

Mostly though, Esther would not leave Cass alone. She had a thousand questions about writing for the papers. And she seemed totally puzzled by Cass's interest in me. But then again, so am I, so it was interesting to hear the answers, even if they were a little sticky—of course those were the ones Cass gave when she knew I was around. By their looks alone, Essy and Cass could be sisters. The voices are another matter, even though they can both talk faster than I can hear.

The dinner on Saturday evening was a lot like a Sunday affair. The table was full. Mom opened a bottle of wine and we had a few toasts at the start. Afterward, Mr. Green produced a bottle of Polish blackberry brandy and there were more toasts. This sent my dad to the basement to pull out something he had stashed away there—an Irish whiskey given to him by a friend. My mom wouldn't drink it, and then Mrs. Green refused as well but both Essy and Cass insisted on trying some and liked it. This was good stuff and that part of the affair went on to midnight, while Mom dragged out every old tale she could about my misdeeds as a child. Mrs. Green, in her turn, seemed reluctant to share such tales about her daughter, but Mr. Green had several to offer.

The best of those was that Cass used to wander off as a child, exploring one thing and then another until finally losing her way. She had been told that if ever she needed help, she was to find a policeman. In time, she was well known to the entire police force and when she got her first job as a stringer for the *Plain Dealer*, she

had a regular source of copy provided by her friends in the Department.

At least Mr. Green had stories that most of us haven't heard,
while my dad's tales were familiar variations on things I already
knew by heart. Mr. Oliphant was quiet as usual, and went to bed
fairly early on. Mrs. Tisdale was out on a date with her new boyfriend, the opera buff, and not there. But Mr. Clurman and Mr. Jenks
were both present through a second pouring of the whiskey. Mr.
Jenks wanted to talk about the Japanese navy because of some-thing
he had read about the numbers of larger ships they were building and
insisted that the Brooklyn Navy yard, where he is working at the
present time, should be expanding to meet this potential threat, but
no one else wanted to pick up on that darker thread.

Talk turned instead to the hunting of rabbits, a sport which
was as necessary in Ohio and New Hampshire as it was in Poland,
mostly because they eat the garden crops. My dad first learned to
shoot that way, as a boy. In western Massachusetts, Mr. Clurman
had used traps for the same purpose. It was agreed that they all
missed rabbit stew. Through most of this, Esther had Cass by the ear
and was grilling her about being a reporter and my mom tried
various lines of conversation with Mrs. Green but none that seemed
to stick.

An evening spent talking about small things can be more
important to the spirit than a discussion of the world's calamities, I
think.

I slept in the parlor. The couch there is too short but it is
plenty comfortable.

Mom got to the kitchen first on Sunday morning and made
spoon bread the way Stacy had taught her, and grits and fried bacon
and eggs, and made battered toast out of the bread she had baked
earlier in the week. This was a far better feast to me than the roast
we had the night before. Breakfast has always been more informal in
our house, with people on different schedules, but it was a larger
gathering that morning. Until Mrs. Tisdale arrived, most of the talk

was about favorite recipes and food. We were then treated to a short dissertation on Wagner which put an end to things.

The plan was that I would take Cass back to her apartment Sunday morning so she could pack a few clothes. All things considered, we thought there was not a lot of worry now that Mr. Neims was no longer around. And we thought any interest in us that the Nazis might have was largely reduced by the busting up of the ring around Mr. and Mrs. Lenz. But I was not confident about either of those developments. That, plus the disappearance of Ted Lorimer had put new thoughts in my head. And this was the state of things along about eleven o'clock Sunday morning when we opened the door on Cass's apartment. The last time she'd been there was to pick up some things on Thursday and I had been with her then as well. Since then, the place had been ransacked.

Here was another puzzle. What good would there be in doing that?

I called the police and we waited for them to come by, while Cass packed what she could. One of the cops who came thought the place might simply have been burgled. But there was nothing missing that Cass could see. Then again, there was not a lot there to take unless you like to wear women's cloths—a few silver hair clips. Some loose change in a jar. A radio. That sort of thing.

It was two o'clock in the afternoon before I put her in a cab back to Brooklyn. Then I went to my place. Though I hadn't said anything to Cass because she was upset, I sort of expected the worst there. And I got it.

The deadbolt on the door was still neatly attached to the doorframe, but both the door and the frame had been kicked in together. It didn't look a lot better inside than it did the night the cops turned the place over.

The sun was blasting the street outside and the apartment was hot with the windows shut, but I had a chill.

I called the cops again. I might have been a little more dramatic with what I said on the phone this time. One of those guys, of the four who came, was the same fellow I'd knocked down the stairs a few months before. He looked to be in good shape again and I told him I was happy I hadn't done anything worse. He appreciated the sentiment.

Our conversation is easy to remember.

"I thought you was just a photographer."

"Just."

"What's all the fuss then?"

"I don't know."

"This wasn't us! I can tell you that."

"I figured."

"What's missing?"

"Nothing I can see."

"When do you think it happened?"

"In the last twenty-four hours. I slept in Brooklyn last night."

"Then maybe, whoever it was, they was after you?"

"Maybe."

I took a hammer to the doorframe and, except for the busted plaster, got that back in place with a few nails, and then packed a suitcase and went back to Brooklyn myself.

But Cass wasn't there. She'd gone in to the *Mirror*.

75. Sunday, August 8, 1937

This was a scene! I can see Barry George standing in the doorway of his office from all the way across the floor. He has his arms folded at the front of him like he does when he is about to explode and he's trying to keep his lungs in. He is looking directly over at Cass's desk. She's sitting there with her back turned to him and her face down in a pile of papers. The Boss sees me and his arms both rise toward the ceiling at once before he waves me directly into the office.

He wants to know, "Does she ever listen to you?"

"Not that I've noticed."

"You know, if you can get that ring back, you could use the money to go to Europe and find out if it's true what they say about the French girls."

"What do they say about French girls?"

"They don't bathe but after a couple of minutes you don't care."

That part of the conversation I remember.

Evidently, he'd ordered Cass to go home. She'd told him she didn't have a home anymore. Some thug had made a ruin of it. She wanted to know why. He had told her that, officially, she did not work there anymore. He had two new guys coming in tomorrow and one of them would be sitting at her desk. She told him to find another desk. I think she said this in other words. Then I told him about what had happened at my place and this had The Boss looking pretty deflated given the circumstances. So I told him that, hell or high water (whatever that means), we would be getting on a train at Grand Central Station tomorrow evening at six o'clock, or else we would both be dead. This did not make him any happier. Especially after I told him that my place had been ransacked too.

Just then the boss reaches out and lifts the strap of my bag off my shoulder. It's an odd feeling to have something like that taken away from you, all of a sudden. Not just the weight of it. It's the presence of it that you become used to.

He says, "You won't be needing that until you get back." He set the bag aside and then reaches over to his hat rack and grabs another little leather case less than half the size. "I was going to give this to you tomorrow, but who knows what she'll be up to by then. You better take it with you now."

I know what it is on first sight. I've read a hundred ads for it and pestered the guys at Burleigh Brooks down on 42nd Street until they look away when I come in the door. It's a Retina II. It's the new 135 that Kodak has the Germans make for them and it's the best thing on the market for something you can easily carry around.

I said, "Wow!" What else was I going to say?

He says, "A bunch of the guys chipped in a dollar each. The others hid out in the hall by the men's room until the hat passed by. It's a wedding present. Now you don't have to drag that beast around with you on your honeymoon. No excuses. We just want lots of pictures."

I had to fondle that for a minute, but my worry right then was about Cass.

I sat down by her desk and waited for her to pay some attention my way. She was feeling a little guilty, I think, for running off and she took her time.

Finally I say, "If it makes you feel any better, whoever it is that made a wreck of your place did the same thing to mine. They even knocked the door down."

For just a second, she looks up at me blank-faced, and then suddenly says, "It's you!"

I say, "I've been here for about ten minutes. It's good to be noticed."

She says, "No! It's because of you! It's not in my notes. There's nothing here! I saw that stooge on the platform at 42nd Street, but he was just the gunsel—that's the word you use, isn't it? But not the boss. The big gun. Not the guy at the top of the stairs. I didn't see him. Not very well, at least. Of course, he doesn't know that for sure, does he? After we chased him in the street the other day, he probably thinks we can tag him. But I still couldn't pick him out of a line-up if I had to. He's tall. Thin. He wears a gray suit. That's about it. But you! You have his picture!"

I say, "When did I get that?"

She sighs, "I don'no. We'll have to figure that out. But I bet you that's why they turned your place over and mine too. Same as the reason the cops did it to you that time, when they were looking to protect the identity of the police captain from Philadelphia. What we have to do now is look in that pile of pictures in the basement at your parents' house."

Our parents had a lot more time to get to know each other as a consequence of all this. Except for about an hour for dinner, late that Sunday afternoon, Cass and I spent most of several hours on the evening before our wedding in my darkroom, in the basement at Sterling Place. (I did not get a single kiss out of that effort.) I have my log of the pictures I've taken there, but I hadn't sorted much lately and the pictures were in the hundreds. Under the circumstances, this was a chore, and Cass did not accept my excuse—that it was because of her, that I'd been too busy to keep them in order.

In the end, what we came up with were only two possibilities. One was in the background of a picture I'd shot at Ellis Island. This guy was an assistant there and stood quickly to turn away when I grabbed a picture of the Director. I suppose he didn't realize I had the camera set. The other picture was not in the loose pile. It was already put away but I found it as I paged back in my log looking for likely circumstances. It was something I took weeks ago when we went uptown to interview Mr. Kuhn. There was a fellow outside the Nazi's office there on 86th Street, smoking a cigarette when we arrived and I was only taking a picture of the building. He just happened to be in it. And looking at it again, I remember that the fellow jumped a little when I snapped it, as if I'd surprised him. The fun thing about this was that they both looked like the same guy.

I enlarged those two and got a couple of extra 4x5s of each and I handed copies to The Boss the next day at the wedding and asked him to send something on to Lt. Barnes.

76. Monday, August 9, 1937

After the fact, I'm a little embarrassed about the wedding too. It had seemed like such a good and efficient idea at the time. But it would have been much better done in a church.

The Brooklyn Municipal Building is one of those enormous places that appears from the outside if it might be large enough to contain all the offices for all the government services in the entire nation—maybe the world. Yet, it's still half the size of the one in Manhattan. Appropriate to such self-important grandeur, it has a row of columns at the front with the building set back behind in such a way they are holding up nothing but air. Hot August air in this case.

We sat first on a bench in the second row of maybe fifty similar oak benches in a waiting room big enough to contain a hundred couples and all their living relatives, but only half a dozen others had shown up for the ceremonies that day, each with its own retinue.

Actually, no. I waited. Cass was not there. My dad and Mr. Green and a few of our friends sat behind. Even so, ours was by far the largest of the groups in the room. Esther kept coming to the door and looking in and making faces I could not interpret. Several times Dad reached forward to pat me reassuringly on the shoulder.

Cass and Mrs. Green and my mom and Essy had come separately in another cab. It appeared that there was some kind of prohibition on a groom seeing the bride before the ceremony that was unknown to the other couples waiting.

Finally, a fellow I had spoken to briefly about the delay came to the door of the adjoining 'Chapel' and said our names out loud as though we were not sitting right there in front of him and asked if we were present. I said yes, and looked over to the doorway but Esther was nowhere to be seen. Our party, maybe twenty in all, followed this man into a room where the light had been lowered to replicate a church, I think. Instead the reduced light and the lack of any height to the ceiling gave the place a dingy appearance and made the air stuffy, more like the basement of a church where the casket is kept before a memorial service. I looked for a window to open and saw none. This sudden close feeling as I stood in front of the assistant clerk, along with Danny Seger, grew by the seconds into one of those eternal minutes you get in life, now and again—usually when you are in severe pain. But I was feeling a little numb. At least my feet were.

I was wearing a rented tuxedo that did not fit quite like the ones Fred Astaire always wears. The sleeves were a little long, the shoulders were tight. It buttoned a little loosely at the front. My shirt collar had a hard grip on my neck and made an extra effort out of every swallow. I do not own a pair of black shoes. The ones I'd borrowed from Mr. Clurman were tight, even though his feet are supposedly the same size as mine and they were well broken in from being worn with his conductor's uniform everyday. But at least they were well polished.

It is a fact that the air conditioner in the Brooklyn Municipal Building was not working that day. No reason for the situation was given. I had the time to consider the idea that Mr. LaGuardia had ordered it to be turned off, having heard that I would be there. Sweat had affixed my shirt to my back while I was sitting and it did not let go of my skin until I removed the shirt itself an hour later along with the shoes, and the rest of it, and climbed into my trusty blue suit and cordovans.

Some time near the end of that eternal minute at the Municipal Chapel, Essy's face appeared again at the near door, and then my mom's, and then Mrs. Green. Mr. Green hustled out of the room. A few long seconds later, he reappeared, with Cass on his arm.

Now, this was the most astounding thing of all. Cass was not decked out in the dress I had seen hanging in the hall closet at Sterling Place. That was something I knew she'd rented that very week at Gimbels. But here she was, dressed in something I had in fact seen before, not once, but for my entire life. It was the gown my mom still wore in the picture that hung in the parlor. Not exactly white, and likely never intended to be, but nearly. It is as much folds of lace as it is satin, with the lace on the outside and the satin in. The neckline is high, with the lace rising up to her chin and the satin falling all the way to the floor, but her arms are nearly bare beneath the lace sleeves. The back, a train of more lace, trailed along on the marble. Not at all like the dresses I've seen these days when out on a wedding assignment for the paper. This was in fact the same one my sister Kate had been married in, and the dress I imagine Essy will wear one day too. But, like magic, it now fit Cass as if it was made for her. (A fact, I later learned, that was made possible through the late-night ministrations of a hired seamstress.)

Our appointment was for 10 AM. We were officially married by 11:30. Ellen Bennett played maid of honor. Danny Seger played best man. The pasty looking fellow who was the assistant clerk that day took about two minutes to check all the lines on two sheets of paper, one for each of us. The legal fact of it took about three minutes, but that was partly because I fumbled the ring. The clerk had his lines memorized. I just repeated the words he told me to. So did Cass. I put the ring on her finger. Cass put one on mine. It was done. I kissed her to some applause that echoed pretty well in that close room and made it sound like more than it was. The larger recollection is vague, but I remember Cass's eyes.

There was very little time for kissing and hugging afterward. The Boss gave Cass a loud buss, and then we were all ushered out of there and the next couple in line was up to bat. But it should have been something more. Ceremonies are worthwhile. I regret the fact now that we did not make more of the occasion when we could have.

But was done.

After that we all went back to Sterling Place and had another feast. The third in three days.

The celebration at the house was better, of course. We had the cake there. And the champagne. But I did not drink very much of that. I was afraid I'd fall asleep. But there were a few dozen more toasts, several involving the anticipation of future McNeills to come. Izzy played the piano, and we danced. And one point I kissed Mrs. Green because she was crying and I thought she needed it. She was pleased with that. But I can barely remember any of it now, less than a month later. Esther took most of the pictures. And then all of a sudden it was time to leave again.

Here are a few of the facts I didn't have to remember.

The *20th Century Limited* leaves Grand Central Station, track #34, every evening at 6 p.m. It arrives at Chicago's La Salle Street Station, track #16 at 11 a.m. the next morning. That's about 960 miles in 17 hours. The fare is $34.40 plus an extra charge of $10.20 (I'm not sure what that one is for), plus the basic Pullman charge of $11 for 'lower birth,' plus an extra for $22.20 for a private compartment. The electric engine that hauls it out of the bowels of New York is changed over to steam up at Harmon on the Hudson. At Albany, the whole rig picks up the New England section coming from Boston. At Buffalo, where the east and west bound trains pass in the night, the crews change. There is a brief stop in Toledo for another crew change to please the Chicago unions. I'm reading all that from the brochure and my ticket stub (except for the part about pleasing the union).

The menu in the dining car (I have that right here in front of me now too) declares a flat charge of $1.75. For this you get sweet pickle chips, Ripe olives, Button radishes, and anchovy olives to whet the appetite. They call those hors d'oeuvres. Then you get your choice of hot clam bouillon, iced tomato juice, canapé of Russian caviar, two-tone cocktail, tomato juice, Virginienne style, fresh fruit cup, or crab Louis cocktail for an appetizer. The main courses offered were something called planked salmon steak, garni (fish with parsley); stuffed eggs with devilled Smithfield ham, braised celery hearts, and Allumette potatoes (?); roast young turkey, chef's dressing, cranberry sauce, new Brussels sprouts with crumbs, sweet potatoes and apples (a turkey dinner); smothered veal cutlet with mushrooms, noodles and prunes, 'minted' new peas; potatoes gratine; roast prime rib of beef, cressons, braised celery hearts, rissole potatoes; or, for an extra $2.35: fresh devilled lobster 20th Century, and again the new peas with mint and Allumette potatoes; or prime filet mignon, shallots butter, grilled tomato, new Brussels sprouts polonaise, au gratin potatoes. We both got the filet mignon. On the side there was a couple of stuffed prunes with orange salad mayonnaise, some corn sticks, assorted bread, pineapple muffins. The pineapple muffins were great. For dessert they had green apple pie; caramel custard; banana shortcake with whipped cream; N.Y.C. French Vanilla ice cream with crush pineapple; melon on ice; N.Y.C. Baked apple; or, Cream Cheese with toasted cinnamon raisin bread. We both had the apple pie. To drink there was tea; N.Y.C. coffee (whatever that is, it tastes just like coffee), or an individual milk.

All the while we get to listen to the New York Symphony orchestra on record. Every guy got a carnation. All the women got a little bottle of perfume. (I can tell you that Cass smells better without the perfume.) And for those who didn't have anything better to do, you get complimentary copies of the New York *Herald-Tribune* and Chicago *Tribune*. We were told there were secretaries and barbers available, but I never saw one. You could get meal service in your Pullman compartment, but that costs an extra buck.

We ate pretty soon after we boarded, so by the time we got to Albany, Cass wanted to wander up and down the train after dinner to see what there was to see. But I think that was only to avoid going to our compartment.

77. Tuesday, August 10, 1937

The honeymoon was just fine. Really fine. Not something I can talk much about, of course, except for the places we went, which were pretty swell too, but all told it was even better than I had expected it to be, and I think I was expecting a lot. The only bad part was when someone tried to kill us.

This is what happened then.

We were somewhere between Albany and Buffalo at the time. Closer to Buffalo, I think. It was about 1 AM. We were both awake but dozing a little. Where two tracks join, the rhythm of the wheels is like the ticking of a clock and there is a gentle rocking that's good for dozing too. Even the extra noise where other train lines come together becomes expected, like markers of your progress. The 20*th Century Limited* is a 'through train' and only has a few stops, but it slows at times. I had the shade up so we could watch the lights we passed and all the little worlds out there that other people are living in. Even late, you see the light on in the upper window of a house and you know something is going on. Maybe someone there is as lucky as I am. Maybe not. At least that was what I was thinking when I hear a click at the door, and in the half-light from the window I see the little lever slide over.

Now I had tried that lock a couple of times earlier. I didn't want anyone disturbing us and wanted to be sure of it. The porter told me it only opens from the inside, unless you have the key, and he was the only one with that and he wasn't going to be disturbing us unless we pushed the buzzer. That button was about three feet over our heads. So I reacted to the click with a fair certainty that it shouldn't be happening. By the time I got my foot out and over to the door it was already open several inches, and I jammed it with my heel about as hard as I could. The door actually bowed a little because there was a hand in the opening, up a little higher from my foot, and it was holding something hard and that was caught there with the fingers for an instant and I thought I heard a grunt before the hand was pulled back and I hear the metal of the thing scrape the door edge. It was just a second. Two maybe. I am sure what I saw in that hand was a gun. Most of a gun. The business end, even if it only looked like some sort of a pipe from where we were in the dark.

Cass was up with a finger to the buzzer and I grabbed a towel from the shelf behind the door because I was naked at the time. We could hear the footsteps of whoever it was running then up the aisle and I opened the door again and looked to see and only caught a bit of a figure at the end of the passage going around the corner where the door to the next car was. Stupid as ever, I ran after him. Bare feet and all. I was holding the towel together with one hand because it was none too large. Modesty is an instinct, I suppose.

The rage of noise between the cars will wake you up if nothing else will, but I had some juice flowing by then. The next car is as quiet as the one I'd left. No sound of a door closing. Ahead of me I see our porter, Jake, hustling down the narrow passage toward me. He says, "Are you looking for the showers sir?"

I say, "Later. Did you see someone come this way?"

He says, "Someone. Someone came through. But I was in-disposed at the time."

"Do you still have your key?"

He pulled it up from a pocket at the end a brass chain. "Yes, sir."

I pushed by him and went on through, with him following and telling me the showers are in the opposite direction.

After another rush of noise between cars, when I opened the next door, I got the smell of cigars and perfume and the recorded sound of Shep Fields and his Orchestra playing *That Old Feeling,* but cut down by a din of loud voices and laughter. Around the corner from the door I can see right away that I am in the lounge car and right next to me at that end is a woman who has just stood up from her seat to leave. She gives me the up and down and a smile. She looks a whole lot like Barbara Stanwyck and it was clear that every face in the car was turned to her until I came on the scene, as naked as I was. The conversations stopped, and except for a couple a giggles, nothing but the rails and Shep Fields could be heard for maybe half a minute.

I looked at every face I could see but there was none that I recognized.

Then some twit standing at the bar, about half way down the way says, "It's about time we had some live entertainment!"

And Ms. Stanwyck says, "I can hold that towel for you if you'd like."

Just about then, Jake arrived behind me, saying, "If you're locked out sir, I can let you back in."

As of yet, I wasn't as embarrassed as I would be later, when I was telling it over to Cass. I was just angry, and I followed Jake back through the cars reluctantly.

We reported all this to the conductor while we waited in Buffalo, but nothing else like it happened again. The conductor was more interested in learning that Barbara Stanwyck was on the train than what he thought were the delusions of an anxious groom on his wedding night. But the dent in the metal edge of the door was there for proof.

78. Tuesday, August, 10 to Tuesday, August 24, 1937

What else? In Chicago, my sister Kate warned Cass I was a very nasty fellow, sneaky and smelly, and that I had many bad habits, some of which she enumerated over a very nice midday dinner at their house in Oak Park. Her husband, Albert, came home from work for the occasion. I've met him plenty of times before and though we get along, he is a bit of a stuffed shirt. Maybe worse in that regard now because he has gained a little weight and has that tendency to lean in when he is talking to you that makes you aware of the poundage. He studied business in college and is already some kind of bigwig at the commodities exchange. I don't know what Kate sees in him.

Her kids are non-stop and mostly avoided me for trying to get them to stay in one place long enough to get some pictures to send to Mom, so they played with Cass instead. But this was a nice thing to see. Cass is often too serious about everything but with kids she gets silly.

Cass's brother Stanley showed up in time for the feast, and left before it was over because he was only on a short recess from court. He is a tall fellow, thin like his father, but apparently more nervous. He had no jokes or stories but seemed at least interested in the ones others had to tell. This was more like his mother, and I thought the blend of the parents in him made for an uncomfortable mix.

And then we were off again. Cass was already taking notes

so I started my own log and began to take pictures of her taking notes, which at least got her attention now and again.

Ms. Stanwyck was on some sort of publicity tour for a new movie called *Stella Dallas* and we encountered her a second time in the dining car on the *Zephyr* the following night. She winked at me as we passed and nodded her approval toward Cass. Good thing Cass missed this.

I have a few notes: If you have seen one part of what they call the Great Plains, from a train, I imagine you have seen them all. Especially as it's getting dark. Much corn. More wheat. Beet fields run away from the eye in low rows like corduroy. Neat white houses in the midst of clusters of trees—islands of humanity amidst the open fields. I will never know the lives that are lived there, unless I get the chance some day to take a picture at less than fifty miles per hour.

We crossed the Mississippi at Burlington in a slow turn but there was very little to grab a picture of except a dozen other tracks laid side by side that were shot just then with moonlight, all converging beside the sheen off the flat muddy water below, and beyond a black guard of low factory buildings hovering at the side in the dusk. We missed Omaha completely because we were already in bed. (I'm told by the porter that there is not much to see.) We had breakfast in Denver without leaving the train, but we got out and ran around the station anyway just to stretch our legs. I rediscovered there that Cass is a very fast runner, which might be why she wasn't caught until I came along. Nice station though. Very large and expansive, bright with beige colored stone instead of gray, but quite empty compared to any other we've seen and fine for echoes if you are of a mind to make some noise of your own, which I was. We missed the stop at Salt Lake City because we were in bed again.

What we saw of the Rocky Mountains and the others of its ilk between Denver and San Francisco was pretty spectacular. But the only shots worth anything through that way were the ones where I could get the train into the picture as it made a bend—for the perspective. Otherwise it all comes out pretty much the same, very nice and very empty; especially while you're moving and can't play well with the shutter speed for depth of field. For awhile I set up in the last car and got the empty rails behind us, but without the right lens, I wasn't going to get much more out of that either.

I liked San Francisco right off. It has its own smell and that is not unpleasant. Cities are like people in that way. Some you can't stand on first sniff. (Though Chicago struck me as smelling a little like New York.) I wouldn't mind living in San Francisco for awhile and mentioned that to Cass out-loud about twenty times while we were wandering around, until she started a count for every time I said it. Maybe this will happen some day. I told her all the stories I knew about my dad's time there after the big earthquake.

That city is a little mysterious. With the ocean close around, the hills break it up more even than the rivers divide New York City, so any one part of it feels a lot smaller when you are in it. And the buildings are smaller, mostly, (maybe because they don't want them falling down on anyone's head again) and that also keeps it from feeling like a city and more like a town when you are standing in one place. Even the shots I managed to get from the roof of the Mark Hopkins Hotel made it look small-townish. A stone gray fog blocked the view from the windows at the hotel every morning and came in on us again each afternoon, so we had to carry our coats with us even when the sun was actually hot enough to bring up a good sweat. The cable cars are fun, as advertised. They are open to the weather and cold if the fog is moving in and you forgot your coat. But these don't carry you very far, or very fast—nothing like a good subway can.

Because every travel article is really about the food, we ate more than we should have. I had crab, which is not as good as lobster, and abalone that was like a large scallop but tougher, squid that was like chewing on a piece of India rubber, as well as salmon and something called Yellowtail that were both terrific. I will stay away from the others next time. Cass and I ordered different things so that she could get a taste of as much as possible to write about. We agreed on the salmon and the Yellowtail but she thought better of the king crab.

The original idea was that we were not going to fly back to New York until September 1st and then figure out our living arrangements. But after about three days Cass was bored with sightseeing in the San Francisco fog, so I found a company that rented cars (a nice little gray Plymouth) and we drove across the Golden Gate Bridge. The sun opened up on us as we passed below the first orange tower and the entire Pacific lay beyond, beckoning westward, and this made us think our decision was good for a time. But we only stayed one night up that way at a very small hotel in a town called Bodega Bay, based upon the recommendation of a fellow I knew who worked at the San Francisco *Chronicle.* He said we could swim near there but the water was far too cold and we just wandered around a bit. It seemed a pity that all of those beautiful beaches are only good for seagulls and sea lions. Much of it is set against high cliffs, with a short hem of mostly empty sand scoured by both the wind and waves. The sea lions lie in clumps up the beach from the water in such a way that you'd think rocks were shifting when they move. The still pictures did not catch that. But I got to see my first living redwood on the way, which is not actually a tree but a building that grows on its own. All of it very fine.

Next we drove out to look at the park at Yosemite. Quite a distance. Over 200 miles and all of a day. But that was splendid too, waterfalls and vistas and all. Very dramatic. But at that point, I was bored as well. All of that near continuous 'spectacular' sort of wears on you after awhile. Sort of rubs your eyes raw. You need a break; some hum-drum to settle your wits.

Now this seemed to be the wrong attitude. Here we were, for the first time in our lives, in the most beautiful state in the United States and I think we both felt a little homesick. I suppose if you lived there you would find the little things to make it worthwhile, other than all that exaggerated beauty, but we only had time to look. That's certainly better than a photograph but not enough. Like The Boss says, one pretty picture after another will put anyone to sleep.

But other things were probably on both our minds. I suggested that if we worked there in San Francisco, at one of the papers, and got all that beauty punctuated by a bloody stiff now and again, or a house fire (they have terrific forest fires, I hear), we'd probably get used to it. This got no smile at all. Cass was already too anxious about getting back. What we'd left behind was troubling her again.

And all the time we were spending money borrowed from our parents because the Hearst people only covered the travel expenses and we wouldn't see most of that back in cash again until we filed for it. (They'll love the bill for the car. That totaled nearly $100 at Los Angeles. We could have bought a good junker for the price).

After a night at a very rustic lodge in Yosemite (you know it's rustic because they leave the bark on the wood inside and out, but they really should bottle the air there and sell it back east), where Cass wrote at least five or six pages of notes before I could get her to turn out the light (and I swear I heard a bear in the night), we drove back to the coast and then on south to Los Angeles. All of it duly beautiful and good enough to fill quite a few more pages. I shot over a thousand pictures with my new camera. Some of those rolls I sent back from a Post Office in Oakland, and another batch from Monterey. (I kept back a few of the rolls that mostly just had Cass on them.)

On the day before our flight home, Cass and I got a tour of the MGM, RKO and Paramount Studios. This was a total waste of time. Because we were reporters with a major newspaper, we got our own guide, which saved some time but this was the sort of star struck young woman who was completely bowled over by getting to see Mickey Rooney wave from a doorway as we drove my. I never got to see Bette Davis, in costume or anything less. But we did get to stand on a sound stage and watch Tyrone Power rehearse a scene. I thought I saw Miss Hepburn once, but it was at a distance.

Two weeks to the day after we left New York, we were on a DC 3, American Airlines' "Flagship Mercury" flying back to New York. We were both exhausted from not doing very much but sitting in a car, but this part of the trip was something else again.

With the smooth lines and aluminum skin, this is a proud looking plane, something like a big brother to Mr. Hughes' Silver Bullet. It has two large engines, one on each wing with the larger wheels on short knees beneath. The wings are broad and the tail wide. It sits right up at the gate, with a smaller wheel at the back under the tail. You board on one side at the rear and walk uphill to your seats. Instead of porters you have a stewardess who is, frankly, a lot better looking.

This costs $135 one-way plus $85 for the sleeping arrangement, and takes about fifteen hours. Plus, you get more food: two meals and a lunch, but these are on the house and served on real china with silverware. For the record, the dinner there was Chicken Kiev, Long Island Duckling with Orange sauce, Breast of Chicken Jeanette, Strip Sirloin, or Filet Mignon, (I had the duckling and Cass had the chicken Kiev) with a choice of salads, and some pastries for dessert. We had a choice of eggs and ham with toast for breakfast, or rice pancakes with blueberry syrup, or two types of omelet. All of it okay, (especially if you considered the fact that we were well over a mile up in the air) but not as good as the food we had on the trains. It reminded me a little of the steam tables at Horn & Hardart. They also had wine and whiskey along with the coffee, tea, milk. No beer. I had a couple of very smooth whiskies.

The floor and seats are level when you're in the air, but trying to sleep in an airplane is still a trick. There are no compartments and no door. Just a curtain across where the seat folds back and they make up a bed for you. The bunks are singles but you can make do in just one with a little effort. There's a steady hum without the beat of the rails to it and the vibration lolls you off until suddenly you get a toss when the plane hits some turbulence. One time the plane started a climb to get around some weather and we felt like we were standing on our heads. But as far as the flight goes, it was generally uneventful.

We were back at Newark on Tuesday, August 24th and home in Brooklyn by for dinner.

79. Wednesday and Thursday, August 25 and 26, 1937

In advance of the expected World Series (bound to be the Yankees or the Giants, or both), Barry George traded any interest he has in Cass's travel articles concerning our Western honeymoon (this now being primarily my photographs and a half-share of the expenses) away to the *Journal-American* for a multi-part series on the successful new rookies for the Yankees, Dodgers, and Giants, plus two sports features to be named later. He got the worst of the deal, to my mind.

I should not have gone into the office my first day back. That sort of behavior can be compulsive. But I just wanted to check on a couple of things. The Boss looked like he was happy to see me though, and when he starts working on sending me up to Hyde Park that afternoon to get a couple shots on Roosevelt, I warned him I had some arrangements to make concerning where Cass and I were going to live, and all of that.

One problem to solve was a sort of 'his and hers' thing between Cass and myself. I felt a pretty strong interest in what had happened to Patrolman Lorimer. So did she. But her loyalties were not the same as mine now. George was not used to handling such conflicts during his tenure as City Editor and I'm not sure he anticipated the matter before this trade for Cass was made. Now he was stuck with resolving it. The *Mirror* had a clear interest in the story itself. They broke it, after all. Naturally, the *Journal-American* thought they'd also acquired the right to Cass's work and anything she did on the Lorimer case was now theirs.

But I warned George, this was more complicated. Lorimer's disappearance was not a one-off. I suspected it was connected to the other matters that Cass and I had been working on. That conversation went something like this.

"Like, what?"

"I'm not sure."

"The lawyer?"

"Maybe."

"Annie Oakley?"

"Could be."

"Annie Oakley, for Christ sake? Why that?"

"It's the politics. The whole place over there is infested with Reds."

"I can name a dozen places like that."

"Not that we happened to be covering right now. I'm not big on coincidences."

"So you've said. But life is still full of 'em."

"There's always a reason. If there is a reason, it's no coincidence. So, can I keep my nose in it?"

"You're not a reporter!"

"I'm learning. I'm writing stuff up almost everyday now."

"I thought I told you we needed a photographer, not another reporter."

"Two for one. But now you've traded Cass away for two more. And I'd say that was a bad deal."

"What do you know! Are you telling me how to run the City Room now?"

"No. I'm just commenting on a picture that is sitting right in front me."

"Keep your comments to yourself."

"Yes sir. So, can you give me a little extra time?"

He folded his arms up for a moment over his lungs and looked out the window.

"You weren't supposed to be back until September. You've

got till then."

"That's less than a week!"

"You were due back the sixth of September. Show me something by then!"

Actually, the living arrangements were made while Cass and I were gallivanting around the West Coast. It was decided that we were going to be living in the basement apartment at Sterling Place now that Stacy and Gary and Mr. White are gone. It was Mom who made that decision.

I said to her, "Who's going to help you with everything?"

She answers, "Let me worry about that."

I say, "We can afford our own place."

She says, "Then you can pay me the rent, instead."

Cass is sitting at the table eating her breakfast and not saying a word. Not looking at me. More interested in buttering her toast. (Or so it appears). It is very clear to me that the decision has been made and I am just being informed. I am very surprised Cass is okay with this.

I say, "Why?"

Cass is not looking at me, but she knows I'm looking right at her.

She says, "We have to pay your parents back for what we borrowed. And we need to start saving something."

This was very 'responsible' of her. I think that's the word.

She turns an eye up at me over a neat slice of toast and strawberry jam. Very cute. From my point of view, it was by far the easiest and best solution to our problem, but if I gave in too quickly, I see the possibility of a pattern getting started—even if this is only the first stitch. I have to protest enough to keep my dignity in the situation.

"I'll have to think about it."

My mom says, "Good. You're father has taken the train to work and left the car. You can pack up the rest of the things at Cass's place and then you can go out to Long Beach this afternoon and cool off. Maybe we can even get your old place all done with by tomorrow."

I say to Cass, "You have to give notice to your landlord."

I'd already sent a letter to mine, assuming we might end up at Cass's apartment for a time.

She says, "I already did."

So it was done. Anyway, I liked the idea of the beach.

80. Saturday, August 26, 1937

I really only knew one person who might be familiar with Patrolman Lorimer, so I went over to Knickerbocker Village to see Grace Williams again. This is Doris Broome's downstairs neighbor and she had been very willing to talk once before. Though I knew that she was wary of us now, my idea is that she might talk to me differently with Cass not around. This was about two o'clock in the afternoon. She was indeed home, but apparently occupied and says only, "Come back later," through a crack in the door. Which I did.

I went over to a place I knew near the old Frankfort Street office of the *Mirror* and got myself a bite to eat, and read the papers.

When I came back at four, Miss Williams is dressed and she let me right in.

"Where's the girl?" was her first question.

I said, "Cass is busy."

Mrs. Williams says, "She said she'd be coming by to talk this afternoon."

"When did she say that?"

"She called me this morning."

So I knew right away I had some competition. I had to get to my points quickly.

I said, "I know you don't want to risk anything with your position here. I promise, whatever you say, I won't use your name or where you live. I'm just trying to follow up on a few things that've happened since. Do you know the cop who used to be on this beat,

Ted Lorimer?"

"Teddy? I've known Teddy for years."

"What do you think of him?"

"Pretty square. On the level. He's always ready with a break if he can give it. And he never asks for anything back, like some of them do. 'Quid pro quo' my friend the judge calls it."

It didn't matter who her 'friend the judge' was. It was just the way business was done in New York.

"Patrolman Lorimer is missing. I'm trying to find him. Can you tell me when you saw him last."

Worry came suddenly into her face.

"No! Sure. He was over here with some coffee cake from the Italian bakery he likes on Pearl Street. He usually does that around Christmas time, but he was trying to work something out and we had a little chat."

"You know him pretty well then?"

"He used to be on a beat up in the Tenderloin. I worked around there occasionally . . . Used to."

"When was that?"

"About six years ago."

"No, I mean when did you have the chat."

"A week and a half, maybe. It was a Tuesday. I have a regular on Tuesday and I had to ask Teddy to leave. Do you think something's happened to him?"

"We don't know. What did you talk about?"

"Things."

"Mrs. Broome?"

"Yeah. Sure. Teddy was a little disappointed in me, because I'd gone back on what I told you guys before. I explained it to him. He understood. Like I said, he's a nice guy. He knows the ropes. I couldn't afford to lose this place."

"Did you talk about anything else?"

"Not much. He told me they'd transferred him out to Astoria. He was pretty unhappy with that. I think he told me that just so I'd reconsider. That's about as close as he got to asking."

"Do you know where he went after he left here?"

"No. Well. He might have gone down to speak with Miss What's-her-face over there. She was sunning herself in all her glory and Teddy saw that pretty clearly from the window that day and he said he'd go talk to her again."

I thanked Miss Williams and went to speak with Lucille Beinecke.

This was a door that Cass and I had knocked on before. Someone was home that time but hadn't answered.

I knocked a little harder to start off. I heard the bare feet on the parquet and knew I was being looked at through the peephole. I smiled back. I suppose she must have considered the situation for about half a minute and then she opened up the door all the way. Thankfully, she was dressed. At least a robe. Maybe there was more beneath.

This is a very good-looking platinum blonde. I don't think the hair is bleached. She has a nearly perfect complexion, which you almost never see, and I don't think she was wearing makeup. But she was wearing a tan and you could tell that because the robe opened up beneath her neck by maybe eight inches. A very nice looking eight inches.

I told her who I was and said, "I'm trying to locate someone and I thought you might have seen him, maybe a little over a week ago."

She was studying my face pretty hard, like she thinks she's seen me before. She says, "Who would that be?" Her words are very exact—deliberate is the word for it, maybe.

I say, "Patrolman Lorimer. Ted Lorimer. This was his beat until recently."

She hesitated again. This was as if she was still trying to remember something. But I had the feeling the matter was not about Patrolman Lorimer.

"Yes. He knocked on my door, a week or two ago. He's come by a few times for the same reason. Some busybodies don't like my habits. I'm a 'naturist.'"

"You study animals?"

She laughed. It was a dry laugh and clearly by way of a comment on my stupidity.

"No. Some of the human kind, perhaps. I'm a nudist."

I didn't say anything to that but I imagine there was some comment on my face because she reacted to with a smile.

I said, "Can you recall what you spoke about with Ted Lorimer?"

Miss Beinecke suddenly frowned at me.

"Where is the girl?"

"What girl?"

"The one you were with, before."

I guessed she must be remembering Cass and me standing there together in front of her door. I said, "I think she's around. She'll probably show up pretty soon."

"Ah. And you're the photographer." She flicked a finger at my bag. "Why are you asking the questions?"

"It looks like I'm not. You're asking the questions, now."

Miss Beinecke gave me a brief squint that I thought might be some irritation at my disagreement. But then she said, "Why don't you come in?" and she stood back from the open door.

Her apartment was what you might call modern. 'Spare' is a word I've heard for it, and generally looked as if she might have just moved in. There was a mat on the floor by the living room window, a thin looking couch that didn't have arms on it, a smallish table by another window with two wooden chairs and a vase of yellow flowers at the middle, and a lamp that grew from the heavy base on the floor into a thin semicircle of bright stainless steel and ended in a light bulb and shade just above another chair that matched the couch. There was also a packed bookcase that filled the back wall of the living room. The overall layout of the interior was much like the Broome's apartment, with a hall at one side that led off to one or more back bedrooms and a small kitchen at the other.

She seemed patient enough to let me look at all that while she sat in the chair by the lamp, and when I looked at her again, she pointed to the couch and asked, "Why are you looking for Mr. Lorimer?"

I sat on command to accommodate her. "It's a legal matter. It concerns a story we did."

"About Henry Broome?"

"Yes. Did you know him?"

"Not personally. He always seemed content just to stand up there by his window and look."

This might be corroborating testimony. I took out my notebook. She waved her hand. "No! I won't testify to that. In fact, if you quote me at all, I'll say it's not true. I'm not interested in sitting in a court."

"Why is that?"

"Why?" She frowned. "Do you like sitting in court? You can make a lot of enemies that way." She flicked a hand in the air, then suddenly changed the subject. "Tell me, do you take good pictures?"

Her English was near perfect, but this was the first time I thought she might not be an American. It was something in the way she had spoken. Not, 'Are you a good photographer,' but 'Do you take good pictures." The difference seems slight enough but then, it did not. Or maybe that was in the precise way she said it.

I said, "I think so."

"Do you take nudes?"

"Only when I have to. No. Just press photos. And a little scenery."

"Ah," she says, and I see then that her robe has parted enough to let me know for sure that there was nothing beneath. "That's too bad. I'm looking for a photographer who can do nudes in an artistic manner. I need to construct a portfolio."

I know the rules about being alone with a woman in a difficult situation.

I say, "That wouldn't be me." Then I nodded towards her robe. "But I think I'm already seeing more than I should. I should probably go."

She pulled her robe together. There was a slight pout at her lips and a crease of skepticism in the forehead.

"I thought you wanted to ask me some questions about Patrolman Lorimer?"

"I do."

"What exactly?"

"You've spoken to him before. Were you friends?"

There were suddenly several creases in the forehead. "Is that a rude question?"

"No. I just wondered if you were friends."

"No, in either case. He only came to ask me to put something over the window when I was sunbathing. But, of course, that would not be sunbathing, would it?"

"No . . . Did he mention anything else that day he was here?"

"I don't remember."

I had let my eyes slide over the spines of the books in the case, mostly to keep them off of Miss Beinecke. Some of it was literature. Some history and biography. There was a row of gray paper covered titles that are the work of V. I. Lenin. I've seen those around before.

Again, as before, she was patient about letting me look.

I asked, "Did he mention going anywhere else after he left here?"

Instead of answering, she asked, "Have you ever read any of Mr. Lenin's work?"

"No."

"A genius. Not for being original, you understand, but for bringing so much together."

I said, "I wouldn't know."

She gave that a pause before smiling, "No. I don't think you do."

Her implication in saying that was clear enough.

So I asked her, "What do you think of Mr. Trotsky?"

It was an impulse question. The answer surprised me by the tone in her voice.

"He is a traitor! Why do you want to know?"

"Just a thought."

She frowned once more. "But you say you don't know about Vladimir Lenin?"

"I don't know much about either of them. Just something that keeps turning up."

Miss Beinecke suddenly sat forward. "The girl you were with before. Is her name Cass Green?"

"Yes. Why?"

She smiled again, oddly this time—more a grimace—and repeated my own words, "Just a thought."

Like clockwork then, there was a knock on the door. Lucille Beinecke's eyes flared. But I already knew just who this was.

"That would be Cass, now."

Miss Beinecke was out of her seat before I finished speaking. Springs in her legs. She didn't bother peeking through the hole first, opening the door right up as if she were anxious to see Cass again.

Cass smiled. I got a scowl, but then a smile later. She says hello to Miss Beinecke, excuses herself for interrupting anything (that got an arch in Miss Beinecke's eyebrow), and then says we have to be going.

81. Saturday and Sunday, August 26, and 27, 1937

At this point we're only a couple of blocks from her new office at the *Journal-American* on South Street, which I wanted to get a gander at anyway, but Cass told me to wait while she went upstairs there on her own, and so I cooled my heels at a cramped little coffee shop across the street filled with a row of stools and a narrow counter that's half occupied with guys that all look like reporters. And these reporters give me the eye as I come in. This is the sort of place that gets bubbles on top of the coffee when they pour a cup and makes you suspect they don't rinse the soap off the dishes when they wash them.

I take a stool at the counter next to a fellow and he gives me the squint. He's a scrawny guy and I recognize him right off. He's packing a camera same as me.

He says, "Do I know you?"

I say, "Sure. We bump into each other now and again."

He says, "But you don't work for the *Journal-American*."

I say, "Neither do you. You're Pinney, with the *Daily News*."

And he says, "You're McNeill with the *Mirror*. Why are you over here?"

I say, "Same question. The answer for me is, I'm waiting on a girl."

He says, "Same thing," and he shakes his head with a smile and then slouches, elbows down on the counter for the duration.

I say, "Lucky for us it's not the same girl."

He quickly answers, "Luck had nothing to do with it."

I say, "Guess you're right about that."

He asks me how things were going. I tell him just fine and let him know I've just gotten married and things never looked better.

He says, "My condolences. The fraternity of bachelors will miss you."

So I ask him about his snakes. He has a reputation for keeping snakes. Some sort of hobby. But now, if the cops get called and find one in a pantry or something, they ring Roy Pinney right up. A lot better than dealing with a zoo. Zoos are more particular. So he tells me he's practically sleeping with them. The bill for the mice he feeds them is leaving him to survive on two meals a day. I ask him about the taste of fried snake and he gives me a weak smile. Worst of all, he says finding a girl who isn't shy around snakes is pretty difficult.

But then he looks at his watch and says, "Let me tell you though, never go out with another photographer. You're always bumping into each other. It's too easy to get your lines crossed."

I say, "Not much different if she's a reporter. I can tell you."

Right then Cass comes walking in and gives me a kiss and says we can go.

Pinney does a low whistle. He says, "Now, that ain't luck."

Now, here is how this problem resolved itself. With a kiss.

There was a little conversation attached to that, but not much. A kiss was enough, and then I spilled the beans and gave her everything I had concerning our platinum blonde.

She was critical of only one thing, "Why didn't you ask her where she worked?"

"I don't know. Maybe I was thinking I already knew the answer."

"Maybe your mind was clouded. Always ask. Sometimes the answer will surprise you."

I say, "My mind has been clouded for months. I was just in the middle of hoping that wouldn't get any better."

But I think she was happy that The Boss had let me do some reporting work. The conflict of interest was not going to be a problem. At least not so long as 'I wasn't holding anything back.' That's the way she put it, but with a smile. I think she already knows I can't hold anything back.

What she had done while up in her office was call Detective Barnes. We didn't have the means to find out all of what the matter was with Miss Beinecke. Jack Barnes did. After all this time, he was hungry for any sort of lead on the Annie Oakley murders. A lack of progress on those killings would eventually reflect back on him. For this, Cass would get a call back from him if he got anything else she might be able to use. And Cass would pass that information onto me.

As far as I was concerned, this wasn't a matter of getting lines crossed, like Mr. Pinney had warned. But it was a matter of fishing in the same pond. If there was only one fish in there, she could have it. She'd earned it. But to carry that metaphor a little further, I thought it was a pretty big fish. Maybe, dinner for two.

I typed up my notes for her that night after dinner. We agreed that too much of what little we knew about Miss Beinecke did not seem quite right. And we agreed we would work on this together, no matter what The Boss, or her editors at the *Journal-American,* said.

Sunday morning Cass was up early and I followed her out the door, still half asleep. The plan today is to take my Dad's A Model and pick up a couple of loads from my old apartment, but she wants to go back to the *Journal-American* office first, to grab some notes she left behind and (just because I'd been asking) to show me around. She assured me it didn't look any different than 45th street. And it didn't. Just a little older and dingier. The place was fairly empty at that hour on a Sunday morning because, even though the *Journal-American* is an afternoon paper, the Sunday edition is out early instead of the usual bulldog and everyone has gone home to get some sleep. No one would likely be asking any questions about why she had a photographer from the *Mirror* in there. Same owner, but the competition is like Dodgers and Giants.

Unfortunately a fellow named Schoenstein was there, doing follow-up, and he's curious. He comes over because he knows my face from somewhere and won't let that go. Cass tells him a few of the facts.

He'll keep it to himself, but he says, "But you better not let Eddie Mahar catch you, married or not. Eddie is a very competitive fellow."

I know Eddie—a little guy but quick, and he uses his size to get in where lugs like me might not fit. His father was a Police Captain and he is famous for using that link to get him in the door ahead of anyone else. He's the photo editor at the *Journal-American* now but he's still a good photographer. If he gets wind of a story like this, and thinks another paper is going to get a scoop, he will be on it like a fly on soup.

We went on our way.

At Perry Street, I had a notice in my box from my landlord for damages on the door. I'll tell him to consult the police report and then stuff it in an orifice as soon as I get the chance. We packed up as much stuff as we could—until the sweat was loose—and went on to Brooklyn for a shower and dinner.

Stenis had a short message waiting for me at home. Detective Barnes had called the *Mirror* looking for Cass. So Cass gets on the line immediately then and tries to get ahold of Barnes. But too late. Barnes has already called over to the *Journal-American,* because Stenis told him Cass had moved over there, and instead, that's where he'd left the message he had for her.

We both knew then that Eddie Mahar would know all about it soon enough. There was nothing to do to stop that now.

The message Detective Barnes left for Cass was that Miss Beinecke had moved out of her apartment late on Saturday. No forwarding address. And she'd left a good deal of furniture behind, so it was definitely a hasty exit. A neighbor said Beinecke had suddenly pulled her car up at the door of the building and stuffed it all by herself. In a big hurry. The car was a dark green Buick sedan. But there was one piece of good news. They had a couple of matches between fingerprints taken from Beinecke's apartment to ones found on the sink at the Hotel Pennsylvania where Police Captain Deems had been murdered.

This last piece of news was, by itself, a good reason to open up one of the bottles we got as wedding presents, but we settled on a couple of cold beers instead and surveyed the chaos of the combined accumulation of boxes in our new 'apartment.'

82. Sunday to Monday, August 29 to 30, 1937

Cass should be a teacher. After dinner she gives a very good lecture, wearing that hat—not simply correcting me for one of my many faults but informing me of something interesting—and she is easy to listen to. There is a fellow that Cass studied in college by the name of Sigmund Freud. He is the psychologist who is the basis for the character with the beard and the funny accent that you often see spoofed in comedy skits. This guy is heavy with theories for why people do the things they do. Most of it sounds like hogwash, but Cass is onto the idea that Miss Lucille Beinecke might be a proper client for this doctor.

We have both settled on the very good possibility that Beinecke is the killer who's been putting bullets through the eyes of half a dozen or so middle-aged men. This alone—shooting out the eyes of these fellows—is the sort of thing that lends itself to some psychological interpretation. The fact that they are middle-aged adds something else to that mix. But Cass thinks the fact that there is likely some political connection to most of them is another matter. That was the actual match that set the fire. The reason for the fire is likely some contest between two gangs of political hoodlums. Thugs always kill more thugs than the cops ever get to. The way of the world. It's just the way that this particular killer has done her job that's unique.

Cass gives me a fair course on all of this Freud business in just a couple hours. Sorting through our separate belongings and fitting them into a new space together is a fine time for such considerations. Otherwise the brain gets caught up on whether some piece of bric-a-brac should be this way or that. Easier just to leave it in a general vicinity and let time and tide dictate where and how it should fill the gap.

The big surprise doing all this comes when I find something I didn't expect. Cass has a gun. It's a colt .22 revolver. The model with the longer barrel. I held that up and looked at it like I've never seen one before.

"Where did this come from?"

"My mother. She brought it with her."

"So you could protect yourself from me?"

"I think so."

She took it out of my hand because I was flipping the cylinder open and shut, just for the sound of it. She checked to see that the chambers were empty and then closed it again and aimed it at a baseball I still have from a Dodgers game and pulled the trigger.

"Peckoo!"

"Is it the one she learned to shoot with? The one she had when she learned to shoot from the real Annie Oakley?"

"The very same one. I'm pretty good myself. My mother taught me."

"So you've said."

"It's true."

"Then you should carry it with you now. You might need it."

"No!" The cute in her face disappeared. "You mean that I should look in my purse and decide whether I should grab my note pad or my gun. No! I can't do that."

"So you think it's fair that someone else should protect you?"

"That's not the point. I shouldn't need you to protect me."

"No? Somebody else then?"

"I don't want to carry a gun just to do my job! That's ridiculous!"

"It's the fact. At least for now. You aren't going to be able to save the world if you're dead."

"That's not the kind of world I want to live it."

"It's the kind of world it is."

"But that's what I want to put an end to."

"Why did your mother give it to you then?"

"She thought—I'm sorry to say, she thinks like you."

"You should listen to your mother."

I stopped my argument right there. We had gone through some of this matter before and it wasn't going to help anything to rehash it. But I told her then that whether she wanted to carry the gun or not, she had better go down to the police department tomorrow and get it registered. We have the Sullivan Act in New York and though they don't enforce it very well, it would make a good story for another paper if she were caught with it.

All this talk nearly made me miss an event taking place over at the 33rd Street pier that very night. Charles 'Zimmy' Zebelman, the 'Legless Swimmer,' was due to dock around six and when I suddenly realized the time I ran out the door almost in mid sentence with Cass right behind me for company. I'd promised Stenis I'd be there because I'd covered the guy before, and it was Sunday and they were short for non-emergencies. We hopped in the car and were there in plenty of time, however. Zimmy was behind schedule and didn't arrive until 10:34, amidst a small flotilla of boats with their red, green and yellow lights hatching the black water around the bobbing of his dark head. He'd swum the distance of 143 miles, from Albany to New York, in 148 hours and four minutes, after setting out the previous Monday at 6:30. There was quite a crowd present and his muscular torso, slathered in grease, and his mustachioed smile despite evident exhaustion made the front page, below the fold. He was, I think, genuinely happy with his stunt. But the sight of him chilled me at first, as they pulled him from the water, manhandling him because he could not climb the ladder. I'd seen one too many bodies lifted from the river in nearly the same way. Luckily, Cass had caught the man's eye as they rubbed him down with towels and she loudly asked the obvious first question, "Why did you do it?" Amidst the hubbub of other reporters, he answered, "Just to get here and see you, darlin'," and blew her a kiss.

This got quite a roar.

On the way back to Brooklyn, I dropped the plates for that off at the paper along with my notes, and all of this activity required another beer so we were not in bed until midnight and not asleep until some time well after.

As usual, at dawn, Cass is up, bright and chirpy. She does not need as much coffee as I do. She's out the door ahead of me and it means I have to get going myself, otherwise she'll have a jump on the Beinecke story that I can't make up. She already has one advantage there. She might get her piece in for the afternoon edition of the *Journal-American,* and except for the bulldog edition, the *Mirror* would not be on the newsstands until tomorrow morning.

She even has a shorter ride on the subway now than I do.

My first decision is to let all that Freud business go. For the most part. I don't feel comfortable playing with it. After all, this Beinecke woman is obviously nuts. The real reason for that is beyond knowing, I think. What's important is getting the information out about it that we do know, so that she might get herself caught. And I also know the first thing that Barry George is going to say when I hand in my copy. 'Where's the picture?'

I have my first attempt at about twelve hundred words done by nine and show that to one of the other fellows who's in the office early and he gives me some fair comment and I knock it around a bit and get a new version ready by ten o'clock that is a third shorter when The Boss walks in the door. He's surprised to see me there and waves me into the office and I show him what I have.

He says, "Where's the picture?"

I tell him the sad fact of the matter. I have seen this face on him before.

He says, "Nobody is going to give a damn without the picture."

Now I've got a very bright idea. I call Captain George Parker in Philadelphia. And I get through to him pretty quick, but right off the bat, Parker says, "What now?"

I start to tell him what I'm looking for. He interrupts me and says, "Your girl already called about that."

Now I have to do some fast thinking. Cass has reached him first. I can't say I'm unaware of what she's up to. He'll probably just hang up.

So I say, "I'm the photographer who was with Cass that day we spoke to you. Unfortunately she gave you the wrong wire number for sending the Beinecke photo up here."

I gave him the number for the *Mirror* instead.

Now, I'm well aware of the trouble I'm getting myself into. All is fair in love and war, but this is something else again.

The facts are: Miss Beinecke was arrested for solicitation in a public place, specifically the George's Tavern at 401 Adams Street, in Philadelphia, on November 12, 1936. It appears she had been bothering a 'foreign visitor.' The nationality of the visitor was given as 'Russian.' That man's name was Nathan Simke. Those charges were later dropped because Mr. Simke did not show up at the court hearing (my immediate bet was that he would not be showing up at any other hearings either). The arresting officer, who just happened to be on the premises at the time of the incident and witnessed the confrontation, was Michael Allen Deems.

This then was the actual link with Captain Deems. His predilections for prostitutes had been his undoing. As for Beinecke, she only knew that Deems could identify her. Their encounter at The Shaw's was likely a happenstance. She probably used different taverns all over town to work for her daily bread. But Deems was a link to one of her earlier murders. The decision to kill him had been last minute and the reason his body had been left conspicuously behind.

The photo that came in with the copy of the police report was more than sufficient for our purposes.

I was not in the office later when Cass called, looking for me. I was actually on my way to South Street carrying a copy of the police report with said photo, right to her desk. When I got there, she was gone, already on her way uptown to speak to me in person.

Her editor is a pleasant fellow named Chester Rice. Mild mannered and low voiced. He eats peppermints compulsively. I'm thinking he would live longer if he just yelled at a wall occasionally. He took the manila folder and told me he would pass it on to Cass.

He asked, "What is it?"

"Something we were working on before she came over here."

"The murders."

"Yes."

"She left here ready to kill somebody. Are you the body?"

"Yes."

"I'll try to calm her down if I see her so we don't have any more cadavers to account for."

I said, "Thanks."

Because neither of us was officially back at work yet, we were both home in time for dinner at Sterling Place. Cass wasn't talking to me. She avoided my kiss. She asked me to step outside for a talk and I refused. If she had been a guy, I would have accepted readily and had the matter worked out in a few minutes. But this was going to be our first real 'fight' since we were married and I was not yet prepared for any verbal fisticuffs. My mom is observing all of this with unusual silence. Dad is keeping his head down.

After dinner we are downstairs together for two minutes before she starts unloading.

The flare in her eyes has turned brown to near black. "Tell me this. Just tell me this. Did you think I wasn't going to give you a copy of that photo?"

I say, "No. I knew you'd give it to me. If you ever saw it. Trouble is, the wire room at the *Journal-American* isn't yours yet. That's still Eddie Mahar's territory."

Amazingly, this stopped her cold. I saw it as merely one excuse among several I was going to use to justify myself. But she sat down on the edge of the bed then as if I had slugged her. So I sat down too.

"What's up?"

She just says, "I didn't think of that."

After a little making up between us, she admits she was miffed at first because I'd figured out the same business she had. She was going to surprise me with it. She said she'd already imagined the look on my face when she handed me the picture.

Unfortunately for the *Journal-American*, they went to press before this was all resolved. The *Mirror* had the first report the next morning.

But I did not get a by-line.

83. Tuesday to Friday, August 31, to September 3, 1937

The *New York Times* gave the story two inches of space on page eight, Tuesday morning—without the picture. The *Post* ran the mug shot with a slightly longer rundown from the Police Commissioner on Monday afternoon, page three. As would be expected, neither paper credited us for putting the story together in the first place. No matter.

Because I happened to be in the office when the call came in, I went out to cover a fire in Manhasset, Monday afternoon. No one died in that, so it didn't spoil things, but it was good to be doing something useful again. However, this turned out to be another inspiration. I talked Cass into going to Fire Island on Tuesday because the weather was pretty fine and warm, but this then required borrowing Dad's car so we could get to the ferry in Sayville. And Dad had deliveries to make. And that brought on another idea. One I'd been thinking a lot more about lately.

Dad has a friend name Harry Bean over in Bushwick. You can't say this man's name without smiling and he makes use of that, plus the fact that you can't forget it, to sell his cars. He advertises in all the papers with a cartoon that features his bald head and an ear to ear grin. Dad sold Harry Bean his first batch of stationery over ten years ago. He's been trying to get Dad to buy a new car ever since. Dad keeps telling him he'll do just that, as soon as the A Model won't start when he needs it. I met Harry for the first time on Tuesday afternoon. I made Cass come with me. She chose the color.

On Wednesday morning we drove to Sayville in a three-year-old, deep blue, 1934 Chrysler Air-flow. Now, I should say something else about that. I have it on good authority (Jim, a buddy of mine from high school who fixes cars for a living now at a garage in Canarsie) that this car had gotten a bad rap when it first came out, and now Bean has four of them on the lot that he can't sell. Unbelievable! It has a look that reminds you of the Chrysler Building, which is the prettiest skyscraper in town. All curves, like a proper lady, and with a chrome grill that bends way back to the sky. Cass thought it was cute and I thought it looked swell and Bean let us drive away with it for one hundred dollars down and twenty dollars a month, which was pretty cheap for a car that has less than a thousand miles on it because it was a 'dealer's show model.' Of course, you hear that a lot from the dealers, but I think it was true in this case because the smell inside reminded me of that big Lincoln that Miss Hepburn drove me home in that day with Mr. Hughes, and it's just about as quiet inside.

Anyway, I suppose it's about time I had my own car.

Because we missed the last ferry home Wednesday evening (not really an accident), we rented a room and stayed there on Fire Island until Thursday. And then, because we were there already, and the weather was still fine, we stayed through and didn't leave until Friday.

Now, I sort of think of this as our real honeymoon. Nothing to do and no place to go for three days and for once I didn't want to be anyplace else. But Cass wrote up our time there anyway and that is supposed to turn up in the travel section pages of the *Journal-American* on Sunday. The pictures are mine but they won't be credited.

84. Saturday, September 4, 1937

When you live in a neighborhood for awhile, you know how it works. Prospect Heights is not the sort of place where you see a fellow holding up the corner lamppost. A kid maybe, waiting on a buddy. But that's a lot more likely down on Flatbush Avenue. Not on Sterling Place. So it doesn't take a genius to figure something's up when you see a guy down on the corner smoking a cigarette like he has all day. Not with it being almost dark.

I was out at the market on Washington Avenue in the other direction, picking up some things for my mom and come back and see this guy down on the corner of Vanderbilt, and right away the hairs are up. I know that Cass is coming home from her lessons at Don Juan's about then, so I set the bag down on the closest stoop and stroll on. The guy does not see me at first because he has his eyes turned the other way and when he does, he sort of shrugs his jacket loose, sticks a mitt in his pocket and starts to walk. I just stay with him. That was a mistake. What I didn't notice but should have expected was a car parked along there and someone else in it.

The street is not busy at that hour. Most people are in having dinner. And beyond this guy, I can see the figure of someone else coming up the next block from Flatbush. It's an easy guess who that is. So now I step a little faster. I have no idea exactly what I'm going to do when I get close—figuring he probably has a gun in that mitt—but at least I can interrupt what he had planned and maybe get out a good shout. And like I said, Cass can run.

Pretty quickly then, I think maybe the shout is better done sooner than later, and I let out the best Tarzan I've got. And with that, all hell breaks loose. The guy I hadn't seen in the car there steps out and takes aim at me over the top of his open door. Cass has suddenly disappeared somewhere and the sidewalk is empty except for the first guy who is further on and he is clearly looking back and forth for her. The second guy is firing something that sounds like a dud firecracker and my idea is it's the gun with the silencer. I'd already dropped to the sidewalk by then but I got a face full of grit from where a bullet grabbed a piece of the cement. Some of that is in my eye as I rolled under the car parked next to me and I tried to wipe it away. Now I can't see much but I hear more shots. At least two more guns. I scoot out on the far side of the car I'm under and look up along the paving bricks and see smoke coming from an open car window closer to me but on the far side. The smoke is not from a cigarette. Up the way now I can see Cass again and she's crouched down low on the street behind a car on this side. The firing continues from the first car on my side to the car across and I can see the metal of the door over there pucker. A real battle. Ten or twelve shots. In the meantime the first guy I saw shows up down the way, right about where Cass was, and I'm pretty sure he has a gun out and he's aiming for her. She's behind him so I can't see that well and my eyes are watering and so I'm up again running and yelling bloody murder, which is what it would have been. There are a couple of louder shots just then from the guy near Cass. The second guy, shooting from the car on my side, starts his motor with a loud grind of gears and backs out fast and keeps it going backward toward Flatbush Ave and toward Cass and the first guy with the gun. There is a screech of breaks. I wipe the tears from my eyes but I can't see Cass. That car starts backing up again then, all the way to Flatbush Avenue, and as quick as that it's gone into the traffic and the dusk. I reach the spot where Cass was when I saw her last and I don't see a thing.

The silence is all of a sudden very loud to me. I just said her name. Those were the longest seconds of my life. And finally I can hear her. She's gasping. She's under another car. As I go down to look, I hear the leather soles on a pair of shoes slapping the bricks, and the private dick breathing pretty hard coming toward us. About a dozen voices start talking at once as people come out of their doors. I'm down under that car by then and Cass sees me and then she starts letting out a real wail. I just laid there on the bricks with her for a while until she calms down. She was not shot. Just scared.

Flynn went down on his knees for a second to see if we were okay and then he stood by on the street until the police cars arrived. Funny thing about that was, the first blood I actually saw was darkening the red paving bricks as it dropped from the limp hand at Flynn's side. The moisture on my face was more of a mix. The cement had peppered me pretty good. But that was the first thing Cass had seen when I went down under there to get her.

85. Saturday to Sunday, September 4 to 5, 1937

Now, here's the thing that kept me awake Saturday night and long into Sunday morning. Cass and I were alive out of dumb luck. I wasn't doing enough to take care of her. I wasn't even doing enough to take care of myself.

The F.B.I. finally shows up again on Saturday night at the precinct station in Brooklyn and wants to talk to us both. We'd already told what we knew to the cops by then, in as much detail as we could, but had to do that all over again. This included everything, all the way back to the murder of Captain Deems at the Hotel Penn.

The F.B.I. finally gets the idea that they are not dealing with one set of thugs here, but two. And that the guy they collared up at Grand Central was not at the end of the line, but more at the beginning. The first two guys we speak to call in someone higher up, and about 11 p.m. we have to go through all this for a third time. And at that point I am tired and a little cranky because these clowns have just figured out that something more is going on here than a local police matter and they should have taken a greater interest in this before.

Still, there are two jokes in all of this.

The better one is that because Cass and I had supposedly been away on a honeymoon, the private dick, Michael Flynn, had taken a little time off for himself and was in the Adirondacks, fishing, which is where he gets word from his office that we are back. So Saturday is the first day he had been on duty again and when he arrived he thought we were both already home, safe and sound, having our dinner, and it being a safe hour, he was sitting in his car, snoozing. He hadn't noticed a thing until I yelled the first time and he was more ashamed of that than he was hurt by having a slug in his shoulder.

And the very reason that The Boss still had the Byron Agency and Mr. Flynn on the payroll was the fact that he'd been unable to get the F.B.I. to keep taking the thing seriously. Our report about the guy who tried to kill us on the train meant nothing to them. They had caught their man at Grand Central Station. Why would the Nazis care about us now?

It makes you wonder.

The other joke is that because of the late appearance of the F.B.I., we both missed our dinner and our deadlines and the story was filed by stringers. Weegee got the photo of the car door and the *Mirror* ran with that.

Cass and I slept late and read all about our escapades in the paper the next morning. Closer to noon. After some delayed breakfast, we went in to our respective offices and filed more detailed stories. I drove Cass to South Street in our new car and then went on uptown to 45th Street. Easy parking on a Sunday and I wouldn't be able to do the same thing any other time.

I had no pictures to add to this latest business, but Stenis dug up some file photos of the collar of the ticket agent up at Grand Central to break up the copy that I handed in. Cass called me when she was done and I drove down and picked her up again. The guys in the City Room were more interested in my car than the shootout.

At this point I have heard nothing about Mr. Flynn, the private dick. Last I saw him he was being carried on a stretcher and put into an ambulance from the Methodist Hospital. I called the hospital and hear he is in intensive care and listed in critical condition. I tell them I'm calling from the *Mirror*, and the only additional information I find out is that the bullet had nicked his left lung and broken a couple of bones on its way through as well as his shoulder blade. Nothing else.

Sunday dinner was pretty good after that. The phone kept ringing until Dad took it off the hook.

86. Tuesday, September 7, 1937

Izzy Baerz calls me on Monday morning. He's read all about it and wants details. I gave him the scoop with a little more color than I used with the cops or the Feds. Then he tells me the real reason he's calling is because he has a guy sleeping on his couch who needs some help. This guy Jerry Siegel has a cartoon character he's been working at for years and he hasn't found a market for it. He wants to get it in the daily strips, but can't get a foot in the door.

Now, I'm supposed to be back at work full-time but one key part to that is Winchell and he's not around for a couple days, so I'm picking assignments off the board like a stringer. I can make a little time between things for this.

My problem with it is that I've been working at the *Mirror* for seven years and I have never actually met a lot of the guys upstairs. Winchell is one of them. Some of them just aren't as friendly as Dan Parker or Charlie Segar. They're both upstairs as well, but in the sports department, which is another matter. Segar was born in England but he actually played baseball right here in Brooklyn for a time himself, and he'll keep you at the bar for at least three more beers with his stories, all of them told with that turn in his tongue that makes it sound like it must be true even if he's twisting the facts to make the story better. He has called downstairs many times to get someone to go with him to the ballpark to take pictures just so they can see a game they'd never be able to get tickets for otherwise. And Dan Parker is everyone's uncle, even the fellows who are older.

Maybe that's because of his size. He's a big man in height and weight, but no flab. Or maybe it's the tone of his voice when he says 'How's it goin'?' He's an easy touch and I'll bet he was in on the hat passing around for my new camera.

Another guy up there is Asher Cohen. He's in circulation. He practically runs it. He has his own office. And he's not fond of the guys downstairs who are always making his life more difficult with delays because of too many words too late or any last minute pictures. But the point is, Izzy wants me to be the one to introduce this fellow Jerry Siegel from Cleveland to Al Capp. Capp is the guy's hero.

I say, "How am I going to arrange that? Capp's stuff doesn't come out of King Features. He's with United."

Izzy says, "Asher Cohen is my first cousin."

Now I am vaguely aware that Mr. Cohen has been seen in the company of Mr. Capp.

"So what's that good for?"

Izzy gives me a couple of beats to catch up and then says, "Capp lives up in Boston these days and comes to town every week or two with his latest strips. He's been buddies with Asher since when they were both down and out. They usually have lunch together. I already talked to Asher. But, Asher doesn't want to be too involved. He doesn't want Capp feeling like he's pushing something on him. Now we need you as a sort of liaison."

So Monday afternoon I go upstairs to see about the arrangements.

Asher Cohen is a thin and wispy sort of fellow. Strikes me as a little shy. Not at all like Capp. I'm thinking they must make quite a pair. And Asher has one of those deep voices you usually only catch in a barbershop quartet.

He says right off, "Al is maybe a little too careful about talking to some people. He's afraid of being set up. Ham Fisher is always looking for a way to screw around with him. And Al's especially wary of other comic strip writers. He doesn't really want to see anything new. He says they're always at the door, like wolves.

He used to be one of them himself. He knows. But now he's afraid of being sued. Since *Li'l Abner* hit the big time he's been in a constant legal tussle with Ham Fisher just because he used to work for Fisher doing *Joe Palooka* strips and Al first got the idea for his dumb hillbilly while he was still doing that."

I tell him that Izzy says, "Siegel worships the ground Capp walks on. The kid needs some advice. He's been beating around the bushes for too long. He's been reduced to sleeping on his friends' couches because he owes back rent. Al knows about what that's like. And besides, the kid is from Cleveland. Everybody I've ever met from Cleveland is as square as toast."

So Izzy makes the call. After a couple minutes he's off again and says Capp's going to be around tomorrow at nine on his way from the Station. He'll talk to the kid then.

Now, I actually called Siegel a 'kid' even though he's only a couple years younger than me. And Asher has used a few of my words on Capp to soften him up. Like, the kid is from Cleveland and 'square as toast.' The only person I know from Cleveland is Cass, but I have no idea why anyone should be as square as toast. That's probably just the word that came to mind at the time. Anyway, Capp bought it. He says he'll see Siegel on Tuesday. But the proviso is that both Asher and me are in the room. He wants witnesses. He's that gun-shy about lawyers.

This thought reminds me, so first chance, I ask The Boss if he knows how Michael Flynn is doing. The Boss says he doesn't know but the agency is sending someone else and they'll be at South Street when Cass leaves work. I got the Byron Agency's number then and called them myself. A secretary answered who doesn't know anything, and after her, a fellow who doesn't want to say anything. So I get The Boss to call them back again for me. This time they seem to know all about it.

It seems Mr. Flynn has been fired for dereliction of duty. I was standing right there and heard George ask again about that. It's clear they are not being helpful. The Boss asks them how Flynn is doing now. They don't know. So I call the Methodist Hospital again.

They have no additional information. But I know that place fairly well. I have been there a number of times through the years starting with the day I was born. At least I know he's being taken care of.

After work, I went down to South Street and met Cass at the door. There were no other private dicks around that I could spot right off. We went over to the Methodist together.

At the hospital we found out that Mr. Flynn was still in a rig to keep his lung from collapsing, and that he would not be able to talk. His condition was now listed as stable. Cass wrote a note and left it for him.

Tuesday, Jerry Siegel is in the lobby at 45th Street waiting for me when I get there at eight. He's anxious. He's thin and looks a little pale. His glasses are smudged. He's shaved but missed a spot on his neck and cut his lip. He doesn't want a coffee—I think he'd already consumed a pot or two—so I take him upstairs to my desk and we chat while I look at the assignment board and figure out what I can handle. Winchell is due back from vacation on Wednesday, so I pick out something that won't need more than a day. There is a funeral that afternoon at Woodlawn at 3 p.m. and the weather is fine. There is a dedication of a new municipal parking lot at 1 p.m. I grab both of those.

By 8:45, I know Jerry's life story. He's a very odd fellow. I haven't met Capp yet but I've spent some time with cartoonists before. They are generally not like artists. More like bookkeepers. They sit down and mark off a day's work on their boards and if you happen by a few hours later they have the squares filled in the way any accountant fills up his sheets. But Jerry strikes me as the opposite case. A freewheeler. He likes to read science fictional stories, so we talk awhile about our favorites. At least we have that in common. But I can't stand *Flash Gordon*. *Prince Valiant* is more my cuppa joe. Jerry likes them both.

We head up the stairs early and sit down outside Asher's office. After twenty minutes or so, Jerry is tired of fidgeting and starts to rehearse what he wants to say to Capp. Despite his looks, he's a pretty accomplished fellow. He has done a number of other strips. I've even seen one or two. *Doctor Occult. Slam Bradley. Sandy Keen and Radio Squad.* It's the sort of stuff you peek at when you're standing around close to a newsstand and waiting for the stiff to be carted away. But Jerry doesn't want to open his portfolio there, so I get the whole load verbally. His idea sounds to me like it's *Flash Gordon* meets *King Kong.* The hero of the piece is a guy called The Superman who is from another planet, looks like Douglas Fairbanks, is strong enough to pull trees out of the ground, or just jumps over them, but disguises himself as a reporter named Clark Kent who works for *The Daily Star* in a place called Metropolis, where he fights crime and evil doers. Fair enough.

Mr. Capp shows up an hour late, shakes hands, apologizes for the delay and blames it on the trains, which he curses in fairly strong terms. I sympathize.

Capp is a swarthy looking fellow. He has a limp because one of his legs is missing, but you can't see that. What you see is that he looks like he's compensated for this discrepancy by pushing weights. Mr. Capp tells us he has another appointment over at United Features, so we have to get right to it.

Asher moves away to a chair in the corner and Capp swipes space clear on the desk with one hand like it's his own and says, "What'da'ya got?"

Jerry opens his portfolio. What I can see there for myself looks pretty rough. There is no color. Jerry is already talking a mile a minute. Capp holds up a hand periodically to slow him down and tries to offer some quick advice.

"Drop the 'the' from The Superman. How does it sound if I say 'The Li'l Abner,' or 'The Dick Tracy?' I suppose you have it alright in 'Terry and the Pirates.' That's one. But Foster doesn't use it on his Prince Valiant series, does he? Clean it up. And what's with the big 'S' on his chest?"

"That stands for Superman."

"He calls himself that?"

Despite the doubt in Capp's voice, Siegel says, "Yeah."

Capp takes a heavy breath, "I understand he's supposed to be very strong and I see you've got him in this circus strongman outfit. I guess that could work. But the 'S' makes it look like he thinks a little too highly of himself. I'm not sure the 'S' is a good idea. So, what would his nickname be? Supe? What would his girl-friend call him?"

"He doesn't have a girl friend. Yet. I'm working on it."

"You gotta have a girlfriend. Even ten-year old boys expect that. But 'Supe,' well, I guess that goes with the nuts. You gotta be nuts to want to do a comic strip, anyway, let me tell you. But this name, 'Superman,' it sounds like Nietzsche to me. You ever read Nietzsche? Shaw? No? You're a Jew. You want to stay away from that stuff. It can be misunderstood. And this line about 'saving mankind from evil'—you're going to have every pastor from here to Timbuktu on your tail for that. They might figure that's someone else's job. Why don't you just settle for 'fighting for truth, or justice, or something a little more ambiguous like that."

Jerry says, "I was thinking his girl friend would be a reporter named Lois, and look something like a Torchy Blane."

And when I hear that, I'm thinking, that's no good!

But Capp says, "Good. She's a cookie. But why does your guy leap? Lizards leap. He should fly."

Jerry holds up his hands in defense, "But he leaps very far!"

Capp shakes his head as if that is hopeless. "You ought to give him some means to fly. Give him a Super-plane. At least something better than Tom Swift."

Jerry protests, his voice weakening "He channels the forces of his alien nature."

"Really? Well, so long as all the Einsteins can't figure out what magnetism is, I suppose that would work. The average ten-year old kid will buy anything, I suppose. But the strength thing is a problem. Popeye is strong. He has to be able to beat Popeye!"

The meeting was over in no time. Siegel seemed awestruck by the experience. I was a little worried. Capp had even used the word 'rough' himself. He told Jerry he liked the look of it but he had to polish it up. 'Supe' definitely needed a girlfriend. Maybe some more superpowers. At least a really swell car. Something like a Duesenberg but with all the edges streamlined.

On the way downstairs I admit to Jerry that when he told Capp that the character for the female reporter in his strip would be like Torchy Blane, he lost me. She's good 'B' movie material. But reporters are tougher than that. And better looking. Blane is okay but she couldn't hold a candle to Cass Green. Jerry says he'd have to see Cass to believe that.

And when we get there, Cass is sitting right at my desk, waiting for me.

This is a moment. These two look at each other with their mouths open.

He says "Sandy?"

She says, "Jerry?"

They already know each other from Cleveland. They grew up a couple of blocks from each other. Once she had to babysit for the guy. For about five minutes it's a reunion. But then Cass says she has a deadline and needs to talk to me. So I take Jerry down to the lobby by myself.

In the elevator he says, "To think, she was the skinny little girl in the shoe store. I'm glad I never saw her later on or I'd never have left Cleveland. You know, you're right. Maybe I'll get Joe to ink in Lois's hair and make her a brunette."

87. Tuesday to Wednesday, September 7 to 8, 1937

Now this is where it gets a little touchy.

I got upstairs again after saying good luck to Jerry Siegel, and Cass isn't at my desk anymore. I look around the office to see if she is schmoozing with any of her old pals and she's nowhere in sight. But I can see that The Boss has his shades down.

I sat and twiddled my thumbs awhile. When she comes out, with The Boss trailing behind, I can tell she is in no mood for kisses. The Boss comes all the way over to my desk with her. He is looking around as he comes, like he's lost. She has a face on that I have seen maybe once or twice before. Most recently, on Sunday, when she wanted to kill me.

The Boss speaks first.

"Hugh. Why don't ya take Cass out to the Palm? Will ya? On me. Talk things over. Please."

I say, "I've got to open a parking lot."

He says, "Give that slip to me. The other one too. I'll have someone else do those. You take care of Mrs. McNeill."

Wrong thing to say. Cass is keeping her maiden name. We had both agreed to that. But given the circumstances (which I wasn't yet fully aware of), this was especially bad at that moment. I see all that business streak across her face, but she holds it in.

The Palm is no place for a private conversation. Instead, I grab a couple of hotdogs and some sodas from the wagon at the corner and we went around to 46th Street where we've gone before.

The tree there is still putting down some good shade and the brownstone stoop has all the edges worn smooth in case she decides to knock me in the head.

But she hasn't said two words.

When we're there and I'm sitting down, she dumps it all in my lap.

"I want to quit."

"Why?"

"I'm sick of it!"

She could hardly speak she was so furious. The words came out between her teeth.

I say, "A hoodlum shoots a couple of rounds your way and you're giving up?"

I figured that would needle the blister pretty quick and she'd get to the meat of the matter.

She says, "I think they had this all planned."

"Who had what planned?"

"Barry George and Chester Rice."

Now, I had met her new editor at the *Journal-American* and he seemed like a pretty square guy to me. If there was any skull-duggery going on, it would be above their heads.

"What is it you think they planned?"

"They're going to stick me on the 'Celebrity Beat.' They want me to interview 'Show Folk' and fucking movie stars! I'll quit first."

I had never heard her use the word before. It was a little shocking. More so because she said it fairly loud. But nobody passing seemed to hear.

I said, "Maybe you should wait until they finish fucking before you try that. You might get them to talk a little more."

She drops her head and I'm a little worried she might start bawling again. Now that I had seen that once, I never wanted to again. And I know that, to her, this situation is worse than getting shot at.

Her voice dropped to a near whisper. "I thought things were

just starting to get pretty good. The Boss was letting me pick more of my jobs than before. And then Rice seemed pretty happy with that idea too. Miss Em is closing shop and she promised to tell me everything she knows about the trade. I have a guy in Harlem who used to work for Dutch Schultz and he wants to tell me his life story. The same old story is going on with the refugee women who are getting off the boats and being told they have to play along or they'll be sent back . . . Hugh. There is stuff to do that matters. Now they want me to interview fucking movie stars."

I could hardly hear the last words but I knew what they were.

I say, "Quit then. Tell them to go to hell. Someone else will want the good stuff."

I held on to her for a minute. There was not much more that I could say.

She finally wipes her eyes on her sleeve.

"You didn't. You didn't quit when The Boss said you had to do that stuff."

"It's different for me."

"How is it different?"

"I still have a lot of stuff to learn. I won't have to take pictures of the 'hams and harlots' for long. I'll get something out of it. And then if they can't find something better for me, I'll go someplace else."

She shakes her head. "It's not the same for you, because you're a guy."

And I shake mine, "No. It's worse. Photographers are a dime a dozen. I'm already getting away with more than most guys do. But you can write. You can write for anyone. Someone will pay for what you have to say and be happy to get it!"

This got her quiet for a minute and we ate our hotdogs. I find myself looking at that tree I noticed before. The metal bands they put around the trunk to protect it years ago are imbedded in the bark now but at one side, I can see that the weld has finally busted and it's coming apart as the tree grows. Still, my metaphor holds.

I say, "You don't need them Cass. They need you. If they

want to play the jack against the ace, that's their loss." When there was no response to that, so I asked, "What did The Boss say?"

"He denied everything. He said he hasn't talked to anyone over there since the deal was made. He thinks they're just trying to protect me. He said I should take it as a compliment. They're just trying to keep me out of the line of fire until things cool down."

"That's probably true."

"It's stupid. If they pull every reporter whenever things get hot, how are they going to get a story? If I was a guy, they wouldn't do it!"

"No. You're right. They probably think it'd look bad if a female reporter got plugged. And for them, it would. You have to see their side of it. That's the only way you can work it out."

"George didn't pull me out of it when he could have. He let me do my job . . . That's why I thought I should talk to him first."

"What was his advice?"

"Stick it out. 'Make yourself indispensible,' he says. You'll get your way and they'll pay you more for the privilege."

"What did you say?"

"I told him," she took a long breath. I braced myself because I saw something coming. "I told him I wanted to have kids some day. I won't be able to work then. I have to get something done before that happens."

Not what I expected her to say.

Now, it is a fact that Cass and I haven't talked a lot about having kids. Not yet. I figured the subject would come up on its own. Naturally. But this was more than a little bit of a knock. She had already talked about the subject with Barry George before she'd talked about it with me. This would need some time to digest. It was something to think about. But as usual, there was no time, and it was clear as day that Cass was right. She usually is.

"Don't quit then. Maybe The Boss is right after all. Maybe you should stick it out."

Those dark eyes flare. "You mean, until I get pregnant and then everything else falls into place and my mind gets made up for me!"

She is not looking to be consoled. She is looking for the fight. I love her for it.

"No! Listen. You do what you think is best. Right? But you'll have more leverage if you're inside than outside. Stick it out awhile. At least until you can get a better picture of things. Talk to Ms. Em anyway. Talk to those women that are just off the boats. Talk to your guy up in Harlem. Get those pieces down. You can talk to the Theatre Folk with your eyes closed and one arm tied. You don't have to work at that. You know what they want there. Give it to them. Meantime, you get the good stuff on paper. And when the time comes, break it to them. Not gently. If they want you to work for them, they have to let you do your job. You'll have something to offer someone else, then. They'll have to listen."

Cass looks at me now with her blank face. Her brain is busy. I wait.

Then she kisses me.

Behind us the door opens and the old gent in the homburg is there again above, and he grunts. This time he stops long enough to let me finish kissing Cass. Then he says, "Pick up your garbage!" as he slips by.

Later, we went over to the Methodist again.

Michael Flynn was sitting up in bed and looking glum. Actually he's suddenly looking a bit pink, as if the blood he's lost had all just returned to his cheeks. He's a ginger haired fellow and the hair is cut short and it makes him look like a kid, sitting there, wearing a johnny and no hat. I figure he is a little shy for having Cass in the room.

We introduced ourselves again as if he hadn't been her shadow for weeks. He thanked Cass for her note. But first thing, as soon as the small talk is done with, I want to know why the Byron Agency fired him.

He says, "It's not a very big outfit. Only four guys. I guess Mr. Byron can't afford to pay me while I'm laid up."

This was a prevarication. I asked again, "But why did they fire you instead of just laying you off?"

"When I told the cops what happened, I told them I was napping in the car before the shooting started."

"Why did you tell them that?"

"It was true."

"Maybe so, but we wouldn't be alive right now if you hadn't been there."

"If I'd spotted those guys when they showed up, I might have stopped the whole thing before it began."

This did not seem like a fair assessment to me.

"Maybe. Maybe not. They weren't there for long. We figure they knew Cass was just coming up Sterling Place from the 7th Avenue stop. Eddy had walked her to the train down at Fulton Street. Maybe they'd tried to get a hold of her there and thought better of it. And Sterling Place is quiet along where they were.

"I shouldn't have been asleep."

"No. Maybe not." But there's more to that. "The Boss says you were fishing while we were gone."

He looked surprised about my knowing this.

"Yeah. Do you fish?"

"No. Where abouts were you?"

"Adirondacks. It's a little far but I figured it might be my last chance for the season."

"How far is that away from here?"

"About ten hours."

"And they got ahold of you on Friday?"

'Yeah. There's no phone in the camp there. You have to go into town. Sorry I didn't know earlier about you being back from your honeymoon."

"So, you drove all night."

"Yes sir. I came as fast as I could."

"Yeah. Sounds like it." I paused a second to let that sink in for all concerned. "So what're you going to do now?"

"Not sure. I'll find something."

"You're going to have to recuperate."

"I'll heal up pretty quick. I'm out of here tomorrow."

"Where do you live?"

"A rooming house up in Yorkville."

"You can afford that?"

"I'll get by."

"I know a place you can stay right here in Brooklyn if you'd like. Better than a rooming house. My Mom will even feed you."

He says, "Nah. Nah. That's not necessary. I'll be okay."

I say, "Yeah, yeah, you will. But you'll be even better if you take it easy for a couple weeks over at Sterling Place."

First thing Wednesday morning, before I can sit down at my desk, Stenis tells me Winchell is in and I have to go upstairs.

It's worth going over my thoughts at that moment. Basically it's everything I said to Barry George a month ago when I was first informed about my new priorities—I thought we had an agreement.

Back then, the Boss listens to my complaint as if I was spitting in his face, which I wasn't. I had said it all very calmly. Cass was there as my witness.

I'd said, "You told me I wouldn't have to do this sort of crap."

That was the sum of my argument.

The sum of his argument was, "You do what we need you to do. I didn't promise you anything. I said I'd try to keep you off that kind of fluff. I've kept my word. But we have a shortage of help on this. Reilly is out and we both know he's not coming back. The guy that usually works on getting pictures for Winchell's stuff, Dick Franks, is out with a case of putting it where he shouldn't have. The budget is tight. Winchell doesn't give us the pics to run with his 'On Broadway' column. That's up to us. And Hearst wants the extra revenue it brings in for his International News Photo service from the other papers that take the column and might want a little dressing to go with it. This isn't the *Daily News* here. I can't afford to be using the latest stuff from the other photo services. They charge an arm and a leg for that kind of new material, but Winchell only wants fresh faces. He goes nuts when we run anything he's seen before. And right now, buster, Winchell is paying both our salaries . . . Now, I have just given you more of an explanation for what I'm doing than I have ever given anyone else in twenty-two years. Even my wife."

He looked to Cass as he said the last part. She offered him no compassion. So it was a kind of irony that now Cass would be stuck in this same sort of muck for a while.

Now, with that in mind, I went along upstairs.

Winchell is not usually in his office. I've looked into that well-appointed space before, like everyone does, and wondered why he doesn't use it more often. But he writes the sort of stuff you can jot on a cocktail napkin at the Stork Club and call in. And that's exactly what he does instead. God save the copywriter who gets it wrong when he calls something in.

The office has blinds on it and the joke is that most of the sports writers go in there to nap when he's not around. Winchell's door is closed when I get upstairs, but the blinds are open and I can see him on the phone inside, and he waves me in.

Walter Winchell is the prima donna of the *Mirror* because he sells more papers than anyone except maybe Dan Parker. He is not a big man like Parker and he is slouching in his seat now, hat on, jacket off, tie loose, and with the phone on his ear while he squints at me like he needs glasses.

Suddenly he says, "Okay, okay, okay. I'll call you back." He hangs the phone up and he is still squinting at me. "How tall are you?"

"Six feet, two inches."

"Are you the only one they've got down there? Anyone shorter? You hurt my neck."

"Sure. Billy. Eddy. I'll tell the boss you want someone shorter."

I turned then to leave.

He's says, "Whoa, whoa, whoa. Hold on there! I didn't say

that. I just asked. These people I write about get intimidated by anyone taller than they are. And some of them are very little people, if you know what I mean. That's how I get in the door. I'm small enough that everybody thinks they can handle me."

I don't believe he meant to say it the way he did. He just wanted to know, right at the start, if I was going to be a problem. There are a lot of guys who'd give an eye tooth to be assigned to taking pictures of movie stars and the like. That stuff can get reprinted everywhere. There's good money in it. That's why the news services clean up on that sort of thing.

I say, "What do you need?"

He nods at me. "I don't need a damn thing. It's our Mr. Hearst that wants something. He wants to sell a few photographs through his I. N. P. service and my column is the train that can pull that caboose. What they want are pics they can match up with the column that don't make it look like *Major Bowe's Amateur Hour*. They want good shots on anyone I'm going to mention. Trouble with that is I don't know just who I'm going to tag until the game starts. They'll typically send out three of four choices with every column. But it would be good to have six or eight, so papers have something to pick from. You don't have to worry about the Hollywood stuff. Hearst has a guy out there for that. We just need to cover Gotham. Can you do that for me for a few weeks?"

"Sure."

"No questions?"

"How much time will I have to get them?"

"I can get you a heads up for some material. But the hot news, as little as an hour. Usually six or eight. Can you handle that?"

I say right out, "I don't think so. Two or three shots maybe. Six wouldn't happen unless they were all in the same room."

He gives me the straight-face in response to my answer.

"How long have you been at this?"

"Seven years."

"You look like a kid."

"I started young."

"Let's hope it doesn't ruin you. Hookers who start young usually don't make it into their thirties."

"That's harder work."

"You think so?"

"I think so."

He nods at me. He's still squinting. I see some of that look in his eyes that Dad often has when he is sizing something up.

Finally he says, "This is what's on the menu for today. We'll want fresh shots of Welles and Houseman. Definitely. Those tyros are starting up a new drama company and somehow they've managed to get a lock on the space at the old Comedy Theatre on 41st Street. One of each is okay but together is best. Definitely Welles. Word is that *The Shadow* thing he's been signed to do for radio is going to be a stopper. And they'll need one each of Robert Taylor and Barbara Stanwyck. The marriage bells are getting louder. I hear Stanwyck is in town. Taylor is in England so forget him because Hearst wouldn't spring for the plane ticket. And here's the thing. You can't tell any of them it's for me. They should never know who it's for. They get gun-shy. And for that matter, no one else should know either. I don't want anyone to know what will be in my column until it's in print. It's just between you and me until it isn't."

"Yes sir. When do you need them?"

He smiles, "Tonight."

I turned to go.

He says, "About the Welles and Houseman thing. Don't say anything about that. I didn't say anything about that! You didn't hear that from me. I just got that tip on the phone, so it's on my mind. I have to check it out first. But we might as well have the picture ready."

I get to my desk and call Jeremy. Jeremy is good for tickets, of course, but he is also ear to the ground about who's doing what to whom and where they're doing it, as far as the theatre folk go. He slips that sort of detail into his reviews and gets good pay for it. Jeremy is loaded with gossip. He tells me that Welles is just back from a quick trip to Hollywood to talk to someone at Warner Brothers, his wife Virginia is upset with him for neglecting her, and also that he's staying with Houseman down in Greenwich Village while they cook up the plans for their new 'Mercury Theatre.' I ask him if he knows the address. I get silence.

After all the other stuff it seemed like a minor detail. So I say, I need to get some pictures, and leave it at that. Finally he says, if I'm careful about it, okay. Welles is a publicity hound. He'll pose for any and all. But Houseman, not so much.

When I get down to the Village, it's about eleven o'clock in the morning. Early for theater folk. No one answers the door. This is an entrance on a narrow alley near Bleecker. First floor. I can hear some classical music coming from a window that's partially open just beyond the doorway.

Above me is a fire escape and someone has put out potted flowers on the metal grate of the steps going up. A different flower in every pot and a different design ceramic pot on every step. A pretty picture but this is against the fire marshal's rules so you don't see it often that way.

I look in my bag. I have about two dozen bulbs in there for the flash. I grab an empty ashcan to stand on and drag it over pretty loudly so it can be easily heard and set up a nice shot on the flowers. The flash fills the alley pretty well. I used up a couple more bulbs before I actually snap a plate in the camera. Pretty soon the door opens.

Mr. Houseman is wearing a paisley silk robe and a gray scarf. He stands in the doorway and watches me take the shot and then says, "Didn't you just knock?"

I say, "Yes sir."

He says, "What are you doing now?"

"I was taking some pictures of the flowers."

The puzzle of it pulls at his face and he sticks his head out and looks upward. Then he nods.

"Very nice. But, why did you knock?"

"I work for the *Mirror*. They wanted some file photos of yourself and Mr. Welles. Nothing urgent. Then I saw those flowers.

Great picture."

He gives me a 'hurumf,' and says, "Well, if it's nothing urgent," and starts to close the door.

I'm about to speak up again but behind him I hear Welles.

"Just a minute Jack. Let me see!"

Welles sticks his head out beside Houseman and looks up.

At that point I had to take my advantage.

I say, "Hey fellas. Can I just take that shot? If it's alright, I'll take your picture the way you are right now if you just hold it a second."

Houseman looks away, somewhat severely, but Welles turns to look directly at me and I snapped it. A nice contrasting composition to the faces. Simple as that.

I'd been hoping one of them would see the flash and come out to the alley and talk to me but this was considerably easier than I thought.

There is more to this story but it will keep for now.

By one o'clock I am in Flatbush.

88. Wednesday, September 8, 1937

Now, here is the situation.

Our new quarters at Sterling Place are great. I have the dark-room right there at the front of the basement. We have our own bathroom, with the world's smallest tub (when Cass sits in it she has to keep her knees up). I brought my rubber hose rig from Perry Street so I can take showers. There are the two rooms as well a sitting area that is also the hallway to the back door. We are using the one with the windows on the backyard for our bedroom. The other one has two small windows up high, facing the air space between the buildings and that has our two desks as well as my old couch (just in the unlikely event Cass ever gets angry with me), and a lot of shelves. The books on the shelves belong to Cass. The intention was that we could both use that room to write but I can't concentrate when Cass is only a couple feet away from me so I have taken my typewriter to the darkroom to write.

Stacy had half a dozen different sorts of flowers going in the backyard but there are just a few blooming now. I don't know the names of many, but the pink and orange ones there now are very nice. The cars, ours and my dad's, are both parked at the back side of the wooden fence that is well covered with blue morning glory vines and mostly white roses in season. It's still the season.

I mention all this distraction as my excuse, because living at Sterling Place means I cannot keep up with this accounting of things the way I did before. Before, when I couldn't sleep I could just sit and type things out. Now there are other things to do and I have to fit this in where I can.

But I was getting to Flatbush.

On Wednesday morning I'd called Jeremy Stern in order to track down Welles and Houseman. Tracking down Barbara Stanwyck is a different matter. She's Hollywood, not Broadway. Who do I know for that? So I called Danny Seger. Danny is a movie fan too. He's alright now from his encounter with the guy in the holdup, but he's still assigned to a desk. This is a matter of concern for him and we have talked about it a couple of times. But at least I know where he is Wednesday morning and I call him at the 78th Precinct. I ask him if he knows where Stanwyck grew up. We both know she was born in Brooklyn and that her original name was Ruby Stevens. That's public knowledge and you can still hear a little of the old hometown in her voice if you listen. But that's about it. What I wanted to figure is where she might go while she was visiting New York. My guess is that she is staying at one of the better hotels in Manhattan. There may be a detail assignment to keep an eye on things, wherever she is. Danny might be able to get me that information if it's a quiet moment and he's sitting on his hands. Danny says he'll get back to me.

So, after I finished with Welles and Houseman, I get on the phone and call Danny back. He's got bad news. There are no detail assignments for Stanwyck that he can find anywhere. But one of the Sergeants at his precinct had duty once concerning Stanwyck and that was over in Flatbush. At least it's something. He'll call the precinct house over in Flatbush and see what he can find out.

I ate some lunch at Morgy's while I was waiting. Doc is busy but I haven't seen him since I moved my stuff out of Perry Street, so I fill him in. And I tell him about Stanwyck. Doc wishes out loud that he was twenty years younger.

Timmy, the old guy who lives in the corner booth, pipes up, "Now, there's a dame!"

This surprises both Doc and me because Timmy looks like

maybe the last motion picture star he'd know anything about is Theda Bara.

Naturally, I've just gotta say, "And she's even better looking in person."

This was a little braggadocio. I was still telling the tale around of her asking if she could hold my towel.

Timmy says, "I surely agree with that. I used to work with her brother-in-law and I got to meet her once back when she was married to Frank Fay. What a dish! The real apple pie!"

I turned on my seat at that. "What's her brother-in-law's name?"

"Bert Merkent. Good fella. His wife Maud looks a lot like Stanwyck but with a few more pounds on the carriage."

"Do you know where they live?"

"Flatbush. Never went to his house though. Stanwyck came to the building where we worked to pick Bert up once."

There is a phone booth at Morgy's and I get on the horn like a flash and call Danny back and give him the name. He tells me he hasn't found out anything else yet but he'll check this for me too. By the time I finished my egg and hash and call Danny back again, he has an address.

By one-thirty, I am in Flatbush. This is a white three-story house cheek to cheek with another three-story house, next to another three-story house. All of them white. You can't tell them apart except by the numbers on the stoop. And I decide the only thing to do is just press the bell.

Someone gets to the door but seems to have trouble opening it up. I hear a 'Damn!'

Finally it opens and there is Barbara Stanwyck scowling back at me.

She has her hair wrapped up in what looks like a kitchen towel, a man's checkered flannel shirt on, and a pair of faded jeans. No make up. You can see freckles on her cheeks I didn't know she had. And she is gorgeous.

She also has a large rag in one hand that looks like an old

undershirt and this has a glop of something at the middle. She's holding that up as if it is a weapon.

I say "Hello. I'm sorry to bother you—"

She can see the press card in my hat and the camera bag so she knows my purposes right off, but she says, "What do you want?"

"I'm from the *Mirror*. They sent me out to get a couple of shots of you back here in the old hometown, if I could. Something candid, if it's possible."

Now, I am very proud of myself for coming up with that line. I had no idea what I was going to say to start with, so I was just winging it. Seeing her there and looking so swell, dressed as she was in whatever she could find in the house, was a knockout.

And she says, "I'm sorry. I can't. I'm trying to help my sister with waxing the floor, and I shut my other hand in a car door recently so it's a difficult maneuver. That's why I couldn't turn the handle just now. I didn't mean to cuss."

I see two of her fingers on the other hand are wrapped tight. I say, "That's okay. I didn't hear it. I'm really sorry to interrupt—"

Then she frowns again and says, "Do I know you?"

I say, "We met once. I'm the guy in the towel."

This gets a quick toothy grin. She has a very nice lopsided toothy grin.

At that point I hear her sister come down some stairs asking, "Who is it Ruby?"

Miss Stanwyck looks up and down the street and then says, "Would you like to come in for a moment? Just be careful. The floor is slick."

So I get to tell her and her sister the whole true account of how I ended up in the club car on the *20th Century Limited* in just my birthday suit and a towel. She thought the story was marvelous. She thinks Cass sounds like the kind of girl she'd like to meet. She even says almost the exact same thing Miss Hepburn said once. "I've always wanted to play a reporter who actually does the work."

I got half a dozen nice pictures of Miss Stanwyck in her work clothes, down on her knees wiping wax on the floor. The one I gave to Winchell is of her looking up at me with that grin.

She says, "My agent is going to hit the roof when he sees these."

I say, "People will appreciate you more when they see how great you look without the pancake."

She says, "I saw your wife. I'll take that compliment for what it's worth."

And I did one more thing.

I told Miss Stanwyck, even though I worked for the *Mirror*, that Cass worked at the *Journal-American* and she's just been stuck with doing interviews until the smoke clears on all the shooting business and she'd love to get a chance to talk to her if there's any time for that.

Miss Stanwyck said she was sailing on the 18th of the month, via Panama for Los Angeles, so the interview would have to be before then. And she gave me the number there at the house for Cass to call. She even says, "Tell her to ask for 'Ruby,' or whoever answers might hang up."

Of course, this was all too easy. I am sure that every picture assignment for Winchell will not go as well. But I have another idea now. If I can get shots of celebrities who might make good subjects for interviews, I can feed those connections over to Cass until they let her roam free again. Sort of a leg up on things. Nobody has to know about it but us.

Back at the office, Winchell is not there so I left a note with the pictures.

So here's the rest of what happened while I was down in the Village.

When I was still standing on the ashcan in the alley after taking the shot of Houseman and Welles together in the doorway, I asked them, "What would you like for a caption on this?"

Right away Welles says, "Brutus keeping his eye on the Ides?"

And I say, "Who is Brutus?"

Houseman does a deadpan and growls, "A murderer."

And I say, "What's an Ides?"

Welles' face lights up. "You see, Jack. That's precisely why we have to do Shakespeare. They don't teach it in school anymore."

In my own defense I say, "I saw Romeo and Juliet. At least I saw the movie, anyway."

I am still standing on the ashcan, mind you.

Welles is not a small man, but he comes all the way out of the door then, dressed in a blue satin robe and slippers. You wouldn't think that would be much of a threat but the scowl on his face was enough to make me consider my position. There are some disadvantages to being a little too high.

He says, "That was a travesty! That was a sacrilege!"

I say, "I agree with that. It wasn't very good either. But wasn't that Shakespeare?"

"No! Lord help us. That was Irving Thalberg!"

I asked them, "So are you doing a Shakespeare play called 'Brutus?'"

Houseman repeats his deadpan.

Slowly, with an obvious effort to keep his temper, Wells says, "We will be doing *Julius Caesar* for our new Mercury Theatre. I'll be playing Brutus. Marcus Junius Brutus the Younger, Julius Caesar's best friend and murderer. That murder took place on March 15th, the 'Ides', way back in 44 BC. That's is, 'before Christ,' if they skipped that titbit at your school as well. As a matter of fact, I think the play ought to have been entitled 'Brutus.' He is the hero who kills the dictator and thereby loses everything he cares about. It is a great tragedy."

Welles' voice had dropped as he spoke, his anger draining, and then he turned to go back through the door. There was no missing the idea that he thought the real tragedy was that I did not know who Brutus was.

I said, "It's true. I don't know a lot about all that. But I'll read about it now. Thanks."

The two men disappeared and the door closed and I was left,

still standing on the ashcan.

I passed the info about Welles and Houseman and Brutus on to Cass.

89. Thursday to Friday, September 9 to 10, 1937

There is a fly in this ointment. The Boss tells me he is having a very difficult time covering assignments with what he has in the way of warm bodies and he needs me to tell him whenever I am between jobs for Winchell, so he can send me out on other things.

Thursday morning I'm back following Dewey around town and stuffing myself into the pool car with six other guys who have various ideas of personal hygiene.

On Friday Winchell has me in his office again.

He's not big on small talk. He puts my picture of Miss Stanwyck, the one they used for his column, down on the desk in front of me and leans back in his chair.

"How did you get this?"

"I went out to Flatbush and rang the doorbell."

"How did you know where to go?"

I shrugged, "She's from Brooklyn."

"And she just let you take that?"

"Well, not just. We'd met once before."

He wasn't buying. He taps his fingers on the edge of the desk. Then he slides over the picture of Welles and Houseman.

"How about that one?"

I say again, "I rang the doorbell."

He says, "You've got a way with doorbells."

I smiled a little, I think. Involuntarily.

"Like my dad told me, when I was shy about doing deliveries, if you don't ring, no one will answer."

He taps his fingers again and looks down at his note pad. "Do you know who George Kondolf is?"

I just shook my head. I'd never heard of him.

He says, "Guy's a producer. I'd like a picture of him. He's just come back from Chicago and he's heading up the Federal Theatre Project here in New York now. He's been brought in against Hallie Flanagan and the Workers' Alliance. That's bound to make some news any day now."

Winchell flipped a couple pages in a small notebook. "Looks like local boy Humphrey Bogart has stolen the show again, this time from Joel McCrea in *Dead End* for Goldwyn. I think he's in town. If you can find him, get a shot where he doesn't look like a hood, . . . and by the way, if he's talking, find out if this means Jack Warner is finally going to let 'Bogie out of bondage.' And let me know how you do on that one so we have time to get the Hearst guy in Hollywood to wire something if you come up empty." Winchell wrote something down on a scrap of paper torn from something on his desk. It was the address for a Maude Humphrey at Tudor City.

That was all he wanted for the day.

I find Mr. Kondolf at the Federal Theatre Project office, which was listed in the phone book and down on East 42nd Street. Easily done. This is a five minute walk from the paper, and I was back in an hour. Mr. Kondolf let me come right into his office and seemed happy that the *Mirror* had an interest in their activities. Nice guy. I had to tell him not to smile every time so that there would be something for Winchell to choose from. But I didn't mention Winchell.

It's Bogart's mother who lives in the Tudor City complex, and it was a fine day to explore that territory. Unfortunately, his mother answered the door.

I got, "My son is not interested in posing for any photographers today," and then she gives me a plug zinc, "Thank you," as she closes the door again. So at least I know he's there.

This place is another development of Mr. Fred French, the

same fellow who built the Knickerbocker Village. But this one is far better looking. They spent a little more money on details and you can see it. The halls are wider. The buildings are taller. It's not the new modern look, but it has style. I sat downstairs for awhile going over my options and thinking it would be a nice place for Cass and me to live someday. High ceilings and chandeliers. Like one of those Tishman apartments you see advertised with a living room you can play ball in. I'd like to see Cass in one of those some day. Then I notice there is a phone booth right there in the lobby and a book on a table with a green shade and the light on. I went over looked up Mrs. Humphrey's number.

I said, "Hi. This is Hugh. Is Bogie there?"

I'd never heard the nickname 'Bogie' before but Winchell had used it and that made me think it must be the right one.

After half a minute I hear the voice. It is not so different from what it was in *Petrified Forest*, but that's probably because he was not sure who the hell 'Hugh' was.

He says, "What can I do for you?"

I say, "You can get me out of a jam. I'm a photograper for the *Mirror*. I need a candid shot of you for a piece covering your performance in *Dead End,* but I won't be able to wait around for you to leave the building because I have to help a guy who's laid up and needs his stuff moved this afternoon. Any chance you can just step out in the hall for a minute and let me do the deed? Promise it won't hurt."

I get complete silence. But he doesn't hang up. I think he had his hand over the receiver and I can hear a little chuckle going on.

Finally he says, "Come on up."

He met me outside the door. Just shirt and slacks. No smile. He let me take two shots and then held up his hand and starts to go inside again. But then he turns to me.

"Why is your friend laid up?"

"He was shot."

"No kidding?"

"He's a private detective and he was trying to save my wife's life. So I owe him."

"What does she do?"

"She's a reporter for the *Journal-American.*"

"Who's trying to kill her?"

"Some Nazis."

"No kidding! I was sure you were just putting me on. It was the best excuse I've had in a month."

"You can read all about it. I think the story's in most of the Sunday papers."

"The real thing then. Not Hollywood?"

"It felt real to me."

"You were there, too. Really? Why don't you come in a minute and tell me a little more about it." He cups a hand at his mouth and whispers, "I'm bored stiff," and then louder, "I can never believe anything I read in the papers these days after reading all the stuff they say about me."

Like Miss Stanwyck, Mr. Bogart also has a crooked smile and he uses this frequently, something you seldom see in the movies where he is usually playing a thug. And he has hound dog eyes. He uses the eyes to keep your attention.

Mostly we talked about the Douglas DC-3. Mr. Bogart had just flown to New York in one and was much impressed by the experience, same as I was. And that got us talking about flying, which he'd love to learn to do, and then about Howard Hughes. Mr. Bogart has met the man several times and found him to be eccentric. While we talked, his mother served us tea. But her face never lost the skeptical glare. Mr. Bogart apologized that he could not serve me anything stronger. So I told him about Miss Em and her Samovar. That got a laugh. We ended up by talking about the Chrysler Airflow, which he loves but doesn't own because Jack Warner provides vehicles from whichever manufacturer is paying the most for the exposure.

I left the place feeling a little better about the job.

Winchell liked the pictures. He looked at me about as skeptically as Maud Humphrey had, but didn't ask about anything else so

I didn't tell him.

Because Dad hadn't left from work yet, he offered to take the El home and I borrowed the A-model and went uptown to the rooming house on 96th Street and grabbed everything that looked heavier than a pound or so. I figured Flynn would be able to handle anything smaller in a few days and the room was paid up through the next week. There wasn't much. Except for a bundle of various sorts of fishing rods and a bucket full of reels and things, two suitcases' worth. Mr. Flynn was living light. He has another gun, a .32 police special and that was the heaviest object other than the suitcases. His landlady kept me there for half an hour more to tell her the whole story again about the shootout.

I picked up Cass on the way to Brooklyn. I still hadn't seen any other private dicks lingering around her office at South Street.

Cass and I both went over to get Mr. Flynn at the Methodist hospital about 6 p.m. We had him up in my brother Erik's old room on the second floor by 6:30.

90. Monday, September 12, 1937

Jack Pines is a veteran crime reporter and knows as much as any man about the dark at the heart of his fellow man. He was a correspondent for the *Telegraph* in the war. Avoided the bullets and the gas on the Eastern front and got as far as Moscow, where he was stood up against a wall by the Bolsheviks everyday for a week, never knowing when they were going to pull the trigger. The *Telegraph* paid an unknown sum for his release. This is likely the root cause of his drinking and the reason he's been married three times (along with his often stated philosophy that what is wrong with most relationships is too little sex and too many tears), and why he has been fired from nearly every newspaper in the city (at least twice before from the *Mirror*). There is always someone like Jack around, but the others (like Phil Smith in the sports department, or Nathan Shultz, who still gets a piece now and again in the theatre section) are usually referred to as 'Jacks,' not for their knowledge of the trade but because they are only lesser versions of the original.

You hear, "Don't be a Jack. Get your ass into a pair of pants and get it done."

As I've often heard it said by others: the hardest part of any job is showing up. The disillusioned reporter is often stymied by the very first hurdle of the day: getting out the door to face the firing squad one more time. This, I believe, was Jack Pines' greatest weakness. The booze only dulled the losses.

Jack Pines' home address has also changed a few too many

times through the years. On at least two occasions I've had to find his current abode, jimmy his door open, pick him up out of whatever piece of furniture he'd collapsed in, dump him into his tub and turn the cold water on his head. Luckily, Jack is not a big fellow and easy to manhandle.

Sam Felt, a towheaded college kid from Columbia University, has been raised a notch by The Boss to take on some of my photographic chores now that I have been elevated to the rarified atmosphere of the fourth floor. Sam acquitted himself nicely during the heavy rains in August while Cass and I were away gallivanting. He got some terrific shots on a building collapse in Staten Island, with the bodies of the recovered dead set out in a row for identification by neighbors. But I've kept my desk downstairs, and Sam now sits in the chair that used to be occupied by Tom Reilly. This is The Boss's doing again, looking to provide a short-cut education. Trouble is, it doesn't work that way. Nothing I say to Sam is going to sink in until he's had to stand outside the Tombs for a couple of hours in the rain on a bad tip. About the fourth or fifth time through, certain things start making sense, even to brains as dense as mine.

I have covered a couple stories with Jack Pines myself through the years, and spent some time with him at several taverns, mostly Dooley's, which is his favorite hangout and where he can most often be found because his ex- first brother-in-law has a family interest in keeping the father of his nephews within reach.

Now The Boss has hired Jack back again to fill in the gaps while the two rookies, Bud and Bob (acquired out of the *Journal-American* trade to replace Cass) get up to speed. Jack knows he's on a short leash. And Bud, a former paperboy with the chub of a fellow who loves his doughnuts, has been assigned to shadow him— ostensibly to learn the tricks of the trade, but I suspect it will more likely result in Bud becoming a connoisseur of the various affordable whiskies that Dooley's is famous for.

This is all preamble toward explaining what happened on Monday.

On Monday, the report came in about some human remains

that were spotted in the City garbage heaps over in Staten Island. Luckily, this did not require another long schlep to that forsaken piece of geography. The remains had been found the previous week and shipped over to the facilities at Bellevue and it was Monday when the wire came through from the police department medical examiner. Despite the decay, fingerprints were recovered and matched to officer Theodore H. Lorimer. He had been shot more than once, not in the eyes but maybe not for lack of trying. Like old Fred Bellows, when Ted Lorimer realized what was happening, he likely tried to escape. The shots were in his back. One in the back of his head. All the bullets were twenty-two caliber and still present in the decay of the cadaver. This was the sad fact we had all expected, though I was not sure we'd ever see the guy's body again. The particular refuse in the immediate vicinity of the human remains were quickly deter-mined to have been removed from the Knickerbocker Village. Miss Beinecke had probably dumped poor Ted right in the chute with the rest of her trash.

A 'wanted' bulletin was immediately, if belatedly, issued for Lucille Beinecke. Now Jack Pines was assigned to doing follow up on this and the links to the other Annie Oakley murders and for that task he comes to see me.

Jack pulls up a chair and asks, "How ya doin?'"

He has his collar pinned tight behind a neat knot of tie just below cleanly shaved jowls, his jacket and vest do not show any signs of soup, his pants are creased, and his shoes shine. I figure Jack is currently on the wagon. Bud Patrick, his apprentice, is leaning up on the edge of the next desk. Bud's eyes are scanning the desks around to see if anyone has left behind any baked goods. The kid already looks a little the worse for wear. Maybe he was up the night before or slept in a chair.

I tell Jack, "Suddenly I'm not feeling so well. Maybe I should go home for a nap."

He gets the apology into the tone of his voice. "Hugh, if it were up to me, I would just leave the whole thing in your lap. I know you want to cover this. But The Boss wants me in on it too. I'm only doing my job. You know your sweetheart over at the *Journal-American* has gotten the same report and she is probably knocking heads to get some space in the next edition over there. But we've got a different paymaster, even if it all comes out of Mr. Hearst's pocket. And remember the *Daily News* and the *Post* are not playing tiddly-winks. So what have ya got for me?"

Now, I have a couple of ways to go on this but I could see it coming when Jack was re-hired and I had already made up my mind. I reached into my top drawer and pulled out the folder with the typed copies of what I'd prepared from my notes for The Boss, whenever he got around to asking. He almost never asks, but I've had my ass in a sling for not doing it in the past and that was enough.

I say, "Just return the folder when you've copied what you want," while Jack gives me the same look that I would give him under the circumstance, asking 'What's the price?' So I add, "I'll keep you posted."

He knows what that means. I'm not walking away from the story. If he doesn't make anymore of it, I will. I'll get back to him for a favor of my own, in good time.

And I know this: that Cass will be well ahead of him.

Actually, when I came in the door, Stenis hands me another piece of an envelope with a couple names scrawled on the back. Winchell is not in the office, but he has called these in: Frances Farmer and Luther Adler. Nothing more. No instructions. Inside the remains of the envelope is a part of a Consolidated Edison electric bill with Stenis' name on it so I know he took the message himself.

When Pines shows up I'm in the process of making my calls for the Winchell job. Sam Felt has been sitting across from me this whole time, reading a comic book, and acting like he is not there. Smart fellow.

With Pines gone, Sam says, "So what are we going to do?"

I suddenly realize I have a small advantage of my own. Pines will be running Bud Patrick into the ground to follow up leads. I've got Sam Felt as my gofer on this.

Now, I tell Sam that, firstly, I want a picture of the scene of the crime. On the day he died, I doubt if Ted Lorimer got much further than Lucille Beinecke's apartment. With a little luck, maybe a lot of her furniture and things are still sitting there where they were. Beinecke had left in a hurry and only taken away what she could fit in her Buick. I run this idea down for Sam and ask him how good he is with locks. He gives me a blank stare. Good man. So I apprise him of the situation. The police have already been in the place—probably more than once. But the building superintendent is not going to just give him a key. He has to make use of his God-given talents and effect an entry on his own that will not damage property or alter the scene in any way. Besides, I say, "The cops probably forgot to lock the door, and even if they didn't, you make sure you say they did, if anyone asks."

The face is still empty. I know the kid is sharp so this is his way of milking me.

I say, "Do you have a fin?"

He shakes his head. A very smart lad, indeed, I think. Never admit you've got any cash to a superior.

I tap my wallet and give him two fins just in case. "First you go to the janitor. Tell him who you are and what you need. He'll have a key for doing repairs. You offer him the fin. If he refuses that, offer the whole sawbuck. If he refuses that, mark him down for a better man and tell Jersey Cohn downstairs in maintenance about him. Cohn is always looking for honest help. Then go talk to the superintendent. Same deal. But if he refuses, don't mention him to Jersey because Jersey wouldn't want anyone who could move in on his own job. Now, if that doesn't work, try the building manager. I think I saw the office on the corner of the building. And if none of that works, try this."

In my drawer I have a steel nail file as well as a small screw-driver for tightening the handle screws on the Speed Graphic. These are legitimate tools of the photographer's trade, but if used properly, can be handy in the case of simple locks. I pass these to the kid and also tell him about the secret properties of a stiff press card.

Finally I had a change of mind, "On second thought, you might try the screw driver and nail file first."

Then I write out the address and send him on his way. After that I finished my phone calls.

It appeared that the two names, Frances Farmer and Luther Adler, neither of whom I knew before, were part of an outfit called The Group Theatre. They have been around for five or six years. Politically, this outfit is somewhat radical—enough so that they are not directly hitched to the Federal Theatre Project. And these guys had just booked the Belasco theatre for November for a new play called *Golden Boy*.

Theatre owners and managers all want to hang around in places like the Stork Club to catch some of the reflected limelight, and this is likely the source of Mr. Winchell's information. But if I was going to track down the principles in The Group Theatre, I would probably find them at a place called the Pine Brook Country Club, which is located on Pine Lake, up in Trumbull, Connecticut.

I should note that all of this information came from one source, but I had to make half a dozen phone calls before I thought of it. My trip down to 42nd Street the previous week to speak with Mr. Kondolf at the Federal Theatre Project had required a very pleasant wait in his outer office chatting with a Miss Finklestein, his secretary. Miss Finklestein's name is Gloria. There I learned that Gloria has her own theatrical ambitions and she seems to know the answer to any question I had put to her.

So I called Gloria. And next I called Cass.

My proposition is that I go to Brooklyn, get the car, pick her up at her office door in forty-five minutes, and we drive out to Connecticut together. She can interview whomever she wants among this thespian crowd and I can get my pictures and everyone is happy. Maybe there will even be time for a dip in the lake. Cass asks if I've heard about Lorimer. I tell her I've sent Sam Felt to grab a couple of interior shots on the apartment just in case The Boss wants them. Cass tells me that she has sent out someone named Perkins for the same job. We both hope they don't surprise each other too badly.

Before noon I've got Cass in the car and a kiss and we're on our way for a drive in the country. The sun is bright, the air is warm and light, and all is well.

An hour later we are still poking along in traffic on the Boston Post Road, somewhere near Rye, and Cass is telling me how she would not mind living in Connecticut, even though that destination is still ahead of us.

Of course, there is a train. The traffic along the way is not the whole story. It's just the smell of the air that does that sort of thing to the brain. The leaves are turning and we have the darker green of late summer on either side with some patches set afire by the first color and all that framing the bright white colonial style houses and small stone-faced shops and the smell of autumn like a deep musk mingled in the exhaust of the car ahead. But something in the way she says this tells me to forget about my thoughts of living in San Francisco or even Tudor Village for the time being. And then she confirms that hunch with her recollections about the day we went to the wedding in Larchmont.

Pine Lake is in the middle of the woods, as you might expect. There is no 'country club' that we can see when we get there. Up a low ridge to the right, shaded into a near dark by a thick cover of tall pines, there is a row of cabins. The main building, which we had passed on the road coming in, is not much more than a wide low barn. The door there is locked. According to the attendant at the gas station, where we had stopped for a soda and a chat out on the paved road, this place is a summer camp for theatre people, but the season is over. The road where we are is rough gravel with the ruts hidden beneath the first fall of leaves. All you can hear when I turn off the engine is the wind in the pines. After a minute Cass says, "I'd like to live right here."

My best estimate is we are at least twenty minutes from the train station in Bridgeport. Commuting to work in New York would be an hour and a half either way.

I say, "It's too far."

She looks at me like I'm a spoilsport. And just then we hear some angry voices coming up the slope from the lake.

Below us, through an irregular barricade of the pines is a sort of natural shallow amphitheater created by the slope of the hill as it reaches the water. In a nest of sunlight close by the water's edge at least a dozen people are sitting around and watching while two of them argue. I grabbed a shot of that on the way in, just to frame the situation.

As we approached, the two guys who were arguing stop and the whole bunch of them look our way. The sound of our steps on the thick mat of the pine needles is a hollow sort of drumming into a near silence, like a proper stage entrance.

One fellow seated at the center of this audience stands.

"Are you reporters?"

His scowl is either a good bit of acting or the real thing.

Cass said, "Yes sir. I'm from the *Journal-American*—"

He interrupts whatever else she was ready to say.

"Did Sandy Meisner call you? I told him I didn't want any reporters yet."

I said, "No, sir. Someone at the Federal Theatre Project—"

He cuts in again, "Kondolf! Now he wants to get a finger in the pie!"

Cass smiles, "I wouldn't blame Mr. Kondolf. We just heard you were doing something interesting and I've been told by my editor to be looking for some fresh faces."

I thought this was a very good line on Cass's part. 'Fresh faces,' are what the younger actors like to have, at least as much as the old ones want to have mugs that are interesting.

We kept walking as we answered and by the time we've reached the perimeter of the gathering, the fellow has given Cass a full inspection.

He says, "You're not an actress looking for a part are you? Because, honestly, we're full up."

She says, "No sir. I'm just a reporter for the *Journal-American*. My name is Cass Green. This is Hugh McNeill," She pulled out her press card for proof.

With that, the fellow waves us off with apparent disgust and says, "Sit down and keep quiet!' But then points at me. "And no flash!"

The flash was not a problem in any case. The light was behind us and the water was a good frame. Nevertheless, I'd brought my new camera with me, just in case, and took some extra shots with that.

For most of the time we sat uncomfortably on the leaves and rocks at the far edge as specific scenes were called out, apparently at random, and various combinations of actors stood in front of the others and delivered their lines. Some scenes were repeated several times, adding minutes to the torment of my rear-end against the particular patch of ground I'd chosen.

All of them look pretty young to me, but the original fellow who had spoken to us, a man I found out later was the director, Harold Clurman, appears to be older than the others. In his mid-thirties, I guessed. He is not tall and commands considerable presence by his voice alone and the exactness of his words, though he never addressed his actors as loudly as he had spoken to us. None of the guys was particularly tall, in fact.

After a couple of hours I had gotten good clean shots on everyone present, and then, with the gathering broken up, I went about my own business getting the names down as Cass pursued the director first and then the two lead actors that Winchell wanted pictures of.

Luther Adler, playing the 'Golden Boy' of the title, is supposed to be a boxer named Joe Bonaparte who wishes he were a violinist—a very unlikely situation if you've ever been around a gym or boxing club. Who writes stuff like that? Miss Farmer plays Lorna Moon, the girlfriend of Joe's boxing manager, and she is the love interest, or maybe Joe is just infatuated. Hard to tell. The manager, a fellow named Moody, is played by the actor Roman Bohnen. Supposedly, Moody is already married and Lorna is waiting for the divorce, but in one scene it sounds like he is trying to get her to seduce Joe, so I don't know.

Joe clearly has an interest in Lorna, but apparently a bigger hankering for money than for either the violin or Miss Moon. I just couldn't buy that. Frances Farmer looked like she might be worth a little more consideration. But this is the old 'threesome' problem again that we had seen before in the movie *Slim* and a boatload of other motion pictures. How was it that this same plot keeps coming up?

The others, none of whom I have seen before, are Martin Ritt, Jules Garfield, Elia Kazan, Phoebe Brand, John O'Malley, Harry Morgan, Lee J. Cobb, Howard Da Silva, Karl Malden, Morris Carnovsky, Art Smith, and Robert Lewis—the most unlikely looking bunch of performers I've ever seen. Except for Miss Brand, and Miss Farmer, of course, not a pretty face in the bunch, fresh or not. But boy can they act up a storm. And they've got the corner on being an unhappy lot.

Cass tells me later that the author, Clifford Odets, has recently been in Hollywood and I figure he was probably just there to steal some more bright ideas from those particular thieves. The really good ideas, like boxers who play violins, must be hard to come by. But Odets is not there at the lake to ask. He's in New York, doing an interview with the *Times*.

During a break in the rehearsal, Cass followed a couple of the lead players up to a nearby cabin to talk. I found a more comfortable spot on one of the logs where the others had been and relaxed there in the sun and chatted with a talkative fellow named Elia Kazan who was nearby. Kazan is maybe the skinniest and smallest of the bunch, with a large head made heavier with thick black hair. He looks like a fellow I used to know named Murray. Murray was so small he once got hit by a coal truck because the driver had missed seeing him over the load. Kazan has just been given a new part to understudy and after reading it through once aloud, he asked me what I thought of what I'd heard so far and I told him that the actors all seemed very good—'strong' I said—but that I did not understand the problem.

He says, "What problem?"

I say, "Any kind of story, even a play, I think, is about a

problem, isn't it? Otherwise there isn't much to say."

He agreed with that, but didn't understand why I couldn't see the problem in *Golden Boy*. He shrugs at me, "Joe's spirit is conflicted by materialism—between doing what he really wants to do and the money he can get from boxing."

I say, "I don't understand that. He's not starving to death, is he? In fact, he looks pretty healthy to me. Especially if he can still fight. If he really wanted to play the violin, he'd just do it."

Mr. Kazan smiled at me in the way people do who think you're an idiot for not agreeing with them.

"Sometimes it's not that easy."

I admitted, "I guess that must be true for some people because you see it happening in the movies all the time. But I've just never seen it myself. Not in real life."

He says, "You must be living a charmed existence. It's not that way for everybody. Most people are not so fortunate."

I answered with my first thought, "Well, that's true. I do live a pretty charmed life, I think. Sometimes I worry about it. Especially when I see other people who're having it rough."

He says, "I thought you just said that you'd never seen that kind of thing before."

I didn't think what I said was all that hard to understand, especially for someone who was obviously pretty smart.

"No. What I said was I'd never seen people who had the choice and didn't do exactly what they really wanted to do. Your Joe there is not starving to death. If he was, or if his family was, I could see him putting aside the violin in order to earn what he needed to take care of things. But from what I've heard, he's more interested in money than anything else. He says that to his father, doesn't he? So I don't see the problem. He goes after the money. He gets what he wants—and that's only what he deserves."

Mr. Kazan shook his head at me. He still didn't get it. He says, "Then I guess you can say he regrets his decision. That's the problem."

This wasn't an answer. That was after the fact.

"Well, in that case, I'd say it comes on him a little late, wouldn't you say? We all have regrets, and it's hard to give a damn about someone who cares so little about the other people in his life, and more about the money. Now, if he just had to choose between the girl and the money, that's no choice at all. No story there. Any fool knows what to do in that case. Especially with someone that looks like Miss Farmer there. So he must not love her. And besides, he's two-timing his friend. That doesn't make him anyone you'd give a break to, does it? In that case he has a problem for sure, and I don't care if he does."

Mr. Kazan was looking at me as if I was kidding him. So before he could make another smart remark I added, "But you know, the actors are so good they make you care about the characters anyway. It's hard not to."

He seemed a little more satisfied with that.

He says, "Did you see *Johnny Johnson* last year?"

"No, I didn't. How was it?"

"Well, I think it was pretty good. I was in it, of course, so that may be an unfair judgment, but others thought so too. It was about the futility of war and death. It just needed a little more of the music that Kurt wrote for it."

He didn't look old enough to know much about the war, but I figured that might be a point for agreement, whoever Kurt was, and even though a musical about war and death seemed like a stunt to me, so I said, "I like the musicals. Say, did you see the new Cagney picture yet? It's called *Something to Sing About*? Now that one's terrific!"

Kazan gets a pained expression, "No. But let me guess. It takes place at Sing Sing. It's a prison musical. What a great idea!"

The sarcasm was thick but I got quite a laugh out of his answer and so did Cass when I told her all about the conversation later in the car.

Cass had some stories of her own and maybe something else that might explain why these people are so taken with this play about a rat. It seems the author, Mr. Odets, is newly married to the actress

Louise Rainer. Rainer is supposed to be top drawer, especially now that she's won the Academy Award, but she's not to my taste. I've never seen her smile. In any case, Rainer is back in Hollywood for a few months and it appears that while she's gone, Clifford Odets is fooling around on her here with Frances Farmer, the blonde who is playing Lorna Moon. That would at least explain some of Mr. Odets' way of thinking for what he writes about. He's a rat too. And it was notable that one of the others in the group was quick to share that piece of gossip. The lot of them should just be happy now that Cass is not about to use the sordid details about that affair in whatever she writes.

It was already dark when we got back. I drove by the office for a minute on the way and left the shots of Farmer and Adler at the darkroom there with instructions to make extra copies and to send one of each up to Winchell's office and another set to Stenis. I also checked on the success of Sam Felt. He'd done very well and turned in a dozen shots of the inside of Lucille Beinecke's apartment and these were safely in Stenis' hands now, out of the reach of Jack Pines. More than enough for my purposes. The kid had even left an envelope on my desk with one of the fins in it.

91. Monday to Tuesday, September 12 to 13, 1937

Cass and I were up late on Monday night, talking. This was the result of some very good cookies as much as the various things that we had to discuss. The thing of that was that Mom has found another housekeeper to help her with things.

My mom's first attempt at replacing Stacy was Mrs. Fabio. I knew her son a little from High School. He was in the grade behind me. Mrs. Fabio is a very nice Italian lady who was born in Palermo, Italy. Plump is a polite description. But she is always moving, so the plump never goes to fat. Her use of the English language is a purposeful confusion of negatives that give her ample room for doing exactly what she wants. "I no think I can't do that, no?" is a favorite. But she has very strong opinions on almost every topic, from making up a bed to the correct way to make bread. Maybe a few more than my mother wanted. She's already gone now and been replaced by Mrs. Nessen.

Mrs. Nessen is a widow, born in Amsterdam, and at least as opinionated as Mrs. Fabio. But Mrs. Nessen knows how to do a proper 'hospital fold' when she makes up a bed and is a stickler for things to be 'clean as a whistle,' which is another expression I have my doubts about. You'll know when she is not in agreement by the fact that she says nothing. And if she likes an idea she is extravagant about telling you, giving it at least three 'Ya's' and sometimes four.

Dad is not getting along with Mrs. Nessen just yet. He was happier with the plump Mrs. Fabio. Mrs. Nessen is square-faced and flat chested. She does not smile more than she has to. She has a very severe appearance and buns her hair tightly at the back in two near perfectly spherical balls, a feat that is accomplished by the use of pearl-headed pins. I've already heard Dad use the term 'big boned' to describe her looks. He has also speculated about the balls on her head in a way that left no doubts about his opinion concerning her strengths.

Now my mom has informed me that Mrs. Nessen already has her eye on Mr. Oliphant's room on the fourth floor. That is, without Mr. Oliphant in it. It appears that he will be leaving us soon. Mom has seen the man moving his belonging out bit by bit, but he's said nothing to her. In the meantime, Mrs. Nessen lives in a rooming house on Bedford Avenue and complains loudly about the walk up the hill everyday so as to make her case.

But here is the deal. Mrs. Nessen has started baking cookies at least once a week. My dad has a great weakness for cookies and now his complaints about our new housekeeper have nearly stopped.

On Monday night we come in the house too late for dinner and the place is filled with the smell of chocolate chip cookies. There is a note and a couple of dishes in the icebox with our dinners, but Cass commandeered the jar of cookies and I grabbed a bottle of milk from the refrigerator and we sat up in bed until three in the morning and talked about what we'd seen that day.

The situation here is this: these actors with the Group Theatre appear to think that their business is not entertaining the public but educating them. Politics before pleasure. Cass thinks there is something very twisted about this and says that it even throws some extra light on our maniac, Miss Beinecke. Cass's interviews with several in the group left no doubt about their political intent and this was oddly repetitive from one to the other, as if they were all singing from the same hymnal. It was the sort of cant you hear from a priest and don't bother to ask yourself where you might have heard it before, or how many times.

As Cass talked about it, I could hear the strains of the piece she would be writing, coming together. As best she could determine, this play, *Golden Boy*, was an attempt to appeal to a larger public after some previous efforts had failed to draw an audience despite critical praise. Two recent dramas, *Johnny Johnson*, and *Waiting for Lefty*, had been much criticized as mere political agitprop. But now both Clurman and Odets had gotten 'a taste of sin' in Hollywood in the past year and wanted more of it. There had been considerable dissension in the group about this and two of the principals, Cheryl Crawford and Lee Strasberg, had left the company this past spring over the disagreements.

One of the actors, Bobby Lewis—this is the fellow who played Joe, the promoter who promises the conflicted boxer the riches he will never have by playing the violin, and a fellow I'd already noted because he spoke with the unmistakable accent of a Brooklyn native—had said that the real reason for the break-up with Strasberg earlier in the year was over the interpretation of something called the 'Stanislavski System.' This is evidently some kind of acting philosophy that seems to drive these people to a near madness over the way they choose to perform their roles. It sounds like more religious dogma to me.

But Cass was more disturbed by the intensity of the argument. There seemed to be very little room for accommodation over differences. Mr. Lewis believes an actor should project his character from both inside and outside, while Mr. Strasberg evidently thinks that the character portrayed by the actor can come only from within. But I know some terrific actors who probably don't know a thing about any of this and never heard of this Russian, Stanislavski, and they do just fine.

I told Cass, the funniest thing was when I mentioned to Mr. Kazan that I'd spoken recently to Orson Welles and John Houseman. I hardly got the brag out before Kazan practically spat on their names and called them "Egoists! Showboats!" This was evidently because they had both already succumbed to the allure of fame and money. His reaction reminded me a little of Miss Beinecke calling the Russian, Leon Trotsky, "traitor!"

The politics of these people was somehow tied up with a

moral belief in the very purpose of their acting. That much was certain. Stanislavsky is their Christ, and like Protestants and Catholics they were fighting it out to the death over who was the better Christian. Christians have been killing each other over that point for centuries, I think, and not so differently than the Stalinists and Trotskyites who are just as willing to kill each other lately over the correct interpretation of what Mr. Marx has said. Wasn't it all about loving their fellow man? Or Woman?

My dad was quite unhappy about the empty cookie jar on Tuesday morning when he packed his lunch, but this was soon remedied by Mrs. Nessen.

92. Tuesday, September 14, 1937

This was a long, hot, and interesting day.

When I get into the office, I see that one of Sam Felt's photos of the inside of Lucille Beinecke's apartment has been used on page one, along with the headline, 'Annie Oakley Killer on the Run,' and right there next to an opening rehash by Jack Pines. However, the kid is not there for me to congratulate him. Under the heading of 'no good deed goes unpunished,' Stenis has already sent him over to City Hall to sit on a wooden bench and watch a ceiling fan turn while one of the City Council members dilates on the need for new garbage trucks.

But two matters bothered me about that photo. One was that the apartment was a mess. The cops had taken it apart, and clothes and things were all over, drawers spilled, and scraps of paper had been dumped from a trashcan. This is a false impression of Miss Beinecke. Even in a rush, I doubt if she would have left anything out of place. The other is that the news is two weeks old.

Nevertheless, our lede beat the *Journal-American*'s, hands down. They had gone with a near standing head, "Jap Guns fire on Chinese Lines," and the sub-head "5000 Europeans and Americans endangered in Shanghai." But that business was half a world away. Below the fold they had a feature on a dog named Socks that managed to climb a tree in the Bronx, probably chasing a squirrel. They tagged that with 'Dog gone it,' along with a photo of the sad eyed pooch out on a limb. The fire department had been called to the rescue and the appropriate pictures taken. No by-line, I was pretty sure who wrote it.

Because it was obviously a slow news day unless you happen to be in Shanghai, I have to forgive The Boss for going with Jack Pine's rehash of the whole Beinecke matter along with Sam Felt's photo rather than letting things go to the dogs.

For my own part, I'd finally finished the books I'd originally bought for the honeymoon trip. I can say for sure now, never take a book with you on your honeymoon. And in my own defense, all I can say about that is, I didn't know what to expect.

Mr. Hemingway is over in Spain again, but I hadn't bought any books that day I saw him at the Scribner's store on Fifth Avenue so I went over there to try my luck again. Maybe his new book would be out. But it wasn't. Instead the place is busy with suits and secretaries and all the things I saw were the same as what I'd seen before. *Gone with the Wind* is still stacked up in the window. *Northwest Passage* is stacked beside that. I don't see another book by Forester, the fellow who wrote *Beat to Quarters*, but there are plenty of books for kids and you'd think it was already Christmas.

So I went on over to the Public Library to look for something else.

The woman behind the counter there looks at me like she knows me. I remember her well enough. She'd made me fill out the paperwork when I'd shown up there the very first time.

I ask her where I can find Mr. Shakespeare.

She sends me away to a corner at the Bryant Park side of the reading room. There, they have at least nine different versions of *Julius Caesar*, and I picked the one with the explanations for the odd words.

Back at the counter, the blonde is there waiting for me now like she has nothing better to do.

"You're the newspaper guy?"

"Yes."

"You haven't been in any more fights lately."

"Not many."

"You like to read Shakespeare?"

"Mostly I just look at the pictures."

She laughs at the joke and gives me a funny face. A nice face. Sky-blue eyes. And I had one of those funny thoughts just then. A year ago I would have hung around long enough to get her name. But everything has changed.

But by that time it's getting late and I know that Cass will get a kick out of the story. So I head home by way of South Street.

First thing I see when I get off the elevator at the *Journal-American* city room is she's on the phone and I take a seat in the waiting area. By the time she hangs it up, I'd already started talking to Mike Sommers, one of the sports writers who happened to be passing by, about the sad fate of the Dodgers. But even across the room I see that look on Cass's kisser right way. A total blank. Then she sees me and comes right over.

She says, "Get in the elevator," so I do.

As soon as we are alone she says, "That was Detective Jack Barnes. He still calls me now and again, you know. He can't figure what I see in you. He's said as much."

I gave that a big shrug. "I have the same difficulty. I figure you must have a lucky blind spot or something. Lucky for me."

She says, "He told me to keep him in mind if I decided to dump you."

"At least he's persistent. That can pay off, sometimes."

I'm just about to tell her about the blonde at the library.

She says, "And just to show that there were no hard feelings, he gave me a little tidbit to sweeten my thoughts about him."

"What was that?"

The doors open and we are faced with a couple of her fellow reporters and she gives them a smile. When the doors close again and we're outside and alone she says, "A murder. In Pelham. Barnes just got the call, himself. Unfortunately it took him five minutes to get to the facts, so we're already late. Come on."

Now I'm all in, but I have to remind her of something she has forgotten.

"Weren't you headed out to Flatbush this evening to talk to Ruby?"

She stops cold in her tracks. Just a second for that. And then says, "I'll call to apologize later."

With rush hour still in progress, we took the El to 14th, switched over to the Lexington Express and then to the Pelham line, and walked from the station there. The murder was already at least an hour old. And it was half an hour before we were on the premises, along with a dozen other newsboys.

Now, in the earlier phone call, Detective Barnes had said to Cass, "I thought you might be interested in the thing because the victim was shot in the right eye." And right off we see Carl Stowe, another *Journal-American* re-porter who works out of New Rochelle and mostly covers Westchester County. He has 'fast' Eddie Pyle with him doing the photos. Carl gives us a dirty look as we come in. He has a right to be there, under other circumstances, and couldn't have missed the first police reports because he has a radio set-up in his basement at home. But later, when we were about done with it, Cass goes over and pins him in the corner like the bug he is and tells him he should have called her the minute he knew what the situation was because it's her story. He mumbles something. Then she tells him to go ahead, file his story anyway, what he's got is his, and lets him crawl away.

The situation there was this: the blonde in the bulky pink terry cloth robe and bare feet with toenails painted red, goes by the unlikely name of Peggy Starr. She's smoking her way through a pack of Pall Malls while sitting on the couch in the midst of all the hubbub, and she has an interesting story to tell.

Miss Starr is clearly pushing forty around and it's getting heavier. She lives in this little one-floor peaked roof Tudor style brick house in Pelham, with her current boyfriend, Stanly Baker. Or did. The house belongs to her, via a previous husband. It's just about a couple of blocks from the end of the subway line. She says she is unemployed, but it's pretty clear she has had a fairly regular horizontal occupation.

According to a local cop at the doorway, she has been busy at this trade for some time, but had only just recently hooked up with this guy Baker. Stanly is a union organizer. A strong-arm. Or was. Just lately he'd been working with the longshoremen. Before that it was the meatpackers down in Trenton. But he's been associated with various and sundry. He's a big fella and that was his primary talent, but he also dabbled in gambling and pimping on the side. Most of that background we get later at the office, but it fits because a lot of the independent party girls hook up with guys like this for protection.

Anyway, Miss Starr says she was in the sunroom at the front of the house, napping on the couch there because of the heat and the breeze from the front windows is better. It is noteworthy that the curtains there are open. And she was awakened just as it was getting dark by the sounds of her boyfriend having sex in the bedroom. She offers this testimony outright. No blush. She said the female involved in the tryst was rather loud about it. Her boyfriend, Mr. Baker, was breathing heavily, as he always did when he got worked up. He has asthma. Or did. She says she couldn't fall asleep again with all the racket and the heat and that is probably what saved her life.

It seems Mr. Baker had come in the back door of the place from the driveway with his new friend. When they were finally finished with business, Miss Starr hears some movement, and then the female voice says, "Did you have a good time?"

Mr. Baker says, "Yes, ma'am. A fine time."

Then the female said, "Do you see this?"

Mr. Baker grunts and his voice suddenly get louder, "What's that?"

The female says, "You see, I have a little gun too."

After which there was the sound of a shot. Just one shot. And Miss Starr hears her boyfriend falling to the floor.

With that, Miss Starr, being dumb but not stupid, was suddenly afraid for her own life and ran out the front entrance into the street. She was stark naked at the time. And that's where she ran right into the headlights of the cop, an officer named Murphy, who happened to be on his regular tour of duty in the neighborhood. Back inside, this cop finds the woman's boyfriend, dead. Shot in the face. But the murderer had already left in haste. The back door hangs open. They are still inside when the cop sees a dark automobile back out of the drive and speed away. He did not have an angle to see a license plate.

It was just about nine o'clock when Cass and I went next door to talk to the neighbor who'd set a kitchen chair out on her front walk so that she could comfortably give interviews to reporters and police. She had many opinions about Miss Starr and wanted to share them with any who asked. Across the street, behind a row of shrubbery, is a three-story apartment building with all the lights on and many of the windows are filled with the silhouettes of interested neighbors. I make my best guess for a clear view of the front of the Peggy Starr house and go across to ring a bell.

This apartment is rented by a fellow name Daikens. I know immediately that he is the right man to talk to and I wave over at Cass who is in the huddle around the neighbor, to get her attention for the added scuttlebutt.

Daikens is a war vet. He is permanently retired now. A smallish man, about forty, with a close cut of black hair. He was gassed three times in four months during the summer and fall of 1918. He breathes with a rasp and talks with a rattle and stands lopsided because of damage to one leg. He leans hard on a neat little bamboo cane that looks barely sturdy enough to carry his weight but is obviously sufficient. He uses the cane to whip the air several times as he speaks. He has his company flag, regimental flag, and the American flag hanging up on his living room wall framed like paintings.

Mr. Daikens says right off, "That guy was scum. Peggy told me he was going to marry her, but I knew he wouldn't. He was a communist. They don't believe in marriage."

"How do you know he was a communist?"

"Peggy told me. She showed me a paper once about his

activities."

"Did you know Peggy well?"

"Occasionally. I get lonely as well as the next man."

"What did the paper say?"

"Some babble about worker unity. The sort of stuff you hear all the time nowadays. But that fella Baker, he was the one who spread it around."

A few minutes later it was clear that the reporters were finally leaving the scene to file their reports so Cass hurried back to the house to have her word with Carl Stowe and then found Peggy Starr still sitting on the couch in her living room, exactly where she had been before. The cops were all outside by that time, either talking to neighbors or amongst themselves. The cigarette pack in front of Miss Starr was empty and lying on a side table beneath the light of the lamp.

Cass asked, "What are you going to do now? Do you need help with anything? Do you have someplace to go? Do you have a friend who can stay with you?"

Miss Starr finally answers, her voice flat and disinterested given what was in her words. "This is my home. If that bitch comes back to kill me, she might as well get me here. Do you have any smokes on you?"

Cass shook her head, so Miss Starr looked at me. I gave her the half a pack of Chesterfields I had left.

The heat of the evening had made Miss Starr loosen her robe and there was a little too much to be seen so I stepped away then into the kitchen, which was small but neat, and then into the open bedroom again. There the blood on the rug reminded me very much of the Hotel Penn, several sections of white tape were still on the carpet where the police had marked the position of the body which had been carried away maybe an hour before. There was no spatter on the wall here. The tape on the carpet hardly defined the shape of a body. I took another picture of that just in case. I had heard that the bullet probably never left the skull.

An open closet was busy with women's clothes. An assortment of shoes were piled helter-skelter onto the closet floor. Several copies of *Life* magazine were stuffed in a bedside table below a clock. The bed was a double-wide and it was disheveled, with one sheet draped to the floor. There was no sign of a man's presence. The conversation in the living room seemed to be going well, so I took an extra liberty and opened the door on the second bedroom.

This was smaller, with a single bed, and smelled of cigars. The closet held half a dozen suits. Several pairs of shoes were lined up at one side. He must have been an orderly fellow. On the wall was a Currier and Ives print of a winter scene like you can buy at Woolworth's, one for every season. The broad sill above a built-in radiator held a stack of magazines and several books. Most of this was the sort of Trotskyite material you can pick up any day in Times Square. There was also a copy of a magazine called *The Nation* on top of yesterday's edition of the *Daily News*, along with several new hardcover books as well. I wrote down the names of the books: *The 3rd International After Lenin, The Revolution Betrayed*, and *Wither France?* There was also one paperback book, crudely printed, but with a familiar name attached, *I Stake My Life*, which purported to be the 'Dewey Report of the Moscow Trials,' and 'an inquiry into the charges made against Trotsky' I picked this up and discovered it was not by Thomas E. but a man named John Dewey. I took a couple of shots on all of that.

At that point we were both pretty tired and we grabbed a cab to get out of there.

93. Thursday, September 16, 1937

Everything started to come apart on Thursday.

This all happened like a dance by the Rockettes, with all the legs kicking up high at the same time.

First thing Thursday morning—it was already late because we didn't get home from Pelham by way of our respective offices till after midnight and then I had taken another cab to pick up Cass at South Street—Winchell wants to see me and I went upstairs. He has a copy of the *Journal-American* on his desk and it's open to Cass's piece on the Group Theatre and the new show, *Golden Boy*.

Before I get the door closed he says, "What the hell is this?"

I say, "I thought it was pretty good. You didn't like it?"

He says, "You went up to Connecticut together, didn't you? These photos in here are yours. I can tell."

I don't answer that. I say, "What's the problem?"

"You know what the problem is. I told you no one else is supposed to know what I'm writing about."

"Your piece was in the *Mirror* yesterday morning. Hers didn't hit in the *Journal-American* until the afternoon. Why does it matter?"

"Because you told her what I was doing! Who else knew?"

I shook my head at him. "I think you know, she's my wife. She knows the score. She wouldn't have jumped you on the story. Period. You should be glad to have the lead on it now that the story is twice as big."

This got him to flex his jaw. "Don't tell me what I should be glad about. Who the hell are you to tell me what I should be glad about?"

"You're right. I can't tell you that."

"You're fired!"

I said, "Thanks," with a nod to make sure he knew I meant it.

Then I went down to The Boss and let him know about that.

For about thirty seconds, George looks up at the ceiling without moving in his chair.

Then he says, "You did this on purpose?"

I tell him, "No. But I should have."

The door was already closed but he looks around me to double-check that.

"Close the blinds. Listen. I'm probably going to get my ass canned anyway. Ad revenues stink and Gauvreau will be needing a fall guy to blame for that. Ex-city editors in this town are a dime a dozen, especially since the *World* closed down and the *Journal* and the *American* combined. I guess it's my turn. But I knew that much going in. I'm not complaining. It paid some bills. I'm just sayin.' There's consequences. Winchell won't be satisfied by firing you and then me picking you up on waivers. He goes for blood. But for the moment, you're hired again. At least for the next twenty-four hours."

This is just the sort of stuff all the reporters talk about over hotdogs and soda on practically every corner in the city. A real donnybrook.

But I was curious, "Whose idea was it to trade away Cass to the *Journal-American* in the first place?"

He says, "Gauvreau's."

I say, "Who knows it?"

He says, "Everyone, I expect. I objected at the time. But I had to make the most of it, or turn in my badge right then. The Hearst people wanted another female reporter over at the *Journal-American* to bring in more women readers there. I think they figure the *Mirror* is stuck in its own rut. Which it is. But that's why they let me pull Cass over here from the *News* in the first place. With this move, Gauvreau saw a way to lower salaries and curry favor. It's still his ass on the line eventually."

I said, "Look. If everybody knows it, maybe that'll be your saving grace. In the meantime, what would you like me to do?"

He does not even bother to catch a breath for that one.

"Write up some additional copy on the Pelham murder and tie some extra strings to Annie Oakley and then pick your own shot to go with it. We'll put it on page one where Winchell can't miss it."

All I could say was, "Thanks."

He says, "It'll work out. Maybe I'll get demoted to the sports department again and get a chance to report on the World Series before this is all over. And one way or the other, you did fine. I sure as hell wouldn't have left that girl of yours behind."

That was the first thing I knew. The second involved Cass.

Cass has kicked up a nice little storm. The Hearst people are very odd about their politics. They generally run stuff from all ends. But these days, politics only sells papers if it gores someone else's ox. In the past they've caused themselves some real damage by reporting on the shenanigans in the Works Progress Administration, and several of the other more corrupt Government programs. Republicans love that. But Democrats, who are plentiful, hate it because Roosevelt is their Messiah. In any case, no one much has tried to take on the Federal Theatre Project or the Writers' Project or any of the artsy stuff.

Critics pan the preachy shows alright, but the idea of the government sponsoring dramas just like I hear they do in the Soviet Union is not really being questioned. Not often, anyway. Maybe they don't care because what they spend on that and other such stuff is only chicken feed compared to the kind of tax money that goes into the building of a single new ship here or another dam there, or how much they're paying the farmers now to quit growing food in some places while people are starving in others. The thing of it is, we live in New York. Here, theatre is big business. And fair or not, what happens on Broadway gets reported on the radio coast to coast.

I don't think Mr. Rice, her editor at the *Journal-American*, was thinking about any of that when he ran with her piece on the Group Theatre. It probably seemed a little like old news to him and just appropriate background detail to her making a point about the 'religious fervor' of the actors. After all, the Reds have been big on Broadway since long before Clifford Odets and waiting for *Waiting For Lefty*. Back in June, Mr. Welles had led his own theatre march to save *The Cradle Will Rock* out from under the politics that's gotten into that stage production. Maybe that was the cause of Mr. Kazan's grievance with him. But Welles wasn't really against the idea of it, just the particular situation. One in-crowd duking it out with another. And I'd heard about yet another of those shows from Gloria Finklestein. The Federal Theatre Project has something called *Pins and Needles* opening soon. She was pretty excited about maybe having a part in it. And this might also be the same production that Miss Tisdale's new boyfriend is in. Or was that the old one?

Cass made a list of the titles of Broadway shows that made no bones about their politics in the past five years. It's long. And like she said in her article, it goes over pretty well in New York because a lot of the anger here is directed toward the Nazis. Everyone hates a Nazi. That's not news in New York. But no one that I know about has tied that together with this new acting philosophy before.

The particular line that appears to have hit the bull's eye reads to me like the sort of hyperbole you see everywhere these days. Different maybe for being a little too true.

She wrote:

> If, as Mr. Shakespeare suggests, 'All the world's a stage, and all the men and women merely players,' perhaps Mr. Stanislavsky is an even better director than Mr. Stalin, or Mr. Trotsky, as to how we should all play our parts. The fervor of the Group Theatre players is of the same sort of ideology that drives at least one mad socialist currently active in New York to put a shot in the eye of anyone else not wearing the proper shade of red. Theirs is a philosophy

that goes far beyond the stage. With this sort of art, the aim
is the only truth. Memorizing the Party line is more important than the text of any play.

Now several editors at the *Journal-American* and at least one
of the higher ups at Hearst has complained. They're getting phone
calls from all over the place, including Hollywood. They say Cass
has given New York theater a black eye. Or worse. And because she
has managed to connect the Group Theatre politics to the maniacal
murders of the Annie Oakley killer, they all now have their noses out
of joint.

As a consequence, Cass calls to tell me that she has been
taken off the 'Lively Arts' beat and put back where "she belongs."
She calls me to tell me about it and she is not sounding the least bit
unhappy, and a thought occurs. Maybe that was also part of the
reason why Winchell was so ruffled. But in any case, it was all to the
good. It couldn't have worked out better if we had planned it that
way. And maybe we should have.

But that's not the end of it.

94. Friday, September 17, 1937

On Friday, I come into the office and find out The Boss is no longer in charge.

In the six years I have been with the paper, I have seen three City Editors. He was the best and in the job for the longest time. But that tells you how that goes. The new goat has not been chosen yet but Stenis is temporarily in charge for now and he is a good guy. It took three of us to talk him out of quitting in sympathy with Barry George. But given the situation, what in hell would we do without Stenis?

At noon, a bunch of us go over to see The Boss at the Algonquin, where we know he'll be hiding out because I called and checked and he was already on his third shot of rye by 11:30 a.m. We managed to pack him into a cab at 3 p.m. and paid the fare to get him home to Port Washington in advance. (The thought occurs that sending him home to his wife is something like a frying pan to the fire sort of deal, but we decide he is better off there for now.)

By that time, Stenis had taken on a load of his own as well, so getting the Saturday morning edition ready by midnight Friday was going to be fun. I just wouldn't be there to enjoy it. Gauvreau, being the standup sort of fellow we all know (if a snake can stand on its tale) sent down an assistant with the good news that I had been dismissed, and this gunsel is waiting for me in the city room as soon as we were back from the Algonquin. There'd been enough disruption to the schedule already so I just left my camera on my desk and went down to the payroll office and made sure they had my correct hours and then left. I could always come back another day to bid adieu to the friends I have there.

And now that I have time to think all of this over again, I've started to get an idea about what makes sense. The first thing is about Cass—and truly, I can thank Mr. Winchell for this. Had I not been exposed to his sort of vindictive nature I might not have seen it coming. The Nazis she had made fools of were not going to leave town without seeing Cass dead. Probably for no other purpose than to quiet some inner bit of hell in their own souls. If they were the cold and calculating fellows the magazine articles all say, they would simply move on to their next assignments. I'd say, the fact that they can take time out from their larger aims to dole out misery on those they hate will likely be the end of them someday.

I got down to South Street shortly after the Friday edition of the *Journal-American* has been put to bed. I sat in the waiting area there until Cass saw me and she is reading minds so she was over pretty quick.

"They did it?"

What can I say? I give her the nod. "Done."

"You want to go out for a drink?"

I admit, "Did that already too. They fired the Boss as well."

"Crap. What now?"

Cass likes to talk over scenarios all the time. Like buying a house in Connecticut. And what kind of house it should be. And what color. All that. I have always been the type to just go about my job and wait for inspiration. And she inspires me pretty well on most days.

"I'm thinking—" and this idea just hit me at that exact moment. "I'm thinking that the Nazis are going to try and kill you again."

This gets a blank stare out of her that lasts nearly half a minute.

"But why?"

"Why would Winchell want me fired? He's vindictive. It's

why no one wants to cross him. And these Nazis seem to want to blame the grief of the world on the Jews. They're a very spiteful bunch. And you may not be heading off to the synagogue right now, but it is Friday, after all. And they hate your guts for a few other reasons. That's why I think maybe we want to keep an eye out." Not exactly the right phrase.

She was skeptical. Worse than that. She was worried about me being worried about her. She thought maybe the trauma of the day had set in on my brain.

But the hairs were up on my neck before we even got out of the lobby.

I managed to talk Cass into waiting for me upstairs again until I get back. She has paperwork to finish up, anyway. People she can call. I made her promise with both hands out where I could see them because she has a way of crossing her fingers on things like this.

Because South Street is close by the East River, and there's no place else to go to the east from there without a boat or swim trunks, there are not a lot of breaks in the buildings on that side. And those are all old and fairly decrepit: some of them still tenements but most of them warehouses. I suppose when the *Journal-American* building was put up on the opposite side of the street during the war, it was thought that things might be looking up soon for the whole neighborhood, but they never really did. Except for Knickerbocker Village, everything else between the bridges ought to be leveled. Just to make the rats find new homes if nothing else.

What this means is that I have a long stretch of street there that is easy to run the eyes over at a glance. Pretty quick I spot the two guys in the car on the far corner on my side and head in that direction. I tried not to show my cards when I cut across to the coffee shop on Clinton. I'd been to this place once before and seen the set-up there, so right in the door I talk to the guy behind the counter as sweetly as I can.

I say, "Can I use your phone."

He says, "There's a pay phone outside."

I say, "There are a couple guys out that way that would like to kill me. I would appreciate the use of your phone in here." And I put down a quarter figuring the bribe might help.

Mike Sommers happens to be there with a couple of the other people from the paper, nursing some coffees, and he says, "Andy! Let the poor guy use your damn phone. The bookie is not going to call you in the next three minutes."

Andy grabs the quarter off the counter and passes the phone to me. I call the cops.

They are all over the corner in about ten minutes. But the Nazis are gone.

I got a cab to drive Cass and me home.

Just for curiosity's sake I called the *Mirror* on Friday evening to make sure Stenis held up under the load and happily hear he's got his old voice back, so I ask him for a favor. A favor might take his mind off himself. I tell him that we had some Nazis waiting on us at South Street and then ask him to find out what happened to the detective agency that was supposed to be watching out for Cass.

About an hour later he calls back with the news. The agency bailed on the job and the Hearst people didn't want to bother with it anymore because it didn't make any sense those guys would be interested in her now.

This one fact lets me know that the Hearst people have no idea what they are facing with these types, and that is just for starters. A thug doesn't make sense of a thing, otherwise they would find another occupation. Doesn't matter if it's a gangster like Victor Neims or some Brownshirt. The only way a maniac like Stalin stops killing is when everyone in his way is dead. And they don't like witnesses.

95. Saturday, September 18, 1937

Mr. Kazan at the Group Theatre has said I must live a charmed life. And I told him that it must be so. This is made obvious once again by what happened Friday. If Gauvreau hadn't fired me, I would not have been at South Street when I was, and never inspired to worry about Cass just when I did. But you can't take such fortune for granted. Like Dad says, good fortune is made.

Saturday morning I drove Cass to work and let her off at the door before going up myself to have a talk with her editor, Chester Rice. I parked in a good spot close by where I could see what I wanted of the street. But this conversation with Rice was just between the two of us.

Chester Rice is a thin man (from forgetting to eat his lunch they say). He is usually dressed down to his vest, shirtsleeves and visor. When he speaks to you, he always takes the visor off which leaves a bright red gash on his forehead. And this only draws extra attention to his lack of hair.

I drew a picture for Mr. Rice concerning the previous day's events. I understood that he was not at the top of the chain. He could only do so much. But either they got someone else—someone good—to keep watch over Cass until this whole thing blows over, or she couldn't work there.

He says that the people in the 'Lively Arts' department all want Cass fired anyway because of the stink over the Group Theatre article. Someone at Actors' Equity even threatened to have the Union put pressure on advertisers.

I say that if he wants them running his paper, fine. That's his choice, but I wasn't interested in losing Cass.

At this point it's in his lap. I could have predicted his exact words.

"I'll see what I can do."

I said, "That's not good enough," and left.

I told Cass not to leave the building until I get back again to pick her up, and this time I didn't have to see her hands to know that she would stay put.

 Rice is a smart fellow and knows that the *Daily News* will not hire Cass back. They'd gotten rid of her once before because she was too much trouble. On top of that they are a union paper and would not be interested in going against Actors' Equity if more of a yowl was made about her article on The Group Theatre. The *Post* is likely to pass on the chance for the same reasons. *The New York Times* had already run an editorial critical of the piece. Where would she go now? The *Herald Tribune*? Or the *Sun*?

Unlike my ex-managing editor, Emile Gauvreau, the publisher at the *Mirror,* A. J. Kobler, is a dapper fellow. There is no garish stick-pin in his tie. His suits are tailor-made. He wears French cuffs everyday. He's been the publisher of the *Mirror* at least since I've been there, and I know he was at one time with the *Globe* before Frank Munsey folded that paper. After that he was with Hearst's *American Weekly*. In six years, I have spoken to the man once and that was to say 'good morning' on a day that I happened to open the door for him. I had no reason to believe he even knew who I was.

I drove up to 45th Street, finally found a space for the car about four blocks away, and get upstairs by ten o'clock. Kobler's office is in the corner of the building and hidden to all eyes by a purposely darkened outer office which is occupied by a couple of stuffed leather chairs, a large mahogany desk, and his secretary, Miss Peterson. This formidable lady is often credited with running the paper, though she could not be over five feet tall, and on first glance reminds me of one of my mom's boarders, Mrs. Tisdale. She sits beside a neat little shaded lamp that casts light only on her desk and hands.

Miss Peterson asks if I have an appointment. I say no, but that the matter is urgent. She looks at me as if the idea of something urgent is unknown to her. She presses the button atop a little mahogany box and when Kobler's voice asks, she says that I am there to see him and that I have said it was 'urgent.' She says the word with the same feeling as her previous look toward me.

He says, "send him right in." Just like that.

The windows in Mr. Kobler's office run from both sides to the corner. Coming from Miss Peterson's anteroom, the light from the windows is blinding. That's why I didn't see Gauvreau until I'd gotten all the way to Kobler's desk to shake his hand.

Kobler rises from his seat and says, "Good to see you, Hugh! Mr. Gauvreau and I were just discussing things."

I turned then and saw Mr. Gauvreau, who had remained deep in the leather cushions and looking very unhappy at my sudden arrival.

Mr. Kobler smiled and held up his hand palm out as if to stop me. "Before you unload on us for our callous treatment, let me tell you that your being fired was a mistake. A misunderstanding. Regrettably, with the necessity of letting Barry George go, an assumption was made. Because you had been the direct cause of the tiff with Mr. Winchell, it was thought that we should part company with you as well. But that is absolutely not the case."

At this point I was still standing, as was Mr. Kobler. I think there was some immediate worry on his part about what I might say out loud in front of Mr. Gauvreau and he wanted to cut off the possibility in case it was something that could not be easily repaired. Gauvreau had sunk further into his cushions. Kobler gestured at a chair on the opposite side from the managing editor and I sat down to listen to what he had to say.

Kobler smiled again. "Hugh, let me give you the big picture on this, if you will. I know you were fond of Barry George. He could be difficult but he was a good man. Our problem with him had

nothing to do with Mr. Winchell, even though that might have sparked things when it did. Barry had his own ideas about the paper and
was responsible for a number of lengthy articles, including several
written by Miss Green, as you well know. It has long been my belief,
as well as Mr. Gauvreau's, that the circulation of the *Mirror* depended more upon emphasizing the pictures, not the writing. That
weighting of space has been the conundrum that has driven us to
drink, since day one. It is my opinion that the success of this new
Life magazine has been wholly on that account. And that is precisely
why your talents are wanted here."

Mr. Gauvreau had not moved. If anything, his face had become more sour.

I said, "Axing Barry George the way you did is not right. But
it's your paper. Fact is, I came here about something else. Cass
Green doesn't work here anymore, but she's in a jam because of
what she wrote for you."

"You mean the attempts on her life?"

"Yes."

Mr. Kobler spread his hands above the papers on his desk as
if these were larger matters than a couple of measly assassination
attempts on a reporter.

"I don't think we can do any more than having the detective
agency keep an eye on her."

Mr. Gauvreau squirmed in his chair.

I said, "But they aren't even doing that! Not now. Those
Nazis tried again yesterday."

Kobler looked at Gauvreau.

The managing editor finally spoke, "I didn't think it was our
responsibility any longer, what with her moving over there to the
Journal-American."

Kobler closed his eyes for at least a second before he turned
back to me.

"I'll speak with Bill Hearst about it. We'll get that taken care
of today."

I simply thanked him. It was as much as I could expect.

Then Mr. Kobler looked at Gauvreau.

Gauvreau squirmed again and spoke directly to me. "If it's alright with you, I'd like to make amends. We'll keep you at the salary we set when you started for Mr. Winchell—" Mr. Kobler cleared his throat. Gauvreau continued, "And we'll add something more to that. Does ninety-five sound fair?"

I left thinking that my good fortune was far too great and I was bound to be hit by lightening or at least run over by a truck at any second.

Instead I got this, when I was driving Cass home.

She was looking very unhappy about something, even though I'd told her about the raise. So I suggested that we'd need it if we were going to save enough for a house in Connecticut.

Out of the blue she says, "Why do you love me?"

Naturally I had about a hundred answers ready for that.

"Because you're a pip!"

She looked surprised at my answer. "You mean like an apple seed?"

"No. That's a different thing entirely. You're a pip. The best there is. The tops. A sweetheart. Hot stuff. A beaut. A peach. The bees knees. The cat's meow. A corker. Cracker jack. Why, you're remarkable!"

That got an "Oh," and shut her up for nearly a minute. Nearly to the top of Flatbush Avenue.

But then she says, with a little hurt in her voice, "Well, don't you want to know why I love you?"

And I told her, "No. I don't need to."

That got her sitting up straight. "Why not?"

"Because I know why. You love stray dogs."

Which got the first laugh out of her that day.

96. Sunday, September 19, 1937

While we were busy Saturday, Police came to the house and worried Mom greatly. She thought at first that it might concern Cass or myself. Instead they were looking for Mr. Oliphant. I found out about this Saturday evening when we got home and so I immediately called Stenis and told him what I knew and he said he would assign someone else to the story. Given that the guy lived here, it would not look good for my name to be on it. Mr. Oliphant appears to have left the state for parts unknown and has taken a significant amount of the valuables from several safety deposit boxes along with him.

Sunday dinner was the first with Michael Flynn at the table. The conversation was thick with the various bits of news. Flynn (as he prefers to be called, even though both Mom and Cass use his given name), looks completely recovered except for the sling on his arm. Apparently he does heal quickly, just as he said. The third degree interrogation at the table for a new guest amounts to the usual curiosity about how he'd gotten into his line of work. But he had little to say other than he'd been a cop for a short while up in Boston. And from something else he mentioned, it was clear his father had once been a cop as well.

He did tell us that he has applied for a personal license to conduct business as a private detective in the City of New York. His intentions are to stay in that line of business.

Being a little too smart-alecky I said, "Do you think there are that many cuckolds out there that need their wives watched?"

Flynn is a very earnest fellow. In a strictly serious voice he says, "I won't be doing that sort of work."

"But I thought that was ninety percent of it."

"Probably is. But I thought I'd try my hand at the ten percent. The frauds and the cheats. There are plenty of finder's fees to be had. For instance, with our Mr. Oliphant. If the police don't track him down within a few weeks, the bank will issue a reward."

This brought a sudden quiet to the table. We had all known Mr. Oliphant for too long. The idea of his being tracked down like a Charles Ponzi, or a Charles W. Morse or an Oscar Hartzell put a damper on all our thoughts. All three names came up in the conversation that followed.

Early Sunday we went over to the rooming house together and Flynn packed up the last of his things. His landlady cried. He seems to have that sort of affect on women. It's fortunate for him that he is unaware of it. He blushes readily.

Sunday afternoon, the police came again and searched Mr. Oliphant's room. It was already empty because Mrs. Nessen had cleaned it thoroughly in preparation for her own occupation, so they left empty-handed after talking to everyone individually about Mr. Oliphant first. The only other fact any of us knew for certain was that he liked to eat.

Also on Saturday we had received several pictures of Detroit, taken by Gary White, with a short note attached saying that he was very happy in his new home. Cass and I got to see those at Sunday dinner.

97. Thursday, September 23, 1937

Stenis is bearing up admirably under his new responsibilities. The week has been relatively calm.

Monday morning, as we left the house, I see a fellow in a car at the corner of Vanderbilt, in exactly the same spot as the two thugs had been that other day. Only this time I have no worry. I winked at this detective as we passed on our way to the El and he scowled back at me.

The new agency has a different system. One guy is at Sterling Place every morning between nine and ten. Another is at South Street between six and seven, at the same time a third guy is at Sterling Place again. I suppose this is done for efficiency. Because our two newspapers have different schedules, my own pattern has been to get to South Street again when Cass leaves work and to stay with her until she is home. Then I grab the car and drive back to 45th Street, if necessary, to finish off whatever I have going there. Parking is easier in that part of town after six.

Another thing is that I have purchased a pistol. I applied for the permit a few weeks ago and that came through. It's only a Smith and Wesson .32 caliber, fairly light, and small enough to fit in my camera bag, even if the weight change is still noticeable. I'd liked the feel of Michael Flynn's second pistol when I first picked it up at the rooming house and that decision didn't take much more convincing. This was the same model that Danny Seger had taught me to handle at a range out in Queens some years ago. I should have bought a gun then, but I'd always found something else to spend my money on instead.

In any case, you'd think that I'd think about some of these things sooner than I do. Sometimes other matters are going on and later is as soon as I can get to them. The gun is one of those. But there is another.

The key to this one is to be looking for the connections, of course. This is not my natural frame of mind. It has always been more my position to take things as they come and mind my own business. But if I want to be a reporter, I will have to get better at this.

Wednesday, I am out in the fresh air for most of the day trying to find good shots at the American Legion parade on 5th Avenue. If you didn't know before, you find out there that old soldiers look a lot like everyone else, but with uniforms on. Their brave deeds are not where you can see them. Just some ribbons. And the uniforms make them all look the same and getting an interesting shot is that much harder.

Thursday morning, standing at a strap on the train with Cass, I am looking at five girls who are scattered in the crowd on the car. They are all dressed in the same maroon outfit with the 'B' emblazoned in yellow on a breast pocket of their jackets, but none of them looks at the other. As if they are all strangers. This was obviously a class outing and they are on their way to the Museum of Natural History or some other such place. All of them were of the age when they want to show their independence. I looked at the adults in the car and it took more than a minute to figure out who it was keeping watch. This turned out to be a smallish woman in a very unfashionable green cloak and matching hat at the far end. I spotted her because of her eyes alone. When she saw me, and realized that I was looking at her girls, her eyes went wide. I turned and whispered all this in Cass's ear.

But I had my idea then. I'd been looking at uniforms. The connections I need to be looking for are not on the outside. Obviously.

The thought was that the murder of Peggy Starr's boyfriend was more than a bit hasty. A little like the murder of Police Captain Deems. The thing was not well planned. It did not seem as orderly as the other killings, just for the fact that she could not have easily moved the body away after the deed. And it was not nearly the effort of someone as careful as the keeper of the apartment I had first seen at Knickerbocker Village. Miss Beinecke is wanted and she knows it, so this murder was done at greater risk. Though there might have been another reason she had done it, other than Mr. Baker's politics. Or at least, an additional one.

I told Cass about my thought there on the train, and that I wanted to go back to talk with Peggy Starr. I had an idea that there may be more to learn. Cass says right away that she wants to come with me.

I say, "You don't trust me?"

Cass gives me the eyes half closed. "I trust you. I just don't trust her."

We switched trains and went to Pelham first thing.

Miss Starr didn't answer her door through several rings, which had us worried at first, but then she finally shouted at us from inside. Whatever she said was unintelligible, but we soon heard her coming to the door.

Not surprisingly, she was in the same robe she had been wearing the last time we saw her. It was also interesting to me then that Cass let me do most of the talking from the start.

Miss Star recognized us, but I figured I needed to work up a better explanation than just that we were doing some follow-up.

I said, "This woman who killed Mr. Baker has killed several others. The cops are not coming up with anything. We've been covering the case for months and we have an idea about it. I was wondering if we could ask for your help."

Miss Starr did not move from her spot in the partially open door. Instead she gives us a "What is it?" that did not seem terribly interested.

At the dining room table inside I can see a small bamboo

cane leaning up against a chair.

I say, "If you or Mr. Daikens wouldn't mind, we'd be very grateful if we could look at Mr. Baker's room again. There could be something there the police didn't notice in there that might help."

This may have been far too direct an approach, but I was feeling impatient. I had figured to scare her a little with the idea that there might be something that would bring the killer back. However, something told me that Mr. Daikens would not be moved by that sort of an appeal.

She stared at me for a second like I was a rat. Then I heard Daikens. From the bedroom, he yells that he had his pants on. Cass had kept a straight face through all of this.

Cass said, "I'm really sorry. We're not trying to cause you any trouble."

We hear Daikens say, "Let'em in Peg. Might as well."

Mr. Daikens limped over to his cane and grabbed it with some irritation. His pants were held up by green suspenders over an undershirt. He nodded at us both as we came in, but said nothing more for the moment.

The Currier and Ives was still on the wall but the rest of Mr. Baker's belongings had already been boxed up for donation. Cass looked behind the picture first thing, and I started going through the boxes. The smell of cigars was still present. But there was no notebook. No letter with a mysterious cipher. Nothing. The stack of Trotskyite magazines as well as the books which had been on the window shelf over the radiator were all in one box and I fanned these hoping to spot something.

Cass dumped an odd assortment of small things onto the black and white stripes of the bare mattress—a cigarette lighter, a cigar cutter, matches, pennies and the like.

The several suits which had been in the closet were folded together in one box and I took these out one by one and went through the pockets. Then another. The jacket pockets were baggy, probably from carrying the printed material Baker liked to hand around. On the third jacket I noticed what looked like a tear in the lining at the very bottom of a side vent that would fall over the right pants pocket. I'd actually noticed this same thing on the first two but ignored it. The coincidence was too much.

Just inside the tear of the lining of one of the jackets was a small piece of paper. Written on this were twelve given names. Beside each was a phone number.

I asked Miss Starr if she knew any of these people.

She held it a minute and then said, "This looks like one of his reminder notes. Stan couldn't remember a number if his life depended—" She shook her head at the thought. "Anyway. He didn't have a head for that. He wrote slips and carried them around. Sure, I know some fellas by some of those names but none that would have been friendly with Stan."

Obviously it was possible that Lucille Beinecke might have taken any other information away with her, but we knew she'd been interrupted by the screams of Miss Starr and the arrival of the patrolman. Perhaps she was not there to get more information at all, but simply to kill Mr. Baker. And the nature of the occasion, as it was overheard by Miss Starr, seemed to indicate that the gaining of information was at least secondary, unless Miss Beinecke already knew where that information was and only needed to eliminate Mr. Baker to get to it. All of that was possible. And too, the fact that Miss Starr had not been revisited by Miss Beinecke since then seemed to indicate she already had what she wanted.

I asked Peggy Starr if she remembered Baker having any sort of address book.

She doesn't answer but turns around and goes to the kitchen and then returns with a cheap monthly pocket reminder from an insurance company.

"You mean, like this? He leaves it by the phone. Used to. That's where he did all his calling. At all hours. Drove me nuts. I thought I'd call some of them and tell them Stan was dead. Just in case they wanted to pay their respects. But I didn't get any answers and then I got one fellow who was pretty rude and a woman who told me that the guy I was calling was dead. So I just sort of lost heart. If you know what I mean? I figured his Union would take care of all that anyway. They paid for his funeral."

Among the fifty or sixty other names, the names on the slip each matched up with a surname and the same phone number, along with an address.

I copied the information for those twelve out twice for both Cass and me to use before Miss Starr tells me just to take the thing with me.

After staying with Cass as far as South Street I went back to 45th, but on the way I stopped by Police Headquarters at Centre Street to leave the original slip of paper and the address book with Detective Barnes. He was at his desk, so I also gave him my own idea of the thing as well. Of the twelve names on the slip, several of these were already crossed out, including one name we knew—Mr. Paul Reagan.

Jack Barnes says to me, "Baker was a union organizer, for Christ sake. He probably knows hundreds of people."

I say, "But the twelve first names on the slip are in there and several of them have lines marked through. I don't see lines like that anywhere else."

He examined the slip again like it was a page. "Look, let us do the police work will you? You just stick to taking pictures, okay?"

If half a dozen guys weren't dead, and more likely coming, I would have taken the advice. As it was, the cops were not doing their jobs and I wanted to do mine.

Back at the office, I called Cass and tell her what Barnes said. We'd divided the responsibilities, and by then she had already starting calling. Because Baker's death had been well reported in the papers, we figured there would be no surprise on the part of those who might answer.

This theory was proved wrong on my first call, to an Edward Sargent. Mrs. Sargent answered the phone.

She says, "Why does the *Mirror* want to know about my

husband? Have they found him?"

I explained as little as I could about the names in Mr. Baker's little book.

She says, "Baker is a bully. He bullied my husband all the time. He'd call up and say, do this or do that, and Eddy would run off like an errand boy."

"Mr. Baker is dead."

"No! Really? Well, good riddance. But I haven't seen Eddy in six months."

"Have you filed a missing person's report with the police?"

'Sure. Lotta good that did."

"How long have you been married?"

"Thirty six years, last May."

"Do you have any children?"

"Four. Why do you need to know all that?"

"I'm looking for some way to track Mr. Sargent down."

"The kids wouldn't know. He hardly spoke to them when they lived at home. I'll bet you none of them have heard from him in ten years."

"Another question, if I may. Do you know if Mr. Sargent has any political interests?"

"You mean, is he some sort of communalist? Yeah. That was his hobby."

Of the six I had to cover, the first call, which had a line through it, was the best. Three more numbers were unanswered, and one of those was crossed out. One number had evidently been given to someone else, and that person was very likely the rude fellow encountered by Miss Starr. His name was Terrell. The number in the little book was listed under Cotter.

98. Saturday, September 25, 1937

Brad Stenis is like the guy on the bicycle with the long pole who rides the low wire at the circus and the clowns are chasing themselves back and forth and climbing all across him and somehow he stays right where he should, on the level.

He doesn't look the type. An average sort of guy. I don't think I appreciated him as much as I should have until we were all at the table at the Algonquin celebrating after The Boss got his notice. I found out then that Stenis is only thirty-two. He has that kind of face. Looks like someone's father.

Stenis told us a story after his third round that no one had ever heard before, not even The Boss. It seems that the guy's whole life changed in one minute, when he spelled the word 'acropolis' correctly in the seventh grade. This was in a spelling bee. The result was that he was involuntarily made the assistant editor of the high school newspaper for the following year. The rest was history.

He raised his glass up after telling that much and said, "I've been 'the assistant' ever since," and downed the contents in one gulp before finishing the story. "The thing of it is, I was going to spell the word wrong. On purpose, you understand. There was this little girl named Connie who was ahead of me in the contest and she got her word wrong before me and if I had gotten mine wrong too, she would have won on points. Connie was my first real crush. One of those girls who develops a little earlier than the others. And she gave me the ogle eyes when the teacher gave me my word to spell and I suddenly knew what that might mean. And to think. If I'd only taken the bait, I could be living in Trenton, New Jersey, today with Connie O'Leary."

That was the exact moment when we had to convince him not to quit. Besides, we all had our own idea by this time that Stenis had another fate in store. Betty Shue had taken to bringing the copy up from the wire room herself, directly to Stenis' desk, instead of waiting for a copyboy. We figured it wouldn't be long now before he was knocked off his balance for good.

But the greater benefit in all this was that suddenly Stenis was fearless. Deciding that he could quit any time he wanted left him free to do his job as he saw fit. Where before he usually waited to have anything important okayed by The Boss, now he had his mind made up and was onto the next thing before you could finish with your excuses.

I said, "It's the weekend so a lot of people are more likely to be home. I'll need to make a bunch of phone calls so that I can get pictures of all the dead guys from their families—"

He just says, "Keep me posted. I'll send The Kid out to cover all the beauty contests."

This was an old joke but basically it meant I was free for the moment to follow my own plan.

However, I was not alone in this, anyway. Cass would not be left out of it. Her first idea was that I take care of my half of the addresses and she would do hers. But I didn't want her wandering around to the homes of a bunch of reds, all by herself. An everyday murder in Queens or Harlem was one thing, but a nest of spies was another.

With Stenis' blessing, and after making my share of the calls, I went back to Brooklyn and got the car. The fourteen names we had—Simon Cotter, Carmine Esposito, Margaret Gruber, Christian Hansen, Gregory Hartunian, Philip Lorenze, John Nagy, George Niemi, Thomas Novak, Nicholas Petridis, Paul Reagan, Robert Rivera, Edward Sargent and Peter Wojak—were scattered throughout the city. We decided to start on the north and work our way down. The number was already reduced to eleven anyway because we had the picture of Paul Reagan from his wife and knew something of his story.

Edward Sargent's name was one of the cross-outs, as well as being on the way to several others, so we stopped by his home in Yonkers first. Mrs. Sargent, a bleach-blond who was carrying well over two hundred pounds on a five-foot frame, had no regrets about the things she had said on the phone. When I asked if her husband had any distinguishing physical characteristics she added some unnecessary detail about his sexual habits. I asked for physical marks that might identify him. With some coaching she came up with a gold molar and a broken ankle. Sargent was 56 years old and born in Boston. He was an accountant, or had been, for an outfit named Haliday, Johnson. He also did work on the side for private clients. Mostly smaller businesses. He still had family in the Boston area but was not on speaking terms with them.

Then she said," If you want that sort of information it means you think he's dead. Right?"

I admitted that I was sorry to say it, but that might be so.

She answers, "Don't be sorry. No big loss there. I just have to notify the Post Office so I can get his pension checks signed over." But then she did have one other possible lead. She was pretty sure that "Eddy used to go to the races with one of his 'communalist' friends. A fellow named Bob," and this guy didn't live too far from there, but that's all she knew. Sadly, the only picture of 'Eddy' she had to give us was at least ten years old.

There was a Robert Rivera on the list, and it was scratched out as well. And he also lived in Yonkers. We had intended to go there next in any case.

This was a tiny house in a row of tiny houses. The size of the old trees from a former estate that had survived the development made the houses look even smaller. Mr. Rivera's little lawn had not been cut in months. A pile of newspapers lay molding on his stoop. His mailbox was stuffed to overflowing.

I rang a neighbor's doorbell and they confirmed that Roberto, as he liked to be called, had not been seen in "awhile." His car was not in the driveway so they assumed he had gone away for some reason. The car was a blue Chevy coupe and this they described as being about four years old. To their knowledge, the man used to work for the Water Department. He had either quit or was fired. They understood that much from a fellow who had come by many weeks before in a Water Department truck to inquire. They never saw any other visitors except for a tall skinny fellow. (That description sounded like Mr. Sargent.) Otherwise, Robert Rivera was never particularly friendly except to share the tomatoes he grew in his back yard. Unfortunately he hadn't been around when those got ripe this year so the neighbors helped themselves.

Because we were already there and Cass didn't want to leave without getting something more, I asked the neighbors if they had ever checked to see if maybe Rivera was still inside. Dead. A heart attack, maybe. Maybe murdered, and his car stolen. This suddenly got the neighbors excited enough to finally call the cops and we waited for them to arrive. The two officers who answered the call looked like we had disturbed their afternoon naps. They were very curious about why two reporters from different papers had already arrived at the scene. We played innocent. One of the officers appraised the situation and went ahead and forced the back door. The smell of rotten food wafted out from the kitchen inside. He held his nose and took a looked around. The other officer wisely stayed behind and kept an eye on us. When the first one returned he told us there was no sign of any foul play. It looked like no one had been home for some time.

We went on our way, hoping the Water Department would have a picture of Mr. Rivera. I called the office from a pay phone and asked Sam Felt to see what he could do about that. Given that it was a Saturday, I did not expect much.

The next closest address on the list was a fellow named Simon Cotter who lived in Riverside. This number was not crossed out, but it was the one which had been answered by a rude fellow named Terrell.

Mr. Terrell is very unhappy to see us. Cass did the apologizing this time. The female touch did nothing to make the man happier. He was tired of getting calls for Mr. Cotter. He had just rented the house in June and was wishing he hadn't.

There was something more to his unhappiness. I promised him I would not use his name, but that this story was very important. If there was anything he could tell us, it might be life and death for someone.

"You won't call me again?"

"No, sir."

"Well, I'll tell you something. Mr. Cotter had enemies. I know that much. And one of those is a little lady who has a gun."

"Did you see her?"

"She was the first one who kept calling. She wanted to talk with me about some damn thing or another. I told her I didn't have an interest. I'm too old for that kind of hijinks anyway. My sister lives down the road here and she's sickly and I just came out from Illinois to be close by. I'm retired so I have nothing else to do. Well, this lady—I'm not sure she was a lady, but we can give her the benefit of the doubt, can't we? This lady shows up at my door one night. I'm sure it was her, because I could recognize the voice by then. She'd called so many times. She stands right there where you are now and looks at me real hard and then asks me my name and I tell her and then she turns right around and goes away. That was the last I saw of her. But I'll tell you what. There was a gun in her pocket. I saw that much. She was wearing a tight little jacket and you could see the outline of that pistol in the porch light as clear as day. I know a gun when I see one."

"What color was her hair?"

"Black as the ace of spades. If that was her hair. Might have been a wig. I've seen a few wigs in my day as well."

Cass tried, "Can you tell us anything else about Mr. Cotter?"

I said, "Does he own the house?"

Mr. Terrell looked concerned, "Believe so. He represented

himself as the owner when he rented it to me."

"How did you find the house?"

"Classifieds. Not a lot of places to rent and I didn't want any sort of apartment. I jumped right on it when I saw it in the paper. He was happy to see me."

"What did he look like?"

"Your average sort. Sandy hair. Glasses."

"How old was he?"

"A deal younger than me. Maybe forty."

"Did he say what he did for a living?"

"No, sir."

"Did he leave an address where you could reach him to make your rental payments?"

"No sir. Said he had to do some travelling for business or another and he'd be by once a month or so, but I never saw him again."

"Did he leave anything behind?"

"Well, I rented the place furnished, you understand. He put some boxes in the basement, I know. Don't know what's in'em."

"Could we possibly look at those?"

"No sir. I don't think that would be right. That's private property."

The next name geographically speaking was Christian Hansen. His name was also crossed out. He lived in an apartment on Amsterdam Avenue at the edge of Washington Heights.

He had not answered his phone, earlier, and there was an envelope from a realty company taped to the door. I knocked loudly a couple of times anyway and a woman came to the door next to his. She had a bib apron on and clearly was in the midst of cooking dinner. She steps right out and says, "He's not home."

Cass asked if she knew where Mr. Hansen was.

"Haven't seen him since sometime in May." She is looking at the press card in my hat and adds. "Has something happened to him?"

"We don't know? We're trying to find out. Can you think of anyone who might be able to help us?"

"He has a sister. I've seen her before. She came by once and knocked. She lives in New Rochelle, I believe she said."

The neighbor knew only that Mr. Hansen worked for the Post Office. "Not much more. He was a private type of man. I think he was shy."

I asked her to describe him. She guessed that he was about 35 years old, but unmarried. Then she quickly added "But normal looking. He's a reader. He has piles of books in there."

She added that he liked to go to meetings in the evening. She didn't know what kind. And that he was a Yankees fan and went to games whenever he could. And she knew he went to some of the marches and sit-downs around town because he tried to get her to go with him one time.

"He asked me once to go to a ballgame with him as well. Maybe he was just flirting. But I couldn't go. My husband had only been dead a year then and I wasn't ready. And besides, he is a little young for me."

We started to leave before I thought to ask again about the sister.

"Any clue at all where in New Rochelle his sister might live?"

"No idea. She was a very good looking girl, but I didn't see a wedding band on her either."

"Was she blonde?"

"Nearly white blonde. Like it was bleached but I don't think it was. She just had that look about her."

Cass and I sat in the car for a short time after that and watched the rush hour traffic push by and discussed what we knew. The cops had told us that the bodies found, or their remains, were those of middle-aged men. Mr. Hansen did not quite fit that bracket. And there was one woman's name on the list: Margaret Gruber. It was not marked out but Cass had called her earlier and not gotten an answer. Her address was on West End Avenue and she would be the next in line.

We were there about 6:30. When I knocked, someone came to the door and looked through the peephole. Then the door opened a crack with the security chain on.

A woman looked out at us both. "What do you want?"

Cass did the talking. "We're looking for Margaret Gruber."

"Who's asking?"

Cass took out her press card and I pointed up at my hat.

"My name is Cassandra Green. We're doing a story and we thought you might be able to help."

"I'm not Margaret. Let me ask."

The door closed and we waited. Shortly the door cracked again and another eye looked out.

"Are you the one who wrote the article about Lucy and Stanly?"

"Yes."

"Is that what this is about?"

"Yes."

"I don't want to talk to you."

The door closed.

I knocked again. I hear someone inside yell, "Go away!" and when I knocked again, the voice threatened, "We'll call the police."

I answered back as loudly as I could, "You should! Lucille Beinecke is going to kill you all. One by one. Maybe the police can save you."

The voice through the door said. "Not us!"

I said, "You're a witness. She'll get to you, eventually."

At this point another door had cracked farther down the hall.

A voice there said, "Leave them alone or *I'll* call the police!"

I spoke out into the hall for anyone to hear, "We aren't trying to hurt anyone. We're just looking for information. The police will be here soon enough."

At that point the crack in Miss Gruber's door opened again.

"What exactly is it you want to know?"

"We have a list. We're trying to find out if she's already killed everyone on that list, or if someone on it is still alive. Besides you, I mean. If there are others, they need to know what's going on."

"What list?"

"A list of names we found at Stanly Baker's home."

"He kept a list?" Then a breathless pause. "What a dope!"

"Maybe so, but it might end up being the reason someone doesn't die."

At this point the door closed again and the chain was slipped loose. Margaret Gruber then opened it all the way and leaned out to yell down the hall to her neighbor that it was okay. Then she let us in.

Margaret Gruber works at Macy's. She had just gotten home when we knocked. Her friend, Dottie, works the ticket window at the Belasco Theatre. Neither of them could be much more than thirty years old. Neither was a beauty but they were both dressed well, hair done in the short fashion of Carole Lombard, and they looked good enough. On the 'it's a small world' list, before leaving we found out that they'd both come to town to get into show business and had tried out at one time for parts with The Group Theatre and been turned down, but it was in the auditions there that they had first met each other.

Dottie added that at least she had managed to get her current job selling tickets that way.

Immediately after we were in the door, Margaret wanted to see our list of names. I gave her my copy of the slip.

"But these are only first names. How did you find me?"

"Mr. Stanly kept that information too, in a little book."

"What an idiot! He had us all skulking around like sneaks, coming in at different times, and going out at different times. Meanwhile, he's got it all written down in black and white!"

As serious as the matter was, I had the feeling that I was talking to a kid who had been playing a game.

Cass said, "I'm not interested in the sneaking around so much. Not unless you were doing something wrong. The matter now is that Lucy is killing people and I'd like to know why, so that the police can stop her"

Margaret said, "She left our group about a year ago. She had an argument with Stanly at one of the meetings. A big blow up. He hit her. Right in front of everyone. And she told him he'd regret it. So I suppose now he has."

We were sitting then in a living room that was only about twice as wide as the hallway. The hallway ran past an equally narrow kitchen. There was one bedroom beyond and a bathroom I could see a bit of beyond that. By the look of the molding I guessed that this was once all part of a single bedroom in the original brownstone, which had been divided to create more apartments.

The two women faced us from a short couch against the back wall and Cass and I used the two chairs from a small table by the window.

Cass pointed at the list in Margaret's hand. "So Lucille Beinecke was a member of your group."

"Lucy? Yes. But she was a big supporter of the reforms. She likes Stalin. She thought Trotsky was a traitor to the Third International. And Stanly was one of the old guard. Trotsky was his hero. So the two of them argued a lot. Mostly it was just Lucy trying to persuade the others, and Stanly arguing with whatever she said."

"Was that only at the meetings?"

"Yes. Mostly, I think. She couldn't see the other's any other way. Not officially. We only used our first names. No one was supposed to make contact except through Stanly. He called the meetings."

"Why didn't he just forget to call her?"

"Maybe because she had some support among the others. The group might have broken up anyway if she hadn't walked out on her own. Or maybe Rottler didn't want that."

"Rottler?"

"Oh. Stanly was the only one who knew Rottler. Rottler is the one up. Rottler is the 'leader' of the next group up, you might say. No one but Stanly has ever met him."

"But Lucy was pushed out?"

"I think she left on her own. She even said it out loud that day. She thought she was being used."

"How was she being used?"

"Stanly was screwing her. We all knew that. But I think a couple of the others were too."

This was said as casually as if it were an everyday matter.

Cass wondered, "But I thought you didn't know each other except at meetings."

Margaret admitted, "We weren't supposed to. But messages were passed. You know. Like in school. I got one once from Christian. I told him I wasn't interested." She shook her head. I see you have a check by his name. Does that mean he's dead?"

"Possibly."

"That's too bad. He was just a lonely guy. The party meant everything to him. It just didn't leave him with much of a social life."

It was eight o'clock before we left Margaret and Dottie and we were both a little tired. We talked on the way home but mostly about the incidentals. I had formed an idea in my mind when we were at Peggy Starr's house in Pelham that we might have stumbled on some incredible spy ring. Instead, it was more likely that these were just the sort of functionaries who did all the legwork, passed out the leaflets, went to the demonstrations, and sat blocking in the doorways. Gofers. So far, the only one we knew for sure to be deadly serious was Lucille Beinecke. And for some reason she was killing the others. Or at least some of them.

99. Sunday, September 26, 1937

     I know a little about cameras, and women, and beer, but not a whole lot about spies. Like any business, a lot of reporting is actually a matter of who you know, not what. And I know someone who does know a little about the subject of secret agents and 'under cover men, or 'operatives,' as the magazines like to call them. At least when he's sober.

     Jack Pines was still sleeping one off about 11 o'clock on Sunday morning when we found him. He's in a rooming house over on 8th Avenue now, which was easy enough to get to. Cass stayed in the car so I could stand over the guy until he'd gotten some pants on and then we took him to breakfast at Morgy's.

     Even with the ache that I knew was pounding at the inside of his head, he has a cat's smile on beneath the shadow of beard on his cheeks. I should have given him time to shave but I knew Cass was waiting. I see the smile and I keep some chitchat going about the Giants and the Yankees just to irritate him. I know he doesn't give a damn about sports. So finally when the eggs are down on the counter and he has swallowed a couple of cups of coffee whole, he turns to me.

     "I figure you've hauled me over here about the Reds."

     "Yes, sir."

     "You want a little help on this one."

     "Yes, sir."

     "What's in it for me?"

"You can share the by-line."

No hesitation. He already has it figured. "Alright. Good. Just so long as I don't have to go running all over the fucking town."

Doc is down the counter serving someone else, but he hears that, "Watch your tongue!"

Jack says, "Yes, sir. Sorry."

I went over some of the details we had from the day before. Cass is quiet through most of it, until the end. Jack has already read my file at the office so he knows a little about it.

Cass says, "The woman might just be crazed. All the political hooha might have nothing to do with it."

Jack says, "You got part of it right. She's crazed. But she's not out drowning her kids in a river, or killing the preacher, or shooting up a gas station, is she? She has a purpose. At least she thinks she does, anyway. My guess is, she's what you call a 'rogue.' She's not doing this under orders from someone else. She's taken a hunting license out on her own account. Most of the fanatics you meet are like that. We don't know what this is all about, but maybe we can get to her by figuring what direction she's headed in."

I said, "I thought that's what we were already doing."

Cass says, "What is it you think we're not doing?"

Jack pours half a puddle of ketchup on his hash and eats his eggs and then some toast to give himself time to think it through. On his fourth cup of coffee he has something else to add.

First he says it to Cass because she doesn't know about all of that.

"I used to tell your man Hugh here to look for the details. Everybody sees the big cheeks in the smile. Look at the eyes. The eyes will tell you if the person is happy or not. Same with everything else. That's what makes your boy here a good cameraman. What are the details here? This lady can shoot. The 'Annie Oakley' is a good tag. Where did she learn to shoot like that? Hugh says she talks like she might be a foreigner. Her English is a little too good. That might be. But it also might be that she's just trying to hide where she's actually from. I'd say from the shooting, it's more likely either the

West or the South."

Cass speaks right up to that. "I can shoot. My mother taught me. And I'm from Cleveland!"

Jack shakes his head, "And I can hear it in your vowels. I never met anyone from the Midwest who thought they talked funny. Nope! The only people I've ever met who're self-conscious about the way they speak are from the South. They get labeled as hicks. A cowboy will tell you to stuff it where the sun don't shine. A girl out of the South who's come to the big city will either try to lose the accent, or else use it on the smitten to get her way. And the women I've known to be the best shots are all from the South. The Carolinas. Tennessee. From up in the mountains. They shoot squirrels down that way for food. If you gotta eat, you get good at what gets you the meal. And a twenty-two caliber is a common choice for small varmints."

This seemed to be a long way from catching spies.

I said, "So this Southern girl comes up North and learns to speak the way she needs to, so as to get her way. That sounds pretty smart. What makes her crazy?"

Jack says the obvious, "Don't mistake being crazy for being dumb. Likely she started off with a load of ambition and she got whittled down real fast by the slick operators. Her real curse would be looking the way you say she does. You don't know what kind of home she came out of, but it couldn't have been all that copacetic, otherwise she wouldn't have left it. My guess is that her name wasn't Beinecke. I'll even go so far as to guess that name might have been taken from a husband. That's the easiest way for a woman to get a new identity. And that's another detail. Along with her looks. And I would make a guess that she started using those looks as fast capital to get whatever she wanted, pretty quick."

Cass says, "That appears to be what she's been doing lately to get these guys to take their clothes off."

Jack nods and settles his thought with one last long draw on his Lucky Strike. "I'll bet. And there's more there. If you think that through. She could have changed her hand along the way. Smart ones do. Most people just sit pat and play the cards they're dealt. Likely enough she had a little experience with men before she ever left home. And the home she left might have given her some other ideas on all that."

And this all seemed sensical, but I was feeling impatient. My plate was clean and three cups of coffee were enough for the moment. "Why Trotskyites?"

Jack looks at Cass, and then at me. "If you let me noodle through a little muddy water here, I might be able to pull a catfish clean out of it, as an old Army buddy of mine used to say."

Jack lights up another Lucky Strike and inhales slowly. I should be used to it from years ago. His mind is on it like a watchdog on the leg.

Finally he says, "She's a woman. Right? She's alone. She's in New York and trying to make a living in the worst way. And she can't shoot her way to success. The days of the real Annie Oakley are over. The gun might even have been some sort of self-protection when she first got here. I wouldn't be surprised if there were one or two fellows who tried to make bad use of her at the time who aren't around anymore. But it's a lonely life. I'll admit to knowing a few of the type myself over the years. They were all very lonely girls. And they can't trust anyone. Every time they do, they get screwed. That's the way they see it. Everything is down to the dollars and cents. And this Miss Beinecke is smarter than most. She's looking for reasons why she's miserable. Somebody to blame it all on. The smart ones are always looking for reasons, but not many are smart enough to find them out. They usually end up wanting to blame their misery on someone else. It's just the way people think. And here you go with this new take on the second oldest profession that blames it all on money. Fits like a glove. Materialism. Capitalists. Bankers. Jews. Whatever. All the same thing."

Jack holds his empty cup up for another refill. I've seen him drink six cups at a sitting, so I know he is feeling better now.

I say, "What about the Trotskyites."

Cass nudges my arm. She's been pretty quiet so far, so I

suppose a lot of what Jack has said makes sense to her.

He says, "It's the same reason some of these girls will stay with a mack—the pimp. It's a home. A place they belong. Why would a girl give up most of what she earns to a madame in a whore-house instead of working on her own? Because it's a rough trade. My guess would be that Miss Beinecke joined her little cell of Reds because it gave her some comfort. She belonged to something. The politics of it jibed with her own ideas about things being unfair. You ever read any of their stuff? It has answers for everything. Just like a Sunday school preacher. It's all in the Good Book. It just depends on how you read it. And as far as that goes, I'll bet you a dollar if you loan that much to me, she got a taste of the Preacher back in the mountains and that was enough of the good Lord for her."

I say, "So why's she killing the other members of her group?"

Jack shrugs. Like just one guess more won't hurt.

"I'll bet it's a matter of betrayal. This Third International is her religion now. The Trotskyites are the traitors."

Lucille Beinecke had said that exact thing to me.

Cass said, "What do you think we should do next?"

"Be careful. At some point she's going to start figuring you out as well. She's going to know you're on her trail. The cops are always going to be two steps behind, unless she stumbles. But if you catch up with her, she's not going to lie down for you."

All this was fine. But I didn't see yet how it was going to get us anywhere. Figuring it might at least be a link on the chain to follow, one more time I said, "What about the Trotskyites!"

Timmy has been sitting quiet in the corner all the while. He looked like he was asleep when we came in, and likely was. But when I said "Trotskyites" a little louder, it woke him up. As if he'd just awakened from a dream, he says, "They was the longshoremens. They wanted to organize our ship onest and refused to load unless we took a vote. Me and the boys all went down to the dock and knocked the sons a' bitches into the water and loaded the damned thing ourselves. Cap'n paid us a good bonus on that, I'll tell ya."

I thought of my father's similar tale. How many times on how many docks had this same thing happened around the world I wondered? I asked Timmy, "Where did you work?"

Timmy says, "Portland. St. Johns. Course, I was born up in Bangor and had family there at the time."

So this wasn't just the same story as my dad's retold in a different way.

Jack speaks up on that note, "That's all changed now. The docks are organized North and South. "You couldn't get a boat out these days without the local tariff."

Timmy laughs at that, "You never met our crew!"

Jack smiles and turned back to his coffee. "They don't make'em like that anymore. And now the Trotskyites are off the perch. They're done for, I think. There's a new strong man in town. Joe Stalin. And he doesn't take no for an answer. Doesn't take maybe. You've read the papers. They don't tell half of it. The *Times* is all wet. Mr. Stalin will keep killing until he doesn't hear a whimper. That's the kind he is. And I think he'd like Miss Beinecke if he ever got the chance. But she'll be dead, sooner than later. They don't want anyone who goes off on their own. Crazy or not. Everybody has to toe the line. You have another thought and you're dangerous. This lady doesn't know the heat of the fire, as my old man used to say back in Pittsburgh. She doesn't understand what kind of metal she's playing with. They'll sweep her away like an ash." He tapped his cigarette in the glass tray as if to illustrate. "But maybe she's useful for the time being. She's doing the work for them. You say, what about the Trotskyites? Forget about them. That's all done for. The whole communist thing is a disorganized mess right now. At least until Uncle Joe puts the pieces back together his own way. Right now it's the Nazis. They're the ones to worry about. Uncle Joe is too busy killing his own. But the Nazis, they want to kill you, Miss."

Jack had turned around on his stool to face Cass squarely.

She said what she has said before, "But why. What good would it do them?"

Jack only says what she already knows, "Because you wrote about something they did and you made fools of them in public. Can you imagine what Luciano would do to the guy he sent out to hit Dutch Schultz if the guy came back and said 'Sorry, I missed?' They don't want any others to get the same idea. That's all. The same thing will happen with all the Reds when Uncle Joe gets his arms around things. All the writers condemning Hitler and his boys now are just a bunch of angry voices, most of them with their own political agendas. The readers know that. They all read the same stuff. But how many news stories have you read about what's actually going on without the writer preaching for yet another solution?"

The question did not require an answer.

I ask, "So what would you do next?"

"You mean, what will I be doing? I'll be heading over to Dooley's to get myself a couple of beers to settle these eggs. Then I'll go over to the office and write up a little copy on what you've told me. I'll leave it there for you to play with when you get in. The one thing I will not do is get myself between the Nazis and the Reds. I've been there before. There's not enough room to breathe."

"I meant, what should we do. Keep following the list?"

"You're too young for this. I'd leave it to the cops. They get paid to be shot at."

"That's not a story. That's a police report."

Jack sighs at me like the hopeless fellow I am. "Yeah. Well, like I said, just don't get yourself between a Nazi and a Red. Stand aside and let them kill each other like they're doing in Spain right now. They have firing squads on both sides over there but you'll only read about the ones that Mr. Hemingway heard the Republicans doing. The ones that someone else saw."

"You don't like Mr. Hemingway?"

"I like him fine. I knew him in Greece when he was with the *Toronto Star*. I had the only room left at the hotel and he was very worried about sleeping in the same bed. I told him, my lice were as good as his. But a fine fellow. Very eager. Brave enough, but knows when to keep his head down. It was me taught him what to say there to get a meal while there were kids and women starving in the street outside. It's what you had to do, or go home. In fact, I was still with the *Telegraph* at the time and on my way home from Russia. I didn't get to stay very long for the fun though." He lit another Lucky. "But I'll tell you this. That novel he wrote about the ex-pats in Paris—that's bullshit." Jack turned his head to see if Doc has heard. Doc has his head under the hood at the griddle, with the fan in his ears.

"That book's all about the scars and the regrets and nothing much about the way Paris really was after the war. Nobody had time for self-pity then. The party was on. There were better things to do. He's better than that, even if he likes war too much. But it's just like a moth to the flame. All about being brave when you're young. From reading what he wrote just lately about Spain, I think he's still in love with the smell of the guns—the conjurer's smoke. The holy magic act. Only he's still surprised to find the bloody body of the lady that was sawed in half lying there beneath the contraption when the haze clears. No magic at all. That cold reserve he uses is just as phony. But he won't be able to explode now because all his dear friends would be aghast at the mess he'd make out of their neat little lives. All of them so critical and so smug. The poets are the only ones who can tell that story now."

Jack laughed, and coughed up cigarette smoke and phlegm, before wiping his face with a napkin. "But you know, I tried to borrow a couple bucks from him one time right here in New York, not long after that, and he looked at me like he didn't know me." He shook his head and gathered a needed breath. "You can't just keep moving ahead and forget what you've left behind."

As I go out the door, Doc yells at me, "Hey Hugh, Goodman's coming to town again. You got another chance!"

Gregory Hartunian's address was at a rug shop on Second Avenue. His name was not crossed out on our list. Because it was Sunday, the shop was closed but there were apartments above. I rang the bells, none of which had names in the brass holder. The downstairs door had a better lock and wouldn't open with my press card, so I kept pressing the bells until finally an older fellow in a white shirt and black slacks, stocky and with half an unlit cigar planted in his mouth, came down to greet us.

"What the hell's with you? Somebody doesn't answer, it means they aren't home."

I shrugged innocently, "But here you are!"

"What'd you want?"

"I'm looking for Gregory."

"He's not here."

Cass handed the fellow a card printed with her name and number with the *Journal-American* logo in color. It reminded me I had to get some of those for myself.

She said, "It's very important for him to contact us if he can. It could be a matter of life and death."

The old man turned the cigar between his lips as he examined the card. Then he looked at me.

"Who are you?"

I pointed at my hat. "We are working on the story together."

He says, "Does this concern the little lady whose trying to kill him?"

I think we both said yes at the same time.

He winces as if in pain, "The cops don't give a damn. He reported it. But what can you do?"

Cass says, "All we can do is write about it. Let people know."

He waved his free hand at us and says, "Bah!"

I say, "The sooner she's caught the sooner this is all over. She's already killed a couple of people who had nothing to do with your son's activities."

This was said with a certain amount of guessing, but I've known a few Armenian families in Brooklyn. They are close. Sons often go into the father's business.

Mr. Hartunian answers, "Bah," again. And then, "What do you know?"

I said, "Not enough. That's my problem."

Mr. Hartunian tapped an invisible ash from his cigar. "Gregory apologized. To me. And to his mother. He's young. He could not help himself. But it was her! She caused it. She seduced him!"

I let Cass answer that, "That's not our concern. This woman is crazy and she's killing everyone that belonged to that group."

"What group?"

We both knew then that old man had no idea.

"Your son belonged to a communist cell. A small group. Your son belonged to it and so did the woman who's trying to kill him."

The old man stared blank-faced out at the street a moment and then at me.

"Gregory told us it was just the sex. You're saying it was politics?"

"Maybe both. But this woman is serious."

"That's where he used to go at night? The political meetings?"

"Probably."

The man held both hands up in dismay.

"The world is insane! Mad! His grandfather and his uncles are all dead from politics. He promised me he would not be a part of that."

"I'm sorry."

Cass said, "It's important that he's somewhere safe until this is over. This woman is a cold blooded killer and she'll likely keep trying to find him until she's stopped."

The old man bit hard on his cigar. "He's safe. But I'll make double sure of it."

Carmine Esposito was next. His name was not crossed out, but he had not answered his phone. He lived on 9th Avenue at 28th street. This was a second floor apartment in a five-floor building, and the front door was wide open to a fairly constant traffic of children and teenagers. His wife came to the apartment door. At least three young children were behind her that we could see.

We introduced ourselves. Mr. Esposito was not home. He had gone on a 'business trip.' She was not sure when he would return. Again I thought it was Cass who would be better at addressing the situation. Cass pulled out another card just to annoy me after having seen my reaction to the first one.

"We're working on a story concerning a woman who is very dangerous. It's important that we contact your husband."

"What does she have to do with him?"

"They were members of a political group that—"

"Communists?"

"Yes. She seems to—"

"He doesn't belong to any communist party."

"This wasn't the party, necessarily. This was a local group."

"He doesn't belong to any groups."

"Whether he does or not is not important. What is important is that there is a woman who is trying to kill him."

"Why? Why would she do that?"

"We don't know. Perhaps just because she's crazy."

Mrs. Esposito looked at me for an answer.

"She said she had something to give him. She wouldn't say what."

I said, "You've seen her?"

"She was here. Last week. Again. She's been here before. My neighbor saw her once but we were away."

I said, "Did you call the police?"

"Why should I call the police? What did this woman do?"

"She's killed several men."

The statement of that at least gave Mrs. Esposito a momentary pause.

"Why would she do that?"

"Because she thinks they did something."

"What did they do?"

"We don't know."

She considered this for half a second more.

"Well, my husband's not here. I told her."

She closed the door on us then. Cass slipped her card beneath it with a note saying to call and I said out loud through the door that it was very important for Mr. Esposito to stay away until this woman was caught by the police

Philip Lorenze had lived on 4th Street not far from where I had found Orson Welles and John Housemen on Bleecker. His name was crossed out on our list. The phone had been answered by his former roommate, Morton Dent, and this was the same fellow who answered the door and said again that Philip had lived there until a few months before. He had disappeared suddenly. That was early June. Because Cass had spoken to Mr. Dent previously on the phone I let her do the questioning.

Evidently, there was a new roommate now and Mr. Lorenze's things had been moved in several boxes to the basement. This had to be done to keep the rent paid. Cass asked if the police had been notified, and they had. A missing person's report had been filed. There had been one phone call from a Mr. Stanly shortly after Philip had disappeared. He had that number written down and this was the same one we had for the house in Pelham. The roommate had called Mr. Lorenze's parents, who lived upstate in Newburgh, to report Philip's disappearance. They too had not heard from him since.

Mr. Lorenze was 50 years old and unmarried. The roommate gave us a photograph of the man taken at the beach the previous summer with several friends.

Nicholas Petridis lived on Broome Street near Broadway. He was the second on the list that we found at home. He hadn't answered the phone before because he worked odd hours. He was a janitor for several buildings downtown. He had not heard from 'Lucy.'

Mr. Petridis was likely about forty years old. Fairly muscular in build. A handsome man and obviously a bit vain about it, considering the amount of oil he uses in his hair. Cass re-explained our concerns, after we had introduced ourselves and seemingly convinced him that we had no interest in his politics, but only in finding Miss Beinecke before she killed anyone else.

He said, "She was an odd girl. But it's hard to believe she would hurt anyone." The statement was made in such a calm manner that it was unsettling. I could see on Cass's face that she was thinking the same thing.

I said, "Fact is, half a dozen people are dead."

He shrugged. He was apparently unworried about his own welfare.

Cass gave him her card and we left with the caution that he should be careful.

From there we drove first to Police Headquarters at Centre Street to see Detective Barnes. He was out, but Cass left a message. From there, on home to dinner.

But our day wasn't over. Cass kept calling Detective Barnes from the house until he called back and then told him first thing about Nicholas Petridis and our worry that he would not survive for long given his attitude.

At least Barnes agreed with that. But he was very unhappy that we had pursued our own investigation. He'd spent the day following that trail of names himself, and he was already frustrated. He lodged the usual complaint about people not wanting to talk to cops even when they were trying to help. But then he wouldn't tell us anything more about his own findings until Cass started bartering information with him. Piece by piece she reported most of what we had found out in return for what little Detective Barnes had learned. As we expected from the line marked through his name, John Nagy was likely dead. According to a sister, George Niemi had left town after speaking with Stanly Baker. Thomas Novak had not been seen for a month. His mother had filed a missing person's report some weeks before and was upset with the police for not doing more to find him. Another name on the list, Peter Wojak, lived in Brooklyn and worked at the shipyard. He had been seen as recently as last week but was not at home presently. His wife did not know where he was, but he'd left suddenly and not returned.

Detective Barnes speculated that Stanly Baker must have figured out something was wrong and started calling the members of his group, one by one. This realization probably dawned on him some time after the *Mirror* reported on Mr. Reagan. Baker obviously didn't know who was responsible for the disappearances or he wouldn't have been consorting with Beinecke when he did. And the thought had occurred to all three of us that Stanly's murder might have been brought on by his own inquiries. Lucille Beinecke wanted to stop him from alerting the victims.

The good thing for us was that Barnes had started from the end of the list instead of the beginning. At least we were saved for the moment from negotiating the streets of the Bronx and Queens after dark.

I found out later that most of this conversation on the phone with the Detective was overheard by our convalescing hero. Flynn's room is right there above on the second floor.

And one more thing. Cass told me this evening that she will carry the Colt revolver with her in her purse from now on, "right next to her notebook."

This was said with about as much regret as she could get into her voice without an actual whimper. All I could do was give her a hug for that, but she wasn't interested. So instead I pulled out the copy of *Julius Caesar* I'd picked up at the library and just started reading that and ignoring her. It took all of five minutes and she was over on top of me.

"Why are you reading THAT?"

"Mr. Welles was acting a little snooty because I didn't know who this guy Brutus was. I thought I'd find out."

She says, "That wasn't acting, I'll bet. Snooty bastard!"

She was probably right about that. But Cass doesn't have a snooty bone in her body. I checked.

100. Monday to Tuesday, September 27 to 28, 1937

Because Cass had risked life and limb by talking to Detective Barnes on the phone, and was the one to go to the precinct house to get the pictures on Monday morning, I let her file the story first. That piece made front page in the regular afternoon edition of the *Journal-American*. My version, greatly shortened by Stenis, but with the pictures much enlarged, first appeared in the 'bulldog' edition of the *Mirror* on Monday evening and then again Tuesday morning for breakfast. The *Daily News* and the *Post* were both left holding hands with stories on page four.

Most of what I offered were the facts of the case, leaving out the names of those people in the communist cell who were not yet dead, or even mentioning Stanly Baker's list and offering brief one or two line biographies of the missing and murdered. I got the front page and a continuation on page three. But that was only a little over seven hundred words sandwiched between the pictures. Nice header though. 'Annie Oakley killer has Reds on the Run.' Cass had two pages as well—but larger pages, maybe 2400 words plus side-bars. Her headline, 'Annie Oakley Killer on the Loose,' was better than most, though the pictures were less than half of one page, including the one on the front. I put the two papers down side by side on the desk in front of Stenis, without saying a thing. He looks back at me and says, "Pretty swell, heh? Great stuff!"

I said, "I handed in as much copy as she did."

He says, "It's all there—just boiled down a bit. Look! Those pictures are worth a thousand words each. Damn! You got two whole pages!"

This was an argument I had conducted with The Boss maybe fifty times, but from the other side. I had no ground to stand on and Stenis knew it.

Sam Felt, good lad that he is, managed to come up with a nice shot of Robert Rivera from the New York Department of Public Works. Rivera had been the Water Department model employee of the month and his picture was featured in some promotion or another they had done the year before. The Post Office personnel department employee picture of Christian Hansen made him look like one of the faces you see on the wanted posters out in the lobby by the letter slots.

Jack Pines showed up just before noon, showered and shaved. He had already seen his name on page one next to mine and he was very pleased. With him wholly sober and gassed up with a full tank of coffee I figured it was the right moment to sit down and go over the situation. Sam Felt sat in on that discussion, looking fairly chipper. The kid was smoking a cigarette, which I had not seen him do before, and just then I figure myself for a corrupter of the youth.

I ran over the few details from Detective Barnes so far and the little additional information I had managed to get on Monday. Cass and I went back to the addresses Barnes had already covered to see if he had missed anything. Few doorbells were answered. I got lost in the Bronx and then caught in the same damned traffic on the Triborough Bridge that I had taken pictures of some months ago. Sitting there, I could imagine myself from high above, just one car buried in the weave of a frayed belt of cars, buckled up over the East River, all of us trying to find some way out and not knowing there was a milk truck turned over in Astoria, which is what we found out later.

John Nagy's apartment had already been rented to someone else. From a neighbor we found out there were bags and boxes in the basement that were his, along with some of his furniture, but all of that had been picked over by neighbors in the last couple of months.

They'd figured he was dead almost immediately because he had not come home one night and his dog had whined until someone knocked the door open with a hammer. They reported him missing to the police in June. They had heard nothing since. The dog, a mutt of no distinction other than a friendly disposition, a cold nose and a very long tongue, was now living with the neighbor and apparently quite happy.

Without asking, we found the basement steps and went down to look at what was left of this luckless fellow's worldly goods. Every box was hanging open and churned. The clothes that remained were all very worn and missing buttons or torn. There was a small empty picture frame on top and I was fairly sure by the size that it was the source of the photo of Nagy that we had gotten from Detective Barnes and run in the papers. In one box there was a short stack of letters held in a rubber band. I 'borrowed' those, just in case.

Both Cass and I had our stories written Sunday night. Hers actually went to press Monday while we were still watching seagulls eat crabs up on the ledges of metalwork on the Triborough Bridge.

George Niemi's sister was not home. Neighbors did not answer their bells. We moved on.

Thomas Novak lived with his mother. She had spoken to the police and did not want to speak with anyone else. The door was shut in under a minute.

Because of the traffic we had not reached Peter Wojak's house in Bensonhurst until sometime after four. This was to be our sole excitement for the day. Mr. Wojak has several brothers and two of them came home from the shipyard about five as we sat in the car trying to work out our next move. A big fellow suddenly tapped on the door with his knuckle, even though the window was open.

He says, "You want something?"

He was eyeing Cass in the seat next to me as he said it.

I say, "Not unless you're Peter Wojak."

"My brother. He's not here. We told the cops that. My mother says she told you that. Why're YOU still here?"

I tried the soft approach first. "We're worried about him."

"Let us worry about him. You get your ass out'ta here."

But I was tired. And the Chrysler has a nice door on it. It opens very smoothly and weighs at least sixty pounds. I let this swing out about as hard as I could and the top frame of the window catches Mr. Wojak in the jaw as he starts to back away. He is on his ass faster than I can get out of the car.

Cass is saying "Hugh! Stop it!"

From the house I see another fellow, a near duplicate of the first, and he's coming down the short walk in a charge. That was no contest. I just kept him going, tripping over his brother's legs, head first right into the fender.

I say, "If you don't do a better job taking care of your brother than that, he'll be dead."

Cass was on my case the entire way home. As furious as I've seen her. I think this might be some sort of delayed reaction to finally giving in about carrying the gun. For a person who dislikes violence as much as she does, she has a hell of a temper. She storm-ed into the house from the car without waiting. I looked up and there is my mom frowning from the kitchen window.

Dinner would have been very quiet on Monday night, if Flynn had not been there to liven things up.

Michael Flynn is a bright lad. He had heard most of what Cass had told Detective Barnes on the phone, and mentioned at dinner on Sunday night that he had some friends. He'd ask around. At Monday dinner he has some ideas. He apologizes for butting in, and then gives himself the excuse that he's itching to work and he hasn't got a case for himself yet. He's got classifieds running in several papers. Not a peep.

I'm feeling a little grumpy over Cass, but I hadn't had a smart idea all day so I ask Flynn to tell us what he's got. Right there at the table. I shouldn't have, but the silence from Cass and my mom had me back on my heels. Mrs. Nessen appears immediately in-terested. At every pause she says, 'Ya, ya," eager for more. Mrs. Tisdale is all ears and can't manage to take a bite of food. Mr. Jenks is ready with his usual opinions. Mr. Clurman is quiet. I have noticed that Mr. Clurman is a lot quieter now that Mr. Oliphant is gone and I wonder if somehow he has lost some funds in that mess as well. But it's not my business to ask.

On about the third interruption by Mr. Jenks, I told him he should keep his opinions to himself, and then had to apologize for bringing the whole thing up.

From the beginning, Dad is looking out from beneath his eyebrows, which is his way of saying he has no part in any of it.

Flynn is saying, "According to my buddy Ned—Ned was my Criminal Law instructor at Boston College when I first met him and now he's with the F.B.I.—these communists are all over the place, but their organization is a mess. One cell doesn't know what the other is doing. He once saw two of them show up at a strike in Worcester carrying signs for opposites sides. And part of the confusion is caused by the crack between the new guys who support Stalin and the old guys that are still backing Trotsky. But it seems the old guys are losing the battle. Stalin is shooting them by the thousands. Thousands! No kidding. The Soviets have something called the NKVD and it's supposed to run these things, but now even that's broken up too, and it's all being re-organized."

Cass said, "I thought it was called the GUGB."

Flynn says "Yes. But that's just part of the bigger organization. What they call the old OGPU. It's all NKVD now, I think. They likely shot the old lot. Really. Or maybe I've got that backwards. Don't ask me what those letters mean. Ned told me something about it but I can't write as fast as you guys do."

I asked, "What are they doing in New York?"

Mr. Jenks answered that first, "Spying. They're all over the shipyard."

Flynn says, "Maybe. But these cells are a political apparatus of some kind. Ned says it's very unlikely this group you broke into would be involved in anything other than putting out propaganda and collecting information. It would be the cell above them that was doing the dirty work. Your Mr. Baker could have been the contact to them. But not necessarily."

Mr. Jenks says, "Spying. Like I said."

Flynn says, "And the recruiting. These lower cells are the recruiting centers for new members because they're out there talking to people and handing out the leaflets and all that. It's just a step away from the Communist Party operation. Mostly just politics at that level. All the assassinations and kidnapping you read about, that's a whole 'nother matter. That's run directly from Moscow. That would have to involve someone more sophisticated."

Mr. Jenks says, "They're in the government too. That whole lot around Roosevelt are Commies."

I spoke then without thinking, "Shut up Mr. Jenks. That's not the kind of talk we're looking for right now."

This brought silence to the entire table and wide eyes from both Cass and Mom. You could hardly see Dad's eyes through his brows. I turned back to Mr. Jenks and apologized. "I'm sorry. Rough day. I apologize. I'm just trying to get an idea about something here. People are getting killed and we'd like to know the why."

Mr. Jenks looks like I'd slapped his face. He's a little stunned and it takes a minute before he starts eating again, but at least he didn't say anything more.

Flynn just ignores my rudeness and pushes on, "The point is, one faction killing another is not on the menu for these guys that you're looking into. My friend Ned's pretty sure what you've found is just a maniac. A psychopath. Someone with their own agenda."

Cass is not looking my way through any of it, but she says, "At least that's about what we think too."

But Flynn isn't finished, "The problem is this, those two guys who've been trying to kill you are a different matter. They have a different purpose altogether. The Nazis don't argue. They're more like a military organization top to bottom. They have one plan. And those guys probably just want to rise in the ranks. And now you've made them look bad."

Cass raises an eyebrow, "With your help."

That brought silence to the table once again.

101. Wednesday, September 29, 1937

My idea then was this. We should separate the list into two groups. The Trotskyites from the Stalinists. If Miss Beinecke's problem was with the Trotskyites, we'd want to break this down that way to see who might be in the greater danger. And we did not have a lot of choices for determining this distinction. Margaret Gruber and her friend Dottie were just about it.

Cass and I had made up some ground on our differences the night before. This had been helped a little by the letters I had stolen out of Mr. Nagy's belongings—the ones we'd found dumped in that basement. The script was in a woman's hand and very small and hard to decipher and we had to put our two heads together on that and it's always good if your heads are together on something. The letters themselves were rather pitiful, I thought. A woman was writing her lover without a mention of her affection for him. There were no envelopes. All of them were dated from this year, and somewhat sadly addressed, 'Dear John,' and then continued on to discuss the higher political aims of their lives—using such lines as 'Our strength will come from sharing our struggle.' Every sentence read like a reworking of the sort of subway pamphlet jargon that litters the floor of the train cars sometimes after rush hour. 'The workers will see the path we have laid for them, and follow us.' I could not help but make fun of it and rewrite the words myself. I said to Cass, "The workers will see the trap we've laid for them, and run for their lives." She did not think this was funny. I might as well be making sport of a line from the Catholic Catechism, she said. And she was right. There was no humor in such religion. No room really for cracking a smile.

The letters were all signed, 'Jane.' There was no explicit emotion or sentiment in any of them, though they all had a tone that Cass thought could be felt between the lines. Yet, the most personal line was, 'When you are back, we can go up to your father's house. I think he likes me, even though you two have argued about it."

Cass had the idea that, because he was the most amenable, we should talk to Mr. Petridis again as soon as possible. I wasn't looking for another argument, so we went there first thing Wednesday morning. But apparently, he was not at home. Or at least, he did not answer the door. Given the time of day, that was not unusual, but the quiet of the place bothered me. Cass wrote a note on the back of one of her cards asking him to please call if we didn't see him first, and slipped that under the door.

I told Cass that the hairs were up on my neck when we were inside the building. She wondered aloud if the guy might already be dead. This ended up with me parking by the phone booths at 14th Street where the pimps hang out in the evenings, while she called Detective Barnes. But he wasn't at his desk.

From there we went up to the Belasco Theatre. Margaret Gruber's roommate, Dottie, works the ticket counter there and it might be a chance to learn more from her with the two women apart. Dottie is sitting alone in the booth behind the grill, smoking a cigarette and reading a theatre magazine. She recognized us right off.

Cass apologizes for the intrusion and then asks, "I was just wondering, did you ever meet any of the others in the group?"

"Margaret's group? No. They weren't supposed to get together except at the meetings. You'll have to talk to Margaret about all that."

"We were going down to Macy's to do just that, but it's likely to be a little busier there this time of day, and she'd mentioned that notes were passed. It occurred to me that you might have been friendly with one or two of the other members."

Dottie laughed as if that were absurd.

"No. You don't know! If she encouraged any of them, they'd come over expecting a lot more than a drink."

"So you never met any of them yourself?"

"No. Well, I did see one of them. Once. Just by accident. Margaret and I were out one night. We went up to the Apollo to see Billie Holiday sing. A guy named Nick was there. Margaret and I were sitting way across from them because she didn't want to have to talk to him. I think, she didn't like him. Next time I looked they were gone, so there was no harm done."

Something made me immediately interrupt to ask, "Them?"

"He was with a girl."

"Did Margaret know her too?"

"I think so. But she didn't say. She was just surprised to see them there."

"What color was the woman's hair?"

"She was a brunette. No. Actually it was black. It had quite a shine."

Cass left another card with Dottie and we went on our way, this time directly to the Police Headquarters to see Detective Barnes. If he wasn't back, and not just avoiding our calls, we could leave a note explaining our thinking. It did not require Sherlock Holmes to wonder if this other person with Nicholas Petridis was Lucille Beinecke. And with the odd reaction of Petridis when we'd spoken to him previously, and the fact that he was still alive and seemingly unworried, my next thought was that the little hairs on my neck were not losing their touch and that Beinecke might even have been at the apartment when we went there earlier. After abandoning her apartment at Knickerbocker Village, she would have needed a place like that to hide.

Detective Barnes was at his desk. He offered us an unhappy greeting, "What do you want now? The *News* and the *Post* are both all over me for giving you guys the pictures first. I can't write the stories for you too."

Cass told him about our conversation with Dottie and my concern. Barnes looks at me like I might have something on my shoe. Then he lights a cigarette and pages through a couple of his notes.

"I actually didn't talk to Petridis. I had another officer go over there. I see here he says the guy was very cooperative."

I say, "Yeah. That sounds right. A Red that's very cooperative with cops."

Barnes gives me a look one more time for the tone of my voice, and then sighs and rolls the eyes like he does and then speaks to his lieutenant and then they make a call to get a search warrant made out for the Nicholas Petridis apartment. This is done in the time it takes to get a cup of coffee.

Detective Barnes ordered us to stay well behind. We followed him and two other cars down to 4th Street. They went in the place so fast ahead of us I hadn't found a parking place and so we were well behind by default. There were no shots to be heard. A sergeant blocked the building door when we got up to it and we stayed outside with the small crowd that began to gather because of the police cars.

After about twenty minutes a patrolman comes out again, and he just says, "The detective says you can go in now. But don't touch anything."

This was probably the first murder scene I'd gotten a look at before the Medical Examiner arrived. The pictures tell the story. Mr. Petridis had not died easily. Miss Beinecke had managed to hit him in the left eye but it had not been enough and he had put up a struggle. Like the others, he was naked. Other entry wounds were scattered over his upper torso. All at the front. If her pistol was a six shot model, she had emptied it. Another officer kept us in a small entry area of the apartment at first, but with the comings and goings we edged into the bedroom and I grabbed as many shots on that as I could before we were ordered out again.

I could hear a neighbor talking to another officer in the hallway. She was an Italian woman, but her English was very good. This conversation was sadly humorous.

She was saying, "I grew up in Naples. You hear the sound of

the guns at night like that and you don't move. You don't say a thing. If they hear you, they will come for you as well. My mother told me that a hundred times . . . I'm sorry. I'm sorry."

This woman placed the shots at or around midnight. She had not turned on her light to look at the clock.

There were a couple more disturbing things about it though—at least to me. The card that Cass had left that morning was no longer there. None of the cops had picked it up or seen it lying around. I looked again just in case. I was thinking of Jack Pines' warning. Now Cass would have another stalker to worry about. And a darker thought attached to the missing card—that Lucille Beinecke had hung around at that bloody scene for hours after she had killed Petridis. Perhaps even taken a nap.

For once I was leaving a scene as Mr. Weegee arrived.

Cass had time to get to her paper and file the story before deadline. I dropped her off there and went uptown to file mine. I had the guys in the darkroom develop the pictures pronto and then went down to the wire room and asked Betty to send Cass some copies of those. Betty tells me then that I'm driving Stenis crazy with this. "He's not happy sharing the wealth."

I was suddenly feeling smart-ass again so I said, "You should be happy about that," and gave her a wink.

The next thing after filing my own copy with Stenis was to go get Cass again and try to catch Margaret Gruber before she left work. Rush hour traffic was the usual but we made it with about thirty seconds to spare. Margaret was literally standing outside the front door at Macy's by the newspaper stand, holding a copy of the *Journal-American* open in her hands, and reading the gory details. I could smell the fresh ink in the air before she looked up at me.

Cass told her we could give her a lift and she accepted. She looked stunned. In the car she offered the information we wanted without our even asking.

"I don't understand. Nick was one of the new guard. A progressive. He thought Stalin was just the kind of strong leader that we needed. Why would she kill Nick?"

I said, "Maybe he knew something else about her. They'd been going out together. Isn't that right?"

"Yes."

Her answer was distracted. She sat silently in the back seat for most of the way. Cass asked her several questions which she seemed not to hear. Then suddenly she said, "I'm afraid for Dottie. She'll kill Dottie too! Dottie saw them together!"

"At the Apollo?"

"Yes! How did you know?"

I explained that we had spoken to Dottie earlier and that it had been the very reason we had gone with the police, and then to the Nicholas Petridis apartment.

She tapped her finger on the paper in her lap, "Those are your pictures?"

"Yes."

"How does someone do that?"

I assumed she meant the shooting and not my taking the pictures.

Cass said the obvious. "Lucy is out of her mind."

Margaret suddenly had panic in her voice. "I have to get Dottie out of there! She's home now. She's there!"

I double-parked directly outside. I was thinking that if Lucy was in the neighborhood and saw the car it might keep her away while we managed to get them both loaded up and out. But I don't really know if I had such a plan. It's just what I thought about later. I did ask Cass to stay with the car and keep an eye out. I remember realizing it was a poor choice of words again.

Margaret ran headlong into the building as soon as the car was stopped. I was left grabbing the gun from my bag and chasing behind. She was loudly saying her friend's name as she took each step, "Dottie. Dottie. Dottie!" but stopped speaking in the moment before the first shot. I think she must have sensed that someone was there in the dark.

The lights inside were off, or the bulbs loosened. I could

barely see my own shadow on the steps cast by the twilight from the windows of the front door. The sound of the shot had come from the upper hall and the immediate echo was shock enough to stop me cold for a split second. There was another shot and the flash as I followed again, taking as many steps as I could at a time without stumbling. That one was aimed at me and came close enough to my cheek to feel.

Dad has a philosophy about shooting which I should mention. He has often said a similar thing in other situations as well. 'You aim if you have time.'

With the sound of that second shot, more a crash than a clap in that stairwell, Dottie suddenly opened the apartment door on the darkened hall above. I saw Lucy then, framed neatly and standing at the rail and I simply fired in reflex. With the hit, she frowned and then fired on me a second time, but I was still moving and that just clipped my leg. I shot twice again before she collapsed onto the tiles.

At the top of the stairs I stepped on Lucy's limp hand to separate it from her pistol and kicked that way. The first blood I actually saw was dripping from my trouser leg onto her hand. Margaret was lying only a few feet away in front of the apartment door. Dottie began screaming and knelt down to hold her. My own breath at that moment was gone.

That was just when Margaret finally opened her eyes and says, "Please Dorothy. You're killing my ears."

Cass comes up behind me then. She has her gun in her hand. And bless her, she has my camera bag too.

And a couple of other things. It amazes me once again, how fast it all occurs. I figured there was less than a minute between the instant I stopped the car and the second I shot Lucille Beinecke and she was dead. I have run through this in my mind a hundred times and I'm sure I'm right.

We'd been looking for Beinecke, or the killer she was, for about seven months. Then the whole thing was over in that one minute. It's as if all time was distorted in some way. All the months were shadowed and forgotten and that single minute was played out over and over. The mind is a funny thing.

A police sergeant caught up to me at St. Vincent's Hospital and took down my rendition of what had happened. They had my gun and would keep that as evidence. I was told I'd probably have to give a deposition to an assistant district attorney to get it back. The Sergeant questioned Cass there at the hospital too, but Margaret Gruber was in an operating room having a bullet removed and couldn't talk. I had less than a dozen stitches. I'd gotten many more of those once trying to jump from a moving newspaper delivery truck when I was a kid.

I made Cass drive me to the Paper after we left St. Vincent's. This amounted to another argument but with fewer words, so I was in the doghouse again after getting myself out so nicely the night before. Jack Pines had me tell him the story with my leg up on his desk as he typed and Stenis told Sam Felt to take the plates down to the guys in the darkroom. Then he ordered me home. I stopped by the darkroom on the way out and asked them to make two copies and take the other set in to Betty in the wire room with the message that she'd know what to do, but Sam had already told them.

Cass had waited in the car, too tired to face the old crew at the *Mirror* just then, and so she was able to hear the first radio news report. They got nearly every particular fact wrong, right down to the name of the department store. They said Margaret worked at Gimbels. My name was now 'McNair.' Lucille Beinecke was named 'Benick'. The complete list of mistakes Cass remembered from the one minute report was enough to make us both laugh, despite the other things. And there was that minute again. Everything in that minute could have gone wrong. It was difficult to feel like I had done anything but get lucky one more time.

The radio report also referred to the whole lot of them, including Lucille Beinecke, as "Reds." This was true, but it left the impression that they might all have been a bunch of psychopathic killers as well, and not just a pack of idiots. Cass thought it might make people think they all had it coming anyway. A sad thought.

And what was more unsettling to me was to think that because of the news on the radio, there were a lot of people out there now who thought they knew the story, even before they got to read the facts.

First thing I did when I was home was thank my dad for his oft repeated advice about taking the shot you had. If I had hesitated or thought for a second to take aim, I am certain I would be dead. He suggested it was more a result of my grabbing quick shots with the camera for all these years. Maybe.

Cass stayed at home with me and called in her story for the bulldog of the *Journal-American* that would not hit the streets until just before noon on Thursday.

As she had shown me on a previous occasion, she is a very good nurse.

102. Thursday, September 30, 1937

Thursday morning I drove Cass to work. Actually she drove, and then I drove over to Morgy's for breakfast. When I'd left the paper the evening before, Stenis had told me he didn't want to see my face for a couple days. I figured to oblige him. But Chester Rice had not said as much to Cass. So I had the day to myself.

At Morgy's I see a copy of the *Mirror* open on the counter so I know there will be no surprises. Doc comes around the counter to take a look and I obliged by pulling up my pants leg and showing off the bandages. Doc has stories from the war, so I know he's not impressed. Someone at a table said, "What'd you do, try to tango with the wrong girl."

I asked him, "How did you know? Who squealed?"

A little laugh ran around the booths.

I caught up on most of my notes in the afternoon and then drove over to pick Cass up at work about six. Now Cass is unhappy with this part too. I suppose it's sort of natural to let down after the last few days. She wants to know when it will end. When will she be able to run around the city again without me on her tail? That put us in the middle of another argument. I like the part where we make up, but the arguing gets to me.

She says, "I have my gun with me now. I'll take care of myself."

"You could. If things were not the way they are, you could."

"They'll have given up on me by now, anyway."

"Would you give up on a story that was important to you? Not likely. And these Nazis won't be giving up on you either."

"They have to, sometime. They must have better things to do than to worry about me."

"They've got nothing better to do. Especially now. You're making a name for yourself. They'll make an example of you. They don't want reporters asking the wrong questions."

"You're telling me it'll be this way from now on?"

"No. Just until these fellows are gone. At least for you. I think Flynn and his buddy the professor had the right mark on that. If these particular guys want to rise in the ranks of their own kind they have to show that they can take care of themselves. They have to show they can't be fooled with."

"You really believe they've thought that through?"

"No. I don't. It's automatic! Like I've said before. They're all thugs. For them it's just the law of the jungle and if civilization's going to rise above it, that law can't be ignored. It has to be dealt with. Like Mr. Van Loon was saying on the radio a couple months back about some ancient civilization they once had down in Central America. The Mayans, he said. They were like the Romans. Roads. Aqueducts. Now the jungle has overgrown the whole damn thing and you can hardly tell it was there. But once it was grand. They built pyramids that rose up high over the jungle around them and they'd built these splendid palaces and monuments. And now they're gone, probably because they forgot some fundamental thing."

"Like Ozymandias."

"I guess. What's that?"

"An Egyptian. He was once king of kings and now he's forgotten too."

"But that's the desert isn't it? I was talking about the jungle."

"It's the same thing."

"Maybe. Except for the water."

But maybe that's just me. I'm probably a little raw myself. So I took her out to dinner and a movie. That settled her down a little bit.

The second feature at the Loews is a bit about a secretary who is such a dish she can't do her job without attracting the attention of every guy in the vicinity and this gets her fired, so she dresses herself down, and guess what? The fact is Marion Davies would look good in rags. Which is probably why my big boss William Randolph Hearst can't get enough of her, but the movie misses the mark. The hero is no better than the others. When she's in her 'disguise' the dolt can't see what every guy in the audience can't ignore. For once Cass agreed with my gripe.

After that she got cute and she says, "Who's your favorite actress."

I say, "Jean Arthur and Barbara Stanwyck."

"That's two."

"Same price."

She puts on a hurt voice, "What's Barbara Stanwyck got that I don't?"

I shrugged. "She's blonde?"

"They're both blondes!"

"That's the power of bleach."

She considered this for an extra beat and then fluffed her hair out with her hand, "Do you think I would look better as a blonde?"

But I advised her, "You already hurt my eyes enough. I might go blind. Blind photographers are not much in demand."

103. Friday to Saturday, October 1 to 2, 1937

Now I know that Flynn has a crush on Cass. There is really no help for that. Anyone would. And he blushes if she says boo. But Cass has a perfect antidote. We talked this over, and Friday afternoon, when everyone is still out of the house, I called my sister at her job in Boston and asked her if she could come down for a visit the weekend before Columbus Day. The holiday this year is on a Tuesday, but maybe she can wrangle the Monday off from classes as well and make it a four-day getaway. This takes her two seconds to think about, before she says she'll do it. I'm thinking Essy is homesick. She'll come down on the train and be here next Friday night for dinner.

That evening, Mom lets it out at the dinner table that she's written my sister a letter and asked her about the same thing. This is not just a matter of great minds thinking alike. Now it's a conspiracy, and as everyone knows, those things never work. I didn't even have to ask my mom how she got the idea. I know she's already taken a liking to Flynn. But the problem is, my sister will figure this thing out in the two minutes after she's in the door, especially when she sees whose staying in Eric's old room and that will be that. She won't be played with.

And I'm not even calculating Michael Flynn's reaction to all this. He may be shy but he's not dumb. He'll figure it out for himself and the whole thing will blow up in our faces. And then if he knows that we can all see that he has had a crush on Cass, he might even move out, sister or no sister. This guy is no wimp like that guy Slim in the movie about the linemen that was played by Henry Fonda. And I'm no Pat O'Brien. Thing to do is get the jump on the situation.

On Saturday I helped Flynn buy a car. He needs one without holes in it now that he'll be working for himself and has no company wheels available for getting around. So, I took him over to Bushwick to see Harry Bean. In five minutes, Bean has just the deal, a nice little 1932 Plymouth coupe, but Flynn is not an easy sell. He wants to test a couple others out. Then he settles on a 1934 Ford Station wagon with 2800 miles on it—a summer car from someone in Connecticut. It's a few years newer, but it has the wooden sides just like my dad's. Though, this one still has the shine.

I say, "All that wood is not going to stop bullets like your old one."

Flynn shrugs his bad shoulder, "The old one didn't stop bullets all that well either."

I call my buddy Jim in Canarsie and we drive it over to his place and he checks it out and gives the A-OK and that's it. $300. Flynn could have had the Plymouth for $200 but he wants to go camping.

On the way back to Harry Bean's from Canarsie, I say, "Camping?"

He says "Fishing. A station wagon like this will hold my rods and gear. And if it rains, I can sleep in the back."

I told him my dad complained all the time about his old Ford. The wood sides let in the cold during the winter.

Flynn says, "That's what coats are for."

So now I'm a little worried about the conspiracy. First thing, whenever Dad took us camping, Essy would always complain about the bugs. The second thing is, I really want Flynn to teach me how to fly-fish. This seems like a very worthy occupation for a gentleman like me—at least the one I aspire to be. And if my sister is around, Flynn's not going to have a lot of time to show me diddlysquat.

I say, "You know, I was thinking, you might like to meet my

sister. But she hates camping."

He says, "The one in Boston?"

"Esther. Essy is the one who wants to be a lawyer."

"I don't like lawyers."

"I thought you studied some law at Boston College."

"That's how I know I don't like lawyers. All I really wanted to be was a cop. Now that's not a door that's open to me, I just have to do what I can."

"Maybe you could get a job with the New York Police Department. I have a friend who could put a word in."

"Like I said, that door is closed."

He's driving and he looks my way and he can see that I want to know.

I say, "It's not my business. You don't have to say anything."

He knows I'm fishing without a hook. He says, "Maybe you should hear about it anyway." He put a mile behind us before he got his thoughts together. "The story is, I was kicked off the Boston force. If I applied here, they'd find out soon enough, so I'd have to tell them anyway."

"I thought you said your Dad was a cop."

"He was. He's retired."

"I guess that makes things difficult."

"Worse. The reason I was kicked off was because I found out my dad was on the take." His face stiffened with the telling. "They just assumed I'd follow in his footsteps. When they told me I was supposed to hide some evidence in a holdup, and I refused, things suddenly blew up. Next thing they tell me is I have to do what I'm told and keep my mouth shut or I'm out. I said nuts to that. So then they tell me my dad was corrupt. What's with me? What did I think I was trying to do?" Flynn grabbed another look in my direction. "What I did was go home and talk to my dad, and he admitted it. He told me to grow up. I wasn't a kid anymore. I wasn't living in a perfect world. All that kind of thing. So I quit." At a stop light, Flynn looks over at me again. "Thing is, I never knew. I didn't know he'd even paid for my college tuition with dirty money. And he really didn't want me to be a cop. He wanted me to be a lawyer. He told me a hundred times that lawyers had the fat end of the deal. When I went against that and joined the force, he had a fit. He knew. He knew then that I would find out about him some day." Flynn stared into traffic ahead like it was a fog. "When I got to New York there were no jobs except with a couple of the private agencies. And as for my getting fired, I'll tell you this, Ted Byron's not such a bad guy. He was in the military. Everything is by the book with him. So I told him about Boston. And it didn't matter. That's why I hooked up there first. At least he's honest. And besides, he's having his own problems. It seems, trying to play it straight in a crooked world is a losing proposition."

I say, "No. Just looks like that sometimes. It'll work out. Things do, if you stick it out. Either that, or you're dead, so then it doesn't matter."

He laughs, "On that bright note . . ."

I had been very curious about the guy, and I was glad I got some of the facts, but there was not a whole lot I could say, so I tell him, "You're going to have to meet my sister anyway. She's coming down the weekend before Columbus Day."

He says, "Maybe I should go fishing that weekend. The season's almost over."

I say, "Good idea. But how about at least you take me along. I've always wanted to learn how to fly-fish."

He says, "Done."

And I'm thinking it's just started.

104. Monday to Tuesday, October 4 to 5, 1937

The World Series is taking up the front pages. I personally think this is a waste of space if the Dodgers aren't in it, but around the office I'm pretty much alone in that assessment. Worse than that, against the guys in the sports department, I don't have a prayer of getting a shot on a page with a single digit unless I get myself into a shootout with Adolf Hitler himself.

Monday, Cass has got the first part of her piece on Miss Em closing up shop in *Journal-American*. Page five. I have a house fire in Fort Greene, page twelve of the *Mirror*. I can see how this competition is going to play out. I think the thing for me to do is fold my hand now and spectate. So last night at the Paper, I went upstairs to see if I could catch Dan Parker at his desk and beg a couple of ducats. 'If you can't beat 'em, join 'em' is the phrase. Anyway, Cass might actually enjoy seeing one of the games. But Parker's not around.

Winchell is in his office though, and he spots me and waves me in.

Right away he says, "Ya' know, maybe I was a little rough on that one, Hugh . . . Bygones?"

He offers his hand.

I say, "Done." I figure I have nothing to lose by letting it drop.

He says, "You have a way with knocking on doors that shouldn't be going to waste. The guy they have doing it for me now hasn't got a clue, much less the knuckles for it. You probably don't want to be working for me again, but remember, the door's open for anything good you might happen onto along the way."

I say, "Thanks."

My mind is already on a couple of things I might pull out of that hat.

A street vendor run down by a taxicab while selling peanuts might make it to page eight but only if he's left a large family behind. Myrna Loy just getting in or out of a cab is an easy page four.

Tuesday afternoon both Cass and I are downtown to give depositions in the Broome lawsuit. The two guys we have to talk with, Larry O'Brien and Bill Murphy, look like the sort of fat-nosed ambulance chasers that give the title 'shyster lawyer' a bad name. They are both regulars at city hall and I've seen them around before. They take twice as long speaking with Cass as they do me. No surprise there.

Their case seems to hinge on just when it was I went into the apartment and restrained Mr. Broome. The *Mirror* lawyers present, Daggett and Thayer, appeared to be satisfied with my answers.

When we get home, Flynn has some good news. He has called around and there is a cabin open in one of the camps he likes at a waterworks called the Esopus, which is the same river the two of us were going to be pitching our tent by anyway, so things are good, no matter the weather. Only five bucks each for the two nights.

I was out in Queens early Tuesday morning to take a few pictures of a couple of kids shot dead in a car out on a lover's lane in Hollis Woods. Both of them lived in Queens Village. The girl was 19. The guy was 20. This gets me down for a bit, but I call in what I have and Stenis sends me right over to Flushing to get some shots on an accident there at one of the drainage tunnels they've put in to dry up the Flushing meadows for the World's Fair. These holes are big enough to drive a truck through and some hapless fellow didn't get out of the way.

For that open door with Mr. Winchell, I hustled my butt

down to the Village again to see if I could get another moment with Mr. Welles. I had heard Welles on the radio doing *The Shadow* on Sunday night and I had a question or two. Besides, now I've read *Julius Caesar*. But he was not at home. Nor was Mr. Houseman.

After Cass's lesson with Eddy Kim this week I took her over to the Gun Club firing range in Bay Ridge and made her give me an hour of instruction on what Annie Oakley had taught her mother. A lot of that is common sense. Getting the feel of the gun in your hand so it doesn't shift a bit when you squeeze the trigger. That sort of thing. But there was another trick that I wouldn't have thought about and Dad will be pleased to hear—Don't hesitate when you have your target in sight. Don't aim more than once. Take the shot before your heart has a chance to beat a second time.

105. Wednesday, October 6, 1937

The value of the World Series is not what they tout it to be. It is not a struggle between the best of teams or even the best players, going head to head on the field of battle. Many times it's only a contest of survivors. Or a rising of the dead. Or a cropper. A wreck. That's the Giants this year. The Yankees may be the best team and might even have many of the best players, but we won't know for sure, because the final test of their mettle was something less than a thriller. Even the best pitcher in baseball, Carl Hubbell, played a lesser game given the quality of support.

The real importance of this is that the contest will not relieve us of our other troubles. It is supposed to take your mind away from all the rest. For that, these games will be a great failure. Think of that. Think about all the other stuff and you go nuts.

There was a guy who was killed over at the 48th Street Pier last night. Actually, early this morning. That's another night's sleep cut to size, but it's hard to feel sorry for yourself when you're looking at some kid's father lying there in a pool of his own blood and urine. I hope the wife has family. But what was he murdered over? An argument? The job, most likely. Likely, with the rackets running the loading on that stretch of the docks. The cops figure this guy for about 35 years old. Looked forty. That's what hard work does. He had a pay stub in his pocket with the name 'de Lillo' on it. I used to know a fellow named Buddy de Lillo who worked the docks in Brooklyn and I hope it isn't his son. Buddy was a good fellow.

Died of a heart attack when he was barely pushing sixty.

But the corpse from the docks doesn't make it to the front pages. Just another dead working stiff. The front page was the pic I took yesterday of the couple of kids, 19 and 20, shot dead in a car at the lover's lane over in Hollis Woods. That should have been front page, true enough, but not for the reason it was. It's the lover's lane aspect that did it. But what about the story of a couple of lives that aren't going to be lived. That's not even there.

What is right there, next to the picture of the car that the two kids were found in, is the headline 'McCarthy's Yanks Look to Murder Terry's Giants.'

That's right too, I suppose. But that's not news of a killing, a wife widowed, and kid without a father. That's news about something that will never matter to the lives unlived of a couple of kids who were probably in love and looking forward to all the things that love can do.

Tonight I see that the police have raided the Oxford Theatre again for putting on burlesque shows. That is a foolish piece of law enforcement, especially given the poor performance of the Giants as well as another season lost to the Dodgers. Where is a lonely guy, or even a kid to go? I am reminded that this fine establishment on State Street at Flatbush Avenue was the first place outside of my own home where I ever saw a naked lady. The perpetrator of that particular incident (there were several more to come) was not a young woman and the fact that her feathered fans did not sufficiently cover her basic attributes was quite disturbing to my fourteen year old mind—more so than the dazzle of sequins on her shifting pasties. And I still remember the question that plagued me then—did women usually apply makeup to their entire bodies? This seemed like a great deal of trouble. I, for one, was certainly willing to have them forego all that. Freckles have their own attraction, mind. So I was very much relieved, some months later when I managed to again come by the necessary quarter (I never once paid the cheaper rate of a dime or sat behind the rail), and discovered that the habit of using makeup below the neck was most peculiar to the older performers.

106. Friday, October 8, 1937

Mr. Flynn is a 'man of many parts.' This is an expression my Dad uses and seems to fit. But I think I might only know the half of it. For instance, he likes to be called Flynn, and not Michael, and I thought this was odd until I found out his father's name was Michael as well. Knowing what I do about that man, I now understand a little more.

I drove to Grand Central Station with Cass and we picked up Esther at six so that all of us were sitting down to dinner by seven. Flynn had been out picking up some supplies for our trip up to the Catskills early Saturday morning and arrived back just in time. So, it was Dad who introduced them. This was a busy moment at the table but I think half a dozen pairs of eyes were paying attention. Flynn smiled. No blush. Essy smiled politely in return. No sudden halting for words from either of them. He shook her hand and then went to the buffet to fill his plate.

They sat on opposite sides of the table. Essy had been in the midst of telling Cass about her job when Flynn came in the room and she picked that account up again without a hitch. I think the previous moment had been what they call an anticlimax, but done in advance. What do they call that?

But not for long.

Esther asks, "Mr. Flynn, what kind of work do you do?"

He says, "I'm a private investigator."

"Whom do you work for?"

"I'm on my own, now."

"How did you get into that line of work?"

"An ad in the papers."

"Do you like it?"

"No."

"What is it you'd rather be doing?"

"Fishing."

"Then, why don't you do that instead?"

"Because I didn't see anyone advertising who'd pay me to fish. It's just the way things are set up. The best occupations are the ones people would do for free, if they got the chance. They'll only pay you for what has to be done but no one else wants to do. But, you probably know about all of that well enough. I'm told you've been studying law. Do you love that?"

He had not asked her if she 'liked' it. He asked her if she 'loved' it.

I could see immediately that this has got Essy in a jam. She's a very straightforward girl, and had to stop eating for a moment to get herself out of it.

"No. I don't love it. It's tiresome. Boring.I suppose if I were in court, pleading a case, it would be better. But I don't even see the clients. I spend most of my time looking up information set in eight point type."

Flynn suddenly turned the tables on her. "Have you looked into other jobs? I hear you already have a college degree. There must be something else you'd rather do than practice law."

"What's wrong with law?"

"Basically, nothing. All that eight point type is the problem. That's all the hooey they've added on top of it. Just another way of hiding the truth. Problem is, most laws are written by politicians for their own benefit and supported by shyster lawyers and judges who'd be out of a job if people knew what that eight point type really says. So they've put it down in words only the chosen few can interpret and mixed in a little two thousand year old language to obscure it all the more. It's a deceit. A fraud. A racket, and a shakedown. Other than that, I suppose it's fine and dandy."

No one at the table was taking a bit of food by the time he got half way through his comment. All eyes were bouncing back and forth between the two of them like we were watching a tennis match.

I learned something new about my sister then.

Very calmly she says, "You seem to know a lot about it."

This was not the sort of tone I'd have gotten from Cass if I'd challenged her like that. It actually sounded like Essy was truly curious.

But then, Flynn turned the table around again. "I'm afraid I know just enough to be rude. I'm sorry."

Instinctively I looked at my dad. His face was up, eyes wide, as if he were witnessing something not to be missed.

After the exchange, Essy was quiet for most of the dinner. From Mr. Clurman we found out a little about the latest strikes. There was a sit-down at Woolworth's that was going on nationally, another walk-out at a General Motors plant in Detroit, and something about timber in Minnesota. Lacking the easy target of Mr. Oliphant, Mr. Clurman had taken to a regular tally of the discontents of others as a source of conversation. I suppose the sense to that is his worry that the world was falling apart and his job might be next. Mrs. Nessen tells us authoritatively that such strikes have been outlawed in Germany, and this example ought to be followed. Norman Jenks predicts a strike soon at the shipyard. Next we learn that Mrs. Tisdale has broken up with her dance partner—or is it the opera buff? He had lost his job. She is now enchanted with an actor named Harry Sullivan. I once knew a fellow named Harry Sullivan but he was no actor. He was a welder. Still is, I thought, but nevertheless, I suppose it could be him. He was pretty good at lying.

Perhaps by way of making it relevant to Mr. Clurman's latest labor news, Mrs. Tisdale ended the revelation about her love life with, "Harry might have a part in a new play about the garment industry. They're always striking, aren't they?"

Trying to be funny, I asked, "The actors or the garment workers?"

But this only seemed to confuse her.

Mom immediately looks at me reproachfully and asks, "Do you fellows really have to go fishing this weekend? The weather looks to be so good. We could all take a ride up to Connecticut to see the leaves instead."

I have never heard my mom make such a suggestion in my entire life. She does not mind the woods so much. She minds the driving. But then, that might be a result of my dad's habits behind the wheel. She's always thought he drives too fast. I immediately suspected her for another motive.

Cass had already spoken to me about my plans with Flynn. I'd told her the details the evening before, and she was none too happy about it. We were "running out," she said. I agreed.

Just about then, out of the blue, Flynn says, "You know, we could all go fishing, couldn't we? I have half a dozen rods. The leaves are turning up on the Esopus, just as well as they are in Connecticut, I think. The camp isn't big but it's large enough for six of us anyway. There are four bunks and I have a sleeping bag." He searched our blank faces and settled on me. "How about it, Hugh?"

Before I can answer, I see Mom's eyes hit my dad hard and then she speaks right up to the latest idea.

"Your father has orders to fill and I haven't finished the bookkeeping. But you four could go, couldn't you? That sounds grand!"

My dad immediately knows his part in this play. But Essy's mouth is open, probably looking for an excuse to beg off.

I say, "Cass? How about it? We could both learn to fish, couldn't we?"

To that, Cass says, "Terrific!" And actually sounded like she meant it.

Still confused by the turn of events, later on I say to her, "Do you think Flynn had any idea?"

Cass just says, "Flynn is no fool."

107. Saturday to Sunday, October 9 and 10, 1937

It was dark when Flynn came knocking. Four o'clock is as black as Brooklyn can get. And as quiet. The garbage trucks and the milkman are not out yet. We piled into Flynn's car in an awkward jumble until things had been squared away at the back and we were on the Triborough Bridge in less than fifteen minutes. I think Flynn was the only one really awake at the start. And I fell asleep again against the door soon after.

When the gray shades of first dawn came up on us, we were in a city again. I opened my eyes to someone whispering and to the hum of the wheels and the squawk of the wood against the metal frame softened a little by the pester of the wind at the windows. It was Esther's whispering. She was at the edge of her seat directly behind Flynn and talking softly, close to his ear, about something to do with differences between tort law and common law. I closed my eyes for a short while more, hoping for something more interesting. Maybe the first hint of a romance. Instead he answered her question with quip about the subversion of common law in favor of syndicates.

"Individual citizens are all second class now." He says. "The syndicate is first."

She answers right back, "But you have to be able to conduct business."

"Not at the expense of the rights of individual people to do the same."

"But society benefits."

"Syndicates benefit. Corporations. Society would be better served by individuals free to experiment—not restricted from the use of their own products by government-made monopolies."

Probably tired of all the shop talk herself, Cass stirred noisily behind me and leaned forward. "Where are we?"

I looked out on the slope of the paving stones to a flat gray sheen of water beneath a pearly mist. This was guarded between the dark brick walls of factory buildings at either side.

Flynn says, "Poughkeepsie! We're about to cross the mighty Hudson. An hour and a half, more or less, to Phoenicia. Who's for a little breakfast? There's a diner up on the other side a little ways near Kingston."

Already there was an edge of excitement to his voice. He got a general confirmation all around.

The bridge there was a cocoon of fog. No grand vista of rising sun over the river like you see from the George Washington.

The first yellow nip of sun reached us while sitting at a small table in a narrow room busy with comings and goings of locals. The air inside was thick as fog with the smells of baked bread and of the eggs and hash sizzling on a wide grill. I wiped one steamy window clear with my sleeve and the sun hit Flynn's face as if he were actually beaming. For all of us, I think, this was the door-way into something completely unlike what we knew day to day and even though Flynn had been here before, he had the voice and appearance of someone who was just discovering a thing for the first time.

"We'll be late for any serious fishing today. Don't expect to be catching much after the sun hits the water. But we'll get our lines wet and then get the rest squared away."

The excitement hurried our eating and the rest of us traded looks like kids on a great adventure.

Flynn had us all casting from the boulders at the banks of the river within an hour of our arrival. This is a delicate operation that requires timing, a flick of the wrist beneath the arc of the rod and a pinch of the fingers more than force. Maybe more delicacy that I am used to. Cass was quickly placing her fly on the water ten and twenty feet ahead of my own. Essy had trouble tangling her line in the reel and Flynn had to help her with that a couple of times but she caught on soon enough.

We had a splendid day. The fog was long gone or somewhere in a valley below us. The sun was buttery. The rush of the water over the shallows and rocks was light and dark at once and moved with a voice like the chorus of a wave at the beach—a choir at High Mass that does not take a breath. Flynn said he preferred this stretch to the quieter waters farther down.

One particular moment, after Flynn had floated the line out in the sunlit air the way a spider might cast himself at the end of his web—setting the fly down exactly where he had told Esther there was likely something hiding in the shadows of an eddy—she asked him, "How did you learn to do this so well?"

"My father. He used to take us up to Maine when we were kids, every chance."

"Does he still fish?"

"I don't know. I don't believe so."

"You don't speak to him?"

"No. Not for years."

"Does your mother fish?"

"No. She reads. She always used to sit in a little wooden folding chair and read while we fished."

"Do you speak to her?"

"Now and then."

Another time, when we were alone, Esther asked me about Flynn's father but I told her it was not something I could speak about.

This was not exactly fair. I had told Cass about my conversation with Flynn. But then, Cass has her own ways. On the Sunday night before, Flynn and I had sat on the stoop after dinner and enjoyed a cigarette or two. It was a warm night and the street was still busy with kids playing a game of stickball and trying to enjoy the last of the best weather.

He had said to me, "Your father found himself a little bit of the good here."

I told him, "That was as pretty much my mom's doing. If it were up to him he'd still be on a ship somewhere between here and there."

"Why did they pick Brooklyn?"

"That was my mom's idea, again. She's told that story a few times. It amounts to the fact that she knew he wasn't cut out to be a farmer. My grandfather had done that and the misery had left its mark on Dad. He'd intended to be a sailor all his life. But he likes cities. He likes ports. And he knew the ways of shipping and trade. Even then his stationery shop was part of an accident. To pay his crew, he once had to sell a lot of those sorts of goods from a cargo that was abandoned. He was working for an independent ship at the time. After the war, mom and dad settled on living here and he got a job with a stationery company downtown. Pretty soon he was in charge of the ordering. Just one thing leading to the other. Only the sorts of compromises people make, I think, to get what's more important to them."

"What was most important to your dad?"

"My mom. And then us."

Flynn studied this idea for a time. I could see that the kids on the street were not the focus of his eyes. He told me then, "My father said something just like that. It was the excuse he made for doing what he did. Stealing. Cheating. Lying. It was for our family, he said. I told him I would have preferred being honest but poor. He said I did not have any idea what it was like being poor. That I had no right to judge him. He was born in Ireland and he had seen things there I could not comprehend. And I told him, his choice was false. As false as he was. As false as he had been. Life was not one way, or the other." Flynn stopped and laughed unhappily a moment at this sad telling. "I'm cleaning it up a bit. My father is given to very hard language when he's angry. His favorite expression is, 'There are as many assholes in the world as there are hearts and brains.' I think your Dad is the better example, at least for what I wish my father could have seen. What he could have been."

I wondered what bond it was to have that Irish poverty in both our histories.

I wondered, "What turned you away from all that?"

Flynn twisted in surprise.

"He did! That was the most amazing thing! He'd always been so strict. About everything. Early Mass on Sunday. Manners at the table. He had me working my first job when I was eight. Eight!"

Another similarity!

"So did I. What did you do?"

"I handed out flyers for the corner market."

"I delivered the morning papers before I went to school."

Flynn shook his head at a memory. "The first time I stole an apple at the market Dad walloped me within an inch of my life and made me go back with the penny. He told me I should offer to sweep the floor there as well, to make amends. The owner, Tony, asked me to hand out flyers for him instead, because the broom was still too big for me. Dad would make us stand in place for hours until he was sure we had told him the truth. Hours!"

This sounded familiar to a point.

"Mom was a softy for that sort of thing. She would end up helping with my chores if she thought they were too much for me. Dad knew he was just giving her more work if he levied too heavy a penalty. The first winter I delivered the papers, Mom came out on the coldest mornings and took half the load."

"Ah! But my mother worked too. And she wasn't there most days. She was a nurse."

That was a thought. What would I have done if my mom weren't there?

"I was luckier. Mom always had her eye on things. You know, someone even told me that recently. And I think it's true. My life has been far more fortunate than most."

"Your Dad did well."

"He did."

And Cass agreed when I told her about the conversation later. And I think she was telling me this was the fact of it, but for the reason of having her.

You have to understand Esther. She has a chip on her shoulder about being a girl. The Merchant Marine would not have her when they took Eric. College was a second choice and she went away for that just to get out from under the shadow of the rest of us.

She had Flynn pegged from the start. He has as many opinions as she does. He's just a lot bigger. On Saturday afternoon, with the four of us standing on a low ledge in a row over the water and trying to imitate Flynn's casting, she keeps up a steady inter-rogation. For the most part, Flynn kept his answers short, and splices them neatly in between instructions.

He says, "Don't reach too far back with the rod. Let the natural spring of it work for you."

She says, "We have two sets of laws—one for the white and one for the negro. How are we going to change that?"

He kept the same conversational voice throughout.

"The law is backward. When did that get turned around? The law is what the government should obey, not the citizen. If a person wants to treat some people differently than others, that's their bus-iness—and likely their loss. It's the government that can't do that . . . But you shouldn't do that. Keep your thumb at the edge of the reel, but don't press down. You'll get a blister."

And later.

"What about the girls caught up in prostitution rackets? All the things Cass is writing about? There have to be laws against that."

"Slavery is already against the law, last I looked. The problem is that the government makes it a crime to sell sex or to pay for sex. How is that going to be stopped any better than drinking alcohol? Can't be done. But if it wasn't against the law, the rackets couldn't take it over, could they? . . . Don't point your rod at the fly. Keep it up."

"But prostitution is immoral."

"Different subject. I thought we were talking about the law . . . If you get a bite, you're going to see the rod bend. You're going to feel that better with the rod up. Bring it back slowly then. Don't jerk it. And don't let it down. The hook can release by itself unless you keep a steady hand."

This contest went on through the evening, over the campfire and into the dark.

108. Sunday, October 10, 1937

The success of a fishing trip is a matter of what you were angling for. Not in the account of what you caught. I suppose this must be a cousin to my dad's repeated advice to us, as we travelled off to the beaches in New Jersey for a week in the summer. We often complained then during the hours in the hot car. He would always repeat his sailor's advice, that it was the journey that was important and not the destination. I answered once in a smart alecky retort that we should just walk around the block a few times then so that we would be closer to home and dinner when we got there. But in truth I was always happier pulling horseshoe crabs from the shallows and swatting the horseflies with my free hand.

The most of our Saturday was spent playing beside the Esopos with cinch knots and dry casting to get a feel for the bamboo rods Flynn had collected.

I asked, "Why do you have so many?"

"Always have extras set aside. I keep half a dozen reels so that I have the dry line I need. The weather is not always like this, and the line wants to sink if it gets too wet."

These rods have a story to them as well, because none were bought new. Flynn had purchased his first rod and reel from a roadside shop when he was twelve. His father had loaned him the five dollars and it had taken him a year to repay. This was just after the war and he was told it had previously belonged to a soldier who had not returned. The brass of the face has browned to flesh tones and the maker's mark there is worn dark like the words on an old penny. The ivory of the knob was yellowed and finely webbed with cracks. All of the others were of a similar type, but without as much brass, and had their own histories—each of them was once the prized pos-session of another fisherman and not given up willingly.

Flynn had given each of the rods a name—Jim and Teddy, Scratch and Bobby, George and Slim. He readily admitted that he did not know about all the previous owners, but what he didn't know he had made up himself during the hours spent in their company.

He said, "They have the memory of good use built into them. They bend as they know they should. They're happy to be useful again."

This was such a sentimental thought that I questioned it without thinking. Though I am naturally sympathetic with such ideas myself, Flynn had not struck me as a very sentimental fellow until then.

"It's just bamboo and glue and a bit of cork."

He laughed at the idea. "You know better! You're teasing me!"

But the romance of it was then in our heads, and when Essy's rod slipped from her hands and dropped into the rush of water below the bank she did not hesitate to jump in after it. Flynn was wearing his waders and standing mid-stream and he picked her up, rod in hand within seconds and set her back. She had to put on some of Cass's extras after that because she had not brought enough clothes with her for the visit.

The weekend was chockfull of good moments. But only one true thrill. In the middle of our first night there, I heard walking in the woods by the cabin. There had been no significant frost there yet and the last of the crickets offered the only other sound. I was on the bottom bunk, having lost the coin toss, and within easy reach of my camera bag. Slipping my gun out as quietly as I could, I tiptoed to a window, but the sound of the intruder had awaked everyone. Flynn was already out on the floor ahead of me, dressed in his long johns, just as I was, and then Cass was down from her bunk as well with Essy following behind. The sound of the footsteps outside stopped and we could hear breathing. The door of the cabin is well greased and opened quietly to Flynn's hand. The sound of walking started again, moving away. We were all on the porch searching the dark before we saw him. I was already fingering the trigger on the gun. A cloud drifted, and a gibbous moon tattered the thinning leaves on the trees close by the water. The figure stopped there, and stood tall and menacing in the shadows between.

Essy flicked the switch on her flashlight, and she was the first to find her voice, "Stop! It's a moose!"

I think the sound of her words jarred the animal more than our weak light. Immediately, it bolted ahead and out across the water in a clatter of small stones, and splashing.

We all laughed at once then. Fairly loudly. Enough to bring a light to the window of the cabin about fifty yards beyond us.

The moment is indelible in my mind now. The three of us, Cass, Flynn and myself, all with our guns out and ready to shoot the villain. The animal stood there for that instant, rump toward us, and turned its head back over a broad shoulder, eyes glowing. There were no antlers. Perhaps it was too young. And then the beast quite smartly ran for its life.

The good of a laugh like that is like the giggles you get after riding the roller coaster at Coney Island. We practically laughed ourselves to sleep afterward, and every time I thought I was drifting off again, someone would say, "Stop! It's a moose!" and the giggles started over.

During our couple of days there I caught one rainbow trout and three browns. Two of those I let go because they were small and in any case we all had done too well and there was more than we could eat both evenings. But I can testify to the fact that there is no difference in the taste between the two fishes, no matter what you hear otherwise. They were both cooked in the same iron skillet in the same lard and consumed with the same corn bread and beer.

The weather was superb the entire time. Though this might be an unfair introduction to the sport. Flynn insisted that it was not always as grand as this. Cold and damp is often the case. But on this occasion the reds and yellows gashed the sky above our heads, and too often, when the eager fish took his bite, I was staring up the slopes at that splendid sight, or down the river at the jewels scattered there, or I would have caught more.

109. Monday, October 11, 1937

It's a funny thing about holding hands. Cass and I had been doing this since May, and just about everywhere we go, except at the office. After a while you don't think about it, unless you aren't, and then it's because you've said the wrong thing or she's just angry with you on principle. But when we all went out to see Benny Goodman at the Madhattan Room on Monday night, Cass and I had a shock. Esther was holding Michael Flynn's hand non-stop. I could see in Cass's look that she was as surprised as myself. The matter of it was this: what had we missed? And when?

There was a note for me at home when we arrived late in the day. Stenis wanted me to go to the Hotel Pennsylvania and take some shots of Benny Goodman for his opening there at the night-club. This brilliant idea had come to him out of a memory of my encounter with the bandleader a few months before. I called him back and told him not to worry and then called the hotel and told them I was covering the thing for the *Mirror* and asked for a table because I was bringing another reporter from the *Journal-American* with me, as well as a couple of guests. We were lucky, I think, that they took the reservation. They were busy and didn't need the extra publicity.

I had missed some good stories while I was gone.

Walter Cravens, 27, an authentic cowboy and roping star, had been trampled and killed at Madison Square Garden by a 1300 pound steer during the Rodeo World Championships. Sam Felt got that picture. British authorities in Peking reported 200,000 Chinese soldiers were dead and 400,000 wounded. That had only made page six. Poison pancakes had killed 3 during a Sunday breakfast in Queens. This, along with the unlucky Mr. Cravens, made the front page.

In the sort of news that had recently become of greater interest to our small clan at Sterling Place, one John H. Ensor of 5 Elm Street in Cresskill, until recently working as a receiver and bookkeeper for the First National Bank of Secaucus, was being held along with an accomplice for 'misapplying funds.'

Detective Joseph Cashman, attached to Special Prosecutor Thomas E. Dewey's office, has nabbed Joseph Gonzales and Ramon Garcia for a policy game operation.

Right in Brooklyn, Radio Patrolman Edward Farrell and Joseph Goldberg of the Empire Boulevard station had finally collared the 'Taxi Robbers.' These fellows were using stolen taxis to rob unsuspecting fares. Dad joked that this was only what happened every time you hailed a taxi anymore and should not be held against them.

Charles Segar, who is still one of the better sports writers in town had a nice piece on the World Series. Dan Parker thinks Charlie must be planning to retire soon and wants to go out with a flourish. Or maybe he's just getting a second wind.

That was just some of the punishment for being gone. But my mind easily drifted over the two days we had spent away and I was happy for it.

110. Tuesday, October 12, 1937

Putting up the pretense of being back at work, I went to the office early on Tuesday morning with the idea of grabbing a couple of easy assignments off the board and disappearing for the day. The official opening of the West Side Parkway was scheduled. That would be an easy one. There are Columbus Day celebrations in every corner of the city where there are more than two Italians present. No problem there. Problem is, autumn has set in, with all of those smells of things that are ripe or overripe and sweet or turning, and the bouquet was reaching even onto the sour and stony streets of Manhattan.

I'm at the office less than an hour, wasting time talking about the World Series with Joe Evans, one of the new copyboys, and suddenly all I really wanted to do was take a walk in Central Park with Cass, so I called her with that in mind. But I catch her just about to leave the office. She's in a rush. Can't talk now.

I insist. "What's so important?"

"I got a call from Greta Sturmgart. She wants to see me."

"The girl we got out of the button factory back in July?"

"Yes. She needs to talk to me."

"Why?"

"She wouldn't say. She sounded pretty agitated."

"Can I go with you?"

"No. She just wanted to see me. She even asked if I would come alone. I think you scare her."

I think I went cold at about that instant.

"Doesn't sound right."

"What doesn't?"

"She wants you to come alone? Have you checked with the Jewish Aid Society?"

"They've placed her at a restaurant out on Long Beach Avenue in Oceanside. She lives near there."

I gave that a beat of time before I asked again.

"Can I go?"

I could see her mind working, even over the phone.

Finally she says, "Okay."

Because they've got lousy buses running out along Atlantic Avenue and Long Beach now from the train station instead of trolleys, I suggested we meet at Sterling Place and we grab the car there.

Back again in Brooklyn, I get in the door to find Cass already in an argument with Flynn. Esther is right there between them trying to moderate. Mom and Dad are away at work so the match is even.

The issue is this. Cass does not want a babysitter. She had gotten to the house before me and made the mistake of telling Flynn why she was waiting. Flynn is ahead of both of us on this. He is laying the facts out for her in detail and she is disputing them as he tries to explain. I sat down in Dad's chair and listened. Essy keeps trying to interrupt, but with Cass she has a worthy opponent.

Flynn thinks he should go as a bodyguard. Now she doesn't want either of us to go with her. But Essy has her own methods.

"Then, I'll go with you," she says.

Cass collapses into a chair like she has been pushed over by a feather.

"This is ridiculous! I'm sorry I said anything to Hugh in the first place. I should have just gone on my way and told you all about it later."

Flynn is a year younger than I am but a few years older in his ways. He gets a voice on that I can imagine he is going to be using someday with my nieces or nephews.

"Sure. Everything I know about this stuff is for the birds. I've never chased down a criminal before. I've never studied his habits. Given that I don't know a damn thing, I can see how you might object. And I'll grant you that you can't be doing your job with someone hanging onto your leg. But grant me this: you're going to have Hugh and me going nuts for the next couple hours if you don't humor us on this. Take us along for the ride. We'll stay out of it. You talk to this woman. Then we can all go for a walk on the beach and we'll apologize for being so difficult about it."

Flynn had put the numbers together even more certainly than I had. These Nazis would still have their vendetta out on her and didn't have a lot of ways to get Cass alone where they wouldn't be interfered with. They couldn't be hanging around on the street waiting for a chance anymore. They would have to be aiming for a set up. And they could read the papers as easily as anyone. They certainly could know about Greta Sturmgart and the button factory. They may even have spoken to Mr. Finckle, who would have only been too happy to share his knowledge of that situation.

This certainly had the right makings for a trap.

Esther says, "Call the police!"

Flynn says, "And tell them what, exactly?"

And I say, "The worst part of that is, if this's some sort of ambush, and the cops scare them away before these guys do anything they can be arrested for, this whole thing is just going to be put off again. For another day."

That much got a nod out of Flynn. But the next problem was dealing with Esther.

She would not be left behind. Period. And besides, she would not mind a walk on the beach afterward if nothing happened. She had to leave that evening on the train for Boston, or she wouldn't have a job herself anymore.

Flynn got his own bright idea for that. Esther could get out on the way, at the restaurant where Miss Sturmgart worked, and inquire about her—do a little extra investigation for us.

His idea was that Cass and I would take the car directly to the house. I would be with Cass, never mind what Miss Sturmgart had said. Flynn would get out a couple of blocks back and walk from there and be out on the side somewhere when we left the car. Esther would have to wait at the restaurant. Period.

Oceanside is an old resort community and many of the houses have the flimsy look of the sort originally meant for use only in the summer months. That was back during the old days but more recently many have been occupied year round, though some were obviously empty for the winter now. Still, midday, midweek, things are especially quiet. It's not yet noon but even the traffic seems light for the time of day. This is the main road to Long Beach and in the summer I know all too well that it's a crawl.

Nevertheless, the restaurant, called the Roadside Rest, is open for lunch and there are at least a dozen cars in the lot beside it. Miss Sturmgart is not there but we leave Essy behind, still protesting, to do inquiries. About a half a mile along, with the numbers on the houses closing, we drop Flynn off. Suddenly it's just Cass and me and I'm not feeling too happy about doing this after all.

Greta Sturmgart is living in a house large enough for multiple families on vacation. There's a wide porch and a barren yard of patchy grass on sandy soil, and at the front the expected rose bushes tightly entwined in a low gray fence that might have once been white.

In the rearview mirror I see that Flynn has disappeared.

I stopped there at the side and we sat for a moment in the car, hoping to give Flynn a chance to do whatever he was intending, and going over what we should be doing ourselves if things are wrong.

The house sits alone under a broad sun. There are few trees close by and these are not large, though they still have their browning leaves. Behind the house a short distance I can see the sort of reeds that grow in wetlands and these run thick and well above head height and they're as brown too as a wooden barricade with the season. The feather tops of the reeds are barely moving and I realize for the first time there is very little wind. The day is quieter for that reason as well. But at that moment, I was wondering how Flynn might approach the house from behind, or avoid being seen, if that was his plan.

There is no fence at either side. The roses are still blooming pink along the fence at the front and the tangy smell of these give the place a complete innocence in the bright sun. The windows, in contrast are dark between the plain white curtains. I am immediately sure someone has peeked at us from an upper room as we get out of the car.

What else can I say here before I dilate on the brief event itself.

There is a sandy driveway at one side, just as there is for all the houses we'd passed. The house closest to this is about thirty-yards away. From the lack of curtains there, I'm guessing it's closed for the season.

Something else. The porch sounded in a hollow drum beneath our feet and that was something of a public announcement of our arrival. Two windows face out at either side. There is a pane of glass in the upper part of the door that shows a dark hall behind it and the light of a smaller window at the back. I'm thinking that window to be in the kitchen and the faint gleam from there reflects off a banister rising on the right side of the hall about halfway. I'm also guessing the room closest at the right had once been a parlor. All I could see now was a closed door with a number on it. The door immediately to the left, also numbered, is cracked, but only just enough to see wallpaper inside.

When I opened the screen and let Cass ring the bell, it's the hall door on the left that opens wider and we can see Miss Sturmgart. She's moving very stiffly for a young woman. I'm certain from the puffiness of her eyes that she's been crying, though her face now is blank. Features rigid. She opens the front door and tries to look angry at seeing me there with Cass. Her voice breaks with nervousness. She says something loud to Cass in German. Cass begins to answer, but I'm not going to allow this to continue. I am sure then that this was the only moment we would have. With the front door swung in and partly blocking the one to the room she'd left, I reached forward, grabbed Miss Sturmgart's arm as firmly and quickly as I could, and jerked her outside.

My thinking was too simple, perhaps. But the hair on the back of my neck was up and giving me few choices. I knew it would be far more dangerous inside. If this was only a false alarm, Greta Sturmgart could yell at me all she wanted to later on.

I'd told Cass to put her hand in her purse the moment she was out of the car and I knew that would be firmly on her gun. She was to step aside from the door as soon as I grabbed Miss Sturmgart, if the moment came. I had repeated that much in the car. In fact, with my hands busy and my own gun still in the camera bag, she didn't have the time to lose.

Farther along the hall there was another door, across from the stairs, and this was already open. From there a man stepped out with his pistol raised to shoot.

It was Cass who fired first then and hit him squarely between the eyes. His head jerked back, as if he had been punched by the sound. She fired again and hit him in the throat as he started to collapse. He never pulled his trigger. I saw all that in those few seconds while I was yelling for Cass to get away from the open door and pushing Greta off the porch and yelling at her to stay down. I grabbed Cass then and pulled her away too. Then I took a hand from each of them and ran for the car.

But there were no shots at us from the house at all. On the far side of the car we opened the doors and I cautioned Cass to stay down there on the inside with Miss Sturmgart, and to keep guard. I left my camera bag with them and went back then with my gun. But I hadn't reached the porch again before I heard several more shots echo from the neighbor's house. All of them sounded like Flynn's .38. At that point I went directly through the building, stepping over the body in the hall, simply as the shortest distance to the sounds. A foolish move, when I thought about it later. Someone else could have been around.

The back door was hanging open and my first view out was another car parked there, and then directly below the back stoop, the gray-suited body of the thin man I had once chased on the streets of Manhattan. I knew it was him, even though I could not see his face. Belly down, he'd hit the sand in the backyard as if he had tried to dive from the back steps. His right hand was twisted at the side under an angled arm, with the elbow bent high. The hand still gripped the same pistol with the long barrel I'd seen before at Sterling Place. His hat, caught on a tuft of grass, lay a few feet beyond his body.

Flynn came from the side of the house, snatched the gun from the man's hand and immediately came up the steps, passing me in rush. I followed him, and the two of us looked around the rooms in the house to see if there was anyone else. Later, Greta told us she was alone that morning when they arrived. The front door had been open. As it often was, with other roomers coming and going.

With the house empty, I waved Cass and Greta inside. Cass was carrying my camera bag again and as she handed it off, she told me in a stern voice, "Don't make a habit of this." There was a smile behind the words that she had not been able to manage in the circumstance.

I went about my business with the camera while Flynn called the police. In the front room, Cass spoke with Miss Sturmgart through her weeping, which did not stop for some time—at least until well after the police had come.

Amazingly, Esther arrived with a cop soon after the shooting stopped. She was in a lone police car with an unhappy sergeant whom she had commandeered in the midst of his lunch at the restaurant. He had not yet even received the call on his radio.

Once again I was impressed by the single thought that this had all happened so quickly, and it took me an hour afterward just to be clear in my head about what exactly had taken place.

111. Tuesday, October 12, 1937

A couple more thoughts.

Death is an instant. Likely, most people never know it's coming. And then it's over. But I did know of a few who had the instant just before to see what was happening and that they were going to die, though I can't say what their own thoughts were in that moment because most of them are no longer dwelling on the matter.

My idea is that it's best to have your thoughts together on things before that time comes. There won't be a chance to reconsider. And perhaps that's even why I was angry when I was at that door. With no chance to think it through again.

My buddy Danny Sager told me his reaction was much the same as mine. When the time came, he was angry. Mostly at himself. Same as me.

That was because I'd gotten myself into this mess. Worse, I had gotten Cass into it and she was going to die just as surely as I was. So naturally I was angry about that too.

I do remember thinking one thing: at least we had gotten married first. But that was not a thought so much as a feeling about it. It's just what you know in that one instant that you have. And it's not like in the movies where the killer takes a little time to explain themselves, and the crime, and their motive for it—just enough time for the posse to arrive.

I came to that door and I was suddenly certain that, despite all my worry and efforts to the contrary, there was a pistol pointed at

Cass and about to shoot. The first fellow, the one in the hall—the one who had been to Sterling Place that day trying to kill Cass once before, and the same one who had been on the train platform getting ready to push her onto the tracks—must have heard me grab Miss Sturmgart by the arm first thing as she opened the door. She didn't make much of a sound when I grabbed her. Just an 'oh' of surprise, as I recall it. That much was certainly fortuitous, as it turned out. The fellow who had remained out of sight to shoot Cass had likely intended to wait just long enough to get her to come inside. But he made his mistake then and turned his gun on me instead. I'm a big lad so he must have thought it was better to kill me first, I suppose. Just in that instant. But that was too long a time. He shouldn't have hesitated. Cass had fired immediately, twice, before I was able to grab her by the arm too and pull her away. I could hear the throttled gasps of the man in the hall as I reached for Cass—sounds magnified in the emptiness there.

I am very certain that man knew he was going to die then. But I can't imagine his mind.

And that makes me think of the frown on Lucille Beinecke's face as well. I don't think that expression was caused by the pain of my first shot back at her. I think it was just a sort of surprise. Maybe she had never considered before that she was the one who would die.

I've read somewhere, dark has many shades. That dark has color and depth. What has no shade, or color, or depth is black. Maybe it was Mr. Conrad who said it. But I do know that the dark at the heart of night is not black.

And something else.

Cass is in bed, asleep. And I am thinking now, here in the dark heart of this particular night, that I am a very fortunate man.

-30-

About the author

Vincent McCaffrey is the pseudonym of a fellow who happens to go by the same name, but has never quite felt like himself. He had once intended to be an author and adventurer. Having paused along the way to be a bookseller, editor, publisher, and more importantly, husband and father, he did finally manage to write a few books. The adventure happened anyway. More about that can be found at vincentmccaffrey.com